COSCON
ENTERTAINMENT

ALSO BY A.P. FUCHS

FICTION

A Stranger Dead
A Red Dark Night
April (writing as Peter Fox)
Magic Man (deluxe chapbook)

NON-FICTION

Book Marketing
for the Financially-challenged Author

POETRY

The Hand I've Been Dealt
Haunted Melodies and Other Dark Poems

Go to
www.apfuchs.com

The Way of the Fog

Volume One of
The Ark of Light

by

A.P. Fuchs

Coscom Entertainment
WINNIPEG

Coscom Entertainment
Suite 2, 317 Edison Avenue
Winnipeg, MB R2G 0L9
Canada

ISBN 1-897217-01-3

The Way of the Fog
Volume One of The Ark of Light

Published by Coscom Entertainment
www.coscomentertainment.com
Printed and bound in the USA

Coscom Entertainment logo designed by
A.P. Fuchs and Roxanne Sorensen

Cover art and design by Sean Simmans
Back cover author photo by Lisa Shauf

Text set in Garamond

Library and Archives Canada Cataloguing in Publication

Fuchs, A. P. (Adam Peter), 1980-
The ark of light / by A. P. Fuchs.

Contents: v. 1. The way of the fog.
ISBN 1-897217-01-3 (v. 1)

I. Title. II. Title: Way of the fog.

PS8611.U34M35 2005 C813'.6 C2005-902358-9

For my wife, Roxanne, my little ladybug.
I love you.

The Way of the Fog

Contents

Prologue: Some of What is Said to Have Happened Since ... 13

FIRST ACT: Leaving Their Worlds Behind

Chapter I: And to the Broken City She Came ... 21
Chapter II: Slummers in the Dark ... 30
Colors Fading ... 33
Chapter III: Come Morning ... 34
Chapter IV: Up on the Hill (Pretty) ... 44
Chapter V: The Blind Man and Catina ... 52
Chapter VI: A Talk Under the Stars ... 67
Chapter VII: When Darkness Falls ... 76
Chapter VIII: Beneath these Ashes ... 82
Chapter IX: The Departure ... 91
Chapter X: Into the Forest-Ring (Spirited Horses) ... 100
Chapter XI: Catina's Memory ... 119
Chapter XII: The Woman in the Desert ... 124
Chapter XIII: Under a Midday Sun (Wesafeld) ... 137
Chapter XIV: A Kind Stranger ... 146
Chapter XV: Peter ... 152
Chapter XVI: At Night (Two Dreams) ... 156
Peter's Journal: Old Earth ... 159
Chapter XVII: The First Sign of Power ... 160
Chapter XVIII: When the Past Takes You ... 169
Chapter XIX: In Darim ... 181
Chapter XX: The Man in the Gray Cloak ... 195
Chapter XXI: The Festival of Armasulia ... 199
Chapter XXII: The Tale of the Ark (Stars) ... 209
Peter's Journal: A Girl like the One I Knew ... 223
Chapter XXIII: Leaving Darim ... 224
Chapter XXIV: The Purifying of the Woods ... 228

SECOND ACT: And it Begins

Chapter XXV: Three Realms (A Fourth Adjoined) ... 235
Chapter XXVI: Onward (Hush-singers and Dreamy Recollections) ... 240
Chapter XXVII: Thalok Moving ... 250
Chapter XXVIII: The Meeting of Mr. Nibbetts ... 253
Chapter XXIX: On the Coast of Seryn ... 262

Chapter XXX: Grek 268
Peter's Journal: A Sad Day 279
Chapter XXXI: The Farewell 280
Chapter XXXII: Between the Purple and the Gray 288
Chapter XXXIII: The Sickness Takes Hold 294
Chapter XXXIV: Gasahd Turns West (The Hunt Begins Anew) 308
Chapter XXXV: By the River 312
Chapter XXXVI: When the Dembatstayr Ride 324
Chapter XXXVII: The Second Sign of Power 327
Chapter XXXVIII: After (Irons in the Fire) 342
Chapter XXXIX: The Haunting of the Minds 351
This Night 361
Chapter XL: A Four-legged Companion (Yaman) 362
Chapter XLI: Stories by the Fire 370
Peter's Journal: Awake 377
Chapter XLII: Villains 378
Chapter XLIII: Healer in the Trees 385
Chapter XLIV: A Talk of Dreams (Blindness) 398
Chapter XLV: The Qinorans Cry 408
Chapter XLVI: Dealing with Death 411
Peter's Journal: Drawing Near 418
Chapter XLVII: Of a Soldier and her General 419
Chapter XLVIII: The Sickness Returns 428
Chapter XLIX: Outside the Whirling Music 438

THIRD ACT: The Ark Calls

Chapter L: Thalok's Arriving (Faces in the Windows) 453
Chapter LI: Back on the Road 462
Peter's Journal: A Few Last Words 469
Chapter LII: From Jakarland 471
Chapter LIII: The Swinging Bridge at Tatamound 475
Chapter LIV: The Third Sign of Power 486
Chapter LV: Reflections 496
Destiny Forging 503
Chapter LVI: Journey's End (And to the Broken City They Returned) 505
Chapter LVII: Carrying On 515
Epilogue: The War is Coming 520
GLOSSARY of Terms 521
MAPS 529

PROLOGUE
Some of What is Said to Have Happened Since

On the End

At the end of Time there was a Great Battle called Armageddon. The Earth was unprepared.

On Good and Evil

The barrier separating the heavenly realms from the Earth had shattered, and the forces of Good and Evil were given free reign to War one final time.

Angels and Demons fought each other; countless numbers of Heavenly Hosts reclaiming all that the Forces of Darkness had taken.

It was the Angels' time for justice, a pure cause. It was their greatest strike.

There had been two sides to the War. One, being composed of Spiritual Powers beyond ordinary understanding, and the other composed of mortal men and women, young and old, fighting in one final blast of aggression. Some knew *why* they were at war and others did not.

On Spiritual Powers

As foretold in the Book of Revelation, at an hour when no one on Earth expected it—when no one on Earth had been *thinking* of it—a trumpet blast echoed throughout the heavens and was heard in all four corners of the Earth. The ground shook from its sound. The mountains bowed down. The seas roared. Even the Earth itself confessed Jehovah was God.

The Archangel, Michael, announced the return of the Lamb.

The sky split open in a blinding flash of light and rolled back like a scroll, revealing countless legions of Angels and Saints. Riding on a white horse ahead of them all, was the Lamb whose name was Faithful and True.

His eyes were like fire, flames blazing in brilliant waves of red and orange and yellow. On His head He wore many crowns, with a name written on them no one knew but He Himself. His robe was dipped in blood, the very blood He shed for all.

Many of the races of Man gathered against Him, and so had the False Prophet, Mandalay. In a mighty display of power, the Lamb spewed forth a sword, destroying all who opposed Him and His army. The Devil and the False Prophet were captured and thrown in to the fiery lake called Hell, where they would suffer for Eternity.

A Note on Future History

There is no solid record of what happened during the End Battle. All there is to rely on is the tongues of Men.

Some say the Battle was over in a day. Others insist it lasted for a thousand years, but one thing is known: the War had ended, or so it was presumed. No one really knows what happened or when the Thunder ceased. Perhaps we were never meant to.

It has been said that some of the Angels and Demons remained on the Earth, waiting until one day, perhaps at a date so far ahead that even the foresight of Man could not see, the War would resume.

The Ark of Light

The Ark of Light stood in between Heaven and Hell, the arbiter of Armageddon, the Battle of Then, the Great War, the Final Conflict. Its task was simple: to be a mediator in the End Battle between Good and Evil.

But the Ark was never opened, its keeper lost somewhere in the chaos, never to be seen again. No one knew what had happened but stories abounded. Rumors. Myths. Tall tales and bizarre ideas.

The Battle continued.

Once the smoke cleared and a Victor decided, the Ark disappeared from the Earth and was lost for more than five thousand years.

Then one day, the Ark, hidden for so long awoke, and wished to be found.

New Creations

The Great and Final Battle was a powerful and catastrophic event, the very Forces at work unlike anything the World had ever seen. And just as a shockwave from a nuclear blast affects Man, so does the fallout after a battle of Spiritual significance.

Mother Nature—the Earth—was tainted the moment the battle hit. Harm, pain, death—continued to fall on her as the battle progressed, was carried out and, finally, was finished. Because the atmosphere of the Earth had changed, because the very balance between Life and Death had shifted, so did the balance that had kept nature in check for more than five thousand years.

Evolution quickly rolled forward and new creatures were born. Some were just mere variations of their predecessors, but in other species, the changes were more severe. These changes all took time, but the end result, after several millennia, finally came to light.

On Moving On (Some Things Never Fade)

Despite the ramifications of the End, the Earth lived on. Time elapsed and centuries passed and the old way of life drifted into the silence of forgotten memory.

Yet something still endured, something had survived—Life.

Life requires food, water, and air to survive. But Life also contains which is unseen: the Spirit. Though suppressed from the onslaught of Armageddon, the Spirit of Life pressed on and found its way back into the World. Perhaps in the way it was originally intended to be—diverse, free, expressive.

History must draw to a close. Though the World is a wonderful and magnificent place, it was not designed to endure forever. The Earth was meant to reach its end at the Second Coming of the Lamb, but the unforeseen had occurred and the Arbiter of the war between Heaven and Hell had left his post. He remained on the sidelines, the Ark of Light by his side, waiting to see who would win.

Angry, God separated the Arbiter from his precious Ark and banned them both from the land of the living. But they did not die; they were only misplaced, left behind as the powers of Good and Evil left the Earth. The Arbiter, with his remaining power, created a Realm where those who died would join him until he was strong enough to make his return. The presence of the Realm on the hidden side of reality, the "Island of the Dead," had given the Earth long life, allowing it to live past its day, until it was time for history to finally draw to an end and for the End Battle to resume. But the Spirits of those who died will not be enough to aid the former Arbiter in his struggle to regain his power. He had been born of the Ark and drew his strength from it.

Now, so long since Armageddon, the Ark has recovered from its banishment and wants to be freed from its hidden damnation. The Arbiter knows this and, when he is strong enough, he will reclaim the Ark for his own and wreak his vengeance upon the powers of Light and Darkness, reigniting Armageddon. This time he will participate in the War, until there is only one Victor.

And so, the Ark of Light has decided now is the time for the last chapter in Earth's dark history.

The Ark of Light wants to be found. To accomplish this, it has made it its business to bring Life to a close so that, once over, Heaven and Hell can continue on as originally planned without the middle-ground of Earth. The Ark has sent a virus out into the World, a plague to erase Mankind—to erase all Life—to prepare a clean battleground for the final clash between Heaven and Hell, Good and Evil.

Though the virus is destructive and lethal in nature, it also has a peculiar side effect: power. Some who will be touched by the plague will perish quickly, others will die slowly, and some will continue living with extraordinary power. Such power will be required if the Ark of Light is ever to be found and brought forth from its hidden resting place.

"In the Last Days the Ark shall rise from the Earth, and a colored darkness will fall on all the lands.

"And in the midst of the Purple Fog, during the Master's Return, one will be born to lead them all to freedom."

- Translated from *The Prophecies of Demnacor the Seer*,
the Year 819 of the Third Aeon.

"In a dream it was spoken to me that a Great Plague shall fall on the Earth, a sign that History is coming to an end.

"The Ark will be a bringer of Light, but also a bearer of Darkness.

"What was once supposed to have finished, will begin anew. And what is supposed to have begun, will end."

- Translated from *The Prophecies of Demnacor the Seer*,
the Year 889 of the Third Aeon.

"The Ark calls from beneath the depths of shattered Time, announcing its rebirth."

- Translated from *The Prophecies of Demnacor the Seer*,
the Year 942 of the Third Aeon.

FIRST ACT

Leaving Their Worlds Behind

CHAPTER I
And to the Broken City She Came

Peter Jones watched the little girl coming toward him. She was still far off, but close enough for him to notice she wasn't from the Broken City of Garathen. It was her dress that identified her as an outsider. More specifically, it was the *colors* of her dress. Though it was night and pretty much everything in sight was hidden beneath a cloak of darkness, there was still enough moonlight to note that what she wore was unlike anything the Broken City had seen in a long time.

There were unwritten rules of dress in Garathen. Every resident of the small city wore black, brown and dark shades of gray. Anyone who wore any other colors was considered an outsider, someone going against the ropes of tradition. The drab colors were meant to show mourning for one's fellow man, a sign to show that each person felt for their neighbor, sharing in the joys and sorrows of their lives. The Broken City was a wretched place to live; the filth of the streets, the decay of the people who roamed them, overtook what was meant to have been a decent, simple society.

The little girl was closer, now, and Peter knew if she didn't get off the road and out of sight, trouble would quickly follow.

As long as he could remember, there had been a sunset curfew in Garathen. It was believed it was safer this way. After dark, and after all were inside and the Dembatstayr—a self-proclaimed Holy army doing the Master's Will—began their nightly patrols. The beasts in the surrounding forests would rise out of their slumber and hunt, looking for anything alive that would make a hearty meal.

Unfortunately, because the Dembatstayr's patrols were done at random, no one knew when they would stop by. If you were caught out in the open, you would be taken away to spend the night in a cold cell.

Also, Peter knew, not all people in the Broken City had the good fortune of having shelter. Most people were poor, many unable to barter their skills in exchange for a home of their own. They were forced to live secretly on the streets, stowing away in dark corners and dank alley-ways, hoping they would live through the night.

The little girl drew nearer. Peter watched her, and knew he wasn't the only person who'd seen her at this late hour. Nearly every night after curfew he would sit alone in the darkness of the small enclosed veranda that ran along the front of his tiny, one-level home, and stare out into the street. Most of the people did this. Many watched just to see which poor Slummer would be captured next for being outdoors and which beasts would roam through the city searching for prey.

In the dim light cast over the street from the moon, something fluttered. Peter thought he saw a shadow skitter across the muddy path that made up the Main Through-way of Garathen, as if someone were keeping stride with the little girl in the darkness off to the side.

The girl kept walking, her pace slow and labored. She appeared to have been walking for days.

The shadow skittered again and Peter was sure that at any moment a palanthora beast would sweep a mighty paw into the available light and steal the girl away into the shadows. A second look showed Peter it wasn't a palanthora beast after all. It was a Slummer and it was watching the little girl.

Peter opened his door, and stepped outside.

The little girl saw something out of the corner of her eye, a flicker of black across the muddy brown of the street. She paid no attention to it, thinking maybe it was the shadow of a night bird flying overhead.

A whisper followed by a snickering laugh came from the side of her.

She stopped and looked to her left. All she saw was darkness and the silhouettes of small huts and makeshift wooden shelters.

She kept going, the noise of her footfalls the only sound in the still night. Up ahead, she saw the silhouette of a man walking toward her. Her heart sped up at the prospect of someone coming to help her. As to what kind of person the man might be, she did not know, but it was *someone*, and that was what was important right now. She had been traveling for weeks, alone across dirty plains and through filthy forests. She needed Human contact. She was just a little girl after all and was not used to being alone for so long a time.

There was another flutter of shadow and patter of feet on the dirt. Before the humanette could stop to see who or what it was, a powerful arm scooped her up from behind and took her into the dark.

Peter ran when he saw the Slummer steal the little girl away. People getting snatched and dragged into the night was somewhat commonplace in Garathen. Many who were out after dark were never seen again. Rumors always circulated, but died down a few days after the disappearance, as if folks were suddenly afraid that speaking of the kidnapping would cause the event to repeat sometime soon.

The little girl was so small, looking so pretty and innocent in her colorful dress, pink flower-like patterns on blue fabric. The very sight of the color was dazzling and that coupled with the fact it was just a child, was almost mesmerizing. Most children were kept indoors at all times in the Broken City, with the mothers and fathers and the older siblings running to and from the shelters on errands or bartering skills for other services. Simply seeing such a young one out in the open was a rare thing, and at night, it was even rarer.

Halfway to where the girl had been taken, Peter stopped a moment, caught his breath, then was running again. He pushed his legs harder, faster, knowing that he had to get to the girl soon before the Slummer had his way with her.

At night the streets appeared the same no matter in which direction you looked. Many of the homes and wooden shelters were of the same design, with planks of wood leaning up against each other in a sort of cone, the huts mere blocks of wood placed cubically, all having the exact same square shape. Peter, like few people, had a slightly larger home, more furnished, and somehow more *complete.* For that, he was fortunate and thankful.

He heard a stifled cry and he veered off the road toward its sound. He was in the shadows now, using the moonlight lining the street as a guide. It was hard to see but Peter knew he had to try and find her. No child deserved to be in the arms of a Slummer. No other person alive did, either. Slummers were ruthless, years of being cast aside by society having built up a merciless bitterness and anger in them, ready to lash out at anyone—and *anything*—that was not of their kind.

There was another shallow squeal. Peter ran toward it and turned into a little nook between one of the cone shelters and a square hut.

Labored breathing and another muffled cry brought panic and anger on full force. The Slummer was hurting the girl, of that Peter was sure.

He hoped he would find her in time.

She couldn't see who it was that had her, but she knew whoever it was shouldn't be touching her the way they were. The person was behind her so she couldn't see her abductor; she was held tightly against his or her body. His or her forearm's tight grip across the girl's neck forbade any scream for help, the sound muted by the rough, callused hand over her mouth. She tried biting the person's thick fingers but each time she tried, her tongue was greeted then repulsed by salty skin.

There, before her, she saw someone coming toward them; the person who held her pulled her further into the shadows. The girl let out a squeal for help, only to be cut off again by a strong hand. The person behind her whispered something in strange gurgled speech. The girl struggled against her captor, her body moving this way and that, only to be restrained by a hand and arm more powerful than any strength she could muster. She resigned she would never be free.

Peter saw them in the shadows. He slowed his run to a brisk trot before stopping completely. They were in front of him.

Slummers were peculiar people. Usually with one stern look could a person quickly disarm them and the Slummer would stop whatever it was they were doing (if what they were doing was wrong). Despite their savagery, they were easily intimated; perhaps years of being an outcast had destroyed their self-worth so much they had given in to their believed insignificance.

But the Slummer who held the little girl had some backbone and would not give up his catch easily.

"Leave her be," said Peter.

He considered his options. He knew that despite a Slummer's occasional cowardice, they were very strong, their strength having been developed from fending for themselves day in and day out, hunting strong beasts and defending themselves against those of regular society, who decided to lash out their disapproval of the Streetfolk. Those of a lesser class were not tolerated by some.

The Slummer enveloped the girl in his arms, as if a prized catch. Taking a closer look, Peter saw the Slummer wasn't a male as he originally thought, but a female. Female Slummers were very rare, if found at all. They usually stayed in the woods tending to any offspring they might have. The prospect that this Slummer was female gave Peter hope and courage. Female Slummers were strong, but not as strong as the males.

The girl's large blue eyes, filling with hope, peered up at him.

"Give me the child," he said.

The Slummer didn't give any indication she would obey his request. He swiftly moved toward her, grabbing the wrist of the forearm that held the girl across the neck. He pulled the Slummer's arm away, pushing her shoulder to free the child. The Slummer took a step back from the force and Peter used his other hand to lead the girl away from her kidnapper. Free, the girl ran off out of the dark nook, her screams sopped with tears.

The Slummer hissed, her bony form visible through her clothes which were no more than filthy rags. Her leathery face and thin lips twisted as she snarled. Thick, matted hair tossed back with a flick of her neck. Arms outstretched, she dove at him. Her hands clasped firmly around his neck. Peter toppled backward and hit the dirt behind him, the sudden thud echoing in his head. The Slummer scratched and clawed at him with her large hand, the other still clasped around his neck, the long nails digging into his skin, piercing the flesh.

Realizing the Slummer's grip was too strong, Peter hooked his fist several times to the Slummer's head, his knuckles connecting hard against her jaw and temple. The

Slummer grunted loudly with each attack, and grabbed Peter by the shirt, lifting him a few feet from the ground before slamming him back down against the dirt and mud of the street. The back of his skull hit the ground with a smack and stars burst before his vision. The swinging of his fists slowed and became more like hard slaps than actual punches. The Slummer screamed and cursed in a messy, almost incomprehensible speech as she assailed him. Another hard smack against his skull and buzzing filled his ears. His face felt fuzzy and fat as if someone stuffed cotton between the skin and bone. The Slummer's angry screeches made the buzzing even worse.

Feeling death creeping up on him, he grabbed the Slummer by the neck. Drawing her in toward him, he quickly gathered his strength and pushed out with all the force he was able, throwing her to the side. He jumped on top of her and with wild abandon, rained blow after blow into the Slummer's head, hitting and hitting until blood splashed up in his face. It wasn't long before the Slummer stopped moving and Peter collapsed on top of her.

Too tired and disoriented to move, Peter took the time to catch his breath before rolling over and lying beside her. Still immersed in the surrealism of what had just occurred, his stomach twisted with revulsion for what he'd done. But there hadn't been a choice. It was life or death.

A few minutes passed before he remembered the little girl. He stood up, legs shaky, and made his way out of the dark nook to see where the child had gone off to.

Peter ran out onto the Main Through-way, frantically scanning for the child. She ran in little steps back the way she had come into the Broken City, toward the Forest-Ring. Peter chased after her.

She glanced back, eyes wide with fear and sped up her pace, running as fast as her short legs would carry her.

Peter caught up to her in short time. Putting a hand to her shoulder, he slowed her run.

"It's okay," he said. "You have nothing to worry about. I'm not going to hurt you."

The child kept trying to run, but Peter kept her in front of him. Tears ran down her pale cheeks. Getting down on one knee, he placed his hands on her shoulders.

"It's all right," said Peter. "I want to help you."

Without warning, the little girl collapsed in his arms, her small head shaking against his shoulder in short, sobbing bursts. Peter held a hand to the back of her head, stroking her blonde hair, soothing her. She was no more than five years of age, six at the most.

He whispered reassurances to her, telling her over and over again she was going to be okay. He didn't know if she heard him or believed him. But that didn't matter. He knew that she understood the calming nature of his touch. She was just a child after all, and children knew that a hug and a comforting hand on the back of the head or nape of the neck meant everything was going to be okay.

After a time, the girl's crying eased and she pulled away from Peter far enough to look at him. Her left eye was swollen shut in a deep pink puff. Her other blue eye appeared healthy.

Her nose wrinkled up in wet sniffles as she wiped the tears from her eyes.

Peter asked, "Are you okay, little one?"

She hesitated then shrugged.

"Can you tell me your name?"

She didn't answer.

In an effort to remedy her silence, Peter placed a palm against his chest and said, "I'm Peter." He then pointed at her. "And you are?"

She still didn't answer. Peter told her his name again and asked once more for hers. She didn't reply.

"No matter," he said, "we can always find out who you are later."

In the gray of moonlight, he saw a red slash near her hairline. "You're bleeding," said Peter. "Here." He pulled his hand into the sleeve of his brown woolen shirt, reassured the girl he wouldn't hurt her, and dabbed at the cut with the cuff, removing some of the blood. The Slummer might have scratched her. He wasn't sure.

"There, much better," he said. He paused; she looked at him spacily. "Now, what are we to do with you? Hm."

And then out of the dark came the horrible shriek of a palanthora beast. It was like one hundred men screaming as loud as possible.

"It's not safe here," said Peter. "Come, we must get you off the street."

He stood and with his hand still on her shoulder, urged her to come with him. Instead, she maintained her ground and her gaze questioned what he wanted.

"I'm serious," he said. "It's not safe here. We must get indoors before something far worse than a Slummer will come and get us both." Peter never had much experience with children so he wasn't sure how to talk to them. He just knew you had to be nice, if you wanted a child to get along with you. You also needed to be assertive, too, so they would listen.

He took her hand. "Come on. It will be all right. Do not worry. I won't hurt you."

When she didn't move, he gave her hand a tug. She followed hesitantly.

Another snarl came from the dark.

Picking up his pace, pulling her along, they stuck to the shadows lining the dirty Through-way of Garathen. They stayed just enough in the darkness to remain concealed, but also enough in the light so any on comers would be visible, namely Slummers. There were other thieves who prowled around at night, but those were few and far between. It was the Slummers one had to worry about, first, and then it was the other creatures that were sometimes out. Most of the nocturnal animals wouldn't attack a person unless under threat. However, there had been attacks in the past and their stories quickly became legendary in Garathen, reinforcing a person to stay indoors once the sun set. Besides, if you weren't attacked by either Slummer or beast, you could get caught by the Dembatstayr and get tossed in a cell for being out after dark. But all knew that such a harsh punishment for being out of doors was actually a kindness, a favor the Dembatstayr did for you by taking you off the streets and into some place safe until dawn.

It wasn't long before Peter and the girl were at the door to his veranda. He led her in and checked the street once more before closing the door.

He didn't see the two Slummers across the way, hiding in the shadows.

Peter lit the candle by the door; he walked in further. The girl stayed by the door, hands clasped in front of her thighs, her colorful dress looking beautiful in the candle's light.

"You can come in, you know," said Peter.

She looked at him with her good eye, its bright blue iris somehow captivating.

"Well, the first thing we need to do come dawn is to find out where you came from," he said. It was more an instruction to himself rather than a statement to her. "I know you're not from around here, at least not with a dress like that. And if you are, your parents are going to be in a fair amount of trouble for creating it, placing you in a higher place than others. Not one man should be put above the rest, you know, and that goes for little girl's, too." Shame struck him, his skin growing hot. The child had just gone through a terrible ordeal with one of the Streetfolk and instead of comforting her, he was reprimanding her over the flowery-patterned dress. He came up to her, noticing the cut on her forehead had started bleeding again. Like before, he dabbed at it with his sleeve.

"We need to get you cleaned up. Are you hurt anywhere else? It's okay. I just want to help."

He looked intently at the eye that was swollen shut. "What happened here?" He pointed to it, the girl recoiling as his finger drew near her flesh. "It's okay. You're going to be fine. I just asked a question, that's all."

Peter wasn't sure what to do. He needed cooperation and it was obvious that she wasn't going to speak to him. Was she not able to talk or was she just simply choosing not to?

He gave her a smile. She smiled back, a moment later wrapping her arms around his neck, squeezing him in a tight hug.

"Mali kwon nali," said the girl.

"What?" asked Peter.

She didn't repeat her words but instead squeezed his neck even harder. She seemed to be thankful for his rescuing her. Peter wished he knew what she said.

He left her at the front door, telling her to stay put as he went to retrieve some wraps and ointment to dress her cut. Though the wound didn't look too serious, Peter didn't want to take any chances, fearing it might become infected if he didn't tend to it.

Peter's home was small yet big enough that he had plenty of space, more than enough for one person. A front landing ran off the veranda—which he built himself—leading into the main living quarters. A small table sat just off to the side of the landing; on the floor beside it, a straw mat served as a bed. In the back of the abode was another small room where he made his paintings and wrote his poetry. There was an easel set up in the corner by a small window, a little gateway to the outside World when inspiration was needed. A low table in the middle of the room accompanied by a cushion was where he put pen to paper. Further in, was a small kitchen and, behind that, a small area for the pottered wash basin and privy. Peter went to that small area, drew back the curtain that separated it from the rest of the home, and stooped down to pick up the small medicine box he kept under the wooden table that supported the basin. He pulled out the medicine box and stood. Mounted above the sink was a slab of Linsheum rock he obtained a year ago. Linsheum was hard to find. Once a year a man would come through Garathen on horseback, hauling a cart of the rock, seeking any who might have use for a reflective surface. And not only was Linsheum rare (unless you wanted to travel far West to find it), it was also expensive. Peter, a poet by trade as well as an artist, had worked for six months painting a portrait of Garathen, venturing most mornings up Shadow's Hill, a large and rocky slope that overlooked the city, for the panoramic view. He also wrote two poems to accompany the piece, enhancing the atmosphere and overall presentation of the painting. The effort was accepted by the Linsheum dealer and an exchange was made for the portrait. The Linsheum dealer chuckled as Peter handed him the painting and the poems, saying that not only did he enjoy coming through Garathen, but he also said the painting compared to works he'd seen in the Eastern cities, places where poverty wasn't an issue and there weren't dress codes. Peter, though glad to receive the Linsheum, felt somewhat uncomfortable having something that few people in the Broken City had—something that served as a mirror. If anyone mentioned his bartering for the Linsheum, he always stressed that he wasn't trying to be better than anyone else. He had only wanted to treat himself to something pleasant and it was as simple as that. People understood the reasoning of doing something positive for yourself from time to time. But *only* from time to time.

Using the Linsheum's reflective surface, he checked himself over for any cuts or scratches from his encounter with the Slummer. Save for the scuffs of dirt on his face and the stinging scratches along his forearms, the Slummer appeared to not have caused any harm. He lifted his shaggy black hair off his forehead and checked for any hidden cuts or bruises. He checked his blue eyes as well, seeing if the area beneath them would turn purple after being struck in the face. The skin around his eyes was red and that was the extent of the damage. He didn't want to take too long in his self-examination for the little girl was waiting for him to bring out dressings for her cut.

He usually kept to himself during the day and obeyed the rule of staying indoors come nightfall. He rarely got hurt. Only once, if he recalled correctly, he had injured one of his fingers while constructing a wooden frame for one of his paintings. And even then, the cut hadn't been that severe. He only needed to wear a bandage wrap for one day, just long enough to stop the bleeding. Fresh air would take care of the rest.

He took the medicine box into the next room. The child had gone from the doorway and had curled up into a ball on the straw mattress next to the table and pair of chairs. Setting the box down beside the mattress, he got down on his knees and looked her over. He could only imagine what must being going through her young mind right now. An encounter with a Slummer was hard on anyone. Peter only knew of two others who had a run-in with a Slummer and each said that all they could think about was death. So for a girl of five or six years . . .

It was a miracle she survived.

A Slummer's strength was their intimidation of others. If a Slummer forced you into believing there was no escape save death, odds were you would die at their hands. Peter was amazed at his own courage for fighting off a Slummer never mind defeating the blasted thing. He'd never had to fight before.

There was something captivating in the way the girl breathed as she slept, how the skin of her young cheeks seemed to look so soft in the candlelight. Peter shook his head, snapping himself out of whatever just had him.

"Are you awake?" he said softly.

The little girl didn't respond. Only slow, shallow breaths escaped her lips.

"Okay, then," he said. "You can sleep here. I don't mind. But come morning we're going to have to find out where you came from. You're not from around here, that much is clear. Maybe tomorrow you'll be able to talk to me. I still don't understand what it was you said. I guess we'll figure something out."

He touched a hand to her forehead then produced a soft cloth from the medicine box and a bottle of ointment. Dotting the bottle on the cloth until he could feel the ointment seeping through the fabric, he sighed with relief the cut wasn't severe. He dabbed the cloth against the girl's cut, disinfecting it. Once done, he put the cloth and ointment away, and closed the medicine box.

He laid down and took one final look at her before closing his eyes.

"Sweet dreams, little one," he said.

He tried to fall asleep, but was having a time of it. He kept expecting her to wake and start crying again.

It was going to be a long night.

CHAPTER II
Slummers in the Dark

Peter awoke to the sound of something scratching at the door. His eyes shot open; the harsh scraping grew louder. A sickening snap came from the bottom of the door as if whatever was out there had broken something.

The scratching stopped.

The door was still intact.

His first thought was it was a palanthora beast searching for something to eat or exploring some amusing scent. His heart rate quickened at the thought.

Peter prayed to the Master it was only a figment of his imagination. If it was a palanthora beast at the door, and if it somehow made its way into his home, he knew he and the little girl had no chance of escape. Though palanthora beasts didn't usually attack anyone without cause, they were still unstable and even the most innocent of movements, like backing away from it, might be enough to cause it to lash out.

The girl was still curled up in a snug ball, sleeping peacefully. He immediately assumed that wherever she came from, she was used to sounds in the night. For now, it seemed, the scratching had stopped. Peter breathed a sigh of relief and closed his eyes. He had finally managed to fall asleep a short while ago after tossing and turning, going over his options as to what he was going to do with her come morning. He knew he needed to find out where she came from and if she could not speak any of the Common-tongue, he wasn't going to figure it out on his own.

The scratching resumed, hard nails on wood.

Peter's eyes opened again.

The scratching moved upwards from the base of the door. Whatever it was must be testing to see how much of a barrier the door really was. There wasn't a lock on the door, just a small iron latch that kept it shut when the wind picked up, to prevent it from flying open. But the latch could easily be torn from its wooden holding should enough force be applied.

The scratching moved along the door to the outer wall toward the window that overlooked where Peter and the girl lay. The window was covered with a blind made of reeds and bark, thatched together in a kind of grid pattern; something to block out the morning light come dawn. Whatever was snooping around out there was in his veranda.

When he'd first built the veranda, the door leading out into the street hadn't had a lock. Thievery wasn't much of a problem in Garathen. Everyone kept to themselves and respected another's privacy and property. Each person, though all having little, made due with what they had accumulated through their own hard work and did not cheat by stealing from another. Exchanging services and products of skill for other goods or services was held in high esteem.

The blind covered a dusty window, its glass not very clear and nowhere near as reflective as polished Linsheum. It was thin and could easily be broken. If it was a palanthora beast outside, it would have no trouble getting through.

The scratching stopped, replaced by a loud tapping at the window. The window rattled in the wooden slot that held it in place.

Blrrm. Blrrm. Blrrm.

Moving cautiously toward the window, Peter hoped he would not alert the intruder that someone inside was awake. And, if it was a palanthora beast, he didn't want the sound of his movement perceived as a threat.

Blrrm. Blrrm. Blrrm. Then a long *Blrrrrrrm* as the window rattled in its slot.

The sound stopped when Peter squatted beneath the blind. He paused and put a steady hand to his heart, calming it some. With one finger he pulled the blind back a crack. Much to his relief, it wasn't a palanthora beast but a Slummer standing on the other side.

The relief quickly passed and a new panic set in because it *was* a Slummer. No, wait. As he looked closer, he saw the Slummer wasn't alone.

There was another.

Peter immediately replaced the blind and moved toward the girl. He was about to wake her when, from behind, he heard more scratching and rattling.

The vivid image of long nails scratching on wood made him cringe.

Jrsh jrsh jrsh.

The window . . .

Blrrm, blrrm, blrrm.

Jrsh, jrsh, JRSH!

Blrrm, blrrm, BLRRM!

Just as Peter was about to wake the girl, the noises stopped. His hand hovered above her head, his neck straining in the opposite direction, looking towards the door. Sweat beaded above his brow. The idea of having to wake the girl and escape into the night made his head hurt. If the Slummers saw them flee . . . . They must have found out about what he'd done to their kin.

Listening intently for any disturbances outside, he sank with relief when all was quiet again. No. They could still be standing outside the veranda or circling his home, waiting for him to come running out with the girl in his arms.

Peter waited some more and, after several minutes of silence, crept back over to the blind and peeked out into the veranda.

The Slummers were gone.

He eyed the veranda for quite some time before deciding it was safe enough to try and go back to sleep. Letting the blind back down so it rested against the windowsill, he thanked the Master the girl hadn't woken up during the whole ordeal. She had already been through enough tonight. He didn't know how he'd handle her should she fall apart because of another traumatic event.

Peter lay back down and stroked the side of her head. Seeing her lying there sleeping soothed his speeding heart, melting away any lingering apprehension the Slummers might come back to visit them again.

Colors Fading

She comes here from afar,
tired, worn thin, needing rest.
The colors on her dress
don't seem that colorful anymore.

Her eye is swollen,
seeming the victim in a losing plight.
A sad look is her smile,
her good eye pleading with me for aid.

For why is she here, this small traveler?
What drove her away
and brought her here
to the Broken City?

- Peter Jones

CHAPTER III
Come Morning

Dawn transformed the Broken City of Garathen from a grimy slum to the cheery place it was during the day. Just before the sun rose, the air seemed to hang, pausing in apprehension, as if preparing to take a fresh breath before launching into a new day. The clouds that dimmed the moonlight throughout the night dissolved, melting away into opposite horizons like a bridal veil parted. The sun rose in the East, a mighty flower of light blooming across the land, eradicating the shadows. The sky lightened; the brilliant blue of day emerged. If there was any one place where day and night displayed their contrasts the most, it was Garathen.

The sun shone in streaks of light through the cracks in the blind, erasing the dark in Peter's home. The heat of its rays warmed his cheeks. He opened his eyes to the girl sitting cross-legged on the straw mat, staring at him. Their eyes locked, Peter taking a moment to remember who she was and why she was there. She stared back at him, memories of the night before imprinted on her face. Yet there was something else there, too. Hope. Her eyes pulled at his heart and he knew she was counting on him to help her.

"Good morning," said Peter and gave her a small smile.

Her eyes squinted—even the one that was swollen—as she returned his grin. Her sore eye didn't look as bad in the morning light. The flesh was shiny, pink and sore-looking, but not as puffy as Peter remembered. He was thankful for that.

I don't want it to get any worse before I figure out what to do with her, he thought.

The cut on her forehead was merely a red line on her skin. The ointment from the night before had taken care of it.

Her dress. It was pale blue with pink flower-like patterns on it, flowers that appeared to be in half-bloom. It was gorgeous; better than the drab grays and browns that he was used to. He envied her for that.

He sat up. She straightened her posture with him.

"How are you?" he asked, creating Common-talk to hopefully get her to say something in return.

She smiled sweetly, telling him she was fine.

"Good, I trust," he went on.

They exchanged stares for a time, Peter not sure what to do with the humanette. He didn't have much contact, if any, with children, so he wasn't sure how to take care of them. The best he'd be able to offer her was the same help he'd give someone his own age.

"Well," he said, "I'm Peter."

The girl looked at him quizzically.

"I see," he said. He put a palm to his chest and stated his name again, hoping she would get the idea. She just grinned again. At least she seemed to be in good spirits.

He tried once more, pointing to himself, saying his name. Then he pointed to her.

The little girl wrinkled her face in thought, and then said, "Teek min som Catina."

I don't think she understood, he thought.

He tried the name-game again.

"I'm Peter," he said, and pointing to her, "you are?"

"Teek min som Catina."

Peter studied her eyes. "I'm not sure what your name is. I don't . . . I don't understand, but you said 'Som Catina' twice now. I'll call you Som Catina, for the time being." He took a deep breath. "I guess the first thing we need to do is get something to eat. But that would mean we would have to go outside."

She stared at him blankly.

Peter continued. "You have nothing to fear though. It's very different here during the day. Much safer and more pleasant. That's part of why we needed to stay inside last night. But you'll like it outside. I promise." He gave her another smile, simply because a smile was something everybody understood. Especially children.

He held out his hand to help her up. She took it.

Awkwardly, Peter asked, "Do you have to, um—" He pointed in the direction of the privy. She didn't say anything.

Peter led her to the privy and pointed to the hole in the ground that was bordered by a sanded-smooth wooden seat, covered with a sanded-down plank of board for a lid. He hoped she would recognize what he was showing her and tell him if she had to conduct her business or not.

She bit her lip and shook her head.

"Okay, then," said Peter, relieved. He didn't want to be responsible for cleaning her up after she was done if she couldn't take care of it on her own. "Um, you'll like what we're going to have for breakfast. I just need to get something."

He took her back to the straw mat, knelt upon it, and lifted up its top corner, revealing the grooves in the flooring where the wooden planks met. He lifted the smallest of those planks by a knot in the board, serving as a thumb hook. He pulled the board up. Hidden within the hole in the dirt beneath was an oak chest with his initial carved in it in a stylized "P." He pulled the box out and set it on the mat. The girl sat down and brought her knees to her chest, looking on with interest. Peter opened the box and inside was a small bundle of parchment—poems that he had written over the past few weeks that would eventually be used to trade for goods, and a leather-bound journal, his personal diary. They were kept there for safekeeping. He wasn't concerned anyone would come and steal them, but the works contained within the wooden box meant a great deal to him, especially the journal as that was where he recorded his most private of thoughts and feelings. The poems, though, were how they were going to pay for their breakfast.

Peter removed two customized poems, closed the box's lid, replaced it in the hole, and then covered it back up with the plank of wood. Som Catina helped by putting the straw mat back over the boards. The poems were specially crafted for Taimus the Baker, the gentleman that Peter normally received his meals from when he went out to eat.

"Ready to go?" asked Peter.

She appeared so. They stood, the girl brushing some of the dust from the floor off her behind. She and Peter went to the front door, the girl behind him. When Peter opened the door and stepped out onto his veranda, she remained in the doorway.

"It's okay," he said. "It's perfectly all right. Trust me." He extended his hand.

After a moment, she took it and stepped out onto the veranda to join him. He closed the door behind them, the latch clicked into place. They exited the veranda and stepped out onto the street. The streets were still made of mud, but because of the hot sun, the mud was already becoming dirty and dusty.

The shadows that hid the other huts and small wooden buildings and cabins last night had been eradicated by fresh splashes of sunlight. The humanette looked up and down the street, her young eyes growing all the wider with the commotion and hustle and bustle of Garathen in the morning. She was checking for the Slummers, Peter knew.

Last night, the streets had been deserted so this was a big change for her. Mornings in Garathen came quickly and, usually, the moment dawn broke, the people came pouring out of their shelters like convicts released from prison. There were people of all heights and widths. Most had darker skin, not brown or black, but tanned like a farmer's egg. Those in Garathen seldom lost their tans. Peter was one of the few whose skin lightened during the Winter. People pushed carts; others had theirs pulled by horses. Shops and stalls were set up along the street, most people conducting business and exchanging their trades right in front of their homes.

Peter said, "Normally I'd be out here myself with my easel and paint tray, waiting for someone to come and perhaps offer me something for a portrait of themselves or a family member. Or I'd write them a poem, if they asked. But today I have to take care of you. It's not a big deal. I usually only work three or four hours a day anyway. I could use a break after last night." He glanced down at her. "You can't understand a word I'm saying, can you?"

She just looked at him blankly.

"Guess not," he said, feeling kind of bad at his sarcasm. It was now a fact that the little girl was not from anywhere near Garathen. People usually spoke the same language for quite a distance from the Broken City. Most people in the World spoke the same language, or so Peter had heard from his friend Alan the Traveler. Unless the girl hadn't yet learned the Common-tongue, she was probably from some far off place of a different culture than any Peter knew of. That would explain why she seemed so unsure about her surroundings and the people around her. Tie that in with what happened with the Slummer the night before, and she was no doubt confused. But, she was a humanette, so she was the same race and species as him. Or, so she seemed, anyway. Yet Peter knew he was going to need help from someone if he were to discover where the girl came from. He knew he'd have to see Alan. If Alan was not out gallivanting across the country, that was.

"Come on," said Peter, and gave the child's hand a tug.

Taking quick steps, they went down the street to see the Baker.

Garathen was busy in the morning. A lot of the people went to work early, hoping to trade for all they might need for that day so they could retire early and use the rest of the day for whatever they wanted. If a person needed something from someone but the other person didn't have need of what was offered in the trade, they would usually trade anyway, for whatever they got in return could then be traded to someone who would have use for it. Most shops and trading posts opened an hour or two after dawn, and most closed an hour or two after midday.

As the little girl walked with him past the array of shops and stands, Peter saw her young eyes couldn't help but take in everything they set sight on. Seeing so many people bustling about in all directions was something she didn't appear to be used to.

He hadn't really noticed before now how busy of a place Garathen was. They passed fur traders and butchers; blacksmiths and horseshoers; tailors and fortunetellers. Though Garathen was a small city, and somewhat alienated from the rest of the World, it was a place one could come to for almost anything they needed. Garathen had three shifts of living, as it were. There was the early shift where the more appropriate goings-ons occurred—the trading and swapping of one service for another. Then came the mid afternoon and evening shift where the darker parts of society would begin to surface—the bars would open along with the whorehouses and those who dealt in substances which would make one feel euphoric and terrible at the same time. Then came the night with the beasts and the Slummers. It was a multi-faceted society, but one that had functioned as such for hundreds of years and had seemed to come along quite nicely despite the sharp contrasts.

Peter was proud to be a part of the Broken City. It was his home and, no matter where his life may lead him, the city would always remain special.

The little girl's stomach growled loud enough that Peter heard it.

"Hungry?" he asked.

Instead of replying, she kept looking around, especially at those who stopped from their work and stared at her colorful dress.

Peter could only imagine what would be going through the peoples' minds right now. No one wore such fanciful colors in Garathen, save for special occasions, and even then, the color was kept to a minimum. Despite the day and night that separated the common man from the Slummers and other Streetfolk, they were still one people and a respect for the more unfortunate of society was always maintained. Usually.

The smell of fresh-baked bread filled the air; both Peter's and the little girl's noses perked up at the delicious smell. It could only be coming from one place: the Golden Bowl, the Baker's station. It was called the Golden Bowl because the Baker was famous for making wonderful bread-bowls, cooked just right, gold in color. Bread-bowls were good for eating along with just about anything, but were even better when filled with fruit, vegetables, or a meat salad. Peter had his heart set on freshly cut bananas and strawberries in a toasted bowl with sugar sprinkled on top. He was sure the little girl wouldn't mind having the same. He'd have to stop elsewhere for fruit though.

The girl tugged on Peter's sleeve, pointing toward the Golden Bowl.

"Yes, that's where we're going," said Peter.

She seemed to understand his smile when he said that, and gave a big smile in return.

There was no line in front of the Golden Bowl this morning, and those who were already awake were busy with their own trading. Peter led the girl up to the wooden table that had a sign draped over its front, a picture of a tan-colored bread-bowl painted at its center. In behind the table, the Baker had his back to them and was hunched over his britches, his big rump up in the air as he removed an iron rack with freshly baked bread from a stone oven. The top of the oven had a grill, and just below that, in a small trench in the stone, were hot coals. At the front of the unit was a stone door on hinges that opened up into the oven itself, the heat from the fire above heating the small space beneath, baking whatever was within. There was a table on either side of the oven. The one on the left for mixing ingredients and cutting dough, the one on the right laid out with racks to set the hot loaves and bowls to cool.

The Baker held the rack from the oven with one mitted hand and removed six loaves with the other, setting them on the racks on the table before replacing the hot rack back in the oven.

"Good Morning, Taimus," said Peter.

Taimus turned around, his big belly turning with him. He let out a jovial laugh when he saw Peter, a big hefty smile rolling his stubbled cheeks upwards, his eyes becoming mere slits on his face. His dark hair tossed back with his head as he said, "Why, good morning to you, Peter. What brings you out so early? I thought you'd be all the way down by your end of the street this time of day." He pointed back the way Peter and the girl had come.

"I've had a change in plans this morning," said Peter, nodding downward, indicating the girl.

Taimus peered over the table. "Oh," he said with a wink, "I see." He didn't seem to notice the swelling on the girl's eye.

Taimus saw many things day in and day out in the Broken City, so an ill-eye was probably beneath his notice. Peter was thankful for that, too, as he didn't want to be asked questions he did not have the answers.

Taimus paused for a moment. "You better be careful, there, Peter, what with walking around with a little one wearing a dress like that. Did you not have anything you could have dressed her in before coming out this way? Folks'll talk, you know."

"I know, but no, I didn't have anything to dress her in. The thought didn't occur to me actually, to be honest."

"Hmm," the Baker considered to perhaps no one but himself.

"She showed up last night and I'm not sure where she's from. We had a run-in with a Slummer and—"

"A Slummer, you say?" Taimus gave a mighty swat down on the table top, startling the little one. "Why, Peter, you ought to know better than to be out of doors come nightfall. You got what you deserved, if you ask me."

Peter took a step closer, so he could speak a little quieter and avoid the eavesdropping of any prying ears. "I was indoors, Taimus. But I saw the little one, here, walking down the Through-way on her own. I saw the Slummer and knew that if I was the only one who saw her, I was the only one who could help her."

"Mighty dangerous business."

"I know. But I'm trying to forget about it."

"I'll bet. Slummers are dangerous business."

"You just said that."

"Huh? Oh. So I did." The Baker let out a chuckle. "Anyway, what can I get you two this morning?"

Having already decided, Peter said, "A pair of bread-bowls, please. I've brought your usual payment."

"I look forward to reading it."

"I've actually brought two poems for you today. One for myself, and the other for her."

Taimus scratched his chin. "Well, I'll tell you what, she's such a sweet little thing, that whatever she wants, is on the table." In other words, whatever she wanted was free.

"Thank you," said Peter.

"But you must tell me what she wants or I won't know what to give her."

"She's doesn't speak any of the Common-tongue or at least from what I can gather. But I'll ask, anyway." Peter crouched down and to the girl said, "You can have whatever you like." Just then the Baker was leaning over them with a bread bowl in one hand and a fair-sized loaf of rye in the other. Peter pointed to the two. "You can have one or the other. Som Catina, which would you like?"

The girl put a finger to her chin, and then with a smile pointed at the loaf.

"Okay, then. That'll be the loaf for her, and a toasted bread-bowl for me," said Peter.

Taimus looked at him and made a face. "I know what the little one wanted, Peter. I'm not stupid."

They both laughed. The girl laughed, too, but Peter was sure she was only laughing because they were. Still, the child's laugh was beautiful.

Peter paid for the bread with the better of the two poems he had brought and bid Taimus a good day. He and the girl, who was eagerly munching on her hot-from-the-oven loaf of bread, made there way back toward Peter's place. He told her not to eat too much as he wanted to take her somewhere special to eat their breakfast. When she seemed not to pay any heed to his words, he let her eat anyway; she had a bad night last night and he didn't want to add to it by stopping her from enjoying her breakfast. Who knew when she ate last?

They had passed a fruit stand on the way to see the Baker, and Peter wanted his bananas and strawberries. He was thankful, too, that Taimus gave him the loaf for free. Now he could use the leftover poem to pay for his fruit.

Peter got his fruit as intended from a lovely young lady named Talia, who was twenty years of age and ran a fruit stand for her sickly father. She blushed when she read the poem he had given her, and though the poem was written for the Baker (it was about friendship and didn't name Taimus by name, so it was just as touching), she appreciated it nonetheless. She had known Peter since they were children and had played together when the chance came. At one point or another, a romantic relationship did cross their minds, but nothing ever came to fruition. Peter decided long ago they would make better friends than something more. She didn't touch his heart the way he hoped his future mate would.

Peter was ill at ease with talking to Som Catina, namely because, so far, she had not given any sign that she understood his words, and only his actions seemed to have been interpreted correctly. He was frustrated, obviously, as he was not used to spending time with someone with whom he could not communicate with. He was sure she was as equally frustrated, but he was surprised as to how willingly she came along with him and how fearless she seemed of being with a total stranger.

The little girl *was* frustrated. There were so many things she wanted to tell him but did not know how. She already knew they did not share the same language when she heard him speak. She had tried saying thank you to him last night. *Mali kwon nali,* she had said. *Thank you.* She hoped that soon she would find some way for him to understand her. She had come to the Broken City for a reason. Several reasons, actually, but one important reason, and it was that reason that drove her to stay with this young man who seemed to genuinely want to help her. She prayed to the Master that all would end well and that somehow He would find a way for them to communicate clearly.

She scratched her cheek and ran her fingers through her long, blonde hair, combing out some of the knots that had settled while she slept the night before. She then rubbed the back of her neck in a futile effort to rub away some of the heat from the sun that was pressing on her skin. Daytime in Garathen was not at all like its nighttime. Yet even as they walked back in the direction of Peter's home, the girl could not help but look at the shadows in between the shops and huts, searching for Slummers.

She ate her loaf of bread quickly, it having been her first meal since sometime yesterday morning. The Ranmorahn Plains that bordered Garathen, and the Forest-Ring surrounding it, had not been a friendly place. Fortunately, she was only six years old and had been small enough to slip beneath the notice of the people she saw. She stowed away in the backs of wagons of those traveling East. Though she was young, she was quite capable and had traveled East to Garathen two times before with her parents, so some of the main roads were familiar to her. She had stopped in three towns on the way over; every time she was seen walking alone in a crowd, she must have been presumed to be a young one who had wandered a ways from her parents, but not far enough for her parents to worry about her. There had been, however, one kind old lady in Wesafeld who took notice she was all alone. The kind old woman had offered her shelter for the night and two hot meals, one at supper time and the other at breakfast. When the old lady went into the other room of her small cabin, the girl had grabbed a couple of apples and pears off the table and scurried out the door before the woman returned. The little one had no way to explain to her where she was going because the old woman spoke the Common-tongue and she did not. As well, though she wasn't sure, the girl thought the old lady was asking the surrounding neighbors if they knew her and if they had an idea as to where the girl had come from. The girl couldn't have that. She had to get to Garathen and it was that thought that pressed her onward as she traveled the great span of miles between the towns and countrysides.

She was glad Peter rescued her last night. She had never been in danger before. When Peter saved her from the Slummer, and after he caught up with her on the street shortly afterward, a small devotion to Peter was instilled in her, a gratefulness that he saved her life—a life-debt, as it were. But she was too young to understand such a thing and simply understood her loyalty to go wherever Peter went as a kind of duty to good company. His presence was comforting, like that of the older brother she never had. Every time he looked at her with those kind blue eyes of his, his eyes always seemed to be smiling at her, assuring her that she had nothing to fear. There was something about him that she did not sense when around others. Almost a paternal quality, a sense of safety and warmth. The people she had passed and encountered on her several-week journey to Garathen never had the same comforting air Peter emitted. She was thankful to the Master that Peter was around and she asked the Master for a special blessing on him.

But she must not let herself fall in love with him, as much as she wanted to. The city from which she came was a duty-oriented society and when you gave your word to someone that you would carry out any given task—you carried out that task, no qualms nor protests. And she had made a promise when she left to go East, and it was that promise she intended to see to its end. She knew that somehow Peter would help in her purpose. She didn't know how, but somehow he would play a role in the reason why she came to the Broken City.

Needing someone she could trust, she clung to Peter like gauze to a wound. Others in Garathen gave her cool stares.

To be left alone . . .

After her breakfast—which was extraordinarily filling and scrumptious to say the least—she would figure out some way to try and tell Peter why she had come to Garathen.

She had come to see her grandfather.

Having been to the Broken City only twice before, with at least a year between visits, she wasn't sure as to where in the city her grandfather lived. She knew it was in a forested area and that there were rocks piled around his home, but that could describe almost any place, especially in Garathen. The Broken City was a strange place geographically. Though its streets were composed of mainly mud and dirt and pebbles and small stones, there was a forested border around it, as if a wall to conceal itself from the outside World. The Forest-Ring. Perhaps that was why Garathen—unless one knew where it was—seldom saw any visitors? Compared to the larger towns and cities, anyway. This left the little girl in a quandary and she was unsure as to where to start looking for her grandfather. Since her grandfather spoke her native language, she'd forgotten the people of Garathen spoke only the Common-tongue, and had assumed that by coming into the city she would be able to find someone and tell them what her grandfather looked like then have that person lead her to him.

Reluctantly accepting the language barrier she now faced, she was scared she would never find her grandfather. She certainly couldn't conduct a search for him on her own. If she tried to search the forest by herself, she would end up doing a fifty-mile search in a circle. Adding to the fact that she was young and could only somewhat fend for herself, the forest was no place for a small child. The forest was where the beasts and the more predatory animals lived, and though these animals and creatures were nocturnal by nature, they would not give a second thought to snaring and killing anyone who accidentally stepped through their nests or dens simply because the person did not know any better. There were not any forests in Grek; she wouldn't know how to care for herself in the wild. All her survival skills were imitations of how she lived her life at home. She knew the basics—shelter, food, water, rest—and as long as she obtained those things, she should be all right.

But she needed her grandfather. There was trouble back home. Big trouble. And her grandfather could help her. He had to. He was family and family always helped each other.

—

The girl glanced up at Peter. He offered her a piece of his bread-bowl, with a couple of strawberries on top of it. She took it, ate it, and smiled big with bread and strawberry seed stuck in her teeth. Peter let out a chuckle. He would take her someplace special.

Perhaps there he could learn more about her and why she was here in the Broken City.

CHAPTER IV
Up on the Hill
(Pretty)

The layout of Garathen and its surrounding area was rather simple. The city was small, only a dozen or so streets and lanes which crisscrossed each other in a grid, creating a square, the bordering trees and rocky slopes forming a natural wall that separated it from the outside World.

Peter and the girl were at the end of his street. Up ahead was a stony slope littered with a few trees and bushes. The slope extended twenty or so paces upward until it plateaued before sloping down to the forest on the other side.

Peter held the humanette's hand, helping her maintain her balance on the rocky slope as they walked up the hill. He saw that her loaf of bread had been eaten, which was a disappointment because he had wanted to take her up to the top to finish their breakfast in a sort of picnic. Since he was not finished with his own breakfast, he decided he would offer her some of his bread-bowl and fruit once they were part way to the top. There was a small level of land there, where he would sometimes come to sit and look down onto the city, spending time with his thoughts. He also went there to write poetry or paint. One of his paintings had been a panoramic scene of Garathen, done with oils and flowered with color around the sky and the surrounding trees. The rest—namely the streets and huts of the city—had been done in browns and grays to depict the people's sympathy for the poorer folk and for each other. It had been traded for a fine, maroon wool quilt and towel set.

The girl slipped and fell to her knees.

"Are you okay?" asked Peter.

She got up quickly and brushed the dusty gravel off her legs and resumed her stride as if nothing happened.

"Here, let me take a look at you," said Peter, stopping her. He checked her over, his eyes stopping at the red skin on her right knee. "We'll have to clean that up when we get back. Are you sure you're all right?"

She smiled and they kept going. He'd always thought of children as frail things, who would cry and complain about injury. But not this girl. Her eye was swollen and, no doubt, always aching. There was that cut on her head from the night before, surely stinging right now as the wound entered the first stages of healing. And now her knee had been scraped. But the little one was not crying; she did not complain. She just kept on living, kept on going. Perhaps he had underestimated the quiet strength of a child. And perhaps this little humanette could teach him something about those much younger than him. Peter was twenty-four years old, and though he had experienced a lot in his lifetime, he still had a lot to learn. Living in the Broken City did that to a person. Being such a sheltered place, not much news of the outside World penetrated the Forest-Ring, and the news that did come through usually caused a bout of surprise amongst its inhabitants, and unfortunately, most of the news wasn't completely reliable. The words had passed through too many ears and out too many mouths to be of great worth.

Leading her by the hand, Peter led the girl round a slight curve in the path they followed.

Peter stopped when they reached a small plateau that was about four feet squared, just off the curved path.

"Here we are," he said.

The humanette looked out onto the city below them, its grid-like patterns of brown streets looking almost like a perfect square from where she stood. The sun was settling in high above them in a rich blue sky. There were a few sharp white clouds in the sky, but nothing that would indicate rain. Her young eyes took in the wonderful sight. Peter could picture her heart singing at the circle of the deep green treetops that bordered the city, and the lighter green of the taller bushes that rimmed its bottom.

"What do you think?" asked Peter.

She pointed out to the city.

"Promno bel tino," she said.

The lilt in her little voice made it sound she liked what she saw.

"Yes, it is pretty," he said.

She suddenly began to cry.

What happened? he thought.

"What?" he said. "Don't you think it's pretty?"

She cried harder, tearing her hand away from him, turning herself away.

She stomped her heels and turned back toward the path.

"Where are you going?" asked Peter, making his way toward her, careful not to drop his bread-bowl.

Her pace quickened. He stopped her and got down on one knee. "Som Catina, what's wrong?"

She tried maneuvering around him. He put a hand to her waist, stopping her.

"Did I say something wrong?"

The tears leaking from her eyes broke his heart. Privately, he went over what he said, thinking of anything that might have come out wrong. There had been nothing.

"I only said that it was pretty," he said. "And—" She started screaming, using her small hands to push his hand away. He caught her hands in an effort to still her and dropped the bread-bowl on the gravel. "Look, it's okay. I'm not going to hurt you. I didn't mean anything by what I said or whatever it was I said that upset you."

Her crying eased some. He thought for a moment. "Okay. I'll be careful what I say." But that was a lie. He couldn't be careful of what he said because he didn't know *what* it was he said that hurt her. Then he got an idea. It may upset the humanette, but it would be the only way for him to avoid causing her to cry again. He wanted to help her but knew that he wouldn't be able to if he kept accidentally saying something that would force tears to her pretty blue eyes.

"I'm going to say some words one at a time," he said, "and I'm . . . . I don't want to make you cry, but I have to see what my mistake was, okay?" He paused. Her crying abated to sniveling. She wiped her healthy eye with the palm of her hand. "Okay. Um, what did I say, now? Okay. Here we . . . . All right." And then he listed off his words, as much as he could remember before she started crying: "Think, yes, uh, is, um, pretty—" And at that last word she started crying again. "Is it 'pretty'?" asked Peter. He cries told him that it was. "Okay, okay. Shhh, it's all right." He put a calming hand on her shoulder. "I'm sorry. I won't say that word anymore. I promise." He tucked his hand in his sleeve— "Here" —and gently dabbed at the tears under her good eye. "Shhh, it's okay, now. I understand what I did wrong." He supposed he did, anyway. For whatever reason, the word "pretty" bothered the humanette. He would be careful not to say it again.

After a time and after assuring her he wouldn't say that word again, Peter convinced her to sit with him on the small clearing part way up the hill. She reluctantly went along with him. Peter didn't say much; he was too afraid to say anything else that would cause her to cry. He would have to take the girl to see Alan the Traveler right away. If anyone in the city could help Peter find out where the girl came from, it would be Alan. His knowledge of what happened outside the Forest-Ring was great and, as far as Peter knew, better than anyone else's who had ventured out into the World.

When the humanette calmed down and any trust that Peter lost from her had been restored, they would go see Alan.

The humanette wiped her eyes, wincing as her small hand brushed along her sore eye. She looked out onto the city. Moments earlier her heart had been jubilant with the hope that the man she was with could help her. Now that hope had diminished because, though she didn't understand anything Peter had spoken to her thus far, she did understand that horrible word—"pretty." She had heard that word spoken a lot over the past several weeks as she traveled. It seemed that almost everyone who laid eyes on her would say that word and if they didn't, she knew they were thinking it. She didn't understand the word was a compliment, an expression that said she was beautiful.

To her, that word meant terror.

Over two hundred miles West of the Broken City was where she had heard the word "pretty" for the first time. Her memories of the moments leading up to that event were quite clear. She recalled spending the morning walking on a winding dirt road after passing through Wesafeld, a city plenty different than Garathen—much hotter and filled with three times as many markets—when, somewhere off behind her, she heard the clamoring of hooves against soil. She stepped over to the side of the road and turned around to see a pair of horses trotting toward her; behind them a heavyset man with deeply tanned skin, sitting atop a wagon. He pulled the horses to a stop when he caught sight of her.

"Hallo, there, little lady," the man had said. "You seem to be a ways off from Wesafeld. Why are you out here all alone?"

She didn't reply. He was speaking the Common-tongue.

"Not much of a talker, I see," he said. "Whatsa matter? Lose your tongue?" She didn't respond. "Not much of a joker, either," he added to himself. "No matter. Let me try this: danna menne com bela?" *Do you understand this?*

Her eyes lit up. She understood him! Thank the Master!

The man chuckled and in her Native-tongue said, "Good thing I am on the road a lot. In my line of work, I meet people of all kinds. You come from Grek, I see. At least, it is only there that the Rolling-tongue is spoken. Mostly. But enough yimmer-yammer. Which way are you headed?"

She pointed Eastward down the road.

"Well, then, time is wasting. Better hop on board before the afternoon sun hits. You will cook out here."

He got down from his wagon, picked her up and plopped her in the seat beside his. "I am going that way myself," he added, "and I would be honored to give a princess a ride."

She giggled at his calling her a 'princess.' Only her step-father called her that and each time she heard it, it made her feel extra special. The man got back on the wagon and, whistling to his horses and clicking his tongue, they were off.

She fell asleep beside him after a few miles, the weariness from her long journey and the fatigue—first starting in her legs but soon spreading throughout her entire body—fully taking her. It was fitful rest, but the best rest one can have while sitting upright. Head drooping, she leaned over and rested it against the man's shoulder, a habit she had when falling asleep while sitting beside her mother.

She awoke whenever there was a large bump in the road. Her eyes would open and, remembering where she was, she would drift back into sleep.

The evening air settled around them, the wind picking up, delivering a swift chill. The man pulled the wagon over to the side of the road and stopped the horses. It wasn't time to stop for the night just yet. She awoke with a start when the man tucked a blanket in around her. She squealed and backed away.

"Gana?" she asked hesitantly. *Yes?*

His eyes were blank, any semblance of freewill gone from his gaze. She shrieked again and scrambled off the wagon, landing hard on the dirt before running frantically down the road. The man immediately tore after her, shouting for her to come back. Her body, still sluggish from sleep, didn't move as quickly as she would have liked. Still, she maintained a goodly speed, powered mostly by adrenaline. She heard his footsteps behind, charging after her. It wasn't long before he caught up with her and wrestled her to the ground. She screamed loud enough so anyone in earshot would hear her. But no one was around. Not at this hour as most supply wagons were usually off the roads before evening struck. The only ones that would be traveling this late would be those who had a deadline to meet or an appointment with a customer.

He straddled her tiny body.

On her back, terrified, she struggled with every last ounce of strength, her little fists trying to strike the man, ward him off—something! With each effort to resist him, the more his assault increased and the further away any chance of escape seemed. She screamed again; he covered her mouth.

"Shh," he hushed. And in her tongue said, "I do not want to hurt you. I just want you to know how special you are. Please do not fight me. You have to trust me." His words seemed far off, as if spoken by another, and they chilled her to the bone. This man, this kind man that had been so nice to offer a ride, was about to do something so despicable, so abhorrent—how could he try and explain that it was in her best interest for her to participate? Try to tell her that she was special and that she could feel how special she was if she would just let him have his way with her?

Confusion set in. He was an elder and seemed to genuinely want to do a great kindness for her. But she also knew if she obeyed him, something terrible would happen.

"Rana Ko!" she shouted. *No!* She struggled some more; he hit her. The shock from his blow dazed her and sent stars flying across her vision.

"Rana Ko," she said, this time more small, weak. "Rana Ko . . . "

If she were asked moments later what happened, she would not be able to give an answer. Her mind had given into the confusion of the moment and, hours later, when the event played over in her mind, she could remember only the glimmer of silver.

The silver . . . . The polished blade of his knife that rocked slightly out of its sheath and then clacked back into place in its holder as he fought with her. She knew what damage a knife could do. She had seen her step-father come home and skin the day's hunt with one or fillet the day's catch. She had never considered using a knife on another Human. She wouldn't even use it on an animal even after it was dead or when her step-father would ask her to aid him in an animal's skinning and cleaning of its hide. But she considered the option of using it right then. It was either that or be a part of what this man had in mind for her.

Hoping that it would not come to that, she gave one last valiant struggle against his hold, squirming and twisting, trying to get out from under him.

It was no use. He was too strong.

Desperate, she grabbed the knife by its smooth, oak handle and pulled it out of its sheath. Swiftly, she drove it home into the man's side, just below his ribs.

His eyes widened, seeming to snap out of his daze. He was too shocked to say anything save for choking gasps. He slouched back on his haunches then fell over on to his behind. He sat there, legs spread out in front of him, his hand holding the knife handle that protruded from his left side. The girl scrambled to her feet and stepped away from him.

In an image that she would remember vividly a day later and then for the rest of her life, the man reached his free hand out to her, pleading with her to help him. Tears blurred her vision. Taking one last look at him, she ran down the road, eyes fixed forward.

An hour later, four miles away, she collapsed on the side of the road and wept. She awoke at dawn, the sun shining brightly over the horizon. Her mind torn, confused, her head aching from the tearshed and dark thoughts and terrible dreams, the little girl continued making her way toward Garathen.

The man—her attacker—was behind her and she did not care to remember him. He would only come to her as a phantom memory of a terrible event, a memory that she wasn't sure actually happened or if it was a figment of her imagination.

Peter looked at her kindly, the gaze in his eyes shaking her from her reflection.

Eyes. Healthy ones. Her left eye was healthy once. Not long ago, as a matter of fact. But about a week or so into her trek East, her eye started to bother her. It grew sore at first, achy and tender. Gradually, over a matter of days, it swelled shut. She became frightened. Nothing like this had ever happened to her before. Occasionally, she also got headaches, the pain centered behind her left eye for the most part. She attributed the bouts of pain to her exhaustive journey. She dismissed the headaches. Her eye worried her, though. She couldn't wait to see her grandfather. He'd know how to help her. Casting her needs aside, she remembered she was here with a much greater purpose. She would gladly bear a lifetime of a swollen eye if it meant that those back home would be helped.

It had been a long journey, but she was capable. Life was much different in her home city of Grek than in Garathen. In Garathen, children led sheltered lives, most often kept indoors while the parents contributed to the livelihood of the family. In Grek, it was almost the opposite. The parents worked hard and so did the children.

Since the age of four, the girl awoke to the rooster's crow. Sleepily, she'd make her way to her parents' bedroom to wake them. It was part of her routine, a set of responsibilities to help form her into the well-rounded, responsible woman she would one day become. The mentality in the household, as it was with most homes in Grek, was to prepare the children to be able to fend for themselves should something happen to the parents. Of course, the children were not aware of this; the thought of losing their parents to one thing or another not only scared them but also induced a state of thought that was too heavy for their young minds.

Through day-to-day observations of running the household and the tasks that needed tending to—like helping her mother cook over the fire in the hearth or carrying horseshoes for her father across their small farm, or brushing the coarse hair off their horse, Lamara. The girl soon learned the value of an honest day's work. Such discipline also formed in her a sense of duty and a mindset that something always needed to be done. This wasn't entirely a bad thing, though rest was frowned upon in Grek.

Part of that ideology pushed her along when she was too tired to go on as she made her way to Garathen. She was going to the Broken City for a reason and she was determined not to rest until that reason was tended to. Her journey taught her a patience that was quite mature for a six-year-old to have. Most children wanted things now, now, now. The humanette wasn't like most children and could wait for days on end for something should it serve her purpose. Besides, her mother told her the ability to wait was a valued thing and that it was selfish to demand something be given to you in an instant.

A cool breeze swept by. She shivered as the wind brushed against her skin. The sun's warmth was barely felt. Peter had hoped to somehow talk to the girl once he had her up here on the hill. He hoped that by her seeing such a great sight it would stir something within her and cause her to speak to him. But that wasn't the case and she remained silent.

After sitting for a time, Peter decided they head back down the hill and go see Alan the Traveler. If anybody could discern where the little one came from, Alan could. Though Alan was somewhat of a recluse, he was also easily accessible when it came to important matters. He had helped Peter last year in crafting a poem, etched in fine wood, which looked like it had been imported from the South. The importance of creating such a thing was found in what it was used for: the purchasing of some supplies for his veranda.

The girl heaved a sigh.

"Just about ready to go?" asked Peter as he turned toward her.

Her attention went back down to the city. Peter took that as a yes.

"Then let's go," he said. "We've got much to do today so we best be off." Then, as if in after-thought, "But it was a good thing to come up here, wasn't it?"

Peter, though he hid it from the girl, was still shaky from the night before. His hands still held the phantom sensations of what it was like to pummel that Slummer. He remembered the fear he felt of going up against her, but also the thrill of knowing he could overpower her, as well. He was not a violent man and, had only been in two other fights his entire life, both of them having been during his youth over matters long forgotten. He had never faced a Slummer before, never mind having to hold his own against one. His thoughts were scattered at the time, his only thought that of the child's safety. Looking back on it, he was glad he had beaten the Slummer. Perhaps the Unfortunate would go and tell her other Unfortunate friends what happened when they troubled one of the Dayfolk. Maybe from here on in Slummers wouldn't stir trouble in the night. No. Slummers were not only angry in nature, but also stubborn. Changing his position, Peter sincerely hoped the Slummer would not tell any of her kin about what happened. Peter shuddered at the consequences should the Slummer come after him. Knowing its ways, it would return with a pack of others and not rest until he and the little one—if she was still with him at the time—were killed.

The two Slummers in his veranda. They must be tied to the one he'd beaten. He didn't know if they'd come back again. He prayed to the Master they wouldn't.

He decided he would hide his fear for the girl's sake. She was seeking refuge in him and he didn't want to show any sign of weakness. He wanted her to feel comfortable in his presence, something that assured her all would be well.

They stood and brushed their behinds, dispelling the gravely dust. Peter took her by the hand and led her back to the main path.

They descended, heading back toward his place.

CHAPTER V
The Blind Man and Catina

The walk home, though a fairly short distance, gave Peter time to think. Having the girl with him gave him a sense of purpose, something to do. Prior to her arrival, most of his days were kept to himself, staying inside after the morning trading and doing the things he enjoyed: writing his poetry, painting his pictures, building little odds and ends that made his day to day living easier. In the early evening he would usually go for a walk if the weather was nice. He didn't have many friends his own age. Most he knew were older than him. He would visit at least one of his neighbors once a week, going over to their homes for dinner, or would have one of them over to his place for the same. All in all, it was a simple existence, but not a fulfilling one. He longed for something to come along and make it interesting, something to give him a reason for why he was alive. He wasn't a believer in destiny or fate; such radical thoughts were seldom contemplated. The common belief in Garathen was that everyone was created to serve each other and aid each other every day. The thought or feeling that there may be more to life was rarely considered. But, being as human as the next person, Peter sometimes found himself sitting on his front step or on his rocking chair in his veranda, questioning why he was alive and what he could do with his life that would count for something. They were common thoughts, but important ones nonetheless.

The little girl gave him a chance to consider those things again. Perhaps there was a reason for why he was with her now? Perhaps this was his chance to find his place in life. The notion thrilled him.

They didn't talk on the way back to his place. He'd given up on saying anything to her as he knew she wouldn't understand. This was a challenge, his helping her without words or reassurances that he *was* helping her, but he welcomed it. The challenge made this task all the more inspiring. If he succeeded in helping the girl then that would mean he could succeed in other things. Maybe even bigger things.

When they returned to his place, he brought her inside and retrieved the medicine box again and cleaned the scrape on her knee, dressing it in another bandage. Then they were off again to see Alan.

Alan lived on the other side of the main Through-way, past the Baker, at the opposite end of the long street. Sure, it would have been much quicker if that morning Peter had taken the girl directly there after getting breakfast, but he had wanted to do something nice for her. It was a successful effort, too, he thought, since he was sure that by the way the girl's eyes had grown so wide when looking out onto the city, she had never seen such a grand sight like it before. Peter was pleased with himself for that and was also pleased that the girl, seeming worn thin from the toll of whatever it was she had gone through prior to coming here, appeared happy he had taken her up the hill and had given her something to eat.

People looked on as they walked down the Through-way, most stopping what they were doing to get a second look at the young girl in the colorful dress.

Without warning, someone grabbed the girl by the arm, pulling her to the side. It was an old woman, someone Peter recognized as being the lady who ran the tailor-stand a few stalls down from the Baker's. He couldn't remember her name. He had only met her once despite how small Garathen was.

"Mind if I have a look at you?" she said to the girl. "My, what a fine dress you have on, little one." She examined the flowery fabric. "Where did you get such beautiful material? Surely not from around here. You know" —she leaned in close— "you shouldn't be wearing this around here. You're bound to get yourself lynched if you do. It's not right to put yourself above others and parade around in something most only dream they had."

"If you don't mind," cut in Peter, "she's not from around here. She doesn't know how things are done. Please excuse us. We're in a rush." Peter pulled the girl by the hand and started walking away from the old woman. The woman pulled the girl by the arm. The girl stopped walking again. The little humanette was clearly uncomfortable.

The woman said quietly, "But I wouldn't mind if I could perhaps borrow some of this material to make me a pretty purse. My, wouldn't the other ladies just be jealous." She snickered to herself.

The girl started to whimper. Peter caught on immediately. The old woman had said the word "pretty" again.

Quickly, he bent down and scooped the girl up in his arms.

"Where are you going?" asked the woman. "I just want to talk to her."

"Not today," said Peter as he took the girl away.

The old woman sneered at him and stormed off in a huff.

Once they were about twenty feet away, Peter said, "Sorry about that. People here don't understand that you're not from around here. They rarely see any outsiders . . . at least not more, um, colorful ones. They don't know any better." The girl's whimpering eased some. Peter smiled. "Don't worry. We'll go get some help now, okay?"

She grinned back.

"Okay," he said.

They continued walking toward Alan's.

Alan lived in an outwardly small, though inwardly spacious, hut at the end of the Through-way. His home was at the bottom of a slope on the other side of the city, jutting out so that only a small portion of the hut's front was publicly seen, the rest having been built into a hollowed-out section of the rocky slope itself.

Peter approached the hut with care, the girl following a step behind.

"Haven't been here in awhile," he said, "but no matter. Alan's a nice enough guy. Strange. But nice."

The girl glanced around at her surroundings and a smile lit her face. She hopped up and down on her toes. Peter got the feeling she knew something he didn't.

Alan's door, a thick slab of oak weathered from age, seemed somehow menacing, as if it kept back something life altering. Peter knocked on it twice, the pulse of the knock echoing in his knuckles. His efforts only produced a soft *cluck-cluck* sound. After a moment and when no answer came, he tried again with the side of his fist, putting more force into his blow. The *cluck-cluck* became a deep *thunk-ka-thunk*.

When it appeared no one was going to answer, Peter took the girl by the hand, about to lead her away.

The door opened.

Alan poked his head out between door and doorframe, his face, mostly shadow, was white against a black background.

"Yes?" asked Alan.

"Alan, it's Peter."

"Peter?" Alan made a face.

"You helped me with a wood carving last year, the one with the poem." Peter took a step forward so that hopefully Alan would get a better look at him.

"Poem?"

"Yes, a poem. I used it to trade for supplies to build my veranda. Don't you recall?"

Alan considered the question a moment and with a shake of his head said, "No," and slammed the door shut, the oak crashing against the stone doorframe.

Peter frowned. So did the girl.

"This is going well," he said, smirking.

The girl crossed her arms.

Peter rapped on the door again. It swung wide open, Alan's thin form coming into full view.

"Blast it all!" he shouted. "I told you I do not know you. Why are you bothering me?"

Peter and the girl took a step back. He guided her behind him with his hand.

Alan stood there, not as the man Peter remembered. He was much skinnier, that was for sure, his gray shirt and black trousers hanging off him like rags on a doornail. His face and hands were very pale. His head was cleanly shaven, where as Peter was expecting a full head of dark blonde hair, as that's what Alan had the year prior. But what struck him the most was Alan's eyes. Though Peter could not recall their original color, they certainly had not been what they were now: white.

Alan was blind.

The girl squealed in delight and ran up to Alan, wrapping her small arms around his legs.

"What is the meaning of this?" he protested.

"Umall cale menne," the girl said.

"What is that? Catina, is that you?"

"Fen som teeka, Catina" she said.

The two of them knew each other?

Suddenly Catina launched into a long slur of words that Peter could not understand. Judging by the expression on Alan's face, Peter knew she was speaking too quickly for him to understand her, either.

"Nu lagnagi," Alan said to her. He then turned his eyes toward Peter but, due to his blindness, looked to somewhere past him. "How do you know my *Shinali*, my granddaughter? I am her *Shinawa*, which means 'grandfather.' You are?"

"Actually, I don't know her," said Peter. "Alan, are you all right? It's me, Peter. We spent a short while together last year. Surely you must remember me."

"Peter, hmm? Peter, Peter, Peter, Peter . . . " His eyes lit up. "Ah, yes, now I recall. Silly me. So sorry. I tend to forget certain things. Not all things, mind you, but certain things. Ah, blast, I guess that is why I am human. As are you, if I remember correctly."

"As human as they come," said Peter. "And as human as you are, too."

"Well, I do not quite consider myself human now," said Alan. "In case you have not noticed, I am blind."

Peter didn't say that he had noticed. He thought it would be rude if he had.

Catina started going on again in her own tongue about something that Alan now appeared to understand. He said something to her, presumably to wait a moment, judging by the look on his face. She scowled. Alan scooped her up in his arms and focused his attention back on Peter. "What strikes me the most, dear Peter, is how you know my little Catina, here."

"As said, I don't know her, well, at least I hadn't until last night."

Alan arched an eyebrow.

"What I mean is," Peter went on, "I met her last night. She came wandering into Garathen and had almost gotten herself killed by a Slummer. I managed to help her and we got away."

"Is that right? Well, I suppose I am indebted to you. And I am sorry for not recognizing your name earlier. Since I have been blind, I have spent a lot of time alone. A lot of things escape me. Anyway, why not come in and fill me in as to how you came across my *Shinali.* Also, I want to find out from her how in the World she had gotten herself all the way out here. Grek is a long way off. Tell me, is her family with her? It would only be a set of parents. Catina is an only child."

"It's just her, as far as I know," said Peter.

"I see. Well, come on in. We have much to discuss." And with that, Alan held the door open for them and they went in.

The interior of Alan's home was . . . different. Most of the homes in Garathen had a similar layout: square, with a main living quarters toward the front of the abode with a kitchen and a bathing room toward the back. Alan's place looked to be something of his own design. The front door opened onto a circular living area about fifteen feet in diameter. Running off from this circle were three rooms: his private chamber, the kitchen, and the bathing room.

In the center of the living area was a hearth with a small fire crackling in it, and above the hearth was a metal cylinder that presumably led to the outside to let the smoke escape. However, this puzzled Peter as he hadn't seen any smoke rising from the home when they approached. He assumed that the smoke must have been channeled via hidden pipes further out into the forest somewhere higher up on the hill before being released. That would be why he hadn't seen it.

Immediately upon entering, Catina pulled Alan by the hand and led him into the kitchen, leaving Peter alone in the room. Since he didn't know Alan all that well, he didn't make himself at home and instead stood there a few paces from the hearth, as though a statue. In the next room he could hear Catina speaking to Alan in the language he didn't understand but had come to recognize as Catina's (and apparently Alan's) Native-tongue.

It was a remarkable coincidence that Alan was Catina's grandfather. Who would have known that a strange little girl with a colorful dress who had a run-in with a Slummer was the granddaughter of Garathen's most-talked-about recluse? For a brief moment, Peter felt something waver inside of him. He had drawn a sense of purpose out of helping the little girl and now that satisfying feeling was abating . . . partly. It was still there but . . . smaller. His time to be involved in the lives of Catina and Alan was not over. He didn't know how he knew this but such knowledge was usually based on premonition and not hard fact.

He took in his surroundings. Sitting before the hearth was a large black chair with a wooden frame, cow skin draped over it, making a comfy seat. Along the back wall between the kitchen on the right and bathing room on the left, was a bookshelf. Peter admired Alan for having what appeared to be over twenty, leather-bound volumes of text. Peter had only one book and, over the course of the three years since he got it, had been content with reading that one story since he could not afford any more books. At least, for the time being.

On the wall between the kitchen and front door were a few shelving units filled with odds and ends, and basic supplies for living, like jars of fruits and vegetables, some rope, some tools. He did notice, however, that on the lowest of these shelves was a stack of paper. A corner of one of the papers peaked out from under its kin. It was a map. Peter assumed the rest of the pages were maps as well. Beside the shelf was a table with short legs, with clothes neatly folded on it; only a few outfits as the people in the Broken City usually wore the same clothes for days at a time.

On the wall that ran from the bathing room to Alan's private chamber was a couple of stools and another table. Against the other wall that ran from his chamber to the front door was a well-painted map of the entire World, with certain key areas highlighted with blue ink. Peter assumed those markings depicted where Alan had traveled. Beneath the map, mounted on nail-hooks in the wall, were mementos from Alan's journeys and things of such foreign culture that Peter could hardly recognize what purpose each served.

Peter heard Catina go on and on about something, her lilty voice rolling off her tongue in a speech more fluent than the Common-tongue. Now and then Alan would interrupt and, it seemed, pose a question or two. For no reason, Peter suddenly thought of how easily Alan moved about despite the fact that he was blind. Peter could only recall having seen two other blind people in Garathen and those two used a staff to navigate their way around town and avoid bumping into things.

It was awhile before Alan, grave-faced, emerged with Catina from out of the kitchen.

"Is everything all right?" asked Peter.

Alan hadn't heard him; he seemed deep in thought. Peter didn't repeat the question.

Catina came up to Peter and took his right hand in hers. She held his hand palm-up and with her index finger drew a small circle on the inside of his palm. "Mali kwon nali," she said. *Thank you.*

Peter recognized the phrase. "Alan?" he said. Alan looked up. "How do you say 'You're welcome' in, um, whatever language you were speaking to her in?"

"The language is called Grescalla, which is the Native-tongue of the city of Grek West of here, where Catina is from. 'You are welcome' is said '*Dana kwon nali.*'"

Peter looked warmly on the girl. "Dana kwon nali, Catina."

She giggled at his effort at speaking her language. Her laugh . . . . It was a good feeling, a sense that the gap that separated them was closing.

Alan felt for his chair, found it and sat down, and crossed his legs. He heaved a sigh and placed his thumb and forefingers over his temples. Peter lifted Catina in his arms. She placed her hand on his neck and held him tight. He went over to Alan.

"Is everything all right?" asked Peter. "I hope I'm not troubling you by being here."

"No, no," said Alan, "not at all. You brought my little Catina to me. It is just that—" He stirred himself from what seemed a painful thought. "I am sorry. Please, grab yourself a stool from over there and have a seat. We have plenty to talk about, you and I."

Peter set the girl down and retrieved two stools from against the wall by the bathing room and set one on either side of Alan.

He sat down and instead of sitting in her seat, Catina climbed on to his lap.

"Is this all right?" asked Peter at Catina's affection for him.

"You ask too many questions, Peter," said Alan. "Yes, it is all right. She likes you and is thankful that you helped her find me. I am glad you did, too. She has just brought me the gravest of news. Grek . . . Grek is under a terrible plague. Catina said she left just after it began to surface. She saw the sickness sweep through her community. Worse, she saw it taking its toll on her parents. She said she did not know what to do and so sought me out. It is remarkable that she is alive. But she, too, is ill. At least, I think so. As you know, I am now blind. I felt her face to get a picture in my mind as to what she looks like since . . . . It has been so long since I last saw her. Her eye is swollen and it does not feel like a mere swelling from, say, taking a blow to the eye. She says that she feels fine, but who knows? I just wish I knew more. And there is that bandage on her head, too. How did she get it?"

Before Peter could answer, Alan turned away.

Catina, appearing tired, still watched her grandfather speak, with interest.

"I think it is best that you tell me how you met Catina, Peter, and then I can tell you what I know. Perhaps then we can form a more coherent picture," said Alan.

"You're going to hate me for asking this but I will anyway. Do you mind me getting involved? You don't really know me, Alan. We only spent a short time together last year, and—"

"Yes, yes. All is fine, Peter. Stop asking so many questions. I am calling on your help because I think you can truly help me. If you do not think you are capable, then please just tell me your tale and be off. Otherwise, sit tight, and do not be afraid to get involved." Alan waited a moment, making sure that Peter understood. "Now," he continued, "tell me what you know."

Peter adjusted himself in his chair and, making sure Catina was comfortable, recounted to Alan all that had happened since last night. He relayed the story of seeing Catina coming into the Broken City and the fear he felt for her for being alone in the night. With hesitation, he told the story of the Slummer and how he caught up with Catina afterwards. There was the night at his place and how he dressed the cut on Catina's head. Peter took extra care to assure Alan that he treated his granddaughter with respect and let her sleep. Though his saying so wasn't necessary, it was good to see Alan's posture settle when he heard that Catina was safe and that the man that had saved her hadn't tried anything . . . wrong. Such acts were not unheard of in Garathen, especially in the dead of night behind closed doors where no one would see the goings on. Peter told of their bread bowls from the Baker and of their short picnic on the hill. He said Catina had fallen while climbing and that he tidied up her wound as best he could. And that brought them up to the Present in Alan's home.

"I see," said Alan.

They sat for a time in silence, each waiting for the other to say something. Alan spoke first. "You shared something, now I suppose it is my turn. I want to thank you, sincerely, for bringing Catina to me. I know you did not know she was my granddaughter but, regardless, you have gained favor with me because of it."

"Thank you," said Peter.

Alan waited a moment then changed the subject: "Catina is the daughter of my late son from his second marriage."

"I'm sorry," said Peter.

"Not to worry. It has been some time since he has been gone. Catina was only two years of age when it happened. One day, he was kicked by a horse while replacing one of its shoes. The horse saw something that spooked it and got all in a frenzy and . . . well, that was it. Things that we do not have control over happen. No one could have stopped the horse from getting scared. There was no warning."

Peter wondered if Catina would ever remember her father when she was older. Sometimes children forgot their father's face or their mother's touch or both, if the parents died while the child was very young. Peter knew because he was very young when his parents died and he began living with his Aunt Silvi. He couldn't remember what his parents looked like or even how old he was when it happened. The thought pained him.

Alan went on. "Catina's mother remarried and now lives with her and her step-father in Grek. A nice fellow, if I recall, though I only had met him once. His name's Michel." He leaned a little closer and whispered, "I needed to know if the little one, here, would be raised in a proper home or not. Often in a remarriage the second father is not like the first and whether that bodes ill or not is unknown at the time. Only the passage of time tells that one." He waited a moment before adding meekly, "I had to look in on them."

Peter wouldn't know. He didn't know his parents. Aunt Silvi raised him until she died one winter four years ago from an unknown illness that could not be cured. He then began living on his own, first as a carpenter, trading his skills for what he needed. It wasn't until one summer when he had been walking home that he began to think about things differently, almost lyrically, his thoughts coming together in *verses* instead of just more jagged ideas and choppy notions. He went home and wrote them down and, after showing a neighbor or two, decided that perhaps he could trade some of his writing for his wares instead of working outside all day in the hot sun, building things for people. He had been the city's poet ever since and, fortunately, Jar Totelum who lived one street over became the city's carpenter instead. Peter's affection for painting had surfaced about a year later when, one day, he had run out of things to say and had given painting a try. He found that he could do that, too, and combined his poetic and artistic talents together, making his skills all the more valuable. The people in the Broken City had a work-oriented mindset—even more so than in Grek—and there was little room in their thoughts for expression and creativity. There were others who were talented with their writing as well. There were storytellers and other rhymers, but the people took more kindly to Peter's work. There were other painters, too, so Peter did have some competition, but there were those that preferred his work above the others'.

Peter thought of Catina. She looked adorable sitting in his lap. He yearned to have children of his own one day. "This is serious business, isn't it?" he said. "Her coming here?"

"It is," said Alan. "Do not think I am taking it lightly. But what I have learned is that one needs to pace themselves when approaching a . . . problem. More often than not we immediately try to remedy it without knowing *how* we will fix it. I am thinking right now as to what we should do. I am still surprised she is here."

Peter watched Alan's blank eyes stare straight ahead.

"I know you are looking at me, Peter," said Alan. "Please do not."

"How—"

"Since I have been blind, my other senses have grown sharper, keener. It is no different than when you know someone is watching you when you sleep. You can somehow *feel* it." He paused and licked his lips. "If you would like to know, a pair of Slummers took my eyes."

"Slummers?" Peter was taken aback. He thought people rarely had encounters with Slummers.

"Yes, Slummers. I had come home from one of my trips one evening last year; it was quite late and almost like ghosts, they just appeared behind me and tried taking the bag I was carrying. I fought back and one of them spun me around. When I resisted and turned back to face him, there was a hot pain in my eyes. I had been stabbed." He pointed to his eyes with his first two fingers. "They left me there on the road, probably hoping I would bleed to death. But not me. I hobbled to our local—now what is that word . . . Helper?—and he . . . helped . . . me before I lost too much blood. He said I was fortunate the blades had not penetrated any further otherwise they would have punctured my brain."

"If I may ask . . . why are your eyes—"

"White?"

"Yes."

"My own doing . . . sort of. The Helper had given me something for the pain but warned that, though the herb focused on the wounded area, the side effect of it was it also bleached that area. Almost a literal erasure of what was once there. An anomaly of nature, perhaps." He smirked. "Does that answer your question?"

"Yes, I suppose it does."

"Good. Now let us put it to rest." Then, "And do not stare at me. I am sure my eyes are wonderful to look at but it bothers me greatly. I will know, Peter, if you do."

"Sorry," he said. It was suddenly uncomfortable in the little room.

"It is okay." Alan folded his hands. "But we should really get to the issue at hand—Catina."

Catina's head perked up at the mention of her name.

Alan continued. "She is here. You are here. And I am here. The question is, where do we go from here? She has come a long way, the little one."

"I'd still like to know how she got all the way over to Garathen," said Peter. "That is, if that's all right with you."

"Of course it is. Why would it not be? You are involved in this whether you want to be or not. Once my family affairs have been fallen into, those involved must stay involved." He looked warmly on his granddaughter. "Catina has only told me bits and pieces, there in the kitchen. But I, too, would like to know the whole story. I am glad she is safe and it is a miracle that she made it all this way on her own." He turned to Catina and said something in Grescalla.

"She will tell and I will translate," said Alan.

Catina's brow furrowed as she called up the memory. So much had happened since she left Grek that all her memories flooded back to her at once. She focused herself, and recalled the morning she awoke to do her chores and went to wake her parents. She remembered the awful smell of their room; the smell of sleep but mixed with something far worse, something like the stench of rotting fish. She started her tale from there.

She said the first thing she noticed was her parents' breathing and how it sounded more labored, as if they were *trying* to breathe instead of just simple inhales and exhales. When she woke them they said they were both ill, but had gotten up anyway. The day began as usual, Catina's mother, Dara, shooing Catina off to do her chores while she and her husband, Michel, got themselves dressed for theirs. After Catina tended to the chickens and cows, Dara tutored her in reading and writing, just like every other morning, with the afternoon spent preparing dinner and other baking. A different meal or variations of a meal were made almost everyday so that one day, when she was older, Catina would know how to cook more than just one meal for her husband. Her step-father came home after working in the fields and they sat down to dinner. Catina had asked if her parents' headaches had gone. They said they felt better but their long faces said otherwise. The next day, when Catina went to wake them again, both parents were bed-ridden, this time their headaches accompanied by an upset stomach.

Catina took care of them that second day, making sure they were comfortable as they slept and got them bread and water from the kitchen when needed. Catina didn't mind the work as it was a pleasant break from her regular routine. Her mother still made her do her reading and writing exercises though. In the afternoon, all by herself, Catina prepared dinner. It was nothing spectacular compared to the meals her mother usually prepared, just bacon and eggs and toasted bread, but her mother was pleased with the result and since they couldn't eat much without risk of throwing it back up, the meal was well accepted despite the little they ate.

The morning after, Catina could not wake them. She tried again. They still did not stir. On the verge of panicking, her heart was put at ease when they finally roused. They explained to her they were very sick and wanted to stay in bed. Dara advised Catina best spend her day outside so she wouldn't get sick, too. Catina obeyed and, to keep busy, did the chores that needed doing outside.

At this point, Alan stirred in his seat at the thought of them being so sick. Sickness in Grek was rare whether it be the common flu or cold. Most folks there were healthy, his late son's family among them, he told Peter.

Catina went on.

On the day she spent outside, she realized how lonely she was when not with her parents. She talked with Susie the cow and told Susie how worried she was. She had never seen her parents ill before.

She spent the greater part of that morning in the barn with Susie and the chickens before returning to the yard. Once outside, Catina noticed a strange silence in the air. Though her family's property was a decent size, the farms in Grek were still close together and not far from the main city. The sounds of people bustling about or farmers shouting orders to their horses or cattle was usually heard—but not that day. The only sound was the chirping of birds and the occasional neighing or mooing of horse and cattle, the clucking of chickens or bleating of goats.

She walked to the city-center and, to her surprise, found few people on the streets, with most of the shops either closed or boarded up. She quickly returned home to report the news. Her parents were just as surprised as she had been and her mother said that perhaps she and Michel were not the only ones who were ill.

"Mel fo galahom co wal gorn," Catina had said. *But not everybody can be sick.*

Her mother had no response to that. Neither did her step-father.

Back in Alan's home, Catina yawned after relaying this bit of the tale.

"Poor thing," said Alan. "She must be exhausted."

"I would think so," said Peter.

"Really, she must be dead on her feet." He then realized she was *sitting* on Peter's lap. With a smirk he added, "You know what I mean."

Peter chuckled.

"The road from Grek to the Broken City is a long one. I would know," said Alan. "I have traveled it a few times. There are things along that path you will not find here."

"Really?"

"Really. Here we are very sheltered. Out there" —Alan glanced toward the door with almost a look of longing written across his face— "out there you see things that, when away from them, you begin to miss."

"It must be something to have lived a little." There was sincerity in Peter's voice.

"Anyone can live or do as they please, Peter, so do not look up to me as though I am someone special. I went out into the World because I chose to, and because I do not believe that a person can be bound to a single city simply because of generations of tradition. There is such a hindering mindset here. It disturbs me greatly. It is a system that holds all things together, this is true—but it still robs humanity of its freedom. It controls you and tells you how to live your life. The whole idea of 'you must do *this* in order to obtain *that*.' But, I suppose, there are a lot of things that are similar out there as well about needing *this* to obtain *that*. Garathen, despite its many faults, and I am talking about the darkness that occurs in the evening hours—it is the best example of what life should be in terms of living from day to day. We should all work to help each other and help each other obtain the things we need. The problem elsewhere in the World, is greed. Humankind seems to have an uncontrollable desire for it and think the more material things the better. You will see this, Peter, should you ever decide to venture outside the Forest-Ring. I wish people could see that they could carve their own path and not have to live for the rules of just one society. I mean, out there, there is so much, so many different ways of doing things. For example, as I am sure you already know, that though there is trading in other cities, giving one service for another, there is also a thing called tradesworth."

"Tradesworth?"

Alan sat back in his chair and slapped his bony thigh. "Oh, come on now, do not tell me you have not heard of it. Drops and droppers. Hay drops and stone drops. People make and sell things for it. Different items are worth different amounts, usually based upon who needs what and when, you know, what it is worth to the person. They pay the worth in drops or droppers of different grades, the high ones being gold and silver drops, and off they go with their new toy. Blast, almost everywhere has tradesworth . . . save here. Garathen is one of the exceptions, I think."

Peter had never heard of tradesworth. As far as he was concerned, people traded goods and services for other goods and services everywhere. "And what makes these . . . these 'droppers' so valuable?" he said.

Alan thought for a moment. "It is said that, oh, I do not know, several thousand years ago, I am sure—that a great man once sat upon a throne made of gold somewhere on the other side of the World. He was the greatest ruler of them all, as history records. And I think that, other than being rare, gold is worth a lot because it was once held in high esteem by this man. He had done many great things, feats that no person alive had been capable of doing. He performed miracles, healed the sick, led all people into peace and prosperity. But that, as history recalls, was before the Darkness fell and the World nearly died. This is before the Master came and saved us. We are lucky to be here, Peter, so lucky." He scratched his nose and arched his eyebrows. "Blast! Here I go again, yammering on when someone else had the room." He told Catina to finish her story.

Catina resumed her tale as instructed. As she spoke, Alan began translating, and Peter lost himself in the story.

She had spent the rest of that day alone, trying to keep herself busy with her chores (as she knew her parents would be pleased if she did them), but instead found herself too upset to continue. Evening came and then night. The next morning Catina awoke again to the rooster's call and when she tried to wake her parents, her heart broke when they opened their tired eyes. Their faces were pale and damp with sweat; their breathing an effort.

This went on for two weeks, her parents being sick. Catina herself felt fine. Then one morning her mother called her to their room. Dara asked that Catina ride into the city and get food as supplies were running low. Her mother gave her some tradesworth and told her to bring back some fresh fruit and vegetables, some milk and honey, and something sweet as a reward for doing so. Dara told Catina it would be best to purchase some food as they had just harvested their garden and the second batch of vegetables were mere sprouts. It was a good thing, too, because Winter only came every other year in Grek. This year was the year it wouldn't snow so it gave them a chance to get slightly ahead for next year.

Catina went to the kitchen where the tradesworth was kept in a jar on a mantle above the stove and retrieved two copper drops. She didn't quite understand their worth but thought it would be enough to pay for what was needed. She ran out the back door and across the property to the barn. She hurried inside the barn and went to the stall where they kept the family horse, Lamara, and mounted the tan-colored mare. Grabbing hold of the reins, she stroked the horse's coarse, white mane and clicked her tongue. She rode off toward the city.

Catina went to the market as instructed and purchased a combination of fruits—bananas, apples, oranges, plums, apricots—and an assortment of vegetables—carrots, lettuce, cucumbers, cauliflower, onions. The man who sold them to her was kind enough to put the fruits and vegetables in separate baskets for her. Catina fastened the baskets to Lamara's saddle and went further down the street to get the honey and milk. She was glad the market's people were able to provide her with change as she went from place to place. In total she had spent one of the copper drops and had gotten change for the second in the form of two hay drops and a five-dropper.

Happy with her purchases, Catina hurried home and, after putting Lamara back in her stall (she knew that if she left the horse tied outside her father would be upset; he always reminded her to put things back where they belonged), she untied the baskets from the saddle, and retrieved the milk and honey from a pouch on the other side. She set the items down, hung the saddle over the wooden beam that made up part of Lamara's stall, and took her purchases back to the house. She went to her parents' room and showed them what she bought and handed the hay drops and five-dropper to her mother.

Her mother was pleased with her honesty as she knew of other children who kept the remainder of the tradesworth from when their parents asked to go on an errand. Her father commended her on bringing back the food. Catina, always eager to please her parents, was glad she had done so again. It was expected.

Dara and Michel sat up in bed and together the three of them ate. Catina ate the most as her parents weren't all that hungry. She was also surprised that her mother hadn't asked her to prepare the vegetables into a salad. It was rare they would eat the vegetables separately when they were from the market.

When the meal ended, her parents lay back down, their stomachs queasy from their unfamiliarly full bellies.

"Are you feeling better?" asked Catina.

Michel smiled warmly. "I am a little better."

He didn't sound it though. And she could tell by the way his eyes seemed a lighter shade of brown than usual, that he was still ill.

"What are we going to do now?" asked Catina.

"I am not sure," said Michel. "Dara?"

"I do not know," she said. She thought for a moment and then said, "I wish your grandfather were here."

It made sense, Alan thought. Catina paused again in her narrative and yawned. Her eyelids drooped nearly closed, her body relaxed as Peter held her in his arms.

"Semba dal umal menne loham," said Alan. "Qu semba nem ro swemitsa." *I am glad you came. And I want to help.*

Catina's eyes widened, joyful. She said she had worried Alan might have been upset with her for taking such a long and dangerous journey on her own. But Alan was a patient and understanding man, despite his outbursts sometimes. He loved his granddaughter very much, and more so, loved his dead son. He wanted to see to it that his only reminder of him had a safe place to live and parents who were healthy. The way Catina described the illness that had come into her household, it was obviously very serious, perhaps even deadly. Alan wished he knew if her parents were still alive or if the disease—if it was indeed fatal—had claimed them or not. The thought of Catina without a home to go back to made him cringe.

Catina leaned her head on Peter's shoulder and closed her eyes a moment.

"Catina?" asked Alan. "Lo menne grul ro ke vol ersa alem?" *Would you like to lie down for awhile?*

She said, "Gana ane." *Yes, please.*

"Lohem cal solm." Alan stood off his seat, went over to her and took her up in his arms. *Come here, then.*

"Mali kwon nali," Catina told Peter again. *Thank you.*

"You'll be all right?" asked Peter.

"Yes, yes, I will be fine," said Alan. "I may be blind, but I know my own home better than anyone. I know exactly how many paces it is to each room from anywhere in here. I had lived here a long time before I lost my sight. The images of this place stain my memory and, with proper imagination, I can almost visualize them as clear as if I could see again." He carried Catina around the hearth and disappeared with her into his private chambers, leaving Peter alone.

Peter wished Catina would finish her story. But, he guessed, she was only six years old and had been through enough as it was. No sense making her relive the whole ordeal over again solely for his benefit. Right now, sleep for the humanette seemed the best option. He could always find out the rest later. And he felt comfortable that Alan was in control now. "Family will do anything to help each other," his aunt had told him more than once. Mostly when she said it, it was because Peter did not want to do his chores around the house, but it was the principle of the statement that he later understood. Things come along that you may have to face, the adversity usually something you wished never to have visited you, but because it had, you must see it clear to its end.

Especially when it came to family.

Peter also knew that, for him, such a statement carried a greater weight. Since his parents had died long ago, he never had a proper family and for him to do something for the sake of family, that made it even more important. It was his chance to make up for lost time and an opportunity to live a life where family came first and all else second. He hoped that he could instill the same principles in his own offspring, should he ever have any.

Alan obviously felt the same way. Catina was all he had in this World in terms of flesh and blood.

CHAPTER VI
A Talk Under the Stars

Peter stood alone in front of the fire for quite some time before Alan re-entered the room, his face long, lined with worry, his lips slightly open as if about to say something. His white eyes, despite being nothing more than white irises on white, conveyed concern and fear.

Alan took a seat and crossed his arms.

The two men sat in silence for a time before Alan spoke. "Something happened to her on the way here," he said. "I am not sure what it was, but I can tell. I apologize I took so long putting her to bed but she told me a little more of her story." Alan scrunched his brow, recalling Catina's words. "She said that she got scared seeing her parents as they were. I do not blame her. For a six-year-old, to see your parents helpless and ill must be a frightening sight. It is just—ah, my thoughts are running away with me. She said she wanted to help them and because of what her mother said about *my* help, Catina went looking for me. She knew that I was far away but as to how far, she did not understand."

Soft whimpering came from Alan's private room.

"Is she all right?" asked Peter.

"I do not know," said Alan. "Lamara, her horse, had an accident on the way over. Thankfully, Catina was not foolish enough to try and walk here. She had set out on Lamara but that damned horse fell two days after she left. Catina had not brought any food or water, at least not enough for a horse that size. The poor horse died of thirst. Catina wept by the body of the sweet animal for a whole afternoon out in the middle of nowhere." Peter's heart went out to her, especially now as she continued to cry in the other room. "She misses her friend, Peter, and by her telling me of the death of Lamara, that stirred her memory and now she weeps for that horse. Excuse me."

Alan got up and saw to Catina. From the other room Peter heard soothing words spoken to calm her and assure her all would be well.

Shortly after, Alan came back out and resumed his seat.

"I'd still like to know how she got all the way here on her own," said Peter.

The blind man shifted in his seat and got himself comfortable. "With Lamara gone, she was alone and had no one to turn to. She was too far from Grek to turn back. She was driven by desperation to find me, I suppose. She made it to Wesafeld and stopped there. But there was more, I knew. I asked but she would not say." Alan sat up more alert. His white eyes locked on to Peter. "I fear something terrible happened."

Peter stayed with Alan for the remainder of the afternoon. While Catina slept, they had tea and ham sandwiches, which were both a delicacy, in Peter's mind. The tea was called Belvada, which tasted like apples and cinnamon and was nutritious. Peter had two cups of it. Alan had three.

Alan seemed a content man and it appeared he enjoyed living in Garathen. He conveyed the image of a man who was done living and was willing to ride out on the waves of knowledge and experience he had accumulated this far in life until the end of his days.

"Why do you live here?" Peter had asked him.

"Simple, really," replied Alan. "To get away."

"Get away? From what?"

"Maybe you are too young to understand, Peter. Or maybe you would understand but would still question my motives."

Peter wished he never asked the question. Suddenly it felt a dumb one and he felt hollow inside. Alan's comment made him feel how most people in Garathen made him feel: different. In the Broken City, life was life and it was accepted that it wasn't going to change. Peter—more often than not—wondered about change and what it would be like to go somewhere else and live there for a time. Or what it would be like to be someone else just so there would be a change of pace, of lifestyle, even in the people you associated with. But in Garathen, there was a mob mentality of sorts and peoples' thoughts and opinions rubbed off on one another, and each—though perhaps they wanted something else—was held back because of what others said.

"I just don't understand why you're living here when you could easily be living in Grek," said Peter.

"I know what you are saying. Why live here where it seems so hard each and every day, whereas in Grek, at least, from what you have heard from Catina, it sounds more like an ideal life. That may be partially true but what is the ideal life, anyway, right? It is different to everyone. To me, the ideal life is to get away from regular life. That is what I meant by 'get away.'"

"I still don't understand."

"Fine, I will tell you. I do not like the World out there, Peter," he said and stuck out a finger, pointing at the door. "It is a terrible place. I am not talking about Garathen and its happy days and melancholy evenings and haunted nights. I am talking about the World that I have seen on my travels. Something is wrong with the

Human race, but I cannot quite place it. I have noticed it all my life, ever since I was little. Like yourself I grew up here, but, ah, I wish it had not been so. I remember quite vividly sitting in a room all alone at home while my parents would spend nearly every waking moment preparing things for Trade the next day. My mother was a knitter. She made sweaters from sheep-wool and my father was a blacksmith. If he was not making horseshoes, he was making kettles. If he was not making kettles, he was making fire stokers. Perhaps that is when I realized something was wrong. My parents were slaves to a system that was overtaking their lives. They were not living, Peter. They were working to live, but never enjoying the fruit of their efforts. As a child I never understood that one could also enjoy life instead of working it away. Then in my early teens when I became curious about the World outside the Forest-Ring, I developed my skill in wood carving" —he must have heard Peter sit up straighter because he said, "Yes, Peter, I am an artist, too. Do not be so alarmed. How else do you think I helped you with that carving last year? Which, by the way, I wanted to thank you for. It was good to do something I love again. I apologize for not remembering earlier. Spending so much time alone makes you place yourself at the center of everything, unfortunately. I tend to forget others now and again. A flaw, I know. But, again, thank you for last year."

"You're welcome," said Peter.

"*Dana kwon nali*, you mean," said Alan, smirking. "Anyway, to finish answering your question, I am here because after I did some traveling, I saw that others were also falling prey to the working system. Especially out in the World since tradesworth exists there and people are quite greedy for it. They work, work, work, never to do what they are supposed to be doing and that is live, live, live. I am here to get away from that. I keep to myself because I do not want to associate myself with it. Sometimes I have to work, like to get food and necessities, but that is where it ends."

"I wish I had your boldness," said Peter.

Alan didn't say anything.

The two spoke well into the evening. However, their conversation kept coming back to Catina and what needed to be done. Alan's plan was to set out for Grek with her the next morning, and if not then, the morning after, depending on how much rest he required and how long it would take to pack for their journey. Alan was going to ask Peter something else but decided against it. He didn't know if he could trust Peter just yet. Sure, Peter had taken care of Catina when she had arrived—had even saved her life—but he wanted to be sure about Peter before he would ask him.

As the sun outside began to dip into the horizon, Alan went to wake Catina for dinner. She told him that she was still tired and didn't want to come out of bed. He told her she should try anyway so she could eat something to help her regain her strength. He said she could go back to bed right after if she wanted to. She reluctantly agreed and came out of her room and smiled at Peter when she saw him.

"Tomi som bena cal?" she asked Alan.

"Fana ko, tomi som bena cal," returned Alan in her tongue. "Semba qoma ma tomi relmi ro wom sim ma neme ro domli zona arna goloha ali." *Yes, he is still here. I told him he had to stay if he wanted to play games with us later.*

He knew Catina would like that.

Over dinner, Catina didn't say very much. Her mind was elsewhere, fatigued and worn. Her journey had been a tremendous measure of character, and of strength. Her mother always told her that even at her age she knew Catina would grow up strong. Catina took delight in knowing that that strength was beginning to show. She didn't know of any other six-year-olds who had crossed such a long way in such a short time and had pulled through. Her journey reminded her of the story of the runaway girl, the one who had fled Grek because she couldn't deal with the responsibilities her parents had placed on her. The girl's body had been found some months later about a hundred or so miles away from the city, decaying in the midday sun.

Catina was glad that she was alive. And she was proud of herself.

Alan had—much to Catina's amazement because she knew he couldn't see—cooked for her and Peter fresh salmon he had caught the day before at a stream that ran along the far East side of the Forest-Ring's inner rim. She was happy he didn't burn himself as he cooked over the hearth. Her stomach growled at the aroma and promise of the meal to come. Alan also served some bread and milk, both of which were hearty and nutritious.

As Alan poured the milk into clay mugs, he placed his index finger inside the rims of the mugs, testing to see when the mugs were full.

For a time Catina's spirits rose and throughout the meal, Peter listened as Alan and Catina talked back and forth in Grescalla. He smiled or laughed when they exchanged something that was funny, seeming to catch on.

Catina grinned as Alan translated Peter's words for her. Using her fork, she prodded at the fish with one hand, her head resting lazily on the other; her fatigue had returned.

"Alan?" asked Peter. Alan looked up. "How do I say 'how was your nap' in Grescalla?"

"*Dom la tinoni menn ka?*" said Alan immediately then resumed chewing loudly on his food.

Peter turned to the girl. "Catina" —she looked his way— "*Dom—dom la ti-tinoni menn ka-a?*"

The little humanette giggled at Peter's effort, the words having come out stuttered and dull. Grescalla was a smooth language, each word flowing into the next. Peter's words sounded more like water crashing into a dam of rocks.

"*Dava lata gi*," she said.

"That means, 'So-so,'" said Alan.

"Sorry," said Peter.

"For what?"

"Just wish I could have said it better, that's all."

"Do not worry. It will come in time."

Come in time? thought Peter. Was he to be spending more time with them? The thought of forming a friendship with Alan was an endearing one. Alan was in his mid-forty years, Peter assumed, and had experienced a lot of what life had to offer. Or, so rumor had it. Alan the Traveler, the man who knew and had seen everything. Peter never had a father-figure that he could look up to. Even now he still wished for someone to guide him and teach him what's what in the World. Then again, in Garathen, "what's what" was usually learned at a young age. You got up, you traded, you spent the afternoon doing as you wished, and then you went back inside. If you were wilder in nature, you visited the pub and whorehouse and traded more of your hard-earned wares for what they had to offer. Peter had never gone in for that sort of thing.

Taking a bite of his salmon, Alan announced, "In the morning we will be leaving." He repeated the same in Grescalla for Catina. An ear-to-ear grin washed over her face.

"Early?" asked Peter.

"Yes, yes, when did you think we would leave? We must get an early start, but not too early. The journey through the Forest-Ring is a relatively safe one, but can still be dangerous if one does not know where to go. Perhaps Catina could show me the route she took. Regardless, after sunrise, we will wait about an hour and then be off. It will give those no good palanthora beasts a chance to settle in for a day of sleeping, and for those blasted Slummers to go wherever they go in the morning. Some of them are still seen that early, skirting the edges of the forest, but they fear the sunlight and dwell only in darkness."

"My neighbor, Mr. Ambelton, said he once saw one when he was setting up shop for the day. He said the Slummer ran into the Forest when the sun peaked over the trees."

"But they stay along the border, along the trees that rub up against the hills. We will still have to be careful."

Peter ripped off a clump of bread and stuffed it into his mouth. "I hope you and Catina will be safe. It'd be a shame for her to have come this far only to run into trouble."

Alan took a gulp of milk. "Agreed. Our journey will be a good chance for her to tell me the rest of her story." Alan leaned in closer. "Especially whatever it is that is bothering her. I know something happened, but I cannot say what."

Peter frowned. Both he and Alan were drawn out of their conversation by the sound of heavy breathing.

Catina had fallen asleep at the table, her arm curled around her plate, her head resting on her bicep.

With a smirk Alan said, "Now look what you have gone and done, Peter. You have bored the poor girl to sleep."

"Sorry."

Alan arched an eyebrow at him. "You know I was only joking."

"Oh."

Alan let Catina sleep while he and Peter finished their meal. Once done and while waiting for the tea water to boil, he carried Catina back to his private room and laid her to bed. He then prepared the tea and invited Peter outside for a breath of late evening air; it was fresh and slightly cool, pleasant against the skin.

The stars came out.

Outside, the two men sipped tea out of clay mugs and watched as the already-deep-purple sky quickly turned to night.

"It's amazing, really," said Peter.

"What?" asked Alan.

"The sky," he replied. "At night I usually sit in my veranda and look out onto Garathen, but I mostly look up at the sky. That's how I saw Catina, by the way."

"You should tell me more about that." Alan's voice was somewhat demanding. "You mentioned an encounter with a Slummer."

Peter told him what happened the night prior between Catina, himself, and the Slummer, with as much detail as he could. More than once did Alan's eyes widen at the tale, especially when Peter said he fought the Slummer.

"It is a miracle you are still alive," Alan told him.

"Thank the Master for that," said Peter.

When the story finished, Alan felt a great pity for Catina. He decided right then that he would send Peter home early so he could pack and then rest for the long journey ahead of them.

After they were finished their tea, Alan thanked Peter again for bringing his *Shinali* to him.

"I'm sure you would have done the same for me, if I had a little one," said Peter.

"Mayhap I might have," said Alan. "Yes. I would have."

A cool whisk of breeze brushed by them.

"It is nice, is it not?" asked Alan.

"What?"

"The weather. Sorry, just creating Common-talk. We have been talking on Catina all night. Thought you might like a change."

"It's all right, really," he said, "I don't mind. If my granddaughter suddenly turned up, that's all I'd be talking about, too. Better, talking *with* her."

Alan grinned a small grin. "Sorry if you felt a little left out at dinner. I know what it feels like to be an outsider in conversation, what with my wandering about and all."

"What's it like?" asked Peter.

"Going about?"

"Yes."

"Not much different than going about town, I suppose. But it is also an eye-opener. Especially—" He stopped there. His trousers had bunched around his ankles. He straightened their cuffs and brushed his hands together, as if dirty.

Peter expected him to resume what he was saying, but Alan didn't. He instead entwined his fingers and lowered his arms. His white eyes appeared lost.

"What's wrong?" asked Peter.

"I am worried for Catina—"

"That's understandable—"

"But more so for her family . . . and everyone else, for that matter." He paused and turned toward Peter, taking a deep breath. "Peter, what I am about to tell you cannot leave where we now stand."

Peter wasn't sure what Alan meant, so he simply said, "Okay."

"All right, then. As you know, I have done my fair share of going from place to place."

Peter nodded.

"And I have seen things. Some of them wonderful, some not as wonderful. But I have also seen something like what Catina described to us. Last summer I was up North, just seeing what I might see; there was a small colony there. Very basic living; probably more basic than here. There were only about fifty people in the village, most of them adults, very few children. While visiting there, after about, oh, three or four weeks, some people there got quite sick. Some of them died a few weeks later; others died even sooner. And others got better and went on living. The point is, what if what has happened in Grek is the same thing that happened up North? What if . . . what if my family is going to die, if they are not dead already? Catina . . . . I felt the puffiness around her eye, though I did not want to say anything to her about it. It appears sick and should be tended to. She came to me for help, and in the mind of a child, a grownup—especially a family grownup—can provide that help. But the truth is I cannot. I am not a Helper and though I do have some knowledge of medicinal herbs and roots, I would not know how to cure a deadly illness should this be what it is."

Just then Alan's appearance changed. He wasn't the wise man that Peter built him up to be. Instead, there was a man who was frightened for the lives of his family. He was a man admitting his own weakness, acknowledging that he will soon have to enter a situation where, though relied on, he wouldn't be able to remedy.

"Is there anything I can do?" asked Peter.

Alan gave him a warm smile. "Not unless you know what is occurring in Grek or of anyone else who might know."

"Sorry, but I don't. I wish I did though. This is obviously something beyond my grasp."

"Do not think inferior of yourself. This is well within your grasp. I do not mean to speak out of turn but you are a little self-demeaning. Do not be." Alan put a hand on Peter's shoulder. "You are a capable young man, Peter Jones."

His face heated at the compliment. "Thanks."

"Which reminds me, why did you bring Catina to me? You did not know she was my granddaughter."

"You're the only one I knew of whom might recognize the colors of her dress. I thought that perhaps you could tell me—that was, if you didn't know her—where she was from."

"That would have been a sound plan, except for one thing."

"And that is?"

"There are many places where ladies wear colorful dresses. But I can see how you came to that conclusion."

Peter felt a little silly for thinking that Alan would recognize the dress. He didn't know *what* he had been thinking. Alan was right. Surely there are many places that weren't as drab and simple-colored as Garathen.

Alan took his hand in his. "Thank you," he said.

"*Dana kwon nali.*"

"Very good. Try accenting the 'L' a little more."

"*Dana kwon nal-li.*"

"See. Told you. It comes with time."

"This illness you told me about, what happens?" asked Peter.

"I was only around it a short time as I did not want to fall ill myself. I spent most of my time away from those who were ill and only visited them once in awhile. They liked me, there, up North. The disease, from what I saw, works like this: it comes on like a common stomach flu or headache, or both. Then you grow weak and are tired most of the time. Much like my daughter-in-law and her husband. Slow but sure, if your body does not beat it, your body becomes so weak that your vital systems begin to shut down and eventually the illness claims you."

Peter shifted uneasily. "I've never heard of anything like that before."

"Myself, neither. That is why this concerns me so. To face the possibility of losing my family even though I rarely see them . . . it is heartbreaking."

With intentional tenderness in his eyes in spite of his friend not being able to see, Peter said, "I'm sure it's nothing, Alan. It'll all work out in the end."

"One can only hope," replied Alan in a grave tone.

The two men stood outside for a while longer before Peter wished Alan a good night. He had to be home as curfew was approaching. He didn't want to be caught outdoors by any early-rising Slummers or any of the Dembatstayr. He wished Alan a good journey and asked that Alan pass on a good-bye to Catina for him. He also requested Alan stop by his home after returning from Grek.

"Just knock," said Peter. "You can come in and I can return the favor of a nice warm meal."

Alan said he was delighted by the offer and that he looked forward to a quiet meal with someone whom he now called his friend.

CHAPTER VII
When Darkness Falls

Peter was careful coming home. It was late in the twenty-second hour as he made his way down the Through-way. Up over head the moon shone through the clouds in a bright circle, a hazy nimbus adding to its majesty. The pub and the whorehouse had already closed for the evening. Everyone was inside. The night air was cool, sending shivers up his arms and legs. But it wasn't entirely the chilly air that caused his shivering. It was also what he knew to be outdoors this hour. He kept watch for any movement.

The streets were cloaked in shadow, most of the homes and shops mere outlines in the dark. Going home would be simple enough though. His place was nearly a straight line from Alan's. He walked quickly, the only sound aside from the occasional gust of breeze was the brushing of the inside of his trouser-legs as he walked.

About a quarter way down the street, he passed the place where the Baker would be serving bread-bowls come morning. His mind chased away his frightened thoughts and he remembered getting bread there with Catina. He was glad the little one was safe and that she had a loving place to rest for the night. And he knew that Alan loved her. During dinner, when Catina spoke, Peter could see the way Alan's face softened when he heard his granddaughter's voice. How Peter longed to see the same expression on a woman's face, the woman he would fall in love with and with whom he would spend the rest of his life. He daydreamed of sitting at the table with her, their children chattering away about children things, her eyes softening at their edges, her cheeks losing any tension they might have from the wears of the day, as she listened to their children speak. What a thing to be, should it ever come about.

Peter was nearly home when he woke out of his daydream. He stopped his pace and turned around, checking to see if anyone—or anything—was coming his way.

It was safe. All was quiet.

He walked on.

When Peter approached the front of his veranda, a sickening sensation filled his stomach. Something wasn't right. A gust of wind swept by him and gooseflesh formed on his skin, the hairs on his arms and legs springing to attention. He checked behind himself once more, but again saw nothing. He held his breath and listened carefully, checking for any sound that might indicate a Slummer or palanthora beast, or anything else that might be watching him.

Again, nothing.

Ignoring his apprehension as mere paranoia, he went to his front door, undid the latch, and entered the porch. The inside of the veranda was black as pitch, the moon outside and behind having gone behind a thick patch of clouds. He went over to the small, waist-high table that was near the window where he sat the night before and spotted Catina. Atop it was a candle and a Rigmata. A Rigmata was a wooden cylinder, about the length of a candle stick, small at one end, wider at the other. On the small end were dried Fala Leaves layered thinly against a rough, sharp-ridged iron surface. Dangling by a string about an inch below the small end was a piece of flint and, using the flint as a striking tool against the Fala Leaves, one would strike the leaves and the tip of the Rigmata would ignite.

Peter struck the flint hanging off the Rigmata against the Fala Leaves. A spark followed then a sprout of flame grew at its end. Peter lit the candle and blew the Rigmata out. He set the candle down in its holder and picked up the holder by its thumb-hook.

He stopped just shy of the door that led to the main room of his home. There was a scraping sound, like something roughing rubbing up against one of the floor boards. He froze, his hand trembling, the candle-holder shaking in his grip.

Finding the strength to speak, he called out, "Who's there?" There was no answer, of course.

"I'm only going to ask one more time. Who's there?" He suddenly felt foolish because if someone was inside his home, he had no way of defending himself. Both his knife and his staff were inside, hanging on a wall next to his painting room.

Still no one answered.

"Okay," he whispered to himself, "and we go." And with that he placed his finger tips on the door and pushed. The door swung open into the dark living area, and, in the glow of his candle, his bedding and table and doorways to the other areas showed up as silhouettes against an orange-colored room, the candle's light bouncing in tanned and yellow colors off the wood. He looked to the floor to see if anything was there. Thank the Master there was nothing.

Peter breathed a sigh of relief. He turned and closed the door behind him and when he turned around again, he saw a Slummer. Then he saw two others standing off to either side of him. Another opened the door behind him, nudging him forward.

Surrounded, his heart sped up to an almost unbearable speed. It banged inside his chest, the *thud, thud, thud* of his heart vibrating in his stomach. His breathing was choppy, each exhale audible, as if he had just finished throwing up and was catching his breath. The candle-holder shook in his hand.

The Slummers had come for revenge. The one standing in front of him, Peter noticed, was the same Slummer he had fought the night before. The Slummer's face was bruised in purple and black patches, her nose broken. This was the first time he had gotten a closer look at the dreaded humanlike creatures that prowled the night. They all dressed similarly, their clothes hanging off them in tatters of ugly blacks and browns. Their hair was long and in tangles and each had beards reaching down past chest level. Even the female had stubble along her jaw. Their eyes were dark, and where the whites should be was only blackness. Their skin was dry and cracked and leather-looking. Peter saw the nails on their fingers were thick and long and claw-like.

The Slummers took a step closer, any chance of escape growing slimmer. They were on all sides: one behind, one in front, one on the left and right. Peter's only shred of hope lay in the fact he had had the upper hand over a Slummer before. But that Slummer had been but one and now there were four.

He wanted to run, flee with all his might. But how? The moment he went to turn, the Slummer behind him would grab him and throw him back toward the others and who knew what would happen then. Peter tried to remain calm, knowing that panic in a perilous situation would only serve against him.

The rampant thoughts of panic and fear in his mind were overtaking him though. Consciously and with effort, he slowed his thoughts. *Think*, thought Peter. *How did I stop her last night?* No answer came.

The Slummers came closer, the gap that separated each of them in the circle around Peter closing. Peter expected them to say something or to growl in fits of anger. But they didn't. And the silence and menace in their presence was what disturbed him the most.

Then it dawned on Peter what had happened the night previous, what it was he had done that allowed him an advantage over the Slummer.

He had done something the Slummer *did not* expect. He had caught her off guard.

Slummers were used to being feared by humans; used to people succumbing to them out of blind terror. Last night, Peter had done the unexpected and had retaliated. His actions had been desperate ones, but the Slummer hadn't known that. That was his edge.

With a flurry of emotion and a sudden sense of understanding, Peter crashed through the small opening that separated the Slummer in front of him and the Slummer on his left, running toward the far wall. Immediately the Slummers followed. Peter went for his staff and knife. He wasn't sure what he would do with them once they were in his grasp, but he wanted protection. Just as his fingers were about to make contact with the knife's handle, the Slummer whom he had previously harmed grabbed him from behind, a thick forearm around his throat. Peter choked under the grip, the pressure against his windpipe making it nearly impossible to breathe. The candle-holder fell to the floor, the candle falling out and rolling toward the straw mats near the table. Immediately smoke brewed.

Legs kicking, Peter was pulled into the middle of the room and thrown to the floor. The female Slummer had been *expecting* a fight. The others, Peter saw, had a look of bafflement in their eyes at his attempt to take them on. If he remained on the floor, he would surely be ripped to pieces. With all his strength, he scrambled to his feet, only to be struck down again.

He had no choice but to stay and fight.

Suddenly there was a loud *whoosh* and the straw mat that was Peter's bed burst into flame. The room filled with thick smoke.

The Slummers, ignoring the fire's threat, surrounded Peter once again, three of them remaining upright while the Slummer that had a grudge against him crouched down over him. The circumstance was astonishing, really. For a brief moment, Peter considered the similarity between that of the Slummers to that of Humans. Humans would be doing the same thing in this situation. If one had something to settle with another—especially a physical score—he would take his friends over to the one he had something against and, while the person was surrounded, he would have first picks at striking the person, while his friends gathered around and watched. It was only if the person meant to be beaten fought back would the friends dive in and ensure that their friend's honor was restored.

Not terribly honorable though, thought Peter.

Not wanting the other Slummers to beat on him, he allowed the female Slummer to get a strike in. The Slummer's meaty hand came down across his jaw with such force that his head snapped to the right from the blow and crashed hard against the floorboards. The Slummer's long fingernails scratched his face on the follow-through. Dazed, Peter hoped that it would end here and the Slummers would leave. But such was not the case with Slummers. The only thing that would restore their honor was that the one who had harmed them perished. Another strike came down, this time across his cheek bone. A multitude of stars burst before his vision; a dull buzzing filled his ears. The Slummer was right over him, now, straddling his chest, the weight nearly crushing him. The heat of the fire that was slowly beginning to overtake the home stung through his clothes.

"Stop," wheezed Peter.

The Slummer paid no heed to the plea nor to the crackles of the burning wood around them.

Just before the third strike came crashing down on him, Peter grabbed the Slummer by the collar of her shirt and, in an adrenaline-charged burst of strength, pushed the Slummer off him and over to the side onto the flame. The three Slummers looking on jumped in as their comrade rolled around on the floor in wild yelps, putting her clothing out. Peter, sweating and fatigued from the sudden exertion, crawled toward his knife belt on the wall, vision blurred, head pounding. The smell of the smoke was nauseating. Legs suddenly seized by claw-like grips he was dragged back to the middle of the room.

He kicked wildly, refusing to let these bastards take him, and managed to kick one of the Slummers off. The Slummer who had caught afire was now fine, only her clothes smoldering slightly about the shoulders. The Slummer came in, her claws outstretched, ready to rip the flesh from his bones. Peter blocked the blow with his forearm. The strike was so strong that his upraised forearm banged against his head. At least he had been protected from the assault. Peter gathered his strength inward, feeling it build inside, then, with a burst of anger and speed, got to his feet and pushed away the Slummer who was about to throw him back down again.

Peter charged for his knife belt. He made it to the wall and when the female Slummer came for him, he kicked her away. The Slummer recoiled but came back with even more intensity. So did the others. Peter grabbed his knife belt off the wall and removed the blade from its sheath. For an instant the Slummers slowed their charge, recognizing the new threat. The blade shone in the fiery light building around them.

A sense of coming victory came over him and the aftershock from the Slummers' assault on him began to ease a little. He felt powerful, but he was careful not to get cocky. There were still four of them and only one of him.

Just then the Slummer whom he had harmed the night before dove at him and in a whirlwind of movement, Peter thrust the blade into the Slummer's middle, between the ribs, up to the blade's hilt. The Slummer's beady, dark eyes grew wide with shock, her large hands clasping around the hand Peter used to hold the blade in place. Then in one powerful motion, Peter withdrew the blade from her, and blood followed its path in a wild gush, coating his hand in sticky red. She dropped to her knees. Peter kicked her in the face and she toppled over onto her side.

The other three Slummers looked on, bewildered.

Peter grabbed his staff off the wall and held both it and the knife up in a ready position, showing the Slummers he was willing to fight them even if he were to die doing so. The three intruders came forward, their steps careful but sure. Everyone in the room stopped and looked when the wall to their right collapsed. Peter's heart sank at the sight. For so long had he lived here; his home was a part of him. Knowing that after tonight it would no longer exist, it angered him even more. How dare these bastards come and invade his home! And now the only place he ever loved was falling to pieces around him. Without his home he had noth—

A Slummer charged forward. Peter brought his oak staff around in a wild arc and caught the Slummer across the face. The Slummer turned to his left from the blow and Peter came up in the opposite direction with his knife, slashing the Slummer's throat.

"Get out of here!" shouted Peter at the other two.

They growled and came at him. Peter didn't know if he could handle two of them but he would certainly try. He was too furious to think otherwise. The Slummers came at him with arms outstretched, trying to grab him. Peter dodged one but was grabbed by the other. His staff fell to the floor with a *thunk!* Fortunately, he still had his knife. The Slummers grabbed him and tried to get at the weapon.

Peter wrestled in their grasp, desperately wanting to get away. Somehow in the commotion, he was able to bring his blade across one of the Slummer's wrists. It screeched and its grip loosened. Peter freed himself and drove his knife into the side of the other. The Slummer screamed and stumbled off into the kitchen, the knife still in his side. Peter moved around and struck the remaining Slummer with a closed fist.

It retaliated, turning Peter around, its claws tearing down Peter's back. Peter immediately felt blood pooling beneath the tatters of his sweater.

Gagging, Peter knew he had to get out of there otherwise he would surely die. The smoke was becoming so thick that he was barely able to see never mind his watery vision making it worse.

He ran, the Slummers following after him. The front wall was covered in flame. The doorway was blocked by a sheet of fire. He had to jump through it. Had to get out onto the veranda and out to the street. Peter charged for the entrance. Just then a Slummer cut in front of him, catching him in its grasp. Weaponless, Peter fought with the Slummer, but to no success. The only thing that saved him was the cries of the injured Slummer still further in his home. The Slummer was covered in flames. The Slummer who had Peter in his hold let go and went to assist his fallen comrade.

Taking this diversion as an opening for escape, Peter ran for the door and dove through the wall of flame. He nearly leaped clear of the interior of the burning veranda, but his foot landed awkwardly on the top step. He toppled forward and landed hard on the dirt. Getting to his hands and knees, he looked back at his burning home. Everything he ever worked for was engulfed in flame. The cries of the Slummers came from inside as they burned alive.

Sweating, panting, and exhausted, Peter got to his feet and stumbled away from the heat of the fire. The night was chilly and dark. A sense of loneliness lingered upon the air. No one had come out to help him.

All he could do was run.

There were others who saw the glow of the flames light up the Main Through-way of Garathen. Both man, woman and child who were awoken by the dancing lights of the fire came forward to their windows to watch. But no one came outside to help.

At night in the Broken City, everyone stayed indoors.

CHAPTER VIII
Beneath these Ashes

Peter's pace slowed about a block away from Alan's home. He stopped, winded and out of breath. He checked over his shoulder, in the back of his mind thinking the Slummers were right behind. They weren't. All he saw was his house up in flames in full roar at the other end of the street, yellow and orange tongues of light licking the dark sky. He bent at the waist and caught his breath. When he straightened, a tingle of sharp pricks raced across his back; the slashes from the Slummers claw-like nails were aching and sore. He heard the growls of a palanthora beast from somewhere far away, its low rumbling growl piercing the night air.

He pressed on to Alan's door.

When he reached it he banged on it with both fists. His arms, weak from the night's ordeal, didn't produce much of a sound against the heavy door. He tried banging again, putting all of his remaining strength behind the blows. The sound was a little louder, but not much.

When no answer came, he shouted, "Alan, it's Peter! Let me in!" He pressed his ear to the door, hoping to hear movement inside. When there was none, he tried calling again, this time with such force behind his voice that it scratched the inside of his throat. "Alan, it's Peter! Open up! Help me!" He shouldered the door then kicked at its base with the ball of his foot.

Tired, his head still spinning from the Slummers' assault, he collapsed on the front step, his knees landing hard on the stone. "Please . . . " His voice was quiet. "Open the door . . . Alan . . . "

Head in his hands, he wept. He thought back to earlier in the evening when he was here, knowing he had his home to go back to when his time with Alan and Catina came to an end. Now his home was gone. He had nothing left. Down the street, his burning home looked so small amongst the others, the huts and makeshift abodes . . . . His place seemed insignificant amongst so many. It was just one house. Surely he could build another. But with what? He had no supplies to create poems and paintings to trade. He had nothing. More tears filled his eyes.

And after a time, when he was almost cried out, Alan opened the door.

"Who is there!" he demanded.

Peter glanced up and his eyes met with the sharp tip of a sword, its end pressing an indent on the tip of his nose.

"Alan, it's me Peter," he said.

The sharp tip lingered a moment longer then was withdrawn.

"Blast it, Peter! What in the name of the Earth are you doing here? You know I am leaving in the morning."

"Can I come in?" asked Peter.

Alan sighed. "Very well." He lowered the sword.

Peter got to his feet and followed Alan inside. Dressed in his night clothes—a long gray gown blotched with black, the hem stopping just above his ankles—Alan looked even thinner than earlier.

"Keep your voice down," said Alan. "Catina is sleeping."

In the middle of the room, the hearth was still lit from earlier, producing a small flame, illuminating the surroundings in a pale orange light.

"Sorry for being short with you," said Alan, "I was in the midst of a good dream."

"It's all right," said Peter. "I'm sorry to have disturbed you. It's just that—"

"What?"

Peter stretched his back again, the skin screaming under the claw marks from the Slummer's nails. "I had a rough night," he finished.

Alan hung his sword on a pair of hooks by the door. Peter realized that he hadn't seen the sword hanging by the door when he was there earlier. He assumed he hadn't noticed it because Alan didn't seem like someone who had need of one. He was glad, though, that Alan had answered the door with his sword at the ready. It made him feel safe to know Alan was prepared.

They sat down in the same chairs as earlier and Peter recounted to him all that happened since he had left—coming home, feeling something was wrong, his encounter with the intruding Slummers, the attack, the fire, the escape down the street.

"A fire!"

"Yes. I lost everything. I have no place to go now. All that I've worked for is lost."

Alan didn't seem to hear that last part. "Nonsense! That simply cannot be. A Slummer would not just come into a home and attack. That has never happened for as long as I have lived here."

"I haven't heard of it, either," said Peter. "But it happened regardless."

"But why? What purpose would it have?"

"Because," said Peter, "I attacked one of there own last night, remember? It was revenge."

Alan folded his arms. "Blast. Yet this is still news. I am, however, glad you are not harmed."

"Actually, I am." Peter turned in his chair so that his back was facing Alan. "One of them clawed my back something fierce."

Alan stretched out a hand and felt along the tear marks across Peter's skin. Peter winced as the blind man's fingers grazed over the wounds.

"Those bastards did cut you up good," said Alan. "Stay there. I will get some ointment."

The blind man left the room. Peter remained and slumped in his chair. He put his head in his hands. "What am I going to do now?" he said to himself.

An ache had been building behind his eyes ever since that Slummer had struck him for the first time. Now that dull pain was in full force. He was exhausted, sore and needed to rest.

Alan returned. "Now, hold still. This is going to sting. I am using a derivative of the Dalcana Herb, which comes from the roots of the Dalcana tree. There are a few of them growing around here. Not many, but some. It will clean the wounds and begin the healing process. When you sleep, though, lie on your side to let the air get at it."

Peter heard a sloshing sound as Alan dipped a rag in a small bowl containing a mixture of warm water and Dalcana Herb. Alan applied the solution to the wound. Peter grimaced as the liquid stung the very insides of the tears. The sensation was like a heated sting. It felt good and painful at the same time.

"There. Done," said Alan.

"Thank you."

Peter turned back to him.

The blind man's white eyes grew tender. "You can stay here," he said. "I will get a blanket and you can sleep alongside the hearth to stay warm. We will deal with the rest of this mess come morning."

"Thank you," said Peter again.

"You are welcome, my friend. Always glad to be of help."

Catina's internal clock woke her early the following morning. Sleeping in was barely an option back home. She stepped carefully over Alan's sleeping body—he was on a substitute straw mat, she having used his bed—and groggily made her way out of Alan's private room and into the main living area. She rubbed the sleep from her eyes, her hand pulling away quickly when she touched the swollen lid of her left eye. It was sorer than the night before. She also had a slight headache. She straightened the bunches in the big brown sweater that Alan had given her to sleep in.

Once in the main room, she was surprised to see Peter lying wrapped up in a wool blanket beside the hearth. She went back to the room to retrieve her grandfather. Alan grumbled a curse in the Common-tongue as she woke him from what had been a deep sleep and led him out by the hand to where Peter lay.

"Ron som Peter cal?" asked Catina. *Why is Peter here?*

Alan pulled her off to the side, away from where Peter lay, so their voices wouldn't carry.

Alan got down on one knee and placed his hands on Catina's shoulders. "Peter boonta ulta firlo tem qu nemme teeka ro swemitsa ma." *Peter got hurt last night and needed me to help him.* His voice was reassuring. Catina didn't want anything to have happened to the nice man who had brought her to her grandfather.

"Som ma gosar?" *Is he okay?*

"Gu amot unba qu blemsha…fana ko, ma li wal gosar. Lohem zel qu san ma kae. Ren bani gu alim sem zora fa golohaa." A few bumps and bruises . . . yes, he will be fine. Come, now, and let him rest. We have a long day ahead of us.

Peter awoke shortly after Catina and Alan had gotten up. When he opened his eyes, it took him a moment to remember where he was. Then he remembered *why*. The night before—the Slummers, the ambush, the fight, the fire—filled his mind. He closed his eyes when a dull pang struck his heart. He was without home, without anything.

He heard voices not far away. He sat up, the wounds on his back tingling as he did. They felt a lot better today, though a bit tender. He stood and put on his shirt and wrapped the blanket around his shoulders to keep warm. He had broken a sweat throughout the night from sleeping so close to the hearth and from the intensity of his dreams—flashes of the night before. His clothes reeked with the thick smell of smoke and burnt wood, but he didn't care.

He followed the voices to Alan's room. Inside, Alan and Catina were tidying their beds, Alan showing Catina how to roll the straw mat into a cylinder and how to tie it so it didn't unroll itself. Peter stood in the doorway.

"Good morning, Peter," said Alan. He must have heard him though Peter could not recall making a sound.

"Morning," he returned.

"Umali ga," said Catina.

"It means 'happy sunrise,'" said Alan.

"Oh, um, uma-li ga," said Peter. His words were a little off; Catina giggled. Peter chuckled, too. So did Alan.

"Did you sleep all right? I hope you were not too warm," said Alan.

"I slept as well as able. Not the best of sleeps. But at least I slept." He paused for a moment. "I'm going to head out to my place and see what's left, if anything. I just wanted to let you know instead of abruptly leaving."

"Very well. Do you want us to come with you?"

"If you'd like. I know you two have things to do. You do still plan on leaving today, yes?"

"If we can pack in time. But we will probably wait until tomorrow. Let us see how the next hour or two pan out, first." He turned toward his granddaughter. "But I know Catina is anxious to leave."

The humanette picked up her flowery dress that was piled in a heap in the corner of the room. She brushed past as she went off to presumably change.

Peter thanked Alan for allowing him to spend the night.

"Not a problem," said Alan. "I guess we are even." He flashed a wry grin and left the room.

"Even?" said Peter.

The early morning sun shone in brilliance. Peter and Catina squinted their eyes, shielding them from the glare. Alan didn't need to. He couldn't see the light but told Peter he certainly felt it on his face. The streets were quiet. Some of the shops and trading posts were already open; others were in the midst of opening for the day. A few early risers left their houses and headed toward the end of the street.

The three of them walked down the road to the end as well, the people they passed stopping whatever they were doing to take in Catina's colorful dress. She clung to the sleeve of her grandfather's loose-fitting black shirt with a small hand. His shirt hung to his knees over a pair of gray trousers. Peter wore the same smoke-smelling clothes as the night before: a brown wool sweater and matching wool trousers.

Alan plodded along, walking stick in hand, feeling his way as they strode down the street. Peter's heart hammered inside his chest, anxious to see what was left of his home.

Alan must have heard Peter's labored breathing because he said, "It will be all right, my boy. You have nothing to worry about. Besides, you know the reality of the situation."

That was true. Peter *did* know the reality of the situation. He envisioned in his mind's eye what he might find once home. He could picture nothing left save for the smoldering ashes of what was once a wonderful place to live. He could already feel his heart sinking with the knowledge that he was going to have to start over again. He was also afraid he'd have no one to turn to once the morning was over. All he had was himself. Alan and Catina would be leaving that day, and if not, then early tomorrow at the latest. There'd be no one. He dreaded the impending loneliness and feelings of defeat.

A crowd had gathered around the smoldering ashes of his home. Peter and Alan and Catina made their way through them, and stood before the ashes and charred boards strewn about. Some folks' attention was directed at Catina's dress.

Smoke hovered about the area.

Peter knelt down and surveyed the one place where he felt safe, where his identity had been forged, where he could go when life troubled him.

Home.

No more.

He placed a thumb and forefinger over his eyes and let the tears well. Alan and Catina remained behind him. All were silent as the people allowed Peter his time to grieve. Like all places, it had its hardships, things that were wished to have gone better, but nothing like this had happened in recent memory. It was as if all of the Broken City's residents had lost something as well. It was a far cry from the night before. Though Peter appreciated their compassion, it felt artificial. Last night . . . . He didn't understand how they didn't try to help him. Though the penalty for breaking curfew was severe, one would think an exception would have been made when your house was aflame.

Then, from behind, "What in the blazes is going on? What happened?" It was Taimus, the Baker. He pushed his way through the crowd and came up beside Peter. His jaw hung open.

"Blast it all," he said quietly. "Peter?"

Peter glanced up at him, his blue eyes glazed over with tears. "Hi, Taimus."

"What happened?"

He stood, brushed the dirt and soot off his knees, and combed his fingers through his hair. Sighing heavily, he said, "It's a long story. I'll tell you some other time. Right now" —he glanced over the smoldering area— "I want to have a look around."

Solemnly, Peter stepped on the ash and wood and dirt, not caring if he stepped on something that was still burning or not. His home had occupied a small area so it didn't take him long to circle it. He walked around and through it two more times, trying to surround himself all the more with the memory of a fine place to live. On the fourth pass around, he stepped into the center of the debris.

"Dear Master," he said. "What am I going to do now?" And as if an answer, Peter went over to his right, to his former main living area, and knelt down. He pawed through the ashes, searching for, if any of it was left, a piece or two of the straw mat he had slept on for countless nights.

"Bele som tan?" asked Catina.

Alan replied something in Grescalla.

Hands covered in soot, Peter yanked his fingers back when he touched a hot ember. He put his fingertips against his lips to cool them. Pulling his sleeve over his right hand for protection against the heat, he stuck it back in the ashes and moved the dust about. When he didn't find what he was looking for, he moved a little to his left and tried again, scattering the soot and ash all over, digging in the mess. He found a curled up, burnt piece of a straw and knew he was on the right trail.

The crowd started talking as Peter continued his search. Their voices were kept quiet out of respect. They exchanged both words of concern and questions, some of the people already having decided to invite Peter back to their place for a good meal and a place to stay. Peter heard some of their talk but it didn't register. He was too focused searching for . . .

Then he found it: the floorboard with the thumb hook. The board was black and gray, part of it already burned through. Peter hooked his thumb in the knot and pulled up, the board breaking in two as his lifted it. He cast the broken plank aside and, with both hands, pulled out the oak chest with the ornate letter "P" on its top. The box hadn't been harmed by the fire. It only had smudges of filth from the ashes that found their way through the knot in the floorboard. The crowd gasped, all seemingly surprised he had a secret hiding place for something that meant a great deal to him.

Alan came over to him. Catina stood for a moment by herself then quickly followed behind.

The blind man crouched beside Peter. Catina sat on her haunches.

"What is it?" asked Alan.

Catina smiled. She already knew what it was.

Peter set the box down in front of them and opened it. His poems and journal were unharmed and in fine condition.

"I keep my poetry in here, as well as a book of private thoughts," said Peter. "If anything is worth saving from this mess, it's this. I never really had reason to keep it safe and hidden, but now I'm glad that I did. At least now I still have something." He wanted to say more but the words eluded him.

"Well, I am glad it is safe," said Alan.

"Me, too," said Taimus.

Peter, Alan and Catina looked up at the big man. The three of them hadn't heard him approach.

"Thanks, Taimus," said Peter. He closed the box's lid, wiped the soot from its top, and stood. Alan and Catina also got to their feet.

Taimus gave Peter a hug. "Look," said the Baker, "I don't know what happened here, but I'll be glad to make you feel better. Have you eaten yet?"

Peter shook his head.

"Then give me a moment and I'll whip up the best fried cakes you've ever had!" Before Peter could say anything to the offer, Taimus was already off toward his bake stand.

"I guess we know what we're doing for breakfast," said Peter, a wry grin on his face.

"I suppose so," said Alan.

Peter surveyed the crowd. They all looked on with expectant faces.

He said, "I know you're all concerned about what happened. I want you to know I'm fine and that I appreciate your concern anyway. I'm not sure what I'm going to do right now, but I'll figure something out. If it's all right with everybody, I would like to be left alone. I need some time to myself."

There were murmurs in the crowd; a few of the folks nodded to each other, understanding the request. The talk began to break up and, after a few minutes had passed, all had begun to go their own way.

"Amazing, really," said Alan.

Peter turned to him. "What?"

"Just like a family. When one of us is in trouble, they all come scooting out."

Perhaps, but Alan's statement wasn't entirely true. "Maybe. Though last night they knew that something was happening here. They saw the fire. But since it was night, they didn't do anything about it."

"Can you blame them?"

"Did you just say, 'can you blame them'?"

"Yes, can you blame them? In a perfect World—rather, anywhere else in the World—they would have come out to see what was the matter. But we live in Garathen, dear Peter. There is a curfew and it is dangerous at night. They were looking out for their own safety."

"But isn't that selfish? I mean, shouldn't you help others who are in need of it. Blast it, Alan! When I saw Catina the other night, wandering the streets alone, I went out to help her, not paying attention to my own skin."

"Peter," said Alan calmly, "I know you are upset. And, yes, it is selfish for one to put their own safety above the safety of another" —he waved a hand at the crowd walking away— "but they do not know that. They have grown up in a system where they stay indoors at night or so the Master help them, they will be punished. And whether they be punished by Man, Slummer, or Beast, who knows? They did not help you out of fear. Please do not hold that against them. They did not know any better."

"But my house?"

"Is just a house. You can rebuild another in time."

Peter thought he should be angry with Alan for saying that. But he wasn't. He was too defeated to care. His mind, body and spirit were exhausted.

There was silence between the two men. Then Peter said, "I'm sorry."

Alan clapped a hand on his back. "It is understandable, my friend."

Peter curled a small smile. Sometimes it felt good to swallow your pride. "What about you and Catina? Aren't you supposed to have left already?"

"You are right," said Alan, "we should have left some time ago." Then, with a smile, "But friends come first."

The three of them began walking slowly away from the smoky area, Peter's heart longing to stay there and dwell over his loss. He chose not to, knowing that if he stayed, he would feel even worse. And he *did* need to get away from there, away from the memories and haunting visions of the events that caused his home to burn down. Then a startling realization struck him: it had been *his* candle that had started the fire. If he hadn't dropped it, perhaps—No, he mustn't think like that. No good could be accomplished by dwelling on the could have and should have beens.

The three friends walked at a leisurely pace, Catina's eyes darting this way and that at the busy street. She turned her head away anytime she saw someone staring at her.

"When do you plan on riding out?" asked Peter.

"I am not so sure, now," said Alan. "Soon, though, as I know Catina wants to be home straight away." The humanette looked up at the mention of her name. "I also do not wish to leave you with no place to go. If you would like, you can stay at my place while we are gone. At least that way you would have a roof over your head. It would not be wise to try and fend for yourself. Not until you have someplace more permanent, anyway."

"Thank you for the offer," said Peter. "That's very kind. I just don't know if . . . what I mean is, is that I wouldn't want it to be an intrusion."

"Nonsense! I am glad to help."

"I know it's . . . " Peter stopped. "I want to come with you."

Alan looked at him quizzically. "What?"

"I want to come with you. I need to get away from here, from this."

"Peter, I do not know. This is something of a personal matter and I do not think that would be wise. We have only begun to be reacquainted with one another."

"Please. If I stay here, I'm just going to dwell on what happened. I need a chance to get away and get a new perspective. I won't get in the way. All I'm asking is to tag along."

"You are running from your problem, then." There was a note of condemnation in Alan's tone.

"I'm not running. But I do need to deal with this and the best way, for me, is to get away. Besides, I would love to see some place other than . . . here. Garathen is all I've ever known. I would like to see the outside World, if it is possible. You said yourself that once someone gets involved with your family, they stick with you all the way through."

Alan placed a hand on his chin. "I still do not think it would be a good idea. Peter, listen to me. You *are* running. Believe me, I know. I wanted to do the same thing when my wife died. Why else do you think I travel so much? It is to *get away*."

"I'm sorry that you lost your wife, but I would still like to come. I don't mean to be demanding, but, please, this would help me."

"Hm. There will be matters I will need to attend to once we reach Grek, and—"

"And I'll stay out of your way," finished Peter. "Besides," he added, looking to the humanette, "I'm sure Catina wouldn't mind if I came along."

Catina smiled at him.

Alan considered for a moment, then, "Why not."

And they walked on.

As they neared the Baker's station, Catina's tummy growled. She placed a hand over it, as if to hush it. Taimus saw them coming, smiling wide as they approached. Peter looked forward to a warm meal.

CHAPTER IX
The Departure

Breakfast had been wonderful. Taimus served up the best fried cakes that Peter and Alan had had in a long time. Catina had never tasted fried cakes before so for her it was a special treat. Fried cakes were made from a similar recipe to that of the bread bowls: yeast, flour, water, but with a lot more sugar. They were deep fried in oil and then, before they cooled, were doused in more sugar and served hot. The four of them ate plenty, Taimus included. Taimus enjoyed this time together with them, he expressed, and also added he was sorry when Alan, stomach full, announced they had to get going. Taimus said that in light of Peter's tragedy, they could come by his station for the rest of the week and receive anything they wished free of trade.

The three went back to Alan's place to pack. Peter waited in the main living area while the blind man and Catina went to prepare what they needed for their journey. As Alan packed he was careful to take only what was essential, being sensitive that Peter had lost all that he held dear. Catina looked on with interest as she watched her grandfather fill a large, single-strapped, brown canvas sack with a change of clothes: a long black robe to keep himself cool from the hot sun, a pair of black trousers and one of his gray undershirts. He also took along his underclothes and stockings.

They moved on to the kitchen and Alan, pushing the clothes in the sack to the side, filled the sack with food: dried salmon he had prepared some weeks before; fruits and vegetables; a skin of water, filled from a pump he kept outside the house; a small change-purse of drops and droppers of various worth, enough to keep them going once supplies ran low. The sack full, he flipped its large flap over its front and clasped it shut. He led Catina out to the living area and over to his desk. Peter stood before it, looking over the various papers and maps from Alan's previous journeys.

"Are we going to need any of these?" asked Peter, pointing to the rolls of maps stacked on the desk.

"Just one of them," replied Alan. He felt the mound of maps with his hand and picked one out of the middle of the pile.

"Are you sure that's the right one?"

"Of course it is. Like I said before, I know this place better than I known the inside of my own head," said Alan. "This is the map we will need. I know the way, but last time I made the journey, I had been able to see. I am going to need your eyes, if called upon."

"I'll help any way I can. It's the least I can do for the hospitality you've shown me."

Alan smiled. "Good. It is always good to be useful no matter your station in life."

Alan instructed to Catina in Grescalla to bring the large black bundle beside the desk, and also the smaller black bundle on its opposite side, to a chair near the hearth.

"Fana Ko, *Shinawa*," said Catina. *Yes, Grandfather.* She looked for the black bundles and when she located them, she bent down to pick them up. As she did, she winced and put a hand to her sore eye. She let out a soft whimper.

"Bel som fen?" asked Alan. *What is it?*

"Nurala," said Catina. *Nothing.* She picked up the bundles in her small arms.

"What are those?" asked Peter.

Catina waddled over, the bundles too big for her arms, and plunked them down on the chairs in front of the hearth.

"A portable shelter and a sleeping mat. We will need the shelter if it rains, which it probably will, or if the winds get high. A lot of the road is open territory and there is not much by way of trees. At least down the main roads, there is not." Alan waited a moment, his blank eyes widening. "I can tell you are excited, Peter."

"Is it that obvious?"

"Yes. I can hear you breathe and your voice sounds somehow . . . different, more urgent."

"What can I say?" said Peter. "I am excited."

"Excellent."

While Alan tied the black bundles to the canvas sack with thin rope, he had Peter take the bucket from the kitchen and go to the outdoor water pump to fill it. Once Peter returned, he told Peter to carefully pour some of the water over the hearth to cool the hot embers. The hearth, by the time they would get back, would be dry and ready to start up its task of heating the home once again.

When all the preparations for the long trip ahead of them had been made, Alan went over to the desk and selected a few of the items he kept in one of its drawers. He placed them in a small brown bag and went over to Peter and Catina, who were waiting by the door.

"All's well?" asked Peter.

"Just fine," said Alan. "What about you? All is well?"

"As well as it's going to be."

"Then let us be off." A second later, Alan slapped his forehead with the palm of his hand. "Almost forgot my walking stick," he said. "One moment." He reached up to where it was mounted alongside his sword by the door. He took it down.

Peter thought they were ready to leave but Alan lingered there a moment longer. The blind man then reached back to where his sword hung and ran a hand along its sheath.

"What do you think?" he asked Peter.

"I think we're going to need it." Then, hands raised, "Just to be safe."

"Me, too," he said and lifted the sword off its hook.

The three stepped outside, secured the door, and made their way out into the street.

As the trio walked toward the Easternmost street of Garathen, Peter asked, "Where are we going?"

"If we are going to make this trip," said Alan, "we certainly are not going to go on our own steam. We will need horses and Mr. Hahdgrove is the man we will see about that."

Peter had heard stories of crazy-man Hahdgrove. His full name was Barmin Hahdgrove and, from what folks said, was a bit of a cow without its bell. He had a stable on the far East of town and loaned his horses to people in need of them. There were stories that, just before the pub and whorehouse closed for the night, old Hahdgrove would take his largest horse out into the city and ride up and down each street, stark naked, singing in a high voice praises to the townspeople, wishing them a good night and pleasant dreams. No one knew why he did that other than he just simply did. Peter thought these outlandish rumors, and nothing more. He'd never seen Barmin do such a thing. No one else in town seemed to have *seen* him do it, either.

"And what are you going to trade for borrowing a horse?" asked Peter.

"Not just *a* horse, Peter. But two horses. And I do not wish to borrow them. I will trade to own them," said Alan smugly.

"Like I said, what are you going to trade?"

"Leave that to me."

Peter rolled his eyes.

Barmin Hahdgrove was outdoors, leaning up against the log fence that bordered a grassy area where a half dozen horses could run and play. The area wasn't as big as the horses would have liked, and it was small for the six of them, but it served their purpose nonetheless. There wasn't much space in the Broken City.

Barmin hadn't seen the trio coming and was startled by their approach. His eyes grew wide under bushy eyebrows when he saw Catina. Though her sore eye made her appear homely, the look in his eyes said she was adorable. He raised his arm at the elbow, greeting his three visitors. His red-brown hair waved in the breeze.

"Why, hello," said Barmin. "And what brings you out this fine morning?"

Alan rested against his walking stick. "We have come to see about a pair of horses."

"Ah, so you've come to old Barmin to borrow a steed, eh? Very good. I'll be glad to loan you my best of what's available. I only have eight and two of them are already out on loan. But there are six left and just as good. Except for the colt, of course."

"Of course."

Barmin looked Peter up and down. He folded his hands across his wide middle. "I'm sorry, Peter, for what happened."

Word of the fire traveled fast.

"Thank you."

"If there's anything I can do—"

Alan broke in. "I do not mean to be rude, but we are in a bit of a hurry. If we could get to business, please. I need two able-bodied horses that can go a great distance and cover a lot of ground without tiring easily."

Barmin arched an eyebrow, presumably surprised at Alan's callousness when it came to changing the subject from Peter's recent tragedy to that of horses.

"Mr. Hahdgrove?" prompted Alan.

Barmin wiped a film of sweat from his coppery face with the sleeve of his dirty white shirt. "Two horses, eh? And where are you going that you require *two* horses? Unless you need one for yourself and the other for your supplies."

"Not just myself," said Alan. "Peter and my granddaughter, here," —he gesticulated to Catina— "will be joining me."

"I see," said Barmin. "Off to see the World again and now you want company? Or is it because of your blindness that you require an escort and—"

"Barmin!" shot Alan. Peter straightened at the volume of Alan's voice. "Do you mind holding back on giving me a hard time? I know we have had our differences in the past and if you want to discuss the issue that is fine, but not in front of these two."

"We have nothing to discuss."

"Then let us leave our errs in the past and get on with it."

Barmin considered for a moment then gave a reluctant, "Very well," and crossed his arms.

"Finally," said Alan.

While Alan spoke with Barmin about acquiring a pair of horses, Peter and Catina strolled alongside the log fence to get a better look at the magnificent animals. Peter—though his time alone with her had been, previously, short—found something stirring within him when it came to being with the girl. He couldn't place it, but a warm sensation was there. Perhaps it was the idea that he would one day like to have a daughter similar to her. And what touched him, at this moment with her, was the way she led him alongside the fence by the hand, her small fingers in his, tugging him along to watch the horses run and play.

They stopped at a place about twenty feet from Alan and Barmin. There were three rungs on the fence: one about knee height on a grown man, another waist high, and another parallel to mid chest. Catina folded her arms and leaned up against the middle rung; Peter, unintentionally, copied her pose and leaned against the top one. The horses ran in circles within the corral, their hooves thudding dully on the grass as they trotted. It was a beautiful sound. Peter watched the expression in the horses' eyes, seeing in them a carelessness and freedom that he longed to one day feel for himself. The hardships of the World and of life were not even a consideration in the horses' minds. They were just there to live and breathe and go wherever their strong hearts would lead them. Their only "limit" was the confines of the corral. It struck Peter these horses were not unlike himself. He was a free man who was capable of making his own decisions, knew the desires of his heart and was able to act on them. His only limit, like that of the log fence, was the Forest-Ring of Garathen, keeping him in.

Catina dug her canvas-shoed toes into the dirt and watched the horses, especially the young six-month-old, tan-colored colt with a white mane that pranced alongside its mother.

"They are beautiful, aren't they?" said Peter. "They sure are pretty."

Pretty. He had said it without realizing it. With all that happened in the past day, he completely forgot about Catina's feelings towards the word. The little humanette's eyes dampened and her lips trembled.

"I'm sorry," he said as he came down beside her, "I forgot. Don't cry."

Catina sniffled some more but her attention on the matter was sidetracked when the young colt came charging along the fence, zipping past, chasing something that was known only to it.

Shaming himself for his mistake, Peter stood. He hoped Catina wouldn't cry again.

She didn't.

A short while later there was a bustling to their left and they could see Mr. Hahdgrove opening up the corral gate for Alan. Alan walked into the corral, his walking stick moving in front of him left to right as he felt his way in, avoiding walking into anything. Barmin, two sets of reins in hand, went and put bridles and reins on two of the horses. One was dazzling white with a gray mane and tail, and the other its opposite, black, with a matching gray mane and tail. Once the horses' bits and reins were in place, Barmin led them over to Alan and, noticing Peter looking his way, waved Peter and Catina over.

Barmin went to a small shed beside the corral and came out with two heavy sacs of horse feed, his stout figure waddling beneath them as he brought them over. He placed the sacs of feed on the horses, one on the back of each horse, tying them with thick twine to their barrel-like bellies, so the rider had something to sit on instead of riding bare-back. The bags of feed weren't too hard so having them on their backs wouldn't bother the horses. Peter was surprised Mr. Hahdgrove didn't have any saddles. Perhaps he had them at one point but then had to trade them away for other necessities. In Garathen, sometimes the supplies required for fuelling your trade had to be sacrificed when times were lean.

Peter and Catina stood beside Alan.

Before Peter could ask about the saddles, Alan said, "You will have to lead them out, Peter. I may know my way around Garathen fairly well, but these horses do not. You do know how to rein a horse, correct?"

"Yes," answered Peter. "It's been awhile but I'll manage."

"Good." He turned to Mr. Hahdgrove. "Barmin, thank you." He handed the horses' keeper a lovely patterned bag. "Inside you will find the items we discussed."

Barmin took the bag, opened it, checked it for what he was promised, and then drew the bag's draw-string closed. "Our deal is sealed, then. Take good care of these horses. They may look friendly but they're filled with spirit. They'll serve you well."

And with a friendly wave, Alan bid Barmin good-bye.

Peter helped Alan up onto the black horse and, once the blind man was steady, he lifted Catina from up under her arms and placed her in front of Alan. Peter mounted the white horse and adjusted himself on the feed bag beneath his bottom. He reached over and took the black one's reins in his right hand, those of the white horse in his left.

He turned to Barmin. "Thank you."

"Remember what I said," said Mr. Hahdgrove, "these two are full of spirit. But sometimes they don't get along. Like day and night, they sometimes are that to each other, like a married couple, hence their names. Day is who you're riding, Peter, and the other is Night. May the Master be with you on your journey."

And with those words, Peter, Alan and Catina rode from the corral, Peter steering them back towards Alan's to finish preparing for the journey ahead.

Catina waved to the little tan-colored colt as they rode away.

Equipping the horses with their things didn't take long. Alan had everything ready to go before they left for Barmin Hahdgrove's. Though Alan's home was at the end of the Through-way, it was still visible by most of the folks who lived in Garathen. Already rumors were circulating as to where the great Alan-the-traveler would be off to next. But once the three were gone, the people would go about their business as usual and forget that the strange blind man had left with his two companions. The people would miss the little girl in the colorful dress, though. Having her there, even if it had been just for a short time, was a pleasant treat and a relieving break from the grays and browns and blacks of the Broken City.

Alan secured the latch on his door and placed a hand upon its entrance.

"Until we meet again," he said.

Peter led him over to Night and helped him up, then tied Alan's walking stick under the big canvas bag that held some of their supplies. He picked up Catina like before and sat her in front of her grandfather. Alan secured his arms around her tiny waist.

"Don menne ta cale gammi?" he asked. *Are you ready to go?*

Catina replied with a delighted nod. Finally they would be off to help her parents in Grek.

Peter mounted the white horse, Day, and grabbed Night's reins. "Where to?" breathed Peter. He was suddenly having second thoughts about leaving. This would be his first time away from Garathen.

"Take the Through-way ahead and we will follow a trail through the Forest-Ring. It is the route I took each time I had gone in the past. I know the path well and can guide you through it. All who reside in the Ring should be asleep as they do not come out until after dark. And unless any of that has changed in the past two years, we should be quite safe. Steady on, Peter, and let us go. We have been dawdling here long enough."

Peter didn't think that they had been doing any dawdling at all, but it was evident that Alan was eager to get under way, and, judging by the way Catina stirred in her seat on Night's back, she was just as anxious to get going.

"Mali kwon nali," said Catina. *Thank you.*

And with a smile, Peter said, "Dana kwon nali." *You are welcome.*

And they were off.

They trotted slowly down the street, Peter getting used to guiding the two powerful horses, directing them which way to go. He was pleased when he saw that once they had been given a direction to go in, the horses began to follow the other's lead; with both currently going straight, he rarely had to correct their path.

As they passed the shops and stalls of traders, they were given waves of farewell and tips of the hat, wishing them a good journey. Some people even came up to them to say good-bye and to wish them well. When they passed the fruit stand, Talia came out, rushing to Peter's side.

"I didn't know you were leaving," she said, walking with them.

"I am. Shouldn't be for too long, though," said Peter.

"Is it because of what happened?" A look of worry aged her beautiful, youthful face.

Alan's words of warning from earlier crept back on him. It suddenly felt as if he *were* running away from what happened. "Partly," he said, admitting his feelings. He knew that Alan was listening to him. "But I also think this will be good for me. Give me a chance to see what's out there. It's strange, you know. For the longest time I've wanted to leave, but now that I'm actually doing it, I want to stay. I didn't realize how much I'm going to miss it here." Then, with a startling realization, "And how much I'm going to miss you, Talia."

Talia's face flushed red. "I know we don't talk much," she said, "but I wish we had. Perhaps when you return? You are coming back, aren't you?"

"Of course," said Peter, grinning. "I wouldn't just up and leave and never come back. No. My heart will always remain here."

She took his hand in hers. "When will you return?"

"I'm not sure."

Alan interrupted. "Probably within a couple of months time. Not too much longer, I should think. We have business elsewhere but if Peter wishes it, he can return whenever he wants."

"A couple of months, then," said Peter, echoing the blind man.

Talia smiled. "I look forward to your return. Stop by my station when you do and there will be a fresh bowl of fruit waiting for you. Maybe we can have a picnic?"

Peter wasn't sure as to where Talia's sudden interest in him was coming from, but it was a welcome one. "I shall look forward to it," he said.

She gave his hand a thoughtful pat and waved good-bye. Picking up her brown dress by the hem, she scurried back to her station.

Peter stared after her.

"Nice girl," said Alan, ruining the moment.

With a feeling of sudden elation about his departure, Peter focused his attention forward. There would be one more obstacle to overcome before they entered the Forest-Ring.

Not far ahead down the Through-way, Peter saw the rubble that was once his home. Unbeknownst to him, he drew back on the horses' reins, slowing their approach, as if in an indirect effort to stave off what was going to be a painful experience.

Smoke still swirled in dull, semi-transparent curls in the mid-morning air, the last of the embers that were still hot finally beginning to cool. Catina's nose wrinkled from the smoky smell.

"Would you like to stop before we leave?" asked Alan.

More than anything Peter *did* want to stop and spend a moment saying good-bye to the remains of his home. But no, he couldn't. He would only be indulging himself in the pain of his loss by doing so. The purpose of his journey to Grek was to move *forward,* and by stopping, he would only be going *backward,* to that place in his heart that was the past.

"It's all right," said Peter. "I think it'll be best if we just ride on past it. I can dwell on it another time."

"I see," said Alan. "As you wish. I will be here for you, though, should you need an ear to listen. I understand loss and am willing to share with you my thoughts should they be required."

"Thank you."

Peter breathed in deep and exhaled an audible sigh as they rode past the site. The powdery gray of the ashes seemed to glitter slightly in the morning sun, as if made of magic, as if his home was saying good-bye to him. In the days and weeks to come, Peter knew, the winds would come along and blow the ashes away, and the burnt wood would begin to return to the earth, and, eventually, after a long while, new vegetation would sprout up in the gaps in the wreckage and leave no trace of his home at all. Thankfully, though, once he returned, he could still come to his homestead and see the scars on the earth from the fire. At least at this moment, as he looked back on the ashes as he passed them, he could take comfort in knowing this wouldn't be the last time he saw the remains of his home.

The burn marks and scars, like all painful memories, would be waiting for him to rediscover again after he returned. It would only be through the passage of time and the living of life that those hurts fade, and he could finally put away his loss in a place that could eventually be forgotten.

CHAPTER X
Into the Forest-Ring
(Spirited Horses)

The trio took the horses up the gravely hill along the same path Peter had walked with Catina the day before. More than once as they ascended, Peter found himself looking back onto Garathen, his eyes wandering over to the rubble of his home. He then made a conscious effort to look forward and leave his life behind.

It was time for something new.

Before long they were at the edge of the Forest-Ring. The horses slowed a little, as though fearing to wade in. Their riders pressed them on, and they entered.

The dense trees of the Forest were menacing, their long and wide trunks coated with a bark so thick it was though a shield to the wood beneath. Higher up the trunks, heavily-leaved branches protruded up and out, reaching dizzying heights above the travelers' heads. There were bushes all around, the undergrowth just as thick as the canopy of leaves above, the ground barely visible beneath. They entered a world of brown and green, the tones light and dark and varied in between. The sun, bright over head, shone holes in the canopy in bold streaks of light, each shaft of luminance stabbing through the leaves like spears, lighting the way through what was normally a dark forest. Peter took this as a sign the weather was on their side. Even the Master. This relieved his nervousness.

They were not on a set path, as there weren't any paths in the Forest-Ring. The Ring seldom saw any travelers. The only guide to those who came through the Ring were the hunting trails made by the beasts that lurked in the forest or by the prey that was hunted, like deer and fopphin and rabbits and jalabes. Peter, Alan and Catina were on such a trail now. Peter hoped he would be able to use this trail to guide them out.

Thinking on this, he asked Alan, "How do I know I'm going the right way? I've never been through here before."

"Not to worry," said Alan, "these trails made by the animals crisscrossing this way and that, run through the entire forest. Or so it is said. The Forest-Ring is broken up into three stages. The first, the one we are in now, is thick, the hunting trails barely visible but visible enough to know they will lead you somewhere. The second stage is thinner and there is a lot of open space beneath the canopy. The third is much like the first, the forest growing dense again until we come out on the other side. All one needs to do when going through here—well, this is what I did—is just maintain your direction and press on in a straight line. That way, you will not get turned around and find yourself lost. I am trusting we have been going in one direction thus far, right, Peter?"

"Yes," he said. "So far. I just don't want to make a mistake and, like you said, get ourselves lost."

"Just keep going straight. The forest will open up in about an hour or so. It will be easier to find our way through after that."

"When do you think we'll be out of the Ring?"

"We left later than I had planned so I am not so sure. Probably just after dinner time. And we had better be out of here by then, otherwise there will be danger. As I said before, the beasts are sleeping for the day right now; that is why our passage is safe. But we must also be careful not to wake them, either. If we do—" Alan didn't finish.

Peter considered the little girl. "Then how did Catina make it through during the night and emerged on the other side into Garathen?"

"Only the Master knows the answer to that. I honestly do not have a clue as to how she survived. Unless, of course, instinctually, she kept to the cover of night and stayed out of sight to the lurkings of the forest. But again, even if that was the case, palanthora beasts have a keen sense of smell and could easily have sniffed her out. Only the Master knows, Peter. I certainly do not."

Peter glanced over to the humanette. Catina's young eyes looked all around at the vegetation and trees and foliage. But her gaze seemed somehow empty, as if her mind was elsewhere.

With a small hand, Catina patted the back of Night's neck, the horse letting out a little gruff of approval of her strokes.

Alan said something in Grescalla.

"What did you say?" asked Peter.

"I told Catina to treat Night kindly and we will be home in no time." Alan put a hand to Catina's back affectionately.

Peter's thoughts drifted to Talia. He had been surprised she had come out and spoken with him. He was equally surprised it seemed she had an interest in him. She hadn't exhibited any interest in him since they were children. This new found knowledge was both exhilarating and sad. He was excited that when he saw her again, they could talk and become friends and, perhaps, something more. Yet he also knew that wouldn't happen for awhile. He would not be returning to the Broken City for quite some time. He was going to miss her. He prayed to the Master to watch over her until he returned. If the past forty-eight hours had taught him anything, it was that Garathen wasn't as safe as he had once thought it to be. He had been attacked by Slummers and, in his mind, that meant that anybody could be attacked. Even Talia.

"You are awfully quiet, Peter," said Alan. "Anything on your mind that you wish to share?"

"No," he replied. "My head's just a little full right now. A lot's happened and I'm trying to put those things behind me, but I don't think I'm finished dealing with them yet. I'm just asking the Master for help in this."

"I see," said Alan. "The Master does give help to those who ask. Though, I am not sure if He has a physical—or spiritual, for that matter—hand in it, or whether it is just our Faith in Him that helps see us through." Alan made a face as he considered what he just said. The muscles around his white eyes tensed with grave seriousness. "When was your Age of Enlightenment, Peter?"

Peter furrowed his brow. "Age of Enlightenment?"

"Yes, yes, your Age of Enlightenment. We all have one. Even Catina, here, has had one by now."

Catina looked up at him from hearing her name then back down at Night's head bobbing up and down as the steed walked through bushes and trees, parting the leaves while he brushed past them.

"I still don't understand," said Peter. "What do you mean the, um, Age of Enlightenment?"

Alan bit his lip.

"The Age of Enlightenment," explained Alan, "happens when you are very young. Usually between the ages of three and seven. Eight, at the latest. You dream of the Master, and meet Him for the first time. It is all in your dream, of course, but upon waking you have a revelation. You awake with a knowledge in your heart, mind and spirit that the Master oversees everything and watches over us all, looks out for us in our lives and aides us when things become hard or unbearable. Please tell me you understand what I mean, now?"

"No, I don't. I've never dreamed of the Master. Not once. I've imagined Him and what He might look like, but I've never gone to bed one night and dreamed of Him. Are you telling me that everyone dreams of Him when they are young and, as a result, have some sort of connection with Him because of it?"

"That is what I am telling you." Alan asked Catina in her Tongue if she had ever dreamed of the Master. He translated for her as she relayed her story.

She had been sleeping in her room at home, and dreamed she'd awoken. She laid there in bed, waiting to fall back asleep when, out of the corner of her eye, she saw a brilliant purple light emanate from the door to her room. Scared, she hid under her blanket but could somehow feel the purple light pouring all the more into her room because she had hidden herself away. The light flashed brighter, engulfing her in a purple haze. She lowered the blanket slowly from over her head and, there before her, was the silhouette of a man standing in the doorway against a backdrop of purple mist.

The Master.

He spoke to her, telling her that He loved her and, because of that love, He was going to preside over her life and see to it that all would turn out well for her. Catina believed Him and just as soon as He appeared, He was gone and she woke up in the real world.

She had told her mother about her dream and her mother explained to her what it meant.

Alan had the same dream when he was small, the only difference being it had taken place in his own bedroom. Over time, when he thought on it and compared the tale of his dream with that of others, he discovered that it was, in fact, the same dream, just altered slightly to fit the person's surroundings at the time they dreamed it.

"See, I told you," said Alan. "Catina has dreamed of the Master, as well. It is an odd thing that you have not. You are not lying to me, are you?"

"No!" said Peter. The sudden loudness of his voice caught him off guard. He spoke softer. "No, I haven't."

The thought of not sharing the same dream as Alan and Catina scared him. Was there something wrong with him? Was that why he had never dreamed such a thing? Peter had always believed in the Master because he heard others talking about Him and had grown up being told that Faith in the Master was what you were supposed to have. Only now did he realize that his Faith was blind. It was based simply on believing what he was told to believe. Nothing more.

Just then Day let out a snort, as if letting the riders know she was feeling left out from the conversation. Catina giggled at the mare's snort. Giving Day a reassuring pat on the neck, Peter ran his fingers through the horse's coarse, gray mane. Then Night snorted, too, as if contributing his own reassurances to his four-legged kin.

"What do you think that means?" asked Peter, referring to not dreaming of the Master.

"I do not know," said Alan. "I have never heard anything of the sort. Maybe you simply do not remember; though I do not know how that could be because those I have spoken with regarding the Age of Enlightenment vividly remember their dreams." He paused. "I do not have an answer for you. I am sorry."

Peter frowned. He felt different from the other two just then, as if he wasn't quite as *human* as they were. "It's okay," he said.

And the conversation was over.

The trail they followed had a slight wind to it, first right then left, but was pretty much a straight path. If Peter felt they were detouring a little too far to the left or right, he would pull on the horses' reins and direct them through the bushes where there was no trail. The new paths he created always rejoined another.

Peter thought it amazing how an animal could create a hunting trail and, if it was effective, could revisit that same trail time and time again without getting it mixed up with another one or get itself lost.

The three travelers rode on in silence for a long time; Catina began to doze as they rode. She was still tired from her long journey two days before and because her headache was returning. She leaned back against her grandfather and he held her as she slept.

The last time Alan traveled through the Forest-Ring, he had been able to see. Now, as he rode Night, he envisioned what he remembered the forest having looked like, at times getting so lost in his imagination that it felt like he could see again. As much as he trusted Peter to guide them through, he was often tempted to keep checking with him to be sure they were going in the right direction. But Peter had been through an awful lot over the past few days and he didn't want to discourage him. He was not used to being dependent on anybody but himself, and would have to learn to trust someone else to see them through this. It was also a lesson in patience.

The horses' ears perked up, their ears twitching back and forth, listening to something the riders could not hear. The horses stopped and wouldn't budge when Peter clicked his tongue to keep them moving.

Alan heard something too. *What—?* Something was following them.

The horses bolted as if death was after them. Peter gripped tightly to the reins, most of his effort concentrated on hanging onto the reins that steered Night, Alan's horse. He didn't want to lose control and have the blind man and his granddaughter become lost in the Forest-Ring, solely on the impulse of a frightened animal. But, that's just what happened. Day and Night's quick strides soon turned into a gallop and Peter lost his grip on Night's reins when the dark horse suddenly veered off to the right.

"Alan!" shouted Peter.

"Blast, Peter, what is going on!" shouted the blind man, turning in his seat as Night took off into the green.

Catina screamed, her small body bouncing up and down wildly as Night tore through the forest.

Day rode ahead full speed, carving fresh paths in the bushes that ran between the trees. Right, left, zigzagging all over, trying to get away from whatever the mare sensed was behind them. Peter strained his head to the right, watching as his two friends disappeared among the leaves, the only sounds of their presence being Alan's grunts as he pulled on the reins, trying to slow Night down, and Catina's squeals. The thudding of Night's hooves along the ground was heard for a moment longer—then faded away.

"Blast!" spat Peter.

He pulled back on Day, the bit straining against the horse's mouth. The mare fought his pull and pressed forward, running at full speed. Thin branches from the surrounding foliage slapped Peter's face; each stinging swat caused a grunt to escape his lips. Just minutes ago, he and his two friends had been moving at a gentle trot through the forest and now, he was riding Day at full gallop, having no control over the horse's actions.

"Alan! Catina!" he shouted into the surrounding trees as they whisked by. His companions didn't respond. At least, not loud enough to be heard; but Peter thought he heard shouts somewhere far away, hidden beneath the clamor of speeding hooves.

Dear Master, watch over them, he thought.

Alan's words from earlier came back to him. Whatever beasts lurked in the Forest-Ring were asleep during the day. Peter knew his shouts would only serve to wake them. He hoped Alan would remember that and would keep quiet. He also hoped Alan would tell the same to Catina.

The thunder of the horses' hooves could not be silenced.

Day's zigzagging eased and she maintained a straighter path, but Peter didn't know how far off course her panic had taken him. She was still at alert; her ears swiveled front to side, listening intently to all around her. Peter's heart raced. He, too, glanced around himself, his eyes searching for anything that might be moving. All he saw was the green and brown of the forest rushing by, nothing more. So badly did he want to shout out his friends' names, but he knew he couldn't. He couldn't risk waking anything that might hunt him—them—down. That was, of course, if something had not been awoken already.

Elsewhere, Night was taking Alan and Catina for a ride. Catina had never been on a horse moving so fast, Alan knew. When she had ridden Lamara back home, the fastest she'd ever gone was a brisk trot. The way Night was zipping through the forest so fast was terrifying, but at the same time strangely exhilarating. Catina squealed and Alan told her to keep her voice down. Alan didn't dare tell her why though, for fear of scaring the poor girl. He was already scared himself. Because of his blindness, he lived in a world of darkness. All he had to rely on when away from his home was his imagination, substituting for sight and other senses. He could smell the very green of the forest, the scent fresh and leafy, and the dew on the leaves. He could hear the air blow past as they sped ever onward and the light swatting of the thin branches as they slapped against his face and thighs. He could feel Catina bounce up and down in her seat as the horse galloped, her small body bumping into him when the horse went over uneven ground.

He had to slow the steed down. If he didn't, who knew where they would end up? And when you're blind, even being just a little lost was a big deal, especially when you were with someone who couldn't help you find your way back.

Catina squealed again. Alan silenced her, this time loudly; she jolted at the command in his voice. Her grandfather had never told her to be quiet so sternly before.

Alan reached around her, fumbling for the reins that were flopping in all directions atop the horse's mane. His fingers entangled in the coarse hair before finally finding purchase on the leather straps. He grabbed hold of them and pulled back. Night's head lurched back hard, the horse's neck arching back at an almost impossible angle. Night let out a powerful whinny. Catina screamed at the sound.

"Wwhhooaa!" he commanded. The horse's pace slowed a little but not enough. He tried again, this time gently, remembering it was useless to further excite an already excited horse with loud words. Night responded quickly to his calm voice and slowed down a little more.

In Grescalla, Alan told her to pet the steed's mane and tell him that everything is going to be all right.

Catina obeyed and, using one hand to hold the horse's mane, she used the other to stroke the side of the horse's neck, reassuring the steed there was nothing to worry about. Alan didn't think she believed the words of reassurance, but she obeyed anyway.

Night slowed a little more, Alan pulling back gently on the reins in intervals, easing the horse back down to a quick trot.

"There, there," said Alan. "Good horse. Good." He then added, "Mali kwon nali, Catina." *Thank you, Catina.*

"Dana kwon nali," she replied proudly. She had done well.

He asked her to look around and see what was around them, if anything was following them.

"Rana Ko," she said. *No.*

"Don menne thim?" *Are you sure?*

"Fana Ko." *Yes.*

They were safe for the time being. The only question being, where was Peter?

At the same time Alan had been slowing down Night, Peter and Day were still moving at full gallop.

Just think of your options, thought Peter. *I have to slow her down otherwise we'll be hopelessly lost. There must be a way to—*

Then it became clear. One of the reasons Day was running so fast was because in the excitement of the commotion and in the fear of whatever had spooked her, Peter's body had tensed and his heels and calves dug into the mare's sides, urging her to run faster. He relaxed his body and almost immediately he felt Day begin to slow down. Peter pulled on the reins softly, this time giving the horse only one signal: slow down. Before, he had been telling her to do two things. Day's head tilted back as Peter pulled on the reins.

"Easy, easy," he said. "We'll be fine. There's nothing to worry about. All is well."

Day let out a snort and slowed to a trot but Peter thought she was going to speed up again. He tugged on the reins a little more, setting the pace for her.

"There we go," he said. "See? I told you. We're okay."

They rode on for a moment, letting the excitement settle then fade. He had to find Alan and Catina before they got hopelessly lost. Surely Alan was capable of taking care of himself. He had done it countless times before on his own private travels. But he had never done it since he became blind. Peter didn't know how well Alan would fare on his own without sight.

Peter scanned the area, searching for anything that might be following him. The Forest-Ring was just like it was when he first entered—green and brown leaves, trees, bushes and the thick shrubbery that made it hard to see the ground beneath.

Peter feared he was already lost.

Somewhere over to his right, Peter heard a dull thudding and the shifting of leaves. Panic immediately seized his heart. Day's ears swiveled in the direction of the sound, but the mare did not change her pace.

Perhaps it's nothing. The thought gave Peter hope.

A horse's instincts, like all animals, were far more accurate than that of a Human's. A Man could be standing next to something evil and not know it, but if an animal were to cross the path of something that intended hostility, it would know and would take action. Usually.

The shuffling of leaves and the dull thudding stopped—then resumed again. Day turned in the direction of the sound. Peter tried to steer her back on course, but the mare fought him and continued going to the right.

Giving in, Peter said, "Okay, though you have not yet earned my trust, I'll trust you in this. But if you get us killed, well, I'd like to say you'll be sorry but you'll be dead and so will I, so there'll be nothing we could do about it. Ah, blast it! You know what I mean. I just hope you know what you're doing, friend. And I hope you also have the sense to run should we encounter something evil."

The horse snorted, seemingly in concurrence.

The shuffling sound grew nearer as well as the heavy pad-pad-padding whatever it was made against the ground. Peter swallowed hard and hoped that whatever lay just beyond the wall of foliage would be friendly.

The leaves brushed past him and Day rose on her hind legs, letting out a powerful neigh.

"Whoa, there!" said Peter. Day plunked back down on the ground. "What's the matter? What do you hear?"

The horse neighed again. This time, somewhere ahead of them, a similar neigh was returned. Day whinnied back at the familiar sound and, as if in conversation, the sounds exchanged back and forth for some time.

Just then Peter saw the sweat-glistened top of Alan's bald head, then, a moment later, the swaying back and forth of Catina as Night rode towards him. The horses continued neighing until they met up with each other, their muzzles nuzzling together.

"There you are, Peter," said Alan. "Still breathing loud as ever. You are lucky we are not hiding from—"

"'There you are, Peter'?" he said. "Is that all you can think of to say to me? I'd nearly gotten lost and all you can say is 'There you are, Peter' and make fun of my breathing? What's wrong with you?"

Catina giggled. Peter shot her a scowl. She didn't care and kept on smiling, evidently happy to see him.

"What am I supposed to say?" said Alan. "Should I ask if you are all right? Should I say 'Oh, thank the Master that you did not fall off your horse and break your leg'? No. It is best to stay calm in alarming situations."

"Yeah, but—"

"Yeah, but nothing," said the blind man. "I admit, if it makes you feel any better, this little episode has caused me quite a stir. But, really, was this life and death? No. So let us move on and get out of this wretched forest before whatever frightened the horses comes back."

Catina giggled again as she watched what looked like the horses giving each other kisses. Day and Night. Not one without the other. They had found each other.

"How do you suppose our big friends found each other?" asked Peter. "It's not like they knew where the other was."

Alan considered for a moment. "But I think they did. Barmin said that these horses are always together and, I think, they just proved that to us. Because of their friendship, I am guessing, they are also not without a sense of where the other is at, at all times. Friends do not abandon each other in times of peril nor do I think these horses would abandon each other in a similar circumstance. Maybe the best way for them to escape whatever they thought was following them was to throw the pursuer off by running in two separate directions, and then meet up again when it was safe."

"Possibly," said Peter. "Maybe that's why it took me awhile to slow her down. But I was also pressing against her sides, telling her to go forward."

Alan cut in. "But I think she has more of a mind of her own than she lets on. Just like Night, here. I am starting to believe that our urgings are more decoration and formalities than anything else. We are more of a simple guide to them rather than a commanding force. And these horses just proved that to us by finding each other—rather quickly, I might add—after scampering off in opposite directions."

Catina said something in Grescalla.

"Hm," said Alan. He glanced up at Peter. "She just asked me if I knew where we were."

"Do you know where we are?" asked Peter.

Alan heaved a sigh. "No, I do not. In case you have not noticed, I am blind." He proffered a grin.

Peter felt his cheeks flush. "Alan," he said, "I've never been to the entrance of the Forest-Ring in all my life never mind into the thick of it. I have no idea where we are."

"Now that *is* going to be a problem." He looked up at the forest's canopy, the sun directly over them, visible through the leaves, coming through in shafts of bright light like earlier, but this time straight down instead of at an angle. The light bathed Alan's white face.

"It is probably around Midday," he said, "though most likely a bit before. Even so, the Forest-Ring is still a big place and we best be on our way. We have to be out before evening comes otherwise we might as well count ourselves as one of the dead."

"How do you know what time it is?"

Alan gave him a knowing glare.

"Sorry. Agreed. So . . . which way?"

They discussed in which direction their horses had traveled while they had been frightened and how much—they guessed—off course they had taken them. It was decided that Night and Day had led them in a fairly straight line and it was only towards the end when the horses met up with each other did their course change. Day had turned to the right and Night to the left. Since they were now facing each other, Peter and Alan decided to pivot the horses in the opposite direction so that Day turned to the left and Night to the right, facing straight, resuming what they assumed was the same direction they had been facing before this detour had occurred.

Catina asked if they would be leaving soon. The leaves were tickling her ankles, making them itch. Alan told her they would get moving in a moment.

And with that, Peter and Alan clicked their tongues and Day and Night trotted on.

Hopefully they would make it out of the Forest-Ring before dark.

They rode on for several hours. It was mid afternoon and they were lost. The horses, as seemingly smart as they were, had led them off course. When Peter started complaining of their circumstance, Alan insisted they maintain a straight line.

"You know the Forest-Ring is a circle, Peter," Alan told him, "and if we continue onward—straight—we will eventually emerge outside of it."

"But will we get out before dark?" asked Peter, his tone an I-told-you-so, trying to prove that Alan wasn't as smart as he thought he was.

Peter didn't know why he wanted to upset the blind man and could only attribute his rudeness to simple selfishness; looking out for his own skin. Growing up in the Broken City, despite the family-like atmosphere, each man was still responsible for his day to day safety and survival. That's just how it was. But, being with Alan and spending time talking with the blind man was changing all that. Alan's experiences of being abroad were showing through and he had a mentality that Peter never encountered before. Alan viewed things with an almost childlike simplicity: black and white; right and wrong; life and death; up and down. Things were either perilous or they weren't. There was no gray area with Alan, even in the things he didn't understand. He always leaned one way or the other, never down the middle.

"If we do not get out of here by dark," said Alan, "then we will ride until we do. And should we encounter any danger, our four-legged companions have already proved themselves capable to get us far away swiftly."

"Far away and lost," countered Peter.

"Why do you always look for the worst in a situation?"

He didn't have an answer.

Before long the First Stage of the Forest-Ring came to an end and an open glade within the dense forest appeared before them.

"At least we are making progress," said Alan.

"Thankfully," said Peter. He didn't even bother to figure out how Alan knew the wooded area had changed.

The open area underneath the forest canopy was a pleasant change from the monotony of the leaves and tree branches they had been traveling through for the past several hours.

The glade was far browner than green, the ground composed of mainly wood chips and decaying leaves. The trees still towered around them but were rooted much farther apart. The canopy of green still remained, the trees; branches longer, maintaining a larger umbrella of leaves than the trees in the First Stage of the forest. All were relieved to be in a much less crowded area.

"Steady on straight, Peter," said Alan.

Peter readjusted his grip on the reins, driving both horses forward. They trotted on a few minutes before a low buzzing began to fill the air. It was a low hum at first, but soon grew louder, almost to a drone. The three companions soon found out the cause of the sound. Piled up against the base of the surrounding tree trunks were decaying carcasses of deer, jalabes, rabbit, fopphins, elks, and even some wild dog. Flies swarmed above the dead bodies like a dense and dark mist. The air smelled of the dead, of blood, thick and tinny and somehow warm.

Immediately Catina wrinkled her nose and covered it with her hand, making a face. "Boola," she said.

"Tell me, Peter, what do you see?" said Alan.

"Bodies," he said. "Animals of all kinds. They're huddled in piles against the bottom of the trees, almost like a blanket at the base. Obviously something put them there."

The flies swirled in black and gray clouds over the bodies, some of them making their way over to the three visitors atop the two horses. Catina swatted them away. Alan did the same and so did Peter. The horses' tails swished side to side, shooing the flies away.

"How far does this go on?" asked Alan.

Peter took Day a little further ahead, glanced around, and then reared the mare back beside Night. "I can't tell. A good ways. I can't see around all the trees but I can see plenty of flies up ahead. Probably a few minutes worth of distance, which isn't so bad."

"Good," said Alan. "Well, steady on, then. I do not wish to stay here any longer."

Catina gagged and for a moment Peter thought she was going to throw up from the stench. Peter guided the horses forward.

Right after the sound of heavy hooves stepping on leafy ground came from the bushes beside them, a palanthora beast sprang out in front of them, cutting them off, sending the horses into a frenzy.

Alan drew his sword.

Day and Night rose on their hind legs, braying as if shouting to the heavens. All three travelers fell from the horses, falling hard onto their backs against the wood-chipped ground. The horses tore off past the palanthora beast and into the graveyard of dead animals beyond.

Catina started screaming.

The beast came forward.

Peter thought they were going to die.

The palanthora's slick gray body moved toward them with an astonishing grace for such a large creature. The muscles in its powerful hindquarters ripple as it moved, its feet long, splayed out before it into two thick toes with equally thick, sharp black nails. The palanthora's powerful shoulders, hunched over its torso, branched out on either side of its neck in an upside-down bow. Its muscular arms hung at its sides almost to its knees, ending with humanlike hands. It had a long face, the top portion above the nose gray and scrunched, like a human face slightly compressed. Its jaws were half its length. The jawbone ran almost twice the length of the face, the mouth rimmed with sharp teeth. The pitch black eyes seemed to absorb the light, creating shadows around the sockets.

The three travelers did not move and remained on the ground as the beast neared them. Peter's back ached, still sore from being thrown from Day. He could only assume Catina was doing much worse.

"What do we do?" asked Peter.

"What is it?" returned Alan.

"A palanthora beast!"

"Blast! How was I supposed to know? This has never happened to me before. This thing is supposed to be asleep."

"Isn't there anything we can do?"

Catina's screams made it difficult for Alan to hear. He told her to be quiet while the two men worked this out. They had to act quickly.

"I am afraid we have no other choice than to fight it," said Alan.

"Fight it? How? With what?"

Alan brought his sword out in front of him so Peter could see it. "With this."

"I don't know how to use—"

"We have no time to talk. Now take this and save us!"

Peter took the sword and got to his feet. Alan moved to help Catina, but instead it was the other way around, the little girl helping her grandfather to his feet. Alan, following Catina's lead, backed away as Peter stood before the palanthora beast.

Peter shakily brought the sword up before him, hoping the way the blade glinted in the shafts of sunlight would be enough to ward off the creature. Instead, the palanthora beast swiped a mighty hand at the sword as if swatting a fly, nearly knocking the handle from Peter's grip. Peter stumbled backward from the blow and wanted to run. He knew that if he did, the beast would no doubt run after him and take him to the ground. And then what of Catina and Alan? They would be next to fall prey to this savage creature. Peter planted his footing and brought the sword back up again, readjusting his grip on the handle so it was firm. The beast came toward him, its weight burly and strong. It swung out again. Peter dodged its arm and moved out of the way, crouching down on his descent. He swung the sword at its muscled legs, swiping in a powerful arc. The beast jumped, avoiding the assault, only the tip of the blade grazing the underside of its foot. The palanthora beast snarled, low and guttural, the growl deep enough that Peter could feel the vibrations in his chest.

Swallowing hard, his heart picked up pace. He had never encountered a palanthora beast before, their existence only reaffirmed time to time by the stories and legends passed down by the tongues of the townsfolk, or by the random growls in the night as the fell beasts roamed through Garathen's streets. He knew the creatures were strong. They were said to have devoured wild horses and avoided the assaults of a dozen hunters. They belonged to the shadows of the night and fear was their ally. He backed up against a tree, his foot coming down on the corpse of a rotting deer. The decaying flesh gave under his weight with a sickening squishing sound.

The palanthora beast dove at him. Peter moved out of the way and the beast crashed into the tree.

It was day and the beast did not have the cloak of night to hide behind, but did that also mean that since the beast was out during the day, it was somehow stronger and more capable of harm? Peter rid himself of the notion. It didn't matter. This was not the time to consider the how and why the palanthora beast was going to tear him to shreds. There would be time for theorizing after.

If he survived.

Catina was shouting something in Grescalla, probably a plea for the beast to leave him alone. Alan was trying to hush her but to no effect.

"Peter, what is happening!" shouted Alan.

"Now's not the time!" growled Peter as he backed away from the beast. To his astonishment, the palanthora beast wasn't attacking him as swiftly as he had anticipated.

It was feeling him out. It was toying with him, testing his strengths and weakness before launching into a full attack.

Peter lunged at the creature, the sword held like a spear. The beast moved, the blade missing its mark. Peter's body moved forward with the thrust, past the beast. As he passed the monster, it threw down a large hand onto his back, knocking him to the ground. He let out a loud grunt when he hit the forest floor. He was lucky the blade was flat when he landed on it otherwise he would have—

Catina screamed again. The palanthora beast grunted and blew hot air from its nostrils.

With a wild shriek, Peter scrambled to his feet and swung the blade at the creature in a mad blur of steel. The sword cleaved a chunk of meat from its shoulder; the palanthora beast howled in pain, its opposite hand immediately covering the wound. Blood sprayed upward and outward. Its large jaws clenched and then released, baring a set of fangs that seemed to have grown since last revealed.

The palanthora beast's prey had proved itself a threat. Death hung on the air like smoke. The monster arched its back, its eyes wild, its jaws wide open, its powerful teeth extending in their roots as it growled.

Catina covered her ears from the sound. So did Alan. The blind man collapsed.

Peter gulped; it felt like a rock passing down his throat. The beast bounded into the air and crashed down on top of him. The monster raised a powerful hand and its nails extended themselves into sharp, thick claws. Peter's world grew silent beneath the crushing weight of the beast. He wished he were already dead so he wouldn't have to witness the beast clawing off his face; he started to shake. The beast's hand came down in a blur; its claws consumed his vision. The mighty hand stopped short of Peter's face.

Catina stood beside him, a scowl upon her face. Peter looked up at the palanthora beast and saw it had locked eyes with Catina. The eyes of the beast held a vacant gaze, as if hypnotized by the little girl.

"Get out of here!" shouted Peter. Then he remembered Catina couldn't understand him. Peter looked about for the blind man but couldn't see him. "Alan!" he yelled. "Alan, tell her to get away! Alan!"

Alan then shouted in Grescalla at Catina and she shouted something back at him.

"What did she say!" asked Peter.

The blind man didn't reply.

The palanthora beast got off of Peter like a horse backing into its stall at the prompting of a carrot. Catina walked toward it, as calm as approaching a dog. The palanthora cowered and sat on its haunches like a puppy. Catina proceeded toward it with an outstretched arm. The beast shut its mouth, hiding its gruesome fangs. She stepped up to it and stroked the top of its head.

Peter got to his feet and picked the sword off the ground. He held it high and was about to bring it down on the beast when Catina stopped him.

"Rana Ko, Rana Ko," she said. "Ment yema li gani yo sei. Ment yomi la gini yo sei."

Just then the beast snarled and moved to attack him. Catina snapped her attention back to it and the beast suddenly stopped its advance, sitting back down. She petted its forehead.

"Peter!" called Alan from several paces away.

"What's she saying?" asked Peter.

"She is telling you not to kill it," he said as he followed the sound of Peter's voice and made his way over to them.

Peter pulled Alan by the sleeve over to the right so he wouldn't walk into the palanthora beast.

The palanthora purred beneath Catina's petting, staring into her eyes.

Still holding his sword at the ready, thinking the beast was somehow playing possum and would strike out at any moment, Peter anticipated an attack. He told Alan, "Tell her to get away from it so that I can kill it while it's sitting."

"Are you sure that is wise?" he asked instead.

"What do you mean am I sure that is wise? The thing tried to kill me!"

"True. But now it is not trying to kill you." Alan straightened his posture. "Do you not think it strange that a palanthora beast has not spilled our insides all over this place? I know we are in the midst of a graveyard, Peter. I can smell the foul air and the stench of decay. But our bodies are not amongst the dead here. Why, I ask you again?" He paused a moment then said, "Now, give me my sword."

"No."

"Peter!"

The muscles in Peter's jaw tightened. This was not a good idea. But, Alan was worldlier than he and, not only that, Alan was his elder. He had to respect him. Peter slowly lowered the sword, and then turned it so the blade was facing downward. He handed Alan the sword.

"Thank you," said Alan as he received it, his voice calm again. No matter how grave the circumstance, there was always an air of serenity about Alan that Peter hadn't encountered with anyone else.

Catina spoke calm words to the palanthora beast in her Native-tongue. Peter found the rhythm of her voice also soothing.

Alan crouched down beside her. Peter took several steps back. To the Pits with them! If the beast suddenly turned from its docile state into something fierce, he was not going to be around when it happened. Alan and his granddaughter conversed in Grescalla.

"Peter?" said Alan.

Peter was over by a tree, looking at the dead carcasses. The sight disgusted him, but not nearly as much as a little girl coddling the beast that nearly killed him. But, his pride aside, he was grateful she had saved his life. Now they were even, he supposed. He reluctantly made a wry grin at the notion. "I'm here," he replied.

"Where?"

Peter turned and went over to the blind man, who was moving in the wrong direction. Once Peter met up with him, Alan told him what Catina had said. "I asked her how she was doing this. She told me she was unsure why the animal was attacking you. They had been nice to her when she came through here before. She does not understand why they are . . . mean . . . now. I did not know what to tell her. As far as I know, palanthora beasts are always 'mean.' But, either way, Catina seems to have an affect on them." He sighed. "These are strange days."

"I'm beginning to see that," said Peter.

"First, Slummers are taking revenge. That has never happened before. They have never harmed a person while in their home. Now palanthora beasts are awake during the day. That has never happened before, either. And now a little girl is calming a savage creature. That, of course, is news as well. Peter, tell me, how is she?"

Peter peered around Alan, checking on Catina. The girl was petting the beast's shoulders.

"We still have a problem," said Peter. "I noticed the moment Catina turned away from the beast, it lashed out at me. We can't obviously stay here and baby-sit all day.

We'll have to leave it alone eventually. And we can't bring it with us, right?—So what are we going to do?"

A short while passed and Alan came up with his answer. "Give me a moment."

Peter stood behind the beast, Alan's sword held discreetly behind his back. Catina still stroked the palanthora's slick skin, the sticky slime that coated it seeming not to bother her one bit. Alan came up behind her and placed both hands on her shoulders. He said something to her, and Peter knew its general meaning, if Alan was following the plan. Alan backed the humanette away from the palanthora, her eyes remaining on the creature. The beast pouted and got up to follow her. Catina held out a small hand, telling it to stay. It took a few tries before it understood and obeyed. Alan stepped backward carefully, as did Catina, slowly increasing the distance from the beast. Peter watched in sadness because he knew Catina was unaware as to what they were about to do. Alan had told her that Peter wanted a moment alone with the palanthora to apologize for attacking it. He knew Catina would think it a delightful idea. Peter felt bad for deceiving her.

Soon Alan and Catina were far away enough from the beast so that when the girl turned her gaze from it, and it lost its docile state and lashed out, they would be safe from harm. It was also up to Peter to see to that. As he stood there behind the beast, he reminded himself to speak with Alan later about receiving instruction on how to wield a blade since he had no experience with a sword.

About twenty yards away, Alan said something to Catina. The beast pouted its last whimper. Catina and Alan turned away under the pretense of giving Peter and the beast their privacy. Like a baby startled from sleep, the palanthora beast snapped out of its serene state and growled out into the forest. It sprang to its legs and as it rose up, Peter swung the sword from left to right, the blade running clean along the shoulder-line of the powerful creature, cleaving off its head. The beast's body staggered a moment before crumpling to the ground. Its head rolled off and over to Peter's right, its large jaw slack, its dark and hungry gaze facing him. In a fit of vengeance, Peter thrust the sword between the beast's eyes.

Catina caught the tail end of the episode and watched from behind a tree as Peter withdrew the blade from the palanthora beast's face. She ran at Peter at full speed, crashing into his legs and knocking him to the ground, crying and hitting him.

"Alan!" called Peter like an older brother calling a parent because he is being beat on by a younger sister. "Get her off me!"

Peter pushed Catina away, but not too harshly as he didn't want to hurt her. Childlike, he ran over to Alan, who made his way in their direction.

"Can't you calm her down?" asked Peter.

"Why? You just killed her friend," said Alan.

"Why do you keep turning things around on me? We both agreed on killing it and now you're making sound as if it's my fault. I—"

"But you also need to look at it from her side, too."

"Then how do you say 'I'm sorry'?" asked Peter.

"*Semba dal Ki*, though I do not think it will do you much good," chuckled Alan.

Peter reached out to Catina but she ran away from him. He went toward her.

"Semma bal Ki," said Peter.

"I said, 'Sem-Bah D-ahl Ki,'" said Alan.

Peter moved toward her. She moved further back. "Semba dal Ki," he said. "Semba dal Ki. Semba dal Ki."

Catina fell down cross-legged and began to cry.

"Semba da Ki," he said once more.

And it was true. He was sorry.

Peter stepped away as Alan consoled his granddaughter. His eyes searched the surrounding trees, past the piles of dead carcasses, hoping to catch a glimpse of their horses. He knew the futility of such a search, but it was all he could do. *Cowardly horses. I hope they come back though.*

After a time, Catina and Alan came over to him.

The three walked on through the gloom of the graveyard for about an hour before the bodies of the deceased animals began to thin and, eventually, were left behind. So much for thinking it was only a few minutes of distance through the heaps of bodies. All the while during their journey—done in a straight line at Alan's advising—they walked ever alert, Peter holding Alan's sword at the ready, eyes peering in all directions for a sign of another palanthora beast. They walked in silence, at Peter's suggestion, hoping to avoid alerting any savage creature to their presence.

Finally, they made it to the border of the Third Stage of the Forest-Ring. The trees and foliage branched out before them, looking exactly like the First Stage. There was a place in the bushes before them about five feet high that looked thinner and more used. They entered, hoping they were following a hunting trail. Overhead, birds chirped as if suddenly coming to life, their sounds having been absent in the Second Stage. Their coos and caws were a welcome distraction to the heavy thoughts of the travelers.

Finally, Peter spoke, mostly to himself, but still hoping someone would hear him. "I wonder where our horses have run off to?"

Alan grabbed Peter's sleeve when he stumbled over a tree root.

"Are you all right?" asked Peter.

"Fine. I just need to be more careful. This is one of the problems of being blind; you never know what is going on around you. Anything can spring up. Thank you for catching me."

"Sure."

"As for our horses," continued Alan, "I have no idea. But, I must retain hope we will find them. We thought we lost them before and they returned. It is safe to say they will return again."

"But how do you know?"

"Because I do not lose hope, Peter. Never."

Peter found Alan's words encouraging. He needed it right now. This was not the little trip he had hoped for.

After awhile Catina's steps began to slow, her legs still sore from her tiring journey to Garathen. Alan and Peter kept their pace with her so they would not get too far ahead. Soon, Catina stopped walking. She stood there, partially hidden by the straying branches of the bushes, watching with wide eyes as Alan and Peter strode ahead. Peter noticed she wasn't with them anymore.

"Alan," he said, stopping his stride.

"What?"

Peter trotted over to Catina and picked her up. She held herself close to him and laid her head on his shoulder. He supposed she had forgiven him for killing the palanthora.

"What is the matter?" asked Alan as Peter returned to his side.

"I don't know," said Peter. "She just stopped walking."

Alan conferred with Catina in Grescalla. And then with a chuckle, Alan said, "The poor girl has a full bladder. But, do not worry, I will take care of it."

Peter put Catina down and the blind man took her by the hand, and had her lead him up ahead and then slightly off the path about fifteen paces away.

Catina relieved herself in the bushes while Alan stood guard.

When the two re-emerged from the brush, Peter caught up to them and they continued on.

An hour later, he had Catina in his arms, her little legs having a hard time keeping up with the two men.

Far off to the side, their came a rustling in the bushes . . . and a loud snort. Peter and Alan halted in their tracks. Peter raised his sword.

"What do you see?" said Alan.

The trees swayed gently in the cool breeze; the bushes shook when the wind caught them.

"Nothing," said Peter.

"Then what made that snort!" said Alan louder than he meant to.

There was more rustling, and this time two snorts, one higher-pitched than the other.

Out of habit, Peter prayed to the Master, asking for it not to be another palanthora beast.

A dark flash appeared then disappeared behind the trees to Peter's right.

It was a palanthora beast. It had to be.

But it wasn't.

It was Night. He trotted out from between the trees, followed by Day, closely behind. Peter had to move out of the way to avoid being hit by the mighty horses. He pulled Catina aside, as well as Alan.

"What is it? Who is there? Blast, say something!" said Alan.

Both horses stopped by them and Night let out a snort, announcing their arrival.

His heart beat frantically in his chest. "It's nothing. Just our runaway horses," said Peter.

Alan grinned. "Thanks goodness."

Catina squealed with glee at the sight of the horses, glad they now had the means again to get to Grek faster than they would on foot.

"Where were you hiding?" asked Peter as he came over to Day. He stroked the mare's muzzle. She whinnied a reply. "I see," he said, happy. "Anything else?"

There mustn't have been anything because Day didn't make a sound.

Within moments the three travelers were back on their horses.

"I wonder where they went?" said Peter after a time. His body swayed from side to side as Day stepped over tree roots sticking up from the ground.

"Obviously to find sanctuary away from the palanthora beast. Some force of good must be with us because these horses returned," said Alan.

"Perhaps," said Peter. "Yes, I agree. But I'm still in awe over it. They left us in a pit of danger and now have come to us again as though nothing happened."

"Strange I know, but I am learning, all things do not necessarily need to resolve themselves in a grandiose manner. These horses simply found their way back to us, though I am sure they had not gone too far from where we were, despite what was seemed. Day and Night are proving to be very spirited."

Makes sense, he thought. "Agreed. Let's pick up the pace a bit and try and get out of here before nightfall."

"Well said." Alan clicked his tongue and Night sped up. Peter did the same and Day kept pace with her kin.

They kept on through Stage Three of the Forest-Ring, maintaining a straight line, guiding the horses down an old hunting trail.

CHAPTER XI
Catina's Memory

Peter and Alan spoke at length about what they were going to do once they reached the edge of the Forest-Ring; unfortunately, Catina did not know what they were talking about. She wished she were able to speak the same language her grandfather spoke. If she could, she wouldn't feel so left out all the time.

Catina watched as Night's head bobbed up and down as he trotted along. She took in the beauty of the forest and the green of the leaves. The forest looked much more different than how she remembered it. But it had been mostly night when she traveled it, and what had just happened, the event with the palanthora beast, stirred an awful memory.

Two days earlier, when Catina had first approached the Forest-Ring, after traveling through a massive expanse of grassland, spanning in all directions as far as the eye could see, it had been evening, an hour or two before sunset. Her small legs were tired, and each step forward an effort. But she pressed on. She knew that Garathen was just on the other side of the forest. How far on the other side, though, she did not know; she just knew it was there and it was that knowledge that kept her going.

Catina had not been aware of the perils and creatures that lay waiting for her inside the Forest-Ring once night fell. The evening wind swept past her, blowing her long strands of blond hair across her face. She pushed them away and curled her bangs behind her ears.

Her grandfather was just on the other side.

At the very edge of the Ring, separating the grasslands from the forest, was a small drop. She stood at the slope, and looked up. High overhead the sky was a deep blue with dark clouds. Off behind the dark blue, the sky tapered down into the horizon in hues of red and orange, the shades of sunset coming to life before her. From somewhere in the dark of the forest, came a foul smell, like that of wet, rotting wood. She swallowed the lump in her throat and entered.

She was greeted by silence, the sounds of the wind that blew across the grasslands suddenly hushed by the walls of the towering trees around her. It was dark, and she was alone. Catina took her time, her small feet finding purchase on the sloping ground as she descended down a muddy trail, and into the depths of the forest.

Being so young, she was not aware of any set direction to go. Instead, she relied on her instincts to go through the Forest-Ring in a straight line. Eventually, she would emerge somewhere, hopefully in Garathen. She walked slowly, her speed determined by both caution and fatigue. How a part of her wished for someone to come along on horseback and offer her a ride. She wanted someone pulling a carriage like that man in—the feeling of need suddenly abated. Her mind had suppressed the memory of the man outside of Wesafeld and what had happened. All she could recall was that she had gotten a ride with someone for a short time. She was unaware of the outcome of that engagement.

The smell of rotting wood grew thicker the further she went in. And, after some time, as the darkness of the tree limbs grew around her, the smell began to change. It smelled like wet animal hair. She glanced up and through the breaks in the canopy of leaves overhead, she could see the stars poking through a matte of night sky. The stars coming into view put a smile on her face. It seemed they were watching over her and she suddenly didn't feel so alone.

Catina could not recall how much time, and how much distance had been covered. Suddenly she heard the scurrying of feet across the leafy ground, and she froze in her tracks. The air grew colder, as if death were approaching. Her heart sped up and her legs began to wobble. She crouched down and hugged her knees to her chest in an effort to abate the chill and rest her muscles. Straining to listen to all around her, she could hear nothing but the trees swaying in the breeze.

She stood, one of her knees clicking in its socket when she did. She took a deep breath before walking again. The bushes here were taller than her, some of their branches blocked her way. Moving them aside, her eyes searched the gloom in front of her for a clearer path. There was none. She would have to remain on the one she was on, if, indeed, it was a path at all.

An owl hooted overhead and Catina stopped her stride again. She looked up and saw the bird flit from one tree branch to another.

"Menne mone teeka!" she said to the owl. *You scared me!*

She kept going. The owl hooted again behind her. She looked in its direction but did not see it. How she wished for the owl to fly down and rest on her shoulder and keep her company. She had been on her own for well over two weeks. It would be wonderful not to be alone.

Darkness settled in the sky above. The starlight muted a little as the moon came out in full. The moonlight came down in streaks through the holes in the leafy roof overhead, similar to the sunlight during the day.

Catina kept walking, moving branches and thin tree limbs out of her way when needed. At one point she had planted her foot wrong and her ankle twisted beneath her. She fell hard to the damp ground, but fortunately landed on her elbows, protecting her face from the fall. Almost immediately she sat up, not wanting to lay there on the ground, feeling exposed to whatever may be lurking in the dark. She rubbed her ankle, the tendons responding to her touch. Fortunately, there had been no significant damage. The muscles had been strained, but she was still able to stand on it. She did not cry. Her mother once told her that crying only showed weakness and that good little girls didn't complain when bad things happened to them. She would brave the discomfort of walking on a sore ankle.

Limping some, she pressed on, praying to the Master that He would lead her to her grandfather.

Off to her left side, she heard something small scurrying away from her into the brush. She stopped, this time glancing in the direction of the sound. In no mood for guessing what was around her, she crouched down and peered into the undergrowth to see what the cause of the disturbance was.

Only black and the outlined silhouettes of leaves stared back. About to continue on her way, she heard the sound again. As she leaned in closer, a blur of fuzzy dark brown jumped out at her.

It was a fopphin.

The small creature, no more than halfway to her knees in height, stood on its haunches before her, its big, floppy paws hanging out in front of it freely, like that of a rabbit. Its face was small and round, with large oval eyes as black as pitch, and small ears pressed flat against its head. Dark, fine brown hairs covered its entire body. Its face was flat, with a small nose that, though Catina could not be sure in such terrible light, seemed to be scrunched, as if constantly sniffing the air for the source of a foreign smell. A pair of bucked teeth stood out in two squares of white against its brown face. Catina realized the fopphin was the cause of the stink of wet fur.

Catina had never seen such a creature before, if, in fact, a "creature" was what it was. The word "creature" seemed too harsh a description though. The fopphin seemed more a cuddly animal than anything else, and would probably make a good pet, if given the proper training.

The humanette found her hand wanting to reach out and pet it, but she fought the urge. Her mother told her not to touch anything she did not know anything about.

"Semba dal mumi mel semba bani ro wal gammiti. Menne wom sorgalo runia," she told the fopphin. *I am sorry but I have to be going. You stay there, all right?*

The fopphin peered up at her in an unspoken question.

Catina smiled at the little animal and kept walking. Behind her she could hear the pad-pad-padding of the fopphin as it followed her along the trail. Each time Catina turned to look at it, the fopphin stopped in its tracks and sat back on its haunches, paws hanging out in front, and sniffed the night air.

"Semba dal wulami. Menne bani ro wom sorgalo." *I am serious. You have to stay there.* She paused a moment, then giggled at the thought of this adorable animal following her.

Catina decided to make a game out of it. She walked on further and the fopphin followed her. She stopped and looked back, and the fopphin stopped, too, and gazed curiously back at her. She walked again, stopped, and turned around. Each time she did, the cycle repeated itself, and each time she saw the fopphin peering up at her, she giggled. The game was a pleasant relief from such a hard journey.

The game continued on for a quarter of an hour until, this time when Catina turned around, the fopphin had a different look on its face—terror.

"Bele som ren?" she asked. *What is the matter?* She stepped closer to the fopphin. "Semba dal fo gammiti ro ulta menne." *I am not going to hurt you.*

The fopphin chirped then whimpered before scurrying off into the undergrowth.

When Catina turned around, she saw a palanthora beast looking at her from between the leaves of a nearby bush.

She screamed. The birds of the forest responded to her scream with chirps and hoots and caws.

The palanthora beast stared at her, its eyes bottomless pits of darkness. The very presence of the beast sapped the strength from Catina's limbs. She felt as if her body would collapse beneath her. The beast moved out of the bush and stood before her, its body hulking and menacing.

More than anything, Catina wanted to curl up into a ball before the creature and submit to its foul desires. Yet her mother had told her never to run from adversity, no matter how terrifying the circumstance may seem. So she stood there, fear encompassing her entire being, waiting for the worst to happen.

Within the blink of an eye, the mighty claws of the palanthora beast swept down, aiming for her head. Catina moved out of the way and started to run. She scampered down the path, not caring about the tree limbs and thin branches lashing against her face and arms and shins.

The palanthora tore after her. Catina looked over her shoulder and saw the beast leaping at her. Just then an immense feeling of power filled her and she stopped running. She turned and faced her adversary. The beast saw this and, as if suddenly afraid that it would run into her, averted its path so it missed her and landed a ways past. Catina spun around, her mind free of conscious thought, survival her only inclination. Instinct took over. The palanthora beast bowed before her, its foreclaws digging into the earth, its hind legs finding purchase behind it, ready to launch another attack.

Catina stared at the creature. Suddenly, the beast's posture changed. It straightened itself and began to back away, seeing a darkness within Catina that was darker than its own. Catina's eyes pierced into it, as if looking straight through the beast, seeing it as nothing more than a creature running on the pure instinct to hunt then kill. The palanthora beast became no more harmless than the fopphin.

The beast let out a fell screech and tore off into the night.

The little girl's limbs suddenly grew weak and shaky, the adrenaline having run its course.

What had just happened, she did not know.

"Finally!" said Peter.

Up ahead, through the cracks in the branches that crisscrossed each other from trees on opposite sides of the hunting trail, was the entrance to the Forest-Ring.

"What is it?" asked Alan.

"The way out, the Ranmorahn Plains. We've made it," said Peter. "Finally. Night is fast approaching."

"I told you we would make it," said Alan, as if he had doubted him from the start.

Day and Night's pace picked up, as if the two horses were happy they would not have to spend a moment longer in the unpleasant place that was the Forest-Ring.

Just then Peter, his mind already reeling at the thought of being outside the Forest-Ring for the first time in his life, thought of something. "Alan," he said, "this path leads out into the Plains. My question is, if the hunting trail, if that's what it was, leads out into the open, don't you think it would be fair to say that perhaps those animals and creatures that live in the Forest-Ring will also be out in the grasslands. I mean, this is a path that leads out, after all."

Alan considered for a moment. "I honestly do not have an answer. Anything could be out there. We best be on our toes, just in case."

"Fair enough," said Peter. "Let's hope that the rest of our journey isn't as hard as it has been thus far. I could really use peace of mind right now."

"And you will have it, trust me. For now, let us ride on." Alan then whispered what sounded like words of encouragement to Catina, and gave her a hug from behind.

The horses plodded up the slope that led into the grasslands outside the Forest. The closer they came to the Forest's edge, the brighter the remaining light of day grew.

They emerged from the Forest-Ring, and the World opened up to them.

CHAPTER XII
The Woman in the Desert

Aiyesha Elnaa moved with swift feet across the Thakari Desert. The sun beat down from the middle of the clear sky. Her tongue was dry; the canteen she had been carrying was nearly empty. Each time she swallowed, her throat pulsed in dry lumps, almost as if she *was* actually swallowing something. She needed water but would not let that hinder her.

Sweat clung to her back, sticking her long black, hooded robe to her naked body beneath. Over her mouth she wore a black veil which served to filter the hot, dry air. Surprisingly, the fact that her garments were black did not have any bearing on the heat of the sun. Though black attracted heat, this material seemed to repel it—wonderful out here in the open desert, with the sun burning so bright overhead.

She was being followed, she knew. A part of her was fairly sure she had thrown off her pursuer, or *pursuers,* some time ago; back at the Great Dune that slipped downward into the open sea of sand that was the Thakari Desert.

Her legs ached, but she pressed on. She had to make as much headway Southeast as possible before night fell. To be caught on the sand out in the open when darkness came would be a cold experience. Her robe would not be enough to keep her warm and she had no other supplies save for the canteen slung over her shoulder. And the canteen had only a few mouthfuls of water left in it. Soon, that too, like her tongue, would be dry. She cursed herself for not being more prepared. She should have known better. But, despite any self-loathing, she had to accept that this was where she was now and could not change it, and any self-depreciating would be a waste of time. Besides, she hadn't had the time to prepare for this journey and had to leave at a moment's notice. She had done the best she could with what she had. There was satisfaction in that.

Two days ago, she had departed from a week's stay in Palatay, a vast city several miles North from the Thakari Desert. She had spent some time there in an attempt to start a new life until she was no longer pursued by the Dembatstayr, an army that seemed to increase monthly in numbers. They had found her whereabouts—she didn't know how as she had been careful to not draw attention to herself—and was forced to flee the city until she could find someplace to try again.

Her hopes of trying anew shattered, she pressed on, her feet sliding in the sand as they propelled her forward.

Southeast. That was where she needed to be. She needed to get herself as far away from the Coast of Seryn as possible. The memories of such a place would surely stay with her; thankfully, *she* herself did not have to be there.

The escape had been a slim one. It had been a successful escape . . . but not successful enough.

Aiyesha, born in Rathern, an expansive and ornate city several thousand miles from where she was now, was raised in Bel Candar, one of three small towns just South of Rathern, the other two towns being Bel Haborr and Bel Jinu. Aiyesha had grown up in a busy household with six brothers and six sisters, she being the youngest of her kin.

Her childhood had been a basic one. Her father was an important member of the government in Rathern, and had spent his weeks in the city, returning home only on weekends to be with his family. Her mother remained at home, her father earning enough to support them all. They were rich and respected. Bel Candar consisted of average folk, so the Elnaa family was amongst one of the wealthiest, if not *the* wealthiest of families in all of Bel Candar.

Days were spent being tutored at home in the little classroom in the back room of their, comparatively speaking, large house. Her father's plans for his children was for the boys to learn of history and geography, matters of finance and real estate and politics; the girls to learn the basics of living and the running of a household, so that they would make good wives to their future mates.

Life had been traditional, sometimes monotonous and mundane, but all in all quite extravagant given the amount of tradesworth Aiyesha's father would sometimes throw around.

When Aiyesha entered her eighteenth year, all of that changed. News of a coming war had spread to Rathern and the surrounding towns, setting all the residents into a stir. Some people had fled the cities to settle where the talk of war wasn't the topic of every conversation. Yet most people remained. And Aiyesha's father insisted that his family stay, war or not. His holdings in Bel Candar and his position in the Rathern government would be too great a forfeit to start somewhere else anew.

That had been twelve years ago. Aiyesha was now thirty years of age. At times she wondered if her choice of lifestyle had been the right one. She knew that if she had stayed and not left home twelve years ago, she would probably be married with a family right now. There was no short supply of men in both Bel Candar and Rathern.

But what she was ultimately to do with her life was up to her. That's what her mother once told her. Her mother said she had an active spirit and knew that she would not be content with being the mere wife of some successful government official, or some other well-to-do gentleman who earned a good living. But all inclinations to follow her own heart and be her own woman aside, Aiyesha still yearned for the quiet life, one with a family and one with love.

Now, a life filled with the laughter of children and the love of a husband seemed far off. She was a fugitive, wanted by the Dembatstayr for escaping their training facility on the Coast of Seryn, also known as the Snake's Eye, or Border of the Purple Fog.

The Coast of Seryn was thought to be thirty or so miles from the Island of the Dead, or Yem Batu, as it was commonly known in the free World. The dubbing "Island of the Dead" was given to it by those in the *know*, namely the officials in the Dembatstayr's army. If one were caught uttering the words "Island of the Dead," they would be executed immediately. And if not that, then long nights in a sealed, deep hole in the ground—called the Pnutar—far from camp, with soldiers standing guard. General Charles Gasahd did not take kindly to any words or phrases that would demean or give the wrong impression of Yem Batu. However, "impressions" or "interpretations" of Yem Batu was all that any in the Dembatstayr army could rely on. As far as anyone was aware, no one had been to Yem Batu, passage into its lands cut off by a purple fog. All attempts to penetrate the Fog had been futile and no man or woman had returned from any efforts to seek what was beyond its border.

Aiyesha had been on the Coast of Seryn for twelve years, having joined, at the time, the secret wing of the Dembatstayr army, a sect dedicated to the breeding and training of female soldiers. The Dembatstayr had felt, according to General Gasahd, that it also required females in its service and not just men.

The Dembatstayr, having never before visited Rathern or the Bel towns that surrounded it, made its presence known shortly after the rumors of war had stirred. The army swept through the city of Rathern and Bel Candar and Bel Jinu and Bel Haborr rather quickly, snatching up any able-bodied male willing to participate in its service. The whole ordeal set the city and towns in an uproar, many of the men choosing not to join the army because their own careers and families were too much to lose for the cause of a war that might never happen. Two weeks after the final male had registered and the army had left, the Dembatstayr returned—presumably because their harvest of male candidates had been so few and had displeased their superiors—and had asked for any females who were interested to join them. It was said that Rathern and its surrounding towns would be the only places asked for this and, even if the war never occurred, the females who returned and had experience in the army under their belts would be compensated generously with gold droppers for their lost time. This gold dropper incentive was offered only to the females because it was known that the females didn't work and it was the males who earned the tradesworth for a household. A chance for a female to be paid for her services was an opportunity that could not be ignored.

Aiyesha, confused about her life and unsure of where she wanted it to go, had opted in to the Dembatstayr's offer and enlisted. Her goal, originally, had been to enlist, try it out, and if she decided that it wasn't for her, would leave the army at the next available opportunity to do so. She had even cleared this question with General Gasahd himself at the time; he had personally supervised the enrolment of the new female recruits. He had said that, yes, should she decide that military service wasn't for her, she could leave and he would personally arrange for a boat to take her from the Coast of Seryn back to the mainland. Aiyesha had been delighted that she wasn't locked in to any set time of service and told the news to the other eleven women who had enlisted. There had been only twelve who had left Rathern and the Bels that day; twelve young women, twelve years ago.

The boat ride out to the Coast of Seryn had been exotic, the boat being of vast size and splendor, with a seemingly unlimited supply of food and drink and male escorts. It was rumored the reason for such extravagance was because once the boat pulled into harbor ten days later, their day to day routines and training would be grueling until they were in shape enough to endure their tasks more easily. Aiyesha ate and drank lots on the journey, but had never partaken, much to her fellow companions' complaints, in the wild parties with the male escorts. Her friends were enjoying their freedom and Aiyesha could not understand why she could not enjoy hers. She would instead, on such nights, make her way to the bow of the ship and look out onto the Rel J'akaar Ocean and almost see, somewhere in the darkness of the night, her home distancing itself from her, drifting away.

Aiyesha removed the black veil from over her mouth and took a breath of hot, dry air. The veil was damp and salty-tasting from her breathing and she wanted to let it dry some before she affixed it over her mouth again. She looked behind her, almost expecting to see a dozen or so Dembatstayr soldiers racing toward her on the backs of their great, gray and black steeds. Instead, she saw she was alone in the desert. Instinctively, she reached for the canteen she had slung over her shoulder and removed its lid. She put the opening to her mouth and frowned when only a small amount of water came out, less than she had originally thought. She cursed herself for finishing off the wonderfully cool water so soon. But she hadn't finished it *too* soon, she knew. She had made that single canteen last three days; but she also knew that if she didn't find a source of water soon, death was not far off. She was already beginning to dehydrate.

The afternoon wore on, each step she took taking her further away from her pursuers. Often Aiyesha turned around and looked over her shoulder, shielding her eyes with one hand from the glare of the sun off the sand, checking to see if the Dembatstayr were trailing her, their mighty horses galloping in her direction at full speed. And each time she looked, she was greeted by the blessed sight of leagues upon leagues of sand, a blanket of gold beneath a clear blue sky. However, though the sight of being away from her hunters was a welcome one, she was also covered with a profound sense of loneliness. Out here in the Thakari Desert it was just her, the sand, the sky, and no water.

At times her body grew heavy, weariness setting in despite her great capacity of endurance. The dozen years of training to be of use to the Dembatstayr army left her with a body at the peak of physical health, but her training had been in a climate of moderate temperature and not under the blistering heat of a desert sun. The hot air sapped her strength and, at times, glancing back to see if her pursuers were behind her, was a task all its own.

Toward later in the afternoon, as evening began to set in, Aiyesha found herself stopping more frequently to catch her breath and letting the muscles in her legs rest a moment before continuing onward.

Southeast. She needed to move Southeast.

She prayed to the Master that this seemingly endless sea of sand would soon end and she would find herself in a more hospitable climate.

She kept moving. Throughout the entire time she traveled, her mind wandered back to the events which brought her here. As she relived some of the events of the past twelve years, her imagination mixed with memory and at times she was oblivious to the desert around her and it felt as if she were actually experiencing the things of the past all over again.

On the Coast of Seryn, along the Rel J'akaar Ocean, were three ports, where those bringing supplies off and to the Coast could dock while delivering the goods. Each port was like a very small town, complete with a tiny docking community whose economy and well-being relied heavily on being hosts to those coming to the Coast, most of the wealth gained from these communities used toward funding the training facility deeper in the Coast's lands. Most of the errands from the mainland were for military purposes. Only some of the boats that docked there were for leisure, people who lived for the Seas and Oceans of the World and lived off their boats, only occasionally coming to a port to stock up again for another long Seaward journey. However, people avoided the Coast of Seryn, if they could. No one wanted to be near the activities of the military, the people of the World not wanting a war, and if they docked there and used the ports, they felt as if they were somehow contributing to the military effort and thus would be held responsible should a war break out. Aiyesha had heard rumors that some of the passers-through had been executed because, once they returned to the mainland, they would report anything they'd seen that they didn't like. The Coast of Seryn thrived on secrets.

Each port-center had a Dock master, who lived in a small shack on the port. If one were to dock, and after making arrangements with the Dock master to hold the boat for a time, they could journey into town and find an inn to spend the night, a pub to have a few drinks, a whorehouse or two to release the tensions from being absent from human contact for so long. There were a couple of restaurants and shops, the shops selling mostly knick-knacks and worthless souvenirs.

One of the small boating towns was named Gal Ulkin, and, like the two others that were on the Coast of Seryn, would sometimes be under attack by Ruggards, by pirates. The Ruggards knew from previous encounters that the Coast of Seryn was used to train soldiers, and would hit the Coast hard. It was their way of stating that though an army was on the rise, they were still the fiercest bands of men alive.

In Gal Ulkin, three days before Aiyesha's planned escape from the Coast, a Ruggard attack took place. Those training on the Coast were summoned to the shores to aid the townsfolk in defending themselves from the ruthless pirates. The echoes of the cannon blasts were heard all around, the smell of sulphur on the air. The wild shouts of savage men and the battle cries of soldiers, the clanging of swords and knives, were like music on the air. The harbor had become a mass slaughterhouse, with the bodies of pirates and townsfolk strewn about in a bloody mess. Some of them were even the highly trained soon-to-be-enlisted male members of the Dembatstayr army.

Aiyesha, dressed in the female training garb—an outfit she detested almost immediately upon receiving it—a gray body suit, rough in texture to toughen the skin, with a deep purple leather breastplate that had two sheaths on the back to house her blades, along with matching arm and shin guards—joined in the fight and with her swords cut her way through the Ruggards who, by the time she reached the docks, were already beginning to surrender.

She fought hard, her training kicking in instinctively so that it was no longer her wielding the blades, but someone else more savage, more ruthless, and more skilled. Each man she impaled with her swords looked at her with wide eyes, shocked they had been bested by a woman. She kept count of the men she'd slain and by the time she reached the edge of the dock where the Ruggards' grand ship floated on the water, her count was thirty-seven. Like a whirlwind she tore through the sea of men, clashing blades and then cutting their wielders to pieces in glorious slashes of red.

The massive ship loomed over her, its masts and sails like blankets of darkness. For a brief moment, she had mistaken it to be night instead of midday, the sails were so big. Behind her the commotion began to settle and she could see her companions yelling shouts of victory as the pirates ran back toward their boats.

This was her chance. *So much for my previous plan of escape,* she thought. You had to take opportunities when they came.

Hoping no one was looking, she jumped off the dock, grabbed hold of the side of the ship where one of the cannons peaked out, and climbed her way on to the ship. When she boarded, she had little time unless she wanted to be discovered by the Ruggards coming back aboard. The ship was abandoned save for a few bodies, all of the Ruggards fighting on the land below. Beneath the ship's deck was a hold for supplies. Aiyesha went down to it and, hiding beneath the boards of the upper deck, could hear the clamoring of heavy boots as the pirates boarded. With remarkable speed, the ship headed out, back on to the Rel J'akaar Ocean.

Inside the cargo hold were crates and chests of who knew what. Aiyesha had a hard time believing that any were filled with treasure. Given the amount of crates and chests and other smaller wooden boxes, she guessed this was a supply ship of some sort. It was dark in the cargo hold, but she did not mind. She maneuvered around the crates and found herself a small nook to rest and plan what her next move would be.

Within a quarter of an hour of sitting there in the darkness, the Ruggards found her.

Survival was key. Living under the iron hand of General Gasahd taught Aiyesha that. When evening set in, the desert was nowhere in sight. She was thirsty and was willing to kill for something to drink. What added to matters was that her bladder was full and each step she took was becoming increasingly awkward. She had thought that having next to nothing to drink would prohibit her from having to relieve herself. It was then she realized that she hadn't relieved herself since earlier on that morning.

Just then a paralyzing thought came to her. She had no means of getting any water and there didn't appear to be an oasis in sight. What if she drank her own—

No! Don't think that! Aiyesha told herself. *That's disgusting. I would never*—but she knew that she would, if it came down to it.

Survival was key.

She prayed to the Master again, asking for a miracle, begging she would find water before she died of thirst and would not have to succumb to the last resort of surviving dehydration.

And if I survive this, what then? she wondered. Each day of her life would be spent running from the Dembatstayr. Once you joined their army, it was difficult to get out. That was, unless, you had fulfilled your twenty-five year minimum of service. You were joining for a cause, General Gasahd always preached. But what that cause was though, he never said. He only spoke of trying to create a better World and to defend the free people from the savages that began wars for no reason other than personal gain. The odd part, Aiyesha always thought, was that there hadn't been any significant wars in over three millennia, and even then, those wars had been small. The size of the army that was amassing, the army she had been training for, was meant for something big, something life altering. And it would alter the lives of everyone on the Earth if a war ever came to pass. So Gasahd said.

Should she return to the Coast of Seryn and pay the penalty of escape? She was top of her class and had excelled in all aspects of the training, both mental and physical. She was a valuable asset to the army. But, she knew, she fell under the same law as the others who were in the army and those training to be a part of it. The penalty of betrayal, of abandoning your fellow man or woman, was death. But if she could somehow escape that fate and return with her tail between her legs and apologize and endure whatever torture they handed her—that would certainly be better than running her whole life. At least, if she returned, and lived, she could finish her service and then lead a normal life, one with a husband and a little house on the top of a hill. She no longer believed in what she was training for. Peace and protection? Yes, she believed in those, but she didn't think they were what the Dembatstayr army was truly after. She couldn't place her conviction, but she knew it all the same. She had joined the army to learn of what was going on and if the rumors of the war were true. She hadn't known that once you joined, your life was forfeit if you didn't complete your service. No mercy. That had been General Gasahd's motto. And whether you were enemy or friend, that motto applied. The more Aiyesha dwelled on it, the more terrified she became of death. Not that she was afraid to die, but because she was afraid to die for the wrong reasons. That would be an even worse fate.

Aiyesha decided to keep going. She couldn't quit. She wouldn't.

She would survive.

The onset of evening, the rising of the stars and moon, and the sudden change to a cooler temperature, invigorated Aiyesha. The heat of day was gone, as was its wear and tear on the muscles, the heat draining them of their strength. For a time she wasn't thirsty. She felt as if she could continue on throughout the night. Shortly, though, dizziness set in and she stumbled as she stepped, each footfall into the sand seeming to last longer than it should, her feet seeming to get caught in the soft sand, as if the sand were grabbing her, pulling her downward.

She fell forward, her hands coming out before her, bracing her fall. She lay on the sand and rested. A chill swept through her as a cool breeze rushed by and rustled her sweat-dampened clothing. She raised her head off the sand. The desert was beautiful at night. The sand was gray beneath the moonlit sky, the stars sparkling in fine white dots against a deep navy canvas. And there, before her, she saw a deeper gray of sand . . . but it wasn't sand. Couldn't be. It rippled and moved and, if Aiyesha was not mistaken, made a subtle whooshing sound.

Water! She crawled quickly toward the oasis, her hands and feet tripping over themselves in a mad effort as she raced forward. For each yard she moved, a yard further the small lake of water drifted away. She scampered harder, not thinking to stand, too excited to do anything but get to the water. Her thirst returned tenfold. Her tongue stuck to the roof of her mouth.

The further she moved, further away the water moved, too. Her breathing quickened. If she could just move a little faster maybe she could catch up to it—

—and just as soon as the vision of the oasis appeared, it disappeared.

Aiyesha was ashamed of her foolishness.

A stinging sensation permeated her loins. She needed to relieve herself. Desperate for something to drink, she knew what she had to do.

The Ruggards gathered around, each one standing before her, some with their hands already unbuckling their belts, others holding weapons: clubs, swords, knives, and chains. One licked his lips.

They wore similar outfits, mostly rags, their loose-fitting shirts dark and full of holes, their saggy pants patched in random places. Their skin was oily, their hair dark, their eyes small and beady, and the beards that hung in mats from their faces looked slick, as if covered in sweat. They smelled like a pack of wet dogs mixed with the sharp, putrid scent of unwashed skin.

Aiyesha was backed against the planks that composed the wooden wall of the inner underbelly of the massive ship. Unfortunately, this "underbelly," this cargo hold, was filled with so many crates there was little room to move.

The men came forward, none speaking. One of them lunged at her. Aiyesha backed herself up against the wall and kicked a leg out, the ball of her foot landing in the middle of the Ruggard's gut. A shocked wheeze escaped his lips.

The moment her kicking leg touched ground again, Aiyesha, from out of the sheaths on her back, withdrew her swords. The razor-sharp blades sprang out before her, emitting a metallic ring. The horde of Ruggards stepped back, both at the sight of blades and also to make room for their comrade who was falling to his knees, his behind landing at their feet.

"Which one of you wishes to die first?" she said.

And with pride-filled sneers, the men charged her.

One of the first rules when facing multiple adversaries, General Gasahd had told her, was to keep moving. Move, move, move. So that's what she did. She kept moving, charging through the men, her blades twirling, wedging herself in between the Ruggards, and cutting them down. It wasn't long before she made her way through them and ran up the steep stairwell leading to the main deck of the ship. When she emerged in the daylight, there were at least four dozen men standing before her.

Beyond, over the heads of men, she could see they were well on their way, sailing into the Rel J'akaar Ocean, the Coast of Seryn a mere blur on the horizon to the West.

Aiyesha poised her swords, one out before her, the other to her side. She surveyed the men around her, all seeming to be clones of the ones she had encountered below deck. Their eyes rested on her in lustful stares and in hatred. She had killed some of their fellow men, and was also one of the Dembatstayr army, or so they thought, and her companions had slain other Ruggards on the Coast. Within an instant, chaos began as the men charged her. She held her ground, cutting those who came forward, impaling her blade into the stomachs and throats of others. For how long the fight went on, Aiyesha could not recall, but a hoarse voice spoke into the confusion, and the men stopped their assault. Some of them lost their lives when they halted because Aiyesha kept fighting, kept cutting them down.

She just finished running her sword through the solar plexus of a man and was spinning around to cut another down, when her sword was stopped in mid-flight by another blade. She looked up and there before her stood a large man, at least a foot and half, if not more, taller than she. His body size was enormous, the definition of his muscles, though covered by a billowy, white shirt, was immediately noticeable. His hair was dark and a long moustache done up in braids hung far past his chin. Her sword was caught against his and when she moved to set it free, he moved with her, locking her in position. She swung her other sword at him and its blade was deflected by the edge of a long knife he withdrew with amazing speed from a sheath at his belt. She fought against him, trying every move she had learned while on the Coast. The big man stopped her each time and, after having fought so hard against so many, Aiyesha's efforts grew weaker. She stopped fighting and stood before him. The man let out a belly of a laugh, his barrel-like chest rising heavily up and down as he did.

"What a feisty kitten we have among us," he said. He let out another chuckle, this one carrying more of an air of defeat over the lost lives of the Ruggards at her feet. "I dare say that we must watch ourselves, boys, should she decide to accompany us on our journey."

A few of the men cheered.

"My name is Morley," said the man, bowing. He acted like a gentleman, which caught Aiyesha off guard as she had expected him to be savage like the others. "Can I have the pleasure of your name?"

Aiyesha didn't give it and instead stood there proud, shoulders squared, mouth clamped shut.

"I see," he said. He glanced about first, then stepped around her, his heavy boots clunking against the wooden planks of the deck. He eyed her up and down. "My, my, my," he said, "what are we to do with you?"

One of the men shouted something rude over the crowd. Morley put up his hand in protest. "We'll have none of that, thank you." Then, to Aiyesha, "Forgive them for that. It has been a long while since they've seen a woman of your, um, caliber."

Aiyesha clenched her teeth at the thought of what must be brewing inside these men's minds.

Suddenly, Aiyesha caught the glint of a knife out of the corner of her eye. Before she could move her own sword to meet it, the knife's blade was already at her throat, Morley having stepped up behind her, bringing the blade around in front, pressing it where her neck met her jaw.

"And it has been a long while for me," he said. "Now, Mistress, tell me your name."

Aiyesha swallowed, feeling the blade of the knife rise and fall with the movement of her throat. "I am Aiyesha Elnaa of Bel Candar. And, Sir, since we are engaging in pleasantries, do you not know that holding a knife to a woman's throat is no way to win her affection?"

For a moment Aiyesha could swear that her sarcasm had been too much and her throat would be cut. The blade pressed against her neck, stinging the skin . . . then released. Morley let out another burley laugh, a laugh Aiyesha would hear often in the weeks to come.

"Very good," he said. "She laughs in the face of death. Very good. Come, Mistress, you will join me in my cabin while my men dispose of the bodies below. And, you will tell me how a woman of your size defeated so many of them at once."

The Ruggards standing around were astonished at the sudden hospitality offered to this stowaway. Some of the men objected to Morley's judgment but he didn't say anything. The fates of those men were already sealed. If one questioned Morley's orders, death would be visited upon them within a day, either by Morley himself or by another one of the Ruggards. And, should you choose, you could walk the plank into the Ocean instead of being murdered but few chose to die that way. They would rather be killed head on and put up a fight then willingly walk to their doom.

That night, while the waves crashed against the hull of the ship, Morley dined with Aiyesha in his cabin. She learned that he had been elected captain of the ship, the *Raven*—the ship given its name because of the large black bird mounted on its bow, its wings outstretched as though it were embracing the air and the World it traveled—when their previous captain had died in their last battle with another ship. Morley explained that the Ruggards were always at war with one another, each ship independent unto itself.

Aiyesha didn't say much as she sat eating fish and bread and drank red wine. Morley was a gentleman the entire time she sat with him in his cabin. He asked her how she could have defeated so many men at once, and she gave her answer simply, that she had been trained to kill multiple opponents quickly and efficiently. He then asked her where she was going and asked why she had stowed away on the *Raven.* She explained that she simply wanted to get to the mainland and that his ship seemed the most viable means of getting there at the time.

"So, you're not a spy?" he asked.

"No, I am not. In fact, I wish to leave this way of life behind me permanently," she told him.

"Why would you want to do that?" he immediately countered.

"What is there to gain from it?" And she knew that she had him because Morley did not have an answer.

Later that night, she slept in a small cabin opposite Morley's. She was awake most of the night, her mind alert to her surroundings. There was only a short period for about an hour where it was completely quiet save for the sound of the Ocean outside the hull. The voices of the savage men were always heard, without break.

And then, like a thief in the night, Morley crept into her cabin.

If she wanted passage on his ship, she would have to give him something in return. Aiyesha knew what that something was and she would not give it to him. She struggled against him as he pressed himself on her. Morely, despite his size and despite the small area, moved swiftly and countered each blow against him, blocking her strikes at first, but when she kept fighting, he struck her back. The blow of his massive fist against her face dazed her. She retaliated but the fight was quickly over. Not since General Gasahd had she seen someone so efficient in hand-to-hand combat.

Morley forced himself upon her and Aiyesha had no choice but to give in.

The remainder of the night lasted an eternity.

Aiyesha awoke, coughing up sand. She must have passed out before filling her canteen with—But she hadn't. Instead, she saw, she had gone on herself while she slept. She remembered the oasis and got to her feet immediately, hoping to see it before her. Instead she saw only sand. It had been a mirage. She shivered.

Above, the sky was still dark but a hint of blue was already emerging. It would be dawn soon and she decided to make the most of the cool morning weather by continuing her trek Southeast because once the sun came out, it was going to be a very hot day.

By the fifth hour, Aiyesha's legs no longer stepped on the sand. They dragged. She had climbed thirteen dunes, sometimes the descent of the dunes harder than the climb up. With heavy feet she pressed on, hoping that civilization would show itself. She had stopped checking over her shoulder long before for any following Dembatstayr. The effort of such a task was too great and she conserved her strength, harnessing it and employing it in her feet, one step at a time. Her tongue was parched, her body sweaty.

Maybe this wasn't such a good idea, she thought. *Maybe I should have stayed on Morley's ship. But, as he promised he would, he had provided me passage to the mainland. Not* my *mainland, but to* land *nonetheless. Maybe I should have found a horse to get me through this terrible place? Maybe I shouldn't have left home so long ago. I wonder what it is like there now? Is it the same, with the same goings-ons as it had been when I left? How are my parents? I'd give anything to see them again. I'd give anything for my old bed.* She adjusted her hood so it sat more properly on her head. *My parents! Bel Candar! Would the Dembatstayr have traveled there looking for me? Would they have captured my mother and tortured her, asking if she's seen or heard from me and where I could be found? Oh, dear Master, I pray You watch over her and keep her safe. I pray for my father, too, and my brothers and my sisters. They do not deserve to suffer for my transgressions. I'm so thirsty. No, don't think about that. It will only make matters worse. Where are the blasted people! Is there nothing but barren desert in this forsaken place?*

She was lost in thought, lost in daydreams, lost in conversations with herself to help pass the time. It had been nearly three days without an ample supply of water. She was told—she couldn't remember by whom—that after three days without water, the body passes into a coma and soon dies of dehydration. Aiyesha was amazed at how far she had gotten. She should have died the day before, given her condition, or at least have passed out, never to wake again. She could only attribute her staying alive to her sheer will to live and find comfort in a small town out of the way and far from the Dembatstayr.

The World around her began to fade as Aiyesha's eyes focused solely on the deep sand before her. The glare of the sun cut into her vision and she had to pull her black veil closer over her eyes to shield them from the light. Her vision now more focused, she kept moving. Soon, her head buzzed lightly and spots of green and red danced before her eyes. She shook her head, trying to snap out of it. Was it her imagination or was the ground coming closer to her face? She discovered that she was stooping low as she walked, the strength in her body gone. The buzzing inside her head grew more intense, the blots of red and green growing bigger. Then she was on her knees. She tried to stand but could not. She fell face forward on the sand and did not hear the approaching horses behind her.

CHAPTER XIII
Under a Midday Sun
(Wesafeld)

Aiyesha's head was bobbing up and down like a lifeless doll when she awoke. She had been unconscious for a little over two hours. She was on a horse and, because of her hood and veil, could not see the rider before her. Her arms were around the rider, her wrists shackled on the other side of his belly. She made a conscious effort to keep still and quiet so as not to alert the rider she was awake.

The first attempt at straightening herself failed; she was too weak. On the second try she managed to straighten herself enough to see that the man before her was clothed in the familiar garb of one of the Dembatstayr army: a dark purple tunic cropped neatly at the waist with a weapons belt carrying sword, knife, baton and other tools.

She had been caught.

They must have found her right after she collapsed. Her tongue was not as dry so they must have given her something to drink as well, or to at least wet her lips with. Knowing her body had been nourished with fluids made her feel better and restored hope. Careful not to stir in the saddle, Aiyesha looked up and, beneath a visor of black, saw they were riding toward a city far off in the distance, visible along the horizon of the Thakari Desert.

Then from behind her, a booming voice, "Behold! She awakes!"

Aiyesha pretended as though she were still asleep but the rider in front of her nudged her with his elbow. "No need to stay still, my lady. I had felt your stir some moments ago."

Feeling defeated, Aiyesha sat up. "Can you please undo these bonds? I can't see. My hood is over my eyes."

The other rider came up beside her and pulled her hood back, exposing her long black hair, which immediately began flowing with the wind. He pulled down the veil over her mouth.

"Is that better?" he asked.

"Yes. Thank you."

She got a clear look at them now, her green eyes taking them in. They rode gray horses with black manes. The men were clothed in standard military garb: a dark purple tunic over a gray woven shirt, the gray arms exposed, with black trousers and shiny black boots that came up just under their knees. Their hands were fitted with purple leather gloves, slightly lighter than the purple of their tunics. Their outfits reminded her of her training uniform (a piece of clothing she gladly gave up when aboard the *Raven*; Morley had been kind enough to offer her other clothes, namely outfits of exquisite design; she had got her black robe, hood and veil from him when the *Raven* had docked on a beach not far from Palatay). The men's heads were partially covered with gray hoods, an extension of the gray shirt they wore beneath the tunics.

She could have gone a lifetime without seeing those dreadful uniforms.

These men were obviously hired hands for General Gasahd. Knowing him, he would have sent several search parties looking for her when she didn't return from battle that day in Gal Ulkin.

"Where are we going?" asked Aiyesha.

Normally, Dembatstayr were not talkative. They followed orders, didn't ask questions and didn't answer to anyone except to their superior. But searching the Thakari Desert is tiresome work and these two men were probably bored with each other's company so talking to anyone other than their comrade was a welcome relief.

"Up to Wesafeld, just over there," nodded the rider to whom her arms were around.

Aiyesha licked her lips. "Do you have anything to drink? I am very thirsty and haven't had much by way of water for some time."

The second rider undid a clasp that held a large canteen to his saddle. He offered it to her, and then laughed. "I guess you cannot drink this on your own, huh? Here." He undid the lid and dipped the mouth of the canteen toward her lips. Aiyesha leaned toward it and drank greedily. The man removed the canteen quickly. "Not too much, now. We wouldn't want you to get all your strength back and become a problem."

The rider in front of her chuckled. The other reattached the canteen to the saddle.

"No, I suppose not," she said. "Yet, I am just a woman, surely no match for such strong men like yourselves."

The two men laughed again. Wesafeld drew closer but it was still a far ways off.

Aiyesha tested the bonds that held her wrists together. The shackles were made of steel and they were warm beneath the midday sun. An escape would be impossible. If she could escape before they reached Wesafeld, if she could somehow rid herself of these two soldiers and make a getaway to the city on one of the horses, she could avoid whatever fate awaited her there by approaching the city from the other side, perhaps the East instead of the West. She would stock up on supplies and then ride out.

She knew the Dembatstayr, if there were any in the city, would be on her trail the moment they discovered that two of their men were missing. But how long would she have until that happened? Who knew that these two were out in the Thakari Desert looking for her? And, who knew they had found her? How were these soldiers so sure they had found the right woman? Then again, how many women were there that would travel alone in a desert on foot? Aiyesha assumed these two would check in with a captain of some sort by nightfall, so she would have until then to escape, gather supplies, and get out of the city.

She checked the men for arms. They each carried a sword and a long knife on their belts. She knew that in their boots they carried knives as well, as was standard practice amongst Dembatstayr soldiers. Other than that, they didn't appear to have any other weapons. And their batons . . . Dembatstayr were too proud to use those. They preferred weapons that quickly drew blood to those that demanded work to cause the victim to bleed. To crack someone's head open was beneath them.

She reminded herself that her hands were bound and were currently around the waist of the soldier with whom she shared a saddle. She would have to move swiftly, before the other soldier could react.

The two men began speaking to each other about how pleased a man named Captain Morris would be when they returned with her.

Waiting until they were preoccupied with their conversation and their minds were busy fantasizing about commendations and possible promotions—Aiyesha slowly intertwined her fingers into a large fist and suddenly lurched her body to the right, forcing the rider in front of her to pull on the horse's reins, steering the horse away from the second soldier.

Aiyesha pulled her hands hard into the soldier's midsection. A wheeze escaped his lungs as she locked her hands underneath his solar plexus. The second he moved to free himself from her grasp, she pulled him close and slammed her forehead into the base of his skull. The soldier let go of his reins and Aiyesha was able to slide her arms up and over him so they were free. She removed his sword from its scabbard and brought it up to meet the blade of the second soldier who had come to his companion's aid. The clashing of the blades made a loud *clang!* The horse she was upon increased its speed to a gallop because of the commotion. She consciously relaxed the muscles in her lower body so as to not resist the movements of the horse.

The second soldier moved his sword and swung at her. Aiyesha ducked as the blade swooped above her head. She slashed at him and missed when he steered his horse away. He turned the horse back toward her.

Given that her hands were still bound, she knew remaining on a horse without control would end in defeat. Waiting for the soldier to get close and then dodging another slash of the soldier's blade, she pushed the man in front of her off the horse. The man fell to the ground with a thud and was trampled by the second soldier's steed. The soldier growled at the sight of his comrade lying dead in a mangled heap on the desert floor behind them. He swiped and slashed at her with renewed vigor, Aiyesha parrying his blows. The two horses ran at full gallop, side by side. Aiyesha came in close to the soldier and, with her elbow, deflected his sword hand skyward for a moment, enough time for her to use her left hand to free the man's knife from his belt. His blade came down and clipped her shoulder. She wailed from the stinging cut. His blade came down again and she moved out of the way, the blade wedging itself in to the saddle, just before her groin. She thrust forward with the hand that held the knife and instead of stabbing the man, she stabbed his horse where the nearest foreleg met the horse's barrel-like chest. The horse whinnied in pain from the puncture and suddenly moved in to Aiyesha's horse. The soldier was momentarily distracted and, using it to her advantage, she thrust her sword into him, through the purple tunic directly in to his heart. The man screamed. He tried to stab at her and instead only made a small cut on her leg. Aiyesha withdrew her sword and in a blur of motion lopped off the man's head. His head spun off his neck in a spurt of blood and landed somewhere on the desert floor behind the two speeding horses.

Aiyesha dropped the sword and grabbed the reins, bringing the horse under control. The other horse still had the knife sticking out of the fore of its chest. Aiyesha felt bad for having harmed the poor animal, but she hadn't had a choice. In a moment of guilt, she grabbed the reins of the wounded horse—which was awkward because of her restraints—and pulled back, slowing it down. The headless corpse of the soldier bobbed up and down, the soldier's feet still caught in the stirrups. After a time Aiyesha was able to bring the horses to a stop. The wounded horse neighed in discomfort of the knife sticking out from it. Blood oozed from the gash, running down its chest and leg as it moved itself forward then back in the same spot, dancing in agony. Aiyesha dismounted her horse and stood beside the other, reins still in her hands. She withdrew the knife from the horse's chest. Blood gushed over her hand on to her robe. The horse moved forward but she held it back.

"I'm sorry," she said. The knife she used to stab the horse was just under a foot long and plenty sharp. She knew what she had to do.

She let go of the reins and stood before the horse.

"I'm sorry," she said again.

The horse, its big eyes dark and wondering, watched as a glint of steel flashed in the corner of its eye, and ended the pain.

Aiyesha removed a set of keys from the belt of the headless soldier and unlocked her shackles. As she rode away, she glanced over her shoulder and watched the headless body of a big gray horse disappear behind her, along with the body of its headless master. Soon, the desert winds would cover most of the dead with sand and hide any evidence of what happened.

She had taken the canteen from the saddle of the deceased horse and drunk it all. The cool water renewed her strength and fought the dizziness in her head, both from thirst and excitement. Her weariness subsided. She set her hood and veil back in place so as to stave off the sun's relentless heat. The horse that she now rode had a canteen of its own affixed to its saddle. She sipped it as she rode toward Wesafeld. About a mile from the city, she steered the horse to the right, riding around the city's borders so she could come in from the East.

The city line of Wesafeld appeared blurry under the glare of the midday sun. Its buildings were short, perhaps the tallest only ten stories high, twelve at the most. They were made of pale gray stone, the windows round at their edges. The taller buildings sat like a ring around the city, the smaller ones on the inside along with the homes of those who lived there. Aiyesha made a decision to ride in quickly and blend in with the people, gather her supplies and rest before heading back out that evening.

Aiyesha turned in the city's direction.

When she came into the city, the streets were crowded with people bustling about running errands and tending to things needing done. And when she noticed that few had their heads covered either by hat or hood, she removed her head coverings, not wanting to attract any attention to herself. The people didn't seem to notice her presence. She knew, from talk of her brothers back at home, that Wesafeld was a busy place and often saw travelers of all kinds. Though slightly relieved at the notion, she remained cautious as she rode, scanning the people moving about, searching for any sign of the Dembatstayr. She didn't see any.

"Blast," she said to her horse. She spoke quietly so no one would overhear. "I haven't any tradesworth to purchase anything. I don't want to have to steal, if I can help it. Maybe if I asked someone for help?"

The horse neighed a response.

"I could do that," said Aiyesha. A conversation with the horse, however silly it was, was a welcome distraction. So far her trek Southeast had been a dangerous one and she could use something to lighten her spirits. "But I'm also thinking that if I did ask someone, and, if the Dembatstayr come around looking for me, they might ask anyone I speak to for help. And if a person didn't answer them . . . "

The horse neighed again.

"Thanks," she said, patting its neck, "you're a lot of help." Another idea struck her. "Do you think anyone will recognize you? Have you been here before and could be recognized as belonging to the Dembatstayr?"

The horse stopped as someone crossed their path.

"Good girl," said Aiyesha (if, indeed, the horse was a girl). She never bothered to check as it wasn't important. The horse was transportation.

They continued on through the crowd, the sounds of multiple conversations filling the air.

"You didn't answer me. Hm, and here I am talking to a horse. I'm being paranoid, I know, but one can never be too cautious." She paused. "This is terrible. I've never been homeless before. Well, I have a home but it's far away from here, and I haven't any tradesworth that could provide for me in the meantime. But I do need something to eat and I know I can't wait until we reach the next city." Then, softly, "I've waited four days already."

She straightened herself in the saddle and peeked around the corners of buildings and homes for the Dembatstayr. So far, she was safe.

Her thoughts went back to the problem at hand. The horse snorted. "You're right," she said. "I do need help. And there's no shame in asking for any. I'll take my chances, should asking for help cause problems."

The conversation ended.

Aiyesha continued on through the traffic of Wesafeld. She searched for kind faces in the crowd, especially the faces of the shop owners she saw standing in their doorways, greeting customers and wishing them a good day.

Up ahead was a large wooden post bearing the flag of Wesafeld. The flag was a monstrous piece of green fabric, with blue and yellow lines embroidered on it that zigzagged up and down, their apexes resembling Wesafeld's skyline. Watching over the lines of the city was a large ornate "W."

Not seeing anywhere else where she could tie her horse, Aiyesha opted for the flag post. She rode up to it, climbed off the horse, and tied the reins around the pole with a firm knot before stroking and patting the horse's neck, assuring it she would be back soon. She said a quick prayer to the Master, asking that no Dembatstayr would come along and recognize the horse. She had no choice but to leave it there. She certainly could not approach each shop or store owner while on her horse, especially if she wished for their sympathy. One without tradesworth did not ride a horse.

Keeping that in mind, Aiyesha saw an alleyway across the street. She crossed over to it, so as to get out of view of the passers-by, and got down to her knees. Using her hands as scoops, she pulled up handfuls of sand and rubbed it on her already-dirty robe. She sprinkled some more sand in her hair and smeared some on her face. Her cheeks turned red as the coarse sand scratched her skin. With two fingers she rubbed her eyes hard, turning them red and puffy. Now she looked like one who had nothing and one who had been crying because of it.

She stood up, dusted herself off just a little, and made her way back in to the street. She was sore so walking with a bit of limp was no task. The people gave her curious expressions as she passed them. Aiyesha did her best to appear innocent, as if her place in life had been no choice of her own. This was partially true.

Her first priority was to get some food. She glanced around and saw a small market set up at the end of the street. She made her way there.

Already she could taste the fruits and vegetables and meats and fish and anything else she could get her hands on. She didn't care what she ate, as long as she had *something*. She passed through the people, her shoulders bumping against many in the crowded streets. A larger built man was walking toward her and when he saw that if neither one of them moved their paths would collide, he negotiated moving to his right. Aiyesha saw the same thing and moved to her left. When they saw that they had moved in the same direction they each moved the other way and faced each other again. The man, seeming to be in a rush, moved quickly toward her and whacked his shoulder against hers as he made his way past. The force of the blow hit her square in the front deltoid and pain shot through her arm. When she turned to look at the man, she saw he had done the same thing again to another woman. The other woman wore a beautiful dress, had a gorgeous figure, a beautiful face complete with pouty lips. The man apologized to her and continued on his way.

That was rude, thought Aiyesha. *Just because I may not be as beautiful as her doesn't give you the right to bump into me and not apologize.* But the man wasn't the only one who had treated her poorly. As she approached the small market, she saw that others were giving her curious looks and sneering expressions. "What is she doing here?" Aiyesha could picture them muttering. "How dare a filthy wretch like that come in to *our* market." "If she had more respect for herself, she would do away with such dirty clothes." "If I wasn't busy on my way, I'd tell her a thing or two about picking yourself up and taking pride in who you are." A few of the younger folk walking through snickered at her Aiyesha blushed with shame. *If you only knew what I've been through,* she thought.

The market was simple: two rows of stands carrying everything from fruit to meat, cheese to herbs. Men and women stood behind their counters and sold their wares with great pride. Aiyesha salivated at the thought of taking a juicy piece of ham to her lips. She approached the butcher, who had a small table set up at the end of one of the rows.

"How much for a slice?" asked Aiyesha, pointing to the row of ham slivers laid out on the table.

The butcher was a man of generous proportion. He had a big belly and big arms. He wiped his hands on his once-white-now-bloody apron. "One dropper," he said.

Aiyesha pretended to consider the price, but was instead thinking of how she could persuade him to let her have a piece even though she hadn't any tradesworth.

The man crossed his arms. "So, are you going to buy one or not?"

"One dropper seems a tad expensive," said Aiyesha.

"Well, I'm not willing to negotiate."

She wanted—needed—that piece of ham. She hadn't eaten in days.

"You see, Sir," she began, hoping to play up the pretend fact that she was both poor and homeless, "I haven't eaten in four days. I don't have much. Actually, I don't have anything. Just what you see here. I was wondering if I could appeal to your kind nature and perhaps have a small piece? I would pay you back, of course, as soon as I get some tradesworth."

The man let out a burley laugh. "Now that's a good one, if I've ever heard. You're a pretty lady and not one of the Streetfolk from around here. They are all as ugly as a donkey's behind, if you catch my meaning. I'd rather make love to a dog than be caught seen with one of them. Regardless, ham is in short supply this season. Some of my pigs have been dying on me from some strange illness. It's going to cost you."

"Like I said, I haven't any tradesworth. If ham is a problem" —she scanned the counter and in behind the butcher was a row of chicken cages, the chickens squawking and fluttering their wings within— "I'd settle for a chicken leg, or a thigh. I'd settle for anything, actually."

He considered her request. "Sorry. Chickens are in short supply, too."

"But you have five there. Can't you spare some?" She was desperate.

He leaned in close to her. "I may—for a price."

"I told you, I haven't anything to pay with ex—"

"Except for what you have there," he finished. "I know." He grinned slyly. "Why don't you come back here in an hour and you and I will go somewhere? And once you pay me, you can have your meat."

Aiyesha knew what he wanted and, despite how hungry she was, would not give in to his offerings. She had enough of that sort of *trading* with Morley.

"No," she said.

The man leaned even closer. "Aw, come on. You're so beautiful. I'm sure you'd be able to pay. Maybe even pay with interest." He stuck out a meaty hand and stroked her cheek.

Aiyesha slapped his hand away. "Take your hand off me!"

The butcher growled and with both large hands pushed her to the ground. Aiyesha, her reaction slow from fatigue, couldn't block the attack. She fell back hard against some people passing behind her before hitting the dirty ground.

"Beat it, Wretch!" the man ordered.

Stunned by what just happened, Aiyesha put her palms to the ground and tried to press herself up. Someone passing by bumped against her and she fell back down. She was astonished that no one would come to her aid and see if she was all right. No one except—

"Are you okay, dear?" came a craggily voice from behind her.

Aiyesha felt a pair of bony hands come under her arms and help her up. When she turned to meet the person, she was surprised when she saw an elderly woman about a foot shorter than her. The woman was hunched over from a hump on her back so she was probably as tall as Aiyesha when standing fully erect. The woman was clothed in a ratty brown dress, with a beige shawl draped over her shoulders. Her hair was long and gray, her skin wrinkled. But it was her eyes that struck Aiyesha. They were bright hazel and glazed over, filled with compassion.

"I'm fine," said Aiyesha. "Thank you."

"You're welcome, dear." The old woman smiled sweetly.

"Come on, you two, get out of here before you wreck my business," called the butcher from behind his table. "Or will I have to come over there with a cleaver and lop off both your heads?"

"Hush up now, you fat bull. We're leavin'," said the old woman. To Aiyesha, "Let's go, dear."

The two women made their way out of the crowd and turned right at the end of the street, where there were less people.

"Terribly sorry about that," said the old woman, "most people aren't like that here. They have good hearts, they really do, but some don't see past the exterior."

Aiyesha dusted herself off a little. "Perhaps."

"Were you askin' him for something to eat?"

"Yes. I haven't eaten in four days and I'm so tired and I just want something to tide me over until I can earn some tradesworth for supplies."

The woman looked at her with such warmth that Aiyesha could nearly feel it encompassing her. "Yes, I see. You don't seem to be from around here. I mean, no one walks about without a little spending tradesworth, and those who are poor don't usually come near this particular market."

Aiyesha was suddenly filled with hope. "Is there another I could go to?"

"There is but you wouldn't want to go there, no matter how hungry you are. The food is terrible and the people circle the tables like vultures. I did the same thing meself once upon a time."

Her hope diminished. The old lady noticed Aiyesha's shoulders sag.

"My name is Samora G'Lammorahon," said the old lady. "What's yours?"

Aiyesha didn't reply. "I can't tell you. It's nothing personal, but I don't think it would be a good idea." This old woman had been so kind to her thus far; she didn't want to give her her name for fear that, should the Dembatstayr come round and question the people and Samora was among them, she didn't want the woman to find herself in trouble for talking to a fugitive.

Seeing that Aiyesha would not respond, Samora said, "Say no more, dear. Come with me. I'll take good care of you." She held out a wrinkled hand.

Aiyesha took it. "Thank you."

CHAPTER XIV
A Kind Stranger

Samora lived in a small home about two miles from where she met Aiyesha. Her place from the outside looked like a large, dusty boulder sticking halfway out from the ground, with all sorts of crags and cervices along its surface, giving it an interesting shape. The inside was small, with only three rooms: one for day to day living, another for sleeping, and another for the privy. It was cozy. The inside was cool, the rock thick enough to block out the sun's heat that was, right then, bringing on a scorcher of an afternoon.

Aiyesha sat at a small wooden table while Samora, on a small stove across from it, prepared a hearty soup.

"Smells wonderful," said Aiyesha.

"Thank you kindly," said Samora. "I may be seventy-three years old, but I can still make a delicious meal, if the mood suits me."

Aiyesha wondered if when she got that old if she would be cooking just for herself, or for a family.

Samora wiped her hands on an old towel hanging on a hook by the stove. "It's almost ready. Just a few more minutes."

"I can't wait."

"Myself neither. I don't receive visitors too often, so it's always nice when I have someone over."

Aiyesha wondered how many poor girls, or boys, Samora had served over the years, or if she was the first. She didn't ask the question.

Once the soup was ready, Samora set the steaming pot before Aiyesha and went to fetch two bowls and two spoons. When she returned, she placed the pottered bowls by the pot and with a wooden ladle served the soup. Aiyesha eyed the bowl hungrily as it was filled. Samora passed the bowl to her.

"Thank you so much," said Aiyesha. "If there's anything I could do to repay you—"

"Don't worry about it, my dear. Just eat. And after, once you're done, you can have a rest in the other room. Or, if that makes you uncomfortable, we can sit and talk awhile."

Just then Aiyesha thought of the horse she had left tied to the post bearing the Wesafeld flag. It was just as well that the horse was left there. By the time she finished her meal and, if she chose, had a rest, it would be evening, if not later, and the Dembatstayr would probably already have found the horse and taken it away. Aiyesha stirred the soup, slices of potato and carrot and chunks of ham coming to the surface. The smell of the steam rising from the bowl was intoxicating; her stomach growled.

Before taking a spoonful of the hot soup, Aiyesha asked, "Does that butcher fellow know where you live, Samora?"

The old woman finished filling her bowl and sat down. She shook her head. "No. I don't think he does. Why do you ask?"

Aiyesha slurped the hot soup from her spoon. "Mmm, this is good. No reason. Maybe I just don't want any more trouble. He said something awful to me."

"He says something awful to everybody, dear. A mean one, he is. Nice at first, but then he turns around and gets ya."

The soup was hitting the spot. Aiyesha could feel herself getting nourished with each spoonful.

The two women didn't talk much throughout the meal, only Common-talk. Samora asked where Aiyesha was from. Aiyesha didn't say from where, but instead said she was passing through and had gotten robbed two days before. She said that two young men had done it. It was be robbed or raped, the boys had told her. Aiyesha was happy to give them her "pretend" tradesworth in exchange for her freedom. Samora made a face at the tale.

When the meal ended, Samora said she would do the clean up and Aiyesha could go on into the other room to rest. Not wanting to be an intrusion, Aiyesha at first passed on the offer, but quickly changed her mind when a sudden rush of fatigue hit her. She said that she would lie down for only a few hours, not wanting to burden an old woman with a stranger in her home.

Samora led her to the other room and showed Aiyesha the cot. Two woolen quilts lay atop it along with a down pillow that looked very comfortable.

"I'll let you get settled," said Samora. She left the room.

Aiyesha eyed the cot then sat down on it. She fell onto her side and was asleep soon afterward, having not bothered to cover herself with the quilts.

Aiyesha awoke from a fitful sleep sometime later to the sound of singing coming from the next room. Peering around the door frame, Aiyesha watched as Samora hummed while sitting at the table, braiding wool into thick strings around a long, ivory needle, before knitting them together to make a blanket. Aiyesha rose out of bed and greeted her.

"How was your sleep?" asked Samora, not taking her eyes off her work.

"Fine," said Aiyesha, taking a seat beside her. "Just fine. How long did I sleep for?"

Samora stopped her knitting, then resumed, and said, "Not long. Maybe three hours. You should go back to bed."

Aiyesha stretched out her arms, warmth pleasantly filling her muscles. "No, I'm all right. Maybe later." What she could really use was a bath to get rid of the dirt and sand from her hands and face. Her robe, too.

"Would you like anything to eat? Perhaps some eggs, bacon, a tall mug of milk?"

The idea of a breakfast-like meal was very appealing, but Aiyesha didn't want to impose on the old woman. "I'm okay," she said. "Maybe just a mug of milk for now."

Samora set her wool and needle down on the table. She started to get up when Aiyesha stopped her. "I can get it," she said.

The old lady gave her a warm smile. By the way she sank back down in her chair, it was evident her bones were sore. "Are you sure?"

"Of course. It was kind of you to offer." Aiyesha stood. "Now where—"

"The mugs are hanging above the stove, as you can see. The milk's in a crate on the other side of the counter." Samora pointed toward it.

Aiyesha went to retrieve the bottle of milk once she saw it. As she prepared her glass, Samora asked, "That's an interesting robe you have on. Where did you get it?"

Aiyesha looked down at her dirt-stained robe. Before she could respond, both the women's heads turned in the direction of the window when they heard shouting outside and the heavy trotting of hooves.

Samora got up slowly, and, with a hand to her back, went over to the window.

"Oh, dear," she said, and covered her mouth.

There, out her window, was a band of four Dembatstayr soldiers riding toward her home. They were still a ways down the street, but would arrive soon enough.

"I wonder what they're doing here?" said Samora.

"Who?" Aiyesha came over and looked out the window. The moment she saw the Dembatstayr she said, "I have to go."

"I know," said Samora. She readjusted the shawl over her shoulders. "Don't ask me how I know, but I do. You're running from them."

Without responding, Aiyesha ran toward the door.

"No," said the old woman, "not that way. They would see you straight on."

"Then which—"

"Out the back."

Hurrying, Aiyesha followed Samora down a short hallway, stooping under it so as to not bump her head on the low ceiling. Samora said the hallway ran under the ground then up to the other side to the back entrance. They approached a small wooden door at the end of the hall. Outside—they could hear the men coming closer.

"You can go out this way," said Samora, "they won't see you. But run." She opened the door for Aiyesha.

Aiyesha, about to rush out, stopped a moment, and took the old woman by the hands. They were cold, even on a day as hot as this. "Thank you for everything. I'm sorry to leave so suddenly. If I had more time—"

Samora gave her a tender smile. "Don't say another word, dear. I was glad I was able to help. Now go."

Aiyesha hurried out the door. Samora closed it behind her.

Suddenly, Aiyesha heard the loud splinter of wood crackle somewhere on the other side of Samora's home. The Dembatstayr had kicked the door down. Samora's screams soon followed.

The rear door from which Aiyesha exited was kicked open and two Dembatstayr soldiers emerged.

"There!" one of them shouted, pointing in her direction. "Tell the others to bring their horses around once they're finished with the old wench. I'll go after the girl."

The other soldier ran back into the house, with the first soldier running after Aiyesha.

"Somebody stop her!" he shouted.

The few people who were around stopped in their tracks and let Aiyesha by, not wanting to get involved. The people in Wesafeld didn't interfere with other people's business. Only a select few, like Samora, helped people when they were in need.

Aiyesha ran hard, the milk in her stomach not quite settled, her stomach aching some. Digging her heels into the ground, Aiyesha sprinted back toward the busier streets, hoping to lose the men in the crowd. She glanced over her left shoulder, checking to see how close behind her the soldier was. He was not far off, perhaps only twenty yards. Aiyesha ran faster.

She turned a sharp corner and headed in the direction of voices. The soldier was not far behind. Dashing down the street immediately became difficult, what with all the people about. Aiyesha had to slow her pace to weave in and around the people, doing her best not to knock anyone over, saying "Excuse me" when she could. She couldn't help but bump into a few people though.

"Hey! Watch where you're going!" said someone.

"Whore!" said another.

"Wretch!" came another one.

Aiyesha paid no heed to their words and kept going. She looked over her shoulder again and saw that the soldier who was running after her was joined by two of his three companions on horseback, one of the soldiers bringing in a riderless third horse by the reins.

The other must still be back at Samora's, thought Aiyesha. *Please, Master, let that sweet old woman be all right. She'd done nothing wrong.*

Aiyesha knew the penalty for housing someone wanted by the law—prison. And, depending on how long the fugitive had been housed, the penalty might be death. She prayed to the Master to watch over the sweet old woman and pleaded with Him that no harm would come to Samora. Sweet Samora didn't deserve any foul treatment. She had been so kind to her, so caring. Aiyesha wished she had been able to get to know the old woman better. Their time together had been so short.

The soldier on foot grabbed the reins of the riderless horse from his comrade and swung himself up on the great steed. The three soldiers increased their speed to a gallop and caught up to her in no time. The biggest of the three grabbed her by the waist and pulled her up toward him, trying to throw her over the horse's back so he could take her away.

As Aiyesha was being hoisted up, she swung out her elbow and caught the man in the chin. The other two soldiers drew their swords. She was half on the horse, the man whose chin had been clipped hitting her hard with a bony fist. It caught her across the jaw. Immediately the taste of blood filled her mouth. She had bit her tongue. She spat her blood at the soldier. The nearest of the other two soldiers thrust a sword out toward her. Aiyesha moved and the blade missed her just barely.

"Watch it, you fool!" growled the soldier who was nearly hit with the tip of the blade.

He kicked, his foot hitting Aiyesha in the ribs. She gasped and lost some of her grip on the horse's saddle and her feet hit the ground.

She ran alongside the horse. People, seeing the commotion, cleared out of the way. Just as the soldier was about to hit her again, she reached down and pulled his boot from his stirrup and swung his leg upward. The man lost his balance and fell off the other side of the horse. Aiyesha swung her weight up and over hard, and saddled the horse. The other two looked back to see their comrade rolling in the dirty street behind them. They turned back toward her, both astonished at how easily she had knocked the rider from his horse. Indeed this woman had been trained well.

The soldier nearest swiped his sword at her. Aiyesha drew her horse away from him. She then turned the steed back toward him and grabbed his arm. He tried to pull away but she already had him in an armlock. About to strike with his other hand, he screamed when she snapped his left forearm, twisting it against the joint and breaking the bone. She took hold of his sword the moment he pulled his broken arm away to nurse it. He rode away from her.

With only one soldier left, Aiyesha, the horse beneath her galloping hard, drove her horse toward him. The swords clashed in the air with a metallic *clang!* Judging by how he moved to strike her, Aiyesha knew he was more highly trained than the others. Not allowing him an opening, she slashed her sword at him, holding the one she stole from the other rider at the ready. He blocked it and parried with another move. Aiyesha stopped his assault. For a short time the two speeding riders dueled, both out maneuvering the other. Aiyesha fought hard and swift. The soldier the same. They were now out of the city, riding out East into the Thakari Desert. Aiyesha considered stabbing his horse like she had done the other earlier that day, but did not want to end the life of another innocent animal. Instead, she rode her horse away from the soldier and, once about nine feet away, hurled one of her swords at him. The blade twirled through the air, the blur of the blade spinning like a metallic disc. Before the soldier could raise his arms to guard himself, the blade removed his head.

Aiyesha lowered the other sword and raced off into the desert. Not long after, up ahead, she could see the sand disappearing in the distance.

CHAPTER XV
Peter

The Ranmorahn Plains went on for an eternity. Peter, Alan and Catina had been traveling West for the past six hours since emerging from the Forest-Ring. The night was clear, the stars decorating the sky in sprinkles of white. Tiredness crept up behind Peter and Alan's eyes, Alan being especially concerned since his entire world was composed of darkness. At times the blind man wondered if he was asleep or awake. Catina had nodded off about an hour ago. She slept with her upper body hunched over, her head bobbing up and down with the trot of the horse. Alan held her tight, and kept her balanced when it seemed she would topple over.

They would go on a little further before stopping for the night.

—

Peter dismounted from his horse and, as he walked over to Alan and Catina, noticed how sore his behind was, aching from the hard sack of oats used for a saddle. The purpose of using such a thing for a saddle instead of blankets, he assumed, was to use its discomfort to keep them awake, thus traveling further at a time, instead of slipping into a slumber atop a comfortable seat. Or perhaps it was a prank of ol' Barmin Hahdgrove's.

Peter went and eased Catina off the horse. Alan insisted on dismounting by himself, not wanting to be the helpless blind man. Peter didn't object to this as Peter knew how important it was for his friend to know he could still take care of himself, despite his handicap.

"We will set up camp here," said Alan.

The area seemed safe enough. All around the trio was an endless field laced with soft blades of grass.

Not wanting to question his friend, but also taking in to consideration he was blind, Peter asked, "How do you know that 'here' is, in fact, safe?"

Alan made a face. "I may be blind, Peter, but I know where we are. I have been out this way before and, as you have already seen, there is nothing about us other than leagues of grass. We will be quiet safe here."

"I'm sorry," said Peter.

"Please do not be. I understand that it must be difficult to leave it to me to guide us. Yes, I cannot see. But I also have a memory as sharp as a dual-edged blade. Though I cannot see what is presently around us, I can, however, see it in my mind. I am sure these plains have not changed much since I have been upon them. Now, if you please, I would like to get settled for the night."

"I didn't mean any offense."

"I know you did not. Once more, let us settle in. Our tent is on Night, here." He patted the horse's rear where half of their supplies were bundled. Day bore the other half.

And with that, Peter lay Catina on the soft grass and let her sleep, while he and Alan removed their tent and blankets from Night, and set up camp. Day and Night were fed some oats from the "saddles" and were given a small amount of water to drink before Peter tied their reins together. The two horses whinnied with glee at their reward for a hard day's journey.

"What shall I tie the horses to?" he asked Alan.

"We have nothing to tie them to. We can only hope they will not be frightened off by anything and will stay the night." Then a smile crossed his lips. "Or, if you want, you can tie their reins to your feet and, if they scamper off, they will wake you and you can regain control over them as they drag you along."

They both laughed. "I'll leave that to you, instead," said Peter.

"Fear not, my boy. They will be fine, as will we. Now, help me finish setting this thing up so we can finally get some rest. We have a long journey ahead. We best start early. We had already lost enough time in the Forest-Ring."

Peter helped Alan set up the tent, a large gray piece of canvas that was sewn in a triangular shape. Three poles about seven feet in length (only half that when collapsed, as they bent in two in the middle on an axis of rope), were used to hold the tent up. Five iron spikes held the tent securely to the ground so it would not fall over, either by the wind or the moving about of someone inside.

The inside of the tent was cozy. Alan brought in a small oil lamp and lit it for Peter's benefit so that he could see what he was doing when rolling out the bedding. Once the blankets were laid, Peter tucked Catina in, and bid Alan a good night. Alan returned the courtesy.

"What about you?" asked Alan. "Are you not coming to bed?"

"In a bit. I think I'm going to stay out here for a short while."

"Suit yourself." Alan retired.

Peter went over to Day and, affixed atop the horse's large rump, was his pack. He opened it and retrieved his journal and pen and went off to think.

Not far from the camp, Peter saw a small bubble of black off in the distance against the horizon of grass. The Forest-Ring. It was an odd sensation to think that, just behind that dark bubble, was his home . . . or what was left of it. Seeing the Forest-Ring from such a distance reminded him of how sheltered Garathen really was and how safe a city it was, being as tucked away as it were. Out here in the open plains, he felt extremely exposed, as if the whole World could somehow see him. The safety of the Forest-Ring, like a warm, securing cloak, no longer surrounded him. He was truly out on his own in spite of being in the company of two others. He didn't know Alan all that well and he had just met Catina. But, he also knew, by the time this was all over, he would feel extremely close to them.

He gazed up at the stars and saw a few deep gray clouds settling in above. The air was warm and fresh and, despite the dark, smelled green. He laid down on the grass, his journal atop his chest, his feet pointing in the direction of the Forest-Ring. He crossed his arms behind his head. The clouds came together and floated apart in the heavens above, creating dark gray shapes and blobs. His mind wandered.

His adventure was just beginning.

One thing stood prominently in his mind. It was his conversation with Alan about the Age of Enlightenment. Though not much was brought of it, Peter did find it strange that he had not experienced it, unlike everybody else. Was he different? Or did he experience it and for some reason could not remember? But that second idea could not be the case as the Age of Enlightenment was supposed to instill in you a dedication to the Master, a loyal Faith in His workings and His Will. Peter prayed to the Master as regularly as anyone else, mostly in times of doubt and trouble. And, like he told Alan, he believed in the Master because He was Whom everyone believed in. Perhaps that last statement carried the answer he was looking for. Did he only believe in the Master simply because that was what you were supposed to do?

His mind wandered to his home inside the Forest-Ring, the pile of ashes that was left of years of work and dedication. His life had been a security to him: wake up, write a poem or two, or paint a picture, trade with others so that he was able to provide for himself until the next day; relaxing at night, the occasional dinner with neighbors. That way of life, to him, had been like a wall to lean upon, a routine that would always be there. Now that wall had burned to the ground and he was forced to stand on his own.

Indeed coming out here beyond Garathen, beyond the Forest-Ring, was a good idea. Already he could feel his old way of life being placed in the Past and a different sort of Future rushing up to meet him. And now, he was in that place in between those two times . . . the Present. He had never really experienced the Present in this sense before. His life had always just *been,* and his tomorrow was always laid out for him. There had been no period of "what if?" Or, "what next?" He was on middle-ground . . . and a part of him welcomed it.

Indeed this would be a time of change.

Gazing at the stars, Peter thought of Talia and the hope he had long ago that they would be together. And with the way she said good-bye to him, the way she took his hand in hers . . . that still may yet come to be. There was something there between them, just misplaced, like a thinly disguised opportunity gone by. "I look forward for your return. Stop by my station when you do and there will be a fresh bowl of fruit waiting for you," she had told him. And Peter knew he would stop by her station when he returned. Suddenly, he wanted to leave their camp and return to the city and see Talia, and tell her that he was there to stay. Then he thought of Catina and Alan and how they appreciated his coming with them on their journey. And then that moment of indecision passed and Peter was glad he was out here in the open on the Ranmorahn Plains.

Something was waiting for him on this journey, something that he could not turn his back on and retreat from. No, he was here for a purpose, and that purpose was to see a little girl home to her ailing parents.

Peter shooed away a fly buzzing above his face. He picked his journal off his chest and opened it to a clean page. He had decided while riding out of Garathen that he would record the highlights of his journey, and, when he returned, compile it into a book that he could trade for materials to build a new home.

Smiling to himself at the thought of having a new place to call his own, Peter began to write.

When he returned to camp, Peter heard snoring from within the tent. He opened the front flap, expecting to see Alan's thin chest rise and fall, the noise of a full-fledged slumber escaping through an open mouth. Instead he saw Catina, on her back, her mouth wide open, as if about to take a bite out of an apple that was too big for her. It was she who was snoring.

Peter smiled in spite of himself and went in, closing the flap behind him.

CHAPTER XVI
At Night
(Two Dreams)

Catina felt herself being moved and when she opened her eyes, she saw Peter over her, tucking a blanket in around her. He hadn't noticed she awoke. Fatigue gripping her full force, she slipped back to sleep.

Her journey thus far had been different than what she expected when she first came to Garathen to notify her grandfather of the perils back home. She hadn't expected Peter to rescue her, lead her to her grandfather, and then, eventually, return with them to Grek. She hadn't expected the encounter with—in her experience—a *second* palanthora beast. She hadn't expected to ride a horse. But she was grateful they were moving along and, soon, would be home. At times she did feel alienated from the two men while they spoke in the Common-tongue, but she felt very much involved when speaking with Alan in Grescalla. The feeling of inclusion was what encouraged her and assured her she had done the right thing by venturing all this way.

Tonight, as she slept, she dreamed of what it would be like to come home with Alan and Peter riding with her. She would be proud to show Peter her home and equally proud to show her grandfather the place he had not visited in quite some time.

In her dream, the three dismounted the horses, she immediately tearing off, running into the house, directly to her parents' bedroom. They weren't in there when she entered and fear gripped her heart. Where were they? She turned around and there, standing in the doorway, were her parents, hand in hand, smiling at her. She ran to them and they fell to their knees, embracing in a family hug. Her parents clutched her to them, they having been worried of where she'd been this whole time. Catina cried, happy she was finally home and that her parents were all right.

Once the embrace ended, she stepped in between her parents, each of them taking her hands in theirs. They went down the hallway leading to the kitchen in their small home and she saw Peter and Alan already in the kitchen, waiting for them. She let go of her parents' hands and ran over to the two men. She took Alan's hand in hers and, paying no heed to his blindness, pointed at her parents, telling him they were all right and there had been nothing to worry about to begin with. When she turned to look in her parents' direction, Catina let out a squeal when she saw they were gone. Vanished. She turned back to Alan and Peter and they, too, were gone, her hand holding nothing but air.

Alone in the kitchen, tears streamed down her face. She went to her knees and cried, afraid and confused.

When the tears finally slowed, she opened her eyes and saw she was kneeling on filthy ground, the house around her gone, and the farmland that was her family's property barren and dead. The sky above was red, orange and yellow, like sunset: brilliant and fiery.

She stood and began running, in which direction, she didn't care. She just wanted to get away. Speeding along the dead grass and dirt, she fell when she tripped over something hard but with a soft covering. She looked to see what had caused her fall and recoiled into a ball when she saw a dead body. The mouth of the corpse hung open, its eyes wide and rimmed with blood, its skin covered in bumps and boils. A foul smell crept into Catina's nostrils. To her horror she saw bodies all around her, all lying there with gaping mouths and leering eyes lined with red, their skin looking as if it had been burned or punctured to shreds.

She screamed . . . and awoke.

The inside of the tent was dark. Alan slept beside her, Peter on the other side of Alan. Catina sat up and shook her head, trying to shake out the lingering memory of her nightmare. She wanted to wake Alan and tell him of her dream, but decided not to, not wanting to disturb him. He needed rest like everyone else. She thought about waking Peter, too, but she didn't know how she would be able to communicate with him if she did so.

Her heart thumping steadily, Catina lay back down. When she closed her eyes, she could see those dead faces staring back at her, those bloodshot eyes peering past her and into her heart. She opened her eyes again and lay awake for a time before growing tired enough to finally fall back asleep. Fortunately, no more unpleasant dreams were visited upon her.

Sometimes Alan could see when he dreamed. Other times, his dreams were an overwhelming compilation of his remaining four senses: touch, sound, scent, taste . . . all except for sight. Those dreams were always in darkness, as if he were lost in a black cave with no hope of escape.

Tonight Alan dreamed such a dream, a dream he dreamed often. He was lost in a murk of darkness, walking, his ears suddenly filled with a female scream, echoing around him. He ran towards the sound, his feet hyper-sensitive in his dream, feeling their way across uneven earth. He could sense a large object falling towards him. He stretched out his arms and caught it, the object lying between forearms and biceps.

It was a body. His wife's body. He could feel her shudder against his arms. A warm liquid dripped out from beneath her, a severe flesh wound in her back.

"Alan," she said, her voice barely a whisper, but to him, he could hear her clearly, as if she were speaking at the top of her voice.

"Aubri, my love," he said.

She reached up and touched his face. The ridges on the skin of her fingertips dragged themselves across his jaw line. He held her hand there.

"I am cold," said Aubri. "I do not wish to leave. I—"

From behind, Alan could hear the footfalls of men. There were at least ten, if not more.

"They are coming," she said. "Do not let them get me."

"I will not let harm be visited upon you," he said tenderly.

But it was too late as the damage had already been done. Long ago, when Alan first married her, he had been seventeen years of age and she had been sixteen. They had been married for less than two years before her death. Aubri had been out after dark, having tea at a friend's down the road. While returning home, walking down the Through-way of Garathen, she had been mistaken for a Slummer by one of the Dembatstayr, who were then called the Guardians, standing watch not far away. Without hesitation, he fired off an arrow from his bow, the razor sharp tip landing between Aubri's breasts, following through clear to the other side. She fell to the ground, stunned, and bled to death soon after.

In the real world, the Guardian never owned up to what had happened, though all in Garathen knew, and when Alan waited up for her that night and she never returned home, he went out looking for her and found her dead in the street. In his dreams, however, he was always in darkness and her body came falling into his arms.

"I know you will not," she said.

"Do not speak," said Alan. "Just rest." When he dreamed this dream, he always sensed the outcome, and each time he prepared himself for its end, and each time he did, he still wasn't ready for it. And when Aubri died in his arms, a part of him died with her.

The footfalls came round and Alan wailed in the dark.

No one paid heed to his cries.

Peter's Journal: Old Earth

Aupil 5, the Year 134, the Fifth Aeon

The Earth is getting old. It's something I can sense underneath *what is seen. Each year vegetation blooms, grows, then decays, or lies dormant for the coming Winter, readying itself to sprout forth from the Earth once more in the Spring. Yet it seems somehow* strained, *this new growth.*

I've never really noticed it before, but now that I think on it, I suppose that the strain *was always there. It's almost as if the Earth is crying out, saying it's paid its dues and is wishing to finally be at rest. "If all living creatures can pass on to the next life, why can't I?" it might say.*

Perhaps we are now reaching a turning point in History. These are strange days we live in. Times are changing. Or perhaps it just feels that way because my own *life is changing. In the past two days, I have experienced more than I thought possible for myself. I suppose it is true when it is said, "Adventure comes from contact," or "Adventure comes to those who least likely expect it."*

This journey West to take Catina to her parents will be an interesting one, I should think. It has already proved itself interesting. I am eager to see what lies ahead.

As a side note, I'm really searching for direction. All that I had worked for back home has fallen to ashes. And it feels that way inside my heart, too. Seems like the old me is suddenly burning away, only to be built up again into something new—maybe even into something better. I hope it isn't arrogant to think that way.

Yes, I'm in tune with the Earth. We're both passing away. I just wonder who will remain behind once all is said and done: myself or the trees?

CHAPTER XVII
The First Sign of Power

Peter, Alan and Catina shared a loaf of bread for breakfast, as well as some cheese, an apple, and water from a canteen. They ate in silence, their bodies still waking from their sleep, their night's rest not seeming to be enough at this early hour.

The sun would rise any moment.

After washing down a bite of his bun with a gulp of water, Alan said they would ride until nightfall, only stopping twice in between to stretch out their legs and eat. Peter added he wished for no more trouble like what was encountered in the Forest-Ring. Catina didn't say anything. She was still disturbed by her dream from the night before. To cheer herself up, she thought of the fopphin she had seen in the forest and dwelled on how cute it was.

All three finished their food and rested for a short while. Just after the sun rose, they continued toward Grek.

Today was cloudy; the smell of rain hung on the air.

To help pass the time as they rode, the three shared jokes and stories, Alan translating for Catina so Peter could understand.

Alan stated how he hated it when people back home named him "Alan the Traveler." He said the name was both ridiculous and foolish. "We are all travelers," he said. "Just on different walks of life. Anyone who thinks one is named a 'traveler' simply because they tour the World, is foolish. If that is the case, then you, Peter, would be 'Peter the Home-stayer,' and Catina would be 'Catina the Farmhand.'" Alan chuckled. Peter did, too. "Why give others labels? It is absurd, if you think on it. I hope you see what I mean. The people back home do it, I think, to provide some understanding of how things work. Garathen is a very sheltered place, as you know, but that is only because the people of it choose it to be so. They hide inside the Forest-Ring, safe from the outside World. Why? No one knows. It has been like that since before the day of my great grandfather. Odds are, I bet, that if the Forest-Ring suddenly disappeared, there would be chaos. But, I think, it would also be a blessing. It would open up Garathen in a way those there never thought possible."

Peter furrowed his brow and looked back at him. Catina was patting Night's neck, saying something to the horse.

"I never knew you were so against home," said Peter. "Is that why you were always leaving?"

"No. My reasons run deeper than that. But I can tell you this, my boy, I left there to help myself move on and remind myself that my identity cannot be formed by my surroundings."

The comment hit Peter hard. He had always relied on Garathen because it provided shelter, like Alan said, and had a set routine of how life was supposed to be. He had thought everyone in Garathen was like him. He was wrong. Alan was a free spirit and he admired that.

Looking back at Catina again, Peter asked, "Are you sure she can't understand me?"

Alan reached out and gave Catina's shoulder an affectionate squeeze. "I am positive. Grescalla is all that is spoken in Grek. Even when I visited, I spoke to her mother and father in the Rolling-tongue. Only at times, when he was still alive, did I speak to my son in the Common-tongue. Grek is a place very set in its ways, and its culture does not welcome outside influence kindly."

"I see."

Peter thought back to the night before under the stars. He wished he was there now. His bottom was sore and he felt ashamed for being what he thought was a weak man. Catina and Alan seemed to be fine riding on such a hard surface. He hoped this journey would toughen him.

Catina put a hand to her eye. The swelling on the eye had gone down a little. She appeared more relieved, but still kept her eye covered.

Catina said something to her grandfather

"Catina has a headache," said Alan. "Me, too."

"Hopefully it won't last long," said Peter.

"Hopefully."

The clouds above grew darker as the morning went on. Intermittently, light drops of rain fell, and when it stopped, the air was warm and humid.

"Do you like the rain, Catina?" asked Peter.

Alan translated it for her and she replied saying that she did. Her home was a dry place so she considered rain a special treat.

They traveled on.

Around mid-morning, Peter asked, "When is our next stop?"

"Whenever we need it," said Alan, "but like I said before, I only want to stop twice. It is too easy to stop frequently when one is tired, and it suddenly becomes hard to get moving again. I am thinking we should stop early in the afternoon, and then have another rest mid-evening so we can eat before going on until after dark."

Peter frowned at the thought of more long hours upon the hard saddle of oats. Already the left side of his behind was numb.

"In about a week and a half we will reach Darim," said Alan. "We will stop there, replenish our supplies, maybe stay the night, depending upon when we reach it. You will like Darim, Peter. I had been there once about twenty years ago, if I recall correctly. A fine place, it is; much larger than Garathen, at least twentyfold."

Peter whistled at the size. Garathen was only a dozen or so streets wide. Any settlement larger than that was almost mind-boggling. He wondered what it would be like to see such a place. He could picture the crowds and buildings, the lack of silence and the abundance of "things to do." Day snorted. Night replied in kind.

Hills began rolling up from the Ranmorahn Plains. The horses took each hill with ease. Peter saw a look of discomfort on Alan's face.

"You all right?" he asked.

Alan swallowed. "Fine." He took a drink of water. "I always hated this part when coming this way. Hills make me nauseous. But it would take too long to go around. Just keep these horses going straight West, Peter. I will be fine."

With the turning of the land, Peter was unsure if they really were going in a straight line. It seemed that with each hill, some bigger than others, the horses would turn a little to the left or right instinctively, to make the climb easier. Besides, the land all looked the same. But Peter tried to obey his friend.

Around mid afternoon, it rained for a short time, no more than fifteen minutes, and the trio was unable to keep themselves dry. Alan cursed at the rain whereas Catina giggled every time the light drops of water sprinkled her face. Peter was indifferent to it.

A short while after the rain stopped, they dismounted their horses at a small dip in the hills and rested. They ate lunch—more bread and veggies, and milk—and lay on their backs on the grass and stared up into the gray sky. The air was fresh and damp; a cool breeze was on the plains. When Alan felt his eyelids droop and knew that he was about to doze, he announced they should be on their way. Hazily, Peter and Catina got to their feet, for they were feeling sleepy as well and yearned for a good nap.

Back on their horses, they resumed their path. An hour later, coming over the hill in the horizon, Peter spotted a dark blotch moving toward them.

"Alan, there's something coming," he said.

"What do you mean?" he asked.

Peter squinted, hoping to see the blotch more clearly. "People," he said, "traveling on foot. Maybe five or six of them."

"You know it is customary to see people when one is out and about, Peter."

Turning in his saddle, Peter furrowed his brow at him. "I know but I thought I should mention it given the fact that we've already run into trouble on this trip and I thought it wouldn't hurt to alert you." He nodded at the humanette. "And Catina."

The humanette, who had been braiding the horses mane, looked up at the sound of her name. Peter smiled at her. She smiled back and then returned to her braiding.

"Thank you for informing me," said Alan. "I do appreciate it. And you are right, this journey has already proved itself to be a dangerous one. It never hurts to be prepared. Always voice your thoughts. It is important so as not only are others aware of what is happening, but yourself as well."

"You're right, but I won't yap too much."

Alan chuckled.

The small band of people grew closer. Peter saw there were six of them, all wearing long brown robes with black cloaks over their shoulders, the thick, long fabric blowing in the breeze. Peter thought it strange they were all dressed alike and described them to Alan. Alan said they were the Velmoras, the Master's Messengers.

The Velmoras were considered a wonder in all the Earth. Though they resembled Man in all ways, they were not considered Human. No one knew for sure the origins of their race, thus adding to their mystery, but a man or woman, when coming across someone of the Velmoras, would know their paths had crossed, whether the Velmoras were wearing their brown robe and cloak or not. The Velmoras were said to be a race who were in tune with the Master. The Master's Mark was upon them, a black or deep purple birthmark upon their left breast, closest to the heart. These were the folk who preached the Faith of the Master by traveling around and proclaiming the Master Lord to all peoples of the Earth.

When Alan explained this to him, Peter wasn't sure what to make of it. Already he was having doubts about the Master's reality because he had not experienced the Age of Enlightenment, but now he was also curious as to who these men coming over the hills were and, if he asked, if they could perhaps tell him why he hadn't experienced the Age of Enlightenment.

"What do we do when we cross them?" asked Peter.

"Depends if they talk to us," said Alan.

When the Velmoras approached them, the man in the front raised his hand in greeting.

"Hail the Master," he said.

Peter tugged on the reins of both horses, slowing them down.

"Greetings," said Alan.

The two parties met; Peter and his company descending a small rise in the land, the Velmoras walking up it.

Catina stirred uncomfortably in her seat.

"Rainy day, isn't it?" said Peter.

The man who greeted them glanced up at the graying sky, as if evaluating if Peter's statement were true. "Yes, it is," he said. "We were caught under some rain a few hours ago. But, no matter. We're used to the weather. Besides, it's all in the Master's grand design."

Peter had never heard the Master brought up this much in such a short amount of time. People back home, though they believed in the Master, never spoke of Him outside of prayer or worship.

"I suppose," said Peter.

Alan, who stared straight ahead over the men, asked, "Where are you folks off to?"

"We have just come from Darim," said the man, "and are now heading East to preach the Master's good tidings. Our next stop is Gnoraveer, I believe." He checked with one of his mates to make sure his statement was true. His companion nodded. "Yes, Gnoraveer." The man then stepped up to Peter's horse. He stuck out his hand, a twinkle in his rich brown eyes. "I'm Rano, by the way, leader of the Men of Humility."

Peter shook his hand. "Men of Humility?"

"That is what we call ourselves. It's our way, as Velmoras, to say that, though we bear the Master's Mark, we consider ourselves no higher than any other living thing on the Earth. We've received a lot of scolding in the past, accused of considering ourselves superior, but that is not the case. Never was. We are only fulfilling our duty, the purpose of our lives, by preaching the Master's Faith."

One of the men behind Rano spoke. "We're glad that you didn't ride on past us, as all who we have encountered since Wesafeld have done so. Thank you for stopping."

Peter noticed the Velmoras carried only themselves and no supplies. He didn't know how he could ask the men about it, so he didn't. But he had no idea how they could survive on their own without any food or water, or even horses for that matter. The distance between place to place was great and it would be a long, long time to get anywhere just by walking.

While Peter and Alan spoke with the men, Catina's headache eased for a short moment, and then suddenly burst into hot pain, the area near her left eye throbbing with sharp aches. Just then the World burst into stars of red and blue, then green and black, then gold. Her line of sight was suddenly drawn to the breast of Rano's robe and the cloak that draped over it. Suddenly, the black of the cloak dissolved, revealing the brown robe underneath. The robe soon began to melt away, displaying Rano's tanned chest. And there, strapped to his body, was a gray pouch, and, tied to its top, where it was cinched together by a canvas string, a Rigmata. The string was thick and had figure-eights etched into it, the figure-eights turned over onto their sides, running the length of the string. Before she could focus on the string any longer, her eyes were drawn to the pouch. The gray material burned away, revealing its contents—a shiny black powder. The pain in her left eye persisted, climaxing into an ache that caused her to whimper.

Rano and his men looked her way. So did Peter.

"Bele som ren?" asked Alan, a hand to her shoulder. *What is wrong?*

The gray pouch restored itself then the brown robe materialized again as well as Rano's black cloak. The girl didn't reply but put both hands to her eye, as if trying to prevent the pain inside from spilling out. There was another burst of stars of red and blue, green and black, then gold. Suddenly, the pain in her eye ceased. Shakily, she removed her hands and blinked the tears out of her eyes.

Alan asked again if she was all right.

"Semba dal gosar," she said. *I am fine.*

Her grandfather double-checked with her to make sure she was okay. Catina insisted he had nothing to worry about.

"Is she doing okay?" asked Peter.

"She is fine," replied Alan. "I am not sure what that was about. Perhaps we best get going."

"Before you go," said Rano, "let me tell you of the Master's Second Coming."

Alan's ears immediately perked up at hearing this.

"What do you mean 'Second Coming'?" said Alan, seeming to forget that he just said they should get moving. "When did He ever come a first time?"

"Oh, He came once long ago," said Rano. His brethren all murmured amongst themselves in affirmative "Uh-huhs" and "Yeses."

Catina recognized the black powder with the subtle shine, in the gray pouch she had seen hidden beneath Rano's robe; though *how* she had seen it, she didn't know. She also recognized the Rigmata. Her step-father had a barrel of the black powder hidden away in the far corner of the barn back home. The black powder was used for lighting fires when the wood for the stove or fire pit outside was wet. Her step-father would stack his kindling and logs and, if they were damp from rain, would sprinkle some of that black powder on it and use a Rigmata or a knife and flint to light it. The flame the powder produced was both bright and very hot. Her step-father said that it got a fire going in half the time it would take for the wood to catch flame and burn on its own, without the powder's aide. But why would Rano be carrying it? Catina wondered.

"When? asked Alan.

"A long time ago," said Rano, "several thousand years." As Rano went on about the Master's first believed appearance on Earth, Catina thought about the shiny black powder in the gray pouch. She acknowledged these men were without supplies, namely wood for a fire. And they didn't appear to be carrying any tools so unless they found dead tree logs or branches lying around, they had no means to cut themselves any wood. Besides, they were out on the Ranmorahn Plains, where no wood was in sight and there was only grass. Suddenly thinking of the Forest-Ring, Catina turned in her seat to her grandfather and grabbed his hands.

In Grescalla they spoke:

"He has some Gero!" she told him.

Alan glanced at Rano then back at Catina. "What?"

"Gero. He has some Gero. I know because Dad used it to start fires at home."

Alan squinted his white eyes. "Catina, I do not understand."

Catina huffed, realizing she wasn't getting through to him. But how could she? She didn't know how she saw Rano was carrying the Gero, but she knew he had it nonetheless.

"Underneath his robe, strapped to himself. I could describe it to you clearly. It is in a gray pouch tied with tan-colored string. The Gero is black and shiny. He has a Rigmata also. What is he going to do with it?"

Just then Alan's eyes tensed even more. "Now, see here. These people have done nothing wrong and I do not want you to go and make up stories about what this fellow may or may not be carrying. I do not know what would move you to do such a thing, but I will have no more of it. Understand?"

"But—"

"But nothing."

Catina made a face and crossed her arms. She didn't know Alan to be so stern. How could he go from a kind, loving grandfather one moment to someone who would not listen to her? She turned in her saddle to face him. "Something happened. I was able to see through his clothes and see what he is carrying underneath."

"Nonsense!"

"It hurt when I did it, that is why I was crying. Why do you not believe me?"

"Because it is impossible. Now, please, turn around, and no more stories."

"Fine," she said, "but if something bad happens, do not blame it on me."

"Nothing bad will happen. Velmoras are a pure folk. There is not one shred of evil in their bodies."

Catina didn't say anything. Fine. If he didn't want to listen, then she didn't want to share any more of it. And now that she thought of it, she may have been mistaken in what she saw. She was still weak from her original journey East to Garathen and, as they had been traveling back to Grek, she had found herself dozing in and out of sleep, sometimes just daydreaming, but daydreaming so intensely that the dreaming felt real.

Rano peered over Peter's shoulder to the blind man and his granddaughter behind, when he heard mention of the Velmoras' name.

"Do you know what they're saying?" he asked Peter.

Peter turned to Alan and Catina, then back to Rano. "Sorry. I have no idea. I was hoping I'd pick up some of it while I traveled with them, but none of it has stuck. Not yet, anyway."

"Maybe in time," said Rano.

"Maybe. You were saying?"

"Yes, I was telling you the Master is returning. You see, we as Velmoras have a special link to Him and occasionally certain things are prophesied to us. Two nights ago, as we camped under the stars, I dreamed of the Master."

"Really?" Peter was interested. "What did He look like?"

The man stroked his chin. "Well, it's difficult to say. He takes on so many forms, some more Humanlike than others. I can only equate this particular instance to that of the Age of Enlightenment, as you Humans experience it. We as Velmoras have no need for such an experience. He is already bonded to us and we to Him, from within. He was like a black cloud against a purple mist. It's strange when one dreams of the Master because once you do, only certain details from the dreams stay with you whereas others are forgotten."

"Hm," was all Peter said.

"But the Master told me that He is coming back and that it is both myself and my fellow Men of Humility's responsibility to prepare the way for His return."

Alan spoke up. "Did He say when He is returning?"

"Well, no. He said He would not reveal the day or the hour. Just to be ready as it could happen any time."

Alan brought Night up alongside Day so he and Peter were side by side. "Then how do you know it was really the Master, and not some strange dream of yours?"

Just then a knowing expression crossed Rano's face. "Because, as you know, Humans only dream of the Master a total of one time in their lives. That's it. Any other dream of Him can only be a message from Him directly."

"But you said as Velmoras you have a special link to Him. That may be true, and if that link permits you to dream of Him whenever or however, then what is to say that residual images of the Master in your memory does not take shape in your dreams?"

"For a blind man you seem to see much. You make a good argument," said Rano. "But you would be wrong."

Peter's eyes darted to Alan to see how his friend would react to someone outwardly saying that he was blind. It didn't seem to faze Alan one bit, his face not flinching, no expression coming through. Catina was oblivious to what was going on. She merely waited patiently for the conversation to end and for them to be back on their way.

"For generations the Velmoras dreamed of the Master, and, somewhere along that Timeline, it was spoken to us that our dreams were not fabrications of our imagination, but rather manifestations of our Faith. Are you aware that the majority of our visions occur when we are awake?" He awaited a response from Alan. When there was none, he said, "No, you are not. But it's true. We have no power over when they come. They simply do and that's the end of it."

When it was clear that Alan could not think of the words to say, Peter said, "That's amazing. Really." He considered sharing with them he had not experienced the Age of Enlightenment, but decided against it. Something within him told him not to, like a frightening voice of conscience saying that if he did, only evil would come of it.

Some of Rano's men shifted as they stood. One of them suggested to Rano that they best be on their way.

"Agreed," said Rano, "we should be off." He turned to the three Humans and said, "Farewell, friends. May the Master watch over you and bless you. And be wary, for His hour could come this very day."

"Take care," said Peter.

Catina waved good-bye to the Men of Humility as they walked past the horses. Alan just stared forward. He didn't even wave.

The Men of Humility were now far behind them, having disappeared over a hill some time ago. Alan and Catina were still alongside Peter. Often, Peter would look over and see Alan looking straight ahead, the blind man's mind off in a place that Peter could only guess at. Peter knew that Alan was hurt. Though the conversation with Rano had been tame, Alan had been left without the final word. And, because he was a smart man who had seen so much in his life, being stuck without an answer, he thought, must be a hard thing to deal with. Peter didn't know what to say that might make his friend feel better.

Before choosing his words carefully, Peter asked, "You didn't believe anything they said, did you?"

"No, I did not," said Alan.

"Which part?"

"All of it. Namely this business about the Master returning." Then, almost ashamedly, "It is not possible."

"Why?"

"Must you ask so many questions!"

Peter cowered at the sudden rise in his voice. Even Catina looked up at her grandfather.

"Sorry," said Peter.

"No, I am sorry," said Alan. "I did not mean to snap at you. It is just there is a lot you do not know about this sort of thing. The Master, I mean. And though I know He is real, and I do believe in Him and ask for blessings, there is a part of me that questions why. Like yourself, Peter, I feel as though I am part of a group, believing something simply because everyone else is. And, like yourself, I am searching for answers. And that is a very hard thing for me to admit."

Peter didn't know how Alan could describe him so perfectly, but that was okay. It brought him great comfort.

"Thank you," was all Peter could think of to say.

Alan turned to him and smiled. "We will talk on this more, but not now. Perhaps when we learn more. Perhaps when we find what it is we are looking for. But let us carry on. We have some ground to cover before dinner. Then, after that, we ride into the night."

CHAPTER XVIII
When the Past Takes You

The small stretch of the Thakari Desert that bordered Wesafeld had been crossed toward the end of last evening, and the land transformed from sand to dirt and eventually to countryside. Aiyesha rode through the night, getting herself as far away from the Dembatstayr as she could. Come morning, she was exhausted but would not rest until she knew she was safe. She decided she would rid herself of the military horse outside the next town or city she approached. The horse would ride off to wherever it pleased, and she would go into the city on foot and, depending on the circumstance, either find a new horse, or perhaps stay for awhile amongst the people and build some semblance of a life there.

And so Aiyesha rode along the countryside, her thoughts wandering, her mind weary but willing to go on. After a time the scenery appeared the same: small rises in the land covered in grass for as far as the eye could see, patches of bush and shrub, thickets of wood here and there. Occasionally there was a stretch of land covered in the gold of yellow grass and its sweet fragrance reminded her of her freedom. Perhaps a temporary freedom, but a freedom nonetheless.

Soon she could see a winding dirt path on her left. A small heap of black humped on the road caught her eye. And when she looked closer, she was startled by what she saw.

A body.

She rode toward it. Once there, she dismounted, and cautiously approached the corpse. A crow pecking away at the body's neck fled when it felt Aiyesha had gotten too close. The dry dirt beneath her sandals crunched as she neared. She stood before the body and stared at it, as if suddenly mesmerized by the sight of the dead. It was a man, rather large in size, and, judging by the gray and wearing of his skin, must have been lying there for several weeks, perhaps a month, perhaps more. His eyes were open, devoid of expression, but Aiyesha assumed he must have smiled a lot in life given the crows feet at the corners of his eyes. His body was clad in a maroon shirt that was darker on the side, once soaked with blood but now dried. He wore gray trousers. Looking further up the road, she saw wagon tracks and hoof prints. Her first thought was this man had fallen off his wagon and the horse had fled, leaving him to die with broken limbs. But that wouldn't explain the blood on his side. She knelt down and examined the wound. She had been around enough blood in her twelve years of military training that she recognized the wound having been caused by a long blade . . . but not long enough to be a sword. It had been caused by a dagger of some sort. Aiyesha looked around the body and, over on the man's other side, was a knife. She went over to it, picked it up. The blood on its blade was streaked down its shaft, having dried in burgundy clumps. The man had pulled it from his body, the flesh open from his wound smearing the blood down the silver of the blade. Her eyes went back to the dirt and she saw a set of footprints; they were too small to be that of a man. They were Human in origin. The man's attacker.

A child.

As if startled out of a nightmare, Aiyesha released the blade's handle and it dropped to the dirt.

Her heart, though callused to the sights of death, twitched in anguish, knowing that someone so small had caused this tragedy. She presumed this was the case, anyway. She wished to know where this person was, so she could hunt them down and wring their neck for taking a life. Aiyesha had witnessed plenty of killing on the Coast of Seryn, so much so she was sick of it and wished never be around it again. But she knew that was impossible. "The Earth is in hard times," had said General Gasahd, "and slaughter, sometimes senseless, and sometimes not, will be a part of those hard times." But Aiyesha did not want to see anymore violence, not just in her own life, but in the lives of others as well.

Compassionately, she knelt down alongside the body and, with thumb and forefinger, closed the man's eyes so he might finally be at rest. She stayed kneeling by his side for a time, asking the Master to deliver the man's spirit into safekeeping in the hereafter.

When she was on the Coast of Seryn, once a month General Gasahd would round the women who were training together and do with them what he called the Exercise of Enrichment, or the Three "E"s, as the women called it.

The women were paired up and, to harden themselves against shame, remove their clothing. One would lie on a custom-made bed of gravel, the sharp shards of rock poking at the skin, sometimes puncturing it. The other woman would kneel beside her partner and, with knife in hand, run the blade along the woman's body, its sharp end scratching the skin. In intervals, the blade would be pressed harder upon the skin until blood was drawn in red lines along the chest and abdomen and tops of the thighs. Once the woman lying down was covered in crisscrossing, red lines, the blade in hand would be exchanged for a much shorter and duller one. Under careful guidance and instruction from General Gasahd, the short blade would then be positioned just under the lowest rib. Slowly, so as not yet puncture the skin, the dull tip of the blade was pressed against the flesh, the ache caused by its dull tip pushing against the skin excruciating. This was the Endurance of pain.

While the blade was pressed below the rib, the woman controlling it would coat the exposed part of the blade with Bertamin, an oily substance that was used within the camp to heal wounds and enhance clotting. Then, the blade covered in Bertamin, was plunged deep in to the other woman. Aiyesha would never forget the cries of the first woman she had pierced. Her name had been Helena and she wailed uncontrollably as Aiyesha steered the blade as far in as it would go, managing to push in the blade up to the hilt. For the one driving the blade into the other woman, this would bring Execution, the dominating of another, being in control, inflicting pain at will. An asset in battle: to dominate and control rather than *be* dominated and controlled. The Bertamin kicked in almost immediately and any blood coming from the wound ceased its flow and the torn flesh remained sealed until the blade was withdrawn. Once the woman with the knife in her side had grown used to the pain (which sometimes would take up to a day or more without sleep or food, only water being administered to both the woman lying and the woman with the knife when needed), the roles would switch. The wound would be dressed with Bertamin and bandages, and it was the other woman's turn to be pierced. The woman who was the executioner would then be the victim to the painful exercise. She would enter the Third "E", and that is to be the receiver of Ensnarement, to be at the mercy of another and to accept the possibility of death. For in battle, should you be captured or slashed when and where there's no hope of escape or recovery, you had to accept the possibility of death, and then, accept the *inevitability* of it. The combination of these three parts, these three "E"'s, were designed to *enrich* you to be the warrior you were training to become.

Aiyesha remembered one session of the Exercise of Enrichment. She had been paired with Helena again. Aiyesha had already undergone punishment at Helena's hands and it was now her turn to put Helena through the process. All had gone well up until it came time to coat the blade with Bertamin. When Aiyesha had been under the knife, Helena had used too much of it and did not leave much for herself when it was her turn for her side to be pierced. Aiyesha noticed this immediately when pouring the liquid in her hand so she could rub it on the blade. Though there had been only a little Bertamin, Aiyesha thought it might be enough to make do, if she smeared it thinly on the blade. Once done, she pressed the coated blade into Helena's side. Helena cried in anguish, the dull yet hot hurt taking her. Aiyesha saw that the blood squirting from the open wound kept pouring forth and would not close. She tried to remedy it by adjusting the knife's position, hoping that if the blade was sitting elsewhere in the wound, it might seal it better. It hadn't. The blood kept streaming from the gaps in the gash.

"Helena, I can't stop the bleeding," she said.

And with a smile, though laden with discomfort and unease, Helena said, "I know. I'm sorry but I want no more of this." Her face winced. "This isn't the way women should be, Aiyesha. We were never meant to perform these bizarre acts on one another. It was never the Master's intention. And if it was . . . " She didn't finish.

"But all our training? The coming war? We must be ready."

"Yes . . . but not like this."

Aiyesha looked up, frantically searching for General Gasahd so she could tell him to retrieve more Bertamin.

"Helena," said Aiyesha, guiding the other woman's hand to the hilt of the knife, "lie here and hold this steady. Do not withdraw it. I'm going to get help."

Helena raised a weak hand to stop her. "No. Don't. Please."

"But—"

"You can't." She coughed. A small amount of blood leaked from her lips. "It's almost over, now. Please . . . please, don't say anything. Swear to me you won't."

Tears welled up in Aiyesha's eyes. "No—"

Helena merely nodded, seemingly agreeing with herself that death would soon arrive. All the World seemed to hush about the two women, the painful cries of the others fading away.

"Good-bye," said Helena.

And with that Aiyesha watched as Helena wrapped her fingers firmly around the knife's handle. She pulled outward and the blade slid from the wound, followed by the dark red flow of blood. Helena's eyes never left Aiyesha's. Aiyesha stayed beside her to the end. Anguished cries came back into being around her as Helena died.

When General Gasahd came to see what kept the two women when they didn't stand when the exercise ended, he stood over Helena's body, his face without expression. The other women came and gathered around their fallen friend. One wept openly. Gasahd told her to be quiet, and back-handed her right cheek.

As punishment for allowing her friend to die, Aiyesha was cast into a deep hole, the Pnutar, as naked as she had been the day Helena died, and remained there for thirty days, a set of heavy, iron bars laid across its top to prevent her from escaping.

After a fortnight in the hole, eating only once every two days on leftover scraps from the camp's mess hall, General Gasahd came to see her. Thankfully she was still allowed to drink every day. Two cups of stale water, one in the morning, one at night.

Gasahd crouched down and leaned over the bars

"You know why you're here, don't you?" he said.

Aiyesha sat with her back against the inside of the Pnutar, the moist dirt cool and soft. She didn't answer.

"Next time think twice about letting a comrade die. I trust you would not do the same thing when the war comes. And I trust you wouldn't want another to do the same thing to you." And with that he stood and left her there.

That night Aiyesha wept. That had been four years ago.

Now, by the body of the man at the side of the road, for the first time since, Aiyesha cried.

—

Aiyesha left the body behind, but not before burying it. She dug a shallow grave four feet from the road, using the man's knife as a shovel. It was hard work and took two hours, but it was the least she could do. She felt it was a penance for taking Helena's life, some sort of "giving back." Fortunately, no one had come by to see her burying him and the road remained empty of all travelers. When the task was completed, she said a silent prayer to the Master for the man's spirit, and left it at that. She kept the knife, having cleaned it by spitting on it and wiping it with the lower hem of her black robe. She might have need of the blade should the Dembatstayr find her again.

And so she continued East for the duration of the afternoon, alone, deep within the countryside, far from the road and out of sight.

A wave of fatigue hit late afternoon and for a moment she thought she would pass out on her horse. She forced her eyes to stay open, and continued on. She would rest at nightfall. Hopefully, she would come across a patch of forest that could provide her with some berries or some game she could feast upon since she hadn't anything to eat since the day before.

Her mind wandered back to the dead man now and again as she rode. And it wandered more so to Helena.

The mind was a fragile thing and though it could be hard with will, it was also soft and could easily be molded and transformed. Twelve years ago, when she had turned eighteen, before she had joined up with that accursed army, she had the revelation that, as one grows older, they are able to think for themselves and the teachings of their youth, namely from parents, no longer needed to form their identity. At this point of self-realization, the mind became temporarily weakened, not having a backbone to lean upon, no set rules of how one conducts themselves in life or how one views things. And it was in this moment of temporary weakness that new thoughts on living were formed and, as times passed, a new backbone, a new wall to lean upon, came into being. But for Aiyesha, during this time of transformation from a young girl to a woman with her own beliefs, she had gone to the Coast of Seryn, unawares that her mind was in a temporarily vulnerable position. And so time passed on the Coast and new ideas and thoughts and beliefs and feelings were introduced and—as more time passed—became a way of life. For twelve long years the ideals and beliefs of the military were drilled into her. No more were these new *teachings,* but a way of *thinking,* her identity forged by what others thought she should be and, eventually, who *she* thought she should be.

This programmed way of thought weighed upon her as she traveled. She felt out of place, her life over the past while not falling into the routine she had lived and breathed for the past twelve years. Even on the Coast, when on her monthly day off, she felt strange and her heart yearned for a set routine of what she should be doing instead of what she wished to do.

A typical day on the Coast of Seryn started with the blowing of a ram's horn before sunrise. Aiyesha, sharing her small hut with five other women, would awake and have to be out on the main field, which was five hundred yards away, to report to General Gasahd. If you were late, you were given fifty lashes with an iron cord. You had to wait two to three hours before Bertamin would be applied to the wounds, prolonging the stinging hot pain of slashed flesh. The wounds never healed completely, though. Aiyesha had only been late twice during her tenure on the Coast. She had the scars on her back to prove it. She had been late the first time by, once waking from the shrill sound of the ram's horn, having closed her eyes a moment to help herself wake up and, accidentally, had fallen back asleep. It was over a week before she could bend properly at the waist.

The second time had been when she fell ill with the flu and, when dragging herself from bed, was immediately nauseated and threw up. And being sick was no excuse for General Gasahd. If you were sick on the battlefield, you were not awarded the luxury of a bed to sleep it off. The lashings from that beating had forbade Aiyesha from bending at the waist for two weeks, the lashings more severe and harder because it had been her *second* time being late.

After reporting to the field for morning training, the women were sent on a four-mile run, without stretching their muscles, jolting their systems, the run a mixture of jogging and sprinting to build up stamina. When the run was over, there was no breakfast. The women went immediately to Service and for an hour, spent on knees, they praised the Master for His wondrous works and amazing grace.

After Service, they ran again, this one only a mile but ran at the fastest speed you could accomplish. And if you completed the mile in over four minutes, you were doomed to repeat it until you could complete it within that time frame. Some of the women who couldn't run it in that time had spent the entire day running, each attempt at the four-minute mile becoming more and more difficult, their legs growing all the wearier with each attempt, their times getting longer and longer and longer. Come nightfall, if you hadn't yet run the mile in four minutes, you were sent to bed, the entire day spent running punishment enough.

And so, if you ran the mile in the proper time, water was given to quench your thirst. Then there were basic strength-building exercises, namely calisthenics and stretching. This lasted for two hours. There was a ten-minute break to use the privy and get more water. On some days, when the air was cool, such intense training was bearable. But on others, when the sun beat down from overhead, the muscles fatigued faster and the physical tasks were at times impossible to complete.

An hour of meditation followed the strength-building exercises, which the women enjoyed because they could rest. During the meditation, they focused their strength inward, picturing their muscles healing, their power being restored. They mentally did the exercises of the morning, all the way from the first run to the strength exercises, imagining them so intensely in their minds it was as though they did them again.

A half-hour lunch followed, consisting of all the right foods, high in nutrition and energy. Lunch was mainly vegetables and herbs and other organic foods. There was also lean meat, usually chicken, not a piece of fat on any of them.

A half-hour rest followed lunch. Though he felt this half-hour of rest would cut into their training time, General Gasahd said it was actually more beneficial to the women's overall well-being and training output. There was no sense training after having a meal because most of the blood in the body was being used to process the food instead of circulating the muscles and replenishing them with nutrients as they trained.

The afternoon sessions, which ran into the evening, focused on combat training. Different types of combat were explored on different days of the week. Monday was wrestling and ground techniques. Tuesday was standing toe-to-toe combat, hand techniques only. Wednesday was toe-to-toe as well, but only foot and leg techniques. Thursday was takedowns and joint locks and bone breaking maneuvers. Fridays were reserved for an art form called Menigi, a slow set of movements displaying all that was learned that week, the techniques being employed in slow-motion so as to enhance precision and muscle control when delivering the techniques. The Menigi lasted for three hours. On Saturday was weapons training, ranging from swords to daggers, to using two swords at once, to using a quarterstaff and batons. Techniques for the weapons were taught as single strikes and blows at first and then, as you mastered the movements, to more complex patterns and routines meant to simulate combat. But out of all the days of the week, the day that was dreaded the most—until you felt secure enough in your skill that you welcomed it—was Sundays. The afternoons on Sundays were a montage of all that was learned the week prior and the women would square off against one another. Protected by thick padding made from chain mail and dense cowhide, and bone helmets, they fought until one of them had a maneuver delivered on the them that would, in real life, render them dead. And recognizing these fatal techniques grew easier over time. So did the skill to avoid them, making the sessions last longer.

Dinner followed and another half-hour rest. Each evening of the week was used for a new challenge, like the combat training in the afternoons. Monday evenings were reserved for the art of man-hunting. Tuesday for stealth training and remaining hidden in the dark, but also being able to shadow your enemy so you had the ability to spring upon him or her at any given moment. On Wednesday was a group exercise. The men from the male training camp would come and the women would be forced to fight off multiple opponents and avoid being dominated by the men who, as preparation, were allowed no self-gratification or any form of sexual release during the week, so that, should they get one of the women in their clutches, they were consumed by the desire to have her. Men—especially the men on the Coast of Seryn—were simple-minded and salivated at the thought of having one of the shapely women either all to themselves or to share her with one of their comrades. The women would have to ward them off, should the man be in a dominating position, to avoid being used for purposes against their will, namely sexual. If a woman was caught, the rule was to let the man have you or it was seventy lashings. Out of all of the women, Aiyesha had been the only one who was never taken advantage of. This made her more desirable to the men on the Coast. Sometimes, during these Wednesdays, the other women were ignored while the men chased after only her. On Thursdays there was riding lessons and how to fight another while galloping on horseback, a tremendous skill needed when riding into battle. This exercise, Aiyesha recalled, was Helena's favorite.

Fridays were painful in the evenings. To get oneself used to be beaten in battle, whether it be by fist or sword, the women would take turns beating on each other, the woman getting repeatedly struck not allowed to retaliate. As the years wore on, getting a strike in the face or a knife's slash to the leg did not hurt as much as it once did. There was one woman you could punch square in the nose and she didn't even flinch, Aiyesha recalled.

Saturdays were a bit easier. General Gasahd taught them how to read battle scenes in the dark, how to determine what happened should they stumble upon a fallen comrade in the battlefield, and how to read the area around the corpse to determine, in detail, the cause of death.

And, lastly, on Sundays, the women, who were greatly outnumbered, would face the men in an exhibition war and practice fighting off multiple opponents.

Then the week started all over again.

The Enrichment Exercise was in there once a month somewhere, often when the ladies least expected it. Also, at any given time, the women were woken in the middle of the night and blindfolded. They would then be taken by wagon deep into the woods and dropped off, spun in circles so as to induce disorientation, and left there to find their way back to camp and survive on their own. Three women had died that way on the Coast, lost, never to return. After a week of them not returning to camp, a search party was deployed and it turned out these women had got so hopelessly lost, so far from camp, that returning would have taken a week should they ever have found their bearings. They had died of thirst, too far from the nearest stream. These women were quickly replaced with others.

Coming to a low part in the land, it surrounded her like a small wall. As she crossed this dip in the land, she felt safe, secure, as if she were in a very large room away from the perils that stalked her. It brought gladness to her heart and a smile to her face. The air was fresh and smelled almost green, like grass on a Spring day. The sky overhead shone blue, with only a few puffs of stark white cloud scattered here or there.

Two hours later, Aiyesha came over a rise in the land. About two leagues away, she saw, was the green mound of a forest. She decided she would go there and find food before resting for the night.

Supper had been hard to find. After tying the horse's reins to a tree trunk, and after surveying her surroundings, Aiyesha found in the forest a small clearing and a stream littered with rocks jutting out all over the place. There was a large flat rock in the middle of the stream, rising a few inches above the water. She went up to it and knelt before the waterside. Using her hand as a scoop, she drank greedily. She went and retrieved her horse and let him sip on the water as she continued her search for food. She had searched the rim of the woods for over an hour before she heard the rustling of bushes, giving sign a small animal was about. Unfortunately, she had no bait to lure the creature. Upset but not beaten, she continued her hunt and soon came upon a bush of fresh Zewlan berries, a red berry no bigger than a small nut, but as sweet as sugar. Using the hem of her robe as a basket, she harvested herself a decent helping. She then rejoined her horse by the edge of the stream and ate her dinner.

After eating, she felt some of her strength return. Despite her battles over the past two days, she had been without exercise, without training. In her mind, she felt weaker for having not trained during the breaks in her journey. She felt guilty for letting her discipline slide. She was so used to constant physical activity that, now, without it, she thought herself lazy and in her mind's eye could see the tautness and strength of her muscles diminishing. Her limbs felt weaker, sluggish, and was attributed to the lack of exercise, not the lack of food or rest.

Guilty, she stood up, dusted off her bottom, and, under the watchful eye of the horse, began a Menigi pattern. As she moved gracefully, her strength slowly returned, the rhythmic movements of the patterns triggering the memory in her muscles and invigorating them. She practiced for three hours, a standard Menigi session.

When she was done she was beat. She took her horse's reins and led him over to the edge of forest behind them, no more than twenty feet away, and tied him to another tree trunk, this one thinner. The ground around was soft, covered in fallen leaves, dry, but not brittle. She lay down and bunched up the hood from her robe about her head and used it as a pillow.

Within moments she was asleep.

She slept lightly, her body used to always being ready, being able to spring to life at a moment's notice. So often in the middle of the night General Gasahd barged in to their dorms and announced they would have to go for a six-mile run then have combat training until dawn. And then they still had a full day of training ahead of them.

There was a sound in the bushes near her head and she awoke, springing to her feet, her knife drawn, like a cat suddenly catching sight of a bird or mouse.

The night sky was clear, the white moon overhead providing clear light, but also making the shadows beneath the leaves and brush darker than they ought to be. The stars stood large in the sky above her.

She wanted to call out and ask who was there, but caught her tongue as she became fully awake. Calling for the enemy would surely bring him or her out. The bushes were silent, the only sound the flow of the stream behind her.

After a time when all remained still, Aiyesha sat down and crossed her legs. She glanced at her horse and saw the most peculiar thing. The horse was lying down, his legs drawn up beneath him. He cocked his head in her direction as if asking, "What?"

Aiyesha smiled at the innocence evident in the horse's big, black eyes. Despite the horse belonging to the enemy, it was, after all, just a horse. When she rode him earlier, she rode him hard, forcing him to pay penance for the crimes the Army set against her. But, she realized, the horse had nothing to do with it. It was just doing what it was told to do, serving whoever was in command.

She came over to him. The horse whinnied softly. She stroked his mane and rubbed the side of his neck, and trailed her fingers down the length of his face, feeling the velvety softness of his muzzle.

"I guess it's just you and me," she said. The horse nuzzled in closer. "You didn't hear anything out there, did you?"

The horse didn't seem to have noticed anything. Aiyesha leaned up against him, propping herself up against his big round body as if he were a pillow. It was far more comfortable than the single blanket used for a bed on a hard wooden floor back at her dorm on the Coast of Seryn. She wasn't used to feeling so snug. She stared up at the stars and wondered how much farther she would have to travel before she would be totally safe from the Dembatstayr.

"But I'll never be completely free of them, will I?" she asked herself. "No, I won't be. Once you commit to them—become one of them—it's hard to get out, probably impossible. Oh, Mom, what a mess I got myself into. What would you do? Hm. Nothing, if my memory serves. You always succumbed to Dad's wishes and I suppose it would be no different here. I want to come back home, but I can't. They'd be there waiting for me, I'm sure of it. Maybe in a few years I could return, if they thought me dead. But that's such a long way off that there's no sense thinking about it. But the hope of home is such a pleasant thought." She turned to the horse. "What would you do? Would you—"

Something moved in the nearby bushes. Back on her feet, knife drawn, Aiyesha espied the forest, waiting for one of the Dembatstayr to jump out at her, or some other fell creature with the lust of the hunt in its eyes. The horse got to its feet as well.

Now I know I'm not hearing things, thought Aiyesha. *He heard it, too.* She silently took a step back. She wanted to draw the horse back with her, but his reins were tied to the tree, and tree was about foot into the bushes where the sound came. The trees rustled. The horse stepped back, and the reins grew taut. He whinnied.

I know, I know. There's nothing I can do though, she thought.

The movement in the trees hushed. After a period of silence, Aiyesha came forward, thinking she could quickly untie the reins and lead the horse back along the flat bed of rock, more towards the center of the forest's clearing. As if in answer to her first step, the trees and bushes shook, harder than before. Her heart leapt in her chest, coming up to somewhere just under her throat. Her knife came out before her, her grip as though holding a sword. At any moment she would draw blood.

Again.

The horse's ears pressed back tightly to his head. Whatever was within those trees were enough to anger him. He stamped his feet, antsy, wanting out.

The trees shook. Leaves fell from the treetops, raining down in a spray of black on the dark brown forest floor.

At any moment something would come.

At any moment.

Her horse stood on his hind legs, his forelegs pawing at the air, a fell bray escaping its mouth. Each time the reins drew taut, so did the horse's frustration at his circumstance increase. He pulled on the reins, stepping one hoof back then the other. Aiyesha saw the top of the tree bending toward him, giving in to his pull. But the tree was too strong and the horse had nowhere to go.

The bushes rustled loud, like someone, or something, unseen were zipping back and forth parallel to the bushes, tearing them apart in its path. Back and forth. Side to side. The whooshing of the leaves grew louder and louder. No matter how hard she tried to focus her eyes on the cause of the disturbance, the dark of the forest stared back at her. The ground rumbled, as if a stampede of horses were drawing near. Night birds burst out of the tree tops, soaring high up, decorating the moonlit sky in blotches of black. They cooed and cawed, screeched and whistled, as they flew high.

Something came to the edge of the forest.

Aiyesha could not see it, but she could sense it. For a long time she stared into the wood. She kept her calm, years of battle training kicking in, apprehension for combat subdued. She stared at the creature. The creature stared back. Aiyesha couldn't recall how much time had passed until she realized she was staring at nothing.

The creature was gone.

A time later, certain it was safe, Aiyehsa went to the forest's edge, to the tree, and untied the horse. The horse snorted, happy to be free. She drew him back, further into the clearing, and soothed him.

Reins in hand, they came to the stream. Both of them drank before she sat on the rock and crossed her legs like before. The horse remained standing. She took his reins again.

Keeping her eyes on the wood, Aiyesha did not fall asleep until sometime just before dawn.

The sleep had been even lighter than earlier and Aiyesha awoke to the velvety muzzle of the horse rubbing up against her cheek. He licked her once. She pushed his muzzle aside. He pushed back, nuzzling in closer. She couldn't help herself but giggle.

"Good day," she said. "Sleep well?"

The horse pressed in to her. She was alarmed to see that she still had his reins in her right hand. She thought she would have let them go in her sleep.

"What? You want breakfast?" The horse eyed her hopefully. "I'm sorry but I have none. Not even for myself. Well, maybe. We can check for more of those berries." She sat herself straight and looked over at the wood. It was so much clearer in the daylight. The forest appeared innocent, as if whatever evil had been lurking there the night before surely could not come from such a green and beautiful place.

Within minutes she mounted her horse and the steed trotted across the flatbed of rock, clip-clopping through the water where the stream ran shallow. They re-emerged from whence they entered the night before. They had come out just off to the side of the forest so it would be easy enough to ride alongside it until the forest withered and turned into countryside again.

She would not take the chance of going *through* the forest. Not with what happened the night before. Not with that creature there.

Over the next several days, Aiyesha traveled far. She crossed the land swiftly and ate well. She had forged a bow out of a branch from another forest she passed and had made the bowstring by cutting thin strips of fabric from her robe with the knife, and braiding them. The arrows were branches as well, cut down to sharp points. She hunted rabbits when she saw them. She didn't go after any big game, like deer, since it would be a waste to not use all the meat and hide. The horse lived off the plush grass of the hillsides. She bathed in the Swani River, a great band of water that ran through the Gorgillian Hillside.

Thus far, there hadn't been any problems. No Dembatstayr, no mysterious creatures from a dark forest hunting her. A great relief.

She had lost track of the days, but on what she assumed to be her sixth day since she left Wesafeld, Aiyesha arrived at Darim. Before entering the city, she dismounted her horse, who she had named Black Brave three days before, both in honor of the color of his mane and of his spirit. Reins in hand, she rounded to his front and put her head against his.

"This is it, my friend," she said. "Thank you for the ride." She stroked his cheek. "I'll never forget you. Maybe I'll see you again one day. I hope so. But I can't have you around for the possibility of a Dembatstayr recognizing you as one of their own." To stop the tears that welled in her eyes, she said, "But don't go telling anyone about me, okay? That's our deal."

The horse dipped his head then jerked it back up, as if saying, "Yes. I'll keep your secret."

She removed his bridle, bit, and reins from his head, and saddle off his body.

"See you later," she said and slapped his side. The horse tore off out into the field, happy to be free.

Aiyesha cast the mounting-gear aside and walked into Darim.

She would stop here.

CHAPTER XIX
In Darim

Darim was unlike anything Peter had ever seen. Likewise for Catina. She hadn't come through there when traveling to see her grandfather. Alan, however, had been to Darim in his youth, and a few other times since then, so he wasn't really missing anything, though the sounds of the early risers of the city brought joy to his ears. At first.

As they rode into Darim, Peter's eyes wandered all around, taking in the sights. The multitude of buildings that lined the streets were over sixty-stories high, sloping inward the higher they climbed. Many more were in the midst of being built further off down the street; an endless sea of construction. The outer walls of the buildings were made of slick marble, gray and glossy, with blotches of light gray and black. They looked hard as stone yet soft as down, all the same. The streets, made of sanded stone, were wide, with only a few people milling about. It was early in the morning and the day had yet to begin.

What Catina enjoyed most, she told Alan—who in turn told Peter—about riding into Darim was that the people did not stare at her. She had been used to receiving looks of wonder and curiosity—especially back in Garathen because of her colorful dress—so being considered lost amongst the scenery was a blessing.

Darim was a busy city. Its people were once nomads called the Darmala, wandering here and there, using up the resources of the land before moving on. For long generations this went on until one of the members of the small band of travelers—their name lost to legend—sometime in the early 100's of the Third Aeon, suggested they stay put and try to grow and multiply and see how much they could prosper. And prosper they had. They established a settlement called Darmalennon. What was once a barren wasteland became one of the finest cities the World over. The Darmala multiplied and an economy was established. They started out farming but soon got into various trades and, before long, selling their goods to places all over the nation. Generations passed and over that time a city was erected, their buildings high and mighty. The Darmala not only grew in population, but also in pride and confidence. No longer were they the Wandering People. They had the respect from other cities and townships, and a lot of their lives revolved around work and tradesworth, making their lives bigger and grander. They had viewed their growth as a second chance by the Master's blessing. And for that they worshipped Him. They were versed in myth and lore and the tales of long ago. Stories and legends were told over the generations of how the World came to be. They celebrated life and lived each day to the fullest, always on the go. And then, in the Winter of the Year 516 of the Fourth Aeon since the Battle of Then, there was an upset and the people began to quarrel amongst themselves, trying to always do one better than the other, eventually leading to a war within the city where many died. After, when the battle was over, and Darmalennon in near ruins, the Darmala realized the foolishness of their pride and began to rebuild their lives. And so they grew again, though some of the families involved with the war still bore grudges against one another. But the good of all society was always put first. They yearned to restore Darmalennon, to what it once was. But that could never be, as that city was in the past. It was renamed Darim, in honor of their ancestors, but still bearing a different name so as to convey a new start as a people. More generations passed and, finally, after over half a millennia of hard toil and labor, Darim had grown to twice the size of its predecessor. Today, the War of 516 of the Fourth Aeon was now but a wrinkle in the past. The people remained versed in legend and lore, and the tales told at dinner time brought much enjoyment. And those legends were treasured deeply, sometimes taken as absolute truth.

Along with their work, the Darmala loved their song and dance and food and parties, but these were only indulged in on special occasions, otherwise their celebrations were usually quite tame.

Inhaling deeply, Peter asked, "Where do we go from here? I'm beat."

Alan considered for a moment. "Let me see. We came in from the East, right?"

Peter did the work in his head. "As far as I can tell. I'm not sure how much we deviated off course on our ride over. East sounds about right, but Northeast feels more certain. Northeast of the city, I mean."

"I wish I could remember this place more vividly," added Alan.

"What was that?"

"Nothing. Just keep riding in. There should be an open space, the city square, somewhere off ahead. Let us get there so I can get my bearings."

A swell of pity for him filled Peter's heart. Here was a man who had been here before, seen the tall buildings and smooth streets, but did not know where he was because he was blind. Peter wished he could somehow sympathize with Alan, but did not know how.

Catina's mouth hung more and more open the further they went into the city. She pointed every which way, commenting on all she saw to Alan. Off behind them the entrance to the city disappeared amongst a clutter of buildings, all similar in height, and all looking the same. One could easily get lost if they did not know their way around. The people wore fine clothing; the women in patterned dresses of all colors, bright and lively, some of the dresses short like skirts, others long like robes. The men wore tidy collarless shirts tucked in to snug fitting trousers. The men's colors were more reserved to tones of black, brown and gray. There were only a few who wore brighter colors like the women. The men's hair was neatly trimmed; the women's hung freely along their slender necks, and over the front of their shoulders. Peter thought some of the women very beautiful. One he saw reminded him of Talia.

"Are we there yet?" called Alan from behind.

"No. I don't know my way around so this might take awhile."

"Well find it. I am tired. And I know the two of you are, too."

And it was true. Peter was bushed. He glanced back at Catina. She looked beat, also.

As the sun settled in above, and the further into the city they went, more and more people were seen, coming out of buildings, going into others. Peter wondered what some of their trades might be. Or did they function on this mysterious thing called "tradesworth" that Alan told him about?

Soon they made it to a large, square area, close to the middle of the city. Peter tugged back on the reins. Day obeyed, Night falling in behind her.

"We're here," said Peter.

"The City Square?" said Alan.

"I suppose. It's a big square in the middle of the city." He made a face, hoping Alan would catch his sarcasm. It was hard to joke with Alan. You never knew when he wanted to be serious.

"This will do." Alan dismounted from his horse, his tall, gangly body looking thinner than usual beneath his baggy black clothes. He withdrew his walking stick from a strap tied to their supplies on Night's rump. He used it to feel his way along the stone ground then stopped a few feet in front of Peter and Day.

"Okay, " he said, "tell me what is on my left."

"A slope in the land about forty, fifty feet away, rising up to a flat surface."

Alan waited, gathering his thoughts. He planted his walking stick between his feet. "And in front of me?"

"More buildings. Well, a street first and then some buildings." His eyes followed the polished gray stone up high, until he could see the tops of the scrapers.

"And to my right?"

"Your immediate right?"

"Yes, yes," said Alan.

"Horse manure."

Alan yelped and jumped over to his left. He scraped his sandal against the ground, as if he'd just contracted a disease.

Peter laughed. Alan spun around.

"And what is so funny?" he demanded.

Peter leaned forward on his horse. "I was only joking."

With a grimace, Alan turned about-faced and said, "Not funny."

"I thought it was," said Peter.

Alan shook his head. Young men.

"You know where we are?" said Peter. "Because I sure don't."

"Kind of," said Alan. "Our main concern is to find a place to stay until tomorrow morning. We all could use a good meal and a rest. We have been up all night."

As if Alan's statement had triggered it, Peter felt his eyes droop. They had ridden all night, and only stopped once for a brief rest before continuing on again.

Behind them came a few people hauling carts, others carrying boxes of goods. They chittered and chattered amongst themselves, paying no heed to the visitors. Big, burly men dragged the carts to the center of the square. Immediately after setting down the cart handles, the men began unloading the goods. The women then came with their boxes and bundles and set them down beside the carts.

"What is happening?" asked Alan.

Peter could tell he was tired of asking what was going on.

"People just brought in some things," said Peter. "Carts, boxes, bags. They're unloading them."

Amongst the convoluted talking of the people, one word was said more often than the rest.

Armasulia.

"Quick, what day is it?" said Alan, spinning around.

Peter had lost track of the days since they left Garathen. After riding all the time, with no routine, Time just blended all together. He didn't know the exact date. "Aupil Eleventh, Twelveth, Thirteenth? Fourteenth at the latest. I think."

"Aupil Fourteenth," muttered Alan. "Aupil Fourteenth. Aupil Fourteenth." His eyes widened. "Of course!"

Both Peter and Catina sat upright in their oat-bag saddles at the sudden loudness of his voice.

"What, 'of course'?" asked Peter.

Alan smiled. "Get ready for the time of your life, Peter. Tomorrow is Aupil Fifteenth, the Festival of Armasulia."

Peter jumped down off his horse and approached him. "The what?"

"The Festival of Armasulia. A very big event here in Darim. I thought it had occurred in Martch. I guess I got my days mixed up."

Peter crossed his arms as he looked about. The supplies from the carts were already unloaded and more were being brought in. "I still don't understand."

Alan reached out and felt for Peter's shoulder. Finding it, he clapped him on the back. "Do not worry. Tomorrow you will know exactly what I am talking about."

"Talking about what? What do you mean? What festival?"

"Later. I am tired. Let us just find some place with a hot meal, a bath, and a comfortable bed."

"Whatever," said Peter.

As Peter turned around to face Catina, he caught sight of a man standing at the entrance to the City Square. The man wore a long, dark gray robe, concealing his entire body, his body looking like a floating piece of fabric, save for the toes of the black boots which poked out at its hem. A long, drooping hood covered his face in shadow. The figure in gray stared at Peter. Peter stared back.

Catina suddenly pointed to something one of the men was doing and said something to Alan in Grescalla. Peter's attention was diverted and he followed her finger. The man she was pointing to heaved a thick, wooden post to a flat place on the rock and tried to stand it upright. When he couldn't do it alone, one of his friends helped him.

When Peter turned to look back at the man in the dark gray cloak, the man was gone.

They left the men and women in the Square to their work and Alan directed Peter to keep his eyes open for a place called the Dimwald, a large inn that he believed to be a few streets over to the left of the Square.

Peter couldn't shake the visual of the man in gray from his mind. If a man was really what he was. Peter couldn't place it, but the man gave off a presence like he didn't belong there. As if he somehow did not have a place amongst the walking, living, breathing people of Darim. Or, the World, for that matter.

As they made their way through the streets, Peter saw a few Dembatstayr walking about, hands on the hilts of their swords, supervising the goings-ons. Peter never knew the Dembatstayr existed way out here. He always thought somehow that they stayed in and around Garathen, coming in through the Forest-Ring, making their random sweeps, and leaving before dawn. Seeing their presence in Darim reminded him of home. His heart ached.

Before long he located the Dimwald and, tying their horses to posts outside, they went in. Alan paid the short, dark-skinned man at the counter for one room.

"We best stick together," said Alan. "Besides, I cannot afford a separate room for you, Peter. We will need our tradesworth for our ride home."

Peter didn't mind. He'd rather stay with Alan. There was something about the middle-aged blind man that was comforting and reassuring.

The room was on the third floor, a small living space amongst the two dozen others on the same floor. The size of the Dimwald was deceptive on the outside. Peter didn't realize it held this many rooms. They entered and dropped their things at the door. Alan went over to the far side of the room to the window overlooking a busy street; Catina was by the bed, a hefty mattress that was in the middle of the room. Peter went to look into a smaller room near the door. It was the privy, complete with a hole in the rich, cedar floor, and a seat. He assumed that whatever was put into the hole was gathered in a tub of some sort and emptied out through pipes that ran down between the floors and walls and lead to somewhere outside. Next to the dunny was a smudged-up mirror, reminding him of the Linsheum he had in his privy back home. To the right of the mirror was a tub.

On a small stone table beneath the mirror stood a basin with a pitcher of water beside it. Peter went over to it, poured some water from the pitcher into the basin, and splashed some on his face. He didn't see a towel or rag to wipe up with. Water trickling down his face, he looked at himself in the dirty mirror. Dark bags hung below his blue eyes—which looked more like a gray-blue than a sky-blue right then. His black hair was in disarray. Weary, he leaned against the stone table. He reeked of his own sweat. A bath would be in order later. He wrinkled his nose and splashed some more water on his face.

When he came out of the small room, he went over to Alan, who was still standing by the window, letting the sunlight warm his face. Peter put a gentle hand on his shoulder.

"Thanks for getting us this far," he said.

Without turning from the window, Alan said, "No. Thank *you.*" He inhaled and exhaled slowly. "I hate relying on people for help but having you guide us here is greatly appreciated. Sometimes, Peter . . . sometimes I wish I could see. It is one thing to get used to going about your business, blind, in a place you know like your own self. Home. But out in the World, it is like, like being a shark guided by scent. You know? It is relying on your instincts to get you around and you hope against hopes that, because you do not where you are and what is around you, you hope that you do not make a fool of yourself by bumping into things, or appear like an idiot because the person you are talking to is making faces at you and you never know it." He cast his blank, white eyes downward. "Maybe I am just paranoid. I do not like people all that much. There is another tale in that, by the way. You did good, Peter. You got us this far and there is still a ways to go. My mind is weary and so is my body. I am not as young as I used to be, when riding all day on horseback was as easy as sitting still on a chair in your own home. And my head is sore from constantly imagining where we are, trying to recall memories of what things looked liked when I came out this way. I—" He didn't finish. For him to have said all that he had, that was enough. Peter understood.

Giving Alan's shoulder a squeeze, Peter said, "I'm going to go for a walk before retiring. I won't be long. You'll be all right?"

A few tears welled up in Alan's eyes. He nodded. "Yes, I will be fine. Thank you again."

With one last squeeze to the blind man's shoulder, Peter turned and crossed the room. When he left he could hear Catina snoring.

By the time Peter was halfway down the street, there were more people than he could count. Most were shorter than he was by about a foot. Some had white skin like he had, others' were darker, and some were even darker still, their skin so black there was a sheen of blue to it. Everyone was on foot and, riding among them, were pairs of Dembatstayr soldiers, on big, gray horses towering above all the rest, yet still dwarfed by the high, gray buildings. Heat came off the stone, making the air dryer and thicker than it ought to be. Sweat trickled down his sides from beneath his arms. He steered himself clear of the Dembatstayr, thinking that somehow one of them might recognize him being from Garathen. Though how they could recognize him, he did not know. It was all in his head.

Just needed to be out, though that's where I've been the past long while. Need to clear my head. Peter could still not shake his mind free of the man in the gray cloak. The man had just stood there so simply, so "put there," and so out of place, that Peter's stomach still swam, disturbed. Seeing that man was like walking in on a conversation between two people and knowing that something was wrong and that one of them was having a bad day. The awkwardness and discomfort the man created . . .

He made his way back to the Square to see how far they had progressed since he saw them earlier. He was looking forward to this "festival." He wished Alan had elaborated a bit more on it. But he said that it would be the "party of his life." There weren't any parties in Garathen. People mostly kept to themselves and the biggest get togethers were between a small group of friends, usually no more than five or six, coming together to eat a hearty meal.

At the Square, the men were still busy setting up posts, some of them laying out a large, blue tarp; a canopy of some sort. The women set up tables with big colorful banners draped over the front edges. The banners bore pictures of fruits, vegetables, and other foods. Others had humorous caricatures painted on them, and others held strange designs, one half of those banners conveying a happy image and the other half a sad one. One such design was, on one side, against a background of yellow, a man wearing a white robe, with wings like that of an eagle. On the other side, against a background of red, was a bat-like creature, its fangs bared, its claws reaching outward towards the man with the wings.

People chattered and children roamed through the Square. Peter smiled as he watched the children play catch-one, zigzagging around and in between the adults. It reminded him of how much he one day wished to have children of his own. And it reminded him of Catina. Such a wonderful child, such a pretty girl. He snapped himself out of his thoughts, realizing that something was creeping into his mind about Catina that should not be there. There definitely was something strange about the humanette. She had an appeal to her that Peter had never encountered in another. And, he admitted to himself out loud, "It's overwhelming at times."

Slouching, fatigue settling in, Peter turned and left the Square. He couldn't wait until tomorrow when he would return bright and early, before they headed out. The Square would be set up by then and the festivities underway.

Keeping his eyes to the street, Peter went back toward the inn. He didn't see the man in the gray cloak coming toward him, but did feel his stomach turn. The man brushed against his shoulder as he passed. When Peter looked up, the man had almost disappeared amongst the crowd. Before he could consider following the man in gray, Peter heard shouts from behind him.

He spun around on his heels.

Still a ways in the crowd, running toward him was a women with long black hair in a black robe. Like he had known about Catina a week and a half ago, this woman was not from around here. She was taller than the rest of the people. A pair of Dembatstayr charged their horses after her. The crowd parted before her, clearing the way. Peter moved to the side as well. The woman came closer, her robe billowing around her as she pushed her body to run as fast as it could. He noticed that, as she ran by, she had looked at him, her green eyes bright and glimmering in the morning sun. His heart jumped at her beauty.

The thunder of horses' hooves shook the ground as the Dembatstayr followed in hot pursuit. They soon caught up to her. One of the Dembatstayr withdrew his sword from a scabbard hanging off his belt. The man's arm rose, about to bring the blade down upon the woman.

On instinct, Peter ran after them.

But he needn't be there to help. With cat-like agility, the woman spun in her tracks, ducked the swoop of the blade coming down upon her, and darted back in Peter's direction. The Dembatstayr turned their horses around and followed suit.

Running off pure adrenaline, his heart pounding from the excitement—and somewhere knowing in the back of his mind that it was a stupid idea—Peter jumped in front of the horses trampling toward him. Both horses began to slide, the forehooves of one and then the other rising high into the air, avoiding hitting him. They whinnied loud and clear.

"What's the matter with you!" shouted one of the Dembatstayr.

Peter didn't answer and moved over to the side. He had bought the woman some time. He hadn't stopped to think she may in fact have been a criminal and that these men were doing everyone a favor by trying to stop her.

The men calmed their horses down enough so they could continue their pursuit. The woman was already gone from sight, more than likely having turned off onto a side street.

Not understanding his desire to do so, Peter took off after the Dembatstayr. He wanted to make sure the woman—should he find her—was, and would be, all right.

He ran up a ways, maneuvering his way past the people, some of them shouting at him to watch where he was going. He passed one street and one alleyway, glancing down both of them both ways to see if he could spot the beautiful young woman with the black hair in the dark robe. All he saw was the folk of Darim, going about their business, a couple of Streetfolk in the alley. On the second street he came to, he saw a blur of black rushing off through the people, far to his left.

It was her.

Peter turned sharply and dug his heels into the stone, paying no heed to his stiff legs from riding all night. He was out of breath before long but he kept going, trying to catch up to her.

"What do I do when I catch up to her?" he muttered to himself. And then, in his head, *I can't just walk up to her, can I? She's a stranger but . . . there's something about her. Something I can't quite place, but . . . . Though I only caught a glimpse of her, it seems she could really use a friend. And what if she is a fugitive of some sort? Then what? I don't want to be involved. Abetting a criminal is a crime. But what would I be helping her with?* His thoughts sped; the woman, up ahead, did not slow her run. She had remarkable endurance, Peter noticed. Already he felt like giving up, felt like putting his head between his legs, catching his breath, and then keeling over and waiting until someone—anyone—picked him up and dragged him back to the Dimwald.

But he persisted.

The rush of hooves clamoring against the sanded-stone street shook him from his thoughts. He watched as the Dembatstayr swiftly caught up to the woman; she kept running until one of the soldiers rounded his horse in front of her, and cut her off. Like a wild cat, in a whirl of black cloth and snake-like grace, the woman moved about the two men, grabbed one of them and tore him off his horse. Once she had him on the ground, she pounced on him before he could produce his sword.

Peter was almost there.

The woman jumped with one foot on either side of the man's head and, gripping his head with her feet, in one quick pelvic twist snapped the soldier's neck. The other soldier was off his own horse in an instant, sword drawn.

They were only twenty feet ahead, now. A crowd had gathered.

As the soldier went to bring his sword down in a mighty arc on the woman, she crouched down, her legs nearly splitting out to either side of her, and the sword, which came across in a powerful swoop, missed cutting off her head. Displaying the same cat-like speed she had seconds before, she spun on her right heel, her other leg coming around from behind her in a strong kick, catching the soldier behind the knees, knocking his legs out from under him. The soldier toppled backward, landing hard, his head bouncing once against the sanded-stone as it hit. It made a dull, sickening sound.

Peter caught up to the crowd. He had made it just in time as people closed in behind him, otherwise he would not be able to see what was happening.

The soldier tried to get up but the first attempt didn't work. The way his eyes rolled back in his head, his brain was obviously swimming from the strike against the hard sanded-stone street. On the second try he was able to sit up, but the woman was already upon him. She gripped his wrist. The woman jerked her hand and cracked the wristbone with an effortless twist. The sword fell from his hand and clanged against the street. The man wailed. She picked up the sword and stood over him, its point at his throat.

"Get up!" she told him.

It took a few tries before he was able to. She kept the blade at his throat. Here he was, a trained Dembatstayr soldier, at the mercy of a woman.

With eyes as cold as a frigid day in Winter, and as green as the grass in Spring, she said, "I will not go back. Do you understand!"

The man didn't reply. With the flick of her wrist, she cut the top three buttons off his tunic. The crowd gasped, thinking she had drawn blood.

"I said—" she started, but was cut off by the soldier.

"I heard you. Yes, I understand. But my understanding won't stop others from coming to take you back to Seryn. You had no right to leave. No right!"

She lopped off another button. "Oh, but I have the right. I was told when I joined that I didn't have to stay longer than I wished. Now I wish to be left in peace."

"You were told no such thing," he said. "We are all bound by our oath to the Master. Once you belong to Him, your life is forfeit." And then the soldier's eyes softened and his voice grew compassionate. "Come back with me. Let's leave this chase behind us. Our cause is peace. Don't you want to be a part of that?"

Her eyes grew taut around their edges, her eyebrows coming down to a point. "Peace? You claim peace? Do you call hunting a woman across hundreds, if not *thousands*, of miles an act of peace? There is no peace in what you practice. Either you go back and tell them I wish to be left alone or I cut your throat right here!"

The crowd hushed, awaiting her next move. Some of them left, not wanting to see blood spilt this day; especially the day before the Festival.

The soldier, from what Peter could see, seemed to consider her proposal. And then, with a dark grin, said, "Then I choose to die here. I, unlike you, have given my life to the Master. I would rather die in His service than anything else. If I go back, like I told you before, it won't matter. They won't heed what I tell them. They will send others for you. And even if you do kill me now, in time others will follow. Do you really wish to run for the rest of your life?"

"I will run until I am free," said the woman.

The man nodded. "Then be done with it." He dropped to his knees and bowed his head before her.

An expression of hurt creased her face. She had given him a chance at life, but the man willingly had chosen death. Peter's heart went out to her. Then her face changed to a scowl and she twirled the blade once in her hand, the edge of the sword stopping at the back of the man's neck, only drawing a thin line of blood. The man shook. He whispered something under his breath. Peter thought it sounded like a prayer.

The woman turned to the crowd, her eyes roaming over all who gathered. And then, with a look that said, "I'm sorry," she dropped the sword and ran off.

The soldier began to cry.

Far from the scene, Aiyesha rounded a corner into a filthy alleyway. Halfway in, she leaned against the glossy, stone wall and put her face in her hands. Some of the Streetfolk in the alley sitting in slumps against the building side looked on.

"He was right," she said to herself. "It won't end."

She heard footsteps, their sound light and slow. Her heart jumped a moment but quickly settled. Whoever was there was not rushing toward her. She looked to see who it was and there, standing with his arms at his sides, his blue eyes wide and tender, was a young man dressed in a brown sweater and trousers, sandals on his feet. His black hair blew as a light breeze swept through the alleyway.

A piece of her heart seemed to fly from her chest and out toward him. At a later time, if you asked what had happened the moment she first laid eyes on him, she wouldn't be able to tell you. But it felt as though a piece of her being had gone out to him, as if a part of her belonged with him. She turned and began walking away. He caught up to her and grabbed her arm.

Instinctively, she grabbed his wrist and twisted his arm around so that it was at an odd angle and he was on his knees, begging her to stop.

"Please," he said, his eyes laden with tears.

She let go and he slumped down, cradling his wrist.

"Thank you," he breathed. With his good hand he wiped his eyes. "I hope . . . I hope it isn't broken."

And then, with a wry smile, she said, "No. Just a little strained. You'll be fine by the time the sun sets."

"How did you do that?"

She wanted to run and disappear amongst the crowd, go back to being alone and fleeing the Dembatstayr—but she also wanted to stay and talk to this man. For two days she had avoided the soldiers. No longer. She decided to stay, yet there was hesitation in her heart.

"I won't hurt you," he said. "Actually, I wanted to help you. But, I see, you can take care of yourself."

She had not felt a warmth coming from another person like this since Samora.

Samora. She wondered what happened to that sweet old woman. Wondered if Samora was still alive or if the Dembatstayr had tortured her, trying to find out if she had said anything to her about where she was headed. Aiyesha took comfort knowing she had told Samora nothing. The old woman was innocent.

Aiyesha gave a small smile. "Yes, I'm pretty self-sufficient," she said. And then her eyes set upon his and her gaze asked if she could reach out and touch him. His eyes said that she could. She took the wrist she had harmed and held it in her hand. Eyes set on her work, she rubbed her thumb along its inside, soothing the nerves and ligaments beneath the skin.

When she was finished, she asked, "Does that feel better?"

He moved his wrist in a circle both ways. There appeared to be little discomfort. "Yes," he said. "It was hot and soothing and . . . yes, much better. Thank you. You'll have to show me how you did that."

"Some other time," she said.

They stood up and he put a hand on her shoulder, in greeting. She looked at his hand there and she thought she saw a glimmer of hesitation in his eyes, one of worry that she was going to render him submissive again. She didn't.

"My name is Peter," he told her. "Peter Jones is my full name."

"Aiyesha," she said. "Aiyesha Elnaa of Bel Candar."

"Where?" he asked. His hand was still on her shoulder.

"Bel Candar, near Rathern, sister town to Bel Haborr and Bel Jinu."

She looked at his hand again. He withdrew it as if he'd done something wrong. He ran his fingers through his hair. Aiyesha noticed his attempt at causality. It was cute.

"Sorry," he said, "but I . . . I don't get out much. This is my first time out and about, in fact."

She looked past him out to the opening of the alleyway, checking to see if anyone had been following her, or if any Dembatstayr had been alerted to what happened. And they would find out, no doubt. The folks in Darim were a talkative people and rumor swelled immeasurably on their tongues. The Dembatstayr would soon catch wind about what had happened a few streets over.

Peter must have caught her gaze because he said, "I don't think they're following you."

"Still," she said, "we shouldn't linger here long." She saw the Streetfolk in the alleyway eyeing her. They would have to leave soon.

"Where will you go?" he asked.

There was something *familiar* about him. Something reassuring. Something that reminded her of the safety of back home.

Instead of answering his question, she asked, "Where are you from? Or are you from around here and spend most of your time indoors?"

"Garathen," he said. "It's Ea—"

"East of here, I know," she said. "I've only heard its name, but never been. From what I know of it, it's pretty secluded, is it not?"

"Ha," he said, "that's an understatement. Only after having been gone from there for some time have I begun to see that. Yes, it's pretty secluded. Our main contact with the outside World is from trading, as is our way there. We don't have this tradesworth stuff that seems to be popular."

She furrowed her brow. A place without tradesworth? Couldn't be. By growing up with her father—when he was home, that was—she had been taught that tradesworth was the be all and end all of life. You were measured by how much you had. On that scale, a she was right then, she was worth nothing, save the value of the black robe she wore.

"Are you serious?" she asked.

"I am."

"Really?"

"Really. We don't have tradesworth there. We trade for what we need."

She thought for a moment, then, "Well, what if you need something from me but I don't need anything from you? Then what?"

He smiled. "We would trade anyway. Usually. You may not have use for what I have to offer right away, but eventually, you will find someone who has something that you need, but who also needs what I gave you. You're allowed to trade other people's goods, if they have given you them. I don't know. It's a good system. It's been around for as far back as I can remember. There's very little greed. Though some has been stirring back home. I don't like it, but I can't change it."

Aiyesha knew of greed, as well. She had learned of its power when she had been with Morley. One night, after using her for his own pleasure, he had gone on and on about how he and his crew were following a map to a hidden island and how it was rumored there was a massive treasure hidden somewhere on it. He had said that some of the other ships out at Sea had caught wind of where he was traveling and how there had been quarrels between the ships when their paths crossed. Morley told her he would stop at nothing to ensure that he found the treasure. He said he would kill any who opposed him, even members of his own crew. When Aiyesha asked why he was so driven to obtain the treasure, he replied by simply stating that with great wealth comes great power and, in the end, that was all he wanted. And he showed her that by how he treated her. Every time they went to bed, he always maintained a dominating position, always reminding her he was the man and she the submissive woman. His actions formed knots in her stomach.

"Aiyesha?" said Peter, stirring her from thought.

"Nothing," she said. "Just drifted off there for a moment. Sorry. About what you were saying, that sounds wonderful. What is your trade?"

When Peter responded, his blue eyes did a little dance. "Well, I do two things. One of them is poetry. I usually write something for whomever I know I'll be trading with that day. I like to customize it because it makes the other person feel special. And the other thing I do is paint."

"Yeah? What sorts of things do you paint?"

"Just about anything," he said. "Mostly scenery though, but I have done portraits of animals. Very few of people. I can't seem to make them look right on canvas for some reason."

Aiyesha's heart fluttered at the thought of all the wonderful pictures. After having spent so much time on the drab grounds on the Coast of Seryn, she much looked forward to the ideas of things with character to it, with real people who were their own and not just drones, brainwashed by a general or a leader, who all thought and acted the same.

Peter, eyeing of the Streetfolk, said, "Not that I'm not enjoying this chat, but I think we should find some place else to go." He leaned in closer. "I don't like the way those people are looking at us."

Aiyesha took notice of one disheveled men staring her way, lust in his eyes, as if he'd never seen a woman before.

"I agree," she said.

And so they walked further into the alley, past the Streetfolk who turned their heads as they walked by, and exited on the other side.

Once out on another street, Aiyesha checked for any Dembatstayr. There were none, just the people of Darim walking by.

She turned to him. "Just so you know, I didn't do anything wrong. Those men—" But she didn't finish. She didn't know how much she should tell him. A part of her wanted to tell him everything, wanted to find shelter with the first person since Samora who didn't seem as though they were after her. But another part knew she couldn't trust blindly. She didn't know Peter and despite how genuine and honest he seemed up front, she couldn't say too much. She knew from past experience that people were not always what they seemed. Like General Gasahd. A man who seemed to be looking out for her best interest, who seemed to have noble ideals and morals, only to turn out to be a merciless killer all in the name of peace. The same man who had ordered hundreds of soldiers off the Coast of Seryn to capture her and bring her back.

"What?" prodded Peter.

"Nothing," she said.

And then there was silence between them.

Finally, Peter asked, "Where will you go now?"

"I can't tell you," she said.

"Why not?"

"Because . . . " He wasn't safe with her. "Thank you for seeing if I was all right. I appreciate it. But there's no more I can say. You've been very kind to me."

"Is there anything I can do to help you?"

"I'm sorry," said Aiyesha, "but those men, the Dembatstayr, they won't stop pursuing me. I appreciate your concern but now I must go. Take care of yourself, Peter Jones. Maybe sometime in the future our paths will cross again. You can tell me more of Garathen and what it's like to live in a place without tradesworth and the greed of Men. Until then, I must be off."

"I don't want to push you," he said, "but it was pleasant meeting you."

"Same here."

He put a hand to her shoulder. "Take care of yourself and be careful."

She smiled. "I will." And she turned and left.

Peter watched as Aiyesha mixed in with the crowd and was gone. With a heavy heart, he turned to go back to the Dimwald. When he couldn't find his bearings, he realized he had gotten himself lost.

It took longer than it should have taken, and after asking directions from a few people, he finally found his way back to the inn.

When Peter returned, he saw Alan in bed beside Catina, the humanette still snoring as strongly as she had been when he had left. Peter went to the window and looked out onto the street below. He searched for Aiyesha, hoping to see her. Much to his disappointment, she was nowhere to be seen.

"I hope you'll be all right," he said.

CHAPTER XX
The Man in the Gray Cloak

Peter went out a second time that day. It was night, the city streets lit up with the gold of flames burning brightly in the lampposts that stood proudly on the sides and corners of Darim's streets.

He had rested well, though he was still tired as he strolled. Alan and Catina were elsewhere in the city, purchasing supplies for the days of riding ahead.

As he walked, Peter thought of home, the long journey thus far, the palanthora beasts in the Forest-Ring, and, at last, Aiyesha. When he had spoken with her, he had sensed a profound air of loneliness about her. She seemed to be yearning for a place—perhaps even a person—to belong to. And what with the way she suddenly took off, she seemed completely and utterly alone in the World, always heading from one place to the next, never to be free of her past.

Peter went by the City Square again to see how far the setup had progressed. It appeared to have been completed though he couldn't be sure. A huge, faded gray tarp hung like a tent over the entire Square, its ends coming to the ground on all sides, hiding whatever was beneath it.

Probably a surprise for tomorrow, thought Peter. He wished they had festivities like this back home. He thought it might have brought the community together even more so, and tightened the sense of family he got from the people in the Broken City.

But, he thought, *they have enough to worry about, what with just making it from day to day. They wouldn't have time to plan a festival. Maybe if Garathen were bigger, more people . . .*

Tonight, he didn't have a destination in mind. He didn't know Darim, so he just wandered about and exchanged smiles with the people—though there weren't as many out this evening as there had been earlier—who took the time to make eye contact. Off to the side, sitting slumped up against the wall of a gigantic building, was a poor man with a tin can set at his feet, his arms hugging his body, shaking. Judging by the way his eyes wandered wildly at the people passing by and how his mouth hung slack, his tongue partially sticking out, Peter could tell the man wasn't right of mind. When Peter passed him, the man looked up at him wantingly; his heart went out to him. Peter patted his trousers, showing the man he hadn't any pockets, thus nothing to carry anything in—no tradesworth. Not even a poem the man might be able to trade for something.

Instead, with a smile, Peter said, "I hope you have a good night, friend." And that seemed to be enough for the needy man.

Continuing on, Peter thought back to a boy he knew in Garathen. His name was Paul and he, like the needy man, hadn't been right of mind. Paul had been of the Colga, Human in appearance but with very yellow skin, almost sickly. The Colga were a race few and far between, an offshoot of Humanity, occasionally born to Human parents but, of course, also to other Colga. They were a remarkable people, if you took the time to know them. Though they were slow of wit and of tongue, Peter knew the Colga were incredibly smart and could calculate numbers at astonishing speeds. They also had a vivid memory and were able to remember everything and everyone they laid eyes on. At the time of Paul, he had been the only Colga in Garathen and, unfortunately—because the people didn't understand him and had a built-in distaste for "what was different"—frowned upon. Peter and few others had been the only ones kind to Paul and treated him as a person and not as one who "didn't count" because he was different. Peter had known Paul for six years and had visited with him often. Paul had lived under a small wooden crate near where Taimus the Baker now kept his oven and stand. Paul had died of an unknown illness in his twenty-third year. Peter had been only sixteen at the time of his passing, but he never forgot him.

"I wish people would treat each other fairly," he said to himself. "I feel pity for that man over there. It's not fair that he has to beg simply because he's misunderstood. True, I don't know his circumstance, but . . . he reminds me of Paul, especially by the look in his eyes, that look of yearning, wanting someone to see him for who he really is and not for what is seen on the surface. I wish people would think better of each other and not run because someone unsettles them." Then privately, *I wish you were here, Paul, now that I'm out here virtually alone. You were always a loyal friend and the listener of many heavy conversations. Your end was an unfair one. Truly.*

He kept his eyes to the ground, his heart heavy with sad memory. He was about to turn back to the Dimwald when he saw the man in the gray cloak.

The man stood amongst the people walking by, the people moving around him seemingly unaware he was there. Heart feeling about to leap into his throat, Peter's legs became weak and his palms sweaty. Fear expelled from the man's presence like a foul wind, his presence darkening the World around him.

Squinting, Peter strained to see the face covered by the large gray hood that covered the man's head. All he saw was eternal shadow, as if the man hadn't any face at all. The World around Peter slowed to a crawl, the people passing by walking in slow-motion.

The man in the gray cloak came forward, moving through the people fluidly, and though he couldn't be sure, when the man brushed past someone, it seemed like the man's shoulder went *through* the person. Seeming to be at one moment far away and the next right up to him, Peter swallowed the stone in his throat, the exhales of his breathing choppy and short. The air grew suddenly cool and his breath became visible.

The people around them slowed their pace even more, then, finally, ceased moving altogether, Peter and the Man separate from the regular flow of Time.

"Wh-who are you," he managed to say.

The cloaked figure remained motionless.

Peter could not find the strength to speak again.

The man raised his hand, his long cloak making no sound as the fabric rose with the limb. Peter tensed and he watched as the man's long fingers rose and were placed upon his shoulder; a Garathen greeting. Thoughts racing, the notion this nightmare of a man was from home crossed his mind. But he knew it wasn't so.

The man's elongated fingers had been resting on Peter's shoulder for quite some time before they squeezed. The rest of his body locking up, Peter felt a heat surge through the thick fabric of his sweater and into his skin, tingling his muscles and bones in the dull pulse of fear.

"I'm coming," said the man in the gray cloak.

Tears spilled from Peter's eyes. He squeezed them shut and forced out the remaining tears. When he opened his eyes, his vision was blurred yet he knew the man, like before in the Square, was gone.

The people around Peter resumed their stride at their regular pace and Darim went about its regular business again. Peter's legs gave way beneath him and he fell on his behind, landing hard on his tailbone. His heart sped and his mouth was dry. *What just happened? What was he? What*—His thoughts churned rapidly for any sort of conclusion to present itself. More tears; Peter wiped them away with his sleeve. When he tried to stand, it felt as though the bones were missing from beneath his skin. His muscles were loose and fatigued. His heart, mind . . .

Just then a pair of shaky hands came up beneath his arms and helped him to stand. When Peter turned to see who had come to his aid, he was surprised when he saw the needy man that reminded him of Paul.

"Thank you," said Peter softly.

The man coughed a response. He gazed in every direction but at Peter. And then he spoke, his voice garbled, speaking through a mouth filled with thick saliva. His breath smelled like garlic. "Yougsh grwished me a goosds nighsht. Bettersh than whatsh I urshgually resheives. Shankss." He swallowed and when he spoke again, his voice was clearer. "You besst be carefulsh around heersh. Folksh are friendshly, but notsh alwaysh. Be carefulsh."

Peter weighed his words. "Thank you," he said again.

Then, without good-bye, the man hobbled passed Peter to another spot beside a building. He carefully sat himself down and set his tin can at his feet.

Gathering himself, Peter headed back to the Dimwald. He would have to tell Alan what just happened. The blind man would never believe it.

Peter didn't end up telling Alan what happened with the man in the gray cloak. When he returned to the Dimwald, the notion he had a real-life encounter with the man in gray began to diminish, as if a dream, and by the time he reached their room, the memory of the man in gray had become no more than the recollection of a disturbing thought. However, a part of Peter did believe that he had spoken with the man in gray, as much as he believed that he had spoken with the needy fellow with the slushy voice. But he didn't believe it was pressing enough to tell Alan—not until he was convinced the event had truly occurred.

When he entered the room, Alan had just tucked Catina into bed. The two men exchanged Common-talk of what each did while apart, and retired early, still weary from their journey.

While Alan slept soundly, Peter tossed and turned and dreamed of Aiyesha, and wondered where she was.

CHAPTER XXI
The Festival of Armasulia

The Festival of Armasulia began just after dawn. The streets filled quickly and the party began.

"Blast it!" shouted Alan, throwing back his sheets. "How can one get any sleep with all that racket!"

Catina was already up, sitting with her hands in her lap, giggling at her grandfather's outburst.

Peter awoke, too. "What?"

Bounding out of bed and nearly tripping over Peter, who was on the floor, Alan pointed toward the window. "That! Do you not hear all those people?" He pressed a hand to the glass. "It is too early to be out and about. Do these people not have any sense! Them and their parties." He turned from the window and placed his hands on his hips. "If there is one thing you will learn about this place today, Peter, you will learn that these Darimeers are a lively bunch and" —he turned back to the window and raised his voice— "do not have consideration for others!"

"Surely it isn't that bad," said Peter.

Alan grimaced. "Oh, but it is. Just wait and see."

The three of them had tried to go back to sleep before getting up for the day, but to no success. The sounds of laughter and shouting and music from the street below forbade that. So, giving in to the joyous pandemonium below, they got out of bed, cleaned themselves up and packed their things. Alan wished to leave right away, but Peter and Catina, despite her wanting to rush home to her parents as fast as she could, wanted to stay for a short while and see what all of the hubbub was about.

They left their things in their room and went out in search of breakfast and sights to see, Alan grumbling the whole way.

The streets were filled with folks dressed in bright colors; the women wearing decorative dresses, the men decorative robes, patterns of flowers and trees, stars and moons and suns. Music laced with the sounds of cymbals crashing mixed itself with the air. Horns blared and bells rang. All were in a merry mood.

Peter held Catina's hand as they made their way through the crowd in search of something to eat. A dark-skinned man, dancing hand-in-hand with a woman, bumped into Alan. At Alan's scowl they apologized and went on their way.

"I tell you, if I had a gold drop for every time someone did that, I could very well own my own city where parties would be banned," he said.

Peter didn't know what he meant by that, and he didn't understand Alan's apparent issue with the Festival. "Oh, come on. Relax. What do you have against this, anyway? You've done nothing but mope and grumble since we got out here."

Alan grabbed Peter's sleeves and caught up to him. "Do you not know what this Festival is about?" He huffed. "No. Of course you do not. But, it is not my place to tell you. Trust me. Today will be a real eye-opener for you. You are about to receive a lesson in History."

Peter still didn't understand what Alan meant and decided not to let the blind man's distaste for the Festival of Armasulia hinder his mood. What Peter didn't know was that Alan hated the Festival because, long ago, when he had been younger, he had been able to enjoy such festivities, no matter to which city he traveled. Now he would miss out on all the colors and wonder, never to experience the celebration like he had before again.

Peter searched the crowd, hoping to catch sight of Aiyesha. There was only a sea of color before him and no one in a black robe. *Maybe she already fled,* he thought. *Well, wherever she is, I hope the Dembatstayr didn't run after her.*

"Kali ta!" said Catina. She pointed to a monkey dancing in the street.

"And now they got monkeys here!" said Alan. Then, sheepishly, "Never mind. I can smell their stink from here."

Peter hoisted Catina up and laughed with her as the monkey walked around on its hands, feet up in the air. Then, with one of its feet, took off the red hat he was wearing and bounced the hat from foot to foot, the bell on top of the hat jingling as he did. The monkey then tipped the hat outward and those who watched plopped a dropper or two into it. The monkey squeaked with gratitude.

Catina clapped, her smile so big her eyes were nearly closed.

"Amazing," said Peter.

Alan fell in beside him. "Let us get something to eat, and then we will look around. Well, at least you will, anyway." He snapped out his walking stick and felt his way through the people. "Come, Peter, steady on."

Peter, Catina in his arms, followed.

They obtained breakfast from a small station just off from where the monkey was doing its tricks. The price was a silver drop. It was evident the man selling the food—

some rice cakes, oranges, and a few meat-sticks—knew Alan was blind and was trying to swindle him one. Though having no knowledge of a silver drop's worth, Peter knew the price asked was far too high.

"This is robbery!" said Alan, shaking a fist at the man. "And you call yourself a respectable seller. You disgust me. Trying to swindle a blind man from his belongings. Blast you! Blast!"

Paying no heed to Alan, Peter called the man on his lie the food was worth a silver drop; the man grinned. Peter thought they could be worth no more than two stone drops, whatever their value was. He was not aware that if this were a regular day, the merchant would charge only one stone drop, if that.

"The price is obviously hiked because of the festival," Alan crossed his arms. "Men and their greed," he added. "And to try and cheat a blind man, no less! Blast!"

The man behind the station scowled at them.

There's always a problem, it seems, thought Peter.

And so they ate anyway, and when they were done they made their way back through the crowd and fed the horses from the oat sacks they kept up in their room at the Dimwald. The innkeeper was kind enough to fill a bucket of water for the horses. Day and Night seemed glad after having not been fed the night before. They ate and drank greedily.

Tired from the commotion already, Alan told Peter and Catina that he wanted to return to their room but they could go look about, if they wished. "But we leave at midday!" he added insistently.

So Peter took Catina by the hand and left Alan to his misery.

Catina seemed to be feeling much better today. Peter saw she could open her left eye some more, the swelling having gone down a bit. It was still early so the two of them had close to five hours until midday.

"Where do you want to go first?" asked Peter.

The humanette glanced up at him.

"Right," he said, "you can't understand me." He crouched down beside her and then, making sure that she was watching, pointed out to the crowd of people. Then he withdrew his arms and made an "I don't know" gesture. He hoped she caught on. She put a finger to her chin. She seemed to really enjoy the music and love all the colors about. In the background people sang.

And the Sun shines down these days
And keeps us safe in all ways
Never to flee from us, on in the night
Where the Moon comes and makes it all right

The harmony—it was perfect.

The voices of the people were lovely. Catina tugged on Peter's hand and led him back into the mess of Darimeers. They stopped and watched the monkey some more before moving on.

They came to a small stage, set up in the middle of an equally small clearing, much like the one that Peter had seen being set up the day before. *I'll have to get back to the Square,* he reminded himself. The stage was wide and about four feet tall and over its edge was draped a blood-red cloth, its ends tapered and smeared with black. On the stage were two puppets: one a dove, the other a bat, the two already in the middle of a story. Catina's eyes lit up and didn't seem to know there was a man and woman behind the stage controlling the characters.

Peter scooped Catina up in his arms and they watched as the bat and dove argued back and forth about many things—which was better? Wings made of hide or wings made of leather?—all of which drew laughter from the crowd. Then the bat attacked the dove and the dove fought back. The dove chirped and whistled. The bat hissed and increased its retaliation. Back and forth the puppets warred, sometimes fighting in anger, sometimes their attacks done comically to get the crowd watching involved. After a time, as the puppets bickered back and forth, a puppet of a purple stallion, with a mane made of navy twine, larger than the two other puppets, rose up and separated the two. The stallion neighed and announced that the dove and the bat should become friends. And they did and the story continued, the stallion always present, watching over the two. But then the stallion became lonely and saw how well the dove and bat got along without it. And so, in a fit of vengeance and jealousy, the horse began telling dark secrets to both the dove and the bat separately, turning one against the other. Soon the bat and dove were fighting again, their war escalating until both of them were dead. And there, standing over them, was the stallion. But then the stallion became sad because he hadn't anybody and he was all alone. Suddenly, tiny puppets of people sprung up all over the stage and the purple stallion was happy again. The story ended with the puppets coming together in a hug. The curtain was drawn and the people clapped.

Catina liked the animals in the story, and clapped enthusiastically to show her support. Peter, on the other hand, partially understood its meaning but not quite. After asking some of the people around him about it, they shared the meaning of the word "Armasulia." "Arma" meant "end," and "sulia" meant "war"—so, Armasulia, in the ancient tongue of Darmaleg, meant the "war to end all wars." What a man in the crowd disclosed to Peter was that the play they had just seen was a child's version of an old legend about that War and about what had happened.

He recalled a similar tale his Aunt Silvi had told him while he was growing up. It had to do with a piece of History that was more story than fact, but involved two friends, one who always wore white, one who always wore black, warring with one another because the one in black tried to best his friend in all that they did. The two had a mutual friend who lived far away, one who always wore colors, usually blues and purples, the color of the sky right before evening turns to night. The friend who wore purple tried to find peace between the two friends but when his efforts failed, he let them be and let them war. But, Aunt Silvi had said, the friend in purple was also a greedy friend and had decided to become best friends with whomever won between the friend who wore white and the other who wore black. The sad part was that the friend in purple had distanced himself from the other two so much that he had lost touch with them and never knew the outcome of their bout. The moral of the story was twofold. One: to try and make peace when you saw those you loved quarrelling. And two: also know when to walk away when or if you stuck your nose where it didn't belong. But don't wander too far or you might miss out on a friendship or important relationship if you do.

They had been having so much fun that they forgot about Alan's insistence they come back to the Dimwald at midday. It was now mid afternoon and there was still so much to see. Darim was a sprawling city and the Festival of Armasulia seemed to cover over half of it.

Peter and Catina, after much happenings in the morning, finally made their way to the Square. The tarp that had covered it the night before had been removed and put away. At the top of the slope, on the small platform-like expanse, was a large display: a massive table with wood-painted-silver posts rising up from its front two corners, with a large wooden panel stretched from post to post. The panel was covered with a light blue banner with spiraling designs in red and pink and orange. Peter found the swirling designs almost hypnotic. Music filled the background: harps and drums, shakers and cymbals, tapping-sticks and whistles. Behind the counter of the large display was a burly man who reminded Peter of Taimus. He was accompanied by a much smaller woman who scurried back and forth in behind the counter, filling little white cups with something from the big barrel that sat in the middle of the counter. The big man hung over the barrel, using a lever of some sort to churn whatever was within. Only when the little woman needed something did he move from his work and allow her access to the barrel.

In the lower part of the Square were other tables and displays, everyone selling something. There were knick-knacks of all kinds, weapons, embroidered quilts and fine linens, trousers and sweaters, food, and a smaller table (that was quite popular), with barrels of wine and ale, that doubled as an outdoor pub. There was even a little pen that was squared off where a man had brought his goat and long-earred rabbit to entertain the children while their parents shopped the stalls.

Catina tugged him in the direction of the rabbit, but Peter was hungry. The problem was, he hadn't any tradesworth. Alan had it with him back at the Dimwald. But Catina in hand, he went up the slope to the big man and his barrel. They came up just as the man removed the barrel's lid and the woman scooped out some frothy orange stuff into a cup.

Taking a closer look, Peter saw the barrel was actually two barrels: a larger one on the outside, with a smaller one within, around the smaller one a ring of ice. Peter went up to the counter just as the man slammed down the wooden lid over the barrel.

"What is that?" asked Peter.

The man looked at him incredulously, as if Peter was completely clueless. The big fella wiped a row of sweat off his brow.

"Hot day, i'n't it?" said the big man.

"Yes," replied Peter. "I've never seen anything like this before."

Catina tugged at his hand. He picked her up so she could see over the high counter.

"Well, hello there, little lady," said the man. He stopped his churning for a moment and rubbed his callused hand on his dirty white shirt, before leaning on the barrel. The people gathered around the counter's sides didn't seem too impressed that he stopped his work.

"I was serious," said Peter. He nodded toward the barrel. "What is that?"

The man straightened himself and began moving the lever again. "What we got here is cream from the finest cows in Darim. And a little bit of ice. Don't ask me how they make it. The only ice I see comes in Winter. The wife here gets it brought in from somewhere North in big blocks. U'Athala, I think it is. Their whole economy is based on ice. At least, I think it is, anyway. The blasted blocks are nearly melted by the time I get them. You add some milk, some sugar, and a little bit of my wife's secret sauce and bing-bing! Bauclabba."

Catina giggled.

"Bauclabba?" asked Peter.

"Yeah, Bauclabba," said the man. "Don't tell me you've never heard of Bauclabba before."

"Actually, I haven't," said Peter. "I'm not from around here."

"So I see," said the man, then to himself, "dressed in rags like that."

"Sorry?"

"Nothing." He stopped again and stared at Catina. There was a long silence, the man looking as if he were about to say something but couldn't find the words. He snapped out of it. "Tell you what, she's such a pretty little thing that—"

Catina screamed and began bawling. The man had said the forbidden word—pretty. Peter tried to calm her down. She pressed against his chest with small palms, wanting to be let down. He set her feet to the ground and crouched beside her.

"Shh, it's okay," he said. "He didn't mean anything by it. He doesn't know."

Catina hid in his arms but didn't stop crying. Peter wished he knew what was wrong with her. "Look," he told the man, "I haven't any tradesworth. Can I have one of those, um, Bock-bac-burk—"

"Bauclabba," said the man.

"Bauclabbas, please. I'm sorry for this. It would take too long to explain."

"And how do I know you're not fooling. Why, you could take her around everywhere and start her up like that, making us merchants feel bad and offer up our goods for free and—"

Catina's crying grew louder. People began looking their way.

"Are you going to help me or not!" snapped Peter, startled at his own shout.

The big man jumped back, his girth seen jiggling beneath his shirt. He sighed, then shouted, "Aye, woman!" Then, when she shot him a hot scowl, he said timidly, "Get a small cup for the little one, here. This i'n't a day for unhappiness, now, i'n't it?" She obeyed and when he handed Peter the cup, there was a twinkle in his eye.

"Thank you," said Peter. He gave the cup to Catina. She took it in her small hands and sniffed it. "Go on. It's okay."

She took a taste and just like that, the rain was gone. Her cheeks, tear-streaked, rose up into a smile, like a rainbow.

"Mali kwon nali," she said.

Peter thought for a moment and then remembered the reply. "Dana kwon nali."

Some of the people gathered around noticed that Peter did not pay for the Bauclabba and began to complain. Peter turned to the man. "Thank you again."

"Don't mention it," he said. "Now beat it. You're ruining my business."

Peter and Catina, Bauclabba in hand, left.

Alone in his room at the Dimwald, Alan paced. He regretted leaving Peter and Catina. But the noise! Oh, the noise! In the past, when he had passed through here, the noise was not nearly as bad. He had only witnessed the Festival of Armasulia once in his travels, and that was in his first year abroad. He'd avoided it ever since. He was not one for parties despite his forcing himself to participate in some in the past.

Today, the noise-level was more intense, more happy, more ecstatic. Everyone seemed to be in the mood for a party. And since Alan had become blind, his other four senses seemed to have awakened to a new clarity. The smells were sharper. The things he touched seemed to be enhanced in texture. The food he ate was fuller, more flavorful. And . . . the sounds were much louder, more clear, and got deep into his head, as if the sounds were inside his head instead of outside it.

"Call me strange," he said to himself silently, his arm resting on the windowsill, "but I am reminded of you, Aubri. Call me silly, but the noise reminds me of the time you shouted at me for not cleaning out our shed. You had said that pigs could settle there and be quite comfortable. Blast. I wish you were here."

Aubri, his poor late wife, nattered at him a lot, now that he thought about it. She would always be complaining about something and her rants were always done at a high-pitched tone. She loved to raise her voice. For awhile there, Alan thought he would go deaf. But he loved her anyway. Aubri and her golden hair, like wheat baking in the sun, reaching for the sky. His home back in Garathen was still filled with her presence, her lingering scent of lilies.

And her laughter.

At times Peter found himself searching the crowd for Aiyesha. Anytime he saw someone wearing black—which was nearly never—his head would spin in that direction, hoping it was her. But it never was. They would be leaving Darim soon and that would be that.

"Blast!" said Peter, stopping his stride. "Alan wanted us back at the Dimwald" —he looked at his shadow on the ground; it was nearly all the way to the right of him—"three hours ago."

Catina looked up at him, her face smeared with orange smudge, all sticky from the Bauclabba. She only smiled and began dancing in a circle around him.

He can wait, thought Peter. *I may never get to see this again. And I doubt Catina's seen this before, either. I'm sure leaving a few hours later won't make a difference.* And then a moment later: *Besides, I might still have a chance to see Aiyesha.* When he realized he thought this, he quickly scolded himself. Who was he to put what he wanted before others? But the Festival . . . . He would stay.

They were only a few streets over from the Square, but he could already feel himself getting lost. He squinted into the bright afternoon sun.

Better not wander too far, he reminded himself.

The crowd began to move and jostle about more than usual. Far down the street, a commotion was headed their way. A parade was coming. Peter put Catina on his shoulders so she could see.

The street quickly filled with dancers, ribbons in their hands, twirling them about as they moved to the music. There were horns and whistles and drums. Darim had a lot of drums, Peter noticed. There must have been fifty dancers, all female, wearing a matching uniform of a pink top with pink pillowy pants, and red slippers. Their faces hidden beneath pink veils, their hair was tied back in tails, the ends of the tails whipping around their head as they moved. The people threw confetti and flower petals into the air. It rained around Peter and Catina in sparkling colors of red, yellow, pink and white. Catina laughed and held out her hands, catching some.

After the dancers came several stages on wheels, all of them filled with colorful characters, many of them dancing. Some wore costumes depicting beasts—some bat-like with horns, the others snakes—and other creatures—lambs and lions. Other stages held people dressed in white, black, and purple, all moving together co-ordinately.

The crowd clapped and cheered as the stages passed by.

Just then a massive stage came down the street. Upon it stood men and women on a set of risers, the men in the back rows, the women more toward the front and the bottom. It was a choir and they were singing.

"Their robes are sensational," said Peter. Each wore a robe that was half white and half black, divided down the middle. Around their necks were color-beaded necklaces, the beads gradually getting lighter the lower on the string: purple, navy, blue, and sky-blue. There was a larger gray bead in the middle.

Their voices filled the air and their song seemed to come not just from the stage, but from all around.

In the days of rolling thunder
The race of Men fell asunder
To the Powers of Dark and Light
Beings both Black and White
In a War lost to legend

The Sun fell and the Moon bled
Counted amongst the rising dead
As Nations warred
As the Lion roared
In a time barely remembered

On and on the Battle went
Swords hewing, armies bent
On total chaos
The World was lost
For a Time unknown to Man

Somewhere in the middle rose a saving grace
To free us from the battle, us, a dying race
It swept along in a Purple stream
And our lives it would redeem
Us from the Battle of all Ages

Perils and doom
The World in gloom
Finally a Deliverer came
Finally we were saved

So let us sing
Let bells ring
Shout out O gladdest of hearts
He has given us a new start
To begin anew a Time of Peace

O so saved
The road is paved
We've learned from the past

That quarrel does not last
And hope always endures

And then in a round, first the men and then the women, they sang:

Perils and doom
The World in gloom
Finally a Deliverer came
Finally we were saved

Perils and doom
The World in gloom
Finally a Deliverer came
Finally we were saved

And together they chimed:

Finally our Deliverer came

The stage, the last of the parade, had now passed them, the melodic voices from the choir already beginning a new tune. The people clapped and cheered once more and threw the remainder of their confetti and flower petals onto the street in another rain of color. Some began dancing and singing songs of their own; others stood and visited and told each other jokes and clinked their drinks together.

"Amazing," said Peter.

Catina clapped quick and hard. She was done with her Bauclabba and handed Peter the empty cup. He took it and found a wastebasket to put it in even though the streets were already littered heavily.

The people around them began to thin. They ventured back toward the crowd.

That's when Peter saw Aiyesha.

CHAPTER XXII
The Tale of the Ark
(Stars)

Aiyesha was beautiful. She looked much different from yesterday. She wore a light beige sweater with a hood hanging off the back, and matching trousers. Brown canvas shoes fit her feet snugly, like stockings. Her long black hair along the bangs and ears was tied back with a string, a ponytail hung high on her head, the remainder of her thick hair hanging halfway down her back. Her eyes shone like forest leaves in the sun. She came over to them, her hands at her sides. She then crossed them behind her back, as if showing Peter she wouldn't hurt his wrist again.

"Hello, Aiyesha," said Peter.

"Hello, Peter."

The air hung between them. Then Peter spoke. "I-I thought you were leaving."

"I was going to," she said, "but I decided not to. Not yet. I—I didn't want to run anymore."

"But won't they come after you?"

"Perhaps. They are looking for a woman in a long black robe. As you can see, I'm not wearing that anymore." Then, coming closer, she whispered to them, "I feel awful about it but I took this outfit from a shop when the lady who owned it wasn't looking. I try to avoid stealing, but after yesterday . . . " She straightened herself a little. "I'll pay her back though. When I can." Her eyes grew tender. "You don't think I'm a bad person, do you? You don't think I'm a criminal?"

Peter had been debating that question since he met her the day before. And her stealing her clothes made her what he thought she never could be. But, he also remembered, if she *was* innocent of whatever crime the Dembatstayr wanted her for, that sometimes those with nowhere to go and no one to turn to do things that go against what they believe in. Sometimes the *uncharacteristic* becomes *characteristic* for a time. The irrational *rational.*

"I'm sure your reason was a just one," he finally said.

Aiyesha smiled softly then bent down to Catina. "I love that dress, little one. It's so colorful. What's her name?"

"Catina," said Peter.

"That's a beautiful name. How do you do, Catina? My name is Aiyesha," she said warmly. "I think that dress you're wearing is very" —and before Peter could stop her, Aiyesha said the one word that would set Catina off— "pretty."

Catina's lower lip trembled and she covered her face with her hands. Peter picked her up and laid her head on his shoulder. He patted her back. That was twice today that someone had said the "P" word to her.

"What?" asked Aiyesha. "I didn't mean anything."

Catina clung to Peter hard and when he moved closer to Aiyesha, Catina cried louder. He took a step back. "I know," he said. "I should have warned you. She doesn't like that word."

Aiyesha looked at him quizzically. "What word?"

Peter mouthed the word "pretty."

"Oh. I see." She didn't say any more.

It took some time but he managed to calm Catina down.

"I wish I could tell her it was an innocent mistake," said Peter, "but she doesn't understand any of the Common-tongue. She's from Grek and only speaks Grescalla. I'm here with someone else and he speaks both the Common-tongue and Grescalla, so he helps with any translation that needs to be done. If he were here now, he could help us out."

"Where is he?" asked Aiyesha.

"At the Dimwald. We had taken a room there. We were supposed to ride out at midday but Catina and I got caught up in the Festival."

"It is something, isn't it?"

"Yes, it is. I've never seen something where everyone comes together to celebrate one thing with such enthusiasm and togetherness. It's like they're all sharing the same thoughts today."

Peter set Catina down. She wrapped her arms around his leg and hung on tight and shot Aiyesha a scowl.

"I guess she doesn't like me," said Aiyesha.

"I'm sure after it's explained to her, she'll know it was an innocent mistake. Just try to bear with her until then."

People began to swarm around them, moving from place to place, always in search of something to see, some new part of the Festival to explore.

"Where should we go from here?" asked Aiyesha.

Peter knew that Alan wanted them back at the Dimwald. But Peter also didn't want to leave Aiyesha. It was a miracle that he saw her again after she said she was leaving. He was sure he wouldn't get the opportunity to see her again if he left her now. He may never encounter anyone quite like her on the remainder of the journey to Grek. He would not let this moment slip away. Alan would have to wait.

"I'm sure there's a lot to see," said Peter. "We can go wherever you want."

Aiyesha smiled. "Why don't we ask Catina what she wants to do? Oh, wait, I forgot. She wouldn't be able to tell us."

"That's okay," said Peter, "when something catches her eye, she usually lets me know. Let's walk around a little. I'm sure we'll find something to see soon." He gave Catina's hand a reassuring squeeze. She squeezed it back.

The three ventured into the crowd. Before long, they were laughing.

There was a man whom everyone gathered around in a circle, watching as he juggled blue, shiny glass spheres, four of them. The people clapped while he kept them in the air with his hands, and they cheered for him when it looked like he was going to drop one but didn't. Every so often, quickly, while two or three of the spheres were in the air, he would remove the big floppy red hat he was wearing and wave it at the crowd.

Peter stood watching, chewing a stick of dried, salty meat that a rolly-polly lady was giving out. Dried meat was his favorite. His aunt made it for him all the time when he was a child, using a variety of spices to give it different flavors. Peter enjoyed the plainer, saltier ones the best. Catina and Aiyesha each had a meat-stick, too.

The man gathered all the spheres, two in each hand, and then told the crowd to watch him closely because he was going to make the spheres disappear.

"I love stuff like this," said Peter.

"Me, too," said Aiyesha. "I have a keen eye and can usually tell how an illusion is done. But some of these fellows still cause me confusion."

Peter bent over and, using hand gestures, asked Catina if she could see. With a big smile, she let him know that she could. The other children around them stood in front of their parents or guardians.

The man began juggling the spheres again, his arms moving swiftly beneath them as they spun through the air. He sometimes caught the spheres behind his back or wrapped an arm under one of his legs, catching the sphere then bringing his arm around again, putting the sphere back into motion. He sometimes used his big hat to catch the sphere and toss it back up in the air. Then, when the man caught one of the spheres, he squeezed his fingers around it, closing it in his fist. When he opened his hand a split second later, the sphere was gone. The people clapped. He said a thank you to the crowd. There was more juggling, more catching the spheres and tossing them up in the air from behind his back and between his legs. And like before, one by one, he made the spheres disappear. When all the spheres were gone, he hopped twice on his toes and did a single flip, and when he landed, he threw his hands in the air in victory. Everyone cheered, clapped and whistled.

The man removed his floppy hat and walked up to the circle of people around them. One by one, holding out his hat to them, they put in a dropper or two.

"Let's go," said Peter.

"Yes. I don't have anything," said Aiyesha. "From what I saw earlier, these people get upset if you can't pay them."

Peter thought of her stealing her clothes. *But she needed them,* he reminded himself.

Peter and Aiyesha were finished with their meat-stick. Catina was still working on hers.

And so the Festival of Armasulia went on into the night. Bands played, people sang and danced. Stories were told and plays performed. People drank. About mid-evening, Catina, from all the excitement of the day, fell tired and said "*Shinawa.*" Peter remembered that the word meant *grandfather* so he took her back to the Dimwald, to be with Alan.

"Wait out here," he told Aiyesha.

She did and when Peter returned, he had a long face.

"What's wrong?" she asked.

He hated getting yelled at and Alan had just given him an earful about how it was now too late to ride out and how they would have to leave in the morning, in turn costing them another night in the Dimwald. Their funds were limited and were not intended to be spent if it could be helped.

"Nothing," Peter told her. "Let's go."

It was different to be walking about with only Aiyesha. Peter felt free to be his own person and not have to worry about baby-sitting anymore. His face itching, over a week of not shaving getting to him, he rubbed a forefinger and thumb across his chin, wiping the itch away. He would have to shave soon. He was surprised that Aiyesha didn't think he looked like a Scruffle.

They walked side by side, not saying anything, just enjoying being out in the night air. There was much less people now than there had been earlier. Those who had little ones were at home, tucking their children into bed. In Darim, Aiyesha said, one parent would stay home to watch over them and the other, should they choose, could go back out and enjoy the rest of the Festival. Most of the parents stayed home together, though. But those who didn't have families favored the night portion of the Festival of Armasulia the most. When the kids were safely tucked away in bed, the adults could then be adults and not guard their behavior for the sake of young eyes and ears.

Besides, at night, that's when the darker tales were told. That's when a more detailed version of the story of the Battle of Then was shared.

And, at night, it was also a lot cheaper to participate, some of the people even daring to miss the day's events and come out at night simply because they couldn't afford the costs during the day. And since most of the merchants' tradesworth was earned during the day time, at night, a lot of the foods and drinks distributed were free, merchants giving one and all a taste of their goods, advertising their business.

Peter and Aiyesha came up to a man with darker skin, who fancily fried meats and vegetables in a pan, putting on a show for those watching. His silver knives gleamed in the glow from the two torches he had at his station as he sliced and diced celery, onions and cabbage, mushrooms and peppers. The meat—pork and beef—sizzled as he flipped them around in the pan. He twirled spice-shakers in his hands and seasoned the meat.

Their stomachs growled as the two of them watched. When the man was finished preparing the meals, with the edge of a big cleaver knife he scooped portions onto small clay plates and handed them out to all who watched him show off his craft. The food tasted delicious and when Aiyesha finished eating it all, she showed Peter an advertisement for this man's business painted on the plate. People never stopped working in Darim.

"Thank you," said Peter, handing the plates back to the man.

"You're very welcome," he said. "Feel free to stop by my place any time, if you want more. I live and work out of my home." Peter's ears perked up at hearing this. He thought that only people in Garathen worked out of their home. "It's called Homung's Frying Palace. Stop by any time," the man finished.

Peter didn't have the heart to tell the nice man that he would leaving in the morning, so he said, "Sure. I look forward to it."

And they went on their way.

Before long they came up to a large, gray stone wall with paintings of doves and eagles and bats and snakes upon it, the animals a dark burgundy in color. Firelight danced along the stone surface from a bonfire set about twenty feet from the great wall. Many people were gathered around the fire. At the head of it, near the wall, was a very tall man who must have weighed close to three hundred pounds. His black, greasy hair glimmered in the firelight. To Peter's amazement, it was the same man who had given him the free Bauclabba.

In a booming voice, the man said, "Come gather, come gather. The time for the Tale is at hand."

Intrigued, they gathered around with the other people. The big man didn't seem to notice him.

When all were seated, the big man said, "Good evening, one and all, and welcome. My name is Pnumar and I'll be telling you a tale this evening, one filled with legend and lore, history and myth, war and danger. It is a story that we've all heard before but never tire of hearing. It is the story of the day the old way of life ended and the new began."

"I love this story," Peter heard the person in front of him say.

"Sounds interesting," said Aiyesha.

Peter prepared to listen.

And so, being the gifted storyteller that he was, Pnumar eyed the crowd, his mouth taking on a knowing smile. He would open his mouth, as if about to speak, but then close it, building up the suspense to hear what he had to say.

When he deemed all were ready, at length Pnumar spoke: "When the Storm came, all the Earth fell under the sounds of Rolling Thunder. The lands shook, the mountains quaked, the rivers roared, the green of the meadows paled—the Earth buckled under the pressure of Powers beyond mortal comprehension. People fled into their homes and hid for days, some say; others, out of curiosity, remained outside to witness what they could from this sudden, and unexpected, event. Much detail as to what had specifically happened has been lost to the years, but some things are still known. It is said that, at an hour none expected, when all who lived on the Earth were going about their day-to-day business, their minds furthest from what rumor was saying was about to occur, there was a great trumpet blast that echoed to all four corners of the Earth. The Thunder began. The sky rolled back like paper from a gift and there, shining in brilliant white, was the Great Lion standing atop a Mountain. The ground split, the mountains of the Earth tore in two, and Spirits who looked like Men but had wings like eagles flew around the Lion. There were three at first. It is told that one said, 'Fear Him and give Him glory.' The second said, 'Fallen! Fallen is the land who made the nations drink of her adulteries.' And the third said, 'If anyone worships the great king, the Beast, let he who does suffer for all Eternity in the Fiery Lake.'

"And then the Lion was sitting upon a white cloud and behind Him were countless thousands of Spirits, descending toward the Earth. This was said to have happened to what was then known as the East, but today it would be called the West, for much of the World has changed since then. Seven more Men with eagle's wings poured out Sickness and Death upon the Earth.

"The Great Lion came down, down, down to the Earth and when He landed, that's when the Thunder rolled louder and the Lightning crashed and the Earth was torn open at the seams. And from the depths, as if from another World beneath our own, rose beings of Darkness and creatures so foul that their appearances, their very presence, caused those who laid eyes on them to tremble and lose way. Their stink tainted the air and all who breathed their funk fell ill. And then it began, the Great War, the Battle of Then, the Final Conflict. Forces of Light, forces of Darkness, clashed and roared. Spirit fought against Spirit. Man fought against Man."

Pnumar wiped the sweat from his brow. Those who were gathered around listened in hushed silence. Pnumar eyed everyone carefully, as if making sure all were paying attention. He took a deep breath and continued his tale. "It has been said through many generations since then that, unbeknownst to Man, there had been three forces at work that fateful day. One of White, one of Black, and one of Gray, though today it has been known as the 'one of Purple' for as time went on, it was learned that that was its true color, not Gray, the mix of Black and White. As the armies of Light and the armies of Dark warred and lives were lost and people slain and the screeching of Spirits both fell and holy filled the realm of Earth, so stood in the middle, upon the Altar of Sovereignce, the Mighty Ark, or, as those at that time called it—and so it has been called since—the Ark of Light, for 'light' is the word for 'redemption,' which I will delve into later in this tale. The Great Ark is said to have been the Arbiter of the Final Conflict, a safeguard set in place so that the War was fought fairly and an absolute truth of which side was the greatest could be discerned.

"The Ark sat in the middle of the place, as it was called back then, Armageddon. It is said that prior to the Battle of Then, it had been there that more wars had been fought than on any other on the Earth." He took a breath. "And so the Darkness and the Light warred. Time was lost and the Battle raged on for an unknown period of time. Some who tell the tale will claim that the War lasted less than a day. So short. Whereas others who tell it will claim that the Battle lasted for an entire generation, some say even longer. A century, an Aeon. It is not known. I'm sad to say that we'll never know which is true. Perhaps it lasted for only half a generation, or half an Aeon, or a mix of all. Either way, the Ark watched over the conflict, keeping those in line who veered from the path of a fair fight, keeping those Spirits, White and Black, straight. But then a piece of knowledge was obtained by the Ark's keeper, Ragmarus."

Pnumar paused and shoved his hands deep into his pockets. He bowed his head and stuck out his lower lip, as though in remorseful thought. "You see, before I go any further, Ragmarus was of neither side, neither White nor Black, Light nor Dark. His origins are unclear, though it has been suggested that he was created by the Force of White and tempted by the Force of Black, but had gone his own way, and so was the perfect candidate to mediate this Final Conflict for he did not belong to either side. He was neither partial to the Light nor to the Dark. Completely neutral. Which, some say, worked against him for the Force of Light was opposed to those who were neither Hot nor Cold and only Lukewarm. It was one or the other for the Light. Same for the Dark. Ragmarus was in a place all his own. It is also said that Ragmarus was tied to the Ark of Light, the Ark being his source of strength and nourishment, his very spirit somehow entwined with the mysterious Ark. One could not survive without the other. It was symbiotic. Back to the tale."

Pnumar removed his hands from his pockets and began walking around the circle of people, sometimes stepping in close to them, emphasizing a part of his story.

"Ragmarus stood by the Ark," he continued, "and did not move from that spot until he saw that the Battle seemed to be going in circles, one side never overpowering the other, both breaking even, equal. Bored with his position in the War, Ragmarus raised his hands, his gray robe billowing around him in the wind, and brought the Battle to a halt. Both sides, both those of Spirit and of Man, looked on him, perplexed, questioning why he had stopped them for this War should not have been stopped. It was the End Battle, after all. And then Ragmarus declared something that neither side expected. He told them he disagreed that, when the war was over, he was destined to side with neither the victor nor the defeated and that he would be doomed to remain on the Earth alone, forever, without anyone. Again, he belonged to neither side but Ragmarus figured, for his service during the End Battle, that he should be welcomed into the arms of the winning side and be treated like a king in their halls for his deeds. Unfortunately, each side didn't see it that way and knew that once the Battle was over, he would remain behind alone, to wander what was left of the Earth for eternity. Knowing that neither side would have him, Ragmarus denounced his title as Arbiter and asked the White to grant him leave of the Battle. The White would have no part of it and so, as punishment, tore Ragmarus in two by severing his connection with the Ark of Light. Once done, the Ark grew cold and faded from its place on the Altar. Faded to where, no one knows. Just faded. Ragmarus, defeated, left the Battle, his spirit growing weaker all the while, his robe transforming from Gray to Purple, his essence showing through, a sign that he was no longer a part of what had once been a sacred task."

"What happened to him?" someone shouted from the crowd.

Pnumar located the person who asked the question: a young woman standing alongside her husband, hand in hand. Peter thought it a sweet sight.

"What happened?" said Pnumar. "Well, that all depends who tells the tale. As I tell it, Ragmarus wandered the ground outside the area of Battle for a time, the sounds of the Final Conflict always echoing in his heart and mind until, one day, he grew so weary of their cries that, with his last ounce of strength, in a flood of power, swept along the Battle, sped it up, until very soon, the cries of War ceased and the Battle was over. And so, too, was the life of Ragmarus. Some say that even though he was cast out of the Battle, he still had a part to play. His presence, however weak his strength had become, was still a part of the Battle, but without his actually being there, both the Light and the Dark were able to attack each other with all their might until, when Ragmarus swept through them once more, a victor emerged. It is believed that the Light overcame the Darkness, like a flame in the dead of night. And so the White and Black left the Earth and went to their own Realms, along with the people who served their sides. But some of the race of Men stayed behind because they had caught wind of Ragmarus's decision and sided with him, agreeing with his stand point, agreeing with the injustice that he should remain alone once the Battle was over. Thus ends this part of the tale."

Pnumar announced there would be a short break before he continued. This was a chance for the people listening to talk amongst themselves and discuss what they just heard.

"What do you think?" asked Aiyesha.

She turned to him and Peter found himself staring into her green eyes, falling, drifting . . .

"I don't know," he said, coming back to the present. "I've never heard anything like it. We have stories back home, of how this World came to be, some of it similar to what—what was his name? Pnumar?—said, but different, as well. Pnumar told the tale of a great war and really stated who the players were. Back home, it was just referred to as a single battle, something far simpler, just two powerful armies fighting for dominion over the lands. I didn't know, or was never told, that the two sides were something of spiritual significance. I always thought them to be mortal and not, as he made it sound, *immortal.* Back home, we're told that after the war was when Time started again and the calendar of years began anew. So, if that's true, what Pnumar said happened, happened five thousand one hundred and thirty-four years ago. That's a long time. I wonder how much of what Pnumar is saying is accurate and how much is what the tale has become over five thousand years of storytelling."

Aiyesha weighed his words. "I don't think anyone will ever know how much is true and how much is imagined, but I'm sure the point of it is the same. There was a war. Two sides with a third party in the middle to make sure no one cheated. Somewhere in the middle, the third party left but because he, she, it—was neutral, it belonged to neither side. As for the Ark—" She trailed off.

"What about the Ark? Do you believe in it?"

She ran her hands through her rich black hair. Peter loved the way it silkily settled back down onto her shoulders.

"I'm not so sure of that yet," she said. "I never heard of it until today, but there must be some shred of truth to it. Just look at the city around us. They have a whole day each and every year dedicated to what happened over five thousand years ago. Maybe the Ark of Light is symbolic of something. Maybe not. But that shouldn't matter. It's the message of the story that counts."

Peter furrowed his brow. "And what message is that?"

"I don't know," said Aiyesha. "Let's listen and find out."

They went to the front of the people around the fire and sat down. Pnumar was in the midst of conversation with another man. When finished, he returned to his place in front of everyone. He threw a few more logs on the bonfire, its flame quickly livening. The bright flame cast his big shadow on the painting-covered wall behind him.

"And so we continue," said Pnumar. He rubbed his hands together and put them over his nose. He blew into them, as if warming them, then sniffled and rubbed his nose. "Sorry," he said, "sometimes smoke bothers me."

The people chuckled. He grinned, and then went on. "So Time passed and many years went by. There weren't many people left alive after the Battle of Then. Just a handful here or there. We started the calendar anew" —Peter's ears perked up at hearing this; this was what he had been told at home, the calendar beginning again—"and tried to start life over. We procreated and created small lives for ourselves. We had to start over for the World that we once knew was incomplete and in utter ruin. And those with the knowledge of how it once was in terms of how far we had progressed as a species were no longer with us, so it was up to those with the basic knowledge of living and survival to start again, to teach us how to live. There is a gap in History here and what had gone on for nearly three thousand years after the Final Conflict is lost to us. To all I know, anyway. It was during that time, though, that Humanity and other species and creatures learned of the omnipotent Master. Bless Him for all He's done for us."

There were some cheers in the crowd at the sound of the Master's name.

"The Master made Himself known to us in our dreams and would not only appear to us there, but would manifest His love for us in our day-to-day lives by providing for us and rescuing us in times of need. Some say that He walked among us for a time, perhaps a hundred years. He left this Earth then, but still continued to work His wonders in our lives. Why, my family and I witnessed the Master's power about six years ago, now, when one of my daughters fell ill. She had come down with an aching tummy, with pain that soon became excruciating. No method known to us was able to heal her and for two weeks she suffered. And so we prayed, prayed, prayed, and a week later, one morning, she awoke and was as healthy as she had been before she became sick. The Master is real, ladies and gentlemen. And He loves us dearly. Perhaps He is a servant of the White who has returned to our Realm to watch over us? Anyway, I'm digressing. Let's continue the tale."

And so Pnumar went on. "As said, many of those three thousand years were lost to us and no accounts of what went on have thus far been found. But there was a Man that came along. He had many names, some of which were Cer'nuem, Halico, Demnacor, Kalimbrim, and Gornash. He had other names but those are the ones that are most remembered. I'll call him Gornash for this tale, for it is my favorite name of the five, but he is more widely known as Demnacor the Seer. Gornash had lived in the lands of the West. As to where, no one recalls, but he began claiming that he would have visions and dreams of the outcome of Earth's final place in History. One of them involved the Ark of Light. He said that one day it would return. So would the Master. And this gives us all hope. I can hardly wait to see what the Master has in store for us and, also, what the Ark has in store for us. Our promised redemption, maybe. The Ark, should it be brought back into existence, will be able to operate without the confines of the forces of Black and White. Truly exciting. As to when these events will unfold, no one knows. I wish that the fine city of Darim would one day learn of any signs, should there be any, of when the Ark will return. There are rumors, however, that have leaked out of the West, where Gornash once lived. Some involved war, others sickness, others the appearance of lights unlike any other in the sky. But these claims aren't taken too seriously because there is no proof for them. Maybe one day we'll learn if they're true or not. One day." Pnumar paused and gathered his thoughts. He mentioned he belonged to a group of teachers who, throughout the year, would talk of the past and of the lore of the Ark. One of the teachers, a woman named Celia, suggested that the Master may very well be tied to the Ark of Light, should the claims of Gornash be true, because Gornash said that the Ark would return around the same time as the Master. This suggestion was scoffed at and still was, except Pnumar had thought about it since he heard the theory two years ago. He was also aware that Celia had committed suicide shortly after telling him. Some thought she was murdered. He hadn't mentioned it during the last time he told the story of the Ark. He mentioned it now but told the people not to take the claim as truth, as he did not want to say anything that was not true.

Pnumar drifted into thought again.

Noticing that Pnumar was distracted, the crowd beckoned him to continue. Pnumar shook his head, snapping himself out of thought. He seemed to see something in the crowd. His mouth hung open. A moment later he said, "I apologize but I cannot finish tonight. My mind has wandered and I suddenly feel ill. I'm sorry."

Quickly, he walked away from the fire and the people and wandered off alone down a dark alleyway just around the corner.

The people began muttering amongst themselves. Some were down right angry that Pnumar didn't finish his story.

"What was that all about?" asked Peter.

"I don't know," replied Aiyesha. "He was right in the middle of it, when, all of the sudden, he just quit. I hope he's all right."

"Me too," said Peter.

Pnumar rounded a corner into the dark alley. He stopped and put a hand to his chest, his heart aching because he couldn't finish the story and give the people what they wanted. But it hadn't been his fault. The moment he thought of Celia's claim that the Master could be somehow tied to the Ark, there, in the area of the circle of people gathered around him, he saw a man standing there, covered in a gray cloak. His face was hooded but somehow Pnumar could *feel* the man staring at him. The presence of the man had caused his knees to buckle.

He felt that same sensation now.

Standing at the opposite end of the alleyway, was the same man, his body shrouded in a gray cloak.

Pnumar didn't return home that night nor ever again.

Peter and Aiyesha left the bonfire and the wall with the paintings and walked around the city. Peter noticed there were no Dembatstayr about. He thought this strange so he asked Aiyesha about it.

"I heard some of the people say the Festival of Armasulia was meant to celebrate freedom and peace and that it was their right to ask the Dembatstayr to leave because the very idea they are soldiers suggest they represent violence and war. The Festival of Armasulia is a sacred event and is not meant to be tainted with anything that opposes what it stands for."

"You must be relieved," he said.

"That I am. It is . . . exciting . . . to walk about without having to look over my shoulder. But they'll be back tomorrow. I'm sure of it. I'll have to leave then."

"I thought you decided you were going to stop running." It was more of a statement than a question.

She made a face. "I did, but my feelings change all the time. I want to stand my ground, but I also want to run and be somewhere safe. There comes a point when you grow tired of running and want to give in, but there also comes a point where you'll do anything to put an end to what plagues you."

Peter didn't want to ask her this, but he did anyway. He hated that this might be the last time he would ever set eyes on her again. "Where will you go from here?"

Aiyesha smiled sweetly. "I honestly don't know, but if I did, I couldn't tell you. If I did, and the Dembatstayr found out I told you, they might come after you. I couldn't allow that. You've been kind to me since we met yesterday and you're the first person that I've spent a decent amount of time with since I began running."

Peter sighed. "What are you running from, if I may ask?"

"You may, but again, I don't want to say too much right now. The less you know the better."

Peter didn't like it but went along with it anyway. "And what of tonight? Where will you go?"

She looked at him and he already knew the answer—she couldn't tell him.

They came out to an open area in the city, the tall buildings not hovering over them as much. They were near a construction area, the buildings only half-erected. It was peaceful in Darim at night. The high buildings provided a non-threatening shelter, reminding Peter of the Forest-Ring. Here in this opening it was almost like being out on the Ranmorahn Plains.

They looked up at the stars. The night sky was clear.

"It sure is beautiful, isn't it?" said Aiyesha.

"Yes," said Peter, "it is."

Growing up, he had spent the majority of his evenings staring up into the sky, looking at the stars. He still did it, sitting in his veranda, peering out the window at the night sky. The sudden memory of his precious home now burnt to the ground stung his heart. He was going to miss those quiet nights alone. Deeply. Maybe when he returned to Garathen he would build another place for himself, one that would be nicer than the one he lost.

But that won't be for awhile, he told himself.

There was a subtle smile upon Aiyesha's lips as she gazed skyward.

"I used to stand outside my doorstep when I was a little girl and watch the stars shine down on me," she said. Peter pictured her, young, gazing up into the sky, the same smile upon her face as she had now. "That seems a lifetime ago. Makes you wonder where the time's gone. I'm thirty years of age but still feel like a little girl of twelve, looking up into the sky, marveling at how deep and ongoing it appears, wondering what else is out there, or if there is someone or something, watching over us."

"I've wondered the same thing," said Peter. "Still do, sometimes. People talk of the Master and say He watches over us. I picture Him sitting on a big chair with the Earth in His hands, He looking down on us, but we never seeing Him." *But I'm not so sure of that now,* he wanted to say, but didn't because he didn't want to say anything against what Aiyesha might believe in.

Aiyesha dipped her gaze from the sky and crossed her arms. "All of a sudden, Pnumar's tale is bothering me. I mean, I always had an appreciation for those things which are bigger than what people can comprehend, but his story unsettles me."

Peter turned to her. "Which part?"

"All of it. I've never heard of 'the White,' and 'the Black,' before. And then that business of Ragmarus's 'Gray' becoming 'Purple.' Sounds far-fetched, a tall-tale."

"I don't think so," said Peter. "Yes, it does sound a little like a tall-tale, but there may be some truth to it."

"And why do you believe that?" she nearly shot.

Peter didn't have an answer. Once again he was caught in realizing that the reason he believed in most things in life was because others had said it was so.

"I guess that is something I'll have to think about," he said. *Boy, that was stupid.*

She nodded subtly. "Maybe. Just be careful what you *do* believe in, Peter. People die for their beliefs. If you were ever faced with it, faced with dying for what you believe in, you better be sure you know why." He must have subconsciously made a face at her comment because she said, "I'm sorry. I didn't mean to come off as critical. It's just that it's been so long since I've had a regular conversation with someone."

"It's okay," he said. "And you're right. I do need to know why I believe certain things. It's something I'm re-evaluating right now."

"Good," she said, "and when you figure it out, you'll be glad you spent the time thinking about it."

They gazed up at the stars some more, Peter pointing out some of the constellations he knew. Aiyesha said they didn't have stars where she had spent the last several years of her life.

"No stars?" he said.

"No stars." She wouldn't say any more.

They left that area after a time. Peter knew it was late and that he ought to be getting back to the Dimwald because he'd be leaving early the next morning.

Unexpectedly, he said to Aiyesha, "Where leaving just after dawn tomorrow. Why don't you come with us? It'd get you away from here. It'd be myself, Catina, and that cranky fellow back at the Dimwald."

Aiyesha seemed flattered by his invite but then corrected her expression, as if she'd just done something wrong. "Which way are you going?"

"West," he said. "We're off to Grek to take the little girl home. Her parents are sick."

"How awful," she said.

"Yes. The other man I'm with is her grandfather and she traveled all by herself all the way to Garathen to come and get him and bring him back so he could help her parents."

"She traveled all that way on her own?"

"Amazing, I know, but it's true. I'm still surprised by it. But, seriously, why don't you come with us?"

She considered. Then with regret said that she couldn't.

His heart sank. He so badly wanted her to come, if for any reason than for some pleasant company and someone to talk to since Alan was already upset with him. "I understand," he reluctantly said.

"Thanks for inviting me anyway," she said.

"You're welcome."

They walked back to the Dimwald in silence, Peter too heartbroken to say another word to her.

Outside the Dimwald, the street out front was nearly bare. A few streets over, the sounds of people still celebrating rang on. Peter stood in front of Aiyesha.

"It was real nice meeting you," he said.

"Same here."

He didn't want to go upstairs but knew he had to. "Where are you going tonight, again?" When she raised her dark eyebrows at his question, he said, "Right. You can't tell me. Well, I hope that wherever it is, it's warm and comfortable and that you have a good sleep."

"Thank you. You, too, Peter. Sleep well." She took his hand in hers and gave it a squeeze.

The air hung between them. He was going to miss her. It had been wonderful to talk to someone who seemed to make the complications of the World fade away, who made the pain of the past seem so much smaller.

"Good night," she said.

Peter saw another flicker of hesitation in her green eyes. Her air of loneliness emerged anew.

"Good night," he returned.

She turned and walked away. He watched her as she went down the street and then, with one final look at him over her shoulder, turned a corner.

Peter noticed she didn't say good-bye.

Peter's Journal: A Girl like the One I Knew

Aupil 15, the Year 134, the Fifth Aeon

I met a girl yesterday. And I saw her again today.

The way she looked at me last night—I could see the loneliness in her eyes. Yet . . . I could also see content, as if she was satisfied of where she was right then. And that she was glad I was with her.

Aiyesha reminded me so much of Talia. Same smile. Same skin. Same glaze of innocence over her eyes. But so different as well. My heart feels torn in two, a part hanging onto the things of old: home, Talia; another part letting go and reaching forward: Grek, Aiyesha.

What do you say when you meet someone and they stir something within you? Aiyesha had me the moment she rushed by me yesterday, running for her life, fleeing from the Dembatstayr. Right then I knew my seeing her was not by chance. But as to who arranged our meeting, I am not sure. I'm not sure of anything anymore, especially when it comes to what to believe in and putting my Faith in a power that is higher than my own. For so long I believed in the Master simply because that was how I was brought up. Now . . . I'm torn. It's like getting told that the sky was never blue and the Forest-Ring was never green. But this is something I'll have to delve in to another time. Maybe when Catina isn't snoring so loudly beside me.

Aiyesha. O Aiyesha. I wish you would have wanted to come with us. Maybe one day our paths will cross again? I hope so.

I'm missing you already.

CHAPTER XXIII
Leaving Darim

Dawn came early for Peter. He had been so upset over never being able to see Aiyesha again the night before, that he had a hard time falling asleep.

Alan awoke him this morning with a hard shake. "Get up!" he demanded. "You have cost us enough time already!"

Tired, Peter dragged himself out of bed and decided it best to stay quiet. Alan had already packed up the supplies he had bought in Darim. Catina didn't have anything other than the clothes on her back.

"Good morning, Catina," said Peter.

She smiled in return, the way her cheeks rose and teeth shone making him feel a little better.

Alan, walking stick in hand, was already feeling his way toward the door, his stick clacking against the wooden floor.

"We are off," said Alan, and he left the room.

Peter felt horrible and didn't want to keep Alan waiting any longer. *Stupid and selfish of me to see the Festival,* he thought. *Aiyesha.* "Come on, Catina, let's go."

And so they left their room and exited the Dimwald. Alan was out by the front doors.

"Do you have any idea what that extra night cost us! In the middle of the blasted Festival!"

"Stop yelling at me," said Peter.

"I will yell at you if I want to!"

To avoid any further conflict, Peter let Alan have his way.

Day and Night were happy to see the three of them. The horses were fed and given water, and the three bundled their things upon them. They affixed the oat-saddles to the horses' backs and were soon on their way. The streets were empty.

Peter led the horses out of the city, the orange light of dawn bathing the tall gray buildings a honey-color.

"Take us West, Peter," said Alan.

With a click of his tongue, Peter steered the horses in that direction.

They hadn't been traveling for long when they heard the sound of hooves galloping behind them.

All three turned in their saddles as the newcomer neared.

"What is it, who is there?" demanded Alan.

Peter smiled first, and then Catina.

It was Aiyesha.

"I decided to take you up on your offer, Peter. I'm glad I found you," she said.

"It couldn't have been hard," replied Peter. "We're the only young man, little girl, blind man on horses as far as I can tell."

"Offer? What offer?" interrupted Alan before Aiyesha could laugh at Peter's joke.

Aiyesha looked at the blind man quizzically. Catina giggled.

Peter brought his horse up to Aiyesha's.

"Don't mind him," he said. Then, looking back at Alan sternly, "He's always in a bad mood."

"That is it!" said Alan. He said something to Catina and the humanette brought Night over to Peter.

When Alan came up to Peter and Aiyesha, he said, "We are not going anywhere until we talk. So, Peter, let us have at it. Who is this?"

If Alan tried to embarrass him in front her one more time . . . "Well, um . . . "

"My name is Aiyesha Elnaa of Bel Candar. I met Peter, here, two days ago. Yesterday, he invited me to join you on your way to Grek."

Alan considered her words for a moment. Her voice was smooth, carrying that distinctive female lilt that sounded wonderful to any man's ears. Then, with a smile, he said, "I see. Now I know why Peter wanted to stay for the Festival."

"You do?" Peter heard himself ask before he even thought to say the words.

"Yes, I do. Obviously she is a beautiful woman. No one with a voice like that could be ugly."

"But—" His heart sped up.

Aiyesha cheeks flushed a light red at Alan's compliment.

"Thank you," she said.

Alan gazed off to somewhere in the distance, his white eyes not blinking as the sun shone against them. "'Aiyesha, is it?"

"Yes," she said.

"Give us a moment." Alan motioned for Peter to steer their horses away from her. When they were about twenty feet away, the blind man said, "What are you doing? This is not some tour where we can gather people on a whim."

"I know, but—" said Peter.

"You know nothing. Not only have you delayed us a whole day, but by bringing her along, who knows how much more time we will lose."

"I know, but—"

"You do not even know her. It is not safe to team with those whom we do not know. The stories I could tell you about being abroad and making friends with those who only hurt you in the end, always going after your tradesworth purse when you are sleeping at night."

"I know, but she is running from the Dembatstayr," said Peter finally.

"The Dembatstayr!" Alan lowered his voice to a whisper. "The Dembatstayr. Are you completely mad? Who knows what they want with her, if what you say is true?"

Catina tugged at her grandfather's wrist; Aiyesha came up to them. "Sorry to interrupt. I don't mean to be a burden. If you don't wish me to come along, then I'll be on my way."

"It is times like these I wish I had my sight," said Alan, his blank stare still on Peter. "That way, I would be able to gauge the look in her eyes and see if I could trust her."

"You can," said Aiyesha. "Trust me, I mean. I want nothing more than to get away from here."

"Peter said you were running."

Aiyesha glanced at Peter. Her demeanor changed. She was no longer just a polite woman asking to tag along. She stood her ground. "I was. But no more. If we encounter them, the Dembatstayr, I'll defend myself. And you. I simply want to start somewhere and begin anew. And one of the best ways, as my mother always said, was to begin by finding some friends. I will be more than happy to earn your trust."

Before Alan could say anything, Peter interjected. "Then it's settled. She'll ride with us." Looking her way, with a wink he added, "And if she tries to steal from us, I'll be the one to get rid of her."

Aiyesha smiled warmly.

Alan grimaced. "Fine," he said. "But I do not like it."

"Then let's go," said Peter.

Aiyesha rode a little past them. Before Peter clicked his tongue and sent Day into action, Alan stopped him. "You are lucky I am a gentleman. We will have words about this later. For now, be a good lad and treat her well. Kindness is repaid with kindness. Right now, we cannot afford anything less. Time is short. Catina came all this way seeking help. We must honor that and do our best to get to Grek in good time."

"Agreed," said Peter.

And on they went, Night and Day falling in behind Aiyesha, who rode a horse she stole that morning.

Not far from Darim, Alan was lost in thought. *I am upset with him, I know, but I have every right to be. He cost us a whole day, and sixteen extra stone drops. But I need him on this journey if I am to make it to Grek on time. I just hope our delay has not caused any problems for my daughter-in-law and her husband. Though Catina does not speak of it much, I know she worries for them greatly. This illness they have come down with sounds serious. It would be no use to make matters worse by being stern with Peter. I am not his father though it feels I am acting like one. Perhaps because it has been so long since I have been around someone his age. He may not realize it, but I can hear it in his voice—he is infatuated with this Aiyesha woman. Peter better not make any mistakes that could cost us dearly in the end. If only I could see . . .*

Catina covered her left eye with her hand. The pain had returned. And the ache not only burned behind her left eye, but felt as if it were traveling in behind her right as well. She had been suffering this pain on and off for the past month and had grown somewhat accustomed to it. But it still hurt. A lot. She didn't know what was wrong with her and wanted so badly to find out. She was scared, thinking that whatever sickness was currently plaguing her parents, was also plaguing her. Back home, when someone in their household got sick, usually the other two members of the family did as well. She was worried because people seldom got sick in Grek.

Her head was full, spinning inside, confused, her mind going back to when they had encountered Rano and the Men of Humility. She still couldn't say what happened and how she was able to see the Gero strapped to his body. She also didn't know if she should tell Alan about it. He had silenced her before, saying that she was telling tall-tales. He would probably say the same if she tried again. Alan was never one for games. And there was another memory before that one, one that was trying to surface but still couldn't come through. Something bad had happened on her way to Garathen, Catina knew. She just wished she knew what it had been.

Catina wasn't the only one who was ailing. Peter, while talking to Aiyesha, in mid sentence had become suddenly nauseated. His head swooned. His stomach felt as if it were being twisted and tossed upside down. The hot sun shone down on them, adding to his discomfort. Not wanting to ruin what was so far proving to be a good trip, he decided to ignore it.

He just hoped it wouldn't get any worse.

CHAPTER XXIV
The Purifying of the Woods

The Men of Humility, the Velmoras, though a group of simple men with good intentions, also held secrets. Though their primary mission was to spread the news of the Second Coming of the Master as Messengers, they were also Executors, doers of the Master's Will, bearers of good in a World of evil. And if the Velmoras found a place where evil was believed to be lurking, they would rid the threat of darkness from that place by any means necessary.

And so, several days since they met with Peter and his two companions, Rano and the Men of Humility came to the Forest-Ring. They were unaware to the existence of the Broken City of Garathen within and debated amongst themselves whether they should round the forest and continue on their way to Gnoraveer, or if they should save time by cutting through the Forest-Ring. After much discussion, and many complaints from the company of sore feet, it was decided they would travel through the forest, shortening their overall journey and save time. And for Rano and his men, saving time was a good thing. It meant that the hours saved by walking through the forest would be additional hours to preach the wonderful news of the Master's coming return.

Rano's dearest friend in the company was Fendomin. He approached Rano, who stood a few feet from the company, his black cloak wrapped around him tightly as if he suddenly caught a chill.

"Shall we rest here before we go on?" he asked Rano.

Rano, his brown eyes squinting, peered at the Forest-Ring. The trees and surrounding foliage stared back at him, the gaps between the leaves and brush dark and foreboding. He turned to his friend. "Yes. Tell to them sit for awhile. We shan't rest long though. I don't know how large this forest is and how long it will take us to cross it. We should go soon so as to gain distance before dark."

Fendomin knew that nightfall wouldn't occur for several hours still, but he also knew that Rano was known to gauge distance and timing simply by looking at the road or path one needed to travel to get from one point to another, whether it be far or near.

"I'll tell them," he said and regrouped with the other men.

The Velmoras rested for an hour before getting back to their feet and entered the Forest-Ring.

Rano led them, stepping down the slope that guided the way into the forest. About fifteen paces in, he stopped, the men behind stopping as well. Rano held his hand up in caution. He felt it first, but almost simultaneously, the Men of Humility clutched at their breasts, their birthmarks near their heart burning with a piercing heat. Two of them grunted from the pain. Both Rano and Fendomin stooped forward, head over their knees, the discomfort . . . . To Rano's eyes—to all their eyes—the green of the forest grew darker, as if each leaf and branch became suddenly dirty. Each of the mens' hearts beat harder in their chest, a sense of panic and caution arising. They looked all about themselves, expecting at any moment that something would burst out from the bushes and slaughter them.

Then the wave of heat and danger passed.

Rano straightened. "Darkness lurks here," he said.

The men murmured, agreeing.

Fendomin was about to say something but Rano silenced him with another raise of his hand.

Then, as though the sun came out from behind a cloud, the colors of the Forest-Ring became lighter, the leaves and branches restored to their regular vibrant green and rich dark wood.

"Whatever it was, it has suddenly passed," said Fendomin.

Rano nodded. He turned back to his men and steepled his fingers together, his brow knit together in thought. Walking to them, and then past them, he prayed to the Master, seeking His Will as to what to do next. And the answer was clear: the forest must perish.

The Men of Humility stood at the border between the Forest-Ring and the Ranmorahn Plains. Rano and Fendomin were in the middle, a pair of men to either side of them.

"What we do, we do for the Master," said Rano.

"Worthy be the Master," said one of the other men.

"Yes, worthy," said Fendomin.

Rano unclasped his cloak and let it fall to his feet. He then lifted his robe over his head and stood naked, his only clothing the strap and gray pouch which bore the Gero and Rigmata. He untied the string holding the Rigmata to the strap and stepped forward, passing the men. The men closed the gap he created and joined hands, the man on either end holding up their free hand as if catching rain.

Rano went closer to the Forest-Ring and, with both hands, brought the Rigmata to his brow. His words were spoken quietly at first, but soon rose in volume; his men remained behind him, eyes closed, listening to his words, absorbing them, then offering them to the Master with their hearts.

Rano prayed openly:

Let Your cleansing Spirit fall upon these trees
In a vengeful, moving, magnificent breeze
And drive out this wretched waste
These evil things created in haste
Bless this work of humble men
And see Your Will unto its end
Dispose the danger, dispose the death
Let Your power come in a vigorous breath
And give life to this flame
Lit upon the wood in Your Name

And the chorus was, with his men humming and chanting:

Be glorifying (We pray)
Be edifying (We pray)
Be purifying (We pray)
Be petrifying (We pray)
Today

Rano resumed:

Remove the perils in Your wondrous creation
For killing those things provide elation
Let them stalk the woods no more
And to this place please restore
The innocent life that it once made
Before the predators came in a bloodthirsty raid
Dispose the danger, dispose the death
Let Your power come in a vigorous breath
And give life to this flame
Lit upon the wood in Your Name

And once more his men chanted:

Be glorifying (We pray)
Be edifying (We pray)
Be purifying (We pray)
Be petrifying (We pray)
Today

Rano collapsed to his knees as his men sang in strange tongues behind him. Like a wild man, he jumped to his feet shouting, and removed the pouch of Gero from its strap, and ran into the Forest-Ring.

Inside the outer edge of the Forest, he ran about, sprinkling the shiny black powder of the Gero on all the leaves and tree trunks and the shrubbery he laid eyes on.

When the pouch was empty, he held up the Rigmata in offering and thanked the Master once more before setting the tip of the Rigmata aflame. He then lit the nearest leaf that had a blotch of Gero on it. The leaf blew up in flame, the flame bright and yellow and hot, the smoke dark. Every dark spot he could see, every black blotch of Gero, he set aflame, the Gero catching immediately in a loud hiss. Rano smiled at his work.

Once most of the Gero was lit, and Rano couldn't bear the growing smoke any longer, he came running up the slope of the forest, out onto the plain. His men continued their song in the strange tongue. Rano stopped, but not out of breath. The peace of the Master was upon him. The men's singing faded and their leader stood before them, naked, sweaty, but glorious all the same.

Behind him the Forest-Ring burned in bright blazes of yellow and orange and red and blue. The dark smoke rose up through the canopy of leaves and floated away in the late afternoon sky.

SECOND ACT

And it Begins

CHAPTER XXV
Three Realms
(A Fourth Adjoined)

In the beginning was the First Realm: the White. Shortly after, there was a rebellion within that Realm and the Black was created. One-third of the White was cast into the Second Realm, the Black. The Earth was formed soon afterward and became the Third Realm, a realm for people and all the creatures of flesh and blood to live within, creatures of air and land and Sea. At the end of Time, in the Lost Aeons, after the Final Conflict, a Fourth Realm came into existence. But the energy flowing through that Realm was not strong enough to stand on its own, so, to compensate, it adjoined itself to the Third Realm, Earth. The First and Second Realms fled known existence and so remained the Third Realm, the Fourth a part of it, but misplaced amongst the knowledge and physical existence of the Third.

The Fourth Realm belonged to the Purple, what was once Gray in the Realms of the Black and the White, at the end of the Lost Aeons. The name of this Fourth Realm is many, those involved with it—whether they know it or not—calling it the Nothingness, or the Purple Void, or, simply, the Purple.

But those, like General Charles Gasahd and those of the Dembatstayr army, call it Yem Batu, or, in slang, the Island of the Dead. But none of these people know of its full significance and what Yem Batu fully represents. Their minds have been closed for sake of loyalty, for if they knew the horrors of what being involved with such a realm would entail, their loyalty would be lost.

The Island of Yem Batu sits apart of reality as it is known, guarded and kept safe from the rest of the World by a Border of Purple Fog, impenetrable and invincible. Only a select few can transcend from this hidden realm out into the rest of the Earth: those who are not of this Earth and what is of flesh and blood, Man or Creature or

Beast, but only those who reside within this Purple Realm, the Fourth adjoined to the Third.

There is one who controls the Purple Realm. He has been given more names than any other in recorded History; Ragmarus having been one of them. But that name is lost to him now, merely something he had been called on a day long ago at a time long forgotten. He prefers to call himself simply the Void-man, for this explains his existence. He is lost to a void of nothingness, without Time or place in either World, either Realm, neither material nor spiritual. However, he is neither male nor female nor any mix of the two. He had once been male but now can choose which gender he wishes to appear. But he prefers, when showing himself, to take on the form of a male, for the male is dominant in nearly all species on the Earth.

And so sits the Void-man, ageless, immortal, hidden from the rest of the World, but not out of knowledge. He is gathering his strength and awaiting the right moment to make his return to the Realm of the Living, the Third Realm.

Since the Battle of Then, since being cast out by the White and not accepted by the Black, he has been in search of his lost Ark. When he was first expelled from the Battle of Then, he scoured the Earth for the Ark of Light, but to no avail. As Time wore on, so did he wear and soon, grew weak. Using what was left of his power, he created the Fourth Realm—which adjoined to the Third as a result of his weakness—and settled there, resting, gathering his strength so he can be well enough to search the Earth once more.

This was shortly after the First Aeon began, right after the Battle of Then.

As the millennia passed and Time wore on, the strength of the Void-man began to return and he, under a guise of an ominous, omnipotent ruler, began to draw the People and Creatures of the Earth to him as their master, visiting them in dreams, granting them their hearts' desires and prayers, enforcing their belief in him. And their Faith in him restored his strength even more. But he will never be complete—never be fully *restored*—until he is rejoined with his beloved Ark, his source of nourishment and power, his very essence and being.

And so, today, just over five thousand one hundred years after the Battle of Then and the creation of the Fourth Realm that is apart of the Third, the Ark of Light, hidden away, has awoken and beckons to be found. The Void-man hears it call out to him, for they are joined, one not complete without the other. The White's severing of their connection not severing enough. But the Void-man does not know where the Ark is, or yet how to gather enough strength to leave the Island of the Dead and begin his search for it anew.

He hasn't told anyone of the Ark's reawakening—no one Human, anyway—for any he told would surely go after it. However, he has set his plans in motion, beginning with his army of Voidsmen—Dembatstayr—many years before, another tool used to control the peoples of the Earth. The Voidsmen are simple pawns and the Void-man found it interesting to learn that the Human mind can be easily manipulated; so can the minds of Humanity's off-shoots, like the Velmoras and Colga, for their hearts and minds are still based upon Human design. They can easily be blinded by believing in a cause or a person or a being that is rumored to be of higher power than themselves. It makes them feel more powerful, more in control—but this is an illusion, of course. One day, perhaps, the Void-man will reveal his intentions of obtaining the Ark of Light to a select few and, because of their blind devotion to him, will hand it over, should it be found, under the pretense that he will share with them the power obtained from such a find.

The Ark of Light is a powerful tool and, once gotten a hold of, the Wielder could determine the fate of the rest of the World and the outcome of the rest of History. Yet, no mortal Man nor any off-shoots of Humanity nor any Creature nor Beast, have the capacity to wield it, for the Ark of Light had been created by supernatural means at its inception and so requires a supernatural being to control it. The Void-man is one such supernatural being who is currently upon the Earth.

But there is one other with the capacity to control the Ark of Light.

His name is Peter Jones.

The Man in the Gray Cloak walked up the stone steps, his cloak around him, covering him fully. The twisting stairs took some time to ascend, but that didn't matter. Here, there was no Time. Eventually, he emerged in a small, round alcove that was no more than a circle about eight feet wide. It was heavily shadowed and a fine gray and purple mist hung in the air. It smelled of filth and rotten eggs—the smell of Yem Batu. When he reached the top of the steps, he surveyed the tiny area for a sign of his Lord. This was where his master would be waiting for him.

"Sir?" asked the Man in the Gray Cloak, his voice low and cautious.

On the far side of the alcove, there was a stirring of the shadows.

His Lord.

"Sir," said the man, his voice low, raspy, like a snake hissing, a panther growling. "I have come with news."

A voice spoke, seeming to come from all sides. "Tell me you have found him, Thalok."

Thalok paused and removed his hood. His gray skin immediately felt the tingle of the foul air around him. "No, Lord, not yet. But I gave him news that I was coming."

The shadows stirred some more, but the owner of the Voice was not seen.

"You gave him news," repeated the Voice. "A waste. Your kind is loud of tongue, Thalok. I should have considered that when I brought you under my employ."

Thalok had no significant words of news; the Voice was right. His people, though few, often ended up speaking when they should have kept their tongues silent.

Ashamed and humbled, Thalok took a step closer. Still his Lord was not to be seen. "He has been traveling with two others. An older blind man and a young girl. They reached Darim three days ago and had just left this morning."

"Which way are they headed?"

"West, as far as I can tell. And they seem to be in quite a hurry. The company had picked up another traveler while in Darim. A female. And I believe you know her. She is the one who had recently escaped your camp."

"Aiyesha Elnaa." The Voice considered this a moment. "When you meet them, kill her, too. But Peter first. It is imperative that he dies, if no other."

It had not been explained to Thalok as to why Peter had to die. The only explanation received was simply that he *did* have to die. Thalok was one of the few races that were able to live on the Island of the Dead, a place of remorse, hopelessness, and extreme anger. His race, the Qinoran, were savage in nature, but extremely intelligent. They were a cross between the Goula—a race that had evolved from random primordial cells on the Island of the Dead—and that of the remaining agents of the Black who had stayed on Earth to tempt Humanity and anything else living that had freewill. The mind of a Qinoran was always in battle, one side leaning toward the Void-man and His ways, and the other to the ways of the Black and the evil they represented. And since the Void-man ruled over the Island of the Dead, all who resided there were bound to Him and had, since birth, carried the desire to see His Will to its end. The Void-man, the Voice, had called upon Thalok to seek out Peter—once Peter had been known to exist in the World, outside the confines of Yem Batu—and kill him.

"Yes, my Lord. Your Will unto its end," said Thalok with a bow. "It shan't be long."

"Before you kill him," said the Void-man, "I would like you to observe him for a time, as you have been doing, and keep me informed. He may leave certain clues that could be of benefit to me."

"Clues? I don't understand."

"And there is no need."

"But I have been asked to kill him. I would like to know why," Thalok found himself saying before he could hold his tongue.

The Void-man's voice grew stern. "You could hardly understand why. Heed my wishes or you and the rest of the Qinorans will no longer have a place within my Realm."

The threat shook Thalok to his core. Though the Qinorans were a strong race, their strength was drawn from the atmosphere of the Island, from the presence of departed spirits from the Realm of the Living. When Thalok left the Island, he only brought the strength he had gathered while there, and the longer away from the Island he was, the weaker he became. Only when returned to the Island did his strength become renewed.

"My apologies, my Lord," said Thalok. He replaced his hood on his head, concealing himself. It was an immediate comfort, as if the Void-man could no longer see him.

"Don't let it happen again. Remove your hood!"

Thalok obeyed immediately. He was on Sacred Ground and respect had to be shown at all times.

The Void-man said, "And what of Peter's awakening? Has he done anything that would show that he knows or feels more than what he is letting on?"

"No, Sir. Nothing that I can gather."

"I see," said the Void-man, "but you would be wrong. Peter knows more about the World around him than he previously did. Already Peter is sensing the World is not as it should be."

"Is there anything else, my Lord?" asked Thalok.

There was silence for a time. Finally, the Void-man spoke. "Nothing for now. But I want to see you before you kill him. And then I want you to bring his body to me."

"Your Will unto its end," said Thalok and bowed once more before turning back toward the stone steps.

Thalok emerged onto a small stretch of rock that was part of a large mountain, a veritable island amidst an endless sea of the Purple Fog. He gazed out into the purple mist and gathered himself before descending the mountain and making his way to the Halls of Time. Being in the presence of the Void-man . . . . The very air around you pressed from all sides. Your legs buckled, your shoulders slumped and all movement felt restricted, as though you were confined in a small space. Out here on the mountain's edge, away from the Voice, liberation was all. Within moments, Thalok felt as though he had never been in the presence of the Void-man, the ruler of the Island of the Dead, at all.

Readjusting his heavy gray cloak around him, Thalok climbed down the mountain, the winds of the Purple Fog rocking him as he moved. Once at the bottom, he would proceed to the Crossing, and continue his pursuit of Peter and his company.

CHAPTER XXVI
Onward
(Hush-singers and Dreamy Recollections)

The four companions went on into the afternoon. They hadn't stopped for a rest and ate while riding, making up for time lost. Peter, on Day, and Aiyesha, on a horse she named Bear—for it was a deep brown color—rode side by side in front, with Night behind, his reins in Peter's hands, Catina and Alan atop his back.

Peter—despite his queasy stomach—and Aiyesha talked that whole morning, exchanging stories of where they were from, sharing the tidbits most interesting, leaving out the details they thought not appropriate (as they were only beginning to get to know each other). Alan kept silent most of the way, only speaking from time to time to make sure Peter was leading them where they ought to be going, and to announce it was time to eat when the time came. When Alan checked to make sure Peter wasn't leading them off course, his tone was condescending, still upset for the whole day of travel-time that was lost in Darim. Aiyesha stood up for Peter each time, saying that while she had worked her way East, she had been down the road they were currently traveling, and that Peter was taking the swiftest route, to the best of her knowledge.

"Just let me know when we hit Peguis Pass," said Alan. "It is best to take the South road if we are to avoid Wesafeld and the Thakari Desert beyond. I refuse to travel in the blistering heat. Besides, it will be quicker if we go South first, and then go Southwest."

"You're in charge," said Peter facetiously. And it was left at that.

Gray clouds settled in above them, the air humid, feeling like a downpour of rain was soon to follow.

Giggling first then sitting up in her seat, Catina began to sing.

Umba velli
Sula belli
Forla cuela la
Umpa scoomba
Sumpa roomba
Forla duelei ra

Cal ren masa
Sumpa rhingsa
Donli ersa galahoo
Rani den sorgalo
Se meva domphalo
Doali ersa galahoo

She giggled again when she finished and began to hum the tune to herself.

"What was that?" asked Aiyesha, turning back to Alan in her seat.

The blind man didn't realize she was talking to him.

"Alan?" she said.

"Hm? Oh. Yes?" His mind seemed to be elsewhere.

"What was she singing?"

"I was not paying attention. I am not sure what you mean."

"How did it go?" said Aiyesha to herself. "Oh, yes. Umba velli, Sula belli—um, I can't remember the rest."

"That is okay. I know the one you mean." Alan smiled for the first time that day, as he recalled the lyrics. "It is an old rhyme-song for children that is sung when going somewhere. A silly song that keeps the children entertained while the mother and father talk about more important matters." He thought for a moment then translated it for her, matching the words to the Common-tongue as best he could. "It means, essentially: Bouncy, jump; Hoppy, skippy; On horsy back; Walking, running; Riding, trotting; On pony behind; Here we go; Riding out; Fun for everyone; Soon we are there; Trip all done; Fun for everyone." Then he added, "It has been a long time since I have heard that."

"Soon we are there, trip all done," said Aiyesha with a smile. "Grescalla, right?"

"Grescalla," confirmed Peter, drawing Aiyesha's attention back to him. It was innocent and by no means did he wish to intentionally stop her from talking to Alan. He just seemed to feel left out when Aiyesha wasn't focusing on him.

It did not rain, thank goodness. Rain would certainly slow them down and time was already working against them. Alan mentioned he was worried about Catina's parents, especially his daughter-in-law. He did not know what he'd do should anything happen to her. More specifically, what Catina would do. Catina loved her parents dearly, especially her mother, and, as independent and capable as Catina was, she relied on her mother for emotional comfort and support—perhaps more than other children relied on their mothers—ever since she had lost her father.

The land around was all grass, much like the Ranmorahn Plains, but the grass here was more yellow and dry in spite of the humidity in the air. They came up over a small rise in the land and, thatched here and there, were bushes, deep green and lush, the grass a bit greener this side of the rise.

As they passed the bushes, Catina let out an "Ooh" when she saw some of them had flowers.

"Gounana!" she exclaimed.

"Flowers," translated Alan.

The flowers were red and white and yellow and pink. Some a powder blue and others a light gray in color. A few bees buzzed around the bushes, gathering pollen.

Peter glanced at the flowers as he rode past. The ones that caught his eye, growing at the base of a small bush to his left, were called Hush-singers, named long ago by the tan-skinned Plains People who roamed these lands before others—those of lighter skin—came and drove them out. Hush-singers were a faded purple, the purple darker around the base of its bell. Hush-singers had long stems and when they bloomed, they bloomed big, their eyes fully exposed. The eyes were a muted gray. At the precise center of the eye was a small white bud and, with enough time, would become a flower on its own within the bell of purple petals; a flower within a flower.

Just then something stirred within him. His nauseated stomach became even more so and he stopped his horse and bowed his head, taking deep breaths.

"What's wrong," asked Aiyesha.

"I'm not sure," said Peter. "I'm suddenly not feeling very well." He swallowed. His stomach swam. A film of sweat formed on his forehead.

"Why are we slowing down?" asked Alan, coming up beside them.

"My stomach's queasy," said Peter.

Alan rolled his eyes. "When did it start?"

"Earlier, when we left Darim. It just suddenly got worse. Just give me a moment to let it settle and then we can continue."

Catina asked Alan what was wrong and he replied by telling her Peter had an upset tummy.

"Do you want to rest?" asked Aiyesha.

"I'm not sure," said Peter. "Just . . . . If everyone could give me some space for a moment then I should be fine."

The company obeyed and Aiyesha took Night's reins and led the horse, along with Alan and Catina, away from Peter. Peter dismounted Day slowly and stepped a few paces away. He put his head between his legs. It felt like someone was churning butter in his stomach. He spat on the ground. A foul wad of milky liquid hit the grass.

A goodly distance away, he could hear Aiyesha talking to Alan. "Was he sick earlier?"

"He seemed fine when we left this morning. I am not sure about Peter. He keeps to himself and to his thoughts. He does not say much voluntarily unless you are talking directly with him. I am will to wager that he is the type of man who does not say he is ailing, and only waits for himself to be truly ill before speaking out."

"He's a tough one, then," said Aiyesha.

"Are not all boys?"

Peter breathed deeply through his nose and slowly out his mouth. He had managed to ignore the unsettlement in his stomach all morning. But when he saw the Hush-singer and their muted purple petals and foreboding gray inner ones, his stomach went taut and the nausea spread all over, his intestines tossing and turning beneath his skin. There was something about the flower that greatly upset him. He couldn't place it. The flower just seemed so out of place amongst the colors of the other flowers along the bushes. He couldn't shake the image of the flower from his mind. And he desperately wanted to.

It reminded him of something. He threw up.

When Peter returned to them, his face was very pale.

"You look terrible," said Aiyesha.

He gave her a wry grin and hopped back on Day.

"Will you be all right?" asked Alan, his voice soft.

Peter swallowed. "I should be fine. Sorry about that. I didn't want to waste anymore time, but . . . " He swallowed, the sour taste of mucus making him wince.

And as if to put their differences aside, Alan said, "Well, we always have time to stop if one needs it. Let us ride a little slower until you feel better."

Peter smiled. "Thank you."

And off they went again.

They had ridden quite a distance and covered a lot of ground despite riding slower for Peter's benefit. But after a few hours since that awful throwing up back near the Hush-singers, Peter's stomach had settled down and he was nearly himself. He kept quiet, not really wanting to talk, thoughts of his home and life before this journey surfacing in his mind more often than not.

Alan and Aiyesha began speaking to one another, Alan asking her question after question, trying to learn as much about her as he possibly could. Most of her answers were vague thus demanding more questions, which Alan seemed to enjoy.

Catina rode in silence. Her thoughts traveled frequently to her parents and what they might be doing this exact moment, and if they were all right. She kept seeing in her mind's eye the image of her parents lying deathly ill in bed, their hair in tangles, their skin pale, their eyes gazing at her vacant and lost.

She missed them.

Then, suddenly, another memory arose and Catina's head began to hurt. And it wasn't the headache that had been plaguing her. Her head felt as if it were pulsing with information, as if she had just learned so many new things and was having a hard time processing it all. The World around her began to drift away and she was lost to a place where only her thoughts existed and nothing more. There was something that had occurred on her journey to Garathen. Something to do with a man. Something . . . . Who was he? Someone that made her feel small and worthless . . . and helpless? When was that?

The man.

The man.

The . . .

. . . man.

It hit her.

The recollection was like a dream; she didn't know if it really happened or not, but it was . . . there. Someone leaning over her, his foul breath blowing against her face, the echoes of his heart pounding beneath his ribs, the beads of sweat running along his brow, the feel of the moist, thin fabric of his shirt as she tried to push him off.

"Rana Ko!" she had said. *No!* The man had persisted, pushed her, forced her to bend to his will. She hadn't asked for it. She didn't even know what *it* was. But it wasn't right. Catina knew that much and it was the *knowing* that pushed her to take the next step to freedom.

The knife in the sheath on his belt. She grabbed it. But what did she do with it? Her mind wouldn't answer.

Catina's experience with death had been limited. She had once watched her step-father slay a horse because it had broken its leg. She had watched her mother countless times lop the heads off chickens before de-feathering them.

Her father had died.

But she had never watched a person die. A person is so much more real than a horse or a chicken despite how much she loved animals. A person is so much more *alive.*

The man.

He had tried to hurt her. Tried to take advantage of her and use her for a purpose she had no idea what, other than that it was something terrible. That look in his eyes, that hint of upcoming pleasure that haunted her now.

The knife in the sheath on his belt.

She had taken it! She had gripped the big handle in her small hand, squeezed it so tight, and had—

The memory burst before her eyes, the sight of the knife quickly sliding in to position just under the man's ribs, tearing through the skin, the muscle, into the soft, squishy stuff underneath. She knew what she had done, but wouldn't let herself admit it. She could still hear the sound of the blade finding its way into the man's flesh, ripping and then piercing its way through the maroon fabric of his shirt. The warm flow of blood on her right hand and how it trickled down her fingers.

Sitting atop Night, her chest ached, dull yet sharp, her heart crying out in pain and torment. How could she have done . . . . It wasn't possible. She would never hurt anything. Each time her mother asked her to help with beheading the chickens, she told her no.

And yet she killed that man.

—

Like Catina, Peter was also lost in thought, thinking of the Man in the Gray Cloak. He didn't know why he was thinking of him or what brought it on, but he was there, before his eyes, in his mind . . . stronger, as if the Man in the Gray Cloak were getting nearer.

I'm coming, is what the man had said. Peter didn't know what that meant or if it meant anything at all. But something about the tone in the Man in the Gray Cloak's voice, something about the ominous shape beneath the cloak made Peter believe this fellow was real and that his warning was not to be taken lightly. But who was he? And what did he want with him?

"It's not real," said Peter quietly to himself. "Can't be." And then he saw a Hush-singer in his mind's eye and the gray of the little flower within the flower, and how the gray reminded him of the Man in the Gray Cloak. The Man's presence also reminded him of a dream he had when he was a child, a dream where he had a brother and he and his brother got lost and fell victim to the Man in the Woods, who lurked within the Forest-Ring. His brother, in the dream, had been slain. Peter had woken up with a start and the Man in the Woods's voice could still be heard, warning Peter that he would visit him again the next night.

Peter swallowed the memory and told himself that it would serve no purpose to scare himself over a dream of long ago. But the haunting air that had surrounded the Man in the Woods, was the same as the air that surrounded the Man in the Gray Cloak. The realization sent a chill up his spine.

I'm coming, the Man had said.

Peter hoped it wasn't true.

—

Catina's hands shook as she realized the truth of her memory and that it had *actually* happened. She glanced around. They were riding three abreast: Aiyesha beside her, Peter on the farthest side. Alan and Aiyesha were still engaged in conversation. Peter was staring at the back of Day's head, his blue eyes seeming to be lost in the horse's mane. Catina had no one to turn to. She wanted to say something to her grandfather but knew that it was impolite to interrupt grown-ups when they were talking. And Alan was the only one with her right now that could understand her. And the last time she said something to him, when she had spotted the Gero beneath Rano's cloak, he scolded her. How she had seen the Gero, she still didn't have an answer, and the further in Time away from that moment she was, the further away an answer seemed. Even the thought the event had actually occurred, the probability that it had actually happened, began to diminish.

For the first time since she left Garathen, Catina felt utterly alone.

They rode into the night, stopping once for food and water and to conduct personal business. They were tired and their behinds were sore, but they kept on. Alan, though blind, was still in charge of leading them where they needed to go and Peter's job was to make sure they remained on course. When asked how much farther until they reached Grek, Alan didn't have an answer. They would ride South and then Southwest. What Alan didn't know was that the road to Grek had changed much since he traveled it last and that, where there was once just open fields, now lived a young forest of trees and shrubbery and bushes of all sizes, planted by a race called the Flistablare.

The company stopped shortly after midnight on a stretch of land in the middle of hundreds upon hundreds of acres of grass. In the light of the moon everything looked the same no matter which direction you faced, so much so that, when they camped, Alan made Peter lay down his sword and staff on the ground in an arrowhead, pointing in the direction they were headed so they would not get turned around come morning and end up going the wrong way.

Alan and Catina shared a bed, using one of the now-nearly-empty oat bags as a pillow and a red and blue patterned blanket they had picked up in Darim as a mattress. The grass was damp tonight and they were all too tired to set up the tent.

Peter, with Aiyesha's help, made a fire to keep them warm. Catina was asleep within minutes.

Once all was set up, Peter saw Aiyesha had wandered a ways from the camp.

"You are not going over to her, are you?" asked Alan.

Peter wiped his hands on his trousers. "I was thinking about it. Why?" It was amazing the blind man knew she was gone even though he didn't see her leave.

Alan rolled over onto his side. "I just do not wish to see you get hurt." An odd statement, for a blind man that barely knew him.

"I'll be fine, but thank you anyway." Peter waited a moment before speaking again. "But when I'm around her—it's hard to explain—but I feel better. Well, this trip, as you know, is hard for me, leaving everything behind. Yet, with Aiyesha around, it's become easier. Smoother. Do you know what I mean?"

The blind man's face became flushed with an almost childlike warmth. "Yes," he said, "I do. But you do not know her, Peter. Be careful. These, as we have seen, are strange times. This has not been a social journey. There has been danger and strange meetings. Do not let her be one of them as well, or both."

"I'll be careful," said Peter and went off toward Aiyesha.

"Young ones," said Alan to himself, making himself more comfortable on his blanket.

Aiyesha stood with her arms crossed, gazing out onto the land, the sweet scent of damp grass alive on the air. She didn't turn to Peter when he approached her.

"Hello," he said.

"Hello."

Without suggestion, they began walking together, further from camp, the moonlight their guide so they would not get lost in the night.

"It's so beautiful out here," said Aiyesha. "It's been a long while since I've been out at night, not worrying that anything would go wrong."

"What do you mean?" asked Peter.

She looked about in all directions except for directly at him. "You wouldn't understand."

Peter chuckled. Aiyesha grinned, too.

"What?" she said.

"That sounds like something Alan would say," he told her. "He treats me as the most naive person on Earth." He changed his voice so it had a bit of a twang to it. "I'm just a simple boy from a simple town so don't put anything complicated on me."

She laughed again and gave him a playful shove to his shoulder.

"I'm serious," she said. "You wouldn't understand."

Peter stood in front of her and crossed his arms. "Try me."

Aiyesha uncrossed her own arms and stepped a little ahead of him. He followed.

"I've only spent one day with you and the others, and it's been wonderful. I'm glad that I was allowed to come along even though I'm still a total stranger." She finally looked directly at him. His blue eyes gazed back at her, innocent and wide. "Why have you been so kind to me?" she asked.

Peter glanced her over, his eyes following the flow of her black hair in the soft breeze, the little gleam of moonlight off her forehead, the way her green eyes were filled with a yearning to understand why something good was happening to her.

"Because you looked like you could use a friend," he told her. "And I wanted to be it."

She took a step closer him, pulling her hands up into her sleeves, keeping her fingertips warm. She felt like a little girl again. No army. No General Gasahd. Just Aiyesha Elnaa, just as she was before she left home.

"Can I tell you something?" she asked.

She wanted him so badly to say yes, wanted so badly for him to say she could tell him anything and to tell him that she was thankful for making her feel a part of something.

His caring eyes lit up. "Anything you want."

Her eyes wandered past him to the sky above. Then, pointing, "There's Quallecor!"

The tender moment was over.

Peter turned to where she was pointing and there, up in the sky, were six stars and, if followed, made the imagined outline of a horse riding towards you. Quallecor, Horse of the Stars. The Northernmost star served as the top of his head, the one directly beneath it the end of his muzzle. Southwest from that star was another, serving as the side of his front hoof, poised in midair as he stepped toward you. There were three stars in the back, one running to the side between the first and second star, signifying the curve of the horse's back. Another, a little further away and a little farther back, was his hind leg. And then another, farther back still and lower, was the end of his tail.

"That's him," said Peter.

The sky was very clear and Quellecor appeared very big and bold.

"Back at home," began Aiyesha, "I used to take my own horse out sometimes at night, when my father was away on business. I'd take my horse out and ride as fast as I could, pretending I was racing against Quellecor, and, of course, I always won."

"Did your horse have a name?"

"No. I wish now that she did. You see, my father believed that a girl's place was in the house and that horses and the danger of riding them was no thing for a lady. I suppose that his wishes stayed in my subconscious each time I took my horse out so I never gave her a name." Then she smiled. "But I shall give her a name now: Fairstar, for that is what she was. Fair and kind, her coat golden like a star." She didn't told him of her father's protests when she joined the Army and his wishes against the violent life that she chose.

"That's sounds nice," said Peter. "I never had a horse when I was young. Garathen is a small place and you could get anywhere on foot. The only horses I saw was when periodically there would be tradesmen coming in through the Forest-Ring to trade with someone there, or pick up some of the crafts we produced. There was, or is, rather, a fellow, Mr. Hahdgrove, and he loans out horses to people, too. That's where we got Night and Day."

"A tradesman, too, huh, Mr. Poet—and Painter."

There was a light glimmer of pride in his eyes. "I try to feel the hidden rhythm in things and people and scenery, and try to translate the feelings I feel to paper or canvas."

"I love poetry," she said. "You'll have to share yours with me some day."

"Perhaps," he said.

The sky settled over the dark horizon in bands of deep purple and black, the light of the moon transforming the purple and black to navy and gray the higher you looked.

"I wish I could paint this," said Peter, "something to remind me how far from home I really am."

Aiyesha came closer to him. "Look around slowly then close your eyes and capture what you see."

The two walked late into the night, sharing more stories of their youth and pointing out the different constellations they recognized. Finally tired, they returned back to camp. Peter set up a bed for her on the other side of the fire, opposite Alan and Catina, and let her use his oat bag as a pillow. For himself, he lay adjacent between Aiyesha and Alan and slept on the grass, which was now dry from the fire's warmth. He bid Aiyesha a goodnight and she said the same.

As Peter lay there, his mind reliving his time with her out here in the open, he thought he saw a flicker of darkness then a flash of gray just above the dancing flames of the fire. He raised his head from his arms and took a closer look. Nothing but empty grassland surrounded him. He lay his head back down and closed his eyes.

He thought about the Man in the Gray Cloak.

CHAPTER XXVII
Thalok Moving

Thalok moved fast. He had crossed over from the Island of the Dead some time ago and was already making his way into the mainland, heading toward Peter, his sense of direction toward his foe based on pure feeling. The closer he got to Peter, the warmer became his fingertips. The further away he was, the cooler they felt, and he knew he had to adjust his course.

His gray cloak billowing out behind him like a cape on a centurion, Thalok ran, his speed equivalent to that of a horse running at full gallop. He stayed mainly to the open land, and when he did venture into any cities, he could always choose whether he wanted to be seen or not. The only drawback was if he wanted to touch something, he had to be seen. He could not touch things when invisible. Thalok was able to place himself in the minds of his prey, haunting them, filling them with the fear of his impending arrival, so that when he did come upon them, they had already surrendered to him, their fear consuming them.

His latest task, finding Peter and then killing him, was an arduous one. But a task that had to be fulfilled. If the Void-man was correct in the little he shared with him, Peter Jones must die. And the first steps in Thalok's hunting strategy were already in motion. By placing himself in Peter's head by concentrating on Peter's name, he also established a link with him and, now, was able to sense where in the World Peter was. But he mustn't confront him too soon. Again, if what the Void-man told him was true, Peter would be difficult to kill; but, as the Void-man also said, killing Peter now would be easier than if he were to try and kill him in a month from now. Even two weeks from now. But he mustn't wait too long. Just wait for clues. Clues for what, Thalok didn't know.

Much of why Peter must die was shrouded in mystery, the Void-man only telling Thalok the basic details without any elaborate explanation. Yet even those basic details were very detailed and each reason carried a tremendous weight.

Thalok Moving

The Void-man revealed to Thalok that Peter was alive by no accident. Partially. Peter's eventual coming into the World was known long before the current Time and the purpose of his coming had been revealed long ago. The Void-man, who was not usually one to state names, let known that Demnacor the Seer was the first and only man to prophesy that Peter would one day come into the World and what his coming would mean to the Peoples of the Earth. Peter's purpose and destiny was to lead a great army to the gates of the Island of the Dead and tear them down and destroy all who resided there. This posed a great threat to Thalok, for the Qinorans, his people, lived on the Island of the Dead, with the Void-man. If Peter destroyed the Island, the Qinorans would die, perhaps even Thalok himself. The Qinorans, as far as any Qinoran knew, were not able to exist beyond the Realm of the Dead thus the Island was the only safe haven for them. Thalok was the only one able to cross the boundary and step out into the World. And there was a reason for his being able to do so. All Qinorans, a race unable to procreate within their own kind were spawned from a parent who was of the Goula and a parent of the Black, fifty-fifty, right down the middle. However, in Thalok's case, his father had been an even Purple-Black split, pure in Qinoran blood, but his mother had been solely of the Black, thus more Black ran through Thalok's veins. It was the first and last pairing between a Qinoran and one not of their own. And the Black, though few existed in this day and age, were able to roam free in the World and linger there until the end of Time. But Thalok had a weakness and that was the further and longer away from the Island of the Dead, the realm of the Purple Fog, the more he would weaken. To regain his strength, he would have to return to the Island to nourish himself.

But now, running across the country in a place called Jakarland, a realm created from his speed, Thalok still had plenty of strength left and would not need to return to the Island for quite some time.

As for Peter, Thalok was *haunting* him, finding him. He would destroy him.

It was the only way to save his people and bring pleasure to his master.

The Void-man sat upon his throne in his cave, gazing at the Great Wall. Upon the Wall he could see Thalok moving like an untamed lion across the grass, in the bubble of Jakarland, moving towards Peter. Thalok was unaware that he was being watched and was equally unaware that the Void-man could watch anyone of his choosing in the World, as long as they had undergone the Age of Enlightenment—which was everyone, excluding Peter. Though he could have used the others—Aiyesha, Catina or Alan—to track Peter, it was also important that Thalok earn a place at his side and not have everything handed to him.

What Thalok didn't know, was that the Void-man had another plan. Thalok was a loyal and faithful servant and found favor in the Void-man's eyes; but the Void-man, in truth, detested those of Qinoran descent for their existence. The Blackness within them reminded him of that day aeons ago when he was thrown from the End Battle and was banished from the presence of the White and the Black forever and was separated from his precious Ark. Yet the Void-man was willing to put his distaste for the Qinorans aside, when it came to Thalok. And because he couldn't leave the Island of the Dead—at least not yet—Thalok was a powerful ally because Thalok could pass through the Crossing of the Purple Fog and enter the World.

However, the Void-man was growing weary of the Island and his damnation to it. He was also sick of the Qinorans lurking there, living their lives as they saw fit—those worthless, yet loyal, creatures who carried the Blackness within them. And, the Void-man thought, perhaps the Blackness was keeping him at bay, acting as the bars to his prison, for the Black, since always, were more powerful than the Purple. The Black visited the Island, mating with the Goula, semi-regularly. The Black tainted the Purple Fog with their darkness, perverting all he built.

The Qinorans and Goula would be banished from the Island once Thalok completed his task, that was for certain. No more would the Void-man's realm be tainted with their filth. Peter would no longer pose a threat and he could then focus all his energy on finding the Ark of Light and using its power to free himself from this wretched place and rule the Earth in a tidal wave of Purple Fog forever. He would rid the World of the Black, conquer them, pour out his hatred and have his revenge. He would deny access to his Realm which would then be the Earth. Those of the White who still remained behind from the End Battle would not be able withstand his power and, like their Black counterparts, fall before him.

And so the Void-man sat upon his great throne and watched Thalok.

The end of the Qinorans was drawing near.

But Peter was still free.

CHAPTER XXVIII
The Meeting of Mr. Nibbetts

They made good time that morning; the land flat, the horses riding swift and sure. The yellow grass had turned to green some time ago. Come afternoon, up ahead on the horizon, Peter could see the lush green of the grass begin to fade and in its place what looked like a dark shadow cast upon the Earth. He didn't think anything of it and assumed that his eyes were fooling him. But the closer they neared that dark place, the more he was able to see that his eyes were not playing tricks on him.

He slowed the horses as they drew up to it, the grass black beneath their hooves, the sharp stench of smoke in the air. Catina wrinkled her nose. They proceeded slowly. There were patches of dead trees, charred, some fallen over in disarray, burnt at the trunk. The remains of burnt bushes and the ash of leaves littered the dark landscape. Gray smoke hung on the air, but there wasn't a blaze anywhere in sight.

"Where are we?" asked Alan.

"Looks like a fire happened here," he replied. "A big one."

The company was already in the midst of the ruin and it would take more time to change their course to ride around and avoid it than riding through.

"Dear Master," said Aiyesha, covering her mouth. All around bodies were stacked in mounds, too many to count. The bodies looked to once have belonged to animals; small ones with a lot of fur. The mounds were everywhere.

"That smell," said Alan.

The scent of charred flesh and burnt hair was enough to turn Peter's stomach. He glanced about. The mounds of bodies were more concentrated on the right than on the left. He dismounted his horse. So did Aiyesha. He wandered away from the company a little, Aiyesha behind him.

"You did not just get off your horse, did you?" said Alan, obviously hearing Peter's feet drop from stirrup to ground.

"I just want to look around," said Peter.

"We are already behind as it is. Blast! Very well, but be quick about it."

Peter and Aiyesha went off and looked over the mounds of smoldering corpses.

"What do you suppose these were?" asked Aiyesha, stepping up to one of them.

He came up beside her. "I don't know. But I've never seen anything like it. Looks like bear cubs. But why would they be piled like this?"

"More importantly than why, but by *who?*" corrected Aiyesha.

The thought of running into someone—or something—sinister sent a chill up Peter's spine. He thought of the Man in the Gray Cloak. Then the sight around him reminded him of the fire that claimed his home. His heart sank.

Shaking him from his thoughts, Aiyesha added, "This is too strange. Someone burnt this place to the ground."

"But why a small forest in the middle of nowhere?" asked Peter, folding his arms under his breast.

"I have no idea," she said. She looked around the disarray. "It's so sad. These animals didn't do anything to deserve this."

The two were not aware that Catina, much to Alan's protests, had followed them, but she lost them amongst the many mounds of dead flesh. She searched for Peter but could not find him. After a few minutes, she went to turn back and got even more lost. She backed up against one of the mounds and recoiled when she felt a patch of burnt, wiry hair brush against her dress, leaving a smudge of ash.

"Boola!" she said. *Ick!*

The humanette rounded another mound and tripped over something lying on the ground. Thankfully, her hands and elbows broke her fall and the only damage was a lung full of sooty air that puffed up when she hit the warm ash on the earth.

"Boola," she said again. She stood and brushed her hands together, getting some of the ash off.

Just then, a voice spoke up from behind and slightly below her. "Gooo awaaay," it said.

Catina turned to see who it was.

She screamed.

Aiyesha came bounding out from behind one of the mounds, appearing before Catina. Peter was a little ways behind her, unable to keep up with her swift legs.

"What's wrong?" asked Aiyesha.

Somewhere from behind one of the mounds about thirty feet away, they heard Alan calling out, asking what Catina had seen and if she was okay and for Peter to come get him and take him to her.

"Go," said Aiyesha.

Peter hesitated. Catina was a few meters away, sitting back on her hunches in a ball, scared out of her wits, her hands over face. She occasionally peeked out from behind her fingers at them.

Aiyesha put a hand on his shoulder. "It's all right. Really."

Peter went to retrieve Alan.

Aiyesha went to Catina and crouched down beside her.

"Catina, honey?" she said.

Catina covered her face even more. Carefully, Aiyesha laid her hands on Catina's and slowly pulled them away from her face.

"Catina, honey, it's okay. You have nothing to be afraid of," she said.

Catina whimpered and pulled her hands from Aiyesha. Aiyesha didn't know what to do. It had been so long since she had to act compassionate toward anybody, but she was determined to do her best and help the little one. She remembered how her mother used to soothe her after she had a bad dream.

"It's okay, I'm here," said Aiyesha and sat down beside her. After a moment, she said, "Do you want to tell me what you saw?" With a pair of fingers, Aiyesha pointed to her own eyes then to the mounds of bodies around them.

At first, Catina shook her head and then, seemingly, changed her mind. She pointed across from her, near the mound she had come round before she had fallen. On the ground near the mound was a heap of brown, all fuzz, like a large hairy bee hive turned over on its side.

"What?" said Aiyesha, pointing along with her. "Is that what you saw?"

"Semba sel gu benda. Fen qola ro teeka," replied Catina, her voice small.

Aiyesha furrowed her brow then went over to the heap of brown fur.

"Was this what you meant?" she asked, pointing to it.

Catina watched her cautiously.

From what Aiyesha could tell, it was just a heap of brown fur, probably one of the bear cubs that had managed to not get burned by the fire. Perhaps the cub had only come in during the tail end of it and remained unharmed but whoever set the blaze had killed it.

Aiyesha turned back to the humanette. "It's okay, you have nothing to fear.

"Gooo awaaay." The voice came from the heap of brown fur.

If it were anyone else, they would have jumped, but Aiyesha was trained for surprise.

"Who are you?" she asked it.

The heap of brown rolled over onto its back just as Peter came back with Alan.

"Me am dying," it said.

It took some time but Peter finally managed to convince the creature to get to its feet. The creature stood just under three feet tall, his entire round body covered in matted, brown hair. Its hands and feet were humanlike, though brown and wrinkled.

Its head was small, the hair combed tight against its skull, like a beaver. Peter couldn't see any ears but the creature seemed to hear him just as well. The creature's deep and dark eyes watered when he pleaded with them to help it.

"Are you burned?" asked Peter.

"No," replied the creature.

"Other injuries?" said Aiyesha. "Knife wound? Bow wound? Sword wound?"

"No, no and no."

"Then what's wrong?" asked Peter.

"Me head's sore. On the inside," said the creature and tapped a wrinkled finger to the side of its head. "Plus me am stiff all over. Me've never experienced anything like this. Me body feels like its filled with sand and moving around takes time and me stomach feels like its lying lifeless on the bottom of a stream."

Peter knew what the creature was describing. He had been feeling the same way earlier. The creature was ill. It had the flu or something like it.

"You're not dying," said Peter. "You're just sick."

"Sick?"

"Yes, you are unwell," said Alan leaning on his walking stick.

"Unwell? Me am always well," said the creature. "Except for now. Me am dying." It sat down on the ground in a slump.

Catina didn't seem so afraid now that the grownups were with her. She came closer to the creature, reached out, patting the fur on its shoulder.

"What? Oh, you like that, don't you?" said the creature. "Yes, me am all fuzzy." Catina continued petting him. The creature grimaced. "But me am not a toy so off with you!" it growled, low and sure.

The humanette ran away and hid behind Alan's leg.

"There will be none of that," said Alan. "You may be new to these parts and were not here the last time I visited, but I know what you are. I would recognize that growl anywhere."

The creature peered back at him.

"A Flistablare," said Alan.

"You know the Flistablare?" asked the creature.

"Well, I know *of* them," said the blind man. "I ran across a pack of your kind on one of my travels long ago. But that was across the Sea of Blue Water, a long ways from here."

This seemed to intrigue the creature. Alan appeared to be the first Human he had ever come across that knew what he was and where his kind hailed from. "You are right. We had lived in Tanturee Forest for ages, near the Kilimin Mountains, but decided to come across the water when times grew dark. This is as far as we came and decided to settle here and plant our seeds and grow our trees because the land felt *right*. We had lived in peace these past sixteen and a half years until last eve."

"What happened here?" asked Aiyesha.

"Interesting you should finally ask that," said the creature, suddenly in good spirits, but at the same time treating these newcomers with a touch of sarcasm.

Flistablare never took Humanfolk seriously. Humanfolk were always too busy thinking on themselves and their own needs and seemed to have no care for the other species and creatures of the world. Humanfolk outnumbered everyone else three to one and seemed to be everywhere, doing their own thing.

"But first, an introduction is in order, me should think." The creature bowed. "Me name is Nibbelus Itelius Telto-um. But 'Nibbetts' is what me go by. Goes off the tongue a little easier, me should thinks. Yes? Yes. So 'Nibbetts' it will be, or 'Mr. Nibbetts' will do just fine"

"You speak very well for a Flistablare," said Alan. "From what I heard, there is usually a drawl to your dialect and a bit of a clacking of the teeth."

"Yes, yes," said Mr. Nibbetts, "that's true. But me, having been young when it happened, was away from me Clan and those me were with spoke a much cleaner tongue. And we'll leave it at that." Then he added, "Don't believe everything you hear."

"I see."

Peter went to Catina, picked her up, and then returned to Alan's side.

Mr. Nibbetts told them the tale of what happened the night before and how the smoke rose and the fire rained down around he and the rest of the Flistablare.

"The night was the same as any other," began Mr. Nibbetts. "Me was coming home back to the forest, after fishing in a stream just yonder." He nodded to his right. Everyone looked but the stream was out of eyeshot. "Then me smelled smoke. And there before me was me forest, a huge wall of flame, fire licking the sky. Me dropped me catch and ran as close as me could towards it. The heat was searing and it was hard to get near. Running from the blaze were a group of Men. At least, that's what me was sure they were. They had already escaped the fire's light and were escaping into shadow when me saw them. But it seemed they were wearing long cloaks, though me am not sure. Then the air was filled with the foul screeching of me friends, unable to escape the forest. Me tried getting in close but it was too hot. Me shouted and screamed for them to come out. No one did. They couldn't. And me watched, watched as all me knew and all me've ever known came to a burning end." Mr. Nibbetts covered his eyes and shook, crying.

After a time, he gathered himself as best he could to finish the tale. "Me stayed for the whole thing. There was no one me could turn to for help. Then me thought of those Men and chased after them into the dark. They were too far ahead and moving too swiftly for me to catch up. And even from that far distance, me could still feel the heat of the fire. Me ventured back, hoping that one of me kin had made it out. Me walked around the whole outskirt of the forest, calling to them, wishing to the dear Master that someone would have made it out alive. No. And so me waited and waited and waited. The fire burned and burned until, like a miracle, it began to drizzle some. The rain quenched most of the flame. Bless the Master. Me fell asleep, too exhausted from everything to keep watch and see who, if any, had survived. Come morning, where we are now is what me found. And what me found was death and ashes. Me am the only Flistablare left."

Mr. Nibbetts sat on the ground, held his stomach and began rocking back and forth. "Ooooh," he groaned, "it comes on again."

His thick brown fur shook on his skin. Aiyesha went over to him and put a hand to his back.

"Leave me be," he said. "Though me was never claimed by fire, Death is coming for me anyway." He lay on his side, and then threw up, some of it splashing against the cuffs of Aiyesha's trousers.

"Boola," said Catina.

"Gross," said Aiyesha.

"What do we do now?" asked Peter, turning to Alan.

Alan didn't say anything.

A short while later, Mr. Nibbetts was feeling a little better and had excused himself from the group. He had duties to attend to, namely finishing piling his lost kin in mounds, as was the custom of the Flistablare when a mass death occurred. However, in the past, any mass deaths always occurred at the hands of Beasts who had hunted out the Flistablare village in the forest and killed many, virtually all. This was the first death-by-fire of Mr. Nibbetts's people. The purpose of piling lost ones in mounds was so that all could be together, even in death, and the display it created would signify to those who happened to see it that the Flistablare were very loyal to each other and stuck together even when their lives were over. Loyal to other creatures and beings, however, they were not. The Flistablare were always first in their minds.

While Mr. Nibbetts was mourning his friends and piling bodies, the four travelers had a meeting.

"I feel terrible," said Peter. "I mean, I know what he is going through. Like him, my home was claimed by fire. Worse, like he, I lost everything."

This was the first time Aiyesha heard this bit of news from Peter.

Peter continued. "I'm not sure how long we should stay here. We're already behind as it is. But we can't just leave Mr. Nibbetts here. We can't just tell him that it was nice meeting him and that we have to go."

"I know what you mean," said Aiyesha. "We can't leave just yet. Plus, as Mr. Nibbetts says, he's dying."

Alan planted his walking stick firmly on the ground and leaned against it. "He is not dying, dear woman. Far from it. The Flistablare do not die of natural causes such as illness. They die of old age and by unnatural death. That is it. And this Nibbetts fellow is not old. His voice still flows smooth. From what I have heard, Flistablare, when they get old, sound very much like an old Human: their voice creaks and drags and craggles." Then Alan furrowed his brow. "What I want to know is *why* he is sick. As said, Flistablare do not get sick. Explain that one to me."

"There's a lot of illness going around," commented Aiyesha. "Mr. Nibbetts, Peter . . . both have been ailing and both had thrown up. Strange."

Though he wanted to say so, Alan kept it to himself that he, too, hadn't been feeling well. He felt weaker, his body more stiff. Thankfully, it hadn't gotten any worse than that. He decided—when he first noticed the stiffness two days ago—that he would only say something should it become unbearable. Alan didn't want to display weakness in front of Catina, not when she was counting on him to get her home.

Just then, a singing rose up from somewhere behind them. It was Mr. Nibbetts and he was singing a solemn tune while piling the bodies.

Tired and weary
Eyes all teary
Wandering this dismal ground

Dear friends, so long
All life gone wrong
You left when the fire came round

Out all alone
Without a home
Once green has now turned black

Wish for a friend
Till me life's end
Now there's no turning back

Dum dee dum
Ho ho ho hum
Doo da dee da da

Lum lee lum
Mo mo mo mum
Loo la lee la la

Mr. Nibbetts paused a moment then repeated the melody.

"We need to come up with a plan," said Peter. Catina was at his feet, off in her own world, sitting on the ground, digging in the dirt, just playing.

"Agreed," said Alan. "I have got to get the little one home."

"And Mr. Nibbetts," said Peter, "whatever he's got, I don't want it. I've already been feeling unwell. I don't want it to get any worse. Especially not out here in the open and while we're traveling. The sooner we get to Grek, the better."

Off in the background, they heard Mr. Nibbetts hacking up a wad of phlegm. The furry creature groaned extra audibly, just so the four would know he was ailing and wanted some attention.

Aiyesha rolled her eyes. "Come on. Let's make a decision."

"Fine," said Alan. "We stay for another half-hour or so, and then we go. That way, we will not be non-sympathetic toward him."

"And Mr. Nibbetts?" added Peter.

"What about him?" came Alan.

"We can't leave him here, sick and alone."

"He will be fine. The Flistablare are determined creatures and can fend well for themselves. They plant entire forests, blast it!"

"But how do you know that for sure? You've only heard about them from people you've met."

The truth of the matter was, Alan didn't want any more company on this journey. This trip was about him and Catina. Peter came because he had nothing left in Garathen and a trip out West would do him good in helping him put his loss in the past. Alan hadn't invited Aiyesha. Peter had, and the blind man didn't like it but entertained it so that Peter would have someone to talk to on the road to Grek, and while he and Catina tended to her parents there. Alan was not about to add another to their band.

"Oh, woe is me," cried Mr. Nibbetts's from behind one of the mounds. He gave an intentional cough. "It would be nice if someone came and stroked me back while me lay down. Me stomach is all topsy-turvy at the moment. And putting to rest me loved ones is only making matters worse."

Alan had heard enough. "He is not coming with us!"

"Then what are we going to do?" said Peter.

Catina stood and went to look for Mr. Nibbetts. When she found him, she put her arms around him and gave him a big hug.

It took the creature by surprise but it seemed to welcome her embrace. "Why, thank you, little one," he said. Mr. Nibbetts looked her over. "Me, me, you're a quiet one, aren't you. Aw, well. Between you and me, me don't care for those who talk too much."

She eyed him quizzically. He gave her a little wink. "Let's return you to your friends, shall we?" And he took her by the hand and they went back to the others.

"Look who you found," said Peter to Catina.

Alan said something in Grescalla.

Catina made a face. She let go of Mr. Nibbetts's hand.

After a moment of silence, Alan said to the creature, "Well, I hope you will be all right. But, we need to be on our way." So much for the half-hour.

Mr. Nibbetts cast a hand to his brow and said, "Oh, me don't know what me'll do when you're gone. Me am not used to all this pain inside." He put his hands to his stomach. "It's so sore." He got to his knees and then lay on the ground, rolling on his back, moving back and forth in mock pain. "Me wish someone would make it go away."

"Blast it!" said Alan, taking a step towards the creature. "You were fine when you told us what happened here."

Mr. Nibbetts stopped writhing on the ground. "That's only because me like stories and company and it makes me feel so much better."

"Then tell yourself a story and start making imaginary friends!" Alan walked off.

Nibbetts looked at the group wide-eyed. Then he writhed on the ground again. "Oh, the pain. Oh, the sickness." He said this loud so Alan would hear him.

Alan turned back, and if he could see, would have glared at Mr. Nibbetts. "Blast," he muttered and stormed off again.

Peter and Aiyesha couldn't help themselves but laugh. Catina giggled too because Mr. Nibbetts looked funny rolling on the ground like he was.

After a moment, Mr. Nibbetts asked, "Is he gone?"

Peter nodded and Mr. Nibbetts got to his feet.

"Why did you do that?" asked Aiyesha.

"Because," said the Flistablare, "me don't like someone telling me how me do or do not feel. Me am honestly dying and me being told otherwise" —he stamped his foot on the ash— "really upsets me!" And then, with eyes so dark and so glazed, added, "Me don't want to be left alone out here. Me have nothing now. Nothing. Can one of you stay, or can me come with you?"

Peter and Aiyesha exchanged glances. And then with a sly grin, Peter said, "Sure."

CHAPTER XXIX
On the Coast of Seryn

General Charles Gasahd drummed his fingers on the night table beside his cot. It was cozy here in his log cabin located at the center of the Officer's Base. He felt "in the middle of it," as though he were at the *core* of the Dembatstayr army. It was a small cabin, as he didn't see the need for any extravagances. The general before him had a taste for the elaborate but Gasahd demanded the old general's cabin be demolished and this smaller, simpler one be put in its stead.

"Plush surroundings are for the weak," Gasahd was known to say to his men when they would complain of the bunks and the thin mattresses they were given. "If you expect a bed of down out on the field, then you've come to the wrong place. Here, I breed men, not children."

The cabin was one room, with the sleeping quarters separated from the rest of the cabin by a beige canvas tarp draped from one wall to the other, three quarters of the way in. The rest of the cabin held a fireplace, a few chairs, a small kitchenette, and a large cedar table that served for meetings when he called his senior officers in for private conversations. The outhouse was outside.

"How difficult is it to find a woman?" muttered Gasahd. "And how many men does it take to bring in one girl?" He heaved a sigh. "Ridiculous. She should have been brought to me by now." He was wearing only a pair of deep purple trousers and a white, sleeveless undershirt. His boots lay in a heap beside his cot. He had been off duty for just over two hours, just after the sun set, and though he had tried to sleep, his patience for Aiyesha's return was running out, and kept him awake.

He picked up the brandy snifter off the night table beside him and took a sip. When he set it down, Captain Frederik Zakmon, his second in command, pushed aside the tarp and entered. Zakmon made two fists, putting each one across his chest to the other shoulder, forming a X; the salute to senior officers on the Coast of Seryn. Zakmon lowered his arms.

"You bring news?" said Gasahd, getting up from his cot.

Zakmon's brown eyes never left the Great Map on the wall opposite to where he stood. "No, Sir. At least none to your liking."

"Then get out. I don't want to hear anymore stories of failure. All week men have been coming in here, telling me they have failed to capture her. No more."

"Sorry, Sir. I didn't mean to upset you," said Zakmon.

Gasahd ran his fingers through his graying black hair, then stroked his thick fingers over his large moustache that hooked down and over his chin in an upside U. "But you did."

"They say she puts up a fight every time they come near her," said Zakmon.

"Of course she puts up a fight. She doesn't want to come back." Gasahd took a step closer. "And, I might add, she's a damn good fighter. The best, in fact. No other has pleased me more. It just goes to show how incompetent a male is at war. Aiyesha trained with more intensity than any man I have ever taught. And because she was female, I had to work her harder so as to bring her equal to that of a man. But she was already strong and quickly grew stronger. Now, it appears, she's stronger than any man sent after her." A thought occurred to him. "Perhaps I should gather my girls to go after her? They seem more worthy of seize-and-capture than you foolish men!"

Zakmon didn't flinch. Like a good captain, he remained motionless—emotionless—and stared at the Great Map ahead of him.

After a time, and as Gasahd returned to his cot to put on his boots, Zakmon spoke.

"What shall you have me tell the others, Sir?"

"Leave that to me," he said.

Gasahd emerged shortly after out of his cabin, dressed in his uniform: purple trousers, black boots with silver at the toes, a purple tunic that fit him snugly and covered his wide frame. Across the tunic he wore a blue silk sash with the Purple Eye embroidered on it, signifying his rank as General and of his loyalty to Yem Batu and to the Master. Zakmon had on a red sash. He still had yet to earn his Purple Eye. If the two were in battle, they would abandon the silk sashes and replace them with wool ones. The silk was worn more for decoration and prestige than anything else.

A loud squawking filled the night sky overhead. A Tharadon screeched down, landing on the dirt before them, folding its wings. The bird hopped directly over to Gasahd, the man it had come to see. The bird came up nearly to Gasahd's waist. The general bent down slightly and removed the piece of parchment clipped to the bird's black leather collar. Seeing that the message was in the hands of whom it was intended, the great Tharadon began pecking away with its black beak at its long brown feathers covering its large frame, seeking out an itch beneath one of its wings.

Gasahd unfolded the message and read it silently to himself.

"More news, more news," he muttered, "but this one is just for me."

Captain Zakmon was well-versed in knowing it was impolite to ask a superior what a private message said, so he waited until Gasahd was ready to talk.

The general stroked his moustache again, as he so often did when heavy matters were on his mind. He read the letter to himself one more time before folding it back up. Zakmon straightened, at-the-ready, when Gasahd turned to him.

"Scouts have spotted her on the mainland. Seems she has joined up with a few friends and is moving West."

"West? Why, that's back our way. Why didn't they approach her?" asked Zakmon.

Gasahd scrunched the paper in his hand. "Because they were afraid."

The Tharadon waited expectantly on Gasahd, thinking that the general would affix a reply to its collar and state who it was going to. Tharadons, trained from the day they first got their feathers, were introduced to their Circle, the five or six people to whom it will be loyal to all their lives. The Tharadon was taught each of the persons' names and had to memorize what each person looked like so that the bird could pick them out of a crowd, if needed be. Tharadons had a keen sense of hearing and were summoned when needed by a whistle made of Telmari tusk that, when blown, could only be heard by their ears.

General Gasahd bent down to the Tharadon and tapped it three times on the head, signaling to the large bird that there was no return message at this time and that it could return to the man who sent it.

The Tharadon turned and stretched out its massive wings, which spanned over six feet across, and flew off into the sky.

"Remarkable," commented Captain Zakmon.

"They've been doing that for years," said Gasahd. "There's nothing remarkable about it."

Gasahd walked further into the camp, Zakmon closely following.

The camp of this wing of the Army was a small one. There were only three hundred men. A set up of stout tents for the lower-ranking officers like privates and sergeants, sat in rows in a square-like grid. The cabins meant for the senior officers like General Gasahd and Captain Zakmon were further away. Typically. But Gasahd liked his in the middle. Fortunately, Gasahd and Zakmon were the only senior officers for this wing and therefore were treated with much respect and awe.

"If I may ask, Sir," began Zakmon, "where are we going? I thought we were going to bring news to the others as to what we will do next to bring Aiyesha back."

"Why? To send out more men to try and capture her and then only have them come back and say they failed? No. I have a much better idea. Come."

Gasahd crossed his arms behind his back and Zakmon followed him through the camp. Men who weren't in training or meeting with others were sitting by fires, winding down for the night. Some were telling embellished tales of the fight against Morley and the *Raven*. Others were telling stories of other small battles and showing each other the scars received from them. When Gasahd walked by their tents and fires, they silenced, not wanting to appear as if they were having too good a time. Gasahd frowned upon leisure, at least in a military setting. He insisted that his men live, eat, sleep, and breathe the Army, nothing more. But his men weren't fooling him. He knew of the stories they told before bed.

I'll let them have their fun, he thought. *For now.* He knew they would not wish to be telling stories after the upcoming war. Most of these men wouldn't return.

They soon passed through the camp and, at the end, took two horses from the corral. Gasahd and Zakmon then rode deeper into the Coast of Seryn, to the female camp.

When they arrived, the girls were in their cabins, in bed. Gasahd and Zakmon dismounted their horses and walked past the female quarters to a small log cabin at the end of the row.

Without saying a word, the general produced a key from his left breast pocket and unlocked the padlock that held together the chain running from the door handle to a tree ten feet away. The door opened inward, so with the chain in place, and should the person inside break the door lock, they would not be able to open it. The chain fell to the ground with a metallic ching-a-ling. Gasahd used another key to unlock the door and went in.

Inside, it was dark, the drapes over the two front windows drawn to block out any moonlight. Beside the door was a small table and on it an oil lamp. Gasahd pulled a match from another pocket and lit the lamp. When the yellow light shone into the cabin, Zakmon gasped.

In the middle of the room, tied to a chair with coarse rope, blindfolded and gagged, was an old woman. Her head was bowed low and she shuttered with each breath she took. The air smelled of a mix of wood and sweat and human excrement. With Zakmon right behind him, Gasahd approached the woman, lamp in hand, and undid her gag. The old woman coughed and opened her mouth wide, stretching her jaw. Gasahd removed the blindfold from her eyes and she winced before squinting against the bright light of the lamp near her face.

"Hallo," greeted Gasahd.

"Who's this?" asked Zakmon.

"Samora G'Lammorahon," said the general, taking a step back when the woman spat at his feet. "At least, that's who she says she is and I'm quite sure she's telling the truth."

Zakmon noted the cuts and bruises all over Samora's face and neck.

"And she is here, why?" he asked, not wanting to question Gasahd too much, for the good general clearly knew what he was doing. He always did.

Samora glared at Gasahd, pain in her eyes.

"She had housed Aiyesha for a short time. A very short time; but a time nonetheless. My men grabbed her in Wesafeld and brought her to me." He turned to Samora. "Housing a fugitive is a high crime, old woman. You should know better than that."

She spat at him again, this time the wad landing on his nose. He slapped her instantly, hard across the cheekbone, stunning her. Gasahd wiped the spit from his face with his right hand then wiped his hand on his trousers. Then he hit her again.

"And what have you learned," asked Zakmon as Gasahd came over to him.

"That she doesn't know where Aiyesha is. She didn't even know who Aiyesha really was until we told her so. But I think this old crone knows more than she's telling."

Zakmon peered around him at Samora. The old woman was shaking her head, trying to clear it.

"What methods have you used?" asked Zakmon.

"Nearly all of them." Then, with a smirk, "If you look closely at the old hag's toes, you will see that her toenails are missing."

Zakmon looked at Samora's feet but because of the way the light was cast from the lamp, her feet remained in shadow and he couldn't see if her toenails were missing or not.

"Keep me here if you'd like," said Samora, her voice thin and weak. "But be careful. There's more here than what is seemed."

"What's she babbling about?" said Zakmon.

"Aw," said Samora, "does the general's pawn not like mouthy old women? Idiot! You house those weaker than you and try to draw information from them by hurting them. Do away with me, if you'd like, but it shan't lead anywhere. You will see."

This time Captain Zakmon came up to her and hit her. Samora screeched when the blow rocked her in her chair. The chair legs on her left side came back down to the floor with a woody *thud.*

Gasahd was at the door. "Gag and blind her," he told Zakmon, "then come outside."

Zakmon did as was told and while he rebound Samora, she hummed the whole while a creepy tune, the pitch of her voice reaching into that secret part of him. Gasahd heard the humming, too. The woman had hummed it when he first went to see her this morning. Once his task was completed, Zakmon told Samora to stay quiet before joining his superior outside. He closed the door.

The night was a warm one, but Zakmon was shivering.

"How did she get here so quick? Wesafeld is a far ride from where we are," said Zakmon.

Gasahd produced a small cigar from one of his many pockets and lit it. "She was brought in through the Back Way."

"The Back Way, Sir?"

A plume of smoke escaped Gasahd's lips. "That's right. I haven't yet told you of the Back Way, have I. Hmmm . . . " It didn't appear as though he would finish but after another puff of his cigar, he said, "We'll save that for another time, but I will tell you that the Back Way makes moving about much easier than on horseback."

Zakmon straightened himself and saluted Gasahd, his arms a X across his chest. "Permission to speak freely, Sir?"

"Always," he replied with a wave of his hand.

"Why did you bring me out here tonight to show me Samora when you could have easily told me about her in your quarters?"

Gasahd turned to him and placed a hand on his shoulder. "Because, my dear Captain, I want you to find out what else she knows." He paused. The muscles in his jaw tightened. "And I want it done tonight."

Zakmon knew what that meant and what he was expected to do to the old woman if she didn't start talking.

The general removed his hand and began walking away.

"Where are you going?" asked Zakmon.

Without breaking stride, Gasahd said, "To retrieve my girls."

CHAPTER XXX
Grek

It had been just over a week, but finally they were near Grek; no more than ten minutes away. And for that, Alan above all, was thankful. He could take no more of Mr. Nibbetts's bellyaching and complaints of feeling either too hot or too cold, too sweaty or too dry. Too sleepy or too awake. More than one hundred times during the past week had he told Peter to "Drop that sack of hair off and let him rot in the midday sun!" But Peter would always come to Mr. Nibbetts's rescue and defend him and ask Alan how *he* would feel if he were dropped off in the middle of nowhere, sick as a dog, with no place to go. Alan had no reply and instead cast his blank eyes in another direction, his chin held high, waiting for his next opportunity to complain about the fell creature and prove Peter's loyalty to Mr. Nibbetts as foolish. But Alan hadn't been completely heartless. The truth was he didn't want Mr. Nibbetts around simply because he didn't want to bring a parade of people into his once daughter-in-law's house. And, if she and her husband were as sick as Catina had said, to overburden Dara with the weight of guests and the bustle of a busy home would not be fair.

Alan knew Peter and Aiyesha enjoyed their time together, traveling the countryside, getting to know one another. However, each time Peter asked her something about what she had been doing these past few years, she always shied away from the subject as if afraid to speak of such things.

He wondered what Aiyesha wasn't telling them.

Catina was so glad they were home, she told Alan. So glad they were finally here.

Finally she could see her parents. Finally she would know if they would be all right or not. Finally there would be no more exhausting days on the back of a horse with little to eat and little sleep. Finally she would have more than one person whom she could talk to that would understand what she said.

Finally.

And so they arrived in Grek. It was midmorning and the sky was clear. The sun was warm against the skin and shone bright behind the travelers, casting their shadows long and deep before them.

Just before they entered the city, Alan's nostrils wrinkled. He leaned forward in his saddle, past Catina, so Peter could hear him.

"Peter?" he whispered.

Peter cocked his head back.

Alan's voice was low and cautious. "Beware of what you will see. There is a fell smell in the air. I just thought you should know."

"Smell? I can't smell anything," said Aiyesha, leaning in her saddle, closer to Peter.

"Alan's . . . gifted," said Peter, "and though blind, can sense things we cannot."

Mr. Nibbetts was sitting behind Peter, sharing the oat bag saddle, which was now empty. It had been for two days and the horses were hungry even though they grazed on grass on the way here.

"My stomach is not so good," said Mr. Nibbetts.

"Not now," said Alan at the furry creature's complaint.

"I wasn't talking to you." Mr. Nibbetts shot Alan a scowl—a bunched up face of fur.

Alan was mature enough not to reply and start childish banter, so the blind man sat back on his oat bag saddle and brought Catina into his arms. She welcomed his embrace.

Grek was deserted. The dusty streets were empty, the wooden buildings and huts and homes all lifeless with their drapes drawn and their doors closed. Peter was expecting to see some color—a lot of color—given that Catina had come into the drab city of Garathen in a such a beautiful and colorful dress. Instead, the homes and shelters and buildings in Grek were the color of the Earth: red and brown, black and gray, pale orange and tan. The houses were small and the buildings were small, too, standing only six feet taller than the houses.

Alan's nose wrinkled again. "It is getting worse," he said.

Peter smelled it, too. So did Aiyesha. The air was warm and the sharp scent of smoke was on the air. But something else was also mixed with that fiery scent.

Death.

The smell, Mr. Nibbetts said, reminded him of the mounds of bodies piled up where the Flistablare Forest once stood. The scent of lost friends and a life burnt to ash. It made his heart ache, he added.

The company kept riding, Catina instructing Alan as to where to go. Her grandfather told her he remembered and assured her they would be there soon.

They rode through the city, the smell of decay all around.

Peter stopped the horses. It was as if the company never left the Flistablare Forest. All they saw—save for Alan, though he knew what they were looking at . . . he just knew—was an open graveyard of men and women and children, all lined up along one side of the street. Their bodies were charred and black, their mouths—what was left of them—slightly open, their hair frizzled and burnt.

All were awestruck at the row of bodies on their right seeming to go on forever down the street.

"Alan," said Peter.

But Alan didn't answer. He was too busy soothing his crying granddaughter who had just gone to pieces at the sight of all she ever knew presented to her dead.

"Don't look at them," said Aiyesha, referring to the bodies.

Mr. Nibbetts hopped off the horse.

"Get back here," whispered Peter.

The furry little creature didn't obey and instead went over to examine the remains.

"What is he doing?" said Peter and he dismounted his horse. He went over to Mr. Nibbetts and grabbed him by his thick, furry arm. Before he could scold the creature, Mr. Nibbetts knelt in the dusty street next to the bodies and wept openly for them.

Looking on, Aiyesha asked Alan, "How far is it?"

The blind man lifted his head from his granddaughter's and said it was still a half-hour ride, as Catina's parents lived just outside of town.

Back near the bodies, Peter put a hand to Mr. Nibbetts's shoulder. "Let's go," he said.

"Me feel so awful," said Mr. Nibbetts as they walked back to the others. "Me've been complaining and complaining, but what that little one must be going through must be far worse."

"I would think so."

"Terrible me. Terrible me."

Back on Day, Peter turned and, seeing that Alan and Catina were sturdy on Night, he gave the reins a tug and they continued onward to Catina's home.

They came upon Catina's house a half-hour later and the humanette was the first one off the horses. She ran toward the house as fast as she could and went inside. The others dismounted and Alan, walking stick in hand, came up behind Peter.

"Thank you for taking us all this way," he said. "But there is one more thing I have to ask of you."

"Anything," said Peter.

Alan took a slow breath and gave Peter's shoulder an affectionate squeeze. "Stay outside. I do not yet know what is within and I do not want you three to see it, should it be anything awful. I had feared we may come upon a silent city, and I was right. I do not wish to be right about what else I am thinking. Stay here with the others and when I have need of you, I will call. Or, I will come out."

"Sure."

Peter stepped aside as the blind man walked past him, toward the house. The gray-paneled, wooden home stood still on the open farmland, the only sound the creaking of Alan's footfalls as he ascended the wooden boards that made up the front steps. On the porch the brown paint was cracked and peeling in places. The gray drapes were drawn and any sign of life the house may have once emitted was no longer there.

Alan went in.

Catina stood in the kitchen at the front of the house. She glanced up earnestly at her grandfather. In Grescalla, the two spoke.

"I did not want to go in alone," she said.

"I know. Let us call out for them."

"Mama! Papa!"

There was no answer.

"Mama! Papa!" she tried again. Still nothing. "Mama! Papa! Mama! Papa!"

"Let us find them," said Alan.

Catina took him by the hand down the narrow hallway that led to the rooms in the back of the small house. Her parents' bedroom was at the end of the hall on the left. The door was closed. Catina knocked. There was a faint moan within, nothing more.

Alan bent down to her.

"You go first," he whispered. "I will be right here."

"I am scared," she replied.

"I know," he said, "but there is no need to worry. Your mama and papa will be glad you are home."

That simple thought made her feel better. With a trembling hand, she reached for the door handle. She turned it and pushed the door open, slightly at first, then all the way.

Her parents lay in their low bed, without any blankets. Sweat glistened their faces and their skin was tanned and bumpy. Catina ran to them and threw her arms around them.

"Mama! Papa!" she said and burst into tears.

It took her parents a good moment to understand what was happening and, when the realization struck them, they weakly put their arms around her and the three cried together.

Standing in the doorway, silent, Alan shed a tear of his own.

After a time the three had no more tears to cry and Catina exclaimed, "I brought Grandfather!"

Dara and Michel looked around the room, their eyes never settling on Alan for they could barely raise their heads to see their own toes.

"Alan?" said Dara.

Alan came into the room and, feeling for the wall, leaned his walking stick against it.

"I am here, Dara. Michel," he said.

"How—" began Michel then coughed.

"Your daughter is a strong one and came all the way to Garathen to get me. She said you were sick."

Both parents fell into another fit of tears. Catina *was* a strong one. And a determined and brave little girl, at that.

"I cannot believe it," said Dara.

"Believe it," told Alan. The blind man, who suddenly appeared older than his years, drew near the bed and stopped when his toe touched the mattress.

"You can make them better, right, *Shinawa*?" said Catina. "Really, really better?"

Alan reached out and probed the air for her head. She took his hand in hers and brought it to her face. "Catina," he said. "Can—" He didn't finish. Painful sorrow with a hint of uncertainty stained his face.

"Catina," he began again, "can you run outside and see to it that our horses have something to eat?"

"But—"

"Please?"

Catina gazed longingly at her mother and father.

"Do as he says, Catina," said Michel. "We can have family-time soon."

"Please, Catina?" added Dara.

Upset, Catina obeyed anyway and went to get Day and Night something to eat. She would have to wait and see what Alan would do for her parents.

When he was sure Catina was gone, Alan turned to Dara and Michel. And in the Rolling-tongue, the two shared with him a tale of death.

Michel and Dara's voices were weak and to speak took great strength, as they were already having a difficult time simply breathing. They told Alan what they could.

It all began about three months ago when Michel had been working out in the field, hoeing the land, preparing it for another plantation. Under the hot sun, he had grown dizzy and fell to his knees. Within moments he recovered and thought nothing of it and went about his day as usual. However, when he returned home that night, he experienced another bout of dizziness. Dara had seen him lean up against the table in the kitchen to regain his balance and asked him what was wrong.

"It is nothing," he had said. "I am fine. I just got a little dizzy, that is all." And it was left at that.

In the days that followed, the dizzy-spells became more frequent and soon Dara was experiencing them as well. Every time Catina was around and one of them felt a bout of dizziness, they masked it by saying they were "thinking"—thus their blank stare when the dizziness struck—so as not to worry her. Soon, the dizziness in their heads ran down to their stomachs and other limbs. Within two weeks after first experiencing the dizziness out in the field, Michel and Dara were both too weak to work and spent their days indoors with Catina.

One day, when feeling better and going to the market in town, Michel caught wind that he and his wife weren't the only ones who had been experiencing unexplained bouts of dizziness and nausea. Nearly every one in the town was . . . except for the children. At least, not yet, anyway.

Another week passed and Michel collapsed in the kitchen while Catina was practicing her writing.

"Papa!" she exclaimed and ran to his crumpled form on the floor. She shook him and when he did not wake, she called for her mother and Dara came running into the room.

"Michel?" asked Dara. When no answer came, she immediately began to panic and as she fled out the front door to get help, a sudden bout of nausea struck her and she fell down the front steps, landing face first into the dirt ground at the bottom.

Catina screeched and ran to her mother's side.

Her parents regained consciousness a few moments after and the two barely made it to their bedroom. Catina tended to them for days, making sure they were fed and had what they needed.

Then that day came when Catina went to the market for her mother for fruit and vegetables, milk and honey, and something sweet as a reward for a job well done. The same day Dara had said, "I wish your grandfather were here."

That was also the day Catina had left home, unable to bear seeing her parents as sick as they were.

That night, when, after calling for Catina over and over with no response, her parents panicked and mustered up the strength to get out of bed and go looking for her. Their search was limited. After spending fifteen minutes outside, the two were too weak to look anymore and had gone in for the night. As the night wore on, the two stayed awake, hoping to hear the front door open and for their little girl to come home. But Catina never came.

The days became a week. A week into two. At the end of the second week, her parents mourned and grieved, thinking that Catina had gone into town on Lamara and fell ill, like some of the other children had, and died shortly after. Catina was counted as one of the lost and was missed, mourned, and fondly remembered. In spite of how desperately they wanted to go into town to find Catina's body, they could not.

However, the sickness came in waves, they noticed, and on some days they felt better than on others. A few weeks ago, well enough to move around, Michel and Dara had finally the strength to go into town for the final time. And it was there they witnessed the burning of bodies and the placement of lost loved ones on the side of the roads, a warning to any who visited the city to be off and save themselves before it was too late. Dara wept as she watched mothers set their dead children ablaze. Michel's heart went out the fathers who outlived their sons, never to teach them how to survive and take care of their women and families. But when Catina's body wasn't amongst the dead, and no one else seemed to have seen her, hope she was alive sparked again.

They retired to their bedroom that evening and hadn't left since, save to get a scrap of food to eat or a small cup of water to drink. Moments awake where spent in prayer, begging the Master for their daughter to be alive. The road that ran past their property, used by travelers and tradesmen, began to be used less and less. Then no one came by the farm anymore.

Not until today.

Alan recognized Catina's footsteps as she came back into the house and sat down on her parents' bed.

"Your eye," wheezed Dara. Perhaps the sickness had gotten to Catina, like the other children.

It had.

"I know," said Catina and covered it. "It hurts sometimes and my head gets sore." She turned to her grandfather. "Did you help them?"

Alan reached out and Catina guided his hands so that one was resting on each of her parents' faces. Their skin was hot and bumpy. Michel coughed.

The blind man smiled warmly at her and hated himself for lying. "They will be fine," he said.

Catina smiled big and wide. "Good. I did it. *We* did it."

Alan stood and straightened his dark clothing. "I am sorry," he said and turned to leave the room. He felt along the wall for his walking stick. When he found it, he turned back to them. "Catina, how about you visit with your parents for awhile and then let them rest and join me outside?"

"Okay," she said.

And Alan left.

Turning back to her parents, in Grescalla Catina said, "Did he help you? Did he make you better? Did I do good?"

Her step-father smiled at her. "Yes, dear. You did good. Very good."

"Thank you, Catina," said Dara.

Then it was worth it. She had succeeded. Her parents were going to be okay.

Just then, Michel coughed, his back arching up off the bed. When his body relaxed, it looked as though the life had been sucked out of him.

The two girls looked on worriedly.

"I am fine," he said after a moment of regaining his breath. He cleared his throat.

"What can I do?" asked Catina. "Can I get you anything? Something to eat?"

"No," her mother said. "Just stay here with us. That is all we need."

"Okay," said Catina and crawled onto the bed and snuggled in between her parents.

"How about you telling us what you have been up to lately and how you found your grandfather?"

"Okay."

She relayed the story of her going to Garathen and how Lamara passed on not far from home. Michel and Dara said they were saddened by the news because they, like Catina, loved Lamara and considered the mare a close friend. Catina explained that losing Lamara was hard for her, too. She told of how she was determined to find Alan and how she remembered the roads fairly well from when she traveled there. She spoke of how she found food—her mother made clear she didn't appreciate the fact that Catina stole the food; after all, Catina had been honest with her by bringing her the change that day long before; Michel, displeased as well, understood that Catina acted out of instinct and desperation and out of her will to survive. Catina explained how she slept on the side of the road and how the occasional passerby would offer her a ride. Catina did, however, keep her encounter with that one man a secret. She herself was still having a hard time believing it actually happened and didn't want to burden her parents with the news that she had taken another's life . . . even if it was out of survival.

Her mother asked her about her eye and what happened to it. Catina didn't know. One morning, after waking up alongside a road about one hundred-fifty miles from Grek, she felt a stinging pain behind her left eye and when she reached up to soothe it, she noticed that it was slightly swollen. Thankfully, today, there in her parents bedroom, her eye wasn't nearly as swollen as it once was.

Catina went on and told them how she met Peter, but left out the part about the Slummer, not wanting to upset them.

Michel and Dara at first expressed their dislike of the idea of their daughter taking a stranger as a friend, but when they heard of his hospitality of taking her in for the night and feeding her the next morning, they warmed up to him. Catina also stated how Peter brought her to see Alan and how they left soon afterward. She got especially excited when she spoke of the horses, Day and Night, and how they reminded her of Lamara and eased the pain of losing a friend so dear.

Catina skimmed over most of the long days on the road but emphasized she was thankful she had found Alan and that she was returning home. She was also quite proud of herself for accomplishing such a task, she added. She left out the darker parts, those of the palanthora beast . . . even the meeting of the fopphin on that trail in the dark. Then came Darim and the Festival of Armasulia—though Catina did not know the Festival's official name so she simply referred to it as the Party. She added that she liked the puppet show and all the dancing in the streets. The dancing was her favorite.

She told of how they met Aiyesha and, with a giggle, mentioned it seemed that Alan didn't like her tagging along but, like the good man he was, did his best not to show it. Catina thought that Aiyesha was just fine (except for that little episode involving the word "pretty"—she didn't tell her parents about that word though).

Peter had been the one to lead them home, she said, for Alan could not see and she didn't want to ask him why he couldn't see because she didn't want to be rude to her elder.

And so, finishing the tale, she ended with the meeting of Mr. Nibbetts and how she thought it was cute the way his face seemed to scrunch up each time he would say something and then Alan would tell him to be quiet. And, sometimes, for Catina's benefit, Alan would tell Mr. Nibbetts, "Cila mon tari!" which was "Shut your mouth!" in Grescalla.

And now she was in the present, lying in between her parents, happy to be home.

In Grescalla, she said, "What do you think?"

Her parents were speechless.

"I do not believe it," said Dara.

Michel was about to say something but his voice cracked. He coughed loudly.

Her parents fanned themselves with limp wrists, obviously hot. Catina was actually finding the room quite cool despite it being a hot day outside.

Dara rolled over onto her side and leaned over its edge. Alongside the bed was a tin bucket. She upchucked.

"Mama!" said Catina louder than she meant to.

Her mother threw up again, retching as she did. When the wave passed, she lay on the bed with her face still hanging over the bucket.

"Dara?" called Michel.

She didn't respond and threw up yet another time. Her lips were red with blood. Her body lurched and she threw up again . . . and again. This time, it wasn't bile or water that poured from her mouth. It was blood, murky red and slightly foamy.

"Catina, go get help," instructed Michel, his voice weak.

Catina sat up and wriggled herself toward the foot of the bed. When her feet touched the floor, her mother managed to squeeze out the words, "No. S-stay. P-please."

Catina didn't know what to do and looked earnestly at her father.

"Catina, go and get help," he said more slowly, emphasizing every word.

Again her mother told her to stay. Michel coughed and a low, rumbling burp escaped his lips. The room immediately filled with the smell of onion and garlic . . . and something else. Something . . .

Dara threw up again. Catina tried going over to her but the sight of throw up in the bucket caused her stomach to lurch and she had to look away.

For almost five minutes, Catina listened helpless from across the room as her mother emptied her guts into the bucket. Then Dara stopped and lay still, her face over the pail. Some of the brick-red throw up had splashed on the floor.

"It is okay, Mama," said Catina. "You will be fine. I will go clean it up. Just go back to sleep."

And Dara lay still and moved no more.

Alone with her step-father, on his side of the bed, Dara's body still lying with face poised over the bucket, Catina and Michel wept together at the loss of the most important woman in their lives.

"Why did she have to die, Papa?" asked Catina, crying into his breast. "She was fine a minute ago and now, and now . . . " It all came pouring out and her heart pounded in her chest. She wanted to get Alan and tell him what happened but she didn't want to leave her step-father because, if she did, what if when she returned the same thing happened to him?

"Do not worry, little one," he said between the tears. "She is with the Master, now."

"I know that, Papa, but it hurts because she is gone. Why did she have to die? What is happening? What, what?"

"I do not know, Sweetheart. Your mama had been sick for a long time. Now she is feeling all better and does not have to worry about being sick anymore."

"But, but . . . "

"Thank you for coming home," he said. "I know your mama was happy. And I know you know that, too."

Catina, despite the tears, forced a smile. It was good to *feel* that her mother was glad she had returned. She gave him a hug. Her embrace loosened when he coughed again.

"Oh, no, Papa. Not you, too," she said.

"I will be fine," he told her. "I will b—" He coughed again.

She stayed by his bedside for an hour after he drifted off to sleep, the time spent reflecting on what just happened, on her journey home, on what she was doing now: waiting by her step-father, hoping—praying—that he would get better.

"Papa?" she said, shaking him.

He didn't stir. It may have been the sound of her own tears that masked it, or it may have been the whirlwind of thoughts that stormed her mind and the memories that seemed so real that they took on a life of their own—but she hadn't realized her step-father had stopped breathing some time ago. There had been no final struggle with the sickness, no display, no sign that this was the end. He had simply died, peacefully.

He had been a good man and a good father though not truly her own.

Outside, Peter and Aiyesha stood away from the house, near the horses. Alan was with them and though Peter expressed that sitting on the front steps of the house would be far more comfortable than standing, Alan said they couldn't for it was customary for those except family to keep their distance from the home when someone within was ailing.

Mr. Nibbetts was lying on the ground near Peter's feet, once again complaining he was dying and there was no hope for him and that, when they left Grek, they should leave him there to rot in his misery.

Alan said he agreed.

The furry creature's complaints stopped when the front door creaked open and Catina came out running, flying into her grandfather's arms, wrapping her arms around his neck and pressing her head into his shoulder. It caught him off guard and he tumbled back with her on top of him.

"You were supposed to make them better," she said in Grescalla. "They were not supposed to die. You lied to me. You lied. You—" Tears poured forth.

Alan knew the onlookers didn't need to speak Grescalla to know what had just happened. Peter and Aiyesha knew. So did Mr. Nibbetts who once again said he was ashamed for talking of his own ailments so much.

And so the blind man and his granddaughter remained on the ground in each other's arms until Catina was all cried out and able to speak without breaking down. They sat up.

"I tried to help them, really I did," she told him.

"I know," said Alan.

"Why did you not save them? That is why I brought you. Is it because you cannot see?"

Alan closed his eyes, hiding their blank white stare. "No. There was nothing I could do for them, Catina. They were sick and what they wanted most was not to get better, but to see you again. And see you they did. I am sure that it was the thought of you, the memories of you, that kept them alive these many weeks. All they wanted was you. They loved you, Catina. Very much. And, I am sure, when they saw you, they felt a whole lot better."

"But why did they have to die?"

"For that, I do not have an answer. But they are with the Master, now. That is all that matters. Now they know you are okay, and they are not sick anymore."

"That is what Papa said when Mama died. He said that she was with the Master and that she was not sick anymore."

"And he was right. Now he, too, is with Him and is happy."

"It is not fair." She stamped her foot on the dirt. "Just not fair!" Thick tears rolled down her cheeks.

"I know, Catina. I know." He reached out his arms and they held each other.

There was nothing left to say. At least, not now.

Peter's Journal: A Sad Day

Aupil 26, the Year 134, the Fifth Aeon

I'm off alone, sitting on a rickety old wagon about thirty paces from the farm-house. Alan is off with Catina. What they are talking about, I don't know, but I assume it's about what just happened.

I wish I could say I can relate to Catina, losing your parents. But I can't. My parents died when I was too young to remember. The only memories I have are from what my aunt told me while I was growing up. I admire Catina. At least she had her parents, even if just for the first six years of her life.

The mood here is a mellow one and today's a sad day. We are all tired from our journey—except for Aiyesha. She acts as if she's used to such hard travel, but she won't tell me anything about herself; at least, the kind of things I'm interested in, like how she wound up in Darim and why. Whenever we start getting along, she distances herself from me. It feels like she's hiding something.

Enough of that.

I'm unsure as to what to say to Alan. His only granddaughter just lost the two most important people in her young life, and, on top of it, lost her father for the second time. Alan will have to take care of her now, I suppose. I wonder what will happen to the farm? There isn't anyone here to take over or pass it on to. They're all dead! I don't know what is happening but one thing is clear: an illness is in the air. And it's not just here in Grek, either. I'm sick, Catina's not well, and Alan, though he doesn't say anything, is looking rather pale. Even for him. Then there's Mr. Nibbetts (at least I think that is how you spell his name, though I've never asked him), a furry little Flistablare (at least that's what Alan called him), who's the loudest, most self-absorbed thing I know. Even he's sick, and he's not even from around here. None of us are. Except for Catina. The only one among us who seems in perfect health is Aiyesha. I hope she stays well. And then there's—

Wait. Mr. Nibbetts is coming over. I'd better put this away. He's probably come to complain.

We'll see.

CHAPTER XXXI
The Farewell

The Farewell took place in the afternoon. The sky was clouded over and all was grim. Peter had dug Michel's grave in the back of the house and Aiyesha had dug Dara's, as was the custom in Grek, where a female would dig the grave for a female, and a male the grave for a male.

"Why were all those bodies burned when we first rode in?" Peter had asked Alan as the blind man watched them work.

"Tradition, Peter, as it is with so many things these days. Long ago, it is said—and I mean a long time ago—seven plagues had befallen the Earth and those who were well enough, in the hopes of ridding themselves of getting any worse, burned the bodies of the sick to dispose of the illness, destroying the body carrying the disease. What you saw when riding in today was homage to that. And, as well, when someone in this part of the World dies because of illness, their bodies are burned so that their spirit, should they have contact with the family after they die, will not pass on the illness to them and risk the loss of another life. Today, I am breaking tradition. No child should have to witness the bodies of their parents being burned, no matter what History dictates. Yes, I could do it in secret while you kept Catina away, but I know that little girl and she would insist on being present as I disposed of the bodies. No. Today we will have a more civil Farewell, and one that will be fondly remembered by all present."

Once the graves were dug and the bodies placed within the holes and covered with dirt, Alan sent Peter to get Catina, who was at the front of the house, sitting on the front steps, wanting some time to be alone. They didn't know where Mr. Nibbetts was, but just as Peter returned with Catina in his arms, Mr. Nibbetts was right behind them. He must not have been far from Catina. Alan muttered to Peter that he hoped Mr. Nibbetts, if he had talked with her, focused his attention on her and not on himself.

Dara's and Michel's graves were side by side, Dara on the left, Michel on the right. Alan stood in the middle at the head of the graves, Catina beside him, his arm around her. The others stood at the opposite end and looked on.

The service was conducted in such a way that it benefited everyone. Alan would say a statement or phrase in Grescalla, and then translate it into the Common-tongue so that the others would understand. Though all save Catina and Alan did not know Michel and Dara, all were touched by what the blind man had to say.

"Catina asked me why this has happened, why her parents had to leave us. I did not have an answer, for Death is such a random thing. It can come at any moment, come to any person whenever it wishes. Is Death a force of its own? Can it decide whom to take away from us next? I decline to think so but that is not to say it does not exist. We live in strange times and anything can happen, including the passing of loved ones when we least expect it." He paused. Moisture rimmed Alan's eyes. He didn't wipe it away and remained strong for Catina. "Michel came into the lives of Dara and Catina when they needed him most, after the loss of my son, Mica. He provided for them, supported them, encouraged them. And he was welcome in their home. Dara, who gave love a second chance after my son passed on, embraced Michel as if he were her first husband and not her second. Catina—my *Shinali*—embraced Michel as a father and allowed her mother to marry him because she knew that Dara needed a friend and a man to hold her heart. Dara schooled Catina and taught her to be independent, responsible, and most importantly above all, she was a perfect example of what a loving mother should be." He drew Catina closer to him and gave her an affectionate squeeze. "I have no answers for this little one. I wish I did, but I do not. But what I do know is this: the Master watches over us all, both in life and in Death. And He cares more for us than we can possibly imagine and for that we are forever grateful. Take comfort, my dear *Shinali*, that your parents are looking at you from the Prairie of Everlasting Peace. They will walk with you for the rest of your days, as do all the spirits of those we love when they pass on. We are never alone."

Alan knelt down and scooped some dirt into his hand. He gave the handful to Catina and told her to sprinkle a little on each of her parents' graves, starting with her mother's. She obeyed then covered her face and cried.

Those watching said their own prayers to the Master for Dara and Michel's souls, and then said a prayer for themselves so that they may live on for many more years to come. The only one who didn't pray was Peter. He still wasn't sure if he believed in the Master or not, but he did take comfort in knowing that, because of what Alan said, his parents were watching him and guiding him through his life. For the first time in a long time, he didn't feel alone.

Rain began to fall shortly after the Farewell concluded. Immediately Mr. Nibbetts ran for cover in the barn at the rear of the property.

Alan picked Catina up and told Peter and Aiyesha that they best get indoors before it started to pour.

"That is one thing about Grek," he said. "One minute sunshine, the next minute a blast of rain."

They walked toward the porch, Alan taking the lead. He found his way across the property with relative ease and Catina guided him toward the rear door. They entered. Peter followed with Aiyesha and before they went up the three steps leading to the back porch, Aiyesha turned back and looked at the property quizzically.

"What?" said Peter.

"Nothing," she said, turning back to him. "I was just wondering, since this is a farm, where the animals are."

"I don't know. Maybe they ran off when their masters got sick."

"Maybe." She nodded in the direction of the barn. Mr. Nibbetts was peeking out from behind one of the barn doors. "Is he coming?"

Peter waved him over. Mr. Nibbetts shook his head furtively and scurried back inside the barn. "I guess not."

"Then let's go in," she said and brushed past him as she went up the steps.

Just before Peter turned to go in, he saw the Man in the Gray Cloak staring at him across the property.

Peter ran after him.

Summoning all strength, Peter ran with abandon, trying to catch up to the Man in the Gray Cloak. The figure stood there, his face completely covered, still seeming to glare at Peter like he had in Darim when Peter spotted him in the Square. No matter how hard Peter pushed himself, he couldn't seem to run fast enough. He dug deeper, his thighs aching, the muscles beginning to burn. Behind him he could hear Aiyesha calling. He didn't look back but kept going, trying to reach this phantasmal figure that had appeared before him more than once, now.

The Man in the Gray Cloak was drawing nearer, but he was still far off.

The expanse of property behind Catina's house spanned some two acres, small for a farm but large for one trying to cover its distance. Faster, now, Peter's legs burned hotter as he pushed himself. He began panting. The Man in the Gray Cloak was about an acre away. The hood over his face seemed to have eyes that peered right through him. He pressed onward. The Man stared. Peter's legs were tiring quick despite his efforts. He couldn't force himself to go faster. But he ran. Aiyesha's voice behind him again, but muted by the whistling of the air blowing past his ears.

"Who are you?" shouted Peter when he thought the Man could hear him.

The Man offered no reply and instead only glared from behind the hood's shadow.

Nearer, now. Almost there. *Come on,* Peter encouraged himself. He dug his feet as deep as he could into the earth, propelling himself forward. The Man was about fifty long-strides away. Peter found himself slowing as he drew nearer. A shock of emptiness filled his chest and gut, the presence of the Man ripping the life from him. He slowed even more. Twenty paces. Almost there. Aiyesha's calling becoming more clear as the air slowed about him. Just as he was about to be face to face with the Man, the Man disappeared and the only thing Peter saw was the empty farmland belonging to the farmer across the way.

Defeated, Peter sank to his knees and caught his breath.

He didn't know what happened.

When Aiyesha finally caught up to him, he had forgotten all about her, hadn't heard her calling his name repeatedly. Peter got to his feet and turned quickly to face her.

Her mouth was creased with concern. "What's wrong?"

"I'm losing my mind," he said and covered his face with his hands.

Peter sat with Aiyesha on the rear porch of the farmhouse, sheltered from the rain by the roof's overhang above. His forearms were on his knees, his head hanging between them. Behind him Aiyesha paced.

"I don't know what to do," he said. "That's three times, now, I've seen him, it, whatever."

"The Man in the Gray Cloak?"

Peter glanced up at her, annoyed. Of course he was talking about the "Man in the Gray Cloak." He had spent the last half-hour talking about him. "Yes, *him.* And each time I see him he has this hood that hangs over his face, hiding his face, though I can still see him looking at me. It's like something out of a bad dream. You know, when you *know* something about something or someone even though you haven't any proof. I *know* this man is looking at me. Even *through* me."

"I know we've been over this already," said Aiyesha, "but I didn't see anything. I went to hold the door open for you and when I glanced back, you took off down the field." From behind, she put a comforting hand on his shoulder. "Peter, there wasn't anything—or anyone—there."

He raised his head. "But there *was* someone there. At least, I think there was. And this happens, too, after I see the Man. It begins to feel as if I *didn't* see him and that it was all in my head. But I know I did. I had to. I've never seen anything that wasn't there before in my life. Why would I start seeing things now? Explain that to me."

"I can't," she said.

"Then what are we going to do?"

Aiyesha peered in through the window. Alan was inside, sitting on a long, cowhide covered couch. Catina was using his lap as a pillow, sleeping, too tired from all her crying.

"We can't tell Alan," she said "that's for sure. At least, not now. This day has already been too much for him and for Catina. We shouldn't add to it; at least not until we know more. The most important thing to do right now is stay calm. You can't let this overwhelm you, Peter. Keep your head clear. There is always an explanation for everything, even for the things we can't explain, as contradictory as that sounds. It may not be an explanation of words but a revelation of some sort. It will present itself to us in time." She then knelt down on the hard, wooden, weathered boards just behind him. She whispered into his ear: "I believe you."

Peter didn't say anything.

The two remained on the porch for the next hour. Slowly, the rain eased into a drizzle, then, finally, stopped. Like a badger out of his hole, Mr. Nibbetts peeked out from the barn and held a leathery hand out to confirm that the rain had completely ceased. Seeming to be satisfied he wouldn't get wet, he marched toward the farmhouse, strutting, proud he had kept himself dry.

"Good afternoon to you," he said to Peter and Aiyesha once he arrived at the base of the steps.

"Mr. Nibbetts," said Aiyesha.

Peter kept quiet.

"Why so sour?" asked Mr. Nibbetts.

When it was apparent that he wouldn't answer, Aiyesha stepped in for him. "Peter isn't feeling too well and is tired. Why don't you go inside and let him rest?"

"Inside? Inside? Why would you stay out here if me'm supposed to 'let him rest'? Besides, me am sick, too, and me need some air as well. So me will sit beside him and together, we'll get better. Why don't *you* run inside?"

Peter laughed. Aiyesha frowned at his chuckle and at Mr. Nibbetts's remark. "Now see here—" she began.

"O, my head!" bellowed Mr. Nibbetts, the rear of his hand pressed upon his forehead. "Me think me am going to faint. Someone catch me."

As he teetered, Aiyesha said, "Fine. Fall over." She looked down at Peter. "I hope you two make each other feel better." And she went in.

Once the door latched closed, Peter chuckled again and Mr. Nibbetts stopped his show. The furry creature came and squeezed himself in between Peter and the left wall of the farmhouse.

"Why do you do that?" asked Peter.

"Do what?" said Mr. Nibbetts incredulously.

"Why do you act so sick? You're not fooling anyone."

Mr. Nibbetts straightened his back and took a healthy lung full of air. "Because," he said, "me don't know how else to handle it. Me really am dying, you know. Me've never felt this way before, not in me entire life. We Flistablare, in our entire History, have never suffered. No war, no famine, no disease, no nothing. We are not built for such hardships. You say me am 'sick,' me say me am 'dying.' Which one is true? 'Sick' or 'dying'? It's the same thing to me."

"But there is a difference," said Peter. "One will end your life."

"No. They both will end your life, depending on the severity of each. Me've heard of Men who've died of the flu. So, they were 'sick' and then passed on. Me've heard of men who were thought dead but only sick." He then whispered shamefully, "Me don't mean to be rude, but look what happened today. Catina's parents died because they were sick. Remember the bodies when we first entered town? All sick. All dead."

"But not all illness kills."

"But this one does, whatever it is. So, to answer your question of why do me do that? Because, if me am to die soon, me'd rather do it with a smile on me face than a scowl."

Then with a grin, Peter added, "But you never smile. You pout and whine."

"Me smile on the inside," said Mr. Nibbetts, "where it hurts the most. Me let you think on what me mean by that."

But he didn't have to think on it. Sometimes things hurt us so much—in Mr. Nibbetts's case, the death of loved ones—that sometimes all you could do to make yourself feel better was to point out the absurdity in a situation that seemed to keep on going wrong. And though Peter had only met Mr. Nibbetts a few days before, he was starting to see there was more to the furry creature than just a belly-aching complainer. There was, he hesitantly admitted, a bit of wisdom.

The freshly fallen rain glistened off the grass. The clouds began to thin.

"You are a strange one, Mr. Nibbetts," said Peter.

And the two didn't say any more.

The world of Catina Nabari had come crumbling down. All hopes of coming home to a warm bed, to good food, to someplace safe, to love . . . had diminished when she first laid eyes on her parents. And now they were gone, too. There was nothing here for her. No family, no future. Just the pain and memory of a life—lives—that ended. Where she would go from here, she didn't know.

It was early evening.

Alan was outside on the front porch, she saw, probably letting her sleep in peace on the couch. But she couldn't sleep. Not today and, she knew, not tonight. Her head pounded from her tears. The flesh at the corners of her eyes stung. She was so very tired but sleep, no matter how hard she tried to relax, would not come. She kept seeing her parents lying there, looking at her, so happy she had returned. But there had been more to their gaze than mere thankfulness for her safety. There had been a desperate plea that her bringing Alan to them would truly make the illness go away.

And Alan didn't help them. Was it because he didn't know how? No matter what words he expressed to her, none of them brought her comfort. She hated him for letting her parents die; but she loved him because simply, well, she just did. He was her grandfather, her *Shinawa.* Yet she had put all her trust in him, all her hope. Catina remembered that long road to Garathen and all that happened along the way. The memory of the man was clear now. How could she lose the two people she loved most after all she had been through? How could it be fair? Couldn't the Master have taken care of her? Shown her love and saved her parents' lives?

No, she decided. He couldn't. He hadn't. If He had, her parents would still be alive.

But her parents were gone.

She sat up on the couch and looked across the hall, past the kitchen, and out the open door at Alan. He sat on the first of the two front steps, his knees up, his hands across them. His sword lay beside him, pointing out toward the road. Alan was the only person she could turn to, even if she was still upset. Where Peter and Aiyesha and Mr. Nibbetts were, she didn't know. They had left some time ago.

Catina lay back on the couch and closed her eyes and relaxed her body. Tears rolled from her eyes.

—

In the blackness that was his sight, Alan replayed his conversation with Dara and Michel in his mind. There was nothing he could do for them, he knew. Not when he was like this, a blind man who was still getting used to not being able to see. If he could have seen her parents, maybe then he could have assessed the problem better. But he had been helpless and was careful not to show it. He also knew that Dara was aware of his condition. He had told her of that terrible encounter with the Slummers in one of the letters he'd written her. He knew that she knew he could not help them. Not without sight. But was there something else he could have done? Could he have asked them to describe the pain they felt? Could they have told him where it hurt the most and what the symptoms were? Maybe. But could he have helped them? He was not a Helper and not a miracle worker. He was just a man, and a simple one at that despite all he had learned while abroad in the days he used to travel. Sometimes illness came and there was no stopping it. But these thoughts did not ease the burden on his heart. Now he had a little girl to tend to.

He was all she had left.

For the first time on this journey, Alan wished he knew what to do next.

Sounds drew him out of quiet thought.

Over there, not far ahead, hooves on the dirt. Alan grabbed his sword and got up with a start. The sound of hooves drew nearer.

"Who goes there?" snarled Alan, his sword held out at the ready.

"Easy, Alan, it's me," said Peter as he rode up, presumably on Day.

The other two were with him, he knew. He could hear Mr. Nibbetts's breathing. And Aiyesha—she smelled like Spring.

Alan lowered his sword. "What did you find?"

"No one. Not a soul. The entire city is empty, save for the bodies along the streets. There were only a few not burned, probably the few that lived long enough to cremate the others."

"The Last Daughter," said Alan, thinking on Catina.

He had sent the three of them into the city to see if anyone could be found and, if they needed help. He also wanted to see if anyone still alive knew Catina and perhaps, if they were well enough, take over the farm once all had settled down. A part of Alan's heart lightened knowing that he would be taking his *Shinali* back with him to Garathen.

"Excuse me?" said Peter.

Alan shook his head. "Nothing. Did you find any supplies?"

Aiyesha dropped down off her horse. "Some, but not many. Seems as though the markets had shut down a long time ago and no one's rode through here for weeks. All the fruits and vegetables were rotten. There was no meat. There was some food, though, like bread and rice, but we didn't want to chance them being infected so we left them. The bread was rotten, anyway. We did, however, get saddles for the horses and some blankets." She gestured towards the horses. Alan heard her arm move through the air. When he arched an eyebrow, Aiyesha said, "Sorry. I forgot."

"It is all right. I am sure the saddles are fine ones."

Mr. Nibbetts plopped off the horse and walked about, the sound of skin rubbing fur loud and clear. "Aye, me arse is killing me."

Like everything else, Alan wanted to say but didn't. Instead, he said, "Good. We have some food left from Darim. We will have to hunt or fish on our way back if we are to stay alive."

"How's Catina?" asked Peter.

Alan turned toward the farmhouse then turned back to him. "She is tired. She is resting on the couch inside. I did not want to disturb her so I came out here."

Mr. Nibbetts yawned loudly. Peter and Aiyesha looked at him.

"What?" asked the Flistablare.

They turned back to Alan.

"How long are we to stay here?" asked Peter.

"Until Catina wakes. I do not want her here any longer than she has to be." The weight of the day settled upon him and a foul taste filled his mouth. He spat on the ground just off to the side. "We leave at nightfall."

Peter nodded. "Good. It's time to go home."

CHAPTER XXXII
Between the Purple and the Gray

With a burst of speed, Thalok propelled himself forward, drawing all the more nearer to Peter. Each time he tapped himself into his quarry's mind, the faster he was able to move, the more he was able to *feel* his prey. The pull came from deep within his chest, a hot, burning lurch, pulling him East, towards Grek. His fingers tingled with heat, as well. But Thalok was still far away. He had strayed North and, for a short time, lost Peter, lost the scent.

Thalok ran, his legs moving swift and sure, never tiring of breath, for he didn't need to breathe. The land opened up in front of him in a lush expanse of green, shimmering under the mid afternoon sun. Mountains lined the horizon, their caps heavy with snow in a dazzling white, their bases creased with dark shadows and sharp turns. And though the scenery rushed by him in a blur, he was still able to see its detail clearly, as if he were standing still, gaping at nature in its finest form.

Thalok moved, his gray cloak billowing out behind him, his head remaining covered by his large hood. He did not like the sunlight shining in his eyes. He preferred a dimmer surrounding, one lined with black and purple and gray. Shadows were his friend.

Peter was near, but how near? Fifty miles? One thousand? It was impossible to tell. At some moments the *drawing* that pulled Thalok toward Peter burned like a fire within his chest, and at other times, the flames cooled, flickered, almost blew out. His fingers sometimes felt as if they were freezing. Why was Peter so hard to track? Thalok began to wonder if he had been away from the Island of the Dead too long and if his strength was beginning to leave him. No. It couldn't be. He was able to be gone for weeks at a time before needing to return to the Island.

As if that notion was a curse upon himself, Thalok saw the air about him swirl and swoon, separating into fine lines of gray and purple mist, like a light rain. The mist wrapped around him. He slowed his run as the grass before his feet disappeared, the mountains in the horizon melting away. Muted purple and gray splashed like paint being spackled on boards before his eyes. Thalok had, unexpectedly, transcended back to Yem Batu.

He glanced down at the hem of his cloak. It hung there, long as ever over slick ground composed of round objects that were eyes, sticky with a clear slime. The Sea of Eyes, the souls of those who died laid out before him, staring up at him helpless, in an endless field of death and longing. Thalok rarely came out here, and when he did, it was not by choice. And Thalok knew that today, he was really here, really on the Island and that this was not some sort of manifestation in his mind. The Void-man had forced him to return through the Border and back to Yem Batu. Borders could exist anywhere. Could.

Thalok turned around and saw that he was not far from the Sea of Eyes's sandy shore. On the shore was a towering mountain, black and terrible, its summit hidden by purple mist and twisted lightning. Thunder rumbled in the clouds. Thalok made his way to it and journeyed toward the Void-man.

He didn't know why he had been called back.

—

On the Great Wall, the Void-man watched Thalok find his way across the Sea of Eyes, back to shore. In this Realm, Thalok couldn't move as swiftly as he could out there in the World. Here, he was just another Qinoran, nothing more.

The Void-man waited for Thalok to arrive.

—

It took awhile, but Thalok was making headway along the Sea toward the shore. Every few feet nearer to the shore, he seemed to move a foot back, as if the shore was pushing him away with a billow of hot air. The Eyes were slick and finding purchase on them was near impossible. But Thalok had once moved along the Sea of Eyes long ago so he knew what to expect when walking upon them. The trick was to step carefully, plant the heel first then the ball of the foot, then the toe, and take your time. The soles of his feet tensed as a charge of static emanating from the Eyes seemed to pull him downward into the Sea. He resisted their tug and kept going.

Soon he would be at the shore.

Time passed, though on the Island of the Dead Time was meaningless and there were only moments and what could be perceived as "time" did not truly exist—in Death there was no Time, only the passage of existence. Thalok took his first step onto the shore. His foot gripped the sand immediately and it felt like he had just made the transition from walking on a sheet of oily glass to walking on wood laced with sticky sap. Why the Void-man made Thalok walk all the way back to Him was not clear. Thalok easily could have been called back, arriving on the stone steps like the last time he was here. The only explanation, at least in Thalok's mind, was that the

Void-man was displeased with him. And if that was the case, there would be no one to help him.

Thalok walked along the shore by the skirt of the mountain until he found a gap in the rock so he could make his way up. Thankfully, the Void-man was not at the top of the mountain but only somewhere in the middle. Thalok could never remember where. It was a trick of the mind the Void-man placed on him so that, should He wish to be left in peace, Thalok could not disturb Him, even in matters of grave importance. Only when Thalok saw the Purple Eye on the face of the mountain would he remember which winding path along the mountainside to take in order to find the way into the Void-man's den.

So Thalok climbed, searching for the Purple Eye.

The Void-man stared at the Great Wall and watched as Thalok drew near.

A blur of deep purple was barely seen just beyond the next turn in the mountain wall. Thalok climbed and kept his eyes on the blur, not wanting to lose sight of it. The Purple Eye was a mysterious thing and, he learned in the past, could easily be lost if one was not watching it, as though it were constantly in motion against the mountain's face, mixing into the lighter purple of the fog on the air.

The dark purple blur fixed in his vision, Thalok rounded the curve on the mountain's face and glanced up to see the Purple Eye standing prominently over a smoothed-out surface in the rock, its glassy stare gazing skyward, almost in longing. The smooth surface on the rock's face was about four feet tall by four feet wide. The entrance.

Thalok removed his hood, as sign of respect for Whom he was about to see. As if acknowledging that Thalok knew he was on Holy ground, the smooth surface coruscated in ripples of black rock and purple glimmers.

The door opened.

The inside of the cave was monstrous. Surely this could not be the same cave he had been in before when speaking to his Master. But it was . . . different. Things on the Island were not what they seemed. They shifted about, moved, what was once a tall mountain could become a small one, what was once a boulder a mere pebble. Storms of Purple and Gray Fog would surface within the twinkle of an eye and diminish just as quickly. Chaos was routine, and Random was order.

It was dark but Thalok didn't need light to see. His eyes, used to the dreary and dim atmosphere of the Island, were accustomed to the dark, as in the dark was where he spent most of his time. Finding his way inside this gigantic cavern would be easy. Besides, he would only need to follow the Voice that called to him in his heart to find the Void-man.

And so Thalok went on.

Inside there were steps of stone, crannies and crevices in the rock and in the walls. The stone was damp and had a fell smell. Thalok minded his feet and progressed up the steps to where he knew the Void-man sat waiting.

Thalok didn't know fear but he was afraid today. Not once in his entire service to the Void-man had he been unexpectedly called back—transported back—to the Island. He decided it best to keep a tight rein on his composure and act as if nothing was out of the ordinary. What the Void-man wanted, the Void-man would surely let him know.

And so on Thalok went.

Not long after, feeling a renewed strength coursing through his body from being back on the Island, Thalok was at the winding stair he had been on earlier when the Void-man had asked him for his report on Peter. Thalok paused a moment and centered himself, drawing on his inner strength and determination. He would get through this. He was Qinoran, strong and proud and did not know fear. The heavy boot of his right foot moved first and planted itself firmly on the stone stair. Then the left one followed, and so on, each step he took growing all the more sure of its movement until he was at the top.

The Void-man sat in a large, stone throne before the Great Wall—which was now just a glossy black surface on the rock face inside the cavern—the chair turned away from the top of the stair so that Thalok could not see Him.

A flash of purple lit up the room. Thalok shielded his eyes at the blast and when he removed his hand, he saw something that had not been in the round room before: a large, beige candle, about two feet high and one foot wide in diameter. Upon it was a brilliant purple flame that did not dance but only stood there prominently, the heat from its flame reaching to where Thalok stood some eight feet away.

Thalok knelt and bowed his head. "I am here, my Lord." A flush of heat swept over his body. From the candle? No. Something else. Guilt perhaps?

The Void-man sat on His throne and did not speak. Thalok was discomforted by the silence.

And then, "Why haven't you killed him, Thalok?"

Because I have not yet reached him, he wanted to say but any slighting of his Lord would end in a severed head. Thalok held his tongue. "I'm sorry, my Lord, but I'm moving as fast as I can."

"No," said the Void-man. "You moved as fast you *wished.* You spend your time planting yourself in his mind, toying with him, before completing the task assigned."

The Void-man's remark was partially true, but Thalok's methods were his own and he did not like them being questioned. If it weren't for his ability to leave the Island then the Void-man would have no one to turn to, no one to kill Peter.

"I'm sorry, my Lord, but as you know, he is hard to track and placing myself in his mind is the only way to establish a link. Without it, I am like a treasure-hunter without a map. I am lost, Sir."

There was a shifting in the Void-man's chair but Thalok could not see Him. "Do not take me for a fool, Thalok. Do you not remember that by you living within my Realm, you are also bonded to me? Have you forgotten that I know the workings of your mind? I also know that this 'link' you speak of is stronger than you let on so don't play me like you would play your prey." His voice dropped low and was as hard as steel. "I want Peter's head before the next full moon, as it is called out in the World. Am I understood?"

Thalok, his head still low, shook. The Void-man was asking the impossible and for the first time in their long relationship Thalok was beginning to see the Void-man may not know as much as he once thought. Thalok was different from the other Qinorans and there was more Black in him than Purple, thus altering his bond to the Void-man. The Void-man was only bonded to the Purple within, and not to the other side and, in Thalok's case, his *stronger* side.

Finding Peter was more difficult than any other being or beast he had ever tracked. Peter's presence and whereabouts were as elusive as a dog trying to pick up the scent of its master who was in a town far away. But the "link" was working. It was only a matter of time.

"Yes, my Lord. I understand," said Thalok and, taking a chance, stood. The Void-man didn't seem to mind his straightening himself.

"Don't fail me, Thalok," said the Void-man. "There is much weighing on your success. More than you could ever dream."

"Yes, my Lord." Thalok bowed and asked if he could have leave. But before he was permitted, the Void-man had one last thing he wished to say.

"The Qinorans are counting on you."

Thalok descended the mountain, moving swifter as he descended than he had when going up.

"Question my methods," he muttered to himself. "You have no idea what I'm capable of."

Thalok had learned long ago to separate the Purple and Black within him into sections. He could bring to surface what he wanted in his Purple side and that which he wished to remain hidden, would remain in the Black. It was a remarkable skill he told no one of, not even his own people. The other Qinorans knew Thalok was different, but as to *how* different, that would remain a mystery until Thalok's last day. He kept to himself mostly, and his ways were a secret told only to himself.

He was soon at the bottom of the mountain and was walking along the shore. His mind busy, he had forgotten to replace the hood upon his head. He pulled it over his head and adjusted it so it sat properly. Now comforted by the concealment the hood brought him, he went along the shore to where he had turned off on it when coming off the Sea of Eyes. He needed to find a Crossing and the one on the Sea was nearest.

A Crossing was a portal into the World. The only others who could cross onto the Island and leave were the Black, but the Void-man wished to have nothing to do with them. However, there was one bargain that had been made long ago. The workings of that deal were elusive to Thalok and he did not dwell on it, but he got the distinct impression that the deal would bring certain doom to the Island should there be a disagreement of some sort. The Black still had a claim on Death. It was a part of them.

Back on the Sea of Eyes, Thalok stepped slowly, preventing himself from slipping across the oily surface.

Spotting a Crossing in the Purple Fog was impossible . . . unless you knew *what* you were looking for. And Thalok knew how to find one. The fog swirled around him in advancing and retreating puffs of purple and gray. Two steps forward, one step back was his walk upon the Eyes. But he would reach the Crossing, and when he did, he would find Peter and act quickly.

A Crossing. A Crossing. A Crossing should be coming up just—

His trained eye could see it in the distance, a fine and scattered mist of navy blue against a veil of purple fog.

He moved toward it.

Two steps forward, one step back.

CHAPTER XXXIII
The Sickness Takes Hold

Catina watched her house fade into the distance as they traveled along the dirt road, the shroud of night stealing it from view. She would never return there again, she knew. At least, not anytime soon. The scent of rain still on the air was doing little to ease her heavy heart. What had it all been for? She had come all this way . . . only to lose her parents. But that's how death was. Catina just wished she knew how to deal with the loss. All she felt right now was a deep remorse for her parents, and a deep longing to be with them, just like before—before they got sick. Little time had been spent with them when she returned home and she would never see their faces again, never feel her mother's touch or see her step-father smile at her, just to tell her they loved her.

Catina prayed to the Master that Alan's love would be enough to sustain her through her grief and replace the void that was now in her heart.

She turned her eyes forward to the road ahead, deciding never to look back. That was the last she saw of home.

Her body wobbled from side to side as they road, Night moving rhythmically beneath her.

She asked Alan, "Don menne tee nawa zel?" *Are you my papa now?*

He gave her a hug from behind. "Rana ko. Semba co rone lanat mon nawa, rosta le Michel rone ru lanats mone. Mel semba li wal mon Shinawa qu li wal rimta cimi Shinawa semba tristah dom ro wal. Fen li yomla unsa coum, mel ren li bani talmo anila. Semba li yomla yu fa menne. Frola." *No. I can never replace your papa, same as Michel never fully replaced yours. But I will be your* Shinawa *and will be the best* Shinawa *I know how to be. It will take some learning, but we will have something special. I will take care of you. Always.*

His words brought a smile to her face. It was what she needed to hear right then. She needed to know that someone would be there to always take care of her and keep her safe.

"Mali kwon nali," she said.

"Dana kwon nali." And he gave her another hug.

She patted Night's gray mane then ran her fingers through his coarse hair.

Suddenly, a flash of white burst before her left eye and sent a shock wave of pain directly into her head. Yelping, she covered her eye.

"Bele som ren?" asked Alan, a hand to her shoulder. *What is wrong?*

The pain melted and a dull ache formed behind her left eye. "Semba danna fo tristah. Tee yili som ultae sa." *I do not know. My eye is hurting again.*

She turned to Alan then faced forward again. Her left eye was more red than earlier. At least, she thought it was. Pain always reminded her of the color red. Tears welled up in her eyes.

"Peter, slow us down. No, wait, stop for a moment," said Alan.

Peter brought the horses to a halt. "Why, what's wrong?"

"Catina," replied Alan.

Catina was bent over, her nose almost touching Night's mane; the dull ache grew increasingly sharper. A light buzzing droned in her ears and her stomach lurched.

"San teeka rol rimta cuela," she said. *Let me off the horse.*

Before Alan could help her, she hopped off and only went a few paces toward the grass that ran alongside the road before falling to her knees. The entire company was already off their horses and were behind her when she began to throw up.

Her head pounded with each upbringing and the buzzing grew louder, as if the air was filled with a swarm of killer-bees. The lurching stopped for a moment and dizziness took her. Sparks of red and gray and white and green danced before her vision. A flush of heat washed over her and she threw up again.

"Is she okay?" she could hear Aiyesha ask someone, though she didn't understand the words.

"Me knows what's wrong. She's sick," said Mr. Nibbetts somewhere behind her.

Peter helped Alan to her side, and then backed away. Alan put his arm around her. She shrugged him off, not wanting to be touched. Her innards shook and the damp air cooled the sweat on her skin, causing her to shiver.

Catina threw up again, this time only a little.

"I'll go get some water," said Peter and took off toward the horses.

"I'll go with you," said Aiyesha and followed.

"What about me?" asked Mr. Nibbetts.

"Just stay there," said Alan.

Catina coughed and lay down on her side at the edge of the road. Alan felt along the dirt until he found her sandal. He patted her leg, feeling his way along the side of her body until he was beside her.

"Shhhh," he soothed. "Fen li wal runia. Ya kae." *It will be all right. Just rest.*

Peter came over to them with a canteen of water. "Here." He handed it to Alan.

The blind man took it and unscrewed its lid and offered some to Catina. She drank a little, just enough to wet her tongue. She didn't think she could keep it down if she drank more.

Alan turned to his right. "Peter?"

"Yes?"

"Is there a blanket?"

"Sure." And Peter went back to the horses to get a blanket.

"Me feet are sore," said Mr. Nibbetts and sat down.

No one commented on his statement.

Peter quickly returned with the blanket and handed it to Alan. The blind man unfolded it and draped it over his granddaughter. He bunched it at the top, forming a small pillow, and placed it under her head so she wouldn't have to lie with her cheek against the dirt.

"What should we do?" asked Aiyesha to no one in particular.

"I will stay with her," said Alan. "If you do not mind, give her some distance. You feel worse when others are too near."

The three others backed off and went over to the horses.

"Flen, simli," said Alan softly. "Galaseme li wal runia." *Hush, child. Everything will be all right.*

Mr. Nibbetts sat his furry behind down on the opposite side of the road and looked on as Alan brought comfort to Catina. "She is so lucky to have someone care for her when she's dying," he told the other two.

"She's not dying!" shot Aiyesha. "She's just sick."

"Like the people here," he said.

"Maybe she caught whatever is causing the illness before she left?" suggested Peter. "She hasn't been feeling well since I've known her. This I know. I know what a healthy child looks like and she, well, she's so pale and you can tell by the way she carries herself that she isn't feeling well."

"All this talk of sickness is bothering me," said Mr. Nibbetts.

"But it's a truth we must face," said Peter.

"I agree," added Aiyesha. "And I don't think it's a common flu or cold or what have you, either. Not this. A flu doesn't kill a whole city."

Mr. Nibbetts shot to his feet. "Do you think whatever she is carrying is contagious? What about us? Me've been sick for a long time. What if me got what she's got? Then what? Oh, Master, save me. Me am dying."

"Quiet," ordered Peter. Mr. Nibbetts shot him a scowl. "Let's not jump to any conclusions. And let's keep our voices down."

Over to their right they could hear Alan hum a calming melody to Catina.

"Let him take care of her," finished Peter.

Why did everything have to go so wrong? Why must she feel this way on top of all the pain and grief she was already feeling? Catina couldn't see the reason for it.

She asked Alan why she was sick.

He told her he didn't know and that he didn't have an answer for her. He only assured her she would feel better soon.

She coughed then followed up with a low belch before rolling onto her stomach to throw up again.

It was hard to speak. "Semba…semba danna fo nem ro…ro sump brina." *I . . . I do not want to . . . to ride anywhere.*

Understandingly, he promised her they'd stay here the night.

Aiyesha came up to them. "Can I sit with her?" she said.

Alan peered up in her direction. "I would rather you did not. I do not mean offence. She just needs a little space."

"I know but perhaps she could use a woman's presence when she's feeling like this. Especially in the company of three males."

"But she does not know you."

"Does it matter? Just let me try."

Alan huffed. "Very well." He let Catina know that Aiyesha was going to sit with her while he alerted Peter that they would be spending the night here.

Catina nodded. She didn't care who was with her, as long as it was someone. The whole World seemed to be shut out behind the veil of ache and discomfort she was feeling.

Alan stood and brushed the dirt off his behind. "If she calls for me, let me know at once."

"Of course," said Aiyesha and sat down and adjusted the humanette so that Catina's head was in her lap. She stroked the girl's blonde hair and whispered words of comfort to her even though Catina didn't understand them.

—

The sky was overcast in dark gray, the moonlight barely getting through the mesh of clouds. Peter had set up camp about thirty feet from the road and was squatting in the middle of the camp before the fire he built. He poked at the fire with a long stick, sparks dancing up into the sky with each prod.

Alan was in his tent with Catina. Mr. Nibbetts snored loudly off to the side somewhere, his furry form hidden by the long blades of grass.

Aiyesha came over with a red and gold-patterned blanket and laid it out on the grass. "Here," she said, "sit on this."

Peter stood up wearily, dropped the stick, and came over. "Thank you." He sat down, his face pale in the fire's light. Beads of sweat glistened on his brow.

"Peter?" she said but could not find the words for more.

He didn't seem to hear her.

"Peter."

"Sorry," he said. He brought his knees up to his chest and wrapped his arms around them. When he exhaled, his breath quivered.

"Peter, look at me."

His blue eyes were glazed over, his eyebrows raised.

"What's wrong? Why are you looking at me like that?" she asked.

He set his gaze back on the fire. "I'm cold. Too cold." He shivered.

Aiyesha reached out and touched his hand. His skin was like ice. She put her palm to his forehead. "You're burning."

"It's nothing."

She brought her hand back and wiped his sweat from her palm against her coarse trousers. "When did this start?"

"I don't know. Awhile ago. Maybe. While I was setting up camp." His eyes were lost in the flame.

"I think you should lie down."

"I can't. I mean, I could, but I'm not tired." He wiped the sweat from his forehead with the sleeve of his sweater. "I am tired but not because I need sleep. You know that feeling you get? You know the one where you're tired but can't sleep? That's the one. I'm just exhausted inside and out. My arms and legs feel like they're filled with sand and my head is cloudy. I can't make up or down of my thoughts. It's like I'm watching myself through a window or watching my reflection in a sheet of Linsheum. I'm me, but I'm not me either. I thought this trip would help me forget the past but seeing Catina lose her parents . . . I don't want to sound selfish, but it reminds me of my own hurt. I lost my home, too. I feel so ashamed."

"It's normal to equate another's loss with our own. Especially in times of death."

Peter's hand began to tremble.

She touched his forehead again. It was hotter than before, or at least seemed so. She was sure it wasn't entirely from the fire. She patted the area of blanket behind them. "Here, lie down."

"Thank you but no. I'd rather sit, if that's all right. I'm not tired." His eyes began to close. He shook his head, waking himself. "I'm not tired."

She looked at him, worry weighing on her heart. "Okay, we'll sit."

The two watched the flame dance. In the background, Mr. Nibbetts let out a snort in his sleep. Neither knew where he went to lie down.

Peter's arms slid down his legs and fell to his sides like dead weight. "What's happening, Aiyesha? What's wrong with everyone?"

"I don't know," she said.

"You're not sick but I . . . but I am. Catina is. I know Alan is and Mr. Nibbetts says that he's dying. All of Grek . . . " He didn't finish. "There has to be some reason to this. Things just don't 'happen.' At least things like this."

The image of dead bodies lining the road burned in Aiyesha's mind like the flame before them. She arched her back, stretching. "I'm not sure why I'm not ill. And I wouldn't say you are, either. At least not like Catina is tonight. You're just tired. We've had a full day."

"But I shouldn't be feeling this way."

"Why? Because you're a man? Full grown and can take care of yourself? We all wear down despite our age or size."

"I'm not used to this. I'm just a simple man from a simple town."

"And I'm just a girl on the run," she said without realizing it until after she said it. Peter didn't seem to have heard her. And if he had, he didn't ask what she meant by that.

Peter coughed and wiped his forehead again. "I'm hot." His legs shaking, he stood and removed his shirt. "Sorry if this bothers you."

With an understanding smile she replied, "I'll turn around if you want."

"It's up to you."

She didn't turn around and instead watched as he removed his shirt and let it drop to the blanket beside his feet. The heavy brown sweater made him look bigger than he actually was. His frame was thin and delicate, his pale skin glowing orange in the fire's light. He didn't look like he ate often.

Peter sat back down, moisture glistening off his neck and shoulders.

"Better?" she asked.

"Yes, much better." The heat from the fire sent gooseflesh racing across his skin.

Again his eyelids started to droop.

"Peter?" she said, a hand to his shoulder.

His head bowed down, lowering, his chin almost touching his chest. When he looked up at her, there were tears in his eyes.

"I want to go home," he said and fell onto his side.

"Peter!" she yelped and tried to shake him awake.

He stirred like one stirring while dreaming a nightmare. Indiscernible sounds escaped his lips.

"Peter, wake up! Wake up!"

His skin was cool and clammy to the touch. Aiyesha grabbed his sweater from off the blanket and draped it over him.

"Aiyesha," he barely managed to say. His eyes opened.

He was awake. Thank the Master.

"I'm here, Peter," she said. "I'm here."

He kept his eyes open and watched the firelight. With strong hands and sure arms, she helped him into her lap and held him there, rocking him back and forth, helping him feel better. He trembled in her arms.

"I'm hot," he said.

She tested his skin and it was still cold. "We should leave the sweater on you for now."

"But I'm hot."

"We'll leave the sweater on you for now," she said.

"Fine. One second I'm hot, the next I'm cold. Sweater or not, I feel terrible."

And this was only the beginning.

The night was becoming a long one. It was late, the sky overhead black as pitch in the dead of night, the clouds having fully covered the moon. The fire was no more than hot embers. Peter remained in Aiyesha's lap; she remained awake. Every so often Peter shook from a strong shiver. She readjusted the sweater draped over his body to ensure he was warm. Periodically, while she sat there she could hear Catina coughing in the tent, followed by the sound of throwing up and Alan saying something to her in Grescalla.

Mr. Nibbetts had been located to a place a short ways from camp, when he would occasionally stand up and, turning in a circle, as if surveying his sleeping area, he would lie back down and go back to sleep.

Aiyesha tried to think of what was happening to these people she had chosen as traveling companions. They were all ailing in some way. Worse, in some *unexplained* way. She thought that maybe she, too, might be sick but didn't acknowledge it because she was so used to pain and discomfort that any symptoms of unease would go unnoticed. She hoped that wasn't the case. What good were five people traveling together if they were all ill? Perhaps come morning she could talk with the others and see how their night went and if anyone had any thoughts. Right now, her mind was on Peter.

He lay with his head in her lap, on his back, asleep. Every so often his brow would furrow in a fit of discomfort. Aiyesha wondered what he was feeling while he slept, if the sickness in this world had somehow transcended into the dream world. She hoped that his place of dream would be a place of comfort and a break from the illness.

She hoped.

"I know I've been very secretive with you," she told him. "And I don't mean to be. I also know that—in all truth—we've just met but you're the first man in twelve years to speak to me without an edge to his voice and without eyes that look at me like some sort of prize, or with greed, as if I were a rare jewel. Is this misplaced affection?" Her feelings for Peter weren't romantic ones. She cared for him like she cared for the others in the group. These were real people with real hearts and real minds. People who weren't fixated on a single goal. Unlike General Gasahd and his men. "I don't know what to call it," she continued. "Truth be known, I'm rather naive when it comes to friendship and relationship with others. For the first time in a long time, being close to someone seems so easy." Then, with a smile, she leaned down closer to him, confiding a secret. "I even have a soft spot for Mr. Nibbetts despite all his going on and on about dying." She sat back up. "Kind of like myself, in the end. It feels like I'm dying. I don't see an end to my . . . running. But yet I do see an end and at that end is a sword and a broken body—mine. I don't think I'm going to be around to see my thirty-first year. Not if I keep this up."

Peter stirred in his sleep and scratched his cheek. He looked like a child dreaming right then.

"Sleep good," she told him. "I'll wait with you until dawn."

His head was heavy and a dull ache throbbed at the base of his skull. Peter knew he was lying down and it felt as if his head was tied down to whatever he was lying on. Whatever it was, it was soft and plush and warm. His stomach swam, something gooey inside it sloshing around back and forth and back and forth and back and forth, turning in circles and figure-eights. The inside of his mouth was moist but the tip of his tongue was dry and would stick to the roof of his mouth every time the two met. The taste and scent of rotten eggs filled his mouth and nostrils.

In his world of darkness, he felt his body shake in numb movement, his arms and legs weighted and filled with pins and needles. He wanted to wake up but didn't know how. His thoughts were scattered, fragments of rational thinking strewn about in a mish-mosh of disarray. Could he wake up? Could he? Wake up to what? What was *waking up?* He was in a dark place; a place far away. Surely there could be some sort of escape from here. Surely this wasn't life, existing in this dark hole of who knows what and who knew where.

The weight holding his head down intensified. A flush of cool moisture washed over his body. A shiver. A shake. A pulse of pure agony beating against his ears, beating in his mind. Wake up. Wake up. Wake up. Heat danced over him and it felt like fire was licking his toes.

Wake up. This wasn't life. There's more, out there, past the black and the weight and the sand that was in him. Wake up.

His head wouldn't move and a high humming filled his ears like the after-echo from his own shout. Wake up.

Wake up.

Wake.

Up.

His eyes opened.

The Man in the Gray Cloak stood over him.

Peter scrambled to his feet, his sweater slipping off his body and landing soft on the blanket. The Man was gone. Aiyesha lay on her side at his feet. The moon was out. It was past the middle of the night, probably close to dawn.

Peter sat back down and crossed his legs. He was feeling better but was still weak. He put his head in his hands then ran his fingers through his damp hair. The fire across from him was no more than ash with a little bit of smoke rising from it, a few red specks of hot embers dotting the ash.

He had seen the Man again.

"He's not real," he told himself.

Remembering that Aiyesha was beside him, he glanced over at her. Her legs were brought up to her waist, her outer arm across her side, her other lying stretched outward, used as a pillow. Her breathing was slow and rhythmic.

Eyes going back to the gray smoke hovering above the ash, another shiver ran across his back. He checked behind himself again for the Man, but no one was there.

Weary, Peter, having forgotten all about it, took notice of his sweater and put it on. It was warm against his shivering skin. The hot flashes seemed to be over. Now he was freezing. He lay back down again and gazed up at the stars. Before any one of them could twinkle back, he closed his eyes, folding his arms across his chest for warmth.

What he would give for another fire. But he was too tired to build one.

The life oozed out of him. Mr. Nibbetts lay on his back, one hand across his belly, the other on his forehead, his cold hand cooling his warm head.

"Me don't know what's happening," he said to himself. "Me so tired . . . but me awake."

A rush of fatigue had come over him some time ago, his insides feeling as if they were losing stability and melting away in a mush of runny liquid. Even the rise and fall of his chest as he breathed had slowed and each inhale and exhale became an effort. His muscles ached, deep, somewhere on their interior in a place he could not name but only feel.

"Me hate this," he said, hoping that someone in the camp would hear him. It appeared no one had because he was still alone. "The little girl gets attention and me do not. Explain that to me, please, because me would really like to know."

He tried to roll over onto his side but he only flopped back onto his back. He tried again and, this time, pushed himself over. With a grunt of effort, he managed to roll partially onto his side, letting gravity finish the job so now his weight was on his right shoulder and thigh.

"Me just so tired." He yawned and after the exhale, tears filled his eyes. His weak left hand came up and wiped them away before flopping down on the grass beside him.

Mr. Nibbetts didn't know why this was happening to him. He was already ill but being around this place seemed to make that illness all the more worse. It was as if Grek—or, at least, its surrounding area—was the source of the illness and that anyone caught in it would be doomed to fall victim to its plague. They had to get out of here, he knew. He just didn't have the strength to call out and tell the others. Yet, he had been sick back home, too. Was it spreading, this whatever-it-was? He didn't know and didn't expect he would ever know. The sickness was an enigma and its very mystery gave it power. After all, you cannot combat that which you do not understand.

A line of drool leaked from the corner of his mouth and gathered in a pool about his cheek.

"Yuck," he said but he was too tired to move his head away from it.

And so he lay there, too weak to move, too tired to do anything but wait until dawn.

Catina had thrown up three times that night and, when she was not throwing up, spent her time dry-heaving. Alan gave her water when he could but still her stomach would not settle. But that wasn't the real problem. It was her eye. A needle of pain was prodding it, poking it, from inside her head. At times the pain was hot, at others as cold as ice, causing a headache like after eating Bauclabba too quickly. When she tried to explain to Alan what was wrong, he told her that she had a severe headache and an upset tummy. But something far worse was happening, far worse than an upside-down stomach or a sore head.

Catina was going blind in her left eye. After all this time of her body trying to heal itself, it could no longer keep up and the illness, which she had contracted shortly before she began her journey to Garathen, was taking hold. It was robbing her of her sight and, she knew, by the time the sun shone in the morning, her left eye would no longer set sight on that blazing ball of yellow in the sky again.

Her stomach swam. Her head pulsed in hollow echoes. Her stomach churned. Her head boomed. She leaned over the bucket they had brought from her farm that was meant to be used to hold water when they stopped for the night, and dry-heaved over it, hoping—wishing—that something would come out just so her stomach would feel better. But nothing came. Just a tense wretch and a small wad of spit.

Exhausted from her efforts, she motioned for Alan to take the bucket away. Though he couldn't see her, he seemed to know when she was done and he took the bucket from her. She collapsed into his lap, too tired to lie back down on her blanket. Besides, lying in his lap, her head being slightly raised, felt so much better.

In Grescalla, her voice weak, she asked, "Why am I feeling this way?"

Alan stroked her hair. "I do not have an answer."

Her heart hurt at hearing this. Alan was a smart man. He was supposed to have an answer for everything. But he couldn't, could he? If he couldn't save her parents, if he didn't know *how* to save them, then maybe he couldn't tell her why she was feeling so sick?

Maybe he couldn't do anything.

She sniffled then asked something that had been on her mind since she realized how sick she was. "Am I going to die like Papa and Mama?"

There was silence for a moment. Then Alan adjusted her in his lap so she was more comfortable. "No, child, no you are not. Not tonight. Not for a long time. You will be fine. You will see. Your tummy is just upset, that is all. Nothing to worry about."

"What about Peter? Is he going to die?"

"No," he said immediately. "No one is going to die."

"But Mama and Papa were sick and they died. Why them and not me?"

"Because," he told her, "they were more sick than you. And they were sick for a long time without getting any help. But I am here to help you so you have nothing to fear. Nothing."

His words didn't ease her concern. His answers were incomplete. What was happening was something she would have to discover on her own.

"*Shinawa*, why is my eye not working?"

As gently as he could, he tilted her head up at him so she could see him.

"No more questions tonight, *Shinali*," he said. "Get some sleep."

Dawn was about an hour away and Catina had just fallen asleep. Alan put his ear to the tent door and listened to see if anyone else was up. Outside, all he could hear was people breathing in slumber and one whimper from Mr. Nibbetts, stirring as he slept.

Finally, Alan was able to face himself and come to terms with all that was within him. Finally, he was able to say to himself that he was feeling terrible, just like the others. Fortunately, it was only one ailment and not a combination of discomforts like what Catina was feeling.

Alan's head was cluttered, his brain sore, as if he had just tried to read as many books as he could and memorize them all. Mental fatigue was his only thought, his only consciousness. His thoughts were unclear. He was tired and wanted to sleep. It took him a moment to realize that he had to lie down in order to do that and that he couldn't sleep sitting up without anything to lean upon.

He felt his way along the blanket beside Catina, and lay down. His ears rang. The pain was *inside* his head and it drummed against his brain like fingers drumming against a table.

"Just relax," he said. "Think of nothing."

Blackness was before his eyes, utter blackness with no swirls of colors or dots of red and green like one usually sees when their eyes are closed. The depth of the darkness seemed to be all the more deep because of the pain.

The stress of going back home also weighed on him, adding to what was already a heavy brick on his mind. He wished he could think clearly, if just for a moment. Everything seemed so scrambled, so lost in nothingness and miscomprehension.

"I could really use you right now, Aubri," he said. The sound of his own voice was a relief to the ringing of silence and the drumming of his thoughts on his weary mind. "I do not understand what is happening to me, to any of us. I am the oldest here, not that that matters, but I feel as if there is a certain paternity I must owe up to. I have to care for the others. Especially Catina. She is the only family I have left. Only her." He took a deep breath. "Hmph, I wish you were here to see her. You would be proud. She traveled for weeks just to get me and bring me to her parents. But" —a pulse of pain against the inside of his head— "but I failed and they were not saved. Yet maybe

I can save her and see her home—my home—safe. Guide me, Aubri. I need your strength right now. I cannot do it on my own."

As if Aubri heard him, a sense of relief came over him. Suddenly what needed to be done didn't seem so impossible and far off.

They would leave in the morning, sick or not.

They had to get away from here.

When Peter awoke the following morning to the aroma of something sweet, just off to his right and down, he sat up and saw Aiyesha squatting before the bonfire, the flames low, a makeshift crossbeam of two sticks with a pot hanging from it, hovering over the flame. What was in the pot, Peter hadn't the faintest idea. Whatever it was, it smelled wonderful. He sat for a moment, allowing himself to wake up and his head to clear. The sun was still low on the horizon. It was only an hour past dawn.

The mixture in the pot bubbled and popped. Aiyesha stirred it with a wooden spoon.

"What are you making?" asked Peter.

"Just stay there. You'll see," she said without turning her attention away from the pot and flame.

Peter scratched his head. He was still chilly but his fever seemed to have abated some. "The others still sleeping?"

"From what I can gather. I heard Catina snoring up a good one just before you awoke. I'm assuming Alan's still in there with her. As for Mr. Nibbetts, I haven't seen him."

"I hope he's all right."

"I'm sure he is. Sleeping outdoors shouldn't be a problem for him. That's how he lived, remember?"

"I suppose so." Peter went to stand but Aiyesha turned around before he did.

"Don't," she said.

"How did you—"

"I can hear you move." She didn't say anymore and returned to her work.

"I see." He stood anyway, his legs shaky. When his stomach swam, he sat back down. Relief came over him when he did.

"I told you," she said. "You'll feel better after you drink this."

Whatever she was making seemed to be finished because she removed the pot from the flame and set it on the patch of grass at the foot of the blanket, and allowed it cool. Peter peered into the pot. The liquid appeared thick and was a pale pink in color. It smelled of strawberries and something else. He couldn't say what.

"What is that?" he asked.

"It's good for you," she replied.

That sounded like something his aunt would say. He leaned back on his hands. "Well, if you're not going to tell me, I'm not going to drink it."

She rolled her eyes. "Fine. There isn't a name for it but it's made from the Vanillaberry flower. They're quite common. At least, I think they are."

"Vanillaberry?"

"A white flower with pink markings near its bud. Smells like strawberries and vanilla."

Vanilla, he thought. *That's what I smelled.* "Uh-huh," he said nonchalantly. "And what else?"

"Well, it's supposed to be mixed with milk and sugar, but that's simply to get rid of its bitter taste. It smells sweet but isn't to the tongue." She wafted some of the steam rising from the pot as if to encourage its cooling. "But it's what's in the flower you want. Cures an upset stomach and a sore head. It helps give you a boost, too."

"How do you know that?"

"My secret." She smiled at him then got up and retrieved four clay mugs: one for Peter and three for the others.

When she returned she took the wooden spoon and scooped out the pale pink mixture into each of the mugs, then handed Peter his. "Go ahead. Drink up."

He brought the mug to his mouth. The scent of the flower was intoxicating and, this close to his nose, did indeed have the rich scent of strawberry and vanilla. He blew off some of the steam still rising from it. "It's not too hot?"

"Just drink it," she said.

"Here we go," he said and he took a sip. It was bitter, bitter as anything he had ever tasted. His face scrunched up. Then, looking at her, he offered a small smile. "It's great."

"Right," she said. "Just do it on the count of three. Knock it all back. Ready? One-two-thr—" And before she could say "three," Mr. Nibbetts came up from behind them and sat on the blanket.

"Where've you been?" asked Peter, taking the mug from his lips.

"Me'd got up early and managed to stand. Me surprised me walked to relieve meself. Me couldn't move last night."

"Rough night for you, too, huh?"

"Yes." He took notice of the drink. "What is that?"

Peter grabbed one of the mugs from the foot of the blanket and gave it to him. "It's good for you," he said, giving Aiyesha a wink.

Mr. Nibbetts cast him a wary glance then smelled the liquid. "Mmmm." And he gulped it down without a word. His face didn't even wince at the bitter taste. "Got anymore?"

"Sorry," said Aiyesha, "we're all out."

Mr. Nibbetts looked off down the road. "Pity."

"Well, here's mine," said Peter and chugged the whole thing back. The thick liquid slid down his throat and he could feel it coat the inside of his stomach. He wiped his mouth with his sleeve once he was done. "Actually, that's not bad. I'd like to try it with milk and sugar some time."

Aiyesha only smiled.

Alan got up shortly after Peter downed his Vanillaberry drink.

"Can you be any louder?" the blind man said. "I can hear all of you yammering as though we were back in Darim, wading in the parade. Too loud!" He made a face, catching the volume of his own voice.

"How's Catina?" asked Aiyesha right away.

Alan seemed disappointed that no one said anything about his subtle insult.

"Not so good. I am afraid all the excitement and weight from yesterday has worn her down." He arched his back, and a small pop was heard by all. His shoulders sank. "And that goes for everyone, too. We are all worn down, and not just from our journey, either. We need to leave this place and the sooner the better."

"Agreed," said Peter.

"Me am expected to ride feeling the way me do?" said Mr. Nibbetts.

"Yes," said Alan. "And you will like it."

Aiyesha stood and handed Alan his cup of Vanillaberry drink.

"What is this?" he asked.

"Just try it," she said, hands now on her waist.

He sniffed it and took a sip. He made a sour face then walked past her. "It is pretty good." Alan stopped himself before walking right into the fire.

"How—"

"I may be blind but I can still feel the heat of flames when I am too close. Now, I will wake Catina shortly. And, Aiyesha" —his white-eyed gaze settled in her direction— "thank you for this. I know we will all be feeling much better once this stuff gets to work."

"You're welcome," she said.

Amazing, thought Peter. *He knows what's in his cup. Better, he knows what it is* for. *According to what Aiyesha said it's supposed to do, anyway.*

And Aiyesha had been right. A half-hour later, Peter was feeling tremendously better, the Vanillaberry liquid having held his swimming stomach at bay. He checked with Mr. Nibbetts and Alan and they, too, were feeling much better.

As Alan was administering Catina her drink—which also involved a debate in Grescalla, presumably about its taste—Peter packed up camp and Aiyesha helped. Mr. Nibbetts was asked to help and when he rolled up the blanket and lifted it, he complained that the blanket was too heavy so he went to take down the tent instead. Fine. Peter didn't care. As long as the furry creature was doing *something.* It seemed that Peter would have to have another talk with him about his complaining.

It didn't take long before the camp was completely packed up and the company were on their horses.

"Ready?" said Peter to all.

"Take us home," said Alan.

Peter glanced at Catina and for the first time since they arrived at her farmhouse in Grek, he saw a look of eagerness on her face.

Content that all was in order, Peter clicked his tongue and beckoned the horses to take them home.

CHAPTER XXXIV
Gasahd Turns West
(The Hunt Begins Anew)

General Gasahd sat atop his great horse—a muscular brown steed with a white mane and tail—and stared out over the plain, alone. A ways back behind him was his company: eleven women and one hundred men. It was extreme, he knew, to bring so many, but if that was what it took to ensure Aiyesha would be found, captured and remained so, so be it.

"Where are you, dearie?" he said out into the open air. "You can't be far."

Captain Zakmon rode up behind him. "I've gone over the proceedings with the men. They won't kill her but they'll bring her to you by any means necessary."

"Good. And the girls?"

"In a party all their own, away from the men. Some of the boys were complaining they found them distracting."

Gasahd turned in his saddle, facing him. "Really? Interesting." The general wore a black leather pouch on his right hip, strung over his left shoulder on a thin strap. From the pouch he produced a letter and showed it to his fellow officer. "Says here that no one's spotted her since one hundred miles West of Darim."

"Is that a Tharadon letter?"

"Indeed. And no one's seen her, Zakmon. Isn't that odd? Makes me wonder why." He paused and let the thought hang in the air a moment. "But I do know why. Where would you want to be if someone was looking for you?"

"In a place where I would not be found, as simple an answer as that sounds."

"Precisely." He stroked his heavy mustache. "And none of the men are going near Grek. Rumors of a plague. Makes you wonder, doesn't it? She was heading West. Grek is West but none of the Dembatstayr are nearing it."

Zakmon nodded. "So I guess we now know where we're going."

Gasahd turned around. "Indeed we do."

He rode swiftly past his men, any who saw him crossed their arms across their wide chests in salute. He didn't acknowledge any of them and kept on. When he passed the last of his men, he rode on about three hundred meters before slowing his horse to a brisk trot.

He approached his girls, a band of eleven women, each on a black horse of their own, sitting tall and proud in their saddles. Each woman was clad in a skin-tight, purple leather outfit, the image of fire swirling embroidered on the leather in purple thread. Each arm bore a band of silver across their biceps, signifying they were still in training. When training was completed, that band would be removed and be replaced by a gray one, showing the difference between the sparkle of a beginner, to the wear and tear of a seasoned warrior.

The women saluted him with crossed arms in the shape of an X when he stopped his horse before them. Gasahd dismounted.

"A word," he said, walking to the middle of them, crossing his arms behind his back.

They turned their horses to face him, surrounding him in a circle.

"We now know where she is going," he said, his eyes on his feet. He moved around them, within the circle. "At least, we have good reason to believe we know where she is headed, especially since I know how she thinks. West of here is a city called Grek, a place rumored to have fallen under the spell of a great plague. She would seek refuge there, thinking that that's the last place we'll look."

"Are you certain of this?" one of the women asked. Her name was Gelera and, in Gasahd's opinion, was the fairest of the women there. Her blonde hair made him swoon every time he set eyes upon it, not to mention her deep brown eyes.

Gasahd glanced at her and took a step toward her. Her hair sparkled in the sunlight. "I am certain enough to go and see what we'll see. What's more, my dear Gelera, is I have you to lead these women ahead of the men, for eleven can move faster than one hundred." He grinned at her.

"Yes, my General," she returned, stone-faced, as one should when talking to a senior officer.

"And," he added, "I don't want any of you to be seen."

"We can handle that."

There were murmurs of agreement among the women.

Gelera asked, "But if we are seen?"

His cold eyes stared at her hard before they were cast downward and he resumed his pacing. "You won't be."

"Sir?"

He glanced back. "You. Won't. Be."

"Yes, my General."

"When she is located, keep watch and wait for me. Decide amongst yourselves who gives me word of her whereabouts. But" —he raised his index finger— "she is to remain alive regardless of what happens. I cannot stress this enough. Under no circumstances is she to be slaughtered."

"But our law says—"

"Tell me, Gelera, why you should be in charge, again?"

She sat up proud in her saddle. "Because you asked me to."

"No, because I'm *telling* you to. I can easily have one of the others take your place, if you wish, but you wouldn't want that. I know you too well."

"Sorry, Sir."

"Don't be sorry. Just do it!"

"Yes, Sir."

Gasahd heaved a sigh and shook his head. The women never took their eyes off him. "Once we have Aiyesha in our custody, she will return with us to the Coast of Seryn and there she will meet the meaning of betrayal." He stopped his pacing again. "Understood?"

"Yes, Sir," they said.

"Good. Now go."

With hoots and hollers, the women kicked their heels against their horses' ribs and turned them West, riding hard toward Grek.

Gasahd mounted his horse and regrouped with Zakmon.

"Everything all right, Sir?" asked the captain.

"Sometimes I feel I'm surrounded by experts in gross inefficiency." Then, to himself, "And I sometimes wonder if enlisting women, though strong, was the right thing to do."

"Sir?"

"The girls have gone on ahead. One will bring word to me once Aiyesha is found. And then we will take her and bring her back."

Keeping abreast to the general, Zakmon asked, "Forgive me for asking, Sir, but why is finding Aiyesha so important? After all, she is but one girl, a long ways from here. Surely she couldn't bring any harm to anyone."

With lightning speed, Gasahd withdrew his dagger and cut the stirrup that held Zakmon's left boot, causing his officer to topple over from the shift in weight and nearly fall off his horse.

Gasahd spoke when Zakmon righted himself again. "Watch your tongue, Captain, or you may soon find yourself scrubbing pots in the mess-tent."

Zakmon was silent.

"It is important to find Aiyesha because she has seen things on the Coast that no one, not even you, not even my best men, have seen. The Master's purpose was revealed to those women. The Master's Mark is upon them and for any one of them to try and abandon that Mark is treason. I will not stand for treason. They are to fight in my army or they will die. If they are not for the Master, then they are against Him, and I will have no part of anyone who does not serve our Lord. Am I clear?"

The Captain cleared his throat. "Clear, Sir. I'm sorry."

"That's not the first time I've heard that today," he said and rode past him.

—

Again Thalok was on the move. There had been no cause for the Void-man to bring him back. If there was anything a Qinoran hated most, it was the questioning of its ways.

"I was on to him," he told himself as his feet moved in a blur beneath him. "And now the Link is lost. Foolish!"

Yet he minded his thoughts and his words. The Void-man had eyes and ears everywhere . . . even inside his head. Though Thalok was mostly of the Black, the Purple in him still succumbed to the Void-man and to the Island of the Dead.

And so Thalok ran, projecting himself out onto the land, feeling his way toward Peter. Like a rush of wind, his insides, his heart and essence, reached out, its fingers crawling along the ground like a spider, smelling the mind of his prey. Then . . .

Thalok stopped and scanned the surrounding area. The sky was bright and clear, the ground lush with green, the rocks of the earth a clean gray under the sun.

"He is moving," he said. "Eastward."

Thalok ran.

CHAPTER XXXV
By the River

Two days had gone by since that terrible night when all were ill. The Vanillaberry flower had worked wonders and everyone was in better spirits.

Even Mr. Nibbetts.

As Peter rode, a foul smell wafted up from somewhere to his right to greet him. He raised his right arm and sniffed his armpit. He made a sour face when the putrid scent of sweat permeated his nostrils.

"I need a bath," he said. He ran his hand over his face, the skin on his palm scraping against coarse stubble. "And a shave." His fingers combed through his hair. "And cut hair."

"Me like long hair," said Mr. Nibbetts, riding up beside him with Aiyesha.

Aiyesha had offered to carry Mr. Nibbetts on her horse so Peter could have time to himself.

"And what brings you to the front, my furry friend?" asked Peter.

"Thought me'd stop me moping and come up and see what the attraction of riding first is. It's different riding further back."

Peter grinned. "I'm riding first because I'm leading us home."

"Me see."

"And how are you feeling today?" asked Aiyesha.

Mr. Nibbetts grimaced. "Well, me tummy is—" He held his tongue and looked up at them: their eyes were wide; they were expecting another complaint. He said, "Me fine. Feeling better. Ghuduff for me."

"Ghuduff?" said Peter, furrowing his brow.

"It meant 'good' in me village. Good for me. Good that me am okay, now." Then, with seeming hesitation, "Thank you for asking."

Peter grinned. It seemed that Mr. Nibbetts was making progress.

They followed the rolling curves of the land. The way they were returning was a different route than by which they had arrived. Alan had told Peter since they were not in a particular rush to get home, they would take a bit of a detour, giving Peter a chance to see what else made up the World, instead of the one path they had originally traveled.

"Why not?" Peter had told him, though he was eager to get home and start his life anew. Yet he did not regret the decision of taking a new road. It was a chance to forget some of the events that led up to Grek and leave them behind.

Peter's eyes widened a little when, peeking out from around the next hilly curve of the land, was the corner of a lake and the tops of trees. Whether a small lake or a full river, he could not tell from this distance. The water glimmered underneath the sun and, even this far away, appeared very inviting.

"Alan?" he said.

"Yes?"

"Let's stop up ahead." He gave a kick to Day's ribs and the mare sped up, pulling Night along with her.

The water was actually farther than Peter thought, but they made it there in good time. And it was a river, not a lake, its end just beyond the curve of the last hill and its length running adjacent to them into a forest quite a ways off.

A perfect place for a rest.

They stopped and all dismounted their horses. Except for Peter. The rest began unpacking what they needed for the short break.

"I'll be back," he told them.

"Where are you going?" asked Alan as he sat down on the river bank.

"For a bath."

"Do not take too long. And holler if something should go wrong or you need help."

"Don't worry, I will, but I don't think there's anything to worry about. We've already had our share of excitement on this journey. Besides" —he glanced over at Aiyesha and gave her a smile— "I've taken baths on my own my whole life. I shouldn't need any help."

Aiyesha laughed. Alan muttered something at the joke. Even Mr. Nibbetts chuckled.

Peter left them.

He took Day swiftly along the river bank, the ground a blur beneath the horse's hooves. The river shimmered under the sun and seemed to be inviting him with outstretched arms. It wasn't long before he approached the mouth of the forest. He slowed Day and crept along the river's edge, into the forest for privacy. Satisfied that he was far enough in and would not be seen by any of the others—should they come looking for him—Peter dismounted Day and led the mare by the reins to the river's shore and let her drink. The flow of the river seemed slower here.

"Thatta girl," he said, patting Day's neck.

When she stopped lapping the water into her large mouth, Peter brought her to the base of a large pine tree, tying her reins to the trunk.

He brought his palm to the horse's muzzle and felt the velvety skin between her nose and mouth. "You be good," he told her.

The horse snorted her agreement and bent down to pick at the long tufts of grass that sprouted out at the tree's base. From a pouch on the horse's rump, Peter produced a small knife, about five inches long with a bone handle; one of the supplies Alan had picked up while they were in Darim. He came to the river's edge and stuck the blade, point first, into the ground.

After dipping a hand in the river to test its temperature (it was cool), Peter removed his clothes and piled them in a heap, far enough from the river bank so as not to get soiled by the damp earth that bordered its edge. He waded in, walking on the tips of his toes until he was comfortable, then let his feet touch bottom. The water was just over waist deep. An unexpected shiver ran through him.

For a half-hour he swam, the cool water refreshing on the skin. It had been so long since he bathed, he shamefully admitted, that he almost forgot what it was like to get himself clean.

Where Peter enjoyed the cool water the most was on his chest and under his arms. He was still a little queasy since last night but with each stroke through the river water, the more refreshed he felt. It felt as if the sickness were being rinsed off him with the paddling of his arms and hands, with each kick of his feet.

Satisfied that he was clean, he swam over to where he had left the knife, pulled it out of the mud and washed the blade clean in the river. He ran a hand along his jaw line, testing the stubble.

He began to shave.

Aiyesha was off on her own, having wandered down the river bank for some privacy. After having spent so much time in isolation on the Coast of Seryn, having to be around people all the time was something she was not used to. Though she had her female bunkmates while on the Coast, there was a sense of detachment about each of the women, a wall built around their hearts so as not to get too close to one another, so, should it happen, losing another in battle wouldn't be as painful. In the end, on the Coast of Seryn, you were alone. But Aiyesha's heart was still partly soft and, yes, she began to care for the other women. Especially Helena.

Far enough away from the rest of the group, Aiyesha sat down on the grass and crossed her legs. She closed her eyes and began to breathe deep and slow, in through the nose, out through the mouth. It was a meditation exercise that she was taught by General Gasahd, one meant to center yourself and regain your internal balance as the day wore on. As she sat, eyes closed, Aiyesha focused on a solitary chair in a small room, someplace far away.

It was her chair.

Her seat.

Her center.

As she continued to breathe and began to wipe clean her mind, the chair in the room grew all the clearer, its wood lacquered to a smooth, golden hue, its legs perfectly cylindrical, its seat contoured to her behind, its back shaped as if formed from her most comfortable posture. The room in the background was empty, the walls gray and smooth. As her mind eased, the walls in the room began to dim, turning from gray to charcoal and then, finally, to black, and all that was left was the chair.

She envisioned herself sitting in it, getting herself comfortable. Her back was erect, her legs crossed ladylike, her hands folded on the tops of her knees. Here, she was in control. Here, she was everything. And here, everything obeyed her.

Something was wrong.

The room began to lighten. Her mental projection of herself faded off the chair. The room grew lighter still. The chair was losing its form, becoming rough and rickety, its golden shine dulling to a light brown.

Aiyesha opened her eyes. Off in the distance, on one of the hills, she saw a female rider.

She knew who it was.

Only a couple of scratches; not bad without any Linsheum, thought Peter, feeling his cheeks and chin, checking for any stubble that might have escaped his blade. There were probably a few stray hairs here and there, but it wasn't like anyone would notice.

He waded back to shore and set the knife down, then turned back and swam out to the middle of the shallow river. He crouched down and dunked his head to wash off the short blades of cut facial hair stuck to his skin. A drop or two of blood leaked from the small cuts on his chin and cheek, mixing with the water.

Something *reached* for him.

While his head was beneath the surface, in the dark of the river, he felt cool swirls of water spiraling above his head, swishing his hair. It was soothing and wonderful.

When he stood to go back to shore, he found the water had suddenly grown deep and remained over his head.

His heart leaped in his chest, nearly catching in his throat. He gasped and, to his surprise, didn't inhale a mouthful of water.

Peter opened his eyes.

The water was murky; a dark green, bits and particles of dirt and bark and algae swimming and floating around him.

He breathed in again, thinking that he must have been mistaken the first time and hadn't breathed in at all. That's why he hadn't felt the cool rush of river water enter his lungs. This time, the same thing happened. He breathed as if he were on dry land. However, the air was cool, just like the water surrounding him.

In a flood of panic, he kicked his legs and circled his arms about, trying to swimming upward. A current of water pushed him back down. Puzzled, but determined, Peter tried again but failed to surface. For how long he fought the current suppressing him, he didn't know, but soon, realizing the futility of trying to swim, his body floated back down to the river's bottom and there he stood, alone in the murk.

Had he drowned? Had he somehow fallen unconscious when submerging his head to rinse his face clean of stubble? Is this what happened when you died? You lingered in the place where your mortal body fell, doomed to spend eternity there?

His upbringing told him no. It told him that when you died, you transcended from the land of the living and into the comforting arms of the Master, to the Prairie of Everlasting Peace, where you would spend eternity with Him in His loving embrace, shielded forever from the cruelty of the World. Yet, Peter had begun to disbelieve in the Master. All the teachings, all the hopes, all the prayers, seeming a memory of yesterday in a life altogether forgotten. Perhaps he was right about one thing. Perhaps he was right about thinking that you spent eternity where your body fell . . . if you stopped believing in the Master.

The murky green of the river grew clearer—blurred still—but clearer. The dirty green was endless around him.

And he still was able to breathe.

Peter walked along the river bed, slow—as it is when moving in water—not really looking for anything but still looking for a way out. He tried swimming upward again and failed.

His heart yearned to be let out of this prison, if that's what it was. How he wished to be back on shore, free, away from the green murk and with the others: Alan, Catina, Mr. Nibbetts and, of course, Aiyesha. But he didn't know how.

He sank to his knees, his kneecaps sliding in the slick, gooey bottom of the river's floor.

Where am I? He needed to know.

As if an answer, up ahead, in the filthy murk, a figure began to form.

Peter pushed himself onto his feet.

"Who's there!" he called out instinctively. He could talk under water? Impossible! But . . . *possible?*

The figure grew clearer and as it did, Peter looked away. He knew who it was he saw.

The Man in the Gray Cloak.

Aiyesha sprinted back to camp to retrieve her horse. It was Gelera she saw, she was sure of it. After seeing Gelera's face day in and day out for twelve years, there was no mistaking it, even in a crowd of people with the same long blonde hair and proud build. She would recognize her former comrade's proud posture, sitting high in her saddle, anywhere.

In one fluid motion, Aiyesha ran and leaped upon her horse, Bear, and rode around the river's edge and tore off down the field to go after Gelera, despite all calls from the others asking her what was wrong and where she was going.

She forced Bear to catch up with Gelera, digging her heels deep into his sides, snapping the reins, hollering for him to go faster.

"Impossible," she told herself. *Gelera can't be here.*

But it wasn't impossible. Knowing Gasahd, Gelera was probably sent to seek her out and bring her home. Then again, maybe Gelera was leading her into a trap? Regardless, she had to know, had to know if she was still being sought out or if Gasahd, having given in, finally let her be.

Being on the Coast, having to always be alert and on edge, had developed her a sixth sense. She was able to sense danger, no matter what size the threat and was able to act accordingly. As she neared the hill, she could see Gelera clearly under the morning sun. Gelera's face was as hard as stone but yet Aiyesha did not sense any trouble from her.

Gelera rose her horse on its hind legs, it forelegs pawing at the air before landing back down. She then tore off and disappeared over the other side of the hill.

Aiyesha pressed on.

"Who are you?" called Peter.

The Man remained motionless in the silent gloom at the bottom of the river.

Peter pushed himself forward, his legs working hard to overcome the slowness of having to walk underwater. "Answer me!"

The Man stood there.

Almost close to him, now. Just a little farther. Peter's feet slid on the river's slick floor and he lost his balance for a moment, tumbling forward in slow motion. But he quickly regained it, slowly straightened himself, and forged on.

"Blast, answer me!"

But the Man did not answer. He only stood there.

This is getting tiring, thought Peter. And he wasn't meaning the hard physicality of making his way through the water. He was tired of seeing the Man and not receiving an answer.

He was almost there, now. Just a few more steps. The Man's gray cloak swirled about him in the gloom but the material of the hood over his face remained still.

Peter stood before him. He was winded from the effort, but didn't let it hinder him. As awkward as it was, he took in a deep breath and again was surprised at not feeling a rush of cool water filling his lungs.

"Who are you, what do you want?" he asked.

The Man raised his hands, as if to move and grab him, but instead merely grabbed his cloak that was swirling about and brought the long gray material back down so his legs were covered.

"I'm coming," said the Man.

"Why? What are you?"

"I'm coming and you will die."

Peter's eyes widened. *Die?* "Who are you?" he asked again.

Without answer, the Man took a step back, then another, and then another, his gray-cloaked body disappearing in the green murk of the river.

Peter charged after him but only found himself treading deeper and deeper and deeper into a world of dark green, without any sign of the Man.

"No!" he shouted and fell to his knees. He remained there at the bottom of the river for a time and when he stood, he re-emerged, waist-deep in the river, in the forest, Day on the shore beside him.

"Gelera!" called Aiyesha.

The woman turned her horse around. Aiyesha caught up to her.

"Gelera," she said again.

"Greetings, Aiyesha," said Gelera. "I bring you news." She sat proud in her saddle.

"Speak," said Aiyesha, wasting no time. *Why are you here?*

Gelera brushed away the golden strands of hair hanging in her eyes. She proffered a smile. "First, let me say that it is good to see you again." Her expression seemed genuine.

"It is good to see you, too, though I wish it were under different circumstances." *You mean good ones. Circumstances were always bleak on the Coast of Seryn,* she thought.

"Indeed. But as I said, I bring you news and in good time, I might add."

Aiyesha kept her distance, skeptical of what Gelera might say. Women on the Coast of Seryn were only privy to little snippets of information and not to the greater whole. What they overheard was usually twisted into whatever they wanted to hear, losing its credibility as the truth, as if those they were eavesdropping on were aware of themselves being listened to.

"Oh, what's that?" she asked.

"As you are no doubt aware, General Gasahd has been searching for you."

Aiyesha's face remained like stone as the memories of her encounters with the soldiers filled her mind. "I am aware."

"And his pursuit continues. He knows where you are headed." The cold in Gelera's eyes told her it was so.

Aiyesha's heart sped when she heard this. How could Gasahd know where she and the others were headed? Spies? Aiyesha would have detected them, if that were the case. Back on the Coast, she was always able to tell when she was being watched.

"And why do you tell me this? Your loyalty to Gasahd runs deep, more in you than in any of the others. Why would you betray him?" said Aiyesha.

Gelera maneuvered her horse closer so that the heads of the two horses were side by side. She seemed to seriously consider Aiyesha's words. "Because, I've seen where his army is headed and the dark turn it is taking. I was blind to it for a long while, but now I see. Like you I want escape but . . . " She gazed downward. "But I can't. I'm bonded to the Coast. My life is the Master's and I must fulfill His will. I have no choice."

"You always have a choice, Gelera, despite what you may think. Look at me—I chose to leave and I got away."

Blonde hair fell over Gelera's face. It was a moment before she pushed it away. "But not entirely. He looks for you and will find and capture you if you are not careful. Besides, if you are caught and taken back to the Coast, the fate that awaits you is far worse than anything you may think of."

Gelera had changed the subject quickly, back to Aiyesha's possible capture. Aiyesha couldn't understand how Gelera could be so drawn to the Coast of Seryn when all it was, was a place of death and never-ending violence. But, she could not force her to change her mind. If there was one lesson she learned on the Coast that still bore weight out here on the mainland, it was that everyone needed to make their own choices about how they would live their lives. No one could make them for you and no influence could be imposed without eventual rebellious results. If Gelera chose the Coast, so be it.

"Punishment?" said Aiyesha. "I am a fugitive, Gelera. My punishment is death."

Gelera shook her head. "That's not what I've been hearing. Despite what General Gasahd is telling any who ask about you and what his plans are for you, he has something far worse in mind. Death would be a holiday compared to what he'll do to you." She glanced side to side, as if to see if anyone was coming. They were alone on the hillside. "There was a woman there, on the Coast. Samora was her name. I believe you knew her."

"Samora?" Aiyesha's voice caught in her throat. She decided it best not to mention she knew the kind old woman and instead prodded for more information. "I do not know that name. Who is she?"

"Someone, according to the general, who aided you in some way back in Wesafeld. She was a difficult one to crack but Captain Zakmon got it out of her. It is rumored that Captain Zakmon held the woman's hands over flame to get his information when all other torture failed." She glanced away. "Some, I fear, worse than flame but it was the fire that made her snap."

Aiyesha, if she were anyone else, would have winced at hearing this, but long years on the Coast of Seryn had hardened her heart and hearing of another's suffering didn't faze her—though she wished it would right now. She kept her expression cool.

"The old woman is now in Beagog Prison where she will spend the rest of her days. No matter. That was not the news I intended to bring. I've already told you what you need to know. I think it best you run, get away from here."

"Thank you, Gelera. I pray to the Master it is not found out by Gasahd that you told this to me. Which way is he headed?"

"West, to Grek. He knows of the plague there and knows of its desolation. None of the soldiers have gone near there. The ones he recruited to go with him to Grek were reluctant but they obeyed anyway, as good soldiers should. I hear that most of them will be promoted simply for coming along."

Aiyesha didn't care of such matters anymore and kept her emotions to herself. "Thank you again, Gelera. May the Master watch over you as you continue to do His work."

Gelera held out a hand. Aiyesha took it.

"You as well," she said. "Maybe I'll see you again one day."

"I doubt that," said Aiyesha. "I need to get as far away from that Coast as I can. Maybe when we're old and have lived out our purpose. Maybe then. Right now, I'm afraid this is our last meeting for a long time—more likely, the final time."

"Take care," said Gelera. "Ride East, away from Grek."

Aiyesha was glad she and the others were already headed in that direction. "I will. Good-bye."

Aiyesha turned Bear to leave and before she could bring him to a trot, Gelera called out after her. "General Gasahd knows of the others, too."

Pulling on the reins, she sat up alertly. "Others?"

"The ones you travel with. I just thought you should know." Gelera clicked her tongue, signaling to her horse to take her away.

Aiyesha watched her a moment, riding quickly over the land. Then, with sudden urgency, she tore back to the camp.

They had to leave.

Baffled by what just happened, Peter stared down at his reflection in the brownish-green water. His mind had turned to clay, his thoughts thick and syrupy.

"Why is this happening?" he groaned.

There was no explanation why he kept seeing the Man in the Gray Cloak. He didn't know who the ghost was or what it wanted. All he knew was that the Man kept haunting him.

What puzzled him more was how the Man somehow manipulated the water where he now stood. It was impossible. No one save the Master Himself was able to alter the physicality of water, and even that instance had only been recorded once in history. It had been the Parting of the Feven Sea so that Harabus, the most faithful servant of the Master's in known History, and his people could cross into the Land of Life.

Had Peter perhaps encountered the Master, though in a different form? But why haunt him if the Master was a being of love? And love did not induce darkness and terror, the way the Man in the Gray Cloak had. Too many questions and not enough answers.

Not any answers.

"It doesn't make sense," said Peter.

Did he dare tell the others? Would they think him a lunatic if he did? The possibility was there. The only person who might believe him was Alan, but Peter knew Alan had enough on his mind right now. Aiyesha? No. He did not want her to think him crazy, not when they were becoming such good friends.

Peter gazed at his reflection. His black hair curled at their ends, his bangs hanging in ringlets just above his eyebrows, longer than they were when he left home.

The weight of confusion settled upon his shoulders.

His shoulders.

Was it his imagination or did they look bigger, more firm and muscular?

"It's just me," he said. *Boy.*

His shoulders drooping, he turned and went back to the shore and retrieved his clothing and knife. Once dressed, he untied Day and got up on her back.

He didn't know if he should tell anyone about what he saw.

Arriving at the camp, Peter saw Aiyesha urging the others to pack their things and get back onto their horses.

"What's going on?" he asked as he dismounted Day. He was still shaken from his experience by the river and did not want any more commotion.

"No time to explain," she said. "But we must go."

"We will, but after. We need our rest if we are going to make it back and on such little supplies."

"Peter is right," said Alan.

"There's no time," said Aiyesha. "Really, we must go."

She was tying her things—which were wrapped in a dark gray blanket—to Bear when Peter grabbed her by the arm. "Aiyesha, listen to me, what's going on?"

She finished tying the cord that held the blanket in place and looked at him. There was urgency in her green eyes. "I can't explain. Really, I can't. I don't mean to be so secretive but I must."

This wasn't making any sense and he would stand for it no longer. His frustration about the Man in the Gray Cloak had worn his patience thin. "Look, I know you have your secrets but you can't expect everyone to jump when you tell them to."

"I know and—"

"And if you think we should leave, you should tell us why. You're not on your own anymore. If there's anything I've learned by being out in a group, is that we have to rely on one another, communicate with one another. We're in this together, Aiyesha. And after all the excitement in Grek, none of us feels like moving right now, especially since we're all not feeling well. We need to take a break."

Peter glanced down at Alan and though the blind man hadn't said anything, Peter knew he was listening carefully. Was that a grin he saw on his face?

"I'm sorry, Peter" —she glanced away— "we can wait awhile."

"Okay," he said, placing a hand on her shoulder. "Okay. Now, let's get something to eat."

The mid-morning snack was a vegetable sandwich: carrots cut into thin strips, celery done the same, potato cut into thin discs and pieces of onion, all between two slices of wheat bread, not dressed with any flavoring. Not the most pleasant of meals but a meal nonetheless and it filled their bellies. Peter was concerned he might not be able to keep the sandwich down, but he did and was relieved it didn't come back out. Another night like the one two days ago was not welcome.

All took a nap in the afternoon except for Peter and Aiyesha. Alan, Catina and Mr. Nibbetts wanted to be rested before heading out that night. Aiyesha and Peter wandered a ways from the camp so when they spoke, their words did not wake their companions.

"Something's on your mind," he told her.

She walked with her fingers entwined, her arms hanging down in front of her. "Yes, many things."

She wants to say more. Why doesn't she? "Like?" he prompted.

There was no answer. Her beginning to say something then cutting herself off was getting to him.

"Look," he said, "I know it's not my place to pry but yet . . . yet I wish to help you if I could."

"I'm sorry, but I cannot tell you. I'd like to. Really, I would, but I can't."

"Why not?" He stopped walking. So did she.

"Please, don't push me."

"I'm not pushing."

"But you keep asking."

"That's only because I'm concerned."

She brushed a few strands of velvety black hair away from her eyes. "I know you are. You shouldn't be."

"But, Aiyesha, how can I not be? You're my friend. At least, I'd like to think you are. And as your friend I get concerned. You seem to always be worrying about something and yet when I ask, you don't say what it is. It's fair to have your secrets but—"

She looked at him earnestly. "But what?"

"It sounds silly to say, but I wish you wouldn't look like you bore the weight of the World on your shoulders. That way" —he grinned— "I wouldn't feel so compelled to ask all the time what's bothering you."

She touched a hand to his shoulder. "I do appreciate your concern. That's being honest. From now on I'll try to not look so burdened."

He glanced at his feet. "That's not good, either. Then you're forcing yourself to mask whatever it is that's bothering you. I couldn't ask that of anybody."

"That's thoughtful, Peter, but I can handle it."

"How can you be so sure?"

When she looked into his eyes, the green of her irises grew darker and were filled with determination and ice. "I can handle it."

A shudder rushed through Peter's arms at her words. It didn't sound like her speaking but rather someone who was much stronger than the woman he saw before him, than the woman he met in Darim.

"If you say so," he managed to say.

Her gaze softened and the green of her eyes lightened. "Thank you."

She walked on ahead of him. He scratched his head, looking after her, and squinted at the bright rays of sun that suddenly pierced his eyes. Aiyesha was a strange one, he was realizing. She was everything a woman ought to be: strong, proud, yet tender and kind, looking after others. Not to mention she was beautiful. Even more beautiful than Talia. Yet she was full of secrets and the queen of things unsaid.

Still watching her walk on ahead, Peter had the distinct feeling that in the days to come, those secrets would be revealed.

CHAPTER XXXVI
When the Dembatstayr Ride

In the midst of thundering hooves, General Gasahd led one hundred men toward Grek. The city was now not far away and discovery of Aiyesha's whereabouts was imminent. With determined eyes and a more determined heart, Gasahd focused on his target. His hatred for her was equal to his hatred for any who would go against the teachings and values of the Master. She had betrayed him by leaving. Twelve years ago, Gasahd let Aiyesha into his circle on the Coast of Seryn, she being the first of the twelve women who would be trained into a breed of killer the likes the World had never seen. The women were a test-force, an experiment, to see if such teachings would succeed and bring forth a new era in military training and the forging of new soldiers. Women were special. Unlike men, women did not have the primal need to dominate, to always believe themselves right when in their heart of hearts they knew they were wrong. Their minds were clear and the division of right and wrong was more apparent. Or, so Gasahd had thought, but as time wore on, he began to see that women were not that much unlike men. And so his motive for training them changed. He was using them as a beacon, a symbol to all women who felt suppressed that a woman could be anything she wanted to, that she could be as strong as she wanted, without succumbing to the ways of men and their, sometimes, laughable and horrendous ideals and behavior. And so Gasahd trained his women perfectly, bringing out the natural perfection within them. All the women, despite their appearance when they began, had grown into perfect figures of beauty, their muscles taut and defined, their proportions as such that would drive any man out of his mind with desire. As their confidence within themselves grew, so did their beauty, their confidence shining forth from their faces in startling brilliance.

Gasahd also knew of the women's one weakness: their love for home and those they left behind. Even the two women who came to him without immediate family, were still hurting over leaving their friends and acquaintances back home. They would never set eyes on them again. To counter this, Gasahd treated the women as family and encouraged them to treat each other the same. They leaned on each other for support through hard times, shoulders to cry on throughout the sad, companions to laugh with throughout the glad. Bonds were formed and intimate feelings and wishes exchanged. They were a family, General Gasahd at the head of the household, his daughters before him, being prepared to carry out the Master's good work. He didn't know that the women still guarded their hearts from one another, didn't know they were still cautious of being attached to one another.

Then one of his "daughters" rebelled and left the Coast of Seryn: Aiyesha, the strongest and most perfect specimen in the experiment. She acted as a leader toward the group, bringing them together when it seemed inevitable they would fall apart. Gasahd needed that nucleus back, needed to bring Aiyesha back under his hand before the other women got any notions of escape.

Captain Zakmon rode up beside him. "Do you think we'll find her, Sir?"

Shaken from his thoughts, Gasahd turned to him. "There was never a doubt in my mind, Captain. We are almost upon Grek. Once there we'll spread out and discover where in that ghost town she is hiding."

"And if she isn't there?"

"Then we wait. She'll make her presence known soon enough."

Zakmon glanced back at the men then back at his general. "Sir? Sir, some of the men have been talking. They want to know why you brought so many of them to retrieve just one girl."

With a sly grin, Gasahd turned to his Second in Command. "They will soon find out. These men will pray they had never set eyes on her once she is found. And, I fear, many of them will not be returning with us. Aiyesha will kill them without thought just as quickly as you blink your eyes."

Zakmon gazed off ahead.

"I'm serious, Captain. It's best you prepare them as they are about to fight off twenty men on their own."

"That's why you brought the other girls, then, isn't it?"

Gasahd grinned. "Precisely. You're catching on. Aiyesha going up against lesser mortals is one thing and, for her, quite easy to accomplish; but for her to go up against eleven just as skilled as she, that is quite another matter. However—"

"However?"

The general slowed his horse a little and adjusted himself in his saddle, turning toward him. "She was also able to best some of the girls. I can't explain how she moved as she did, so fast and smooth, her actions preceding her thoughts. She was trained on the same programs as the others. Somehow, in the midst of the training, she must have realized her astounding ability and trained even harder, at a level higher than the others without my knowledge. These eleven girls, to her, will be more like six, seven at the most."

Zakmon remained silent. Then, "I will go back and tell the men to be wary when we come upon Grek."

"See that you do but do not scare them. After all," he said, "it's still just one girl."

Off in the distance, some four hundred meters ahead, a horse galloped toward the company at full speed, its rider's golden hair bouncing up and down, the wind rushing by her blowing it back. The horse seemed to pick up speed the nearer it got to them.

Seeing it was Gelera, General Gasahd called out to his men to stop. Behind him he could hear "Halt!" shouted throughout the company, and the rumble of hooves as Zakmon ran his horse up and down the line of men, telling them to bring their horses to a stop.

As the men slowed, Gasahd rode up ahead to meet with Gelera. She came up at full speed then stopped before him abruptly, her horse's head jerking back when she pulled on the reins.

"I have news," she said.

It was all Gasahd needed to hear.

CHAPTER XXXVII
The Second Sign of Power

It was four days since the river, since encountering the Man in the Gray Cloak. Peter and his companions were tired, but the thought of going home alleviated their weariness. Since that night just outside Grek, none had felt as ill. The only complaints among them were the bouts of the Sickness' tiring effects, the strain and drain on the body. Catina had complained to Alan on the second day since the river that the muscles in her abdomen were sore, strained and fatigued from all her exerting whilst throwing up. Mr. Nibbetts, well, he complained of continuously feeling sluggish . . . but his complaints weren't as frequent as before.

So Peter led them on, over land and hill, past rocks and forests, moving toward the Broken City of Garathen. How he longed for home and for the opportunity to begin his life anew. He looked forward to painting again and writing poetry and trading his skills for what he would need to begin construction on a new home.

Aiyesha rode alongside him, Mr. Nibbetts sitting behind him, Alan and Catina behind them on Night.

"How much further?" asked Mr. Nibbetts, shielding his eyes from the sun.

"Still a ways, I should imagine," said Alan. Then, with a grin, "Start asking your question in a few days time."

"A few days! Me should be dead and withered in a few days."

"No, you won't be," said Peter, turning back in his saddle and giving Mr. Nibbetts a reassuring glance. "You'll be just fine."

Mr. Nibbetts didn't reply and only fixed his gaze forward.

"This is longest me've ever traveled," he muttered.

"Not even when coming overseas from the East?" said Alan.

"This is the most me've ever traveled at one time," said Mr. Nibbetts. "When me traveled from the East, me came by boat, then when on land, me walked with the others but stopped every few hours for a break."

"Do all Flistablare move in such small increments?" asked Aiyesha.

"Mostly," said Mr. Nibbetts, "our legs are short so what is a short distance for you, is a long distance for us."

"But a horse is doing all the work for you right now," said Peter.

"Even so," said Mr. Nibbetts. He left it at that.

They continued on into the afternoon. The land around was flat save for a rise in the land about one hundred feet ahead, masking what was on the other side.

When they approached the base of the hill, Peter noticed Aiyesha sit up alertly in her saddle.

"What's wrong?" he asked.

"Pull back your horses," she replied, her voice as cold as steel.

Peter halted the horses and drew them a few steps back. The company sat in silence. The rustling of the grass in the wind became all the more clear from the absence of stepping hooves.

"Why did we stop?" asked Mr. Nibbetts.

Aiyesha hushed him and took her horse a few steps up the hill. Peter saw Day's ears perk up, rotate forward, then to the side, then as far back as they would go before standing alertly, facing the front again. *What's she*—Night let out a snort of discontent behind him. Day concurred with him with a snort of her own.

Peter watched intently as Aiyesha rose in her saddle, standing in her stirrups, her neck straining upward, trying to peer over the top of the hill. It seemed she couldn't see anything because she seated herself and drew her horse back beside him.

"Let's ride along the bottom on this side," she said.

Peter looked to his right and saw that the hill went on for a good mile, if not more, before tapering off into flat land.

"Why?" he asked.

She side-stepped her horse so she was right next to him. She leaned in and whispered, "There's something on the other side."

Other side? "Do you know what it is?"

"No, but it's not just one thing there, either. There are a lot of them. How many I cannot tell but more than our company here. I suggest we try going around, far to our right so we're a good ways from here before moving East again."

"If you say so," said Peter.

"I don't know. But something *alive* is over there, at any rate. Let's go."

He trusted her judgment. More so, he trusted the tone of her voice. She spoke with such conviction that threat or no on the other side of the hill, she believed that something was there, seemingly with her whole heart.

Peter turned in his saddle and faced the others. "We go right and then we'll resume our course."

"And the reason?" said Alan. "I could hear you two speaking. What is on the other side?"

"I don't know," said Aiyesha. "Whatever it is, everything inside me tells me we need to avoid it."

Mr. Nibbetts was looking off somewhere. Peter knew he wasn't listening.

"Very well, then," said Alan.

Catina said something to him in Grescalla, presumably asking why they had stopped. He answered her question. She seemed content with his answer.

"Then we go right," said Peter and began steering Day along with Night in that direction.

"What? Why are we going around?" asked Mr. Nibbetts.

"Shhh," said Aiyesha, a finger to her nose. "Quiet."

"Don't tell me what to do. Me want to know what's going on, why we're changing course."

"Does it matter?" asked Aiyesha.

"Yes, it matters. Me want to go home with Peter quickly. Not longer."

And before Aiyesha could tell him of the believed threat on the other side, Mr. Nibbetts reached around Peter and gave Day's reins a mighty tug and a call to go forward.

"Wait! What are you doing!" shouted Peter, trying to regain control of the reins. Night's reins slipped from his hands from the sudden lurch forward.

"No, stop!" called Aiyesha after them as their horse ran up the hill. She rode after them.

Day took Peter and Mr. Nibbetts to the crest of the hill. The mare suddenly stopped abruptly on her own accord; the momentum sent Mr. Nibbetts crashing into Peter from behind.

Mr. Nibbetts let out an "Oof!" as his jaw rammed into Peter's back.

"Ak!," cried Peter.

"Sorry," said the furry creature, sitting back up in the saddle as if nothing had happened.

When Peter straightened, his eyes went wide. Aiyesha came up beside him on Bear.

Mr. Nibbetts screamed.

The army, at first, seemed to spread out for miles before them, but it was really less than that: four rows of twenty-five men in purple uniforms sitting atop large gray horses with black manes, as calm as a flock of birds on a beach. All were staring at the three companions on the hill. In front of the mass of men were eleven women, dressed in tight purple uniforms that, even from where Aiyesha sat in her saddle, hugged their figures, revealing their curves. In front of them were two men: General Gasahd and Captain Zakmon.

Aiyesha immediately picked Gelera out of the eleven women in the front.

Gelera had betrayed her! Curse her!

"Let's turn around. Now!" she told Peter.

Mr. Nibbetts yelped again and Aiyesha's hot glare rendered him silent.

"Good idea," said Peter. His voice creaked.

Just as they turned their horses around, a low, booming voice called out from the bottom of the hill. It was General Gasahd.

"Come down, Aiyesha!" he said. "I wish to have words."

"Who is that? How does he know your name?" asked Peter, turning back in his saddle, glancing at Gasahd.

"No one of consequence." And Aiyesha turned and rode down the hill, back toward Alan and Catina.

Peter followed.

As they neared the bottom of the hill, there was the mighty thunder of the soldiers' voices, shouting from the other side and the sudden rumble of hooves, tearing up the ground. Within an instant the men came pouring over the hill.

"Alan, ride!" called Peter.

Alan grabbed Night's reins and steered he and Catina away from the monstrous sound. They tore off as fast as Night was able.

The men rushed past Aiyesha in a blur of gray and black and purple and went off after Alan and his small companion.

"No! Stop!" she shouted after them but, of course, they didn't.

She was surrounded by men. She looked over her left shoulder and saw that a group of twenty soldiers had surrounded Peter and Mr. Nibbetts as well.

Where were the women? Aiyesha suddenly wanted to see her friends from the Coast of Seryn, the women she had spent day in and day out with for the past twelve years. In spite of what was happening, she missed them.

The men, proud in their uniforms, glared at her but did not approach. These were the men from the Coast, she knew. The men on the Coast wore a slightly different uniform than those on the mainland. The men from the Coast wore purple tunics and trousers made of a flexible canvas, strong and not given to tear but easy to move in. They wore glossy black boots with silver buckles at the top, by their shins. Their elbows sported black patches with the outline of the Blue Eye on them. None wore helmets. Those from the Coast seldom did as they believed they were superior to those on the mainland and did not need the protection of one unless going into battle. And capturing a single woman was not deemed a dangerous task.

The men began to part as General Gasahd and his captain rode toward her. When Gasahd drew near, she locked eyes with his, her face as firm as if cast in iron. The muscles around her green eyes tensed.

"At last I find you," said General Gasahd.

She did not speak. She would not give him the pleasure of hearing her voice. Never again. She didn't want anything to do with the Coast of Seryn or its officers. She would not contribute any part of herself to their cause unless it was absolutely necessary. Even then, she would rather die.

"I see," he said, glancing down, "she remains quiet. No matter." He looked up at her again, his lips a grimace beneath his mustache. "You will come with me back to the Coast of Seryn and continue serving His Lordship."

Aiyesha said nothing.

"If you resist, those two over there" —he nodded toward Peter and Mr. Nibbetts. Peter appeared to be remaining calm in his saddle though Aiyesha knew his heart must be beating faster than a Tharadon's wings. Mr. Nibbetts seemed to be in a daze from this sudden surprise. "And those over there" —he nodded the same way to somewhere behind her. When she turned to look, she saw a group of men bringing Alan and Catina back. Alan did not move. Catina was crying. "They will die. I don't believe in big drawn out speeches about ultimatums so I suggest you tell me what you will do. Shall you come with me or will they die? Answer quick before I kill them anyway."

Her heart sunk in defeat. She could not allow Gasahd to kill the others. She knew that he would end their lives if she did not obey.

She didn't have a choice.

"Very well," she said, "I will return with you."

"Good," he said with a terrible grin.

"But you must let them go, first," she added. *You better let them go, first.*

He cocked his head to the side and peered up at her. "What kind of a fool do you think I am? If I let them go first, there is no guarantee you will come with me."

"Please, they didn't do anything. Just let them go." Though anyone else's voice would be pleading by now, hers remained calmed.

"No," he said. "Now, come with me."

Head bowed, Aiyesha took one last look at her friends.

Friends.

That's what she called them, now. Her friends. She had friends. And she would never see them again. She gave her reins a tug and rode past Gasahd and Zakmon and into the swarm of men to where the women were.

"Good to have you back," said one when Aiyesha grouped with them.

She looked at Gelera. She saw the shame in Gelera's eyes for betraying her.

"I'm sorry," said Gelera.

"Your words mean nothing to me," said Aiyesha and turned her head away.

Just as she was about to ride away with the other girls, a foul shriek filled the air.

It sounded like Mr. Nibbetts.

Two minutes prior, while Aiyesha was exchanging words with General Gasahd, Mr. Nibbetts had disconnected himself from the reality he was facing and was somewhere inside his thoughts, a dark place where he was his only company. There, in that terrible place, all his fear boiled like a kettle over a fire, its flame hot and blue. He thought of home and the Flistablare forest. He thought of his loved ones burned to ash in the field. He thought of the look on Catina's face when she acknowledged that her parents had died. He saw Peter's smile when Peter encouraged him and told him that he wasn't dying, only ill. Mr. Nibbetts's insides shook, trembling under the weight of suppressed emotions and frustration. He had been selfish this whole journey, complaining at every chance he could, paying no heed to the needs of others. Shame added itself to the feelings compounding inside that dark place where he was alone with himself. He knew what was happening. He was experiencing the Change, the release of emotions pent up inside. The Flistablare were very emotional creatures, their thoughts and feelings amounting to more than a Man or Woman could muster in the most painful and stressful of circumstances. But the Flistablare controlled their feelings, for if they did not, their society would surely have fallen apart centuries ago, their emotions having driven them to madness. But, every so often, when called upon, a Flistablare could go through the Change, a shift of internal balance, removing the chains that kept these dark emotions at bay, and release them in any manner they chose, without going mad.

The Change was happening now, here, in this place of blackness and solitude, away from the World and the men in purple outside his realm of consciousness.

The Change was happening and Mr. Nibbetts reveled in it, joyed himself on the feeling of the imminent release of fear, frustration, anger, anguish, pain, the helplessness of being ill because he was not used to it. It was building inside him, pulsating, his feelings begging for him to set them free and pour out from this furry shell of a body.

Mr. Nibbetts kept the emotions down, waited, allowed the Change to occur. The darkness inside him, before the eye of his mind, flashed red, a flush of heat coming over him. He trembled and shook, his muscles tensing, a low gurgle forming in his throat, turning into a low, rumbling growl.

Almost there. The emotions had built up to the top of his neck. All the pain. All the hate and discontent of his unfair life. All the grief over friends and family burned and gone. All the loss. All the frustration of succumbing to an illness, a state of being, he knew nothing about.

The Change was happening.

And it happened now.

With a growl louder than ten lions, Mr. Nibbetts stood up in his saddle. Peter yelped, caught off guard from the rumbling sound. The men about them, all of them, dropped their jaws, their eyes widening so that the whites outweighed the color of their irises.

The Change had occurred and Mr. Nibbetts, transformed from a complaining, timid furry, little creature, unleashed the wrath of a pack of angry wolves. His teeth and claws elongated to twice their size, straining to be released from their fleshy cradles, he tore into the men.

The battle began.

Everything changed.

Using Mr. Nibbetts's growl as a diversion, Aiyesha leapt off her horse and darted in between the men surrounding her. Only when she ran past three of them did the others notice and began chasing after her. The familiar metallic ring of steel brought forth from heavy sheaths filled the air, but still Aiyesha ran. It was no use being surrounded, being confined. Now, gaining some distance from them, she was free to move. Instinctively, her training kicked in and she was no longer the Aiyesha she had been moments ago. Now she was Aiyesha Elnaa, warrior of the Coast of Seryn, the finest soldier out of all the women. And she was aware of her skill. While training, the techniques, the discipline, came to her with ease and so she harnessed it and trained harder, longer, and soon became unbeatable.

She was exercising her training, now. This was for real. Nearly sixty men came rushing toward her on their horses. How could she, being just one, conquer so many? And where were the women? There! Beside her, just off to her left. They had been hiding behind the other men this whole time. And they were riding toward her, their steeds at a full gallop.

Aiyesha dropped into a crouch when the first of the male soldiers came down on her, the sharp edge of his sword just missing her. She grabbed his arm and, using the momentum from his swing, pulled and dragged him down off his horse. With a quick twist of her hands, she broke his wrist and removed the blade from his fingers and kicked him in the face, breaking his nose. Just as soon as that soldier was down another was upon her. She twirled and ran the blade through his middle and stole the sword from his hand so now she had two.

The shouts of the soldiers fell silent on her ears, her thoughts and feelings slowing so that all around her were moving in slow motion, her concentration the only task at hand: survival.

The women were beside her now, all eleven leaping off there horses, some landing on their feet, others in fancy rolls to the ground. The women each drew two blades from sheaths mounted on their backs, the blades about six inches shorter than the swords Aiyesha held in a relaxed yet firm grip. And so the women surrounded her, warding off the men, telling them to keep their distance.

Gelera was in front of her, the other women on all sides and behind.

"I'm sorry that it had to come to this," said Gelera.

Aiyesha did not reply. Her mind was alert, conscious of the women circling her from behind, of the men who had just surrounded her gone off to aid their comrades who were dealing with Mr. Nibbetts and Peter. Aiyesha was even aware of Alan and Catina, Alan swinging his walking staff wildly, beating off any who touched him. Alan mustn't have been able to get to his sword in time. It must have been tied in with their bundles on Night's rump or he surely would have used it.

Behind her, someone moved. She heard the wind from a blade slicing through the air. Aiyesha spun around to meet it and deflected the blow using the sword in her right hand. The wielder of the blade, Nomara, fell to her knees with wide eyes when Aiyesha ran her through with the sword in her other hand. It was a signal to the other women that despite their long years of companionship on the Coast, she was not afraid to kill any of them.

Gelera rushed at Aiyesha from behind. Aiyesha spun to meet her and steel clanged against steel as the women matched each other's moves until Aiyesha saw an opening when Gelera's right arm was raised, and struck her with the front of her elbow across the jaw. Gelera took a step back and the other women rushed in. Aiyesha warded them off, her blades a blur of silver, clashing against theirs. She moved among them like a cat dancing in a room filled with mice. Many of the women found themselves turned around as they spun to match Aiyesha's movements, trying to match her speed.

Move smoothly and rhythmically. Let them do all the work. Tire them, thought Aiyesha. And so she obeyed her thoughts and moved about the women, their swords crashing together when a strike was made, their ring loud in the air . . . but not to Aiyesha. She was one with the battle and the battle was one with her. She was now in the Silence. She could hear the blades ring as they clashed but the sound was not outside her ears but inside her head, inside her heart.

She tracked each of the women's movements, her mind anticipating each lady's move, her limbs reacting quickly, countering each strike against her. Her blade jutted out, as if on a will of its own, and she ran one of the women through the chest. Her blade swung out again and another woman was cut in two.

Lara, who was evidently angry for having been elbowed in the nose a moment ago, attacked and Aiyesha countered each swing of her blades with ease. Lara was the least-skilled of the women. Aiyesha spun and caught her right leg behind Lara's knee, taking the woman's leg out from under her. A downward stroke of the sword and Aiyesha's blade planted itself in Lara's center.

Three dead.

Eight alive.

Aiyesha, motivated by how well she was doing, fought harder, her moves faster. Two of the women came at her at once and swung their swords, two of the blades heading for Aiyesha's middle, two for her head. Aiyesha fell onto her belly, narrowly missing the four blades as they swiped a mere foot and a half above her. She rolled onto her back and stuck a sword in each of the women from behind. Both women turned and looked down at her and moved to strike their final blow. Aiyesha somersaulted backward and the women missed her before falling down dead.

Five dead.

Six alive.

Gelera was on her again, putting her in a choke hold from behind. Aiyesha stuck both her blades in the ground and grabbed Gelera's forearm and, with one swinging movement, heaved Gelera over her hip. The woman fell to the ground with a hard thud just in front of Aiyesha's blades. Aiyesha recouped them just in time as the other five women ran at her. With fluid motion, she knocked two of the women's blades from the air and lopped the head off one of them. Another came toward her and she, too, was beheaded.

Seven dead.

Four alive.

Gelera was back on her feet in a flash and Aiyesha kicked her back down just as quickly. One woman came at Aiyesha from either side. She ducked as the blades just missed her head. Then when another came at her from the front, she rolled along the ground, out of the way and kicked the legs out from under her attacker. Aiyesha's sword came down in a blur and severed the woman's legs. Blood sprayed immediately and covered the beige of Aiyesha's sweater, turning it a brick red. The smell of blood excited her and she leaped over the legless body and ran another of her former companions through.

Nine dead.

Two alive.

Gelera, while Aiyesha was fighting the other woman, slashed at her. Aiyesha saw the blade coming and moved . . . but she didn't move fast enough. A thin sliver of meat was shaved off her shoulder in a tear of fabric and flesh. The pain lasted for less than a second and was then lost to a world of numb feelings and the thrill of the fight. Another blur of blade swept across her vision. Aiyesha didn't realize she moved as the woman tried to cut her. Without thought, Aiyesha thrust out her sword and tore into the woman's hips. Gelera came at her from behind and was struck by the heel of Aiyesha's foot across the jaw. Aiyesha withdrew her sword from the woman's hip and ran the other blade through her throat. A squirt of blood sprayed Aiyesha's face. She spun around to face Gelera just as the other woman fell.

Ten dead.

One alive.

Two fighting.

The heat of the battle was over and Aiyesha and Gelera circled each other slowly, Aiyesha still lost to the Silence of the fight.

"You killed them," said Gelera. "After all they've done for you, after all those nights we sat together by a fire and supported one another through our torture. After all the times they were there for you when you cried you wanted to go home. You killed them."

"They wanted to kill me," said Aiyesha, and that was reason enough. *They would have killed you, too, if our positions were reversed.*

With a scream, Gelera lunged at Aiyesha. Steel rang on steel. The women struggled with one another, their blades clashing together with more fury than when Aiyesha fought the other ten women. Within moments their blades were driven from their hands, each knocking the blades away from the other in heated fury, thrown away to somewhere beside them, amongst the bodies of fallen friends. Gelera kicked at Aiyesha's knees and Aiyesha blocked her and delivered a few round kicks of her own, aimed at Gelera's head. Fists flew. Gelera executed an open palm and caught Aiyesha in the nose, breaking it. The pain flashed inside her head in a brilliant red striped with white, but soon faded away. Aiyesha opened her hand, keeping her fingers tight together so her hand was like a knife and, from the side, went for Gelera's throat, hoping that the arch between thumb and forefinger would act like a board crashing against Gelera's neck. Gelera blocked and Aiyesha came with an upper cut, connecting hard against the underside of Gelera's chin.

Aiyesha sprang on top of her and threw her to the ground, next to one of the fallen swords. When Gelera struck out to get Aiyesha off her, Aiyesha quickly moved Gelera's fast hands away with a swipe of her forearm and grabbed the sword that lay on the grass beside them. The blade came down and in a spray of blood Gelera lost her head.

Without stopping to examine what she had done, Aiyesha got to her feet and went to aid her friends.

Ten minutes earlier, as Mr. Nibbetts screeched and sprang off Day and onto the nearest soldier, Peter's legs felt as if they had just been filled with water. Fear gripped his heart as he watched two soldiers go to their comrades' rescue as Mr. Nibbetts bit and tore flesh from the soldier's neck.

Somewhere, over to his right, Aiyesha was surrounded by men. He looked past the men and saw eleven women, watching. Then the women moved toward the crowd. He wanted to call out to her, wanted to see if she was all right. When he opened his mouth to speak, all that came out was a hoarse whisper. There was a pinch at the back of his throat. He cleared it.

"Come along, now," said one of the soldiers to his left, producing a pair of shackles.

Shouts of men filled the air. Peter's thoughts were lost to the din. He saw Aiyesha drop off her horse and move away from the other soldiers. She darted in between the horses, trying to evade them. He had seen her fight before but he was still amazed at how smoothly she moved. He knew she would be safe.

When the soldier to his left came up to him, shackles in hand, Peter turned to him with hard eyes. The soldier reached out to grab him and Peter came with a right hook, setting the soldier in a daze. Adrenaline pumping, Peter felt the strength return to his legs. He grabbed the reins and beckoned Day to ride. Day took off and the soldiers followed him.

He glanced back and, behind the ten soldiers on Day's tail, he saw Alan and Catina being bound with rope.

Alan! He has no way to defend himself. He can't see. And Catina—Peter turned Day around and came at the soldiers full tilt. Some drew their swords, others gazed on in bewilderment at the man riding toward them. Peter moved away from the soldiers with the swords and kicked one of the unarmed soldiers off his horse. Peter laughed at the small victory.

He saw Mr. Nibbetts—who was now a fierce and uncontrollable animal—make his way from man to man, clawing at them, biting them and their horses. No more could he ponder on the sudden change in his friend's appearance and demeanor when two soldiers came up beside him and forced him off Day. Peter fell off the mare and landed hard on his behind, banging his tailbone. A numbing pain shot up his spine.

"Ahh!" he cried and immediately went to feel the wound. It was sensitive to the touch.

The two men dropped off their horses. One drew his sword.

Peter got to his feet and he didn't need a slab of Linsheum to know all the color ran from his face as the sword came down on him. Just as the blade bore down, its path shifted and went off to the side, grazing Peter's right shoulder, down along his bicep and forearm, tearing the brown wool fabric, but no harm was done to his flesh. The soldier toppled forward, Mr. Nibbetts on his back, the furry creature digging his teeth into the soldier's neck. The other soldier looked on, his eyes dull, filled with bewilderment. It seemed to Peter that he had never seen a Flistablare before.

Heart racing, Peter took the diversion for his own and ran from the scene, confident that Mr. Nibbetts would be able to care take of himself. Off to his side he could hear men shouting and calling out hideous curses as they tried to rescue their comrade from the rabid Flistablare.

A soldier's fist caught Peter square in the jaw and he fell onto his behind, stars of red and green bursting before his vision. A droning buzz filled his ears as three soldiers grabbed him and hoisted him to his feet. Blood dripped from the corner of his mouth. The soldier stood before him, a twisted grin on his face, his eyes dark and menacing, gazing deep into Peter. The soldier struck him in the throat; Peter gasped and coughed, choking from the impact. When he swallowed the blood in his mouth, it was like swallowing a stone.

His arms bound by a soldier on either side, and a meaty forearm around his chest from behind, Peter watched in stupefied horror as another fist came rushing toward his face. It landed with a wet slap, as if he had just been hit open-palmed instead of with a closed, gloved fist. Peter's world became a blurred, sloshy mix of teary vision, watery thoughts, and a damp consciousness, as if he were looking at the soldier in front of him from underneath the surface of a rotting lake. He was barely able to stand, his legs bent at the knees, the soldiers that bound him keeping him up so their comrade could deliver punishment for a crime Peter did not know what. His limbs were heavy and sore, aching still from that lonely night when he and his company, save Aiyesha, had fallen severely ill.

Peter struggled, fought against the forces holding him at bay. Somewhere in the background Mr. Nibbetts was tearing someone to pieces. How many soldiers Mr. Nibbetts was destroying, Peter didn't know but by the sounds of the struggle, it was more than just one person. He heard Catina crying elsewhere in the background and Alan speaking in his smooth voice in Grescalla what sounded like words of comfort and reassurance about the outcome of the fight.

The soldier kicked the inside of Peter's left knee and in a heated moment where a white flash burst into his mind's eye, he thought something in his knee had been momentarily put out of place and then slipped back in its proper position again. He tried to shake his arms free but to no avail. The soldiers were laughing; at least, he thought they were. He could not tell amidst the din of his thoughts, amidst the headache caused by the involuntary tears running down his cheeks. He never knew battle could be like this: so hypnotic in its presentation despite the pain felt. Peter watched all that was going on around him seemingly all at once: Aiyesha off to the side, driving a sword through the belly of a woman dressed in a tight-fitting purple outfit; Mr. Nibbetts tearing the arm off a soldier who flapped around on the ground like a fish out of water; Alan being tossed from soldier to soldier, exploited and mocked because he was blind; Catina bound and gagged and blindfolded off to the side in the company of two men on horses, presumably the leaders of this rabble.

His arms were heavy. His legs were tired. Just moving demanded more effort than Peter thought possible. Another fist to the face, a stamp on the foot, a shot to the solar plexus and a sharp burst of pain echoing in his middle. He wanted to throw up.

His limbs were so heavy, so weighted they might as well be dead. So heavy. So hard to move. Peter envisioned burlap bags tied to his wrists and ankles and in each of the bags a load of fifty bricks. He could not move. Could not fight. Could not.

Could not.

He didn't know how long he lost consciousness but he thought it was no more than a few seconds. When he regained some understanding of where he was and what was happening—

—something happened.

The weight in his arms was slowly being lifted and Peter thought someone was untying the brick-filled burlap bags from his wrists. The weight keeping his legs down was also being undone and, if he did not know any better, he thought he might float off the ground.

The soldiers still held them in their grasp, the soldier who had been hitting him gone off somewhere, probably to inflict damage on another of his company.

Peter's arms and legs were light, no longer carrying the weight of fifty bricks each. A sudden and unexpected energy filled his innards, pulsated in his muscles; his joints jittered, yearned to be free and moving.

And move they did. Peter closed his left arm and his right arm together, the soldiers who were holding them coming crashing together in front of him, obviously not expecting him to suddenly move and with such strength. The soldiers' heads banged together and the echo from their skulls crashing still rang in Peter's ears when the soldier who held him from behind strengthened his grip. Peter grabbed the soldier's forearm and dug his fingers into the meaty area between bicep and wrist. The man howled and kicked Peter from behind. Peter fell forward, face first, his hands outstretched, bracing his fall. His palms hit the ground and he lowered himself, as if from a push-up, and then pushed against the ground and sprang back to his feet. The soldier came at him and, without any conscious effort, Peter grabbed him and hoisted him off the ground and threw him over ten feet and into a crowd of soldiers who were trying to have at Mr. Nibbetts.

The furry creature growled as some of the soldiers fell on top of him. In a burst of speed, Peter charged towards them and, with each hand, threw the soldiers off his furry friend, tossing them back several feet behind. A hot sting struck Peter's leg and when he looked to its source, he saw the fabric of his trousers had been torn, someone having sliced him with their sword. Looking for the one who hurt him, Peter then saw Alan lying on the ground, soldiers kicking him in the stomach.

Peter charged over to them and leapt at them from behind. Five men piled on top of him. Beneath the weight of the bodies, Peter was in a world of his own, his mind scrambled, only thinking of one thing: survival. He brought his arms inward and summoned all his strength. The bodies of the soldiers pressed in from all sides. He waited for a weakness in their force upon him and when the time was right, he pressed both his arms out, pushing three out of the five soldiers off him. He swung out wildly at one, his fist catching the soldier across the temple. He swung out again, his fist crashing into another's ribs, snapping them like dry branches. One soldier tried to jump on him but Peter kicked him off.

Getting to his feet and with ease, he picked up Alan and drew him away from the battle. When he felt Alan was a safe distance away, he glanced around for Catina and saw her still with the two men who presided over the battle like a pair of priests presiding over a Service to the Master. He took a step toward them but stopped when he heard Mr. Nibbetts howl.

Peter ran.

Mr. Nibbetts was being overtaken by at least thirty men. Peter jumped into the middle of them and fought.

Gelera's head was still rolling along the ground when Aiyesha ran to help her friends. In a flurry of movement, she hacked her way through the soldiers, getting all the nearer to where Mr. Nibbetts was fighting off men like a rabid dog would a burglar. She saw Peter, his arms swinging out wildly, hitting anything that moved. She made her way to his side and handed him one of her swords.

"Thanks," he said and stood back-to-back with her.

The men moved in toward them, circling. Mr. Nibbetts growled. Aiyesha noticed Peter glancing her way, his eyes asking for direction as to what to do next. She kept a calm expression on her face and simply said, "Don't move until they come."

But Mr. Nibbetts moved first and tore at the men. This was a gutter war and Aiyesha was excited. No form of movement. No set pattern of how to fight. No specific routine to anything.

It was about survival.

Her blade carved the air in a silver arc and removed the head of a soldier coming in with a blade of his own. A twirl of the wrist and her blade found its way to the middle of a man behind her. The sloshy sound of his guts spilling open found her ears, but her expression remained hard.

Another swipe of the blade and another man down. Then another. Then another.

Soon, some of the men began to back away. Off behind them General Gasahd called out for them to finish the job. Aiyesha lunged at the soldiers in full fury, cutting away at them before they had time to move.

Attack when the enemy is preoccupied, she remembered.

Peter grunted off to her side. Mr. Nibbetts snarled.

The battle was coming to an end. The men were falling more quickly, now.

"Keep going!" Aiyesha shouted to Peter. *They know it's a lost cause. They're losing hope.* "Don't give up!"

Someone came at her from the side and tackled her to the ground. A hard fist came down, landing on the bridge of her nose, aggravating the already-broken cartilage, the knuckles scraping along the tops of her eye sockets. Aiyesha stuck her sword into the man's side and felt the immediate warm rush of blood gush out onto her hand. She withdrew the blade and shoved the man off her and got back to her feet.

Many of the men were retreating, jumping back onto their horses and riding off toward the hill. A few disappeared over its horizon. General Gasahd called out to them but they didn't listen and kept riding.

Aiyesha looked over to her former general. He stared back at her.

She made her way to him.

Catina sat on the ground, blindfolded, hands and legs bound together, on a patch of grass between the two great horses that bore General Gasahd and Captain Zakmon. When she approached them, she lowered her sword but kept it ready, should the need arise. She could feel the knife she had taken from that man on the side of the road while traveling, pressed between the waist of her pants and the small of her back. She had forgotten all about it. That was not like her. *Blast!*

Gasahd clapped slowly, dramatically.

"Well done," he said.

"Well done?" She did not follow.

"Very well done. I don't suppose it would do me any good to come down there and try to take you back with me, now, would it?"

Aiyesha didn't need to respond. She knew he knew the answer.

"I thought not," he said. "You definitely are the finest, that much is clear."

She glanced down to Catina. The child sat there, her body hunched forward, her chin above her knees, the ties from the blindfold hanging over her ears. Her breathing was quick and shallow—Shock.

"So you've come for the girl," said Gasahd. "This I know. Go on. Take her. She is of no use to me. A little young for my taste."

Aiyesha's eyes tensed around their edges. Men and their perversions. She raised her sword and held the tip out to Gasahd and Zakmon, keeping an eye on them while she bent down and put her arm around Catina's waist.

"It's all right, Catina. It's me, Aiyesha," she said, hoping the girl would recognize her voice.

Catina squirmed but Aiyesha held her still. She backed away, sword held out in one hand, the little girl in the other.

"I want to be left alone," said Aiyesha. And she meant it. She hoped the battle today would prove that she could not be overtaken and that any future efforts to take her back to the Coast of Seryn would be futile. And if not that, then at least anyone who came looking for a fight would not live to tell the tale.

"So be it," said Gasahd. He gave Zakmon a nod and the two rode toward the battle site, telling the men that remained fighting with Peter and Mr. Nibbetts to be on their way and to return back over the hill.

When they were gone, Aiyesha set Catina down and, using her sword, cut the bonds that bound her. She removed the blindfold from the girl's eyes.

Catina sat on her behind, rocking back and forth, shaking.

CHAPTER XXXVIII
After
(Irons in the Fire)

The bloody bodies of men wearing torn hides of purple canvas lay about, their limbs strewn at odd angles, some headless. Others, too weak to speak and only able to wheeze their breaths, lay still, waiting to die. Blood colored the deep green of the grass an awful brown; the scent on the air was that of iron and sweat and lingering death.

Peter sat on his haunches, catching his breath, while Mr. Nibbetts was several paces away, seeming to shrink from a hulking menace of death and destruction right before his eyes. The Flistblare's claws began retracting, his sharp teeth shrinking back into his gums. He was too tired to ask what happened to his furry friend and why the Flistablare had turned into a monster.

Off a little ways to the side, Aiyesha was with Catina. Peter could tell the little girl was traumatized by the whole ordeal. He was traumatized himself, in shock, completely in awe that he had survived an attack that out-numbered he and his companions twenty fold. He spat, the wad a mix of saliva and blood. The foul taste of iron and copper circulated inside his mouth. Mr. Nibbetts groaned off to his left. When Peter looked upon the furry creature, he was just Mr. Nibbetts again, a small furry thing that, by his posture, could barely carry the weight of his own body.

Alan. Where was Alan?

Peter got to his feet, his arms and legs shaky, and surveyed the area. Alan was about thirty yards to his right, the blind man cowering in a ball on the ground. As Peter walked over to him, scenes from the battle flashed before his mind's eye, the grimaces of the soldiers' faces, the grunts and growls as blades were swung and thrust at him. The high-ringing clash of steel on steel that still screamed in his ears.

"Al—" He coughed, not getting the man's name out. He tried again. "Alan?"

The cowering figure stirred, his body shifting beneath the folds of his black clothes.

"Alan? It's me, Peter," he said. He was only a few paces away, now. "Alan?"

Alan peeked up at him from beneath his arms slung over his eyes. "Peter?"

"It's me, Alan. It's Peter." He knelt beside him and helped his friend sit up.

"Peter," was all Alan said.

"It's me, it's okay." He sat down beside him.

"Catina. Is she all right?" Worry filled Alan's face.

Peter stole a glance and saw Aiyesha sitting on the ground, Catina in her lap, rocking her back and forth, soothing her with soft pats and gentle strokes to her back.

"She's all right," he said. "Aiyesha's watching over her."

"Take me to her," he said and held out his hand.

Peter took it and helped him up. Alan's legs wobbled when he stood. He led Alan to his granddaughter and, guiding him, placed the blind man's hand on the little one's shoulder.

"Catina?" said Alan.

The little girl looked up and grinned when she saw who it was. As best she could, she left Aiyesha's arms and fell into her grandfather's. Catina began to cry. So did Alan.

Seeing the two reunited brought a smile to Peter's face. He could only imagine what being a part of something as violent as this along with someone you love would be like. Even he, who was not as attached to his friends as Alan was to Catina, was filled with joy and relief that they were still alive, still breathing, the wounds small.

Still alive. He was still alive.

How? How could he have survived with as many men attacking him as there had been? Aiyesha, surviving, yes, he could see that. She was obviously capable of taking care of herself when it came to combat. And Mr. Nibbetts, what he witnessed from him was extraordinary. Alan had been drawn off to the side, he had noticed, when he was fighting the men. Alan was safe once Peter got the soldiers off him. Catina, well, he did not know where she had been but she was obviously safe. As for himself, how he had managed to fend off man after man, blow after blow—how he had freed himself when the three soldiers held him—this he did not know. It was impossible. Wasn't it? Adrenaline, maybe? Maybe, but even that explanation was unlikely. Adrenaline was good for short bursts of strength and energy and Peter knew that his strength had lasted for a good while during the fight. His energy, too. He had only grown tired once the men fled and the rush of fatigue from all his exertion hit him like a stampeding horse. His survival was a mystery added to the other problem plaguing his mind: the Man in the Gray Cloak.

Aiyesha. She had some explaining to do.

Peter turned toward her, his expression hard. Since he had known her, he always made an effort to be polite, courteous, gentle with his words. That was his way. Now, his mind full of overwhelmed thoughts and questions that demanded answers, his shy nature melted away.

She owes us an explanation, he thought.

"Who were they? What was that about?" he asked her.

She stood and brushed the dirt off her behind. "Dembatstayr. The Void's Army."

When it appeared that that was all there was to her response, Peter placed his hands on his hips. What did she mean by "the Void's Army"? "I know. The Dembatstayr. But what did they want with you? You have to tell me, Aiyesha. I saw them come after you in Darim. I was there, remember? Are you in trouble with them? You have to tell me—Tell us." He swept a hand out, gesturing toward the others.

Aiyesha took a long breath and exhaled slowly. She folded her arms beneath her breasts. "You're right. As I'm sure you've known, I haven't told you everything about me. And after what just happened, you four are entitled to an explanation. Why don't you gather Mr. Nibbetts and I'll tell what I can."

"Not *what you can,* Aiyesha. Everything. I don't want a detail left out. Secrets are what brought this upon us. I don't want to risk anyone anymore. I have a responsibility to get Alan and Catina safely home. As for you or Mr. Nibbetts, you're welcome to come. And I don't want you two to get hurt, either. I want the truth."

She turned away, her eyes looking out onto the field, their greens clashing with the brown of the grass. When she spoke, her voice was low, sounding almost ashamed. "Then you shall have it."

The company gathered away from the battle site, sitting in a semi-circle, Aiyesha standing at its center.

"I'm glad everyone's all right," she said.

The wounds had been small: a cut here, a cut there, nothing to cause worry. Peter's lip was swollen and there was some bruising around his eye. Alan complained of a sore arm, the muscles strained from all his lashing out at the attackers he could not see. Catina, Alan reported, was fine and no harm had come to her. Though, she also told him, she didn't like the way the men were looking at her. They made her feel like a slab of meat, gazed upon by the eyes of starving wolves. And Mr. Nibbetts, well, no injuries could be seen, but with all that fur, who was to tell? He said he was fine but there was an air of dishonesty to his tone. And when Peter insisted that he tell the truth of his injuries, Mr. Nibbetts maintained that all was well and that the Change had kept him free from harm. Whatever that meant. Aiyesha seemed relatively fine, too, but her nose had been broken, Peter noticed. It didn't seem to bother her though.

And so Aiyesha stood before her companions, like a criminal on trial. She did not pace or move around when she spoke. Instead, she stood in one spot in the center before them, hands folded over her thighs, her face expressionless, as if admitting to a crime.

"Those men had come for me," she said. "And" —she eyed Peter— "as some of you know, I've kept things from you."

"We know that," said Alan. "You should have been honest with us."

"Let her talk," said Peter. *Please, Aiyesha, say something we don't already know.*

"Why?" the blind man shot back. "It is because of her we were nearly killed. It is because of her that our blasted horses have fled and my granddaughter is in shock. I was right about her, Peter. She has just proved that."

"Let's wait until she's finished and then we'll make our judgment."

Alan wrapped his arms around Catina, who sat between his legs. She was still shivering and her teeth chattered.

"I want to say I'm sorry for what happened," said Aiyesha. "It was not my intention to allow things to occur as they had. I did not expect this to happen. Those men were after me."

"Why?" came Alan again.

"Because I'm one of them, Alan," she said calmly. "I'm one of the Voidsmen— Voidswomen. Twelve years ago I went to the Coast of Seryn, the Snake's Eye, to train. In Bel Candar, where I'm from, there were rumors of coming war. Soldiers were needed, so I went."

"There has been no war," said Peter.

"Please, let me finish." A look of regret came over her face. "No, there hasn't been one. At least, no battle that would compare to what is rumored to come. My land was filled with the talk of it and, I heard, women were wanted for a secret wing in the army, women who, unlike men, would not be expected to be a part of a war as great as the one said to come. Their purpose was more elite, meant for missions of higher importance. There were twelve of us on the Coast. Those women there" —she nodded in the direction of bodies behind her— "were with me. I killed them today. I don't want to go back. I left because I no longer wanted to be a part of something I didn't believe in, a cause that held no meaning to me. Well, that's not entirely true. I believe in its cause but its methods I don't. No longer could I stand another morning on the Coast of Seryn. No longer could I stand another drill. So I fled."

She told of the battle at the harbor and her meeting of Morley. She told of her running along the Thakari Desert and the men she encountered there. There was Wesafeld and Samora. There was that night in the forest. There was Darim and her meeting of Peter.

"The army is here for a reason," she said. "What's more, the army belongs to the Master. They're there to carry out His work and bring the people together, enforce laws that will bring the Master glory and set in order a race of people who have lived lives unworthy of the Master's notice."

Peter thought of the curfew back home. Rules to keep the people in Garathen in check (as if they needed it; they were such a quiet and peaceful folk . . . except for the Slummers).

At hearing this, Alan shot to his feet. Catina nearly fell backward when his support left her.

"Alan, sit down," said Peter, surprised at the sternness of his own voice.

"This is an outrage!" exclaimed Alan. "Blast, woman! How dare you say that what happened here today is of the Master's work. Do you honestly think He would allow the bloodshed of those He loves? Do you honestly believe the way these men treated us brings Him glory? Nonsense!"

"As I said, I no longer agreed with the army's methods and that's why I left. It wasn't making sense to me. My leaving cast me a fugitive. Apparently once you sign on with the Island of the Dead, your life belongs to it."

"What did you say?" said Alan.

"I said my leaving cast me a fugitive."

"No, after that."

"Once you're a part of it, your life belongs to it."

Alan shook his head. "No. You said 'Island of the Dead.' You said 'once you sign on with the Island of the Dead, your life belongs to it.'"

"So?"

"So!" Alan spun in a circle. "My dear girl, you are in grave danger."

"Okay, that's enough," said Peter, getting to his feet. He put a hand on Alan's shoulder and eased him back down.

When Alan was seated, Peter bent at the waist and spoke into his ear. "Please, let her finish and then we can ask questions. There's no sense in interrupting until we've heard all that she has to say."

Alan huffed a response.

Peter took that as a concurrence to his request. "Thank you." He sat back down.

Aiyesha went on. "They've been hunting me ever since I left the Coast. As I said, my life belonged to them, to the Coast, to Seryn, to all of it. To General Gasahd."

"General Gasahd?" asked Peter. A part of him was fascinated by all of this. Tales of things unknown. He was only aware of the going ons in Garathen. This journey was teaching him things he only dreamed about: a bigger life beyond the confines of the Forest-Ring.

"My commanding officer on the Coast, and my trainer. He's the one who said a war is coming. He was the one I reported to the first day I decided to be a—a Voidswoman. But there's more. And, to be honest, I don't know all the details. A lot of what went on at the Coast of Seryn was kept secret. Only bits of information here and there were disclosed to the soldiers and to the women I trained with. It was said that another of the army's purposes was to pave the way for the Second Coming of the Master."

There was a gasp by all at hearing this. The Master? Coming again? Immediately Peter's thoughts went back to Pnumar and his tale of the Ark of Light and the Master, the war between the Black and the White, the Purple that mediated it. The Master. He was there; that war had been His beginning. He was coming again. Peter also remembered that Rano, the leader of the Men of Humility, had mentioned it.

"Sheep-folly," said Alan with a wave of his hand.

"It's true," said Aiyesha. "At least, I'd like to think it is. The Second Coming of the Master would mean a better World for us all. Just imagine Him walking among us, talking with us, being with us. We won't be alone anymore. We won't need to wait to pray to talk to Him. He'll be here, with us. That's very exciting."

"But why would the Island of the Dead be mixed up in it? What does the Island have to do with the Master? The word 'dead' has no place with Him."

"Yem Batu is where the Master is. The Coast of Seryn is close to it. It's hard to explain but while I was on the Coast, I could feel this energy permeating me in every way, a sense of something alive on the air. It was like after praying to the Master, that sense of calm and peace that comes over you, yet that feeling of excitement that your prayer is not falling on deaf ears."

"I'm confused," interrupted Peter.

"As you should be," said Alan. "Matters to do with the Master are seldom comprehensible." The blind man looked in Aiyesha's general direction. "Can I interject?"

"Not yet," she said.

"Yuh, me want to hear more," said Mr. Nibbetts.

Aiyesha went on. "It was said that this war that's coming will be huge, larger than any war in recorded history, larger than the Aeons have seen. There will be many who will oppose the Master. General Gasahd said that another army will rise up to counter the Dembatstayr, the Voidsmen, preventing them from paving the way."

Peter didn't know of any such army other than the Dembatstayr. He was relieved there was only one, as far as anyone was aware, anyway. Having just one known army in the World was already intimidating. Just having one was already seeming to put a roof on freedom. The looming presence of conformity hung over him.

"I'm still lost," he said.

"Perhaps the less you know, the better," said Alan.

Peter smirked at the remark.

"But, and before Alan speaks, I want to say I'm sorry," she said. "I didn't mean to drag you into this. I had no right. I'm confused myself and everything that I've been believing for the past twelve years has suddenly taken a turn. I want peace for all. Who does not wish that? I thought I could contribute to that. I thought that by being on the Coast I *was* contributing to that. I was wrong. The methods that were in play to bring about that peace—I don't know—didn't sit right with me. My spirit has been uncomfortable for a long time." She paused, took a breath. "Again, I am sorry. I know there's no way I can make it up to you. If you'd like me to leave you, I will, and I'll understand and not bear any ill will. We were lucky today."

"We were," said Peter quietly. *I don't think 'luck' is even the right word for it.*

A long silence hung on the air. What Aiyesha said had opened up a flood of questions in everyone's minds. It suddenly seemed that all their beliefs of how the World worked, how the Master worked, had lost credibility.

Alan was the first to speak. When he did, his head hung low. "I am no theologian. I have only my heart to guide me in terms of what I believe. Yet it is safe for me to say that I know enough about the Master in terms of what He stands for and in terms of what exists beyond our mortal World. At home, I have an extensive library of books on the subject. It was a hobby of mine before I lost my sight and I accumulated as much written knowledge as I could while abroad." He sighed. "When you said Island of the Dead, Aiyesha, my heart jumped in my chest. Worse, it jumped even more when you said that the Master resides on Yem Batu. And, further, that Yem Batu is here, in our World, in our plain of existence."

"That's right," she said. She remained standing though Peter thought she would sit after her apology had been made.

The blind man glanced up but then covered his eyes with thumb and forefinger. "In some of the texts I have, it does speak of Yem Batu being here, on Earth. Others say that only a portion of it is here on Earth, the other in a Realm that none can get to. And some say the Island belongs to a place of its own, and the latter is the most popular theory. It is actually the foundation of what most believe; the Master being somewhere that we can only communicate with by prayer. Your words alarm me. It was said, long ago in a year forgotten, that the Master would come again. I read that in a book and I look forward to that day. What concerns me is the term 'Island of the Dead.' Even more so, the word 'Void.' These are dark words to be associated with a kind and loving Master."

Aiyesha nodded.

"And since, it would seem, that the Island of the Dead is a part of our World, then we are all in trouble. You have given the army that has surfaced a name: Voidsmen. Or, in your case, Voidswomen, a name other than that which we are familiar with: Dembatstayr." Alan removed his fingers from his eyes and wet his lips. "This poses a great threat. Now, I do not know how much of what I have read is accurate or how much is merely the imagination of the author, though how the arguments were presented, I do believe the writers were of credible note. However, this 'Void,' this term 'Island of the Dead,' was always used in a negative context. They said that once those words were uttered here in our World, it meant that the End was coming. It meant that the Master would finish His work from long ago, walk among us, be everything we thought Him to be." Alan grinned a knowing grin. "What is interesting to note about someone believing in the Master is that we do not know His history, at least, not precisely. We do not know of His factual beginnings. We only know of His legend, of the Battle of Then, of the Black, the White, the Purple, the Purple being the Master."

Peter's ears perked up at this. Again he thought back to the Festival of Armasulia.

"The truth is," continued Alan, "we do not know much of what we believe. We base it all on our Faith and that is where we leave it." He rubbed his temples. "All this is giving me a headache and I fear I may have confused everyone even more."

"No, I understand what you mean," said Aiyesha. "You're essentially saying how can a cause that is supposed to be so noble and just be filled with so many holes and inconsistencies. How can it be presented to be standing on a solid foundation when, in fact, that foundation is as unstable and slippery as a rocky cliff and as hidden as your shadow in a dim alley."

"Exactly," said Alan.

Peter furrowed his brow. "What I would like to know is more about this counter army. The one that's supposed to rise up to meet the Dembat—Voidsmen, or whatever they're really called."

"I can't give you a solid answer, Peter," said Aiyesha. "By the time the words came round to my ears on the Coast, the tale and facts were probably exchanged by so many tongues that the truth of it was lost. What I do know is that someone—or *someones*—will come along and make a stand. General Gasahd didn't seem to be too concerned with this resistance. He is confident in his men and is sure they will prevail over any threat."

"Yet today we beat them," he said.

"True."

There was another pause. It was as if the truth of them, a mere five people, having stood there ground to a crowd of men one hundred strong, was finally beginning to take hold. All were clearly in a state of disbelief.

"How did we beat them, anyway?" asked Peter. "I mean, it's impossible. There is absolutely no way we could have done it. Not when the odds were twenty to one, give or take. And Mr. Nibbetts" —he turned toward his furry friend— "you still have to explain what went on there. If anything, it was you who warded them off."

"Me did nothing of the sort," said Mr. Nibbetts. "It was the Change. Not me. The Change, thank you."

"The Change?"

"A Flistablare instinct. It's something that happens to us under times of great stress and physical threat. But there is a catch. It has to be a threat that we know we can fight off. If me people had gone through the Change during the fire . . . they would have survived. Easily. But how could they have warded off flames that came from nowhere and towered over them like a mountain? They couldn't have. The Change couldn't be triggered. Today, the Change was triggered. In me. Me knew there was a chance to save meself from those men. It happened and here we are. Also, me can't remember much of how me did it. When in the Change, the Change does it for you. You don't do anything for it."

"Incredible," said Peter.

There was another lull in the conversation.

"Irons in the fire," said Alan.

"What?" asked Peter.

"There are too many irons in the fire. There is too much going on. And the irons are getting hot or so it seems. I suggest we stop talking for now and think on how we are going to get back home."

"All right." Peter glanced around, absentmindedly checking for Day and Night. All he saw were bodies, dead men lying in a bloody field before a hill.

Catina got to her feet and began walking toward the hill.

"Catina?" said Alan. "Rin don menne gammiti?"

She stood before the hill. All eyes were upon her. And, as if she had been calling them, Day and Night rode over the hill toward them. Aiyesha's horse, Bear, was not with them.

"Amazing," said Aiyesha.

The two mighty horses galloped toward the company full speed and slowed at the last moment before stopping in front of them.

"Cowards," muttered Alan.

"At least they came back," said Peter. *Thank the Mast—Thankfully.*

He turned toward Aiyesha.

"What about me?" she said. "Should I remain here?"

Peter turned toward Alan, again forgetting the man was blind and could not see the questioning in his eyes. When Alan didn't respond, Peter asked, "What do you think, Alan?"

He took a long time to consider. Then, hands on hips, said, "She can come. Who knows what else she knows. Maybe there is more she can share that can shed light on these strange days."

Mr. Nibbetts laughed a belly laugh. "Then let's be gone. Me do not wish to stay in this graveyard any longer! Me've seen enough dead bodies to last me a lifetime."

CHAPTER XXXIX
The Haunting of the Minds

With an ever-darkening rage, Thalok reached out to them. He was getting closer. *Peter. Peter. Peter. There are others with him. Peter. Peter. Others.* His thoughts echoed in his head like the steady beat of a drum, each reverberation a desire to accomplish his task. *Peter. Peter. Others. There are others.*

He was alone. It was night, the sky clouded over in an unsettling mix of murky gray with patches of even darker cloud blotted on it like a filthy quilt.

Thalok stopped running. Inside his dead heart, cold to years of hateful thinking and perverse desires, a hunger brewed. Hatred for the Void-man lurked in the background, a shadow covering him internally, a desperate yet savage desire to prove his master wrong. Prove to his master that *his* methods were best. A thought struck him. Perhaps it was the Void-man's intention to get him angry? Perhaps it was no accident he was motivated to accomplish the task of killing Peter quickly. Perhaps the Void-man orchestrated it so rebellion would bubble within him. But that was perhaps and "perhaps" was never definite. Thalok would call forth darkness, one that would not only affect Peter, but also the company Peter was with.

The Man in the Gray Cloak stared out onto the prairies, images of his prey filling his imagination as if Peter was out on the prairies with him; far away but almost within reach. Thalok closed his eyes and stretched himself outward, *reaching* to find Peter's location. The grounds around him filled his vision, his mind speeding over the landscapes like a lion chasing its prey. Blurs of dark green grass danced before his mind's eye, mountains with summits higher than anything he had ever set sight upon rushed by him, rivers sitting still in the night, their surfaces glistening like finely polished Mica.

Peter. Peter. Peter.

Others.

There are others with him.

And he found them. They had been moving, Thalok knew, but now they had stopped. He couldn't say how he knew but he read their expressions well. Their faces were long, weary, their eyes carrying a twinkle of gladness that they had stopped for the night. Thalok was pleased he would reach them in a few days, if that. This newfound realization they were so close made the weight of his dead heart lighter, as though filled with hot air, an excitement that soon this hunt of his would be coming to an end. The excitement of the euphoria he would encounter once returning to the Island of the Dead, his body being replenished after what would be—if the Void-man was right—a draining fight with Peter. A fight out here, in the World, away from the Purple Fog.

Thalok stretched himself even further, his thoughts and feelings encompassing Peter and the rest of his camp, watching them as they lay down for a night's sleep. His finger tips heated then burned. He was close.

Tonight Thalok would come to them. All of them. Not a one left out.

The flames were everywhere, on all sides, left, right, up and dow—no, not beneath him. Peter wiped the sweat off his face, his skin sweltering in the heat. He was in his house, back in Garathen, lying on the ground, watching helplessly as his home burned around him.

Memory of being out in the open, of having left Garathen to take Catina home to Grek was gone. He was always here, in his house, watching it as it burned.

He flipped over onto his stomach, his lungs thankful for the floorboards and the absence of flame. He could breathe, the heat from the flames all around him gone as he pressed his face to the floor, his hands cupped around his mouth, allowing only enough room for small sips of air. Yes, he could breathe.

Above him he heard a beam in the roof snap and fall to the floor beside him with a crackling thud. The air reeked of smoke. The wood of his house snapped and crackled beneath the roar of the flames.

He wasn't supposed to be here, he knew, but yet—it felt right to be here, to be home. The shirt on his back stuck to him, the flames above him heating his sweat, his skin burning like a pierogi boiling in water. Peter turned himself over and allowed his back to cool on the yet-un-burnt floor. It wasn't strange to have flame all around him except for that one spot where he lay. It all seemed perfectly natural.

His heart broke as another beam fell from the roof, narrowly missing him. He choked back his tears, telling himself to remain strong. Why did it matter? It was only a house. He could always build another. Who set this place ablaze? Had he been careless somehow and left his fireplace go unattended? He didn't think it likely but did consider the possibility.

His head full and aching, his thoughts scattered, his comprehension of the World around him slowed, he sat up. He glanced behind himself and saw the flames on the floorboards quickly swallow up the area where his back lay just seconds ago. Now he would be stuck sitting. He so desperately wanted to lie back down again. All strength had left him and his lower back ached. The muscles in his body felt suddenly weak.

The wall of oak burned slow before him, with a patch here and there completely burned through so he could see the porch of his veranda and out onto the main Through-way beyond. And there, out on the street, was a familiar sight: the Man in the Gray Cloak. The Man stood there, watching Peter through the gray hood that covered his face. This time Peter stared back, remembering the Man and the many times the Man haunted him.

"What do you want?" called Peter, past the flame.

The Man stood there, like he always did, with no response.

Peter stood, the floor behind him where he sat swallowed up in flame like it had when he sat up after lying down. Flames swirled about his feet, fanned by a wind he could not see but only feel. Swallowing hard, sweat running off his forehead, Peter hopped through the flame on his tiptoes toward the door. Once there, he saw the handle was completely immersed in swirls of yellow and orange flame. He looked around for something to perhaps open the latch with, but could find nothing. Just more fire.

Peter raised his knee nearly to his chest, and then kicked outward as hard as he could. The door splintered on the first try but did not break. Peter's sandal caught fire, the flames already licking his toes. He stamped his foot, trying to put it out but soon realized the futility of the action; the floor was covered in flame. He looked down and, suddenly feeling the heat because he realized that he *ought to be*, saw his other foot was catching fire. Peter quickly kicked at the door again. It splintered some more but was still not open. He kicked again. Almost, but not quite. And again. The door splintered and, putting his shoulder into it, Peter burst through the broken doorway and out past his veranda, through the opening where the veranda's door had burned away who knew how long ago, and into the street. Peter fell to his hands and knees, kicking out and downward wildly, smothering the flames on his sandals.

The Man stood before him, this time looking down at him through the thick, gray hood.

"Who are you?" asked Peter.

In a low, rumbling voice, the Man said, "Thalok, Qinoran of the Purple Fog. Your time has come. It is time to die."

Peter awoke with a start, sitting straight up from beneath his blanket. The sweat on his forehead, hands and forearms glistened under the moonlight. He used some of the slack in the blanket to wipe it away. Glancing around, he saw the others were asleep, all lying in their favorite positions, none stirring, only lying still. Peter flopped back down and said ouch when, forgetting he didn't have a pillow, his head hit the grass hard. He rubbed the back of his head and out of nowhere, thought it funny how rubbing your head after you bump it suddenly made it feel better.

After a time of trying to go back to sleep but with no success, Peter got up and wandered a ways from the camp. When he glanced back at the others, he could swear he saw a blur of dark gray glide over them.

Morley loomed over her, his massive form writhing on top of her as he breathed heavily from his effort, his sweaty skin glistening in the pale yet warm golden light of a lamp in the small cabin beneath the deck of the *Raven.* Aiyesha was helpless. She needed passage to the mainland, needed to be free of the Coast of Seryn. She had to oblige to Morley and his nightly giving of what was supposed to be pleasure but was instead hours of awkwardness and humiliation.

With every ounce of effort, Aiyesha tried to pretend she was enjoying herself, tried to make Morley feel as though he were doing her a favor by gratifying her. But Aiyesha knew Morley saw through her disguise and was well aware she was humoring him so that she could get what she wanted: a ride to the mainland. And Aiyesha knew that Morley didn't care she was humoring him. Either way, he was still getting pleasure from his taking advantage of her and, if she wanted to continue as a passenger on the *Raven,* she had no choice but to let him have his way with her.

He grunted, she countering his groans with moans of her own, hoping that somehow her sensuous noises would excite him and aid in him in completing his lovemaking sooner. But this was not lovemaking. This was rape! But, Aiyesha wondered, did rape mean that she had to be *forced* into sex with him. She was lying there, *allowing* him to do as he pleased with her. But this *was* force, wasn't it? She had to obey if she wanted a ride on the Sea. She had to let him do as he pleased. It was rape, and it shamed her, humiliated her. All those years of training could not have prepared her for this. Handling a man in combat, that was easy. But in bed? Under circumstances in which she had no control? Circumstances that led her to allowing herself to be defiled by a sex-obsessed beast? Nothing could have prepared her for it.

She was weak. She could not defend herself.

Morley grunted and groaned, his movement above her quickening as he approached climax. Aiyesha rocked her body along with his, moving her hips faster, hoping—like her throaty moans—that it would speed up his release.

But it didn't speed it up. Morley seemed to be taking longer than usual tonight. It was as if he somehow thought that morning would never come and that he had a night with her without end.

"Come on, you're almost there," she coaxed, urged.

He grunted louder. The floorboards of the deck above creaked and groaned. Aiyesha thought a shipmate would intrude on them at any moment. But no one ever came and she was doomed to spend eternity beneath this man, succumbing to his whims, an endless night of forced sex.

She continued to urge him on, praying all the while to the Master that He would deliver her from this. He didn't, and Morley was still on top of her. For what seemed like hours, Morley had his way with her body. His pace never slowed and Aiyesha was growing sore between her legs. She closed her eyes, tired, hoping that she would fall asleep and would not have to endure this anymore, at least, not consciously, anyway.

Morley's movements quickened. The ropes beneath the thin mattress of the cot rubbing against the iron bars they were tied to made a rough scraping sound.

"Grrr, hrrr, hrrr, grrruh . . . oh . . . mmm . . . grrgh . . . mmph . . . " And on like this he went, his groans becoming suddenly hypnotic.

She kept her eyes closed, not wishing to see his face contort as he, hopefully, approached climax. And then, with a deep, throaty moan, Morley released himself inside her. She got visuals of his vile seed pooling between her loins, inside that place that was supposed to be meant for only one. Her stomach twisted and she wanted to throw up.

He collapsed on top of her, his large head beside hers, breathing hard and deep into the pillow. His cheeks were cool from the sweat and, after all the heat from their bodies moving together, refreshing.

After a time he pushed his arms out and hung over her. She felt his eyes upon her. Digging to what seemed like the pit of her stomach for strength to face him, Aiyesha opened her eyes. Instead of seeing Morley, like she had expected, she saw that he was replaced by a man covered in a gray cloak, his face hidden beneath large folds of the thick, gray fabric of a hood. Yet, she knew the man was looking at her, straight through her.

Her insides went hollow and then she awoke.

She lay there, looking up at the stars, seeing her breath float up into the cool night air. She sensed the others lying nearby. Rolling over onto her side, Aiyesha thought back to her dream, to Morley, to the man wearing the gray cloak.

It may only have been a feeling, but she thought she could sense someone else in the camp there with them, someone who didn't belong to the group. For the first time since she could recall, she was too afraid to face it.

All was dark around him, blackness on blackness, so thick, so deep. Alan's only window into the outside World was the sounds it made . . . but tonight there was no sound. Silence. Nothing.

Then . . .

The edges around his field of vision blurred and a murk of gray swirled around the corners on the left and the right, circling around a cloud of dense black. The cloud became smaller, forming odd shapes, the gray around it growing clearer, images of a starry night sky at the borders. The cloud became even smaller, twisting, contorting as his sight was restored until, finally, the cloud was gone and Alan was on his back, lying on the main Through-way in Garathen, looking up at the night sky. His wife, Aubri, loomed over him. She held him in her arms, her tear-stained eyes staring down on him.

"Aubri," he said, his voice barely a whisper, but he knew she could hear him clearly, as if he were speaking at the top of his voice.

All suddenly became familiar. He had done something like this before, been with Aubri this way before—*exactly* this way before—but he couldn't place it.

"Alan, my love," she said.

He reached up and touched her face, tracing her jaw line with his fingertips. Aubri held his hand there.

This was so familiar. Alan glanced down at his chest and saw an arrow—a Dembatstayr arrow—protruding from between his breasts. He could feel its tip digging into the dusty ground beneath his back.

"I am cold," said Alan. "I do not wish to leave. I—"

Aubri cocked her head to somewhere behind her. Footfalls.

"They are coming," he said. "Do not let them get me."

"I will not let harm be visited upon you this night," she said gently.

Alan remembered what he had just been doing. He had been returning home and—he didn't know how he knew this; he just did—was mistaken for a Slummer wandering in the dark. A Dembatstayr had spotted him and in an instant unloaded a large arrow at him, the arrow piercing him mid chest, tearing its way through his body straight through to the other side.

"I know you will not," he said.

"Do not speak," said Aubri. "Just rest."

He listened to her and a sudden coolness came over him. A swirl of purple filled his vision and he watched a trail of purple smoke drift over his body, starting at his toes then making its way along his legs, past his stomach, his chest with the arrow sticking up from it, towards his face and then over his eyes. The purple smoke, mist, fog—was damp, cold, yet welcoming.

A hot pain filled his eyes and it felt like they were being sucked from their sockets. All went black again, just like before, just like before Aubri was hanging over him, cradling him in her arms.

He had died, he knew.

In the blackness a new shape came. A rush of relief washed over him, happy that he could see again. There, in the distance, he saw what looked like a long gray coat, hanging on a coat-rack, bunches of material hanging in loose slumber, waiting to be worn. The coat got closer and soon its flowing gray fabric was filled out with the body of a man. A man in a gray cloak.

The image of the man turned so that he faced Alan. The Man's face was hidden beneath a large hood, yet somehow his eyes were seen through the fabric. Alan, in the dark, tried to move, but he could not.

No one heard his cries as the Man continued to stare straight through him.

Catina sat on a chair in her kitchen back home, staring at the table, not knowing why she was staring at it. It suddenly seemed like she had always been staring at it and up until now realized what it was she was doing and decided to stop. She averted her eyes to the plain wall ahead of her then over to her right, to where the hall led to her parents' bedroom. Her parents were in there, sick, dying, with no one to help them. They had told her to stay out there in the kitchen, where it was safe. Catina didn't understand the request, but she obeyed anyway. She always obeyed her parents. They always knew what was best for her.

But she was going to argue today. She stood and made her way down the hallway to the bedroom, the hallway seeming somehow longer today, its walls more blank than usual, more plain than usual, more *not-the-same* as usual. When she reached the end, she went to her parents' bedroom on the left. Their door was closed, the big brown panel of wood shielding them from the outside World, blocking her out.

Catina knocked on the door and waited. No response. She knocked again. Same thing. Thinking her parents were asleep and didn't hear her, she thought she should open the door and check on them. Her hand poised above the door handle; she stopped, and knocked one more time.

Her mother's melodious voice was heard from the other side of the door. "Come in," she said in Grescalla.

Catina opened the door and entered. She stood dumbfounded in the doorway from what she saw. Her parents who, at a time she could not recall, had told her to sit out in the kitchen where it was safe—were dancing! Dancing on top of the bed, as if the mattress were a ballroom floor!

Michel held Dara's thin waist with one hand, his other hand holding hers at shoulder level, spinning his wife around to the melody of a waltz that Dara hummed.

"I thought you were sick?" said Catina.

Her parents kept dancing.

"We were," said Dara, "but not anymore."

"No. We are fine, now, Honey," said Michel. "Just look at your mother. She is dancing like a woman on her wedding day!"

Catina grinned from ear to ear and came further into the room.

Her parents continued their dance.

Catina watched, nearly mesmerized by the spectacle. She could still not get over the fact they were moving about when before they looked to be doomed to spend the rest of their lives in bed, their thin bodies beneath the sheets, their faces pale, their eyes hollow and seeming to cave into their skulls.

Michel, leading his wife, slowed the waltz. Then they stopped. He hopped off the bed and quickly went over to his little girl and picked her up and spun her in his arms. Catina giggled with glee. She always loved getting picked up and spun around. Michel laughed. So did Dara.

As Catina was spinning, she reveled in the firm grip her step-father had about her waist. He was so strong, always taking care of things, always had everything under control. Her mother clapped in the background. The room spun about her.

Her step-father's grip began to ease. Catina thought she was going to fall but he sometimes did that to get her heart going and make the ride more exciting. When she thought his grip would reaffirm itself . . . it didn't. The grip continued to loosen until Catina was sure she would fly out of his arms.

About to ask him to hang onto her, her father vanished before her eyes and, in her peripheral, she could see her mother had suddenly vanished, too.

Catina flew threw the air, tumbling. She landed on the mattress and bounced for several seconds before she sat on her rear, dazed, and acknowledged she was safe and hadn't been thrown across the room or onto the hard floor.

Forgetting her parents had suddenly disappeared, she slid on her bottom toward the edge of the mattress, about to leave the room.

Standing in the doorway was the Man in the Gray Cloak.

Mr. Nibbetts didn't know his right from his left as he ran through the fire raining down around him. His friends. His family! Where were they?

"Where are you?" he called out into the flames.

The forest burned all around in brilliant displays of red, orange and yellow, the underside of the flames bright blue and green.

He was on a path in the Flistablare Forest, the path covered in wood chips and dead leaves that were quickly curling from the heat. The sides of the pathway were covered with trees and bushes aflame, creating a sort of tunnel that led to where Mr. Nibbetts could not tell. The sky overhead was dark. The flames made the normally brown pathway an eerie orange, like the remaining burning embers of a large bonfire.

Mr. Nibbetts ran down the path, his short legs not carrying him nearly as fast enough as he wished.

He was running from something but from what, he did not know. But whatever it was, it was gaining on him. Stumbling and pawing at the ground to regain his footing, he pressed himself to run faster and harder, digging his stumpy legs into the wood chip pathway, taking him further down the road to the abysmal dark at the end.

It was gaining on him.

"Confound it! Get going or it will get you!" he told himself, over and over until he was nearly sick of hearing his own voice (which was a feat all its own).

It seemed no matter how hard he ran, no matter how far away from the haunted thing pursuing him he thought he was, it was still on his heels. His legs began to fatigue and a sharp pain hit his lungs. But he ran harder, his footfalls growing louder and louder as his feet slapped the pathway with each stride he took.

It was gaining on him.

A hot breeze touched the fuzzy brown hairs at the nape of his neck. But it wasn't a breeze. It was breath; hot breath from his pursuer behind him. Spine tensing, his legs slowing from the realization of this, Mr. Nibbetts forced his head to turn on his shoulders and glance behind. He didn't know what to expect: a frightening face, perhaps? A gaunt face with hollow eye sockets and pale, gray lips outlined with the red of blood? Maybe. And when he looked behind, that was what he prepared himself for:

some sort of haunting visage or face of a ghost, its appearance scaring him out of his furry coat.

Instead, when he glanced behind, he saw nothing, just an endless tunnel of dark outlined by the fiery orange of the flames, spanning out down the pathway, leading to who knew where.

He ran a little further until his legs gave out from under him and he fell face first into the wood chips. The taste of sour saliva filled his mouth, so he spat it out and, face against the inside of his right forearm, tried to catch his breath. His body tensed, ready for whatever was chasing him to suddenly land on top of him and rip him to pieces.

Behind, he could hear the roar of the fire as the flames engulfed the forest, the sizzling of the leaves cooking, the snapping of branches as they popped under the heat of the flame. The *whoosh* and *whoomph* as the trees burned grew louder and louder . . . and louder . . . until . . .

Nothing. Silence. Absence of sound.

The heat against his back had cooled to a soft breeze and the orange flickers of firelight dancing around the gaps between forearm and ground as he hid his head began to diminish until there was utter darkness.

Breath caught, Mr. Nibbetts closed his eyes and wondered why he hadn't gone through the Change. It was, after all, a time of great stress and his survival had been on the line. There was no explanation except perhaps . . .

And before he realized he was in a dream and in a dream a Change was impossible because the dreamer, no matter how terrifying the dream, no matter how desperate the situation, knows they will be all right—Mr. Nibbetts heard the crunching of footfalls on the wood chips behind him. The footfalls rounded him from the back until they stopped before him where he had his face hidden beneath his arms.

Moving his right arm a little beside him, he opened his eyes and saw a pair of black boots and there, draped beside them, a long gray cloak.

Mr. Nibbetts surrendered.

Peter was by himself away from the camp, alone and awake. The field was peaceful, the grass standing on end; there was no wind. The sky was dotted with dark clouds and half the moon was showing in a bright semi-circle of white.

Nothing made sense. His head hurt and there was a dull ache behind his eyes. He didn't know what he had seen, that swoop of gray floating by his friends. There was no explanation but, though he wouldn't admit it, he knew that it was the Man in the Gray Cloak. Knew it was Thalok, or so the Man called himself. He had said in the dream that he was a Qinoran of the Purple Fog. What did that mean? What was the Purple Fog? Unless . . . no, it couldn't be. Master-lore said that the Master lived in a world of purple mist, a color free of the plainness of black and white, a color with meaning. A color that was there during the Battle of Then.

But why would anything from the Master want to kill me? Peter wondered. He hadn't done anything wrong.

Is Thalok part of the Voidsmen, and is he after me because . . . . He couldn't finish the question because he didn't know *how* to finish it. The Master's ways were, and have always been, shrouded in mystery. He wished he had some answers. He'd give up his very *being* for some right now. What Aiyesha said about the Master's coming, about the Dembatstayr—the Voidsmen—preparing the way . . . Peter believed her. But did he believe in the Master? He didn't know. A part of him did. A part of him didn't.

Maybe Thalok wants me dead because—at least, I think I'm right about this—I didn't go through the Age of Enlightenment? Am I somehow set apart from everyone else because of that? Am I somehow different? I'd give anything to be ordinary right now.

Anything.

And right now, I wish none of this had ever happened. I wish Catina hadn't come to Garathen. I wish my house didn't burn down. I wish I didn't go with them to Grek. There's been nothing but confusion. Nothing but secrets and mysteries and near death experiences. Nothing but problems, sickness, just . . . . I hate this!

I want to go home.

This Night

A night of darkness
A night of change
A night of possibility
A night of strange
Things occurring

This night will be remembered
This night I look upon
This night something is stirring
This night shadows are on
These strange things occurring

- Peter Jones

CHAPTER XL
A Four-legged Companion
(Yaman)

All overslept that morning and the journey home got underway around the tenth hour. They ate their breakfast as they rode: biscuits with a little bit of honey smeared over top, and water. None were in the mood to eat much. Not after the night before.

"You are awfully quiet, Peter," said Alan from behind him.

It was true, Peter realized. He had hardly spoken a word all morning.

"I'm all right," he said. "No, I'm not all right. This is the worst morning of my life. I'm beginning to wonder—actually, beginning to wonder *again*—if coming on this journey was the right thing to do. I'm wondering how things would have turned out if I'd have stayed home."

"But you will never know, will you? There is no way for us to find out what might have been unless we actually had lived it. Even imagining would not convey the truth."

"I know, but—"

"I know this trip has been hard on you. It is not easy to leave everything behind. I remember the first trip I took. After making it through the path in the Forest-Ring—and this is well before those palanthora beasts stirred up any trouble; besides, they sleep in the day, or are supposed to, anyway—I remember turning back home because I had gotten homesick once out on the Ranmorahn Plains. I must have gone through the Forest-Ring and then gone back home two times before finally leaving."

He's kidding, thought Peter, but it brought a smile to his face. He hadn't pictured Alan as being one who got homesick.

Alan went on. "But I forced myself to go on, to see the World because that is what I wanted more than anything. Just like you forced yourself to go with me and Catina to Grek."

"But you needed a guide."

"True, but you still could have said no. There would have been no hard feelings if you had. But you came with us anyway, left your life behind to aid someone else in theirs. I remember on that trip of mine, when I finally got myself to leave, that I kept wondering, 'What if I stayed behind?' And that is when I realized anything I came up with in answer was merely an imagining and that was all it would be. Because I had left, my life had grown all the more richer. When you get home, Peter, and sit on your new porch, you will look back—and this is a good thing, mind you—and feel more mature, more wise, all that you learned on this journey coming at you like a stallion on the tear. You will feel like a man who has realized his worth. I promise that."

"I look forward to the day," said Peter. *If it ever happens.*

They continued on for two hours, most of that time spent in silence. Peter thought about asking why everyone was so quiet but decided not to, simply thinking they were all tired.

It was midday when they came upon a wood, its trees towering, reaching for the sky, their branches long fingers trying to grasp at the clouds. Their tops were full of dark green leaves that spanned a quarter of the way down their trunks then, the lower they went, slowly became a darker gray dotted with brown.

"The Calahudron Woods," said Alan when Peter described the trees to him.

"You've been out this way?" he asked.

"Once, long ago. I am sure it has not changed much since then."

"I wouldn't know. I wasn't there when you were here."

Aiyesha stepped a little closer to the wood and peered in. Bear hadn't returned that day on the Hill. So, making the best of it, she and Peter took turns walking beside Day while the other rode.

Mr. Nibbetts shifted in his saddle. Somewhere on the flat land of grass behind them a couple of wild dogs barked, their banter carried on the wind.

"Me don't like the looks of this place," he said. "Sends a chill down me back." And it was true. The hairs on his back were standing on end.

"I'm sure there's nothing wrong with it," said Peter.

"Says you," he retorted.

Of a sudden, there was a whimpering coming from inside the wood. Its pitches would go high then low in labored whines, then high again. The leaves of the undergrowth rustled somewhere within the wood. Night let out a snort.

"We shouldn't go in here," said Aiyesha. "These woods are not empty."

Alan brought his horse up beside Peter and leaned in toward him. "If we do not go in, then we will have to ride around. That goes without saying. But this wood is large and to go around it would add at least three days, if not four, to our journey. The question is, Peter, how quickly do you wish to go home?"

Peter thought for a moment. He wanted to go home right away. He was growing tired of being on the road, tired of riding a horse day in and day out, tired of eating simple foods, always worrying about how much he ate so there would be enough for the next day. After a long, decisive sigh, he said, "Let's go in. Whatever's alive in there, it can't be dangerous, can it?"

"I would not know," said Alan. "I went around it the last time I was out this way."

"Aiyesha?" Peter brought Day up beside her. "What do you think? Is it safe?"

"There's a foulness on the air. I can't place it, though I ought to. I can sense danger usually quite well. This escapes me."

The whimpering resumed again, this time louder, more persistent.

"Alan says riding around the forest will add three or four days to our journey. Personally, I'd rather go through. I'm sick of riding." The whimpering continued. "What is that?"

She smiled warmly at him. "Let's look and see. Sounds like an animal of some kind."

Aiyesha stepped in. Peter led the others in after her.

The light inside the forest was darker, struggling to touch ground after being filtered through the forest's thick canopy two hundred meters overhead. The vegetation inside was a lot sparser than in the Forest-Ring. There were bushes and shrubs and patches of long grass all over, but the forest was not dense. Too much of it was taken up by the massive tree trunks. The further the group got in, the louder the whimpering became. There was more movement of brush somewhere off to the right.

From behind, Peter could hear Alan pull his sword free of its sheath.

"Cannot be too careful," said Alan.

"Me agree," said Mr. Nibbetts.

"It's probably nothing," said Peter, trying to ease their concern for what they might find.

They followed the whimpering sound until they came to a small patch of bushes next to the trunk of a tree that had fallen over long ago. The leaves on the bush moved side to side, as if waving at them. Whatever was making that whimpering sound was underneath the brush. Aiyesha drew a short sword she had taken from the battleground that she kept strapped to her back. Peter eyed her as she moved closer and paid special attention to the way her feet moved. Her right foot slid forward silently along the ground then set itself, her left foot brought up so that her left heel was touching her right heel in a L. She repeated this sliding walk until she was at the bush.

Whatever was under the brush was moving quickly. It yelped and then barked.

A smile coming to her face, Aiyesha put her sword away and peeled back the top leaves of the bush and peered in.

"It's a dog," she said, a small giggle rising in her throat.

There was a collective sigh of relief. After all the excitement while on this journey, it was easy to get worked up over what turned out in the end to be a small matter.

"It's trapped," she said.

Peter dismounted Day and came beside her.

"Once it's free, me say we have it for lunch. Me starving," said Mr. Nibbetts.

Alan turned his blank eyes in the Flistablare's direction.

"What?" said the furry creature. "You didn't know that Flistablare eat dog? And you call yourself a traveler."

"Do not call me that," said Alan. "And I do not call myself that, either."

The dog's big, black, glossy eyes peered up at Peter and Aiyesha from under the bush's leaves. It yelped again and barked once more. Aiyesha parted the leaves further.

"Its foot is caught," said Peter, seeing the dog's hind left paw trapped in a snare of some sort. He leaned in over the branches and leaves and examined the trap. "No problem. It's just a rope. A good knot, though."

"Here," said Aiyesha. She drew her sword again and handed it to him.

Peter took it and leaned over to cut the rope. The dog cowered away from him at the sight of the blade.

"Don't worry," he said, "I'm not going to hurt you."

The sword's sharp edge cut the rope easily and the dog's hind leg jerked free. It ran out from under the bush and did a dance in a circle before stopping to look at its rescuers. The dog was about knee height on all fours, its body white with two blotches of brown fur, one on its right side, the other on its rump. The eyes and ears on its face were covered in brown fur like a mask, and there, on the top of its head, surrounded by the white fur that ran down the top of its head to its muzzle, was an oval patch of brown.

"Is it big?" asked Alan.

"No, not really," said Peter. "Why?"

"Catina asked me if she could pet it."

"Petting wild animals isn't a good idea," said Aiyesha. "You never know what they might do."

"Oh, I am sure it will be all right," said Alan. He spoke to Catina in Grescalla and, using his right arm, helped her down off the horse.

As Catina neared the dog, her hand outstretched, the dog looking up expectantly at her, two men jumped out of the bush, their makeshift spears—long, straight branches with razor-sharp tips—pointing at the little girl. The dog barked first then growled.

Aiyesha was on them before Peter could even acknowledge their presence. She ran in behind one and locked her forearm around his throat, closing off his air supply. She dug her knee into his back, causing him to arch backward with a frightened yelp. Her leg then spun out and kicked his companion square in the throat. He dropped to his knees, his hands to his throat as he gagged. She pulled back on the fellow in her arms and Peter heard a crack. Had she just broken his neck? No, he didn't think so. The man was still breathing. She must have temporarily dislocated some of the vertebrae and then put them back again, the pain from such involuntary movement in his bones causing him to go down on his knees. Aiyesha released the man and pounced on the other, kneeing him in the face. Taking the spear from his hands, she snapped it in two. It all happened in a matter of seconds.

It took a moment for the company looking on to realize what just occurred.

Feeling suddenly useless, Peter went over to the first man and picked the spear off the dirty ground. He pointed the spear at him, now feeling involved.

"Who are you?" demanded Aiyesha.

The men, topless, wearing only tattered browny-gray loincloths, their skin tanned, their hair long and dark and scraggled in knots, glanced up at her. Their lips moved beneath thick mustaches and long beards.

"We . . . we are . . . " The one on the left coughed. Before his sentence could be completed, ten more of these bush-men jumped out of the woods, each carrying spears identical to the two men whom Aiyesha had just subdued.

It was like being on the Battle on the Hill again, the threat of attack, the inevitability of physical conflict to come. Peter's heart sped with a surge of adrenaline and he raised the spear. The ten men neared the group. Peter noticed a sly smile spread across Aiyesha's lips. She was enjoying this.

And like before, in a whirlwind of motion, with movements more graceful than the sleekest of felines, Aiyesha moved into them. In the span of seconds, Aiyesha had four of the men down. In another two seconds, three more came down. The three that were left stopped their advance and, as one, went to their knees before her.

Peter handed her the spear. She pointed it at the men.

"Forgive us, Lady-girl, for trying to harm your friends," one of them spoke. He was the biggest of the three left. Upon further examination, he was actually the biggest of the bush-men there. He had long blonde hair that fell in a mat halfway down his back and a long, scraggly, dirty blonde beard that hung down to his collarbone. He had blue eyes, which was different because the other bush-men's eyes were brown.

"What is your name?" she asked him.

The entire company—Peter, Alan, Mr. Nibbetts, even Catina—listened for his reply.

"My name is Yaman, First-man of the Calahudron Woods. Those around me are my Hunt-group. We were out in search of our half-day meal and set our traps." His eyes peered up at her under bushy brows. "We like dog and" —he nodded toward the dog that was now at Peter's side— "were coming to check our trap because we heard squeals. But then, hiding in trees, we saw that our meal had been freed. We tried to rescue it but you have already proved anymore attempts at that would be futile. If I may say, you move like a fox on the prowl. And I've seen a fox move, mind you, out there on the plain." He then stood up and stuck out his chest proudly. He stepped up to Aiyesha so he was no more than a few inches from her. He stood at least two heads higher, his shoulders twice the width of hers. Aiyesha eyed him steadily, her jaw cast in iron, her face bearing no emotion. She sheathed her sword in the short scabbard that was tied to her back with leather straps. "I am Yaman, First-man of the Calahudron Woods," he said. "You have shamed my men and I must reclaim that loss. May I have your name?"

Peter watched with stunned amusement. Likewise, he knew, so were the others. He thought even Catina knew what was going on.

Green eyes firmly set upon Yaman's, Aiyesha spoke. Her voice was cool, backed with steel. "I am Aiyesha Elnaa of Bel Candar." She paused, and then seemed to assign herself a label to which Yaman could relate. "First-woman of the Coast of Seryn, mightiest of its ranks."

Yaman rose up on his tip-toes then came back down again in a sort of huff. "Aiyesha Elnaa, I tell you to come with me!" Then to all, he said, "Clear the way. I will reclaim our shame."

Aiyesha gave her group a look that said to listen, that she knew was she was doing. Peter and his company obeyed and stepped to the side. Catina drew the dog aside by the scruff of its neck then giggled when the dog licked her hand. The men got off their knees slowly and, not bothering to dust themselves off, followed Aiyesha and Yaman out a ways back toward the entry to the forest. The company followed as well. Peter led Alan by the arm.

"What is happening?" whispered Alan.

"I don't know other than I think they're going to fight," said Peter. *I think.*

"Oh. Great."

"Me thinks this will be amusing," said Mr. Nibbetts with a chuckle.

"Why?" asked Peter, a few paces in front of him.

"Just you watch. You remember the Battle on the Hill?"

"Yes, but you don't."

Alan barked a laugh and, unbeknownst to him, drew eyes toward him.

When Mr. Nibbetts didn't reply, Peter knew his tease had worked. The Flistablare didn't remember much while in the Change.

They came to a spot where—and it could have just been their eyes playing tricks on them—the trees were arranged in a circle, with only a few smaller trees in the middle of the round clearing. Yaman's men went to one side of the circle and Peter and the others went to the other. Aiyesha and Yaman were in the middle, far enough away from everyone so that one had to strain to listen to what they were saying.

I hope she knows what she's doing, thought Peter. *This looks like some kind of rite . . . or some sort of tradition, anyway.*

Aiyesha slid the straps holding her short sword to her back off her shoulders. It landed at her feet. She kicked the sword to the side. Yaman tossed his spear to one of his men.

"You handle yourself well, Lady-girl," said Yaman.

"I know what we are doing," she replied. "It does not take a Wise-man to figure it out. Flesh against flesh, no weapons. I read you like a book."

"A book?" He seemed not to know what a "book" was.

"Never mind," she said.

They stepped a few paces away from each other and each performed a short set of exercises. Aiyesha stood in a sort of X, her legs spread wide, her hands outstretched skyward. She arched backward until Peter thought she was about to bend in two then bent forward and touched her head to the ground. She executed a few kicks and punches, the fabric of her wool clothes snapping as she did, and then straightened; her legs brought together, her hands at her sides.

Yaman moved in a thuggish dance, bringing his knees chest-high then moving them in a half-circle outwardly before stepping to either side. He moved in two rotations to his left and right before standing normal again.

The two faced each other.

"Ready?" he asked her.

"Move at will," she said.

His hands hooked like claws, he jumped into the air toward her. Peter suddenly got a vision of a panther attacking its prey. Worse, a palanthora beast. In the half-second that Yaman was in the air, Aiyesha spun on her left heel, bringing her right leg around and, with more power than a horse kicking, she threw her right leg out when her body faced forward again, into Yaman's middle while he was still in the air. Yaman's entire body lurched forward, his upper torso and legs closing around Aiyesha's right leg in a U. He let out the loudest yell any of them had heard and it wasn't a yell of attack or triumph. It was pain.

Aiyesha pulled her right leg back and planted it firmly on the ground. Yaman fell and hit the forest floor with a loud thud, his body still folded in half, his upper body hanging over his legs. He fell onto his side and his men rushed to his aid.

Aiyesha, a glimmer in her eye, picked up her sword and straps off the ground and returned to her companions.

"Are you all right?" asked Peter when she returned.

"Fine," was all she said and moved away from them.

"Now what?" asked Mr. Nibbetts. No one gave him an answer. No one had one to give.

Catina was sitting cross-legged on the ground, the dog on its haunches beside her. She had her arm around the dog and a worried look on her face. Peter gave her a smile, letting her know everything was fine. Alan came over to his granddaughter and talked to her in the Rolling-tongue. He seemed to do a good job because when Alan stood beside her, Catina had a grin on her face. She then returned Peter's smile to him.

"Aiyesha Elnaa of Bel Candar, First-woman of the Coast of Seryn!" came a booming voice through the wood. It was Yaman.

Peter moved toward the call but Aiyesha motioned for him to stay where he was. He watched her go back toward the bush-men.

"I don't have time to keep fighting you," she said as she walked toward them.

They exchanged words silently; Peter could not hear what they were saying.

"If you ask me, she should wipe the forest floor with him again," said Mr. Nibbetts, his arms crossed across his chest.

"Why?" asked Peter.

"Because," said the furry creature, "she can. They attacked first. We should have gone around. This is stupid."

"Just because they attacked first and she defended us, doesn't mean we should beat them up simply because we can."

"This is coming from the guy who stood his ground against a bunch of Dembatstayr not too long ago?"

Mr. Nibbetts reminded him of how the Voidsmen crowded around him, some holding him, and his mysterious ability to throw three of the large men off as though children. Peter still couldn't say what happened that day or how he was able to do what he did.

Aiyesha returned to them, Yaman walking unsteadily at her side.

"We've been invited back to their camp," she said.

"Why?" asked Alan.

"Because we want to repay you for our trying to harm you," said Yaman. "Calahudron people are a proud people and don't take kindly to outsiders, except for those who prove themselves worthy to be near us."

"What makes you better than us?" demanded Mr. Nibbetts.

Yaman didn't seem to hear the question but instead kept talking. "And perhaps, by spending time with Aiyesha of Bel Candar, First-woman of the Coast of Seryn, we can learn how she can fight so well so that we, too, may fight so well. She says that you are on a journey going home, and that all of you could use a hot, filling meal and a warm place to sleep for the night."

"I am not eating dog," said Alan.

Peter had to bite back a laugh. He didn't know why that was so funny, but it was.

"There is more to eat than dog. Even that dog there, the one you rescued, can come. And trust me, no harm will come to it. I will make it clear to my people that the dog is to be unharmed. I am First-man and they will listen."

Aiyesha must have seen Peter's indecisiveness in his eyes because she said, "You wanted to experience everything you could while out here, Peter. Now's your chance."

"Alan?" asked Peter.

He tugged with both hands on the loose fabric of his shirt. "Why not? Let us see what happens next. And, if these bush-people try to harm us, Aiyesha could take care of them."

"That I will," she said.

So it was decided they would follow Yaman back to his camp for a hot meal and a warm place to sleep. It was also agreed they would stay for just one night and leave in the morning.

Peter still wanted to be on his way home.

CHAPTER XLI
Stories by the Fire

They had gone back to retrieve the horses, accompanied by Yaman and his men, before returning into the Calahudron Woods. Leading the horses by the reins, they followed Yaman and his fellow bush-men deeper into their forest to the camp hidden within.

Yaman and Aiyesha walked in front of the company, followed by Peter and Alan and Day, then Catina, then Mr. Nibbetts and Night, with bush-men on either side of them and in behind, as if protecting them from a threat that loomed somewhere in the towering trees. The dog wandered ahead and all around them but never strayed far, sniffing the ground, smelling some treat that escaped everyone else's notice. Every now and again she—at least Peter was pretty sure it was a she; he didn't really look that closely—would come and walk beside Catina, and Catina would pet her and run her hand from the top of the dog's head all way down its back to its tail. The dog's tail wagged with each long stroke.

Watching Aiyesha and Yaman yammer on about combat, Peter found himself getting jealous that she was spending so much time talking to Yaman instead of him, which he wasn't used to. Usually he was whom she spoke with while riding.

Don't complain, he told himself. *You don't own her. She's found someone who she has something in common with.* He noticed that Yaman had his hand against his left rib, as if cradling it. His hand moved slightly now and again from his rib cage as he walked, and Peter could see that a deep purple bruise bordered by a sickly yellow had formed on the skin. *From Aiyesha's kick.*

The journey into the forest was longer than Peter had expected. They walked most of the afternoon, mostly in silence. Alan had a hand to Peter's shoulder, following behind, using Peter as a guide. Every so often Mr. Nibbetts would mutter a complaint about the walk to the "bush camp" taking so long and how his legs were tired and that he wanted to sit down and rest. "Or at least let me ride one of the horses. Me can't stand this," he said more than once.

Every so often Peter glanced back at Catina. And, most of those times, she walked with a hand to her left eye, covering it, as if shielding it from the sparse yet sharp rays of sunlight piercing through the tree's high canopy.

"Is she all right?" he asked Alan, nodding toward Catina, again forgetting that Alan couldn't see the nod.

Alan let Catina catch up. He checked in with her then gave her hand a thoughtful squeeze. "She will be all right. Her eye is bothering her again. I would like to say I should have a look at it, but you can see the conflict in that. Let us just hope it does not get any worse. She has already been through enough."

The trees all looked the same, just big old trunks of rough-looking bark with giant knots, reaching up to the heavens. All the trees had long, bright green leaves that draped down to the ground like a fat woman's skirt. Bushes about waist height were set in patches along the path they followed. Peter knew that if the bush-men suddenly decided to leave, he and his friends would be hopelessly lost.

Let's just hope that after tonight, these people are willing to lead us out or we may never leave the forest, he thought. *We would never have made it through here on our own.*

And so the afternoon wore on and they came to a man-made clearing in the forest where the big trees—after a long and tedious effort, Peter assumed—had been chopped down so as to allow room for the bush-men's village. The village was set at the bottom of a shallow dip in the forest floor that served as a mini valley. A canopy of tree leaves and limbs still covered the ceiling of the forest despite the absence of some of the trees.

It's a city of trees, thought Peter. "Alan, if you could see this," he heard himself say.

"That is okay. I can certainly smell it. Smells green, full of life."

Peter glanced back at him, wondering what he meant by that remark. Alan, somehow sensing he was being looked at, gave Peter a grin.

Remarkable. The bush-men village indeed was a city of trees. Each of the big trees had been hollowed out into dens with open doors, at the trunks. Bush-men, wearing nothing but loin cloths and their own skin, ran about, all seemingly on errands for the bush-women, who stood in those doors, barking demands at their mates. Naked children ran about beneath the bridges higher up on the trees, linking one to the other, where there was a second level of homes hollowed into the trees. There was also a third level and a fourth, and a fifth. People swung on ropes from one tree to the next like apes, carrying bundles of who-knew-what from place to place. There were small huts made of sticks, square in nature with leaf-thatched roofs, with small bonfires burning outside each of them. The smoke from the cooking fires rose straight up instead of to either side, as smoke often does. There was no wind in the village.

Its simplicity, its air of naivety of the outside World, reminded Peter of home. It was as if the Calahudron Woods was a world all its own.

Everyone stood with jaws agape. Even the horses seemed in awe, what with the snorts of content they each made. The dog barked once.

A chill ran up Peter's back when he saw a bush-man on the stick-made balcony of a fifth-level home, swing out and down to a fourth-level balcony. It was such a long way to the ground from up there. He shivered again. High places terrified him.

"Welcome," said Yaman. Then, with a booming voice, shouted out over the village, "We have visitors! Let them be welcome and treat them well!"

Everyone milling about, even the children, stopped in their tracks and eyed their guests. Then as one they rushed toward them. It seemed these bush-people had never seen any outsiders before.

Before anyone knew it, they were being mobbed by long-haired men and women and naked children, the bush-people's hands pawing at them, wanting to touch the outsiders. Peter raised his hands, as did the others, protecting themselves from the fingers and palms touching them all over. Peter noticed that the men and women and children all had dark hair and dark eyes. Yaman was the only one with blonde hair and beard, and blue eyes.

Is that why he's called the First-man? wondered Peter. That *was* why. Once unto every generation to the bush-people, Yaman would later reveal, was born one who was different from the rest. He, or sometimes she, was always marked with blonde hair and blue eyes, a sign of the Giver of All, that this person was chosen to lead them for the duration of their lifetime, or until they were too old and passed the mantle onto their first born, who was also born different than the other children the First-man or First-woman might have, the child the only one of its kin with blonde hair and blue eyes.

"Yaman, what's going on?" demanded Aiyesha.

"We have never had guests before. They are all very excited." He chuckled. "There was only one other time a hundred years ago. That was when we learned your language. That is enough!"

And the pawing and touching stopped and the people backed away. It was remarkable, his command over them. First-man of the Calahudron Woods indeed.

Yaman led the company down the slope and took them to a place—with all the villagers following behind, of course—where they could stable their horses and give them some feed and water. Once this was done, he took the guests into the heart of the village.

"Go back to what you were doing. There will be plenty of time to visit later," Yaman told his kith.

Peter wondered what that meant. He had enough of people touching him for one day. Maybe even for the rest of his life.

Dinner was a party, with dancing around bonfires and songs that sounded more like a combination of hums and random vocal sounds than coherent lyrics, sung in all pitches yet in harmony all the same. Peter, Aiyesha, Alan, Catina and Mr. Nibbetts were seated at a long uneven table made from a tree that had been chopped down and then, as Yaman explained, cut down the middle lengthwise with a large hand-saw and then tipped on its back so that its outer round edge was the table's legs and its flat side was its top. It didn't rock back in forth like a cradle. Its tremendous weight had already settled it into the forest's floor. Yaman sat at the head of the table, a king entertaining his guests. For dinner they ate deer and rabbit, berries and nuts, a plain salad and potatoes and Heraseah feet. Heraseah, Yaman told them, were little creatures that looked like tiny chickens with their feathers plucked off. They were without arms and were only found at night. It tasted like liver, a taste Peter didn't care for. Aiyesha said she enjoyed the tough texture and didn't mind the bland taste. All of this was washed down with blackberry juice, which was more bitter than sweet but surprisingly did quench your thirst.

When dinner was ended and all stomachs were full, a large bonfire was set, a heap of wood piled four feet high and a dozen feet in diameter, with flames higher than the travelers had ever seen.

"Me don't like this," said Mr. Nibbetts. "Reminds me of home. At least, what happened."

"Sorry," said Peter, though he didn't know why he was apologizing. It just felt like something he had to do. Perhaps because he understood what it was like to see your home engulfed in flames. His mood suddenly sunk and it took awhile before it perked up again.

The villagers gathered around the fire and, as best as each of the travelers could, began sharing some of the tales of their journey, each leaving out the incidents with the Dembatstayr—the Voidsmen—and the personal story of Catina's parents passing away. They also left out the sickness and death in Grek, and their sickness so as not to ruin the festive mood. The bush-people seemed to find the stories from the Festival of Armasulia in Darim the most intriguing. Some of the villagers told tales of their own, "The Legend of the Shadow Figures," "The Tale of the One-legged Boy," "How Gurg Treeha Beat the Bear."

"But there is one tale that demands telling this evening," said Yaman, getting up off the tree stump he sat on. "This is the story of 'The Gray Man.'"

Everyone hushed at the mention of the story's title. Even the kids—Catina included in that number as she and the dog were playing with them—went silent.

Peter, who was drinking blackberry juice out of a wooden cup, nearly choked. *The Man in the Gray Cloak,* he thought. *Thalok?* A few eyes darted toward him as he coughed and tried to get his breath back. He noticed that Mr. Nibbetts's dark eyes widened to an almost impossible size. So did Aiyesha's. *Why are they surprised? Do they know of Tha*—Before he could finish his thought, Yaman was speaking again.

And so he began the tale.

Yaman stood proudly as he spoke, his arms moving to the sides and out in front of him, emphasizing his words. His tone jumped and lowered at the appropriate points, making the tale more exciting and real. "They say that the Gray Man moves at night, like all the things we fear, and watches us while we sleep. Alone he stands, with no movement. Just him, watching us, watching you, watching me. He comes to our village on the cold nights and also comes when it's too warm and we cannot sleep. He watches us, waits on us. Long ago, when my father's father was First-man of the Calahudron Woods, the Gray Man stopped his watching. All were asleep and all were awoken by a shrill screech in the night, like a flurry of bats tearing through our village. It was the Gray Man, his long gray cloak flapping as he moved, like a multitude of bats with their wings a blur, flying as fast as they could to escape the oncoming dawn. The Gray Man moved throughout our village in a whirlwind; the huts shook, the ground trembled, and he, after so many years of waiting, watching, biding his time, snatched men and women and children from my father's father's generation. Like the strong First-man he was, my father's father sprang out of his hut, spear in hand, ready to dispose of the threat. And there, the clatter of the flutter of wings suddenly ceasing, stood the Gray Man, waiting again, waiting on my father's father. The First-man lunged at him, his entire body putting power behind the spear, aiming for the Gray Man's heart. The spear impaled the Gray Man and the Gray Man staggered back. Just as my father's father thought the Gray Man would fall, the Gray Man let out a viscous laugh, one that to this day haunts me, a laugh that is said to be the high-pitched scratching of nails on stone mixed with the low scraping of a saw on wood. The Gray Man drew the spear from his body, the spear clean of blood. He laughed again and the First-man stood in awe, amazed that this thing had survived such an attack. And then" —Yaman, a man who appeared to be strong beyond the measure of the word, wiped a tear from his eye— "the Gray Man dove at my father's father and tore him limb from limb. It is said that the day after, the entire village remained inside due to the horrific sight of his body lying on our grounds. Just over there" —he nodded past the fire to an area where a group of huts circled an opening on the forest floor— "was a display of more blood than one, even one from as strong a people such as we, should see in their lifetime. The blood somehow, through the Gray Man's power, had been multiplied and littered the streets in a circle wider than a line of thirty men all linking arms across; blood on the walls of the homes, on the trees, on the bushes and even blood covering the undergrowth in the places of shrub that no eye in this generation has set sight on. There's more. The blood was not the deep red as the dried blood on a dead dog's hide. No. It was darker than that, almost gray. Gray blood from the Gray Man, but not from him. No. His touch poisoned his victims; turned their blood a dark gray."

Peter shifted uncomfortably in his seat. He saw that Mr. Nibbetts had done the same. Aiyesha's face remained calm, cool, as if hearing of such gore was common to her. Peter wondered if Alan could envision the tale in his mind. Alan proved that thought when he let out a long sigh. He was seemingly able to see in his imagination all that Yaman was saying. Glad that Alan wasn't translating the tale to Catina, Peter resumed listening to the rest of the story.

"And even now," went on Yaman, "the Gray Man watches us. Why, you ask, do I tell you such a dark tale before we lie to sleep? Why scare the children? Because . . . we fear nothing! To erase fear, we must first face it. We must first see it for what it is. The Gray Man is real and he is out there somewhere in our forest, waiting on us, watching us. What some don't know is that, by my father's father's body, was a symbol drawn in the dirt which, in our language, means 'two,' and another symbol which means 'son.' The second son. No one knows what it means but I suspect that it means every second generation the Gray Man will return and kill again." He paused and cleared some of the stray hairs from his mustache from his lips. "I never told you what else happened that night. Children went missing. Parents, who had moments earlier visited their child's bed, had seen them there sleeping peacefully, fell apart, breaking into tears, when the children were suddenly gone from where they slept. All knew it was the Gray Man who did it. All knew that the Gray Man haunted the woods, first in tales like this one then, over time, in their minds until one night, he did come and killed my father's father and stole the children. Where those children are now, no one knows but, I suspect, if they are still alive, that wherever they are is not pleasant. Perhaps they are the Gray Man's spies and, like him, watch us, wait on us. Tonight, when you lie your heads to sleep, pay attention to what you feel surrounding you. Tonight is a cold night. The Gray Man may yet visit us."

Yaman sat down. The crowd was silent, their eyes glassy, staring at the branches popping and crackling in the massive bonfire. Children hugged their parents and, if they weren't near their parents, quickly made their way to them. Peter saw Catina look around and, copying the others, hugged Alan.

Later, when most of the crowd had cleared and gone to bed, those who remained visited; those of the bush-people talking mostly amongst themselves, leaving the outsiders alone.

Yaman was now sitting beside Peter. Watching the bearded man, Peter couldn't shake the story he had heard.

The Gray Man.

Thalok? Had to be. But if Thalok did come to the village two generations ago, how old was the Man in the Gray Cloak? And those symbols drawn in the dirt, the symbol for "two" and the symbol for "son." Did that mean that the second generation from the First-man, Yaman's father's father, would be slain? If that was the case, that would prove why the Man in the Gray Cloak was suddenly around.

Perhaps Thalok is haunting everybody, thought Peter.

He turned to Yaman. "Why did you tell that story?"

Yaman glanced at him then back at the flames, its light dancing in his blue eyes. "Everyone here has heard it before. Actually, they are all tired of it. I told it to you and your friends because it is one of our most entertaining tales and it will send chills up your spine. It will keep you alert, and in the woods, being alert is an asset. You never know what's out there waiting for you."

Good point, thought Peter. The dog they had rescued earlier came up to him. He scratched it behind its ears. He didn't know how to ask Yaman this so he just came out and said it. He had to know. "Is it true?"

"The tale? No, of course not. It's an old story, older than what I made it out to be. I said my father's father, when describing the events. It keeps it more immediate. If it were true, it would be more like my father's father's father's father's father's father."

"That's a lot of 'fathers.'"

"Yes, it is," said Yaman. "It's a story I never grow tired of. I like to scare people sometimes, plus it strengthens the young ones, hearing such dark tales when they're so young. Gives them a respect for fear and teaches them how to deal with it on their own. Very important when growing up to be strong."

Peter nodded. "I see." The dog left him to go sniff around the base of a large tree behind him and off to the right.

Mr. Nibbetts was curled up beneath another tree off to the side, the glimmer of the fire shimmering against his matted brown fur. Catina was talking away to Alan about something. Peter couldn't see Aiyesha. Just before he asked Yaman if he knew where she was, she came and sat down beside him.

"Hello," she said.

"Hello," said Peter.

"Lady-girl," said Yaman.

"Yaman," she replied. "How's your rib?"

The First-man straightened in his seat and touched a hand to the bluish-purple bruise under his left rib. "Sore. I think you broke one but, no matter, our Healer will be returning to our village shortly. He is gone out to seek the Giver of All and find wisdom. When he returns, he will heal me."

"How do you know?" asked Peter.

"Because the Healer is anointed by the Giver of All, that's how I know," said Yaman, his voice sure and solid.

Peter yawned, entwined his fingers together and raised his arms above his head, stretching. "It's getting to be that time."

"What time?" asked Yaman, obviously not knowing the old expression.

"Time for bed," said Peter.

Yaman stood. "Let me show you and your friends where you will stay."

Peter rose. So did Aiyesha. She went and gave Mr. Nibbetts a nudge and told Alan and Catina to follow her.

As Yaman led the outsiders to their hut, he leaned in and said to Peter, "I want to apologize."

"For what?"

"I lied to you."

Lied to me?

"The story of the Gray Man is true," said Yaman. "Old but true. And it was two generations ago that he came. You best sleep tonight with your guard up. He could be out there tonight."

Peter's Journal: Awake

Mae 5, the Year 134, the Fifth Aeon

Yaman's tale sickens me. Though it is no more than a story to keep your heart pounding, I still find it disturbing. How could he have told it to the children? I worry for their young minds. Yaman said it gives them a respect for fear. I suppose this is true but it still does not ease my worry for them.

I can't sleep so I'm writing this down. It's sometime into the new day, but it's still dark outside. All five of us—six, including the dog—are in a small hut with walls made of sticks piled on their sides, one on top of the other, held together by mud and clay. There is a window where some of the torches burning outside allow some of the light in. It is by this light I am writing this. The others are sleeping in a row on the ground next to me, but I don't think it's a peaceful rest. I look at their closed eyes and, by the expression on their faces, it seems they are forcing their eyes to stay closed, as if they're trying to grasp at sleep, as if they are still awake, with images from the story of the Gray Man playing on their minds. I would have to agree for that story is also keeping me awake. Especially what Yaman said to me afterward about the story being real. I wonder why he told me otherwise? When he said it was an old tale, it eased my worry, but now . . .

The shadows press in upon me and the muscles around my neck tighten. It feels like at any moment, the stick-made door to this hut will swing open, the roof of what Yaman called Gallow Leaves will come crashing down, the long leaves burying us as we gaze up at the Gray Man standing in the doorway.

Is this even the same Gray Man as I'm thinking of? Is he the same man as Thalok because I don't think Thalok is *a man. He must be something else, some other being if he could show up in my dreams and in this World. Unless I was dreaming when seeing him in this World, of course.*

Alan was right. These are strange days. There is no way to express the confusion I feel. I try to hide it when I ride with the others but the truth is, I'm terrified. All that I was led to believe about life, about my existence, has suddenly been brought into question. I know I've said all that before but I must repeat it for it is true.

The Master help us.

If He exists.

I pray for our safety tonight.

CHAPTER XLII
Villains

"Fools!" shouted General Gasahd. "Vile, incompetent fools! All of them. How could so few defeat so many? Impossible, I tell you. Down right unfathomable. Yet . . . it happened."

Captain Zakmon only stood and nodded at his commanding officer. The two were in the Golden Barrel, a pub in Fangheld, a small town about three hundred leagues North from where the battle with Aiyesha and her companions had taken place. The Golden Barrel was small, a room no bigger than twenty large paces wide and about thirty long. They sat on stools at a high wooden bar, each with a mug of ale in their hands. Laughter and music filled the place, bouncing off the walls, making it seem louder than what it actually was. The Golden Barrel was nearly at capacity with folks visiting after a hard day's work. Though most appeared tired, some were in the mood for dancing.

In the golden light from torches hung in ornate iron holders on the walls, Gasahd's face appeared almost bronze. So did Zakmon's.

Gasahd slammed his tin mug down on the counter, frothy ale spilling over its edge. The barkeep didn't seem to mind the mess. "Still unbelievable. All of it. And now . . . " He knew what he was going to say. He was going to admit disgrace, defeat, and all his feelings thereof. This fifth mug of ale made all his feelings seem that much more stronger now.

"It seems bad, now," said Zakmon, "but that's only now. Who knows what tomorrow will bring."

"Terrible words," said Gasahd. "I don't know how you could say such a thing at a time like this. They've all gone, all of them. All the men. It's just you and I, now, Captain. You and I."

"The men only went back to the Coast because you ordered them to." Then, after a pause, "Sir."

"Did I? Oh. I suppose you're right." Now he remembered. He had ordered everyone back to the Coast of Seryn after the disgrace on the Hill. The truth was, he had ordered them back simply because he was too ashamed to ride alongside them. He, the big general, unable to take down a simple woman. No. Not just any woman. Aiyesha Elnaa. The greatest warrior ever to come down the paths of creation.

Fuzziness filled his head. Too much ale. He poured the rest of his mug down his throat and ordered another. When he forgot to pay the barkeep, the big man behind the counter leaned forward and, with one hand, waved his fingers inward, silently saying, "Pay up. Pay up. Drink all you want but pay up."

Gasahd slammed a silver drop down on the countertop. "This should cover me for the evening." It seemed that it would because the barkeep snatched it up and brought the general another mug of ale, setting it beside the one Gasahd already clutched in his hand.

"Well," he said, turning to Zakmon and giving his first officer a clap on the back, "at least I have you."

"By your side till the end, Sir," said Zakmon. He eyed his general—obviously not used to seeing such a great man in such a state—as Gasahd tilted his head back and took a large swig of his drink.

There were some angry shouts off to the side. A couple of men got in a scuffle but it soon ended and the two men were friends again. A common sight at the Golden Barrel.

"What are we doing here?" asked Zakmon.

"What?" said Gasahd.

"What are we doing here? Look at us! Two of the highest ranking Dembatstayr, sitting in a smelly pub, wallowing." He glanced down at his uniform. It looked as if the once sharp purple material was beginning to fade, the fabric still filthy from the battle. Gasahd's uniform was in the same shape, if not even more so. "I say we try again!"

Gasahd straightened himself in his seat. His head was tilted down but he peered up at Zakmon with eyes both glassy and inquisitive. The stare lasted a good while before he spoke. "Try again?"

"Yes, Sir."

"Try again, try again." Gasahd nodded to no one, just himself. "Try again." He stood. "You're right. You're absolutely right."

Just then a big man pushed his way past the crowd and walked up to the bar. His shoulder bumped Gasahd and the general fell back onto his chair.

"Watch it," said the man. The man smelled like a sack of old fish that had been rotting in a cellar for a week.

Suddenly, there was a blade at the man's throat. Gasahd's blade, the steel of his sword glinting in the golden light.

"I beg your pardon," said the general.

The man went to move—the many long coats and cloaks he wore giving away his movement even before he raised a finger—and Gasahd slit his throat. Everyone in the pub stopped what they were doing and watched as the man, eyes wide with shock, hands trying to catch the blood spurting forth from his neck, sunk to the floor in a heap. The laughter stopped. So did the singing and dancing. Then, as if nothing out of the ordinary had occurred, they all resumed their drinking, their telling of jokes, their dancing to the music.

Gasahd sheathed his sword, not bothering to wipe off the blood. "Manners, manners."

Zakmon seemed pleased with his superior and side-stepped around the man on the floor. He went up to Gasahd. "Then we go?"

"Yes," said Gasahd and stood. His legs faltered beneath him and Zakmon caught him.

"Perhaps a night's rest, first," said Zakmon rather than suggested.

Gasahd considered it for a moment. He had had a lot to drink. "Yes, I suppose you're right. We'll get one of the rooms upstairs. And we'll get it free, us being Voidsmen and all. Part of our alliance with Fangheld." *Voidsmen,* he thought. *How dare I use that cursed word. And in public no less! That name is not for unknowing ears. Too much ale, that's the problem.* "Dembatstayr, I mean."

"Alliance?"

"Relationship. Now" —Gasahd looked around— "who do we see about a room?"

As Zakmon searched about, the barkeep no longer behind the bar, Gasahd eyed a young red-haired girl in the corner. She must have been no more than seventeen years of age. Every time his eyes rested on her, she looked away shyly but then would glance back with a sly grin across her lips. Being looked at by anyone in the Dembatstayr Army was indeed an honor.

Perhaps she should come upstairs with him? Gasahd wondered. After all, it was a cold night tonight and no one deserved to be alone in a cool bed.

Deep gray shadows danced along the ceiling of the suite, a small cramped little hole of a room on the second floor of the Golden Barrel. The shadows moved, the wooden ceiling a muddy mix of brown and gray, doused in the moonlight that came in through the windows. The moon always seemed bigger in Fangheld, Gasahd noticed. Zakmon was one room over and Gasahd could hear him snoring loudly through the thin walls separating the suites.

The general lay awake, the red-haired girl wrapped around him beneath the down sheets, her smooth naked body against his, sleeping soundly. One of her arms was slung over his chest and, in his stupor, seemed to weigh far more than it actually did. He moved it so it rested on his shoulder instead. He resumed watching the shadows move on the ceiling.

Shadows.

Danger, was what it was. He had failed in capturing Aiyesha, but that was not what bothered him the most even though it did bother him greatly. No. What weighed upon him more was that he failed the Master. Failed his oath that he would breed an unstoppable group of women who could lead the World back into the Master's arms.

Thirteen years ago, a year before the first—and to date, only—group of females came to the Coast, the Master had visited him. Gasahd wasn't even a general then. He had been only thirty-two years of age at the time, young, working at the dockyards in Port Eril'ov as a Loader, one who would aid the crew of ships passing through Port Eril'ov in loading and unloading their cargo.

One night, while loading crates of oranges onto a small rickety ship, grumbling to himself that the work could have easily been done by the ship's crew—who were drinking down at a pub two gels away—Gasahd took a moment to rest and, looking out onto Lake Eril'ov, he saw the impossible. On the smooth black surface of the water beneath a sky lit with stars, was a man walking toward him, walking on the water. He had shook his head twice and closed and reopened his eyes several times before acknowledging that what he was seeing was real. Mesmerized by the man walking on the water, Gasahd stepped up the ramp leading from the cargo hold onto the main deck of the ship, then up to its bow. The man was walking toward him on the water as if treading upon a street as strong as stone. Flowing purple material—a robe—covered the man and moved fluidly in the subtle breeze that ran across the lake. The robe's material didn't get wet when it touched the water, he remembered vividly.

Then the man was gone and the lake was empty.

Not sure what happened and also not wanting to tell anybody for fear of being called a lunatic, Gasahd turned to go back to his duties. When he turned around, the man in the purple robe stood before him. The man's hair was long and gray, as was his beard and mustache. His eyes—they were bright blue, no whites, just blue, as if his eyes were the portals to a clear summer sky—looked deep into Gasahd from beneath a pair of bushy gray eyebrows that seemed more like one eyebrow than two.

It was at that moment Gasahd knew who this man was, and it was at that moment that everything changed.

"And now I've failed You," he spoke into the darkness of his room. The red-haired girl, whose name he couldn't remember, stirred beside him and then rolled off him, onto her back. "You gave me everything—You made me what I am now—and I've failed You. Forgive me."

There was no peace after this request. Normally, asking the Master for forgiveness bestowed upon you a sudden sense of calm, an assurance that, though you erred and strayed from His path, He had forgiven you and allowed you to walk with Him once again. But not tonight. Not for Gasahd. The creation of a female army for the Void were orders demanded by the Master Himself. The women, all of them, were important. And now all were gone and, unless he waited twelve more years to train others to match the strength, speed and skill of their predecessors, they would not be replaced.

Especially Aiyesha.

His head still spun from the ale. There was so much going on. He had to make it up to the Master; had to correct his wrong. Had to get Aiyesha lest he pay the price for failure. The Master had given him specific orders to recruit and retain the females, women hand-picked by the Master Himself.

"I couldn't even do that right, could I?" said Gasahd.

He felt like he were back at the dockyard, a worthless nobody stacking crates for ships' crews who couldn't care what his name was. He winced, a reaction to the feeling. It was a terrible thing feeling this way, a terrible thing feeling as if you were nothing.

"But in Your eyes I am nothing, aren't I?" he said.

The shadows danced along the ceiling. And then, as if an answer to his question, the shadows curled into dark tendrils, long limbs, perhaps fingers, pointing to the bedroom window to the right.

Gasahd followed the trail of shadow along the ceiling until he was looking out the window. A purple-gray mist was settling down on Fangheld, dense and thick, the streetlamps glowing dully in the fog.

The red-haired girl sighed in her sleep. When she spoke, her voice was barely a whisper.

"I'll never forget the water," she said.

The time was drawing near. Thalok was growing eager. Attacking all of them in the night—*reaching* out to them—drew him all the more closer. He had shifted his course three hours ago and already he picked up their scent on the air. The company was near. How much further? Thalok both knew and didn't know. They were just closer, and *closer* was a good thing.

Something was amiss.

All Qinorans were connected. Some more than others, but the connection was always there, like a baby to their mother. One Qinoran could always sense the presence of another, in some way, shape or form, no matter the distance. Here, as Thalok moved like a mighty steed along the horizon of Jakarland, a sort of realm created when he ran so quickly—he could feel the other Qinorans on the Island of the Dead. Though, out here, out in the World, it was a little different. Their presence—their air—was fuzzy, distorted, as if his feeling of them was like looking at another through the veil of muddy lake water, as though the other Qinoran was beneath the water's surface.

The connection between all Qinorans began at their beginning, during the fallout of the Battle of Then. The Purple had been cast out. Some of the Black followed, pitying it. And so began their alliance, their union, some of the Black pairing with some of the Purple: the birth of a race—Qinoran. And since all of the Purple were loyal to the Void-man, and since He ruled them all, He was in tune with them and they with Him, He their link to both Him and each other. He was their mother and, as a parent to a child, and a child to their parent—connected.

But something was wrong. Through the murk of his connection to the other Qinorans, Thalok could sense their unease and an impending feeling of being lost with no place to go. For Thalok, though, his connection with his kin was slighter than other Qinorans to each other. Thalok was more Black than Purple and so was different. But he still sensed them.

And today—if the idea of a "today" could exist on the Island of the Dead—his kin were screaming, calling out to each other, pleading with each other for suggestion as to what to do. *Do about what?* Thalok didn't know and he cursed himself for it.

His thoughts then shifted to the Void-man and the altercation on the Island about how he wasn't going about the hunt as he should. Though this was, really, a trivial matter, it still bore upon him.

"Curse Him," he said, adjusting his cloak on his shoulders so that it blew more comfortably with the wind he created. "Curse Him. I've been doing this longer than any other of my kind. Better than any other of my kind." And that was true; he was the greatest hunter on the Island.

"He detests me, I know it," he muttered. "More Black than Purple. More Black than Purple. Even though those colors no longer have meaning, the Black in me is filthy in His sight. I was there the day those shades were given label four Aeons ago. Before then, after the Battle of Then, the colors weren't yet defined. So much has passed since then." Thalok stopped his monologue, realizing this was the first time he had truly begun talking to himself. He also realized this was the Blacks' way, always muttering on and on to themselves about something that wasn't going to plan. And the Black still existed in the World. Thalok knew because he had seen them, watched them, studied them, in the hopes to learn more about their existence as it truly was and not how the Void-man painted it to be.

His memory of the past was a distorted one. How much had the Void-man created as past moments in Thalok's mind? How much of it was true? Poisoned memory was what it was.

Thalok stopped his stride, the wind billowing around him as he came to a halt. He was out of Jakarland, back in the World. His thoughts changed again and settled on Peter, then . . . the girl, what was her name? . . . Aiyesha . . . the little humanette . . . who? . . . Catina . . . the old fool . . . blind Alan . . . and the complainer, the one with the long name who liked to be called what, again? . . . Mr. Nibbetts.

Thalok reached out, across landscape and lake, mountain and hill.

He found them. They were in the Calahudron Woods, not far from his present position.

The hard part was over. He knew where they were. The rest would be easy.

Thalok sped on, Jakarland building up around him until it was everywhere.

It wouldn't be long now.

On the Great Wall the Void-man watched Thalok move. Though a part of Him hated to admit it, He was proud of the Qinoran for his defiance. No one dared stand up against Him. Especially a Qinoran, the spawn of His blood, His life, His very essence. They were all a part of the Purple. But they were tainted, those Qinorans. They were touched with the Black, the other side of the White, from that battle long ago.

With a mere thought, the Void-man changed the image on the Great Wall and saw the Qinorans in His holding cell in the heart of a mountain, far from His throne. Most of the Qinorans were there, with only a few still roaming about the Island. Soon, once Thalok completed his task, the Qinorans would be eliminated, as they should have been at the moment of their creation. The reason He hadn't slaughtered them at birth was because He had hoped, since Qinoran blood was half of the Black, He could create some sort of alliance with the Black and have a place to go instead of remaining on the Island in exile. But that never occurred. The Black Powers detested Him for tampering with the course of the Battle and disturbing what was supposed to be a straight forward outcome: the End of Time, the finale of the then-tiring war between the White and the Black, between Good and Evil, Light and Dark. Only a few of the Black took pity on the Purple and formed a separate alliance; again, the birth of the Qinorans, a race that was a mix of sides.

Now, though, that mix would end and there would be nothing left but the Island, the Purple, free of the taint of the Black. But not yet, not while Thalok was away. And not while Peter still lived. Once Peter was gone, however, then the Qinorans could die. The Void-man could not leave the Island Himself. Not yet, anyway. Perhaps one day, with the finding of the Ark of Light.

One day.

On the Great Wall, the Qinorans in the holding cell slid back and forth across the floor, their way of pacing.

It would only be a matter of time.

But Time did not exist here on the Island of the Dead.

CHAPTER XLIII
Healer in the Trees

Yaman woke Peter with a sharp poke to the ribs.

"Get up," said the First-man.

Peter blinked his eyes open with a quiet grunt. The inside of the hut was blurry. Yaman stood at his feet, his blonde, hairy face looming over him.

"I've been trying to wake you for the past while. All the others got up without a problem."

Tiredness hung over Peter's head as if someone were pressing their palms hard against the sides of his temples. *Why am I so tired?*

"Sorry," said Peter. He slowly sat up, the cobwebs still hanging thick inside his skull.

Yaman straightened. Behind the First-man was a rectangle of morning light decorated with the green of the leaves and bushes beyond and the deep brown of massive tree trunks—the doorway to the hut.

Peter glanced around the inside of the hut. Yaman was right when he said the others were already awake. The hut was empty except for him. Why had he slept so late? Too tired to think on it any more, Peter stood and walked slightly hunched over, past Yaman, out the door. The First-man followed like a parent supervising their child, making sure they got out of bed before a full day of chores.

The city in the trees was empty save for Alan, Catina, Aiyesha, and Mr. Nibbetts, and the dog, her tail wagging. She barked a high-pitched bark that rang inside Peter's head. His companions were already on their horses, packed and ready to go. They all looked at him as if they had been waiting long for him to rise. Where was everyone else? *Sleeping,* thought Peter, *where I'd like to be.*

"Sorry," said Peter to the others.

"We thought something was wrong," said Aiyesha, bringing Day toward him.

"No. I just overslept, that's all," he replied and then yawned.

The two looked at each other for a long time, like long lost friends. Aiyesha was the first to glance away. Peter thought he saw her blush but couldn't be sure. His head was still a little cloudy.

Alan cleared his throat loudly, stealing the moment from them.

"I guess we better be going," said Peter.

"We should have got going an hour ago," said the First-man, walking past him to stand with the others.

Peter apologized again.

"Here," said Aiyesha. She dismounted Day. "You can ride her first. You look tired."

"Thank you. But what about you?"

"I'll be fine."

"Are you sure?"

She smiled at him. "Positive."

He felt unworthy, as if *he* should be the one walking. A gentleman always lets the lady ride. He could tell by her gaze that he wasn't allowed to say no.

"Thank you," he said again.

He mounted Day, sitting in front of Mr. Nibbetts, and thought being seated on her back never felt so good. He was grateful to Aiyesha for allowing him this comfort.

The company arranged their horses so that he was on foot in front of Alan and Catina, who were on Night, the black horse's reins in his hand, ready to lead it. Aiyesha walked ahead of them along with Yaman.

Yaman took Day by the reins and began leading the group to the right of the hut and past a few others. Inside one of them, one of the bush-people snored loudly.

"Me wish me was doing that," grumbled Mr. Nibbetts.

"Me, too," said Peter. *Boy, do I wish it.*

The Calahudron village was small so it didn't take them long before they were back into the thick of the woods, the tall trees, the dense thickets. Behind Peter, Alan yawned. It was contagious. He did, too.

Yaman walked slowly, leading the horses, negotiating his way around the massive trees with the ease of having walked through these woods countless times before. For the first hour of their journey, the company was quiet and only spoke in short sentences, all seeming a little down-trodden because they were back on the horses, back to traveling.

Peter thought again about Yaman's tale of the Gray Man and the similarities between the tale and what Peter knew of Thalok. And Yaman's mentioning that the story of the Gray Man was true, didn't add to anything. His eyes wandering about the path they traveled, Peter would not have been surprised if Thalok jumped out from behind one of the trees and had at them. It was almost as if he was expecting it.

Thalok, if he was real, was getting close. Peter could sense it, like knowing it was going to rain just by the smell of the air without having to look at the clouds. Thalok was out there, of that he was certain. Wasn't he? Maybe. The dreams—It had all been too real. But dreams were like that sometimes, he knew. Too real. Dreams were the way the mind dealt with the troubles of life. They helped you cope. But even now as Peter rode Day, out of the corners of his eyes . . . . He could feel Thalok looking at him, watching him, waiting on him, ready to strike at any time. Knowing about Thalok's reality was like the feeling that comes after being at a funeral: your life suddenly becomes more precious because you realize your own mortality and, more than anything, you hope that your time to die doesn't come soon. But Thalok was near. This thought, this idea, rang loudly in Peter's head and in his heart, his very *being*.

Up ahead, Yaman was speaking to Aiyesha about the rules of combat and how you should not plan your movements but react instead. Aiyesha said that it should be a combination of both, to just react when on the defensive, but to also search for openings on your opponent so you can get a strike in.

Peter was never one for fighting but given what had occurred since he had left Garathen, he paid attention to all that was said between the two warriors. The information might come in handy should he ever find himself fighting for his life again. He hoped he wouldn't, but then again, he knew he probably would. If Thalok were real, that was. He *was* real, wasn't he? Yes, Peter thought so. No, he didn't.

"Peter, where are we?" asked Alan from behind.

"In the woods, Alan," he replied. The dog barked twice then padded up beside him.

"I know that, you fopphin. What does it look like?"

He hadn't noticed the transition while his thoughts wandered but Peter saw the leaves on the bushes and the leaves of the treetops way overhead had become brighter, a more brilliant green. In fact, all of the colors around them became more pronounced, enhanced, more vivid. Even the brownish-gray of the tree trunks was deeper and, seemingly, more colorful, richer. Streaks of morning light came through the gaps in the canopy in bright shafts of white, giving a sparkle to the edges of the leaves.

"It's amazing," said Peter after a time and explained to Alan what he saw, how the trees had suddenly changed color.

The entire company, except for Alan and Yaman (who had seen this part of the forest many times before), were looking around, their heads angled up and rotating on their necks like a cat eyeing the flight path of a bird.

"This is the Heart of the Woods," explained Yaman. "Here is where the Giver of All's blessings are."

"Then why didn't you build your village here?" asked Mr. Nibbetts.

"Because we didn't want to be selfish of the Giver of All and live in a place where Her blessings continuously flow. My people—and myself—did not want to be spoiled by being used to splendor. No. We camped elsewhere so, when we needed our spirits lifted, we could come to this part of the woods and marvel at the Giver of All's magnificence."

"It's beautiful," said Aiyesha.

"Sure is," said Peter.

And on they went, Yaman leading them, walking proud as he took them through the best part of the Calahudron Woods.

An hour later Yaman slowed them. Eventually they came to a halt.

"Why are we stopping?" asked Alan.

Yaman hushed them and lowered the reins in his hand slowly before letting them fall completely. He crouched down and crept up behind a bush. From where he was sitting, Peter couldn't tell what Yaman was looking at, but he knew that the First-man sensed something. Yaman was sniffing the air like a dog sniffing the ground, seeing who had gone there before. Aiyesha moved behind him smoothly, her footfalls not making a sound as they touched the ground, and came up beside Yaman. The two exchanged whispers. Aiyesha only glanced back once at the group before turning her attention to whatever it was Yaman was looking at, and, judging by the expression on her face, Peter knew that something was wrong. He hoped it wasn't anything serious.

He didn't notice it until a moment later but Yaman had disappeared and Aiyesha was walking back toward the group. She crossed her arms under her breasts.

"Something's out there and he's gone to make sure the path is clear before we continue." Her tone was somber, like one reporting bad news.

"Does he know what it is?" asked Alan.

Aiyesha shook her head. "No."

"Great," said Mr. Nibbetts. "Me knew there was going to be a problem. There always is."

"Quiet, you!" snapped Alan. "I have had enough of your belly-aching and your childish complaints."

Mr. Nibbetts wrinkled his nose and bore his teeth, something Flistablares did when upset at another.

"I'm sure everything is all right," said Peter, trying to ease everyone's worries before they even began.

The dog padded up to the bush that Yaman disappeared into. She stood alert on all fours, her eyes focused on the bush. Her ears perked up and stayed that way.

Catina called out to the dog in Grescalla but Alan said something to her and she quieted.

After waiting for what felt like an hour but was really only about ten minutes, Yaman emerged from the bush, his face long.

"The Healer is dead," he said. "Aiyesha Elnaa, come with me."

Aiyesha glanced up at Peter, then at the others. "All right." And she disappeared with Yaman into the bush.

"Where are they going?" asked Mr. Nibbetts.

"I don't know," said Peter.

"The Healer is dead," repeated Alan softly.

Catina said something in Grescalla. Peter didn't know what. The dog remained by the bush, eyes fixed on something. After a moment, Peter got off his horse.

"Where are you going?" asked Alan. He must have heard Peter walking away.

"Just going to take a look," said Peter and, walking past the dog, gave her a pat on the head. The dog licked his hand but stayed where she was. Peter entered the bush.

He didn't know where Aiyesha and Yaman were but presumed they went straight ahead. So straight ahead he walked, parting the branches with his hands. One swung back and slapped him in the chest. Beyond another bush, the big trunk of one of the towering trees was in his way. He rounded it and, on the other side, heard Yaman speaking.

"I've never seen anything like it," said the First-man.

"Who or what do you suppose did it?" asked Aiyesha.

"I don't know. This does not comfort me."

Peter followed their voices until he emerged from behind a bush to where they were. The two stood before the trunk of a wide tree. Yaman's large form blocked whatever it was he was looking at. Aiyesha was beside him. She turned to meet Peter.

"I didn't want to sit there and do nothing," he said.

Aiyesha didn't say anything and moved over to the side to allow Peter room. As he came beside the First-man, Peter felt the strength run from his legs.

"Our Healer," said Yaman with a nod toward the tree.

The Healer's body was impaled against the tree about a foot off the ground. The skin at the corners of his shoulders and the bottom of his shins was stretched outward and, for each stretch of skin, held to the tree by what appeared to be wooden spikes, no thicker than a bush-man's arrow. Whoever or whatever had used those spikes to nail the Healer to the tree must have used a force or strength stronger than anything that could be imagined. Peter didn't know what kind of strength would be needed to drive wood through wood. The Healer's body hung limp, his head bowed, long, dark hair drooping over his face. His tanned skin accented the deep brown of the trunk and seemed to sharpen the nooks and grooves on the bark's surface. His middle was slashed open, his guts spilling out and hanging over his groin like a second loincloth, strings of red and maroon and an out-of-place gray dangling like chimes on a tree. Flies buzzed around the open flesh. Above the Healer's middle, on his chest, was an engraving in the muscles and skin. Peter noticed the color was not the color of blood.

Disoriented, Peter didn't make out the writing and, gagging, turned around and covered his mouth. Stomach swimming, head suddenly feeling fatigued, he prepared himself to throw up.

He didn't and, a few moments later, his stomach settled, as if he had never looked at the Healer's dead body.

He turned back. It wasn't as bad the second time, looking at the Healer. The torn-open gut, the dark dried blood oozing from around the wooden spikes holding him against the tree didn't seem as disturbing. Peter examined the writing on the Healer's chest. The writing was jagged, plainly slashed into the flesh with haste and carelessness, but with enough effort to make it legible. The color of the writing was the dark gray of stone but still liquid-looking like dripping blood.

I'M COMING, it read.

Gagging again, Peter turned and spat out a wad of bile. He stared at its yellow, murky form as it hit the ground. Aiyesha came up behind him and put her arm around him.

"Are you okay?" she asked.

Peter spat again, this time just saliva. "Yes. No. I don't know." His thoughts gelled and a sudden feeling of disbelief came over him. Words from the Square in Darim flooded his memory. *I'm coming.*

Thalok.

He wanted to tell her everything, wanted to tell her of the Man in the Gray Cloak. Tell her of Thalok and how he had been haunting him. Tell her Thalok was re— "Aiyesha, I—"

Yaman came up behind them. "Are you all right, there, boy?" He slapped Peter on the back.

Boy? Peter hated the name and stood. "Fine." He gave Yaman a hard look because of the slap. He was not in the mood for it. Turning back to the Healer, a foul taste filled his mouth.

Fear.

It tasted like the water by the river. Peter shuddered and looked at the writing again.

I'M COMING.

"The Gray Man is real," said Peter, not realizing he said it aloud.

"What did you say?" asked Yaman.

"What?"

"You said, 'the Gray Man is real.'"

"I did?" He supposed he had. "Yes, I did."

The dog barked again somewhere behind them. The three turned to the sound then Yaman and Aiyesha's attention returned to Peter.

"I've been seeing the Gray Man," said Peter. Saying it aloud suddenly made him feel ashamed. He didn't know why.

"That's impossible," said Yaman. "The Gray Man is real, yes, but only in stories. I told you that he was real just to scare you."

Aiyesha looked on in intrigue.

Peter shook his head. "No, he's real. Very real. I can't explain it. I've seen him. I've seen him throughout most of this journey. It started in Darim. It happened again in Grek. It happened by the river." His shoulders sagged. "I even dreamed of him."

Aiyesha's green eyes shot wide. "You dreamed of him?"

Peter met her gaze. "Yes. A couple of nights ago. I can't remember which night. I've been trying to forget it."

She bit her lower lip, her eyes to the forest's floor. When she glanced up, her gaze was that of grave concern—and, though Peter couldn't believe it, not after what he had seen of her—fear.

"Did he wear a gray cloak, so large, so smooth, that it almost looked alive?" she asked after a moment.

Peter nodded.

"What are you two talking about?" asked Yaman, taking a step closer, coming between them.

The knowledge that Aiyesha had either the same dream or had a similar dream, didn't surprise Peter as much as he thought it would. Throughout the whole journey, it had been one surprise after another, one amazing event after another. He supposed he had gone numb to surprise, at least when it came to things that couldn't be explained or events he thought would never happen.

"We've had the same dream," he said, his blue eyes never leaving Aiyesha's.

"Darkness, is what you're talking about if you're telling the truth," said Yaman, scolding. "No one has the same dream."

"I was on a boat," said Aiyesha, "with Morley. He—"

Yaman cut her off. "I don't want to hear it. Keep that Darkness inside and don't spoil this place where the Giver of All's blessings flow."

Peter glanced back at the Healer, the words I'M COMING standing sharp against the rest of the sickly flesh.

"We have to go," he said quietly. "We—we have to go."

It looked like Aiyesha had more to say but she didn't speak further. The three, all taking one last look at the Healer's impaled form, returned back into the bush and a short while later emerged where the others were waiting.

Peter came up to Day and paused before mounting the mare. Mr. Nibbetts wasn't around but Peter hardly noticed.

"What did you see?" asked Alan.

He leaned against the mare's back then stroked her mane. "Their Healer," he said. "He . . . " An image of the Healer nailed to the tree danced before his eyes. "He . . . "

"He is dead," finished Alan.

With weary eyes, Peter looked up at him. The blind man was able to sense the gaze.

"I may be blind," said Alan, "but like I always say, I can sense things. Sound, touch, the mere feelings of another. Call it a gift from the Master, if you like, to compensate for the loss of my sight. I can hear the weighted breathing of you, Aiyesha, Yaman. But the fate of the Healer was known when Yaman told us. What happened?"

"What is this? Who's dead?" asked Mr. Nibbetts, emerging from a bush off to the side.

"Our Healer," said Yaman, overhearing.

"There's a body over there!" The furry creature glanced around.

"Where were you?" asked Peter.

Mr. Nibbetts hopped up atop Day. "Why, can't a simple creature like me relieve himself?"

Without meaning to, Peter chuckled. "I'm sorry," he said and got atop Day. "What will you do with the body?" He didn't want the Healer's mangled form left out in the woods to rot.

The First-man, grabbing the reins in hand, said, "He belongs to the Giver of All now. There is no better place for him to be other than here. This is the Heart of the Woods, the place in the forest where the blessings flow. The Healer wouldn't want me to take his body back to the village. Now . . . now he can become one with the forest. The others will come, eventually, once I give them the news. Respects will be paid." He gazed back into the bushes. "We go around."

Guess I was wrong, thought Peter.

And with that, Yaman gave Day's reins a tug and began to lead the others around the place in the Heart of the Woods where the Healer's dead body was nailed to a tree.

Not much time had passed before they were out of the Heart of the Woods. They must have crossed most of it before discovering the Healer's body. Once they were back in the "regular" part of the Calahudron Woods, the change in the colors of the trees, their leaves and the bushes, was noticeable. All—despite before seeming beautiful—was drab and plain, the green just the natural green of leaf, the brownish-gray of tree trunks just the same old brownish-gray of tree trunks.

Shaking the silence, the dog barked again.

"Quiet, you, or I'll have you for dinner," said Yaman.

The dog barked again. Peter saw a smile cross Aiyesha's lips. She looked so beautiful out here in the woods; the softness of her skin, the richness of her black hair, the brilliance of her green eyes. She seemed to make the plain of the forest more attractive again.

"Aiyesha?"

She cocked her head back toward him.

"Your dream. Are you sure about it?" He had to know. The idea of her having the same or similar dream hung over him like a persistent headache.

"He had a gray cloak, did he not." It was more of a statement than a question.

"Yes, he did. A long gray cloak," said Peter.

Mr. Nibbetts started to say something but was cut off by Yaman.

"I don't want to hear of your Darkness. Any more talk of this dream you folks say you had and I'll leave you here to be lost in the woods."

"Why can't we talk about it?" asked Peter.

"Because it is Darkness. It is not of the Giver of All and Her ways. No one dreams the same dream."

"How can you prove that?" asked Aiyesha.

Yaman was silent for a time, seeming to be stuck on an answer. Then he spoke. "Because . . . . Remember that story I told you? Of the Gray Man? It is real."

"Is it or isn't it?" demanded Peter. "You've changed your mind on it being real or not real every time it is brought up. Which one is it? Real or not real? What are you afraid of?"

Yaman shot him a hot glare. He spoke one word through gritted teeth. "Real."

"People had the same dreams when the Gray Man visited this forest last, am I right?" came Alan, joining the conversation.

"Gray Man?" said Mr. Nibbetts. "The one with the long gray cloak? Me dreamed about him, too. He's real?"

"We all had a dream," said Peter, "though I'm not sure of Catina."

"She had it, too," said Alan. "She told me the morning after. It was about her parents. It seems we've all dreamed of this man with a gray cloak."

"He's no man," said Yaman. "He's a being of the Mist, opposed to all the Giver of All stands for. There is another story about the Gray Man, if, the one you dreamed about is the same Gray Man I'm talking about. It is said that he used to be at the right hand side of the Giver of All. It is said that he used to be a messenger of the Giver of All. When this was, no one knows. A long time ago. There was a falling out. It is said that there were more like the Gray Man. How many? Again, we don't know, but there were others and the Gray Man was the finest of them and so earned the Giver of All's respect." He negotiated a turn around the base of a big tree. The ground was uneven here and they descended down a small slope in the woods. "But they had a disagreement and their relationship has never been the same since."

"How do you know that?" asked Alan, running a hand over his head. It was no longer smooth and bald but rough with the dark blonde stubble of hair.

"My people used to leave the village quite a bit. They would go on walks for days, seeking out the Giver of All, hoping to be more in tune with Her. When they returned, they reported scratches in the trees, markings blaspheming the Giver of All."

"Those could have been made by anybody," said Alan.

"Not my people," said Yaman. "We love the Giver of All with all our hearts. No one would ever—and no has ever—written such a thing. Besides, the writing was written in blood from some of the animals around here, namely bears. And the blood had a taint of gray to it. Not as much as the Healer's blood had been, for we believe that because he is a man, because he had an Eternal Life-strength within him, that was why a man's blood will turn to gray. Like in the tale of the Gray Man. Bears, animals, they do not have the Eternal Life-strength and are here instead to help provide us bush-people with the means to live: food, clothing, tools from bone. But that is the story, in summary. Something happened between the Gray Man and the Giver of All. They do not get along as well as they once had and so, because the Gray Man is bound to the Giver of All, he still tries to redeem himself. But, at least in my people's history, each time he has come around these parts, he has left violence and destruction in his wake." He led them round another tree. "So, for that reason I do not wish to hear of your dreams of him. It is Darkness. It goes against the ways of the Giver of All. She deserves glory in Her forest, not words about Darkness."

Not wanting to test Yaman's threat about leaving them in the woods, Peter said, "Very well. We'll talk no more of it, out of respect."

"Thank you," said Yaman.

They rode on and, from behind, Alan leaned past Catina and whispered, "That was very wise of you, Peter. I know those dreams—the idea we have all dreamed of the Gray Man—is pressing on you. We will talk more of it once we are out of the woods."

Peter nodded. Midday was approaching and they still had quite a ways to go.

The further they got from the Heart of the Woods, the further the memory of the Healer's body spiked to a tree fled from Peter's mind. It was as if the physical distance of being away from the site pushed away the event in Time, like something that happened long ago and was on the verge of being forgotten.

Catina let out a squeal, then, "Boola!"

Yaman stopped the horses. No one had really noticed it until Catina yelled. The leaves of the trees at some point had turned from green to black with only a few small blotches of green still visible. But it wasn't the leaves that were black. It was what was *on* the leaves.

Caterpillars. Long dark caterpillars with a hundred legs moving quickly on the leaves, crawling up and down the branches of the trees and bushes, up and over and around each other, a mess of caterpillars feasting hungrily on what leaves remained.

The dog moved around in circles, trying not to let the caterpillars touch it.

"Where did they come from?" asked Aiyesha.

"I don't know," said Yaman. "They were never here before. In fact, I've never seen so many."

"Get me out of here! Get me out of here!" yelled Mr. Nibbetts, rubbing his hands all over his body as if there were already caterpillars crawling on him.

Peter grabbed the furry creature's shoulders, discouraging his movement. "Sit still!"

"What is wrong, now?" asked Alan.

"Boola!" said Catina.

"Caterpillars," replied Peter.

"A lot of them," said Aiyesha, keeping a fidgeting Day in check.

Yaman wiped a caterpillar off his chest. "Here." And he shoved Aiyesha further back. She blocked his pushing hands instinctively, but then allowed him to push her aside.

Yaman climbed on Day, nearly shoving Peter off the horse. The mare whinnied at the crowded weight atop her. "Aiyesha, take the dark one."

Aiyesha helped Alan and Catina further down Night's back, and she mounted the horse and grabbed its reins.

Yaman turned back to Peter. "Ready? We ride quick."

"But the trees—" he began, but Yaman tore off into the bush before he could finish.

"Where did they go? Where did—" started Alan but then leaned back in his seat when Night lurched forward as Aiyesha snapped the reins. Alan clutched Catina and then eased his grip when she squealed because he had grabbed her too hard.

"Hang on," said Peter as they tore into the bush.

Mr. Nibbetts yelled the whole time while they galloped, past the leaves coated with caterpillars, in between the caterpillars that dropped from the branches overhead like rain.

Yaman's blonde hair bounced up and down as they rode, the matted locks swatting Peter in the face more often than not. Each time he shoved them away and gave Yaman a nudge between the shoulder blades. Yaman didn't seem to notice and only kicked Day's sides harder and told Alan to do the same. Night must go faster if he was going to keep up.

"This is terrible," said Mr. Nibbetts.

The dog, without being coaxed, kept pace with them the whole time, darting away from the bushes when she got too close to the caterpillar-coated branches.

"Ugh," said Peter. *They're everywhere!*

"I hope you know what you are doing," said Alan.

And they rode. The caterpillars fell from above. Some seemed—despite how impossible it was—to jump off the branches at them, but missed because they were riding past so hard. Yaman took Day, Night following behind, around the trees, jumping over some of the bushes.

The sound of the horses' hooves galloping thundered around them. Branches with caterpillars began slapping against their chest and faces. Some of the caterpillars stuck to them and they all tried to maintain their balance on the speeding horses while trying to pick the caterpillars off. Mr. Nibbetts yelped even louder when some of the caterpillars got caught in his fur.

Catina covered her eyes then pulled her hands away to frantically brush the caterpillars off, then covered her eyes again. Alan kept wiping them off himself as best he could without seeing exactly where the insects were against his dark clothes.

Peter brushed his own caterpillars away.

Just when he thought the rain of caterpillars was about to get worse, the insect's presence on the branches and leaves began to thin and the forest soon grew clear. Yaman and Aiyesha brought the horses side by side and dismounted.

Mr. Nibbetts was off Day in a flash and danced around as he tried to get the remaining caterpillars off himself. "Me hate this! Me hate this! Awful critters, they are."

Peter got off Day, wiped himself off, and then helped Catina and Alan do the same. Aiyesha and Yaman had already picked the caterpillars off themselves.

Peter noticed that someone was missing. "I think we lost the dog," he announced to the others.

Just then, the dog tore out of the bush and, wagging its tail, stopped in front of him. Only one caterpillar was on the dog's back but was quickly snatched up by its teeth and swallowed.

Peter made a face and, looking at Yaman, pointed back to the place in the forest that they just left. "What happened in there?"

The First-man pulled at his long beard. "I don't know. I've never seen anything like it. It was as if all the caterpillars in the forest had come to one place."

"Can you make it back?"

Yaman considered the question for a moment. "I will try. I may have to go around."

The dog barked and Yaman shot it a hot glare. "Sure, you're fine. What about the rest of us?"

The dog merely eyed him curiously.

"I can't believe how many there were," said Aiyesha.

Alan shivered. "Just thinking about them makes my flesh crawl. Sorry, but can someone check me over once more. I need to know there are none on me."

Aiyesha came over to him and looked him over. Peter had missed one caterpillar when he had brushed Alan off. Right after Aiyesha wiped the caterpillar away and it fell to the ground, Mr. Nibbetts came over and stamped on it.

"There! That'll teach you!" he growled.

Aiyesha looked at him with raised eyebrows.

"Well, it would," said Mr. Nibbetts and went back over to Day.

"I'd like to leave, now," said Peter.

And off they went.

An hour later there was a breaking in the trees and the light of day came through the leaves like sunlight through a series of small windows. They were almost out of the forest.

As if echoing Peter's thoughts, Yaman announced, "We're almost there."

Peter's heart speed up at the idea of being out on open country again. The caterpillars had been too much.

Before long they were out of the trees, much to everyone's vast relief.

"Finally," said Mr. Nibbetts.

The dog ran out into the field and chased a rabbit for a short while but when the rabbit disappeared into its hole she returned to the group.

Yaman, who had stayed on Day, dismounted and landed with a thud. "This is where I leave you."

They all got off their horses for the good-bye. Peter came up to him first and put a hand on his shoulder. "Thank you for taking us through the woods. I had a good time." He waited. "A real good time." *Save for the darker parts. It was an . . . an eye-opener, though. Didn't know there were others who lived inside a forest.*

Yaman, seeming unsure as to what to do, put a hand to Peter's shoulder. He didn't know this was the Garathen way of saying hello and good-bye. "You are welcome in my woods whenever you pass by." He dropped his hand and stood an inch away from Peter. His breath was hot and smelled of rotting wood. "But leave your Darkness behind before you come. I will not have it in my forest. Not near my people."

Peter grimaced and made way for the others to say good-bye. Catina wasn't given a farewell by Yaman. It wasn't the bush-people's way to say good-bye to children, not until they were old enough to be revered as a "real" person.

When Aiyesha came up to Yaman, he swung out in a wild arc, and, in the split second before his fist connected with her jaw, Aiyesha moved to the side and deflected the blow. She countered with a strike of her own, her hand coming around to the side of his neck. A ridgehand, the thumb tucked in, the fingers like a board of solid oak. It was only a soft hit but strong enough for Yaman to immediately clasp his hand to his neck, cradling the tender flesh.

He coughed. "I wanted to remind you to be alert. Instead, you showed me that I am the one who needs to be more aware."

"You'll be all right," she said and walked away. It was a warrior's way. No sympathy, even in exhibition.

The First-man coughed again. His skin along the side of his neck was already bruising.

Mr. Nibbetts let out a laugh. "He didn't see it coming! He didn't—" Like a wolf lunging at an unsuspecting deer, Yaman dove at Mr. Nibbetts and tackled the furry creature to the ground.

Yaman had his fist cocked over Mr. Nibbetts's face. "Get. Off. My. Land."

Aiyesha came up behind Yaman and whispered something in his ear. Yaman's posture eased and, finally, he got off the Flistablare.

"Did you see that? Did you see?" asked Mr. Nibbetts as he got to his feet. "If it went on any more, me would have entered" —he scowled at Yaman and, when he spoke, his voice was low and foreboding— "the Change."

Aiyesha walked Yaman to the edge of the forest. The dog yipped.

"Quiet," said Yaman, "or I'll skin you."

And just like that, the First-man left and disappeared into the forest as though the trees were a fog.

When Aiyesha returned to the group, Peter asked, "What did you say to him? He looked ready to kill Mr. Nibbetts."

"I simply told him that, if he killed him" —she glanced around, making sure Mr. Nibbetts was out of earshot— "he would actually be doing Mr. Nibbetts a favor."

"A wise move," said Alan, walking slowly toward them.

The sun shone in the clear blue sky. Only a small mist of clouds hung in the East.

East.

That's where they needed to go.

CHAPTER XLIV
A Talk of Dreams
(Blindness)

It was night, two days since leaving the Calahudron Woods. Catina was ill again. So was Mr. Nibbetts. Camp was set in a rocky cove up on a hill not far from Hillmalen, a small village known for its simplicity and the kind folk who lived there. From the cove, the hill tapered down into a grassy field, littered sporadically with stones. It was said that a great graveyard once lay there. As to what it was called or when, Time seemed to have forgotten. All that remained was a single pillar, no more than four feet high, perhaps a gravestone at one point. Still, being there intrigued Peter. He was developing a keen interest in culture and History and how the World worked outside the Forest-Ring.

While Aiyesha tended to Catina and Mr. Nibbetts—whose small bodies lay around a bonfire—Peter led Alan by the arm down the hill and the two went walking. The horses were tied to the pillar, nibbling at the small patches of long grass that grew along its base.

The dog was curled up by the fire. Catina had named her Belina, after, Alan later revealed to the group, a squirrel she had named Belina back home. The name in Grescalla meant "small and cuddly."

"Watch your step," Peter told him when Alan slipped on a stone and Peter caught his arm.

Alan didn't thank him. Peter could tell that his friend was growing weary of being helped all the time.

Peter was tired, too.

The past two days had been building up to this moment. The weight of the thoughts, the dreams, of the Gray Man—Thalok—had been pressing upon him. So many times had he wanted to talk to someone about it. So many times did he want to talk to Alan because Alan seemed to know everything when it came to, well, knowing everything. Now that the time had come to talk about the dreams, he wished he were up on the hill with Aiyesha, helping with Catina and the Flistablare, instead.

"There is no way to introduce the topic, Peter," said Alan after a time. He clasped his hands behind his back and his slow walk slowed even more. "So we must begin with a question, instead. The Gray Man, as Yaman called him. You dreamed the dream. So did Aiyesha. And so did Catina, Mr. Nibbetts and myself. My dream was different than what Catina dreamed. She told me hers. It was about her parents. Mine was about Aubri. Aiyesha . . . you said it was about Morley, that pirate on the *Raven.* Mr. Nibbetts, after overhearing him talking to himself about it, his dream was about his home in the Flistablare Forest. The burning of it. You . . . "

"Was about the burning of my home, too." Peter's heart sank. He thought he had gotten past losing his home. He was wrong. It was nearly sickening him, thinking about it all the time. *I wish I could just let it go. Enough already.*

"All of these dreams centered around painful events. Events, in our dreams, that have been twisted and turned . . . but painful nonetheless. I have given this a lot of thought."

"That's why you've been so quiet."

Alan smirked. "Yes, maybe. And they were thoughts worth thinking. Thoughts that needed to be thought upon—more importantly, thoughts that needed to be analyzed. Again, these are strange days. Especially strange when a group of, in actuality, five strangers dream similar dreams. I have no doubt that this 'Gray Man' is real. The tale Yaman told us is true."

Peter stopped him. "But how can you say that? You've always seemed to question things you weren't sure of, and that goes without saying. Now you're believing this?"

"How else would you expect me to react to it? Five people, Peter. Five people dreaming similar dreams in one night. Though it is conceivably possible for five people who know each other to each have nightmares on the same night . . . . But to have five nightmares with a common thread? A common image? A common Creature of the Night? The odds against that are more exponential than I care to think. I would rather believe that this gray-fellow is real and try and understand how it was possible for him to invade our dreams than to brush this off as coincidence. To me, that is even more disturbing."

"I suppose you're right." *I guess.*

Furrowing his brow, Peter gave a tug to Alan's arm and the two began walking a bit faster. "Have you ever seen anything like this while on the road, away from Garathen?"

The blind man shook his head. "No. Nothing like it. I have only heard one story but that story took place at the beginning of Time. The story, as much as I am able to recall, said that at the Birth, when Life came to be, there were two forces, now commonly known as the White and the Black. It is said they warred and, while they did, people—all Life—thought about them. Dreamed about them. They were everywhere. When the war ended and the Master came and saved us, recreated us as we are now, He annihilated those repeating thoughts of Black and White from our minds, filling us with the Purple of His Holy glory, His peace. The Black and the White fled and we have been in the comforting arms of the Master ever since." He sighed. "That is the only thing I know of that can parallel our dreams now."

"The Gray Man . . . he has a name."

"Oh?" Alan's white eyes widened.

The name was on the tip of Peter's tongue but, for the life of him, he had trouble saying it. He felt ashamed to be saying such a name out loud. He swallowed and when he spoke his voice cracked. "Thalok."

"Hm," was all Alan said.

"I saw him in Darim, Alan."

The blind man stopped walking. "What do you mean?"

"I saw him in Darim. In the crowd, at the Square. He was there for only a short moment before . . . . When I looked away and then looked back, he was gone. He told me he's coming."

Those words must have crippled Alan's tongue because the blind man didn't speak for a long while. When he did, his tone was flat. "When is he coming?"

"I don't know," said Peter. "Those words—'I'm coming'—were on the Healer's body when we found him. His blood had turned gray, like in the story of everyone in the village getting killed, the one Yaman told us. I believe the Gray Man is real, too. Thalok" —he swallowed; his heart sped up— "is real." He hated saying that name.

"So he is," said Alan. "Let us pray he doesn't come for us again."

Somewhere . . . somewhere far away but seemingly near, Mr. Nibbetts's snores droned in Catina's ears. Where was he? Surely close, yet . . . he was so far away.

Blackness. The purest dark. That was all she saw. She was awake; at least, conscious enough to see the darkness before her eyes but her body felt as though it were one hundred miles away, perhaps further. There was no sound in this place, in this dark, save for Mr. Nibbetts's snoring. Where was he? Certainly not here. It was just blackness, an abysmal dark. There was no body beneath her, no ground beneath her head. But she knew she was lying down. Somehow she knew.

Somehow.

Catina savored the serenity of this place—no more humming in her head, no more ringing as if someone had just shouted in her ear. Quiet. Mr. Nibbetts's snoring—but quiet.

The blackness before her eyes took on a new form, swirls of red peppered with pink flakes twirling, tumbling, moving all around. The colors were few at first then grew in number. Streaks of red, twisting like string, dancing to an unheard song. Pink dots popping in and out of her vision like sparks from a fire. The darkness took on dimension, instead of just a flat mat of black, but something with depth, as if it went on forever.

The red swirled and moved, the strings growing bigger as they neared. Each pink spark transformed from small, far away dots, into larger bursts until they were so near Catina thought they would hit her in the face.

She didn't need to scream. She didn't want to.

Mesmerized by the dancing strings of red and the sparkling of pink dots, she felt safe, secure; nothing could harm her. Mr. Nibbetts's snoring faded away and there was only silence, only blackness, only red twirling strings and little pink fireworks.

Then the humming began and Catina knew she was waking up. So hard did she try to relax and fall back asleep. So hard did she fight the consciousness that seeped back into her body. So hard did she not want to leave this place of serenity and comfort. So hard did she not want to lose the vision of dancing red lines and pink sparks.

The humming grew louder; a ringing came into her ears. The darkness began to be taken over by the swirls of red, growing fatter, blocking out the pink, until . . . . She was looking at the inside of her eyelids and—just beyond, she knew—through the skin of her lids to the bonfire on the other side.

The dull droning persisted inside her head, culminating behind her left eye. It pulsed, it pushed, throbbed as if someone was poking the backside of her eyeball with their finger, tapping it, irritating it. The pain was hot. She began to sweat.

More consciousness, almost awake. The heat of the fire beyond felt on the skin.

The pulsing.

The pain.

Red skin and the want to not open her eyes.

She was awake.

She opened her eyes and the bright flash of the fire's flames caused her to close them again. Her eye hurt more than words could express. All she could release was a whimper. It hurt so much that she couldn't hear Mr. Nibbetts snore anymore. She didn't know if anyone else was awake and she didn't care.

She wanted to be alone.

She needed someone.

Anyone.

She wanted to be alone again.

The pain continued behind her left eye, now feeling as if someone were digging their index finger into her eye socket, trying to hook their finger behind the back of her eye and pluck it out. For a moment, Catina thought that her eye *would* pop out. It didn't, thankfully.

Her head ached, ached more than any other time she had been sick. She could not recall when her head had hurt so much, even after when she had slipped in the barn back home and banged her head against the floorboards. Nothing she had ever known compared to this.

"Swemitsa," she managed to say. *Help*. But no help came. She was alone.

Wait, not alone. Something was shuffling behind and off to the side of her. She opened her eyes and saw Mr. Nibbetts roll over in his sleep. Where were the others?

Her grandfather? Peter? Aiyesha? No, wait. Aiyesha was on the other side of the fire, sitting with her legs crossed, staring blankly at the flames.

Catina wasn't sure if she had said "swemitsa" at all. Aiyesha surely would have heard her if she had.

"Swemitsa," she said, trying to say it as loud as she could. The pounding in her head, the pulsing behind her eye, drowned out most of her voice. "Swemitsa. Swemitsa. Swemitsa."

Aiyesha's eyes wandered over to her. Catina felt a tear run down her cheek. The finger that felt to be trying to pull her eye out grew stronger in its efforts.

The pain.

The pulse. The bright flame of the fire and the droning in her head. Catina opened her left eye for the last time . . . and it saw no more.

Peter and Alan were making their way back to the camp when they heard: "Alan! Peter, come quickly!" It was Aiyesha.

Giving Alan's arm a tug, Peter and the blind man hurried their pace, Alan moving as quick as he was able without stumbling and falling down.

"What is it? What has happened?" asked Alan the moment Peter let him know they were back at camp.

Catina was crying.

Aiyesha sat on the ground, cradling Catina, rocking her back and forth.

"What's going on?" asked Peter. "Is she all right?"

It was right then that Mr. Nibbetts rolled over in his sleep. When he spoke his voice was thin and weak. He was obviously ill. "Pleeaase be quiet . . . mee sleeping . . . mee dying . . . " And he went back to sleep. Come morning, he probably wouldn't remember ever waking up.

"Aiyesha?" said Alan.

"I was sitting there," she said, "on the other side of the fire, when Catina started to say something, I can't remember what. I couldn't hear her. Swem-something. Swem-swemi-swemi—I can't remember."

Alan walked slowly in the direction of Aiyesha's voice, his hands reaching out. She touched them when he was near enough. He came close to her and sat down and she handed his granddaughter to him. The way Alan's gaze set on Catina, it was as if he were looking right *at* her, instead of just past her like he always did because he couldn't see her. For a moment, Peter swore Alan could see.

Catina's crying began to ease and she cradled her left eye with her hand.

"Shhh," soothed Alan. And then, when he spoke, he spoke in Grescalla what sounded like more words of comfort and concern.

Aiyesha moved from them and came over to Peter. He watched as Catina clutched Alan's sleeve with her right hand, her hand opening and closing around the black fabric of his shirt in agony. The way those two were near each other, the way Alan leaned his head down to her and the way she snuggled up against him—Peter could sense their bond. There was an air of unity around the bonfire that night.

"Is she all right?" asked Peter again, softly.

"I don't know," said Aiyesha. "I was sitting there and she began to cry inconsolably. I don't know what's wrong. She fell asleep just after you and Alan left. When she woke up, she was crying."

Though Peter could not understand Alan and Catina's words to one another, he stayed and listened to them talk.

He wished he could understand.

Catina's voice was barley a whisper. The Rolling-tongue came slowly from her lips.

"I cannot see," she said.

"What do you mean?" asked Alan.

"My eye, this one" —she removed her left hand and pointed to her left eye with her index finger— "I cannot see out of this one. All I see is black. It hurts. It hurts so much."

"I do not know which one you mean. I cannot see it."

"My left one. It hurts so much. It hurts real bad."

"Did this just happen?" Alan leaned in closer for her response.

"It has hurt for awhile. I feel so icky. So sick. My head is so sore it feels like I banged it, but worse." She covered her eye again.

"Keep it closed," he said. "I will need someone to check it for me."

"Why can I not see? Why does it hurt?"

Alan was silent for a long time. When he spoke, his voice rang with defeat. "I do not know. Just try to rest."

"It is too hard to sleep. My head hurts too much. Make it go away. Make it go away. I do not want to be icky anymore. No more. No more. Please no more." Tears rolled down her cheeks.

"I wish I could take the pain away. I really do. But I cannot." He rocked her in his arms. "But I cannot." Then, "Peter?"

Peter came over to him and bent down so his ear was level with Alan's chin.

"Bring me a blanket and something for her head. Put some water on a rag or any soft material so I can cool her forehead." Alan wiped a thin film of sweat off Catina's brow.

"Sure," said Peter. He retrieved a cloth from one of the two bundles a few paces away and poured some water from a canteen onto the cloth. He brought them back to Alan.

"Thank you," said Alan and laid the damp cloth on Catina's forehead.

"Mali kwon nali," she said.

"Dana kwon nali," replied Alan.

All through the night, Alan never left her side. Peter forced himself to stay awake so he could be ready if Alan needed anything to properly tend to his granddaughter. Every so often, Catina would manage to sleep. But more often, she was awake, her voice weak, her body twitching from the pain. She and Alan would speak and Peter would be left wondering what they were saying. Whatever it was, it didn't appear to be good. He hoped Catina would be better by morning. She didn't deserve to feel this way.

Aiyesha slept intermittently and when she awoke, she came by Peter for an update on Catina. Also for an update on Mr. Nibbetts. "He's just as important as she is," she told him.

The dog, Belina, awoke now and then and had a walk around the bonfire before stretching and finding a new place to curl up and return to sleep. But before she closed her eyes, she would glance in Catina's direction, concern in her gaze, as if she understood something was wrong with her friend.

While Catina slept, Alan relayed to Peter what she told him and how, for the first time since his wife died, he felt helpless, not knowing what to do to aid someone in need.

"We must get home as soon as we can," urged Alan. "This sickness or whatever it is has not gone away. It is back and this time, I fear, more stronger than before. Let us hope that the rest of us will not suffer. But if I could take her pain" —he bowed his head— "O, how I would. I would give anything to take this from her. Anything."

"I know," said Peter. "I know you would."

The night was long and morning seemed like it would never come. But, just after four hours into the new day, the sun appeared, its bright smile peeking over the horizon in a glare of sharp yellow. The bonfire was just smoldering ash, now. Peter was tired and, he could tell, so was Alan. The poor man sat with his head bowed, his granddaughter in his lap. She had finally fallen asleep again about fifteen minutes ago. Alan said he'd remain sitting with her because he did not want to wake her.

Mr. Nibbetts awoke. His sitting up roused Peter.

"Good morning," said Peter to the Flistablare. "How are you feeling?"

Mr. Nibbetts wiped his eyes with his palms. "Me tired, but me better. Still woozy. But better."

"I think that's the most positive thing I've ever heard you say," said Peter. The Flistablare looked at him as if he didn't know what Peter meant. "I'm just saying that it's good to hear you're feeling better."

A grimace crinkled the furry creature's face. "But me still ill." Mr. Nibbetts looked like a child who had just broken its toy.

Peter glanced back at the smoldering ashes of the bonfire.

"Some things never change," he said to himself.

Aiyesha awoke and came over to Alan and helped him with Catina, moving her so she could take the child in her lap. "You need to sleep," she told him.

Alan pinched the bridge of his nose with thumb and forefinger. "Yes, I do." And so he did.

The day had been spent there, out on the field, Catina not wanting to move from that place, not wanting to travel. She was blind in her left eye. Something bad was bound to happen to it, she knew . . . but not this. Not blindness. She had never considered that. Her eye had been sore, swollen for awhile, then fine, then sore again. Now she couldn't see out of it. And even when the swelling had abated some, she still wasn't able to see. Not fully, only a small amount through squinted lids, the image blurred by the outline of skin and tears. But she had seen through it, she remembered. Seen through it clearly. She had seen through it when they had met Rano on that day so long ago. She had never seen so clearly in her entire life, not even when both eyes worked together to produce a clear, single image. There had been something more to her sight that day. Something far more. She had been able to see *through* Rano's cloak, to the pouch of Gero and the strap that held it in place across his body. She had seen everything that day.

Now, sitting silent beside Alan in front of the bonfire, the dark of evening setting on, the others of their company giving her and her grandfather distance, she would give anything to see how she had the day they met Rano. She would even give anything just to see through squinted lids, through the blur of skin and tears. Just to see again.

Just to see.

She put a hand to her left eye, covering it, picturing in her mind that, when she drew her hand away, she would be able to see again. Of course, that wasn't the case. When she removed her hand blackness was still before her vision, her sight a split between the bright orange and yellow dancing flames on the right, and the utter darkness on the left. Thankfully, her headache had eased enough so she was able to sit here, upright, without feeling the pain draw her head back down to her blanket.

Alan's smooth voice and well-articulated Grescallon tongue was pleasing to her ears. She no longer heard the humming that echoed inside her head throughout most of the day.

"It really is not so bad," he said in the Rolling-tongue. "It takes getting used to. And it takes time."

"How much time?" she asked.

He sighed. "That all depends on you and how much you want to get used to not being able to see. How much you will allow your other senses to take over." He paused. "It took me a long while to get used to it. Weeks passed before I fully accepted my circumstance. I did not leave home, I was so afraid. It took a good while for me to trust myself to move without bumping into things or tripping over my own feet. But you, Catina, are fortunate."

"I am?"

"Yes, you are. You have only lost sight in *one* eye. Not both. Your right eye will serve you well and, in time, I am sure, provide you with enough sight so that it will be as if your left eye was not blind at all."

She drew her knees up to her chest and hugged them. "I do not like not knowing what is going on to the left side of me." She motioned to her left, forgetting Alan couldn't see her gesture. "I feel like something—anything—will creep up on me and tackle me down. It is like being in the dark but there is no lamp to light."

"I suppose it is a lot like that, being in the dark. But you still have one lamp lit. That is good. That is the side of things you must look upon. Not all is lost."

"But it feels like it is. Lost. I am not all me anymore."

"That is not true. You are every bit as Catina Nabari as you were yesterday." It sounded as if he was going to say more but no words came.

Catina considered Alan's words for a time. He was right. She was every bit herself as she was the day before. Every bit. But she was also different, she knew. There was no other way to look at it. She could no longer see out of her left eye. Of course she was different. Yet . . .

"I do not understand why my eye stopped working," she said, furrowing her brow. She raised her palm and covered her eye. When she removed it, she was still blind on that one side. "I have not been able to see out of it for awhile, ever since I left home." She thought of the farm, her parents, how they died. Her eyes watered. And it was a relief to know that, despite not being able to see out of one of her eyes, both eyes still worked in producing tears. "But I saw out of it for awhile. Just a little even though it was all puffy and sore. Then I saw out of it for real, not just a little bit. A lot. Like normal. But more . . . "

"When?"

"When we met that man with the black cape and the brown robe." How could Alan not remember? He shifted in his seat beside her. "For a moment I saw fine even though my eye was sore and puffy. But then I saw through him, into his clothes and saw a pouch with black stuff in it."

"Catina," said Alan. His tone was almost condescending. "You know that is impossible. You could not have seen through his clothing."

"But I did!" She stood up, arms straight at her sides. "I saw something. I know I did. Everything blurred and changed and his clothes disappeared away and I saw a pouch with black stuff in it. Gero, he had. Papa used to use that stuff. I know what it looks like."

Alan didn't look her way. "I do not want you making up tall tales. I know that what just happened is upsetting but you cannot use it as an excuse to make up stories."

"But I was not blind when I saw what the man had. I was not! Now I am blind but I was not before. I know I saw it. Really, I did!" Tears welled up in her eyes. She put her hands to her face.

"Catina." Alan reached out to touch her.

When his hand grazed her arm, she turned away. "No!" She started sobbing. "Why do you not believe me?"

When he didn't answer, Catina lowered her hands and walked away. Her left foot tripped over a rock and she fell. She curled herself up into a ball on the ground and wept.

Alan found his way over to her and they cried together. Somehow, they would figure this out.

CHAPTER XLV
The Qinorans Cry

Everything that Thalok knew about awareness—about life, knowing the Qinorans were always there in the back of his mind—suddenly ceased. He didn't know how long ago he had fallen over. A day? Two days? A week? It was all the same. However long, it had been a long time. Jakarland had vanished long ago and now he lay on the slope of a mountain, faced-down, his chin between the crevice of two rocks. Another large rock was by his foot and his right hand lay atop another. He didn't know what time it was, only that it was later in the day, perhaps early evening.

Something had happened to the Qinorans. What—he didn't know. He only knew that it was bad, terrible—something that should not have occurred. When did this happen? A day ago? A week? It was too hard to tell. Trying to reach out to a Qinoran while on the Island of the Dead was one thing, but to pinpoint there place in Time was difficult, if not impossible, especially out here in the World. How long ago had his kin suffered? How long since their combined cries pierced through his heart, into his soul—his Being—into Jakarland, pulling him out so that he was in the World again.

His eyes closed, he reached out to his kin, to the Qinorans, waiting on some sign that they were okay.

They were *alive.*

He needed to know. Reaching, searching, waiting on them to reply. Waiting for anything. Waiting for a sign that they were still alive, if "alive" on the Island was a possible thing. On the Island of the Dead, it was more an existence of *being there,* nothing else.

Thalok reached and reached far, himself forgotten, his surroundings vanishing around him, no rocks, no towering mountainside. No Peter. No Aiyesha. No Alan, Catina, or Mr. Nibbetts. Nobody.

Nobody but the Qinorans.

His consciousness retreated inward, finding a calm, then surged forth, reaching for the Island. In his mind's eye he could see the silhouetted memory—glimpses—of Aeons past on the Island, imprints of Time spent there, in a sea of eyes where there was no Time, only *being*, existing, nothing more. Shadows of Qinorans, their pale gray faces, their lean and muscular naked bodies wearing purple cloaks, walking in and out of view, never fully coming into focus, but Thalok knowing all the while they were the Qinorans and not the other fell creatures that lived on the Island.

Another cry pierced the gloom of his Reaching, screaming out, crying out in terror as the life was drained from the Qinorans who called.

Something terrible was happening on the Island. Something terrible *had* happened. Something terrible *will* happen.

Something . . . . A voice. A whisper calling out, pleading for help, begging for Thalok to return, begging for not just him but anyone who would come and provide aide.

The tone was hushed, as if the Qinoran speaking was afraid to be overheard by someone or something. "He comes . . . no warning . . . . The sky splits and the fog divides then comes together in a tornado . . . comes towards us . . . . No one can stand against Him . . . no one can stand ground . . . one by one He is killing us . . . destroying us . . . there is no hope . . . " The words slurred and became incomprehensible. Just murmurs, droning sounds, low and deep and dark. Then came clear: "Anyone! Help us! He comes as if we've done Him the greatest wrong. No explanation. Only destruction. Qinorans no more. No more. No more."

Thalok shuddered under the power of the words and the urgency behind them. He knew whom this Qinoran was talking about . . . but he wouldn't believe it.

The Void-man. The Void-man was doing something terrible on the Island of the Dead.

"The sky splits open above my head . . . dark waves of a purple storm . . . the Sea of Eyes bubble . . . some pop and splash in a slop of goo . . . the clouds are joining . . . only a matter of time . . . they clash . . . tornadoes form . . . whirling, whipping . . . no way out . . . it's coming for me . . . it's coming for me . . . it's coming . . . it's . . . " And the voice spoke no more.

Thalok shook again, both in anger and in pity.

Pity.

He never thought he would feel pity for another. Never had to. And never had a Qinoran died unnaturally. Never had the Being been sucked from them and then been lost in a sea of madness and purple mist. What had they done that upset the Void-man so?

"What have you done?" spoke Thalok into the darkness between the two rocks. "What have you done?" *There must be something.*

A gust of wind blew across the mountainside, the rush of wind twisting his cloak and blowing it over his leg. He kicked his foot against the ground. Should he go back to the Island? Should he find the Void-man and seek out answers? But, this event may not have happened now, while he was here, out here in the World. The absence of

Time on the Island made knowing that near impossible. The Qinorans' cries could have come from sometime in the Future, perhaps echoing back on the chords of Time, cries so powerful that they could not be contained in their Time Period and so came back as a warning or desperate plea.

But . . . this had never happened before. Not once had Time gotten mixed up and twisted on the Island. There simply was no Time, just the passing of moments without the feeling of *passing*. Just existing, just being.

"It could be wrong. It could be a mistake," he told himself. But was it a mistake? There was no way to find out. No way but to go back to the Island without—

Find him! It was the Void-man. *Find him and kill him! Now!*

Peter. He was talking about Peter.

"But my kith? What happened to them?" asked Thalok. His face was still over he arms, looking into the dark between the crevice of the two rocks. There was another gust of wind across the mountainside. His cloak flapped. He didn't notice. "What happ—"

Kill him! Finish this! He has already discovered a portion of his power. Go and end this. Now!

The desire to carry out the task ran strongly through him. Loyalty to the Void-man was something not easy to go back on.

"My kin . . . "

Now!

"But . . . what about . . . "

I said, 'Now'!

Using his palms, Thalok pressed himself away from the rock. He had been on the mountainside a long time. At least, he thought it was a long time. He had been so lost in the Reaching that he didn't know how much time had passed. A day? More? Still impossible to tell. On his knees, he glanced up. The sky was a mix of purple and gray cloud, appearing so much like the sky on the Island of the Dead. It was early evening on a day he did not know.

Now!

Thalok stood, his cloak collapsing at his sides, covering him completely. He drew his hood over his head.

He began to Reach.

Peter and his company were close. So close. At least, Thalok thought they were. Reaching out to his fellow Qinorans had drained him more than he cared to admit and his senses were not as sharp. He still had his instinct to go on though.

Mind torn between learning of what had happened to his kin and carrying out the Void-man's wishes, Thalok fled down the mountainside in search of his prey.

They were close. No longer far away. He would be with them soon.

CHAPTER XLVI
Dealing with Death

It was all surfacing, now. Vivid memory. For the last three days Catina had been thinking heavily on the Battle on the Hill. As much as she tried to chase the memories away, they haunted her, rang in her head. So much violence. Even from the distance she had been from the battle, sitting between the horses of two men, she could still see her friends fight. Still see the blows exchanged and the flesh torn open. Still see Aiyesha tear into those women with the purple uniforms. At least until she had been blindfolded by those two big men. That was what triggered it, now that she thought about it. The Battle on the Hill. That's what triggered the memory, the vivid recollection of what happened on the road to Garathen so long ago.

Catina remembered the man, the one who had attacked her. She didn't know why he did. But there was something in his gaze that was dangerous. Something foreboding yet almost . . . lustful? Was that the right word? Maybe. Many have looked upon her that way. All who she had encountered since she set on her journey on the ninth day of Febwary. The only people who hadn't looked at her with that hidden glint in their eyes was Alan, Mr. Nibbetts, and the dog, Belina. Peter, as well. Even her parents had looked at her in that strange way. But that was only a day or two before she left for Garathen. Catina didn't know why. At her age, only six years old, she did not understand what lust was. But she was still able to recognize it, just not to the extent of the full meaning of the word. Why did people look at her like they wanted her, as if to own her? What was it about her they found so . . . wanting?

The man had looked at her that way. Maybe that was why he had offered her a ride. Maybe that was why things turned out like they did. Maybe. She wished she could understand his actions. She wished she could understand hers.

She killed him.

Catina could see him, as if it were happening all over again.

He was big, his belly broad and large and, when he sat, it bunched up under him like a stuffed sack around his middle. His jovial laugh was what she liked best though. His kind words and offer to help her and allow her a ride on his wagon were also welcomed and made her feel warm inside. Such a nice man.

He was leaning over her, a blanket hung halfway over the edge of the seat at the top of the wagon. Hot breath, a terrible smell, his eyes lost in her. She screeched and jumped off the wagon and ran down the road. Footsteps clamored behind her as he chased after her. The run—this time, in her mind's eye—seemed shorter than it had in reality and, within an instant, he was on top of her, wrestling her to the ground. She screamed and he was on top of her again, straddling her. She couldn't move. A meaty hand covered her mouth.

"Shh, I do not want to hurt you," he said in the Rolling-tongue. "I just want you to know how special you are. Please do not fight me. You have to trust me." His words seemed as if they were coming from far away. She managed to turn her head hard to one side and removed her mouth from under his hand.

"Rana Ko!" she shouted. Wriggling and squirming beneath his weight, she saw the bright glimmer of steel, the blade of a knife, rocking in its sheath.

A knife.

Even now, in this recollection, she still felt the debate if she should grab it or not. Still was unsure what she would do once it was in her hands. But she knew what she had to do.

Had to.

It was either that or be victim to whatever he had planned for her. Either try and escape or . . . she shuddered at the thought of what else. The oak handle of the blade spoke to her, pleaded with her to grasp it and draw the blade from its sheath.

Catina obeyed.

The man didn't seem to notice what she had done. Probably, he didn't expect it. Knife in hand, she plunged the blade into his side. Immediately, warm, dark blood oozed onto her thumb and forefinger, beneath the handle. He fell backward and sat with his legs splayed out in front of him.

The image that Catina knew so well but tried so desperately to bury in her mind occurred. The man, knife protruding out of his left side, reached out to her, desperate, pathetic, his eyes questioning, *What have you done?*

Even in this memory, she felt the warmth of tears swelling in her eyes as she looked at him. Then she ran away and never looked back . . . until today, in her mind and in her heart.

Alan sighed after she relayed him the tale.

"I understand, now," he said after a time. Catina liked the way he spoke Grescalla. His way of the Rolling-tongue seemed more trained, more pure than her own.

"You do?"

"Yes, I do." When he looked at her, his white eyes seemed to disappear for a moment and they were blue like they once were. Catina knew this was only her imagination playing tricks on her, but still . . . his gaze made her feel safe. Finally, safe.

"I am so, so sorry, Catina. This never should have happened to you. So many things. So many terrible things. You do not deserve any of them." He leaned in closer and his eyes were white again. "Do you understand? You do not and did not deserve any of this."

"I thought maybe the Master might be mad at me. Maybe that was why He let me do that bad thing. Maybe that was why He took Mama and Papa away from me." Tears swelled in her eyes. She wiped them away. She wished her left eye would work, if just this once. To see her grandfather with both eyes again—if only.

Putting his arm around her, Alan slid in closer. "It was not the Master. Nothing evil comes from Him. As I have told another of our friends, these are strange days. Things are happening that we cannot explain."

She rested her head against his breast. "Like when I saw through the robe of that man?"

Alan nodded. "Yes. And I know you saw through it. At least, I would like to believe you did." He looked off to somewhere past the fire. "This man that . . . died—you did what you had to do. Anyone here would have done the same. He was trying to hurt you and wanted to do something terrible."

"What was he trying to do?"

"We will discuss that another time."

Catina sat up from underneath his arm. "No. I want to know now!" No more covering things up. No more half-truths.

Heaving a sigh, Alan leaned closer to her so that the others, who were sleeping around the fire, would not hear his words should they awake and begin to ask questions. He told her what she wanted to know.

Catina's eyes widened when he was finished. She was silent for a time then said, with finality, "Then, I am glad I killed him." And with concern, "I should be, should I not?"

"Now that is a question I do not have an answer to. Who are we to take a life, even when ours is threatened? There are two sides to that argument, young one. One, say, from Peter, which would be very different than the one you would get from Aiyesha."

"I think it was her who made me remember. She killed-she killed people, too. She killed some girls."

"I know," he said. "And there are reasons for her actions, too. Hers are similar to what you had to do."

"I do not like seeing people die. And now . . . . It makes me think of Mama and Papa."

He turned toward her. Tears rolled down her cheeks. He put his arm around her again. "It makes me think of them, too."

"Really?"

"It does. Too much has happened on this journey. Too much. I pray to the Master that we never go through such things again. It is more than anyone can bear."

The surety in his voice brought her comfort. There was so much she needed to express but could not find the words. How could you tell someone that you killed another and then talk about it? How could your actions ever truly be justified? There will always be an argument, both with others and within yourself.

"Has anyone told you that, I am not sure, that . . . that I look different?" she asked.

"I do not know what you mean."

"Has anyone, like Peter, said anything to you about me. That somehow I look different than everyone else?"

"No," he said. "Other than, in some places, your colorful dress stands out against more drabber colors. No. He has not told me anything. What makes you ask?"

"Everywhere I go, people look at me strange. It is like they cannot stop looking at me. The man was the same way. He looked at me but I do not think it was him looking at me."

"Then who was it?"

"I do not know. Someone else. Not him."

The words hung in the air like the knowledge it was about to rain. Alan didn't have an answer for her.

They talked for an hour, Catina repeating the story of how she killed the man, dwelling on certain parts more than others. She had a lot inside and much more needed to be released. In the end, she realized, she would never get entirely past it. At least, not yet. Who could? Unless you were trained to murder in cold blood, the death of another would always weigh upon you. It always did, even if someone died of a cause that was not your fault. Death by old age. Death by illness. Those bothered you and made you consider your own mortality. To kill someone with your own hands . . . it made you wonder if you would die the same way. Catina didn't like the feeling of that.

An hour later, she finally yawned, the weight of the discussion having drained her.

"Just remember," said Alan, "I will always love you, no matter what you do."

"No matter what?"

"No matter what. You are my *Shinali* and I am your *Shinawa*. We will always be together. We will return to Garathen where I will take care of you. All will be right in the end. You will see."

"I hope so," she said. "I hope so."

"It will, my dear. It will."

They retired to bed shortly after. Catina tossed and turned the whole night. Alan woke her up once to see what was the matter.

"I had a bad dream," she said. "About the man and he was lying on the side of the road. I was walking toward him and, when I walked up to his feet, he sat up. He sat up! And he looked at me. His eyes were the same when he was on top of me, that look of . . . wanting. I was scared. He gave me the knife I used to . . . to . . . to stab him with. Gave it back because he said he did not want it. I did not want it, either, so I threw it away and it fell in the dirt. The man lay back down but kept his eyes open and watched me."

Alan held her and rocked her back to sleep. She dreamed that same dream a second time, but this time didn't wake up from it. She spent the night trapped in her dream, looking on as the man watched her. The only good part was, she knew he was dead.

Waking for Alan always came in two stages. The first was the *awareness* of waking, watching whatever he was dreaming fade away into total darkness, and the opening of his eyes. The second was the *acknowledgment* that he was awake. The acknowledgment of the sounds around him, the knowing of the pillow beneath his head, the smells on the air—all of these too vivid and too real to be a dream. Each morning he awoke—and even after all this time—he yearned for an image, a picture, something before his eyes so that he knew he was awake and not lost to pitch black sleep. Over time he had gotten used to waking to total darkness and learned to tell the difference between being asleep and being awake.

When he awoke shortly after dawn, he waited, and then was aware he was awake. Birds chirped high and over to the left of him, their morning calls a pleasant thing to wake to. Mr. Nibbetts was snoring, with effort, as if he were *trying* to sleep instead of just merely sleeping. The steady breathing of the two girls, Catina and Aiyesha, was also heard. He wondered how Catina's dreams were and what she was seeing. He prayed she would be all right and could carry on through the day. With his left hand he felt the spot next to him and found her small body. He rested his hand on her shoulder, the warmth of her skin coming through the fabric of her colored dress, letting him know she was still alive. Alan didn't know why he thought she might be dead and was ashamed of himself for even considering it. But with all the death since setting out from Garathen, the idea of either he or his companions falling on the road home always lingered in his mind, either falling victim to the Sickness or to the blade of a sword.

He knew that Peter wasn't with them this morning. Somehow he knew.

But last night, his own sleep had been a fitful one. Even now, lying on a rolled-out blanket next to the cooled embers of the bonfire, he was still tired. Damp clothing clung to his skin and as though acknowledging this, a chill swept over him, his skin turning to gooseflesh. He wiped his forehead with the sleeve of his shirt. He wished he had set up his tent instead. It would have been much warmer.

"Fever," he muttered. *It has come back and I know I am not the first to feel the Sickness return. Mr. Nibbetts has been ill since last night and Catina was sick the night previous and last night, too. Being around each other—all of us—might mean it is contagious.*

He sat up and brought his knees part way to his chest and rested his forearms upon them. Gathering the images of what he thought their camp site looked like—he on a blanket, Catina beside him, the bonfire in the middle, a blank sleeping spot for

Peter to his right, Aiyesha one spot down and then Mr. Nibbetts one spot further still—he stood for a time, letting his body fully awake. Once satisfied he was up and ready, he turned one hundred-eighty degrees and left the ring of friends around the fire.

Wandering away from the camp, he was mindful of his steps and, with his foot, felt along the ground for its slope and slowly descended down the hill. He was determined to make it without his walking stick. Perhaps it was his own way of combating all the hindrances on their journey by believing he would make do without it.

The descent down was slow but, once used to the gradual slope of the hill, each step became easier. He made it to the bottom without any trouble.

"That's good," he heard Peter say.

"Good morning," said Alan.

"Good morning. How'd you sleep, all right?"

He thought of the fever. "I have had better nights, if that is what you are asking. I slept all right. Could have been better, but all right. And you?"

He heard the grass crunch beneath Peter's feet as Peter neared him. "It was not bad. Had a headache for part of it and, while I lay there, it felt as though my arms and legs were pinned to the ground, like someone was holding them there." Peter took a breath. "We've all got something, Alan. Something that we can no longer ignore."

"I have never ignored it." He reached out to test how far away Peter was. Peter grabbed his hand.

"I'm here," he said.

There was silence between the two men. Peter spoke first. "What's happening to us? It seems like there's too much going on, like the World has thrown everything it has at us. How much have we encountered while we've been away? What we've seen isn't normal. No one leaves their home and encounters problem after problem after problem. And if they do, they certainly aren't potentially fatal ones."

"No, they are not," replied Alan. "The truth of it is, I do not know what is happening to us. I just know to trust that all will work out in the end."

"But how do you know that? That it will work out in the end?"

"I do not know, but I trust that it will. It is a fine line but a very important one in difference." He crossed his arms behind his back. "Catina told me something last night that I was not prepared to hear. I, being her *Shinawa*, had to be strong and, seemingly, wise, trying to provide her with some answers. But our talk last night was only the first of many. One discussion will not fully cure the wound she has endured."

"What did she say?"

"She killed a man, Peter," said Alan immediately. "She killed a man in order to protect herself." It was obvious by Peter's silence that he was taken aback by this. "It is okay. She is fine and is unharmed. She is also not dangerous. But the wound from killing someone runs deep."

Peter breathed in deeply then exhaled audibly. "But how do you know? You've never killed anyone."

"No, I have not. But I have met men who have. Some, yes, do it without remorse or regret. But others . . . well, they told me that they would rather be the man in the ground than the one on top. No one has the right to take a life. No one."

"But Catina did."

"And so is the dilemma. Was she justified in her action? Yes, some would say. No, would say others. I am afraid there is no easy answer to that question. At least, none that I could give. Perhaps Aiyesha would know, perhaps not. Her situation is much more different. She is different. I do not even wish to think how her mind works and what manipulation has been done to it."

"I still can't believe Catina killed someone," said Peter. "Yet, I'm also not surprised. Not at her for doing it, but because of all that has happened, even news like that is beginning to become common place. The extra-ordinary has become ordinary, you know?"

"I know what you mean."

The two men stood, each taking in a face full of the morning sunlight. Its warmth permeated Alan and he envisioned the chills from his sweat-dampened clothing being chased from his body.

"You didn't dream of . . . Thalok . . . last night, did you?" asked Peter.

"No," said Alan. "Not last night. There was only that one time, and I am thankful for that. Did you?"

"No, but I fear he is drawing near. I can hear him, inside me. Not a voice but a . . . presence. He's out there and . . . "

Alan felt his muscles tighten. "And?"

"And I'm afraid. I'm afraid he'll kill us all."

Peter's Journal: Drawing Near

Mae 13, the Year 134, the Fifth Aeon

He's getting closer. Thalok is coming. I don't know how I know this. Perhaps it is simply paranoia. Perhaps it is because I'm succumbing to the fear, the idea, that this man, this thing that has haunted each of us, will come for us soon. He is real. Yaman said so.

There's a fell presence on the air. The wind blows thick and warm, not thin and cool as a breeze should. And there's a smell, one I can't name and can't place but only try to explain. It is the smell that was present when we entered Grek, the smell of decaying bodies. It is the smell of sweat after a day's work of sitting outside under the hot sun, painting the passers-by. It is the smell of a hard sleep, the kind where after you wake up you feel almost burdened and there's an awful taste in your mouth. What is strange about all of this is that this sensing of an evil presence, my sensing of Thalok, seems more internal *than* external. *None of the others have commented on the laughter in the air, the almost palpable fear that wraps its horrid fingers around us.*

Perhaps they are afraid.

I know I am.

I wonder when the Man in the Gray Cloak will come. Tomorrow, tomorrow night, the day after that, or the day after that still? Not next week, though. It will be much sooner than that.

Thalok, if that is even his or its name, is everywhere. I can see him out of the corner of my eye, see him before I go to sleep. He's here.

He is everywhere.

The sun is slow in rising this morning. I'm up early because I cannot sleep. Not with the way I'm feeling, at any rate. The Sickness is back. It's setting on and, I fear, will be much worse this time round than the last. Mr. Nibbetts is already under its hold. He complains of a headache and extreme fatigue. Catina was sick last night and has gone blind in her left eye. She's seems to be doing better, now. I glanced over at Alan when I awoke last night. Sweat glistened off his face in the remaining light of our fire. A fever has come upon him. Aiyesha, well, she's something altogether different. She hasn't shown any signs of illness as yet (I hope she never gets sick), but with her, who is to know if she is truly all right? She has been trained to not show feeling or discomfort of any kind. She could be as sick as the rest of us and we would never know it.

Back to Thalok. He's here, not far from us, waiting to strike. He must have passed through the Calahudron Woods, knowing that we would venture there. What is his game? Why the warnings? Why not just come out and kill us? That is a secret, I fear, that we'll never know. Something is pushing him toward us.

I just wish I knew his purpose. I'd give anything to understand.

Thalok draws near.

CHAPTER XLVII
Of a Soldier and her General

Ever since the Battle on the Hill, General Gasahd had remained in Aiyesha's thoughts. He would not go down without a fight and the Battle on the Hill was not nearly enough of a blood bath to appease his desire to right a wrong. Why he had run off once it was over, she did not know. It was not his style, yet perhaps Gasahd really *was* afraid of her? Her lips curled up at the thought.

They were on the road to Hillmalen, now, Aiyesha and the others. Alan said—if their pace remained constant—they would make it there by the end of tomorrow. Aiyesha looked forward to being around people again, like in Darim. All those years of isolation on the Coast of Seryn was finally taking its toll on her.

As much as she tried to ride comfortably and pretend everything was okay, everything was not okay. Something tugged at the pit of her stomach and she knew it wasn't the sickness that was going around. She felt fine. Nor was it her concern for the safety of the others. It was something else. Unfinished business. There was still Gasahd. He wouldn't give up on her, she knew. He never had. As much as he hated her for leaving the Coast of Seryn, she knew she had won a place in his heart, in a strange and almost perverted way. He loved her for what she had become, the warrior that was bred through twelve years of intensive training and suffering. She was what he had yearned to create. She was the perfect warrior. And Aiyesha knew this because he told her two weeks before she left the Coast. The sky was clouded over that day and it was raining heavily. But it was also warm and the air was humid.

Not far off from where she and the other women slept was a Training Square, a simple slab of dark gray clay, sun-dried and hard as stone, for ground. In one of its corners was a large wooden post with a canvas, sand-packed dummy in the shape of a person strung up against it, meant for practicing strikes and toughening the skin over the knuckles and insteps and balls of feet. There were three other devices as well, each in the remaining corners. There was an iron-dummy, a metal-man made of pipe, with working, locking joints so that it enabled him to be positioned into any fighting stance desired. His purpose was for practicing blocking techniques. In another corner was a system of iron plates on pulleys, with a frame of wood with two ropes running through it, running over the top of the device, through the pulleys and tied to the weights on the ground. Each rope had a noose on its end for easy grabbing. Taking a noose in each hand, you would pull on it and lift the iron plates off the ground. It was for practicing throwing techniques and strengthening your execution of any desired move. The last corner held a series of sandbags hanging from another arrangement of posts so that, standing in the middle of it, you were between the bags. Since it was such a small area, being in the middle of it helped you learn to move in a circle, around your opponent, when fighting. Each sandbag would be struck with any move that seemed most efficient, depending on where you stood, you not being allowed to move out from the center of the sandbags.

It was morning and, while it rained, Aiyesha had been practicing on the iron-dummy, focusing on her blocks. Over time she had gotten used to the drills and her forearms quickly numbed to striking the hard, rusting bars. Her skin, however, always turned red. The other girls were inside the mess tent, eating and visiting. It was lunchtime. Aiyesha had chosen to practice instead. She paid no mind to Gasahd when he approached her.

"Aren't you eating?" he asked.

Aiyesha countered an imaginary right hook with her left forearm against the dummy. "No."

"Are you sure? The food's hot and it's mighty wet out here."

Another imaginary strike. Another block. "It's also warm out here."

He came up close and watched her as she practiced, hands clasped behind his back. "Are you sure?"

She countered two strikes in half the time it took a normal Dembatstayr soldier to block just one. "Leave me alone."

Gasahd glanced up at the rain pouring down. His hair was matted to his forehead in wet curls. "Why do you drive yourself so hard?"

Aiyesha continued her drill, her pace never slowing as he spoke. If anything, her speed in her blocks increased. A part of her wanted to impress him. The vibrations from her forearms hitting the bars caused her words to sound as if someone were patting her back fast and hard while she spoke. "The Master has called me to this. I have a purpose."

Her words sounded false even to herself, as if she didn't believe them.

Gasahd took a step closer. "Uh-huh. Is there more?"

"I must bring peace and order to a fallen World where darkness is spread faster than light." She struck the bars more furiously, a grimace on her face. Her long black hair danced with each movement.

Beside her, now, next to the iron-dummy, Gasahd grabbed her by the wrist and moved to strike at her head. She countered him and the two fought for a time before Gasahd bested her by slipping his right foot in behind her left ankle, causing her to trip backwards and fall on her tailbone. Aiyesha shot up like a coiled spring, but Gasahd raised his hand, palm open, stopping her from coming closer.

"But what is the real reason? Why do you do this? Honestly," he said.

Her shoulders sagged and her eyes cast down to the splashes of water as the rain hit the Training Square. When she looked up, her green eyes were alive, as if Spring was in her gaze.

"Because. Because I need to," she said. "When I practice, when I move, I finally feel alive. I finally have purpose. There is nothing grander than that, to know why you're here. And I know why I'm here. I'm here to help. That's what this army's for, is it not? To help? To spread the Master's Will?"

Gasahd smiled. "I am fortunate to have found you. I tell the truth when I say you will do great things. You're perfect. And you have purpose. Never forget that. Never lose that. Ever."

She didn't answer but she promised herself that day to never lose her sense of purpose, her sense of why she was here.

She had meaning.

Ignoring the pellets of raining pounding against her, Aiyesha crossed the Training Square to the canvas dummy on the opposite end. She practiced all her punches, kicks and strikes until the rain dwindled and the sun came out. Gasahd supervised her all the while, driving her to train harder, to make herself even better than she already was. Gasahd seemed to have forgotten all about the other girls that morning, and they wouldn't have sought him out if he didn't retrieve them from the mess-tent.

A lot has changed since then, reflected Aiyesha, gazing at Day's flowing mane. *So much has changed. I now know how he felt about me. I wasn't merely a soldier to him. I don't know why I didn't see that before. Blind, perhaps? So driven to become physically perfect that I missed myself losing . . . myself?* Admitting that possibility made her jaw clench. *I have purpose. I'm not a soldier. But I am . . . I am . . . .* What was she? And then, in an instant that broke her heart, she realized she didn't know *who* she was. She was just a girl from Bel Candar, wanting to play in the Army, to play war. Time away from the Coast of Seryn, away from the lectures of Gasahd and the grueling training, began to change the way the World looked. It wasn't such a bad place after all. Aiyesha just wished she knew where she fit into it.

Day neighed and let out a snort. Peter walked alongside her.

"You said it," she said, patting Day's neck.

She glanced down to the dog and then up at Catina, then back to the dog again. *Those two share something,* thought Aiyesha. *They seem to understand each other in a way that the others do not. Perhaps it is because they are the only two here that do not understand the Common-tongue. They have their own way of communicating, that's for sure. Silent nods and secret gazes.*

I fear for the others. Peter is very pale and gray circles are forming beneath his eyes. Mr. Nibbetts is falling asleep in his saddle and Alan, well, he's awfully quiet, even for him. Catina. She can't see anymore out of . . . . Aiyesha dropped back a little to where Alan and Catina were and, when the little girl looked over at her, Aiyesha gave her a smile. Peter remained ahead of them.

Aiyesha ran a hand through Catina's blonde hair and then, motherly, kissed her own fingers and placed them on Catina's left eye, as if saying she would be okay and there was nothing to fear. Catina smiled ear to ear at this and, Aiyesha assumed, told Alan what she had just done.

"Thank you, Aiyesha," said Alan.

Aiyesha did the same to him and a puzzled look came over his face.

"Why did you do that?" he asked.

"Just because," she replied and then moved Day away from them and back to her place in line.

Peter looked on in interest. Mr. Nibbetts was dozing and didn't seem to notice. The dog padded along with her nose to the ground, as if discovering secrets in the earth.

Stomaching rumbling, Aiyesha looked longingly at the saddlebags on Alan's horse behind her. The remaining food from the supply purchased in Darim had run out yesterday morning. They hadn't eaten since and here, on the trail in the forest surrounding them, there was nothing to eat, just oak and birch and shrub brush. None of the bushes carried any berries, at least none that were eatable.

As if reading her thoughts, Mr. Nibbetts roused from his stupor. "If we don't find anything to eat soon, me is going to die of starvation!" And then he closed his eyes and went back to sleep.

Peter burst out laughing. "What was that?"

"He has been rambling now and again, waking then saying something, then falling back asleep," said Alan.

"From the Sickness?"

"Maybe." He reconsidered. "Most likely. He has got something. He probably was not even awake when he said that. Just murmurs—loud murmurs—in his sleep."

"Me am not sleeping," came Mr. Nibbetts. "Me is just resting me eyes."

"Why, did all your looking around tire them out?" asked Peter. He chuckled to himself and patted Mr. Nibbetts on the back.

Mr. Nibbetts didn't seem to notice, seemingly already back asleep.

Aiyesha's stomach rumbled again. Not only was she hungry, but she was antsy. After so many years of getting up at dawn and training until late in the night, her body was used to expending so much energy during the day. Now, all that energy was being pent up inside her, without outlet for release. When she had fought the men in Wesafeld or the soldiers in Darim, or on the Battle on the Hill, or with Yaman, it had felt so good to release all the energy inside her, driving it forth and into something else instead of within. She could hardly wait until they got to Garathen to train again, if only to expel her energy.

Peter walked beside her on the wide trail. "Do you think the army will come for you again?"

Amazing how he knows what I'm thinking, she thought. *Were my thoughts that obvious?*

"Perhaps," she said. "I know General Gasahd and I know he won't rest until he's brought me back."

Brow furrowed, Peter scratched his nose then put two fingers to his temple.

"Are you all right?" asked Aiyesha.

"Just a headache," he said. "My stomach is beginning to turn upside down again."

"Do you want to stop?"

He looked off into the trees passing by and Aiyesha knew that he wanted a break.

"No," he said. "I just want to go home." He took a deep breath, held it a moment, then exhaled slowly. "Why does this Gasahd guy want you so much?"

"I'm his most prized soldier. He wants me to train a new recruit of females since I performed best out of the women he trained. At least, that was the plan, last I heard and, of course, before I left."

"There must be more," said Peter. "He wouldn't have confronted us like he did on the Hill if that was the only reason. He could have gotten the second-best girl in your group to train the new recruits if that was the case."

"He also wanted me to train the men," she said almost immediately.

"Even so, he still could have gotten the second-best to do it."

She shook her head. "Not Gasahd. He wants the best and only the best. He said a war is coming, a war to end all wars."

"Kind of like the Battle of Then," mumbled Peter.

"What?"

"Nothing. Just thinking back to a tale I heard in Darim. Are you sure there isn't more as to why Gasahd wants you so bad?"

She cast her eyes away and a pang of hurt pierced her heart. "My leaving the Coast of Seryn was also an act of treason."

"Against who? The Army doesn't belong to any one country, as far as I know. Then again, I don't know much about such things. The Voidsmen just made sure everyone was in bed on time back home, to keep us safe from the Slummers."

"Slummers?"

"Evil Streetfolk. Essentially. Not human though."

She reached up and pulled on the tie in her hair, tightening it. She picked up her reins again. "No. It's not treason against any specific country. It's treason against the Master."

Peter's eyes widened. "The Master? How?"

"He speaks to Gasahd, apparently. The Voidsmen are there to pave the way for the Second Coming. The Second Coming is after the war, of course. If it was before, then there wouldn't be a war because we'd all be delivered to safety by the Master. But now, what I've come to realize along with my reasons for leaving the Coast, I don't think that what Gasahd says about the Second Coming is entirely true. His orders change often. It's 'Do this because the Master said so.' Then it's 'Do that because the Master wishes this instead.' We all followed Gasahd blindly. Being on the Coast of Seryn is hypnotic. When there, you are compelled to believe whatever is thrown at you. It's only when you separate yourself from all the talk and the hype of the coming war do you see the folly in the way they are going about it."

"I'm confused," said Peter.

"Me, too. That's also one of the reasons I left. I wanted to find out about the Master on my own, away from all the clutter of religious belief. I wanted to learn about life on my own and not within the confines of some Coast near a border of purple fog."

"That must have been amazing, seeing the border all the time."

"You got used to it."

"But a great wall of purple mist, just hovering there, no one getting in or out. Amazing, really."

Peter, you have no idea. "Perhaps." She glanced up ahead. The forest was breaking up. They were almost out.

"And Gasahd? Any other reason?"

She looked at him, both sternly and gently at the same time.

"Sorry," he said. "I'm just curious and I also don't want to get into another fight with him. I still can't explain what happened that day on the Hill and how we survived. How can five people overtake one hundred?"

"Never mind that. How did the *three* of us do it? Alan and Catina didn't fight. Not really. Not Catina, anyway."

"True. Then how did three people overcome it? I mean, I was able to fight off the men as if fighting off children."

"Seriously?"

His hands rose, palms up, and he looked at them as if they held precious stones. "I was—I was so strong. Somehow . . . I don't know. I can't explain it."

"Neither can I."

His blue eyes held an air of fear in them. "What's happening to me?"

"I don't know," she said.

"Well," he began, as if they hadn't just spoke of the miracle on the Hill, "if Gasahd comes for you again, I hope I'm able to leave alive. I hope I can do what I did again." Then, after a pause, "He won't come, will he?"

She put her tongue between her teeth then wet her lips before she spoke.

"I don't know," she said. "He loves me."

Gasahd and Zakmon rode side by side.

"How do you expect to find her?" asked Zakmon.

"The Master will provide," said Gasahd. "He always does."

"You realize, of course, that she could be anywhere by now."

The general kept his gaze straight ahead as he spoke. There was bitterness in his tone. "Yes, I do. But I won't rest until we bring her back to the Coast of Seryn. She must join us again."

"And if you never find her?"

"To accept that possibility is admitting defeat. I *will* find her, Frederik."

The men rode in silence for a time. The land was open and flat. There was nothing in sight, not even a tree or a shrub, just leagues of open yellow grass. Briefly, Gasahd considered they might be lost but soon chased those thoughts away. Part of his duty as general was to study the maps of the Fellamoor Continent, never mind the maps of the other continents he also studied. His mind was sharp and he easily committed things to memory, a gift that aided him in securing his post as general. He had battled with the best of them, but it was his intellect that got him the position. And a little influence on the decision-makers from the Master. To go from a no-name soldier to a general in a year…

They rode on for a time before stopping so Zakmon could relieve himself. As Zakmon returned to the horses, a Tharadon flew down from the sky and landed before them. It folded its enormous brown, feathered wings and waddled over to Gasahd. He got down off his horse and removed the letter from the Tharadon's black leather collar. He unrolled it and read it silently to himself. The Tharadon waited expectantly at his feet.

"Who's it from?" asked Zakmon.

"Lieutenant Allise," replied Gasahd. "He mustn't have heard of our encounter with Aiyesha. He suggests, here, to rally my men and bring them East. His scouts say they caught sight of her not far from the Calahudron Woods. The path they are currently traveling is leading them to Hillmalen. Lieutenant Allise thought I should know. Remind me to thank him when I see him next."

"Yes, Sir. So, then, we are going to Hillmalen?"

Gasahd rolled up the letter and stuffed it in his pocket. "Yes." He bent down and the Tharadon came even closer to him. He tapped the giant bird three times on the head, letting it know there wasn't a reply message. Like that day on the Coast, the Tharadon turned and spread its massive wings and took off into the sky.

Hillmalen. That's where we'll meet, thought Gasahd as he watched the Tharadon fly West, presumably toward the Coast of Seryn or to wherever Lieutenant Allise was right now.

Mounting his horse, Gasahd turned to his second in command. "Shall we be off, then?"

"Absolutely," said Zakmon as he mounted his own large stallion.

The two horses, trained for war and traveling at high speeds, tore off toward Hillmalen. Gasahd hoped to make it there before Aiyesha did. *If* she was going there.

He wanted to surprise her.

This . . . quest . . . to find Aiyesha was a harrowing one. Gasahd knew *why* he was doing it yet . . . he didn't know. There was just this pull in his heart, this desire to see her again and bring her back. Some, like Captain Zakmon, might call it obsession. There was a point, Gasahd didn't know when, when he lost all reason as to why he was doing this, why he drove himself to madness to bring her back. There was a strange duality to his thoughts. He was aware of his reasons: she being the finest warrior out of all the women, she being the best of the bunch and a tremendous asset to the Void's army. But Aiyesha had also made it very clear that she did not want to go back. If he caught her, if he somehow convinced her and/or captured her and took her back to the Coast, what could he expect of her? She certainly would not go along with him on anything he would suggest. She, evidently, had already made up her mind about that.

This last attempt to find her and bring her home suddenly seemed futile.

An hour had passed since receiving the message from the Tharadon. General Gasahd and Zakmon had remained silent for most of the journey.

His captain broke the silence. "You're awfully quiet, Sir. Is there anything I can do?"

Gasahd looked off longingly at the horizon. All he saw were open fields and, frankly, he was getting sick of them. They were so plain—like the Coast. "No. But thank you for asking. I'm just concerned about what we'll do once we reach Hillmalen. And, if she'll even show up."

"I understand." And the short conversation ended.

Captain Zakmon was a good man. This, Gasahd knew. Despite being the best soldier working under him, Zakmon was not all about the war. He was also a friend, the only one Gasahd could confide in. And even though Gasahd kept secrets about many a thing, Zakmon was always there by his side, ready to do what his commanding officer ordered, even if, at times, he didn't agree with it.

Aiyesha.

She was like Gasahd, too. Dedicated. Driven. Never settling for anything less than the best. He saw a part of himself in her and, he supposed, that was why he had devoted more of his time to training her than any of the others. As if she needed the extra time. Aiyesha always put in the extra hours when it came to her training, but he would encourage her and correct her form when she made a mistake and, even though some of his lecturing had been harsh, drove her to proving him wrong by showing him that she was capable of everything he said she wasn't. At times he felt like a strict parent toward her. Perhaps it was because he didn't have any children of his own. At least none that he was aware of. There had been a handmaiden here or there, all young women, of course, when on occasion he would come to the mainland for supplies for the Coast or to recruit new men in the cities and villages. There was that red-haired girl he had just gone to bed with. The Master help him if he could remember her name. If he had even asked it. But Aiyesha, well, she was just . . . better than them. More pure. More deserving of affection. Gasahd was ashamed he wasn't as loyal to her as he would like to be. It was hard to do so when there was no established relationship that would forbid any other woman.

Being out here, away from the Coast did, however, show Gasahd one thing: the World knew of the Voidsmen, the Dembatstayr. They were no longer a small presence, as they had been for over one hundred years. In the past ten years alone, their numbers had grown over tenfold, men joining them from all over, banding together in what was seen as a holy cause: preparing the way for the Master's Second Coming. Gasahd just hoped the Second Coming would happen in his lifetime so that he could see all his dedication and hard work come to full fruition.

Gasahd considered himself something of a holy man, one who conversed with the Master regularly. There were others like him, as well. Going from town to town he would overhear other men speaking quietly amongst themselves, some of them saying the Master had given them a revelation the day previous or in a dream the night before. Speaking to the Master, *knowing* that you were truly talking to Him was something that had little proof. It was a matter of knowing in your heart of hearts that it was Him you had spoken to. Just like being in love. You just knew. No ifs, ands, or buts. You just knew.

And Gasahd knew he spoke to the Master. He *knew* it. And he knew he loved Aiyesha. But as to what kind of love, that still eluded him. He didn't know if his feelings were more than platonic or not. Yes, she was beautiful and, yes, who she was made him wish he had never joined the Army and had instead settled down with a girl like her. But, he also thought, his feelings for her could simply be the byproduct of spending so much time with someone, like a close friend you've known for many years. In Gasahd's case with her, twelve.

So when he reached Hillmalen, and Aiyesha did show up, what then? He would try to talk her into coming back with him first, hoping the confrontation on the Hill suggested to her that, though she escaped, and if she didn't come back with him, he would return to the Coast of Seryn and retrieve two hundred men, even three hundred if necessary.

Her escape still eluded him. She was good, that much was already known. But to wipe out more men than he had ever seen her encounter? Kill eleven other women who were almost her equal in fighting skill? All as quickly as she had? There was no explanation for it. At least, not yet. Perhaps the Master would reveal an answer to him in time.

Right now, he focused on his goal and that kept him going, despite his bouts of not knowing why he was doing it.

Soon the land began to roll and the horses seemed to enjoy the small challenge of going up and down hills. Dark clouds built overhead and covered the sky like a gray cap. Soon it would rain.

Gasahd welcomed it.

CHAPTER XLVIII
The Sickness Returns

Forty or so miles outside of Hillmalen was a small lake about thirty feet across and twenty or so feet wide. It was evening and the company had ridden all day. They stopped there by the water because, well, there was no other place to go. The land around was flat and there weren't any trees in sight. There was just this lake, out here, in the middle of nowhere. Rain splashed heavily against the lake's surface, the drops fat and thick like globs of syrup.

For Peter, the coolness of the rain was welcome. He had fallen ill again sometime in the afternoon. It first built in his stomach, upside down and nauseous. Then it escalated into a full blown stomach ache, like having the flu but more nauseating. Hot flashes came over him frequently and, he thought, they also caused his head to ache, right on top in the middle. The heat from his ailing stayed all afternoon so when it began to rain about fifteen minutes ago, he welcomed it willingly. Even now as it poured on him, he still felt hot, as if sitting on a heap of coals, heating him through and through. And he wasn't the only one who was sick.

Alan had fallen ill, too. He complained frequently of a fever and, for awhile, removed his shirt and rode topless as they traveled. He had his long black shirt on now, though.

Mr. Nibbetts was still sleeping. About once an hour one of the others would wake him—despite his grumbling protests of being disturbed while he slept, and his foul language—just to make sure the Flistablare wouldn't sleep forever. Before, the furry creature would complain of always being hungry; now, he hadn't eaten a thing since their supply ran out.

No one was in the mood for food tonight. They were just thirsty and Aiyesha filled their canteens in the small lake and handed the canteens out to be shared amongst everyone. She seemed to be feeling all right.

Catina huddled by the dog as Peter tried as best he could to help set up camp. The blankets were brought out and the saddlebags removed from the horses. With the bags he made a small wall and, on either end of that wall, were two makeshift posts. One being Alan's sword, stabbed into the earth, the other being Alan's walking stick. The blankets were hung across from the walking stick to the sword and draped over the small wall of saddlebags, like a poorly made tent. It wasn't much but at least it would keep them out of the rain for a short time before the water soaked through the thick blankets. At their last stop, Alan discovered his tent had gotten a hole in it from being bundled next to the sword. Though the sword was in its sheath and the end of the sheath was dull, it still wore a small hole through the material over time, rubbing against it as Night rode. The small hole soon wore to a large one and, in a fit of anger, Alan insisted they burn it, as if he were having revenge on the tent. No one understood his reasoning but they let him have his way anyway. Aiyesha expressed her disapproval because the black smoke generated from the burning tent might alert any Voidsmen to their whereabouts.

The four Humans and one Flistablare went under the makeshift tent. The dog came in soon after getting a drink of her own from the lake.

Peter lay on his side, toward the back of the small encampment. Alan was at one end with Catina, and Mr. Nibbetts was curled up sleeping at the other. Aiyesha sat on the soggy ground next to Peter, the dog at her feet. Outside the tent, the horses whinnied at the rain but didn't seem to mind it too much. Day would often stamp her foot on the ground then Night would do the same, splashing up mud, as if proving his stamp was harder than hers.

The company sat shivering under the canopy, waiting for the rain to let up. But it kept on throughout the night. It drummed down, as if it had something personal against them. Peter found the beat of the rain against the blankets overhead somewhat therapeutic and its tid-tid-tid-tidding sound calmed his aching head.

And so the night wore on. All slept intermittently; Aiyesha slept the least.

Mr. Nibbetts stirred in his sleep and raised a heavy head. "Me dying," he said then lay his head back down against the wet earth.

So are we, thought Peter, surprised he had just thought such a thing. It certainly felt like it, though. Dying. "I hate feeling this way," he complained to any who were listening.

"I know," said Aiyesha. She brushed away the hair hanging in her eyes.

Peter rose and leaned on his elbow. His arms were so weak that he was having a time holding himself up. "And you're not even sick." He voice cracked. It was coming on strong now. His stomach swirled, a sharp ache somewhere in the depths of it, feeling to be toward his back rather than right in the middle of his stomach where it should be. His head pounded, a dry hurt, one that, even after closing his eyes, wouldn't alleviate. He was hot then cold. Hot then cold. "I . . . I hate this. It isn't fair. No one did anything to deserve . . . to deserve this." Babbles. Babbles and complaints he couldn't control, just had to get out.

Aiyesha listened courteously as he complained, as he told her how he felt empty inside, as if his innards had been left somewhere behind on the path. His eyes were closed as he spoke. It was a habit, closing his eyes when he had a headache—which was rare, having a headache. At least, until lately, that was.

"I want to throw up," he said. "But I can't. There's nothing there *to* throw up." A shiver rushed through him and the hairs on his arms rose on end, standing straight up on gooseflesh.

Mr. Nibbetts's snoring wasn't helping any, either. Neither was Catina's.

Well, at least Mr. Nibbetts isn't complaining, thought Peter. So he himself was, instead. He had to tell someone how he felt. How ill he was. Why wouldn't anyone understand? Why didn't they see he was suffering? Why couldn't anyone do anything? Angry, he grimaced and spat on the ground, narrowly missing Aiyesha. Realizing what he had just done, he apologized.

"It's all right," she said.

His words came out broken, spoken between labored breaths. He stretched out the arm holding up his head and lay down on it. "No . . . no it's not." *I'm not the only one feeling this way. Have to remember that.*

"Is there anything I can do?"

He focused on the darkness before his eyes, hoping that by keeping them closed, away from any sight, his headache would ease. It didn't. "No. Unless you have some of that . . . some of that Vanillaberry stuff, that is."

"No," she said. "I do not have any. I don't even know if it grows around here. Probably not. Maybe. I'm not sure."

"That's okay," he said. "Thanks for listening to me, though. I know it's not my place to complain, what with how the others are doing. I just hate feeling this way."

"You already said that." Aiyesha grinned.

Peter chuckled softly. She had made a joke. He put a hand to his eyes. "You're right. I did. Goes to show how much I hate this."

"It will pass." It was Alan. He was sitting cross-legged, hands resting on his knees. His head was bowed, eyes closed. Drops of rain that had seeped through the blankets above dripped off his head, which now was a brush of deep blonde hairs on a receding hairline, the hairs one quarter-inch long.

"I know," said Peter. *Tid-tid-tid,* came the rain. Peter tried to let its beat soothe him to sleep. Instead he found himself counting the beat, like the drum of a monotonous tune. *This-is-bad; I-hate-this; let-me-out; no-more-now*, were the words to the song. Over and over it played in his head. It made him feel a little better.

"My heart hurts," said Alan, head still bowed.

For a moment Peter feared a heart attack. Alan sighed and said, "Like someone broke my heart."

Peter's worries ceased, but he thought Alan sounded like one does when they're about to cry.

"Aubri," said Alan. "Why did you go?" The blind man then growled, his sorrow suddenly replaced by anger. "Blast it! Why this foolish journey! Nothing but sickness and death. Fear! Terrible things and things unwanted." Back to sad again. "No one wants me. I am just a blind, old fool."

"You're not a fool, Alan," said Aiyesha.

"Am I not?" he asked.

Peter just lay there and listened, too weak to even speak. Like that day on the Hill, his arms and legs felt weighted, as if someone had cut them open and filled them with sand and then stitched them back up again. He could picture the stitches there now, all in a row, mocking him, keeping him pinned down. He didn't care. He was too sick to care.

"No, you're not," said Aiyesha. "If it weren't for you . . . " It seemed like she had something to say but couldn't find the words.

"If it were not for me, what?" he demanded.

"If it weren't for you, Catina wouldn't have made it home. And to come all that way, to drop everything you were doing back in Garathen, to come to her side . . . you have done plenty, more than most people would do. Many would not brave such a long journey under a disability, even if it was family who had come for their aid. But you did. *You* did, Alan."

"But she is my granddaughter. I have to help her."

"Then you forget you have a choice. We all do. It is up to us what we do with ourselves and our lives. There are no obligations. We choose to do or not do. And you chose to help her. And if you hadn't, we wouldn't be here, together, in the presence of others whom, I think, have now become friends. It was your choice to go. Not Catina's. Not Peter's. Yours."

Peter listened and Alan remained quiet. He wasn't sure, but he thought he heard him crying.

Catina awoke right then and said a few things to Alan in Grescalla; words of sympathy, it sounded. Peter opened his eyes and, looking down the length of his body to where the two were, saw that she had her arm around Alan in a sort of half-hug. Alan returned her embrace as best he could, as distraught as he was.

"Aiyesha," whispered Peter, glancing up at her. She slid her behind closer to him and bent her head down so she could hear him. "What's wrong with Alan?" he asked.

"I don't know," she said. "Could be a fever of some sort."

"I wish this sickness would go away. Not just for myself but for all of us. I was never this sick back home. It's been getting worse."

She put a hand on his shoulder and rubbed circles against it with her thumb. Her touch was soothing, reassuring, a mother's touch. Aiyesha was gentle.

"Thanks," he said.

"Shhh," she said. "Just go to sleep. I know it's raining and Mr. Nibbetts is loud. Just try. Sleep. You'll be fine before morning."

Her voice was so smooth, so sure, so calming. Peter, right then, couldn't get over it. He wanted to touch her hand with his own but couldn't find the strength to move it. He was at that place between being asleep and being awake. There was consciousness of his surroundings but that was as far as it went. A humming built in his ears, his head pounded at the top, in the center, like something was inside his head, thudding against his skull, wanting to get out. Thoughts muddled, he thought of home and how his house used to look before it burnt to the ground. A hot flash rushed over him and, shortly after, felt a trickle of sweat roll down the small of his back.

Everything went black for awhile, the sound of the rain and the droning hum inside his head was absent for a time. For how long it was quiet, he didn't know, and then soon he realized he had fallen asleep. He was aware of the World again and remembered where he was. He looked around and found Aiyesha lying in a fetal position against the soggy ground. Mr. Nibbetts was in the corner, his snoring finally at a tolerable volume, barely moving. Alan lay in a heap close to Peter's feet and Catina lay against her grandfather's legs. Belina was curled up near Mr. Nibbetts, her snout sticking out a little from the blanket-canopy, rain splashing against her black nose as she slept. Thankfully, the rain had thinned. It still came down hard but the drops weren't as fat.

Peter's arms and legs were all pins and needles. He wanted to move them, to stretch them out, but they wouldn't budge. *I can't move!* The thought seemed fresh, as if he hadn't acknowledged it before. His heart sped up and he feared he was paralyzed. *No! Don't be silly. You're not paralyzed. Just tired. Yes, that's it. Tired. Too tired to move. Your stomach hurts, your head feels like it's being squished in a blacksmith's vice. Sounds ring in your head like the echo of thunder. You're sick. That's all. Just sick. It will pass. It did when you were a kid and Aunt Silvi brought you fired-bread and juiced-apple to make you feel better. You're fine. We're all fine. Just ill. But fine. We'll be fine by morning.* Many more thoughts of this sort followed, assurances that everything was going to be okay. His heart rate began to slow. It made him feel better.

The night wore on again. The longest and darkest night ever on this journey. Peter had trouble falling back asleep. He kept wanting to throw up. He rolled over nearly onto his stomach so that his face was only a few inches from the ground, one arm under his stomach, waiting for something to come out. Nothing did but he wanted—needed—to let something out. Anything. He considered forcing his legs to move to get him out from under the makeshift tent and to the lake, so he could have something to drink and in turn have something in his stomach to regurgitate. He also knew he wouldn't be able to maneuver around Aiyesha and the other four cramped in that small area, never mind getting his legs to move. Out of desperation, he tried moving once but to no success. He remembered this same "non-movement" from before on the Hill and how it had went away after a time. He hoped it wasn't a recurring thing, something that would plague him for the rest of his life.

He prayed it wouldn't be. *Master or not, I've got to try. Please, heal me!*

He rolled back onto his side. Body suddenly feeling like it was dropped into a tub filled with ice, he shivered, the shiver racing through him like a swarm of tiny needles. He wanted to bring his knees to his chest to help himself warm up, but he couldn't. His legs wouldn't move.

Catina coughed in her sleep. Alan did the same, as if in response. Aiyesha, thought to be asleep, moved.

"Aiyesha?" asked Peter. His voice was barely audible even to his own ears.

"Yes?" she said.

How did she hear him? His voice had been so soft.

He waited a moment. Closing his eyes again, he said, "Nothing." And then tried to go back to sleep.

It was still going to be a long night. Peter was anxious for morning. Things always seemed better in the morning, even if you were sick.

—

The morning sky was gray and overcast, the scent of moisture on the air. It was still raining, but only scattered drops. The worst of it was over.

Peter slept horribly, waking up every hour or so, looking around, remembering where he was and how terrible he felt, before going back to sleep. One of the first things he noticed when he got up was Mr. Nibbetts was gone. So enthralled by his own problem, Peter didn't care where the Flistablare had run off to. Peter's first priority was to see if he could move or not.

Gathering his strength, channeling it into his limbs, he went to move his arm. It twitched slightly, and it ached. He tried again, this time with more effort. His arm slid off his side and landed in the wet dirt. He wiggled his fingers.

Finally.

His knees bent slow but they were working, too.

Finally.

Very slowly, giving it everything he had, he managed to sit himself up. Once upright, he paused and caught his breath, amazed at how hard of a work it was to do something he had done thousands of times before: get out of bed. He peered out from under the canopy, between the drips of water rolling off the blanket overhead. A mist rose off the lake. At least it was warm. As if acknowledging it was warm were a trigger, a shiver ran through him. He hugged his arms to himself. His insides shook, the Sickness still within him, hanging on, having not yet passed.

Alan coughed in his sleep beside him. Catina was asleep with her head on Alan's lap. Aiyesha was at his right, curled up. She seemed to be sleeping peacefully.

He was thirsty and so, carefully, inched his behind closer to the opening to the makeshift tent and, once at its edge, gathered his legs up beneath him. With a mighty push, he dug his heels into the mud and stumbled back a step once upright. Arms moving, trying to maintain his balance, feeling as though he held an iron brick in each hand, he managed to catch his balance in time so he wouldn't topple on top of the tent and cause it to collapse. He waited, reassuring himself that his legs were under him and that they would not give way. Confident he wasn't about to fall over, he slowly took a step, his foot feeling heavier than lead. One step. He took another with his left foot, this one, too, slow. Two steps. Another. Three steps. And another. Four. With each step it became easier, the pins and needles diminishing from his muscles as the blood flowed back into them.

At the lake, he got to his knees at its shore and rested his hands upon them, catching his breath. *That was only about ten feet and I'm already winded. Blast it! You've ridden for days and you were just fine, no pins and needles. What's wrong with you?* He pawed at the water, testing its temperature. It was cool, refreshing. He splashed some on his face and washed his hands. Eyes suddenly pinching at their edges, he sneezed, and then wiped his nose with his sleeve.

"Boy," he said and sniffled. *Now I got a cold.* A rain drop hit him on the nose. He wiped it away.

The lake rippled in the subtle breeze, its water dark and gray. Peter watched his reflection change on its surface, becoming lost in its rhythmic movements, his wavering features. He was able to see himself clear enough though, in terms of detail. His hair was a mess and stuck out by his ears. His skin was pale, his blue eyes seeming darker in the watery reflection. Deep purple bags were below his eyes, making him look like he hadn't slept in days.

"Boy," he said again quietly. He scooped some of the water into his palm and, after smelling it, took a sip. It was refreshing to his dry throat but it still tasted like metal. He made a face after he swallowed it.

There was some stirring behind him. Before he could turn around to see who it was, Mr. Nibbetts was at his side. The plump Flistablare plopped down on his heavy behind and gathered his legs up to himself, almost sitting cross-legged but not quite.

"Guh" —Peter cleared his throat— "Good morning."

"Morning," said Mr. Nibbetts.

"Where were you just now?" His eyes ached with fatigue.

"Me needed to stretch me legs. Me didn't realize me slept that long."

"Do you remember anything else?" asked Peter. He wanted to know if Mr. Nibbetts remembered waking up now and again and muttering something before falling back asleep.

"No. Just sleep. A black one, too. The kind that makes you wish you could sleep some more."

"I know the feeling," said Peter. *I guess he* doesn't *remember.*

Mr. Nibbetts clicked his tongue, his mouth slightly open, a pondering expression on his furry face. "Me hungry," he announced. "Me haven't eaten anything in a few days. Three, me thinks. Me can't remember."

Peter noticed his own emptiness in his stomach. "Me neither. A day less than you though. I'm starving and there doesn't seem to be anything around here we can eat."

Mr. Nibbetts splashed at the water with his toes. "No fish?"

"What would we use to fish? Worse, what would we use for bait? Even if we made a fishing pole, we'd still have nothing to lure them. All the food is gone."

"You're right. Bad idea."

A wave of nausea passed through his stomach, causing him to wince. He grumbled and closed his eyes, letting the moment pass. Mr. Nibbetts didn't seem to notice his discomfort.

"We're close to Hillmalen," said Peter. "If we can hold out until then, then we can eat something there. Alan still has some tradesworth left. We could also get some supplies and that should last us until we get home."

"Me looking forward to a good meal," said Mr. Nibbetts. "Me looking forward to it very much."

The two stayed by the side of the lake for a short time before Aiyesha awoke and came over to them.

"Good to see you're up," she told Mr. Nibbetts. "Morning, Peter." She laid a gentle hand on his shoulder.

"Morning," he replied.

"Feeling better?"

"A little," he said. "Nothing I can't handle. Better than last night, at any rate."

"Do you think you'd be able to make it through the day?"

"Just the thought of a hot meal will make me do anything," he said. "I'm starving."

"Me, too," said Mr. Nibbetts.

"You're always hungry," said Aiyesha.

"Stop teasing me." The Flistablare scrunched his face up into a knot, his nose nearly up between his eyes.

"I'm not teasing. I'm just saying how it is."

"You're still teasing me."

Aiyesha rolled her eyes.

"He has a point," said Peter.

She didn't comment.

Alan and Catina were up a short time afterward. The consensus among everybody was to clean up, pack up, and get moving, despite how unsettled everyone was. No one wanted to be caught out in the open should it start to rain full force again. The rain had pretty much let up now and that made everyone happy. The horses seemed to be glad at the idea of getting underway, as well. They snorted happily as the bags were affixed to their big behinds. Peter wondered how they weathered the night and if they would be mad at their riders for leaving them out in the rain. *Don't be a fool. They're animals. They've been out in the rain before.*

Aiyesha, taking Catina by the hand, led her to Day and Night in turn and showed her how to grab a handful of grass and feed it to the horses without them nipping at her fingers. She didn't know Catina once had a horse back home and already knew how to feed the animals. Catina giggled each time one of the horses' sloppy tongue licked her hand.

Peter led Alan by the arm over to them. He was walking better and it didn't take as much effort as it had earlier. His grip on Alan's bicep was still weak though. Before they approached Catina and Aiyesha, Alan stopped Peter.

"Do you ever feel like we will make it home?" he asked.

Peter turned to him. "I've never doubted it, if that's what you mean."

"I do not know what has come over me but I know fear is a part of it. I am scared, Peter. And I am sad and angry, all at the same time. I do not know where these feelings are coming from. My head hurts. I will be glad to get underway."

"Then let's get going," said Peter and he took the blind man over to the horses.

The moment Peter was in close proximity of the horses, the smell of their wet hides made his stomach lurch. Letting go of Alan's arm and quickly covering his mouth, he turned and threw up.

"Peter?" he thought he heard Alan say.

Someone was at his side. It wasn't a man. It was a girl. A woman. It was Aiyesha. He didn't remember falling to his knees but he was on them now. A small pool of pale yellow throw up was between his knee caps. He had narrowly missed kneeling in it. His insides trembled and his head felt as if it were being pulled toward the ground by a string. Aiyesha said something to him. He didn't pay attention as to what. Heat covered his entire body and his damp clothes clung to him even more as he began to sweat in a combination of cold and hot flashes. He coughed, threw up again, and fell over onto his side. There was nothing after that.

Aiyesha loomed over him when Peter opened his eyes, her beautiful face coming into focus. It took him a moment to realize who it was.

"I threw up," he said.

She nodded, rubbing his chest and stomach soothingly.

Peter glanced at the others. They were standing several feet away, as if afraid to come near. They all looked at him with concern. Even Alan's blank gaze carried a sense of worry.

"What happened?" asked Peter. His voice was hoarse. He cleared his throat. "I feel better. A bit."

"Can you sit up?" she asked.

"I think so."

Slowly, Aiyesha helped him sit up. His head swam when upright.

"I hate this," he said.

She smiled. He did, too. He had said the same thing several times the night before.

"Maybe we shouldn't head out right away," he said.

"What?" came Mr. Nibbetts.

"If you don't think you can manage—" said Aiyesha.

Peter reconsidered. "No. He's right. We should get going. We need something to eat. All of us. Just give me a moment to get myself together."

"All right." She stood.

"Can I be alone?" he asked her.

She bit her lower lip. Her green eyes were flushed with worry. "If that's what you need."

"Thank you."

And she left him.

There, alone by the lake, Peter waited, waited for some sense of "center" to come to him.

It was a long time before it came.

CHAPTER XLIX
Outside the Whirling Music

Since arriving the day before, General Gasahd spent most of his time sitting in the pub that was part of the Whirling Music, an inn on the Main Road of Hillmalen. The pub had a large, single window that overlooked the Main Road, making it easy to watch the passers-by. Best of all, Gasahd and Zakmon were able to stay at the Whirling Music, an inn known for its celebration of song and nightly sing-alongs, for free. The Dembatstayr were highly regarded in Hillmalen, something which brought a smile to Gasahd's face every time he thought of it.

Our presence is growing, he thought. And he was right. The moment he and Zakmon had set foot in the door, their deep purple uniforms worn proudly, all who saw them and walked passed kept their distance, not out of fear, but in awe and respect. They were a part of the Dembatstayr, the deliverers of the free people of the World, bearers of the Master's Good News.

He and Zakmon sat at a dark, cherry-wood table, each hanging over a pint of ale. It was now mid-afternoon and the two hadn't moved from that spot. They were the only occupants of the tables which ran along the window, everyone else keeping their distance and sitting at the tables further away. The only persons that approached them were the innkeeper, a scrawny fellow with a dirty yellow shirt named Henri, and the blonde-haired, young maiden who served them, named Elnya, who seemed quite taken by Gasahd's charm each time she came to refill their glasses or see if they wanted something to eat.

Zakmon took a sip of ale. "Do you think she'll show?"

Gasahd steepled his hands and leaned forward on the table on his elbows. "Without a doubt. As long as they kept on their course, as stated by Lieutenant Allise, they should be here soon. We'll keep our eyes sharp."

They had been over this conversation many times before but Gasahd found it comforting that Zakmon kept checking to make sure he knew what he was going to do the moment Aiyesha came into town.

"And when we see her?" asked Zakmon.

"I'll decide at that time. I don't want to jump out at her like a wolf out of a bush. I will try to resolve this peacefully. Last time we met her with hostility and she overcame us."

"Still a miracle," muttered Zakmon.

"What?" He didn't hear his Second in Command.

"Nothing. I think that's the best course of action: talking to her first."

"So do I, Captain. And if she refuses to listen, we'll address it at that time. I know she is prepared to fight for her freedom. She's already proven that much." He leaned closer. "Tell me, should she not listen and should we have to take her by force—do you think you would be able to handle her? Given what happened on the hill?"

"I think so," replied Zakmon without taking a moment to consider the question. "And, if I get struck down, I know you'll be able to handle her. After all, you were the one who taught her everything she knows. Second-hand knowledge and skill is no match for first-hand knowledge and skill. Like myself, you taught me everything I know and despite how well-developed my skills are, you are still able to best me when we practice. It should be no different with Aiyesha." Then quietly he added, "Hopefully."

"You're right." He was about to say more but the words eluded him.

"What if the others she is with decide to jump in, especially that Flistablare that's with them? I don't trust him or her or whatever it is. It lashed out at the other men and tore them limb from limb. I'm not prepared to die that way, if you ask me. That blind fellow that's with them and the little girl, they're not a problem. Even that other chap, the one in the brown clothes, he's a skinny one and doesn't seem too much a threat."

"Or do you forget that he threw three men off him like they were dolls?"

Zakmon waited, and took a sip of his drink. Gasahd did the same.

"Right," said Zakmon, "he did do that, didn't he. But maybe that was just a one-time thing? No one of his size should be able to do that. Even men three times larger than he could not do that. His strength must have been driven by fear and panic or something. You and I both know what it's like to be in the heat of battle. Sometimes we feel like our strength is doubled, even tripled. All part of the thrill, in the end."

Zakmon had a point. Many times while fighting, Gasahd had felt himself stronger than he actually was. Survival. That's what the boost in strength was attributed to. The desire to do anything—do whatever it took—be capable of whatever it took—to survive. The human body was an amazing thing, when you got right down to it.

The topic changed. "If she doesn't show in four days," said Gasahd, "then we'll start tracking her again. Until then, we'll stay by this window sill, waiting."

"If that's the case," said Zakmon, "then I'm off to our room for a sleep. Henri said, since we told him we were tracking a fugitive, that we can have access to the pub during the night. 'A Dembatstayr privilege,' I believe he called it. A return for the hope we've restored to the people." He gulped back the rest of his ale. "I'll take the nightshift." He stood up and scraped his chair along the wooden floorboards so he could get out. "Wake me if you see her. Or have Henri come. I'll pass word to him if I see him on my way upstairs."

"I'll keep you posted," said Gasahd, reclining back in his chair, and watched as Zakmon left the room. Others turned their heads as the soldier departed. When he was gone, the patrons returned to their chatter and drinks.

The remainder of the journey to Hillmalen went a little slower than expected, what with everyone feeling so ill. Peter was to blame for their slowness. Often, after an hour or two of riding, his stomach told him he better get off his horse lest he throw up all over Mr. Nibbetts, who sat in front of him. It always took fifteen to twenty minutes after throwing up for Peter to feel well enough to continue on. The good news was that everyone else felt a bit better. Not one hundred percent, mind you, but better. For a time, Alan appeared almost jubilant as his mood improved. At one point he had even cried out that his heart no longer felt like it was breaking and chuckled out loud to himself. Mr. Nibbetts, too, seemed more lively.

Perhaps he overslept, thought Peter, *and now he has the energy given from two nights of sleep?* Either way, it was good indeed to see the others were feeling better.

Catina was slowly getting used to her blindness, Aiyesha informed him. When they stopped so he could throw up, Alan got off Night with Catina and helped her to get used to seeing with only one eye. Having the dog around also helped her with this. Aiyesha reported she had never seen the young humanette so happy since the dog had joined them. Belina was a blessing.

Now, an hour or so outside Hillmalen, Peter's head swam, his body feeling as if someone had stolen the bones from beneath his skin. It was from hunger, he knew. Anything solid—if there had been anything solid—in his stomach was gone a long time ago, lost when he threw up. He could tell the others were woozy as well. All needed a meal. For awhile on their journey, everyone was ill tempered, snapping at each other over little things, reaming each other out when one complained of one thing or another. But all understood it was because they were hungry and tired and so it made the arguments that much easier to get over.

"I have to stop," said Peter, his voice quiet. No one seemed to have heard him. He swallowed and told them again, this time a little louder.

"Okay," said Aiyesha and she told the others to stop their horses.

Peter hopped off Day and went a short ways from the group. He put his head between his knees and waited as his stomach gathered itself into a knot, preparing to push out some of the water that was in there from his drink a couple of hours ago. Arms shaking, Peter waited. His feet were hot even in his sandals. Another flush of heat wrapped over him and he felt the beginnings of sweat on his forehead.

"Just breathe," he told himself. "Breathe slowly." And he did, slowly, in through his nose and out through his mouth. Each breath made him feel slightly better.

Mr. Nibbetts said something behind him but he couldn't make it out. His head dipped forward, that invisible stringing pulling it toward the ground again. It was almost time.

His insides locked and he opened his mouth, ready to do what he hated the most. Instead, he dry-heaved and for some reason or another thought of Thalok. Thalok's haunting presence in his mind caused his arms to shake even more. *Where is he now? He's coming. I know he is. He has to be. He's behind me. He's in front of me. He's on either side. He'll confront us before we reach Garathen. He'll kill us, too.* Peter didn't know where these thoughts came from but just merely thinking them made everything so much better. It was as if the *act* of thinking the thoughts that had been stewing in his subconscious was like him throwing up: expelling the garbage from the body.

He coughed and his stomach settled. He waited and when it was apparent he wasn't going to throw up this time, he carefully straightened. When he did, green stars danced before his vision. He waited some more and the World around him was clear again. Spitting once, he returned to Day.

"Feel better?" said Mr. Nibbetts.

Peter recalled thinking on Thalok. "Not really. But better for now, I guess. I just need something to eat and a warm bed. I think I caught a cold from that rain." He sniffled.

"Me, too," said Mr. Nibbetts.

Grinning, Peter got back on Day. He didn't know why Mr. Nibbetts's comment was so funny.

They proceeded to Hillmalen.

Evening rolled around and Gasahd was finishing a plate of roasted chicken, steamed carrots, a side of ground-potato, and a tall glass of milk. The grease from the chicken coated his lengthy mustache. He dabbed at it with his napkin. Reclining back in his chair, he let out a sigh at a meal well done and well received.

Zakmon should be up soon, he thought. *Getting tired of all this sitting around.* He glanced out the window. The bustling of people that had been present all day was finally diminishing. He thought the markets in other cities were busy, but in Hillmalen, they seemed to be even busier, everyone in need of something.

Elnya came by and began cleaning his plate and glass off the table.

"Eat well?" she asked. Her smile was small and kind.

"Very," he replied, reclining back in his seat even further. He found himself gazing at her, her blonde hair in ringlets, her bright green eyes. Dear Master she was beautiful. *No,* he told himself. *You're here for one person and one person only.* Then, almost as if another voice, *That hasn't stopped you before. Go on. Ask her to sit down for a drink.* Then the other voice: *She's working, you fool. Besides, Zakmon will be back shortly. You don't want him to see you with yet another one. What kind of general do you think you are, anyway?*

Elnya must have seen this debate going on behind his eyes because she asked if he was all right.

"I'm fine," he said. "Just tired." *Liar!*

She gave him a cute smile then scurried away with his plate and mug. Gasahd slapped a hand over his eyes.

"When are you going to learn, old boy? When are you going to learn?" He straightened and leaned over his table.

Outside the window, a few people were chatting. He watched them. One was a woman, the other a man. The woman wore a tall hat with a bright, red-petaled rose sticking out of its top. The man wore a tall hat of his own, large and black, its brim wide and floppy. Gasahd thought the hats looked ridiculous.

As the two outside the window spoke, Gasahd looked up and down the street.

That's when he saw her.

Aiyesha.

She was here.

Gasahd, heart pounding with excitement and victory, jumped from the table and stormed out of the pub. He bounded up the creaking stairwell—nearly crashing into another handmaiden who was coming down the stairs with an armful of laundry—in search of his first officer. Zakmon better be awake.

Aiyesha didn't have to be one of those fabled Seers to know that something bad was about to happen. Call it premonition, but she knew that something terrible would occur before the day was out. Years of training, years of always being *alert* and *aware* told her this. Her flesh crawled and her breath caught in her throat. She gripped her reins hard and scanned the Main Road of Hillmalen. There were many people about, none seeming to be paying attention to any of the outlanders. The first thing Aiyesha picked up on was the amount of tall hats she saw. The men wore mostly tall black ones with floppy brims, and the women wore similar versions, theirs of assorted colors with various colored flowers sticking out from their tops. Aiyesha thought they looked ugly and wondered why anybody would want to wear such a thing.

Keep your eyes open, she told herself.

Peter glanced at her. "Something on your mind?"

Aiyesha's gaze remained calm, cool. "Not really. I have a bad feeling about this place though. Best keep your eyes wary, and keep to yourself. I don't know how I know this, but we should get indoors as quick as we can."

"Alan?" called Peter.

The blind man cocked his head in the direction of Peter's voice.

"Alan, do you know anything about this place? Like where we can find somewhere to rest?"

"Sorry," said Alan. "I took the countryside the last time I was out this way. Same thing when we passed by on our way to Grek. I do not know this place. Just watch for an inn or a hanging sign indicating one. It should not be hard to find. Every city has an inn." Then the blind man said, "Well, there is one thing I do know and that is Hillmaleners are quite fond of hats. The hats, according to what I have read, signify stature. The taller your hat, the more important you are."

Peter glanced around. "But all their hats are tall."

"But if you look closer, you will see—at least, if my books are right—that some hats are slightly taller than others, and others are slightly shorter. Just a way of saying, 'I am that much better than you,' as is common in the minds of Men these days. Pride. Greed. Every man looking out for just himself."

"Not in Garathen," said Peter.

"Even in Garathen," said Alan. "Just not as obvious as other places away from there."

Maneuvering the horses through the crowd of people was tricky, but was managed nonetheless. A few rude glares were shot their way when it appeared one of the horses might step on someone.

Aiyesha eyed the buildings all around, many of them short buildings made of stone with wooden roofs and dirty windows. One, up ahead, had a large window running along its front and . . . a hanging sign. Focusing her eyes, Aiyesha made out the words: WHIRLING MUSIC. An inn! Finally.

"Alan, there's an inn up ahead. It's called the Whirling Music," said Aiyesha. Right after she said those words, the muscles in her shoulder blades and neck tightened. *What's wrong?*

As if in answer, General Gasahd and Captain Zakmon stepped out in front of the Whirling Music. A sharp pang spiked Aiyesha's heart. Gasahd grinned at her.

She wasn't as surprised to see him as she thought she would be. The others, almost collectively, turned on the backs of their horses and looked at her. All except Alan who looked on straight ahead as if nothing was wrong.

"Aiyesha . . . " said Peter, his voice shaky and unsure.

Aiyesha walked quickly to the front of the line, as if to shield the others from the two men. The people in the streets scurried off to the sides and stood in a row, watching whatever was going to happen next.

She remained motionless, her face calm. No emotion whatsoever. A quick flash to the Battle on the Hill went before her eyes and, just as quickly, was gone. This is the man who had been hunting her. He was the one who she knew so well and, for a brief time in her past, thought she couldn't live without. And now he was with her again. Here, amidst the eyes of strangers, all looking on, preparing for bloodshed. She drew her fingers into a fist, her nails digging into her palms.

And so it comes to this, she thought.

Gasahd took a step closer and a jolt shot through Aiyesha's chest, an ingrained reflex to be ready for anything, at any sudden movement. Gasahd stopped, brought his feet together and held up his hands, as if in surrender.

"Hallo, Aiyesha," he said. His voice was smooth but had a rough undertone, like there was gravel in his throat.

A subtle grimace creased her lips as she eyed him intently. The company behind her sat still atop their horses. Even the horses were like statues, waiting to see what would happen next.

Gasahd met her gaze with an equally hard stare. Then, suddenly, his expression lightened to something warmer. He was almost smiling. "I said, 'Hallo, Aiyesha.'"

Still she did not reply. She wanted to take the horses around them and, once around, dash off to someplace far away from the two men.

Zakmon was eyeing her, too, obviously waiting to see what Gasahd was going to do. Gasahd, with thumb and forefinger, parted his dark, bushy mustache away from his lips. Hands now crossed behind his back, he began to walk around her, slowly, like someone biding their time before something big was about to happen. As the general moved around her, Aiyesha kept her eyes on Zakmon. Should Gasahd try anything, she knew she could turn to meet him in a flash. She also had the others to rely on to warn her if and when he would do anything. She wanted to keep Zakmon in her sights should he lunge at her.

"I often wondered what I'd say when I saw you next," began Gasahd. "And now that we are here together, I am not sure what to say. I don't suppose there's anything I could say that would convince you to come back with me, now, is there?" Her lips were sealed. "No, I guess not. No matter. Just listen and let me speak." And so she did. "You left the Coast. No warning to anyone. That's okay. Other men have tried it before. And they left . . . but they were found, brought back, and, now, they are some of my most loyal men. The Master has His Mark on you, Aiyesha. And it's a strong one, at that. Do you think it coincidence I had found you, or that you came to the Coast, after praying to Him for guidance and direction? Praying for a group of women who would be more skilled than anyone else I've ever trained? In all honesty, I thought so at first. It's sometimes hard to believe it when prayers are answered. But, as time went on and you and the others showed what you were capable of, the more I believed that, yes, my prayers *were* answered." He was coming up the right side of her, now. He didn't pause, even when he looked up, and kept his slow stroll. "But then something happened. I began to pray for something else. I began to ask the Master for someone who could not only lead the women I recruited, but also the other men, as well. Someone who, when all was stripped way, was a better soldier, a better warrior, one whose skill surpassed everyone. And guess what? That prayer was answered, too. Answered in you." He was in front of her, but not for long before he started moving around her again.

She could hear the heavy breathing of her companions.

It was fear.

Zakmon's eyes went from Gasahd to hers, his gaze knowing, like he had some dreadful secret up his sleeve.

Gasahd went on. "And you proved that when we fought on the Hill. You bested not only my men, but the other girls as well. Something I thought could never be done. After all, my girls were supposed to be more well-trained than my men. I was wrong. But you . . . you, Aiyesha. You're what I need to further the Master's cause. Someone to show what is now a poor excuse for an army the proper way to do things."

Her jaw clenched. She did not believe in the Voidsmen's cause anymore.

Gasahd rounded behind her—She could tell by the sound of his boots crunching the dirt on the Main Road. She kept her eyes forward, as if fixed on something seen only to herself.

"There's no 'proper way,'" came Peter. His voice was a ripple in a heavy-mudded pond.

Aiyesha turned to him, her arms ready should Zakmon decide to attack from the front.

Gasahd eyed Peter. "And then there's you. Another one worthy to join the Master and I. You managed to toss men around like dolls. Care to explain how you were able to do that?"

"I . . . I . . . " started Peter. Then, with defeat, "I can't."

"Either way," said Gasahd, "it was extra-ordinary. But my affair today is not with you." He turned to Aiyesha. "So what do you say? Come to me, and you, the captain, and myself can return to the Coast of Seryn and finish what we started."

His face was as hard as steel. So was hers.

"No," she said. Her words were ice.

Gasahd nodded, as if approving her decision. "I see. Very well." And he came back around to the front of her.

Mr. Nibbetts groaned. Alan told him to "Hush up."

"Why?" said Mr. Nibbetts, hand outstretched.

"Quiet!" said Peter.

"Why? Why should we sit here and do nothing when we know what's going to happen. Me don't want to repeat the Hill, please. Me knows what happens when trouble starts."

"And what is that, my dear Flistablare?" asked Gasahd.

Mr. Nibbetts fell silent. Aiyesha knew he didn't want to mention the Change.

"No answer." Gasahd glared at the furry creature. "Coward."

"Leave him be," said Aiyesha.

Gasahd waited a moment. Then, "Make your decision. I may not be able to talk you into it. But I will take you back." He sighed. "I need to."

"Why? Why am I so important?" she asked.

"I just told you."

"That's not a good enough reason. If you need someone to lead your men, or so you think, then why don't you do it yourself? I left the Coast in search of a life away from what the Dembatstayr stood for." There were some gasps from the people around them, as if they could not believe she would say such a thing. "I don't want any part of it, General. None."

"You will come," he said. He nodded to Zakmon and the captain lunged at her.

Aiyesha moved out of the way swiftly and Zakmon missed grabbing her. He pulled out his sword.

"What is happening?" called Alan.

Aiyesha was at the blind man's side in an instant and told him to stay where he was. From the saddlebags fastened to Night's rump, she drew Alan's sword, something she had been yearning to hold since she first laid eyes on it. The sword she had stolen from the Battle on the Hill was something she did not want to touch right now. Using it to try and defeat her enemies . . . . She didn't want to have anything to do with the Voidsmen or their weaponry.

Zakmon was on her the second she drew the sword. Steel clashed against steel and a metallic ring filled the air. Zakmon pushed his blade against her and she pushed back, equally hard if not more so. Knowing that he was stronger than she was, she dropped to one knee and whirled her other leg along the ground, sweeping Zakmon's legs out from under him. Gasahd already had his blade drawn and was coming after her. Aiyesha did a backwards somersault on the dusty street and got her distance from them . . . and from her friends. She didn't want them caught up in this. She didn't want any needless casualties. But Gasahd and Zakmon . . . they could die today. *Gladly.*

On her feet, she brought her sword up, ready to meet Gasahd's blade that was already bearing down on her. The swords clashed and Aiyesha felt the reverberation all the way up to her shoulder. Peter shouted something at her but she was so lost in the battle, so enraptured by the fight, that she could not make out his words. Something about looking out?

Gasahd took another mighty swipe at her. Zakmon was behind him and then, suddenly, at Aiyesha's side, taking a stab of his own. She moved, Zakmon's blade narrowly missing her. She pushed Gasahd away and delivered a side kick to the small of Gasahd's back once she was behind him. That was the thing with these two men. She had never known any two warriors who fought almost exactly alike, a combination of quick and smooth, calculated moves, and simple, harsh brutality.

Mr. Nibbetts was covering his ears, crying out something, something like, "Me hate this."

Catina spoke in a high-pitched voice, all Grescalla. Even amidst the confusion, Aiyesha had a moment to think that she wanted to learn the language so she could understand what the little girl was saying.

Her former general and his captain were on her before the thought even ended, their steel a blur, coming at her from every angle. She countered all of their attacks . . . except one. Gasahd's blade nicked her on the shoulder. She didn't flinch. It was just a quick zing, telling her she had been hit and that was all.

Not good enough, she thought. And she wasn't talking to Gasahd, either, but to herself. It was her way of pressing herself harder. Nothing was ever good enough for Aiyesha Elnaa when it came to the Fighting Arts. She had to be the best. She *needed* to be.

Zakmon's sword came over head and Aiyesha ducked under it and caught his arm, entwining it with her own. She stuck her sword in the dirt road with a hard thrust and, with her right hand, slugged Zakmon two punches in the gut and one in throat in the time it took the average Dembatstayr to deliver one strike.

The crowd lingering in the street shouted at her, at the soldiers, at everything. It was a fight and people tended to shout when watching a fight. People were cheering for both sides, as if, in this instance, speaking against the Dembatstayr was allowed despite how much Hillmaleners appreciated the army.

Gasahd hooked her one in the jaw and another in her kidney. She thrust her leg out and caught him clean in the chin with the ball of her foot. It didn't slow him. She let Zakmon go and picked up her sword, whirled around, and sliced a chunk of meet off Zakmon's calve and gave him a shove to the ground with her shoulder. Immediately, her blade clashed with Gasahd's and she kicked the inside of his right knee. He let out a squeal, then, almost instantaneously, regained his composure and came at her with even more vigor.

In the flurry of blades and the blocking of punches and kicks, Aiyesha saw Peter was off his horse and cautiously nearing the fight.

"Get back!" she called out to him.

"But—" he started, but she cut him off with a, "Go away!"

Peter teetered back but was still too close. If she was not careful, one of the soldiers' blades would surely take his head clean off.

Then, from behind Peter, "Get back here!" It was Alan and he was motioning for Peter to return to the horses.

Aiyesha blocked another punch and delivered one of her own to Zakmon's kidney. Peter looked at her as if it were the last time he would ever see her again. The crowd's shouts grew louder. Some shouting, "Dembatstayr! Dembatstayr! Dembatstayr!" And others shouting, "Girl! Girl! Girl!" They didn't know her name.

Peter didn't seem to know what to do with himself. Aiyesha saw fear in his gentle blue eyes.

Peter, get away! she wanted to cry out but could only think. Her voice was being used for grunts while exchanging blows with the men.

Zakmon somehow got behind her without her seeing and she felt a sharp pain in the back of her knee. Something had cut her. She collapsed to the ground, dirt spilling up about her. She dropped to her belly, rolled over and delivered her heel straight into the soft spot under his chin. Zakmon staggered back, coughing. The point of Gasahd's sword came driving down. Aiyesha rolled onto her right side just in time as its point barely missed her. Gasahd kicked her in the shoulder blades, causing her to roll over onto her stomach. She got up but was kicked back down. And now, not just one boot, but four were slamming their heels into her back, the rear of her thighs, her arms, all over her, as the soldiers delivered her punishment for betraying them.

"Get up!" shouted Peter from somewhere.

She could not see him. Her face was in the dirt.

Gasahd straddled her back and sat down and grabbed her ponytail, yanking her head back.

"You will return!" he shouted.

Never!

She grabbed her sword just as Zakmon rounded to the front of her. She jerked her wrist in an upward thrust and drove her sword home between Zakmon's legs, penetrating his groin and running deep into his insides.

The captain didn't make a sound. Aiyesha watched him as he looked down on her, eyes wide. Blood spilled forth from his lips, his eyes remaining on her. Gasahd held her in his clutches but didn't do anything further. Zakmon's legs wobbled and could no longer hold him up. His knees bent, his body sinking even further on the blade until the hilt was right up against his privates. Aiyesha released the handle and let Zakmon fall backward onto the filthy street.

Then, as if it never happened, Gasahd's focus was back on Aiyesha. He pulled back on her hair even harder.

Palms shoulder width apart, she pushed up and arched her back in the process. She was strong and Gasahd's balance teetered, but didn't teeter enough. She fell face first to the street again, banging her nose against the hard, dusty ground. The already-broken cartilage flared with a spike of heated pain. Dirt got on her tongue but she didn't spit it out. Not until she could spit it on Gasa—

His fist came down on the back of her neck. She heard a crack but nothing was broken, just a vertebrae getting pushed out of place then falling back in line again. She was suddenly thankful for all the lessons in bone-breaking techniques back on the Coast, all those painful days of training. From time to time, when some of her bones were slightly out of place, she would remain in discomfort for a few days before learning how to set them in their proper place again. She was used to the pain.

Centering herself, taking as many deep breaths as she could with her face pressed to the ground, Aiyesha gathered her strength, her will, her power. She would not go out like this. Not at the hands of who was proving to be more of a dictator than a leader.

"Aiyesha!" called Alan.

"Aiyesha, please get up!" cried Peter next.

"Hurry!" came Mr. Nibbetts.

"Coona ma ta!" said Catina.

Aiyesha glanced at Zakmon's body, his feet close to her, his head somewhere on the other side of his torso, blood oozing from his lips, but not leaking out as quickly as the blood from between his legs.

No more, she thought. *It ends now, no matter what the consequences. The others can hunt me for the rest of their days if they want to, but I will not run from Gasahd anymore. No more. Time to finish this.*

With a quick jerk, she twisted her body so she was on her back beneath Gasahd's heavy build. His fist landed square in her face the second she was fully rolled-over. Her broken nose blazed with the fire of hot pain again. When he went to hit her again, she blocked him, her forearm slamming into his wrist, pushing his arm away. She did a sit-up and at the same time pushed as hard as she could against his chest. The force pushed him onto her thighs instead of on her hips like he had been when she had rolled over. She hooked him twice across the temples, then twice from the other side, dazing him. She pushed again and got her legs out from under him. Then, within the longest half-second of her life, she got to her feet, spun around, withdrew Alan's sword from between Zakmon's legs, and whirled around again, driving the blade home through Gasahd's chest. The blade pierced through him like a sharp knife gutting a pig. She held the blade there, her arm locked, gripping the handle so tight that she thought she might squeeze the steel handle into a noodle. Gasahd looked up at her and, amazingly, began to laugh. His head rolled back and he closed his eyes, laughing.

A grimace on her face, Aiyesha forced herself to withdraw the blade. Then she drove it through him again . . . and again . . . and again . . . until Gasahd was no more than a Practice Dummy from back on the Coast. All sound around her abruptly ceased as she poured out twelve years of pain into each of her blows. Again . . . again . . . again. She was destroying the man who destroyed her, the little girl from Bel Candar.

Blood spattered onto the street, onto her arms, onto her face. Again . . . again . . . again.

She didn't know how long she had been stabbing him before a pair of gentle hands touched her shoulders. She kept on stabbing, cursing the general.

"Aiyesha," said a gentle voice.

Tears rolling down her cheeks, she kept on with her assault.

"Aiyesha," said the soothing voice again. It was Peter's. "Aiyesha, it's over."

It took a moment for those words to sink in. *It was over.* Finally. It was over. Her assault eased and after she withdrew the blade for the final time, Gasahd fell backward, his torso a bloody mess of slaughtered flesh and purple material. He hit the ground with a soft thud, like a sac filled with sand.

The sounds of the crowd picked up and then tapered off into gasps and the occasional scream for more blood. Then everyone was quiet.

Aiyesha stood motionless, staring at his mangled, bloody form. Peter's hands were still on her shoulders. He stood with her, silent. Just like everyone around. Alan's sword dropped to the ground and Aiyesha waited for her rage to pass.

THIRD ACT

The Ark Calls

CHAPTER L
Thalok's Arriving
(Faces in the Windows)

Night. A dark sky, with gray puffs of rain-filled clouds on a sheet of charcoal black. Barely any moonlight reached the Second Main Road of Hillmalen this night. The streetlamps were lit, the flames standing proud inside their metal casings, the lamps twenty feet apart, lining the street.

In this part of town, known as Beggar's Foot, Hillmalen was its opposite to where Aiyesha had mutilated Gasahd. The Second Main Road was on the downside of the Main Road, as if on a slope. From the sky, you could see the division more clearly, one side—the Main Road—higher and mightier than the other.

There, on that other side of Hillmalen, the brick that made up the walls of the buildings were a light gray, their rich shade still seen even during the night. The brown of their rooftops still vivid and deep. But here, in Beggar's Foot, it was the reverse, no matter how much the buildings on opposite sides of the city looked almost alike. The gray of the stones here was tarnished, old, second rate. It was as if the stones were chosen out of the reject pile when the builders constructed the buildings on the Main Road. Down the Second Main Road were the same types of businesses: florists, barbers, fruit and vegetable markets, butchers, blacksmiths. But these were your second-rate tradesmen, the ones who didn't quite make the cut when it came to opening up their shops on the other side of the city. There was even a "parallel" Whirling Music, but on the Second Main Road it was called the Singing Dangler, "singing" because that's what the men there liked to do when tying on one too many, "dangler" the slang term for drunkard. Homes lined the street as well, squat buildings that were miniature versions of the business buildings they stood beside: dark gray stone for walls, brown shingles for roofs.

Thalok walked among them and knew that Peter and his friends were on the Second Main Road, not the Main Road, and Thalok favored it. It was much darker here, more gloomy.

The street was bare this late hour, all who lived on the Second Main Road behind closed doors long before. It was unsafe to travel unguarded or unarmed down the Second Main Road at night. He walked, his long gray cloak gliding out behind him, almost majestically. He kept his pace slow, savoring this moment of finally being in the same place as his prey. The satisfaction of nearing the completion of his task filled him with what could only be called jubilation, mixed with relief. He looked forward to the kill, and looked forward even more to returning to the Island of the Dead for its replenishing nourishment. He had been away far too long and could already feel the effects of the outside World weighing on his body. Would the Void-man summon him back—transport him back—just before he would complete his task so that he would be at his strongest when he confronted Peter? Thalok thought that would be a wise move, but he also equally doubted it would come to pass. Once the Void-man assigned you to a task, He liked to see you complete it on your own strength, without any aid. Then why had the Void-man called him back to "correct" him? Wasn't that *aid?*

Thalok's eyes glanced around from beneath the shadows of the big hood that hid most of his face. Most of the windows of the establishments were bare, not a soul in sight. But there, up ahead, was that someone? Someone leering at him behind a pane of glass, wondering what this strange phantasmagorical figure was, coming in the night? Thalok stared straight through him, through his dirty face, to deep within him. The man vanished from the window.

As Thalok proceeded down the street, he caught the gaze of others, those who couldn't sleep and had nothing better to do than look out the window at this strange figure that had come into the city. Thalok eyed all of them. The moment his eyes met with theirs, their eyes widened, their mouths opening, as if about to speak, but no words came. They all disappeared to further within their homes.

No longer needing to Reach, Thalok followed the pull as it led him to the Singing Dangler. Peter was there. So were his friends. They would die, too, Thalok knew. It was no longer Peter that he intended to kill. The others, if they lived, would surely report that the once thought mythological Qinorans were on the rise again and, shortly after, a hunt would begin. True knowledge of the Qinorans' existence was something the Void-man did not want, hence the killing of Pnumar in Darim. He had *known* of Thalok and his kind. Perhaps, too, had known more about the Void-man than he ought to.

The Singing Dangler was drawing near. Thalok's insides shook with apprehension. His fingertips pulsed with heat. Finally. His search was over. It would all end soon and he could return to the blessed comfort of the Island. More importantly, he could prove that fool Void-man that he could achieve any assigned task on his own terms without His interference!

Without realizing it, Thalok's pace sped up and soon was standing before the entrance to the Singing Dangler. Darkness came from the large window on the main floor and the same with the four windows that lined the second floor, likewise with the third. Three horses were tied out front. This close, Thalok even knew their names. Day, Night, and . . . well, the third didn't have a name. But it didn't belong to the party he had sought and now found.

Everyone was sleeping. Even Peter. He knew that. The same went for the others. But there was a disquiet about the group. Thalok smelled fear but not the kind that one gets from seeing a bear rise on its hind legs, about to tear you apart. No. This fear was something far worse. It was the fear of your fellow Man or Creature. Something had happened earlier that day. Something that set the others off, causing them to be wary of one of their companions.

A girl. The little one? No. The older one? Yes. She had done something. Aiyesha. That was her name. Earlier she had done something so terrible the others could not believe it. Yet . . . there was something else there. Love? Yes. Love. They loved her anyway and there was a collective understanding that she did what she did because she had to. She *needed* to.

The scent of new death was suddenly on the air and Thalok inhaled it deeply. Soon there would be more suffering, more pain, more death. The scent would be intoxicating.

Euphoria would come.

Peter pulled the white blanket over his mouth, trapping in the heat. He was still chilled from the rainy night prior. He was with the others in a single room on the third floor of the Singing Dangler.

After watching Aiyesha stab Gasahd over and over again, the group had wanted to leave, get away and not linger amongst the Hillmaleners. But they also knew they had to stay. They needed food. They needed rest, and it was over one hundred and twenty miles to the next town, and going there would also be going out of their way because they were pretty much on a direct path back to Garathen. Pretty much. And with Aiyesha—who had studied maps on the Coast of Seryn—helping with leading them, their journey home was coming along a little quicker than when Peter and Alan and Catina set out for Grek. Staying with Yaman had set them back a day, so it might work out to the same in the end though.

When Aiyesha's fight was over, the crowd had begun to shout curses at them, screaming that these outlanders had killed two of the valued Dembatstayr. The Voidsmen. Soon they were chased from the scene and fled to the other side of the city, to here, to the Second Main Road. Judging by how *outcast* everything seemed, they figured it was the best place for them to stop for the night. Everyone they encountered there seemed to have no idea who they were and were also not aware of the death of the Voidsmen, despite the rumor that news fled through Hillmalen like wildfire. It seemed the people didn't even care that they were even there. It was perfect. They could be left in peace long enough to catch their breaths and fill their bellies.

Using most of what was left of Alan's tradesworth, they got a room and spent most of the evening inside it, only leaving once to go down the stairs to the eating area for a hot meal of meat stew and thick slabs of bread coated with butter. A salad was also served with the meal. At extra charge, of course. But it had been worth it. They needed the nourishment the greens would bring. Milk was drank and, when the meal ended, all were too tired to sit around the table and talk, so they went upstairs and retired early.

Peter slept for a few hours before waking to the sound of Mr. Nibbetts snoring. That's when he noticed he was cold and pulled the blanket up over his mouth. Alan lay beside him on the massive bed, Catina beside Alan, and Aiyesha at the end. Mr. Nibbetts slept at their feet with Belina, the two curled up the same way. Moonlight came in faintly from the room's window, its light casting shadows from the folds of his blanket across his thighs and middle. He watched them change shape as the clouds in the sky blocked the moon then moved away. Their dance was almost hypnotic and he saw shapes he recognized as the shadows formed one thing then another. A tree, a mountain, a face with one eye missing, something resembling a sword, a horse with only two hind legs, its front two hidden in the patch of another shadow.

Then Peter saw something else. A patch of shadow as big as a Human head, bigger, growing, as it drew across the blankets. His body immediately locked at the sight. The shape grew, the head becoming pointed at its peak, fanning outward like a rounded pyramid. Peter didn't need to look to the window to know what it was.

It was the hood of the Man in the Gray Cloak.

He began breathing hard through his nose, his breaths audible and shaky. Everyone's breathing in the room seemed to quaver, as if they all knew there was something there that didn't belong.

Peter's first hope was that someone would awake. No one did. Not even Aiyesha. He expected her to, her being the warrior among them, able to move stealthily, pick up on sounds, *sense* when something was wrong, as warriors should. But she remained deep in her slumber, the day's events, the slaying of Gasahd, no doubt having drained her. But she had been trained to kill without thought. Would Gasahd's death really have fatigued her that much? Even Zakmon's? Peter didn't think so, but also presumed that since Aiyesha had spent so much time with Gasahd, she had grown attached to him, whether she had wanted to or not. It might have taken more out of her than he realized.

The shadow in the shape of a hood stirred on his blanket. He gripped the blanket, so much so he felt his fingertips dig into his palms through the fabric. A flush of heat enveloped him and he closed his eyes, hoping that when he opened them, the shadow would be gone and it would only be his imagination playing a trick on him. But when he opened his eyes, the shadow was still there. And now there was nothing left to do but look to its source simply because, maybe, if he did look, he might see that it was not Thalok, but something else, perhaps a crow or raven perched on a building top across the street. Maybe it was only his mind playing tricks on him.

The very idea that it was Thalok preyed on his mind. He had to give in. Needed to, if he wanted to go back to sleep. Body still stiff, hands still gripping the blanket, he rolled his eyes over to the window.

Empty. Just charcoal sky and pale moonlight. Thank the Master.

Peter removed the blanket from over his mouth and breathed a sigh of relief before looking away from the window.

Nothing. I don't believe it. Thank the—But the shadow was still present across the blanket, draped over it like a second blanket of dark gray. It was still in the shape of a hood. Peter glanced toward the window again and—nothing.

Peter. A hoarse whisper in his mind, more so echoing in his heart, the very core of his being. It was Thalok's voice, though Peter had never heard it before, at least, not in this World and only in visions.

Peter.

"Go away," said Peter and pulled the blanket back over his mouth.

The shadow was no longer on the blanket, just the regular shadows created by the folds in the blanket remained. Nothing more. Heart racing, he closed his eyes and tried to relax. He finally managed to doze off for a time before suddenly waking again.

Peter.

"Not again," he muttered. The blanket was no longer over his mouth. He must have pulled it off while he dozed.

Peter.

Then, without thinking, on pure instinct, he glanced toward the window.

Thalok stared back at him.

Peter screamed and awoke everyone in the room. Aiyesha was at his side faster than a rabbit darting away from a hungry dog. It took him a moment to realize that she had indeed gotten up and was beside him as quick as she had.

"What's happened?" She was gripping his hand. Hard.

Peter swallowed a stone and could almost feel it plunk into the pit of his stomach. "He's here," he said. "Thalok's here. He's here. I saw him. The window."

The others were up and were getting to their feet as Aiyesha looked out the window.

"There's no one there," she said.

Peter covered his head with his blanket. "Look again. Don't tell you me you can't tell he's here. You know when danger comes about. You're the fighter, here. There's someone very bad outside, Aiyesha."

"What's that supposed to mean," she asked, "me being the 'fighter'?"

"You tell me. I saw him. He is out the window."

"Me see nothing," said Mr. Nibbetts.

Peter hadn't heard him go over to the window and stand beside Aiyesha.

Alan was explaining something to Catina in Grescalla, and then said, "Catina wants to know why you screamed, Peter."

Peter pressed his hands to his eyes through the blanket's fabric. "I don't want her to know why. It'll scare her. She's seen enough as it is. I don't want to paint pictures of my nightmares for her."

Aiyesha returned to his side. She tugged at the blanket covering his eyes. "Listen to me." When he fought her pull on the blanket, she pulled even harder—and quicker—pulling it back so his face was staring up at the ceiling. "Peter, listen to me. There's no one there. You have to trust me that there isn't."

He eyed the window, expecting to see Thalok there, grinning at him, a face that only he could see. But Thalok wasn't there. Just like before, there was only a mat of smoky night. Peter took a deep breath. The exhale was relief. He sat up, one knee drawn, one leg outstretched, and rested his forearm on his knee.

"I swear to you he was there," he said. Sweat glistened along his hands. A chill swept through him, the hairs on his arms and neck standing up right.

"What do you think we should do?" asked Alan calmly.

"I don't know," said Peter. And he didn't know. They couldn't just leave. Thalok would surely follow. The Man in the Gray Cloak had been following them this far. What was to stop him from following even further?

He turned toward the group. "Did anyone just have a bad dream? Remember we all dreamed about that man with the big, gray cloak? Did anybody just dream about him? Please, someone tell me they had. I don't want to be alone in this."

They all shook their heads.

"I *am* alone in this," he said. "I thought before I was going crazy . . . then all of you knew he was real. Now I'm alone again. I wish I knew what was going on."

Aiyesha crossed her arms. "Me, too."

"What do you mean?"

"I want to know what you saw. Obviously we're facing something—someone—very real. I think we should all believe Peter saw what he saw."

Peter let out a huff, but it was meant in fun instead of frustration. "What made you change your mind? You just said there is no one there."

"Because you said *who* it was you saw. If living on the Coast had taught me one thing, it was to believe in the things that could not be explained. I witnessed miracles while I was there. Horses with a broken leg suddenly being mended. The girls I trained with, beaten beyond recognition, healed. And not through natural means. Prayer. The Master's blessing. Even I was healed; often, too, I might add. Despite how much I don't agree with the army's message, I do agree with the Master. In that regard, anyway. Not the domination part of it. Not what I've seen anyway. I just wish I knew what He was really like." She came to the left of him and sat down. "But I believe you. I'd be a fool not to. All of us would be."

Mr. Nibbetts's brow was drawn down in concentration. "Me don't want to die."

"Myself neither," said Alan. "I wish I could see what you saw, Peter. But I cannot. I—cannot."

There was a tap at the window. When they looked toward it, they all jumped out of their skins.

Thalok smiled at them.

There was a collective yelp from everyone in the room. Thalok loomed in the window, his shrouded face glaring at them even though none of his features was discernible.

The Man in the Gray Cloak.

Thalok.

The moments ticked away for what seemed like an eternity. Even the smoky clouds that made up the sky outside the window seemed more gray, but not nearly as gray, not nearly as deeply gray, as Thalok's cloak.

Peter didn't know how much time had passed before he realized that he, and the others, were looking at a window with nothing behind the glass but the top of the building across the street and a cloudy sky with a gray that seemed to have lightened.

Thalok was gone.

They were all there. A satisfied smile curled on Thalok's lips, then a frown. They were all there and he hadn't done anything. It would have been so easy to smash the glass and enter the room. It would have so easy to go up to each of them and in the span of an instant, snap all of their necks. Peter's first, of course. But he hadn't and he didn't know why. Something held him back. How long had he hungered for this moment, the moment right before dismembering his prey and tearing them apart, watching them die at his feet. Still, he hadn't gone after them.

For a moment Thalok felt his blood course through his veins, feeling the life—and death—within him. He was a mile away from the Singing Dangler, in an alleyway, shrouded in darkness, concealed from anyone who might be taking a late night stroll.

"They were there," he said aloud. He didn't like speaking to himself. It was a sign that something was so wrong that it couldn't be thought through, but rather spoken out, as if hearing it would bring on a new clarity. But for a Qinoran, their thoughts were always clear. They were a very silent race. Even their conversation was quiet, mostly nods, the other knowing just by reading the other's facial and bodily expression, what the other was saying.

You had them!

It was the Void-man. He was in Thalok's head.

"I had them," echoed Thalok. "They were there."

You did nothing! You fool!

Preparing himself for an instant transport back to Yem Batu, Thalok straightened, ready to meet the Void-man head-on, ready to be reamed out for not acting like he should have. But the transport never came and Thalok remained in the alleyway.

"There'll be another time," said Thalok.

When?

The Voice was loud and it wasn't just in his head. It was everywhere within him, from his toes right up to the top of his head, and all around.

"Soon, my Master," said Thalok, his voice barely a whisper.

The response was slow in coming. *I will not tolerate failure. Especially not from a Qinoran who lives on my Island, under my power. If it weren't for my land, my realm, you would have died long ago. You have three days.*

The Voice left him and Thalok was alone. He could feel it, as if a part of himself had suddenly drifted away. There was an emptiness inside that he found uncomfortable, but he brushed it aside and stepped out onto the street, anger surging up inside him. Anyone who happened to be passing by as he emerged would be torn to shreds, should he encounter someone. But the street was empty, nothing but drab buildings with dark windows and the pale light of the streetlamps.

Thalok glanced in the direction of the Singing Dangler, picturing Peter and his friends in that cramped little room, all looking at each other in horrid shock, all speechless as to how to explain what they saw that night through the room's window. How to explain how someone—something—could appear in a window that was three floors from the ground.

"Three days," muttered Thalok, and he glided down the street, sticking to one side, staying within the shadows.

There was a reason why he hadn't struck tonight. There was something wrong on the Island. Something was happening. The other Qinorans were suffering. He stopped his movement and Reached.

Reaching, from out here in the World into the Island, was more difficult than it was to Reach from one place in the World to another place in the World. To Reach into the Island, Thalok had to Reach through the Border of Purple Fog. The Fog was thick, dense, like trying to push a pin through a slab of iron. There really was no way to do it without imminent failure. It took effort and skill and, most of all, Desire and Will, so much so that if Reaching into the Island was successful, it always left a Qinoran drained and left them with a ravenous hunger to return to the Island to replenish, nourish. But tonight, Thalok Reached anyway. He had to know his kin were all right.

He closed his eyes and let himself drift away, his Being seeking out the Purple Border, determined to make it through. It had been easier before, when the Qinorans called out to him. They had combined their strength, making the task of penetrating the Border easier. Yet Thalok was but one and he was the only Qinoran who could cross the Border and make it out into the World. So Thalok Reached, Reached, and Reached even further. Finding the Purple Border, out here, was easy and it quickly rushed up to meet him.

The wall of the Purple Fog stood before him, spanning high, so high that it seemed to go on forever, past the sky and into the stars beyond. The purple murk was thick and all enveloping. So he Reached further, his Being swimming through it like a man swimming through a lake of syrup, but even thicker still. Already he buckled under the strain, but still he pressed on. Clouds of purple swirled around him, purple spanning forever in all directions. Thalok didn't know if he was even going the right way. All sense of direction was lost. There was just purple fog, and that was all.

He was so small, so—off in the distance, was a high-pitched sound, at first quiet, droning and humming at the same time. The more Thalok swam, the louder it got. It was screams and anguished wails from a pain that Thalok did not dare to fathom. The screams surrounded him and wracked him from all sides.

The Qinorans.

The Purple Fog swirled around him and, in a blast of hot wind, dissipated and Thalok was back on the Second Main Road, only faint gusts of purple smoke dancing at his feet. He dropped to his knees and put out his palms to meet the dirty street. The moment his palms made contact, his arms could not support his weight and he collapsed, his face hitting the ground. For a long while he stayed like that, face down over bent knees, catching his breath and gathering his strength. When he felt he could stand, he pressed his palms against the ground and pushed with all he had. He straightened, knees still bent and gazed up into the sky. The cloud cover had cleared. He must have been down there for awhile. He was surprised no one had come along. If someone had, though, he hadn't noticed them. If they saw him, they would almost certainly have fled, unable to handle the trembling darkness of his presence.

"Three days," were the first words out of his mouth. *Three days, what?* Then he remembered. Three days to kill Peter. Three days to murder the others. Three days until it was all over. But it didn't have to be three days, he knew. It could be sooner, should he choose. Yet he may need the next three days to recover from trying to Reach into the Island.

Suddenly, he felt eyes upon him. He glanced around and there, in the darkened windows of the buildings and homes that ran along each side of the Second Main Road, he saw the faces of the Qinorans, one to each window. Helplessness was in their gaze, all of them pleading for Thalok to please the Void-man and finish his task and return to them.

Finish it. Finish it and come home. You must. He'll kill us all if you don't. He doesn't want the Black on his Island anymore. He doesn't want us anymore. He's growing stronger. Finish it. Finish it and come home.

The faces faded from the windows and a cold chill swept through Thalok's bones.

Finish it.

CHAPTER LI
Back on the Road

No one slept that night. The haunted memory of seeing Thalok's face in the third story window plagued them all. Each time their eyes closed, they saw Thalok's hooded face. He was looking into their hearts, laughing, making them feel worthless, without power and that their lives didn't matter. Not to each other. Not to the Master.

Not to anyone.

Sleep finally came in the wee hours of the morning, after the sun had already risen and its light shone brightly through the window, the dust on the glass making the shine brighter. They slept with the sun's heat upon their faces and their bodies. But it was a restless sleep, one not nearly sufficient enough to allow them to recover from such a hard journey.

When mid-morning approached, they began to wake one by one, all with tiredness in their eyes. It showed in their moods when getting ready to head out and how they snapped at one another over trivial matters.

It wasn't until they were all mostly awake did they speak of Thalok and what they had seen the night before. Talking about it brought on a peculiar feeling. It felt like they had been talking about it since it happened and did not have the break of sleep in between. Thalok was all they spoke of after he vanished until they had nodded off one by one, overwhelmed with fatigue from the hard days previous.

Peter had said the least when they talked that night. The whole time, while the others talked, he thought of Thalok, dwelled on him. That hooded face glared at him in his memory like the angry eyes of a bear: pure rage, hate, the desire to kill. As the scene of Thalok glaring at him through the window played in his mind, that picture of the hooded man staring at him, Peter noticed something. It was memory-by-association, he knew. Around Thalok's hood, like a halo, was a ring of purple smoke. Peter recalled Pnumar's story in Darim about the Battle of Then, the final conflict between the White and the Black. *Is Thalok some sort of holy messenger?* he thought. *No, that couldn't be. If he were, why do I detect such hate in him? Holy people do not hate. They love. Right?* Peter didn't have an answer to his thoughts, yet so badly he yearned for one. Even a partial answer would suffice. He just needed some light shed on that mysterious Man in the Gray Cloak.

"Though I did not see him, I could see him," said Alan. "It was like it was in my dream about Aubri. That Man was there. His presence brought his image forth in my mind as clear as if I could see, if not clearer. It is hard to remember, sometimes, what it was like to see."

"There is more to him, too," said Aiyesha, her voice calm yet as cold as a winter's night. The warrior in her speaking. "He fears us, somehow. At least, that is what I perceived."

"But you don't know him!" shot Mr. Nibbetts. "How can you even say that? He's going to show up time and again. What is he? He was in our dreams. He's real. How can someone step out of a dream, anyway? That's impossible! Me know it is. It has to be, right . . . Peter?"

Peter had been sitting against the wall at this point, lost in his own thoughts. "Wha—Oh, yes."

"Were you even listening?"

"Sorry. My mind's preoccupied right now. I—"

"The main question is," began Alan, cutting him off, "is what does this fellow want?"

"He's wants us," said Peter. "He . . . he wants me."

They all looked at him like he had grown a second head.

"I don't know how I know it. I just do. I was seeing him before any of you dreamed that dream. Back in Grek, I saw the Man on Catina's property. Back in Darim was when I first saw him."

"He did," said Aiyesha.

"And you never told anyone?" asked Alan.

"No," said Peter. "What could I have said? I didn't want anyone thinking I was losing my mind. I didn't want to think *I* was losing my mind. It's a relief, though, to know I'm not . . . not crazy. I'm not the only one who saw him. But I saw him first and that's what worries me. Why not any of you? Why me? I'm just Peter, some random fellow from Garathen. Out of all the people in the World, why choose me? There's no reasoning behind it." He sighed and put his palms to his ears, shutting out the noise of his thoughts.

"I should have believed you—fully—when you told me you saw him," said Aiyesha.

Peter glanced up at her. His eyes watered. "Would it have made a difference? Would he have gone away if you had?"

She didn't answer.

"I thought not." He paused. "Look, I'm sorry. I'm just so confused."

"So are we all," said Alan. "Catina is frightened. Look at her."

He did and when the little girl looked back at him, his heart broke. He had never seen such pain in one's eyes before. Her cheeks were tear-stained; her lower lip trembled when she inhaled. The poor girl. It was all coming down on her. Her parents, loss, fear, and now the haunting from someone whom she didn't know.

"Will he come again tonight?" asked Mr. Nibbetts.

Belina groaned right then, as though a response to his question. Peter suddenly wondered if the dog had seen Thalok, too, or if Thalok only appeared to more intelligent beings.

"I don't think there's an answer for that," said Aiyesha. "But I do know we should get out of here. Quickly, too. We've all had next to no sleep in the past few days. I suggest we try to get some before first light. Talking about what happened is fine, but it solves little. It just helps us deal with what we feel inside." She came over to Peter and slid down against the wall, sitting beside him.

They remained silent for a time. Belina came over to Catina and licked her hand. It seemed to make Catina feel a little better because she smiled at having the dog nearby.

"Aiyesha," said Alan, breaking the silence, "would you be so kind as to go downstairs and see if our horses are all right? When we do leave, we will obviously need them with us."

"Sure," said Aiyesha. She stood and made her way for the door. Once at the door, she took one last glance at them and then went off down the hall.

Peter's head was pounding, partly from fatigue but more so from confusion. He could not shake Thalok's image from his mind. He assumed that neither could any of his companions. There was just so much menace to the Man in the Gray Cloak. But, there was something more to what he saw. It was as if Thalok were pulling at his heart, tugging at it, nudging it toward meeting him. It was like Thalok was *reaching* toward him, bringing him closer. Maybe not in a physical sense, although Thalok was obviously very near, but more in a spiritual sense, like Peter *had* to meet Thalok and confront him. Peter prayed he never would. He knew he would surely pay for any encounter . . . with his life.

He just knew it.

When Aiyesha returned a short while later, they all looked at her with worried eyes. They were certain Thalok had done something to the horses.

"Everything's fine," said Aiyesha. "They were a little jumpy, but they are fine. We'll feed them before we leave in the morning. I know they'll appreciate that."

"Feed them what?" asked Mr. Nibbetts. "All their food's gone."

"I'm sure we can find something for them even if it's not exactly horse food." She came over and sat back down beside Peter.

Later, after speaking of Thalok some more, and everyone acknowledged that at least they were safe and no harm had come to them, one by one they nodded off. Peter and Alan were the last to go to sleep.

"I'm scared, Alan," he told him.

"Myself as well, dear Peter. Very much so." He breathed in deep and exhaled through his nostrils. "Makes you wish we could just figure this out and solve it, does it not?"

Peter couldn't help but crack a smile at the comment. "It sure does. But there are no answers, are there?"

"I am afraid not," said Alan. "At least, not yet. But if there is one thing I have learned since losing Aubri and losing my sight, it is that answers do come. Some sooner than others. But they always come."

It was an encouraging thought. "So have . . . did you find an answer as to why you . . . you lost Aubri?"

"Partly," said Alan. His voice carried an overtone of confidence. "It came to me just after we left Grek. I realized that, by my missing Aubri, by so badly wanting her to be alive—that I truly valued her love, and my love for her. I will admit I was not the most perfect husband. There were times when I was certain she would leave me. But she did not and stuck by me. Imagine her, sitting at home alone, while I was out and about, getting a taste of the World. As you know, I did most of my traveling after she had passed on, but even though sometimes I was with her physically, I still was not completely there for her. I was distant, plagued by my past, and it weighed me down. Back to our journey home. When I realized how much I missed having her around, I mean truly realized it, I had a renewed love for Catina and a new appreciation for family. She is all I have, now. And I her." He paused. "Like I said, it is a partial answer. Perhaps more of it will be revealed in time."

Alan was right. He did seem to appreciate Catina more. During the journey to Grek, Alan, though caring in his approach to her, still seemed kind of *distant.* But on the journey home, Peter noticed, Alan seemed so much closer to the girl. Peter suddenly wished his parents were still alive. It would be comforting to have a family.

"If Thalok comes again—" said Peter. He couldn't help but bring up the Man in the Gray Cloak one last time. "If he comes again . . . I just hope I'm ready for it. Like I said earlier, I think he's coming for me."

"What makes you say that?"

His stomach twisted into a knot. "I don't know. It just seems that is the case. I saw him first. He was in Darim, in Grek, by that river we stopped by before getting attacked by those men, the dream—He's all I think about now. It's like he's calling to me." His heart sank. "I just wish to be left alone."

"So do I," said Alan.

They sat in silence and, eventually, fell asleep.

Now, in the morning, even though Thalok was always on his mind, the problem didn't look as big. Peter was rested . . . rested enough. There was nothing he could do about Thalok for the time being; he resigned himself to that fact. As they left Hillmalen, Peter noticed it was not just he who kept looking over his shoulder. The others did it, too, as if expecting Thalok to jump out from behind a building and slay them all. But Thalok never came and they were safe. For now.

Peter hoped he would never see the Man in the Gray Cloak again. But he knew that he would, and he also knew that it would be soon.

The first part of their journey was in silence, all of them taking their time waking up. A weight settled about them because they were back on the road again. The good news was their journey home would soon be over. Peter enjoyed the route they were taking back to Garathen. He didn't want to pass through Darim again, as much as he took pleasure in the Festival of Armasulia. But even then, he was a different man back then. So much had happened since and those events had changed him. Life didn't seem "all figured out" anymore.

He munched on a smoky-flavored meat stick as they rode. Earlier that morning they had gone to the first market open before leaving and gotten enough food to last them the rest of the way home. Alan had grumbled as to how he was nearly out of tradesworth and it would take him awhile to replenish all he had spent.

When he finished the meat stick, the dog looked up at him wantingly, her hope that Peter would share some of the meat stick with her suddenly diminishing when he glanced her way.

"Sorry, girl," he said. He showed her his hands were empty. "Got nothing left." Her big, dark eyes peered up at him. They seemed glazed over in disappointment but Peter knew that's how a dog's eyes always looked. He reached down and the dog licked the juices from the meat stick off his fingers. Once done, without any gratitude, she went off and walked alongside Catina and Alan, hoping they would share some of their meat sticks with her.

"Sure, don't say anything," he said quietly and smiled.

As the morning progressed into afternoon, so did the flat land progress into rockier terrain. The land began to roll and, embedded in some of the grassy hills they rode in between, were large boulders.

"Are you sure we're heading the right way, Alan?" called Peter.

"Well, what is around us?" said the blind man.

Peter and Aiyesha explained their surroundings to him. There weren't any trees. The next patch was far off in the distance and they wouldn't reach them until evening. They were on a path, the grass worn, as if many had traveled this route before. Ahead, there were more small hills with rocks embedded in their sides. Even further away, the rocks grew more frequent and a few boulders were on the side of the path, as if markers, encouraging you to go between them, to stay on the path.

"How did we wind up here?" asked Alan. "You should have been watching the road, Peter. And Aiyesha, I thought you knew where we were going. You were just as much a map hound as I was."

"I only know the main roads, Alan. Not these side ones," she said.

"So what's our next move?" asked Peter.

The blind man thought a long time before answering. "I do not want to double back. You say we are on what looks to be a path or trail, so it must lead somewhere."

"But it could keep going. Who knows where we'll end up," said Mr. Nibbetts.

"There might be signposts. You can watch for them, to help us get our bearing. There is nothing worse than being lost. Believe me, I know," said Alan.

"Let's go a little further," said Aiyesha, "and we'll see where it takes us."

Murmuring agreements among themselves, they took the horses down the path, all eyes searching for a road sign to let them know where they were going.

"Me hate being lost," said Mr. Nibbetts. He seemed more "awake" today.

"We're not lost," said Peter. "Just a little sidetracked. We'll be heading back in the right direction before you know it."

Mr. Nibbetts frowned and crossed his arms. "This is all your fault."

"My fault!"

"Boys," said Aiyesha, coming up beside them.

They silenced like a couple of children being told to behave by their mother.

"Bush-man," muttered Mr. Nibbetts. It was directed at Peter.

Peter rolled his eyes. He wanted to give the Flistablare a shove but held back. There was no sense in furthering the argument. Mr. Nibbetts was a complainer and that's just how he was. Peter was getting used to putting up with it.

His neck and shoulders suddenly tensed. The hairs on his arms and neck stood on end and a chill swept through him. His heart sped up and his hands began to shake. His breathing suddenly became short and choppy.

Someone was watching them.

Peter kept focused ahead at first, not wanting whoever was watching them to see him looking around. Then, ever so carefully, still keeping his head forward, he glanced around. The rocks in the hills were bare of life. No animals. No shrubbery. No sprouts of green growing through the cracks in the rocks' craggy surfaces. Nothing. There was no one around. But someone was watching him—watching them. He already knew who it was.

Thalok.

It had to be. The Man in the Gray Cloak was drawing close. Was he following them? Had he been behind them since Hillmalen? Peter thought he would have seen him if he was. How hard could it be to spot a man in a long gray cloak?

He might be able to turn himself invisible, thought Peter. *Nonsense. That's impossible. Then again, has anything Thalok done been* possible? *He's done things that no one can do. How can anyone show up inside someone's mind—in their dreams—at any moment? How can they appear to you then suddenly disappear?* Peter swallowed the lump in his throat.

Aiyesha must have noticed his distress because she asked him if anything was wrong.

"Don't tell me you can't feel it," said Peter. His eyes darted around again. His legs grew wobbly as he walked beside Day.

Aiyesha glanced at Mr. Nibbetts first before speaking.

"There's something behind us. I didn't see anything when I looked. But something is definitely there. I've been trained to sense when someone is coming near. I'm quite good at it, actually, and can usually tell when someone is not far off."

As casually as he could, Peter turned around, pretending to fidget with something on the saddlebag on Day's rump, and glanced down the path behind them. It was just an empty road with hills and rocks on either side and a cloudy sky. The gust of wind rustled his hair and blew some in his eyes. He brushed it away when he faced forward again.

"How far behind us is he?" he asked.

"How far is who?" said Mr. Nibbetts. "Is someone back there? Oh, dear Master, me is going to die for sure."

Paying no heed to the Flistablare's comment, Peter asked again, "How far back there is he?"

There was a quick calculation behind Aiyesha's eyes before she spoke. "Not far. Perhaps one or two gels."

Where's Thalok hiding? There's still not much to hide behind out here, hills or no.

"I just hope he doesn't come for us," said Peter. "Tell Alan."

Aiyesha nodded then took her mare down the line to Alan.

"What's going on?" demanded Mr. Nibbetts, calling back to Peter as Aiyesha took him and Day to Alan. "Who's back there? That Man? Is it him? Come on, answer me!"

"We don't know for sure," said Peter. "But, yes, I'm almost certain it's him. Who else would it be?"

Alan leaned over to Aiyesha as she whispered something in his ear.

"Maybe it's just someone coming down the road like we are, going home," said the Flistablare.

"I wish you're right." There was that pulling at his heart again, that *reaching* from Thalok. He was calling to Peter.

I'm coming.

"He's coming," echoed Peter softly.

"What?" said Mr. Nibbetts.

"Nothing. Just talking to myself." *He's coming!*

Peter's Journal: A Few Last Words

Mae 15, the Year 134, the Fifth Aeon

It will happen soon. Thalok is coming. I'm writing this as I walk toward a forest ahead. We're lost. Well, not lost, but we've somehow lost our sense of direction. It could be because my mind was so preoccupied when we left Hillmalen that I didn't pay attention as to which direction we were headed. Aiyesha doesn't know this area. Not well, anyway. Her mind is busy, too. I can tell when I look at her. And, of course, Mr. Nibbetts and Catina don't know where we are so they won't be able to help us get back on the right path. I only hope we come to a signpost soon and hopefully it will say a name that Alan will recognize and help set us back on the proper course.

But there is a more pressing matter than even this one. Thalok is following us. I didn't see him, at least, not yet. But he's here. The same fear I felt last night while seeing him in the window, I'm feeling now. There's a difference between being scared and real fear, too. "Scared" is when you see something the shocks you and frightens you. "Fear" is the trepidation that something terrible is about to happen. I do not know what Thalok will do once he confronts us.

I'm coming. That thought—that feeling*—has been present ever since I laid eyes on him in Darim. It grows, day by day, as if I'm walking toward the blade of a sword, about to be impaled. There's something else, too. I don't think the others are as affected by Thalok as I am. I see caution in their gaze as we ride on, but not genuine, honest-to-the-Master fear.*

As for myself, I'm terrified. This little journey is not what I had expected. That is obvious. Should this be the last time I write in this book . . . well, what can I say for my last words? Perhaps I can say that I miss home. I miss Talia. I can also say I'm thankful I've made it this far and have remained alive in spite of the battles we've encountered.

And, Aiyesha, should you read this (which I have no doubt you will, should I die at Thalok's hands; you'll surely defeat him as you are the warrior in our little band), I want to say that I value your company and each day when I awake, I get excited because I get to spend it with you. I truly hope nothing changes much once we reach Garathen. Getting to know you has really opened my eyes into seeing there is a lot happening in the World that I was not aware of when living back home. I hope to learn more from you.

Alan, thank you for teaching me many a thing along the way. I'm sorry that, when living back home, we didn't speak more often. I didn't realize that the reclusive hermit living at the end of the Through-way was such a fascinating person and a wise one as well.

Catina. You came to me first. You set us out on this path. Though there have been hardships, I wouldn't trade these experiences for anything. I'm glad to have met you. You feel like family to me. Alan, please translate these words for her, please.

Mr. Nibbetts. Though we banter back and forth, I'm finding I like being around you and, reluctantly admitted, enjoy your complaints. They are funny and humor is what is and was needed on this trip.

I don't want to end this journal with a "final word" or "statement" because that would mean I've already resigned to Thalok killing me. I'll end by saying that these are strange days we live in. Nothing is what it seems.

Something is rising.

CHAPTER LII
From Jakarland

From Jakarland, Thalok watched the company ride between two hills, the rocks from them jutting out at odd angles, dark crevasses scattered here and there about the hills' faces.

With swift legs and great speed, he ran up one of those hills, keeping his pace. He could not slow down. If he did, Jakarland would fade and then vanish around him and he would be seen by Peter and the others. In order to maintain his invisibility he had to run back and forth alongside the company, his only glimpse of the five companions his glances at them as he passed by. But he didn't mind. His heart raced—the area in the chest cavity where a heart should be—throbbing—excited for what was to come. There was a thrill in those final moments before engaging an enemy, an expectation that all—despite any pain endured—would work in your favor and you would stand victorious. There was the satisfaction of carrying out the Void-man's will, and great pleasure in the reward of being allowed passage back onto the Island of the Dead.

But Peter wasn't really *Thalok's* enemy, was he? No. He was the Void-man's and, as yet, Thalok was unaware as to why. Yet there was something that poked at the back of his mind, something that traced back to the Battle of Then and what occurred. But that was a long time ago. Thalok wished he could remember the rumors that circulated about the Island back then. There had been rumors, of that he was certain. Something about the Purple being holier than the White or the Black. Something about the Void-man being unjustly cast away from what was supposed to be a pure cause. Thalok just wished he could clear his mind and recall what those rumors had been. That was the problem from having spent so much time in a place where all that made up your surroundings were one person's desires, morals . . . power. The Void-man ruled the Island of the Dead and his taint was everywhere and on everything.

A well of hatred brewed inside Thalok as he sped back and forth, keeping Jakarland around him. And it was not his hate . . . but someone else's.

Kill him now.

The Void-man.

"Three days," said Thalok. "I have three days."

Too long. Now! No longer.

He grunted and continued his run. Peter and the others were a short ways away from a forest at the end of the road.

"Three days," maintained Thalok.

Today. Not a moment more! Menace coursed through the Void-man's voice and at the same time, its sound was soothing to the ears as it pulsed through his heart in a hypnotic beat.

Thalok didn't know what to do. Three days. He had been given three days. Not one.

Then suddenly Jakarland changed and Thalok skidded to a halt. Jakarland, strangely, was still maintained around him, something he never thought possible. Before him, no more than twenty feet away, stood a line of Qinorans as far as the eye could see to either side, their hands joined together. Their gaunt, gray faces and dark eyes were blurry, as if Thalok were looking at their reflections in a murky lake. It was as though every Qinoran residing on the Island of the Dead were present.

They were.

He turned and checked behind, just in case he was in fact looking at some kind of mirror; but there was none behind. Just Jakarland, its impression upon the landscape skewing how it truly was, the land's colors and detail muted, like a painting washed over with dirty water. Back before him, the Qinorans, their torn cloaks hanging limp at their sides, black ones, brown ones and gray ones, stood before him. Across each of the Qinorans' faces was a look of helplessness, their normally deathly stares made innocent.

Fear.

"Today!" they chorused, their voices like gravel; rough and throaty. "Today!"

Confusion setting in, Thalok rubbed his eyes, hoping that when he removed his hands, Jakarland would return to normal and the Qinorans would be gone. Yet when he removed his hands, the Qinorans seemed to have come closer to him, now no more than ten feet away. Thalok smelled their fell breath from where he stood.

"Three d-days," he managed to say. His voice was soft and shaky.

The eyes of the Qinorans went as black as midnight and grimaces graced their faces. "Today!"

Head bowed, Thalok wrapped his gray cloak around himself tightly. "What has He done to you? Why are you here?"

Before the Qinorans could respond, their eyes shot wide open and their jaws stood agape. In a blast of thunder, one by one they dropped, at first to their knees then finally keeling over onto their sides, writhing in pain on the ground, strained coughs escaping their lips. Thalok rushed over and knelt beside one of them. A heat burned through Thalok's heart and a jolt of numbness coursed through his bones when he turned the Qinoran over. He was dead. His eyes remained open, his mouth hung low to an impossible size, his body rigid. Qinorans entered rigor mortis immediately after death. Within a few seconds of holding him, the Qinoran crumbled to dust in Thalok's arms, and the debris from the ash-like body blew away as a powerful wind swept through the scene.

And there, standing behind the row of bodies, was the Void-man, his silhouetted form leering at Thalok.

Getting to his feet immediately, rage pumping through him, Thalok flared out his cloak and summoned his Qinoran strength. He charged at his Master. Before he could even come near, the Void-man raised His hand and in a blast of air blew Thalok backward. Thalok toppled along the ground like a leaf in the wind before skidding to a halt over forty feet away. The Void-man was beside him in an instant.

"Today," said the Void-man, and was gone.

Jakarland shifted and became the Jakarland that Thalok knew. Since he was not moving, Jakarland began to shimmer and fade away and Thalok was left out in the open. He was on a hill, over looking a path, Peter and his companions about sixty or seventy feet away, maybe more. Thalok dropped to his belly to get out of sight. Just before he hit the ground, he saw Aiyesha glancing back his way. He was certain she did not see him.

Mind reeling over what just happened, Thalok looked to where the Qinorans had lain while inside the Void-man's Jakarland. He could imagine that blank patch of grass around their bodies, as if they hadn't disappeared along with Jakarland, they lying there, eyes wide with open mouths, a look of desperation on their faces. He shot to his feet. Thalok ran and in a blurry rush of speed, Jakarland formed around him like a bubble. He hoped to see the Qinorans and examine their remains to determine precisely what had happened. But the Qinorans were gone, the Void-man having taken them away. Back to where? To the Island? Most likely but Thalok knew that even the Island's power could not restore a dead body.

A harsh pang surging through his heart and chest, Thalok arched his head back and growled at the sky as he ran back and forth. In a tidal wave of painful emotion, the cries of the dead Qinorans, their Beings shouting out in anguish, poured into Thalok and drove him to his knees. Jakarland dissipated around him and he was in the World once more.

Dead. They were all dead.

Pounding his fists against the dirt, Thalok wailed and his screams echoed in the air.

It was a message from the Void-man, showing him what would happen if he disobeyed. And instead of killing just one Qinoran, as great a crime as that would be, the Void-man had annihilated all of them, with no less effort than a bear swatting at a fly. The Void-man would pay for what He had done.

In a rustle of leaves out of the treetops ahead of them, birds raced for the sky at the sound of the scream, their wings flapping wildly as they climbed higher and higher. Peter stopped his stride and Aiyesha and the others halted their horses and glanced around, trying to determine the direction of the sound. It seemed to come from all sides.

"What is that?" demanded Mr. Nibbetts, covering what, Peter assumed, were his ears, though no ears were seen on his furry head.

Catina began to whimper and Alan wrapped his arms around her. The dog barked madly, as if she had just seen an intruder. Except, no intruder was present. At least none they could see.

Peter about-faced and stared up onto the hills. The scream's echo began to die down and, eventually, all was quiet again.

Aiyesha rode up beside him.

"He's coming," said Peter. "Be ready."

"Then let's go," said Aiyesha and she helped guide the group down the path toward the forest.

They would be there shortly. They could find shelter there.

Glancing over his shoulder often, Peter saw the Man in the Gray Cloak watching from atop one of the hills. The Man didn't move.

CHAPTER LIII
The Swinging Bridge at Tatamound

Catina watched as the forest neared. Its trees were nothing like the trees of the Calahudron Woods. These were just average trees, about thirty feet high, maybe two feet around. Average trees. But they were dense and stood close together, three maybe four feet apart, their branches and lower limbs intertwining with each other as if holding hands. You could very well climb one of these trees and walk around the whole forest just by stepping from tree limb to tree limb, she reckoned. That would be fun. If the branches supported you, that was.

She glanced back at Peter and saw that he kept looking over his shoulder. He caught her eyeing him. His eyes suddenly cast down, as if uncertain what to say.

"Sorry," he said.

But she didn't understand that word. He gave her a smile. Peter always looked better when he smiled and his blues eyes seemed to glisten with gentleness when he did.

She smiled back. Again eyeing the forest, the dense woods where shadows made up the gaps in the trees, Catina focused her right eye, practicing "seeing" with it, strengthening it because, in her left eye, all she saw was black and it always felt as if it were *relaxing*. But she could see out of it, couldn't she? She had seen out of it when she saw that pouch of Gero beneath Rano's cloak.

Imagining that she could see out of her left eye, she squinted, pretending to focus it, hoping that, somehow, her sight would return and whatever had happened that allowed her to see through Rano's cloak would happen again and she would able to see. Her breathing slowed and she tensed her eyes. On the right side of her vision, the details of the forest grew more acute. She saw the odd shapes and patterns in the bark, the deep knots and crevasses upon its surface. The different shades of green on the leaves. But her left eye still saw darkness. She wished she knew how she had done it, how she had seen through that man's clothes. The problem was that she had just *done* it, without thought, without meaning to, without even knowing she could do it. How could you make yourself do something if you didn't know what you did? You couldn't and Catina hated the thought.

Maybe with practice she would figure it out. Maybe.

Thalok had vanished from the hilltop about five minutes before. Peter didn't know *when* he had vanished but just that he had. He could remember seeing Thalok, standing there, gray cloak hanging off his body, then . . . then he was gone and, even now as he looked back on the hill, he could envision Thalok standing there, watching, waiting.

"The path leads in there so we might as well take it," said Aiyesha, pointing to the forest.

"Is it safe?" asked Alan. "I hate going into places I know nothing about."

"Never mind that," said Mr. Nibbetts. "Me just hate the dark."

Belina padded up to the entrance to the forest and sniffed around at some of the fallen branches and the dead leaves scattered at its mouth. Her sniffing stopped just as it began and her head jolted upright, her ears perking up. For a long time she stood, body ridged, staring into the forest. All looked on her expectantly, as if, when she turned around, she would share with them what she saw. Instead, after a time, Belina barked once then turned and padded back to the group.

Alan said something to Catina. Peter thought it had to do with asking her why she was staring at the forest. After Alan spoke to her, Catina glanced around again, following the conversation from person to person. Peter thought he saw disappointment in her blue eyes, as if she had hoped for something but it never came.

"What's that?" said Mr. Nibbetts and lifted Aiyesha's arms—that were around him, holding the reins—over his head and dropped off the horse. He landed with bent knees and when he straightened he walked a few paces forward and dug around in one of the bushes near the forest's entrance.

Mr. Nibbetts parted the branches of the medium-sized bush in front of him and revealed a signpost made of wood.

Peter went over to him.

The sign was old, the wood rotten around the edges. Its color, which looked to be at one time a deep tan color, was now a light beige. Weathered and faint letters were carved into it. They were somewhat unclear, but still legible enough.

"Tatamound," said Peter, reading the sign. He turned to the blind man. "Alan, do you know what or where Tatamound is?"

"No," he said. "That is a new name to me."

"Anybody?" asked Peter. "Aiyesha?"

She shook her head.

"The sign's pretty old. Who knows how long it's been here. Maybe it's the name of the forest, like the Calahudron Woods or something." He examined the sign further. "I wonder what it means?" Absentmindedly he glanced back at the hills, thinking Thalok might be there. He wasn't. Where was he?

"It's just a name," said Mr. Nibbetts, scratching his belly.

"If that's the case, then we have nothing to worry about," said Aiyesha. "Come on. The sooner we get going through the forest, the sooner we'll get to the other side." She took in the forest. "The path seems to run all the way through despite how close together the trees are."

Peter helped Mr. Nibbetts back on Day. Aiyesha returned her arms around the Flistablare.

"Then let's go," said Peter.

And they entered the forest.

They traveled for an hour, always sticking to the path as best they could. The only time they left the trail was when a tree stood right in the middle of it and they had no choice but to go around. Riding through here reminded Peter of the Forest-Ring and the Three Stages within it. He wondered if this forest, too, had three stages: one thick with trees, one thinly populated with trees, and then one thick with trees again. So far the trees had all been close together. Getting the horses through was a challenge and sometimes they would have to stop while the rider coaxed the mare or steed through. One of Alan's saddlebags caught on a low branch that was sticking out and Peter helped him free it so they could continue on.

As he walked, Peter kept checking behind him. He imagined Thalok darting around the trees, watching from behind them, waiting for the perfect time to strike. Often Aiyesha would flash him worried looks, questioning ones, asking him if he knew if Thalok was near. Each time she looked back, he shook his head, announcing that, as yet, they were safe. That was, until . . .

Thalok stood in the middle of the path some ten spans behind them. Peter's heart leapt.

"Run!" shouted Peter.

All in the company looked back, even Alan whose blank white eyes shot open horrifyingly.

"Listen to him! Go!" he yelled.

In a fit of panic, Peter spun around on his heels, checking to make sure his friends were kicking the horses in their sides, urging them to run faster. Aiyesha had spun Day around, ready to charge back and ward off the Man in the Gray Cloak.

"Aiyesha, no!" came Peter. "Leave him! Let's go!"

"Yes, go!" shouted Mr. Nibbetts. "Me don't want to be that man's supper!"

Belina growled and barked loudly at the Man in the Gray Cloak. Thalok just stood there, as if there was no hustling and shouting ahead of him.

The company took off through the trees as quick as they were able.

Damn these trees, thought Peter. The woods were so tightly packed, there was no way to take the horses up to their full speed. He hoped for a clearing, or at least a thinning of the trees. Low branches slapped him in the face and chest, as well as the others, as they hurried through. His legs were already tired from running. Constantly looking over his shoulder at the Man in the Gray Cloak, checking to see if he was following them, Peter urged Day and Night forward, as well as himself. He even whistled at the dog, who had a tendency to run a few paces, stop, turn, and yelp at Thalok.

They had to keep moving. Keep going. Get as far away from the Man in the Gray Cloak as they could. There was no telling what he would do to them once, and if, he caught up.

But he will catch up, won't he? thought Peter. His heart lightened when he saw the trees ahead beginning to thin a little. *Thank the Master.* He was suddenly struck with the searing memory of the Forest-Ring back home. Home. How he would love to be there right now, on his veranda, late at night, looking out onto the main Through-way, feeling the comfort of being inside, away from the Slummers. Being safe.

The gaps between the trees were about four feet wide, just enough room to squeeze the horses through. Peter slapped Day's side and Aiyesha tugged on Night's reins, urging the big gray horse behind her forward.

"Peter, don't lose the path!" shouted Aiyesha.

"I won't!" he called back.

"Ah!" yelped Alan as a branch slapped him across the bridge of his nose. He kept his head low from then on, his body hovering over Catina, protecting her as they sped through.

Behind them Thalok was nowhere to be seen. Wait. There, off to the side. A gray blur in the trees, speeding past.

Keep going, Day. Don't forget the others, thought Peter. *Don't forget Night.* Then, a thought that was not his own: *I'm here.* His breath caught in his throat and to get the spittle down, he had to swallow hard.

He didn't know if they were on the path anymore. The ground rushed by too fast and it all looked the same. There was no way to tell which part of it was more worn than the other, which part was the path. Peter thought back to the Forest-Ring and the hunting trails they'd followed to get out onto the Ranmorahn Plains.

Check for gaps, he reminded himself. *Look low. See where smaller creatures have run before. Just look closely. You'll be able to tell. Can't lose the path, for the sake of the others.*

He looked down Day's flank and saw the lower branches of bushes and the base of the trees as they went by. *Focus.* Consciously, he paid careful attention to the scene rushing by, hoping that by focusing, the "seeing" of the ground would become more clear. It did, a little. Some parts, especially alongside the underside of the bushes, were a little thinner in foliage than others. He kept to the thinner bushes, praying that he was indeed on the path.

His legs burned and were fatiguing quickly. Peter wished he was stronger.

He straightened and, suddenly, his shoulder tagged the side of a tree trunk as Day squeezed through the opening, pushing him into the tree.

Another gray blur to the side of them then yet another crossing the path twenty or so feet ahead, and then disappearing into the forest on the other side.

"Aiyesha!" called Peter. "Do you see him?"

"He's everywhere," said Mr. Nibbetts.

"He's around us. Don't get us lost!" said Aiyesha.

Catina began to scream from all the excitement. Alan murmured something to her and her screaming grew to whimpers instead.

Wait! Where's the dog? thought Peter. He couldn't see her.

"Belina!" he called. As if the dog knew its name. "Belina" was only something Catina had named her. Peter very much doubted the dog had learned her name already, but he had to call her something.

Glancing behind, Peter saw Thalok standing on the path, staring at him. A dark glare emitted from the non-existent face beneath the shadows of his hood. The Man in the Gray Cloak moved back into the trees.

Beads of sweat dripped off Peter's brow. Belina suddenly darted out from behind a tree and rejoined her companions.

What's she doing!

Up ahead, the forest became considerably thinner, almost as if in just a few short moments they would emerge on the other side of it.

"We're almost out!" he called back to the others.

"Thank goodness," said Mr. Nibbetts. "Ow!" And a branch whipped him across the cheek. He rubbed the pain away with a pair of stubby, brown fingers.

"How soon?" asked Alan.

"Not long. It's coming up right—" began Peter and then he saw why the forest had appeared to be "over."

"Pull back on your reins!" he shouted.

Day brayed as Aiyesha pulled on the reins. So did Night.

When they came to a halt, Peter ebbed back alongside Day. "Hold still a moment," he said. "Aiyesha, watch for Thalok."

She turned her horse around and stood guard, Mr. Nibbetts complaining they were facing the "wrong way." Peter didn't have to be looking at her to see the anger upon her face.

He took a step up to the edge of the forest. There was a patch of brush, almost like a wall, at the forest's end. Just past that small wall was blue sky, as if the top of the small wall of bush was an open window, looking out onto a field of clouds. Peter carefully stepped closer to the edge. Just beyond the small wall of bush was a wooden plank, about five feet wide and one and a half feet deep. Then there was another plank. Then another. Then another. It was a bridge and it spanned some two hundred meters to the other side, which appeared to be a mirror-image of the edge that Peter now stood. On either side of the bridge was a rail of rope, held up by thick, foot-round posts on either end of the chasm. Every four feet or so along the rope railing were rope beams connecting the railing to the faces of the planks for stability. At least Peter hoped it was stable. Beneath the bridge was a drop several hundred meters down. They must have been traveling on a shallow incline when speeding through the forest and not realized it.

"Peter!" called Aiyesha.

He turned and saw Thalok standing fifteen or so paces from the group. Peter's breathing accelerated, his heart palpitating inside his chest. A flush of heat washed over him. Fear. The others felt it, too, he knew. Thalok took off into the trees again.

"Let's go," said Peter calmly. He surprised himself that his voice had been so quiet.

Aiyesha came up beside him. "Is it stable?"

"Should be. I don't know but it's better than sitting here and letting him get us. He kept his distance thus far. But I also don't want to be here when he strikes, when it comes down to it." He eyed the bridge once more. It seemed both inviting and foreboding at the same time.

"Me not crossing that!" said Mr. Nibbetts and moved to get off the horse.

Aiyesha grabbed him by a furry shoulder and pulled him back into the center of Day's back.

Peter said, "Would you rather stay and fight off Thalok? Can we rely on the Change for that?"

"You're crazy!"

"But at least I won't be dead."

"Suit yourself. Me hope you drop to your doom."

"That's no way to talk," said Aiyesha and she gave him a light shove on his shoulder.

Alan cleared his throat. "People, if you do not mind, we have someone closing in on us, if he has not done so already. I do not wish to have my *Shinali* fall prey to him." His white eyes seemed to be looking straight at Peter. "Now, Peter." His voice was steel.

"Okay," breathed Peter. He carefully went first, very slowly, testing the stability of the bridge. It seemed strong enough. He wondered if it would support the horses.

The moment Day's hoof touched down and found stable footing, relief came over him. Day took another step then another, then another.

"Seems all right," said Peter.

Aiyesha handed him Day's reins and Peter coaxed Day forward, Aiyesha holding Night's reins, leading the steed behind.

Alan drew his sword from the saddlebag behind him and handed it to Aiyesha.

"Be careful with that," he said.

"Don't worry, I'll be careful." And she held the sword at the ready.

Alan gave her a knowing grin. Then, to the dog, "Belina, come on."

The dog had her back to the bridge and was eyeing the forest, with ears perked, a low growl bubbling in her throat. Alan whistled. Belina turned and followed behind them.

Now with the two horses on the bridge, the bridge rocked, causing a yelp from everyone. The forested ground below seemed to grow farther away because of that, seemed to spin for a moment. Peter checked for Thalok and didn't see him. They went forward slowly, careful not to rock the bridge anymore than necessary.

"Easy, now," said Alan to Night. He gave the steed a pat on the neck.

Catina mimicked him.

Soon Peter was lost in the rhythmic clip-clop of the horses' hooves against the wooden planks of the bridge, getting to the other side without toppling over the side of the bridge his only concern. His focus on Thalok began to diminish and he almost forgot about him until a blur of gray rushed past them along the top of the rope railing to their right. His heart stopped, and then picked up its beat again.

The bridge before them was empty. Aiyesha held Alan's sword up high as she rode, eyes ever-watchful.

They were only thirty feet or so to the other side. There was much more ground to cover. Belina padded alongside the horses, sometimes stopping to wait for whatever horse she was beside at the moment to catch up with her when she got ahead.

Peter was ready. Any second now, Thalok would appear. He was sure of it.

Another blur of gray across the rope railing, this time on their left. The air rippled around them briefly, after the blur passed.

Clip-clop, clip-clop, carefully down the bridge.

Suddenly, the bridge tipped violently to the right and Peter was sure he would slide off the wooden planks and plummet down to the forest far below. He clutched Day's mane to prevent himself from falling, nearly bringing the mare with him.

"Whoa," said Alan.

"Peter!" shouted Aiyesha, hand outstretched. She tried to move toward him but the bridge was so narrow, any more movement would send the horse over the edge.

"Don't bump into me!" growled Mr. Nibbetts as her shoulder briefly pushed against his back. Day let out a shrill bray at the commotion.

Belina yelped.

Peter leaned as hard as he could to his left, Aiyesha drawing Day in that direction, too, righting themselves. He, Aiyesha and Mr. Nibbetts and Day swayed side to side on the bridge for a moment before finally settling upright. They stayed like that for a moment, catching their breaths, before continuing on.

"Are you all right, Peter?" asked Alan.

"Fine," he said. "Sorry, Mr. Nibbetts." And he gave the Flistablare a pat on the back.

"Me am now thinking we should have gone over," he replied with a gruff. "There would be less effort if we did. Me was never good at keeping me balance."

Alan and Catina had teetered on their horses, too, but not nearly as severely as Aiyesha and Mr. Nibbetts had. Aiyesha was able to help them right themselves by pulling on Night's reins in the opposite direction that they swayed, setting them straight again. Peter felt the boards teeter beneath his feet.

Another gray blur sped up the right side of the rope railing. The blur skipped over to the left side and darted back down toward them.

Thalok. Peter grimaced. He was even more determined, now, to make it to the other side.

They were half way across the bridge when the gray blur rushed up the right side for the last time. Instead of jumping across to the left railing, it instead jumped into the bridge's center and Thalok materialized before them. The Man in the Gray Cloak stood there, face shielded by his hood, the hatred in his eyes still felt nonetheless. Aiyesha yanked back on Day's reins, startling the mare and it took a few steps backward before it stopped. She, like Night, began stamping their hooves, heads bobbing back, trying to ebb away from the Man. They neighed and snorted, the stamping of their hooves growing all the louder. Aiyesha whispered calming words to Day.

Peter wished she was whispering them to him.

Aiyesha had Alan's sword drawn again, raised, ready for action. Peter could tell she wished she was at the front of the line instead of him. She would be a much more suitable candidate to handle this.

"Move us back! Move us back!" begged Mr. Nibbetts.

"No," said Peter. "We've been running from him too long." *But perhaps not long enough?* His knees suddenly felt hollow.

Belina snapped and growled at Thalok. Her claws curled hard against the wooden planks of the bridge, her body arced, ready to pounce should Thalok come an inch closer. It was obvious she would not be making the first move though.

"Peter?" It was Alan. His voice was frail, filled with fear. The poor guy. He was trapped in a world of darkness, with no idea as to what was happening around him. Peter glanced back and saw two single tears spill from Alan's eyes.

"What's wrong?" asked Peter gently. He was hoping his taking the time to ask Alan what was the matter would show Thalok that he didn't have the power over him he thought he did.

"Sadness, Peter. Sadness," replied the blind man.

"Just sit tight, okay? Don't move."

He gave Aiyesha a glance which read for her to tend to Alan while he faced Thalok. He could see reluctance in her eyes, her desire to be up front, confronting the enemy.

I'm here. It was Thalok's voice and it rang inside his head, low and grim. *I told you I was coming. Now, I'm here.*

Jaw clenched, teeth grinding together, Peter faced the Man in the Gray Cloak.

"Move back, Peter. Move back!" said Mr. Nibbetts, panicking.

"Please, just be quiet," he told him, raising a hand.

He watched as Thalok stood motionless, his gray cloak hanging limp around him in spite of the breeze this high up.

I will kill you.

Peter swallowed and tears welled up in his eyes. He didn't want to die. Not after this journey, not after proving that there was more to himself than just Garathen, safely tucked away within the confines of the Forest-Ring. More than just paintings and poetry. More than the childish longing for the past.

"No," said Peter. With shaky legs, he took a few steps closer.

"What are you doing?" whispered Mr. Nibbetts. "Are you crazy? Get back here."

Peter dismissed him with a wave of his hand. Thalok didn't move.

"What is happening? What is going on?" Peter could hear Alan ask Aiyesha in the background.

"Bele som tan?" came Catina's voice.

Thalok's cloak parted slightly and his black-gloved hands were shadows against a uniform of dark, dark gray, a body-suit of some kind, looking to be made of scales, like that of a crocodile but much more jagged, more sharp. But it wasn't a body-suit. It was skin. His hood remained over his face.

Come forward, said Thalok's voice.

Compelled to listen, Peter took a step forward, then another, then another. He stopped. "Speak," he said. "Get out of my head." Despite the iron he tried to give his voice, it still came out weak, almost spineless

Raising his gloved hands slowly, Thalok grabbed either side of his hood, about to draw it back. *I found you, out here, in the World. I found you and I will kill you.* He pulled his hood back and revealed his face. His gaunt gray and cracked skin made his sunken eyes appear dark, like those of a skull. His thin lips, lined pale pink, remained closed. Peter saw that his eyes had barely any whites, his irises like black marbles in his eye sockets. Even out here beneath the sun, neither the details of his face nor his body cast a shadow.

He began to shake. He had never seen anyone who looked as decayed—looked as *dead*—as Thalok.

"I found you and I will kill you," said Thalok aloud.

His voice was less haunting when spoken out loud. But it was still low, still seemed to sound as if it came from inside Peter's head instead of from Thalok's mouth. Peter couldn't see Thalok's teeth when his mouth moved. There was only darkness when his lips parted.

"Why?" asked Peter. "Why me? I haven't done anything. You've . . . you've haunted me since Darim, and you . . . you've stalked the others. How did you do that? Why do you want to kill me?"

There was a long pause before Thalok answered.

"Because I have to," he finally said. "You've killed thousands whether you know it or not. Thousands, each of their lives ten times more valuable than your own. Twenty times, even."

"Says who?" It was Aiyesha. She came beside Peter, sword cocked, read to deflect any blow that came their way.

Alan muttered something to the others. Peter wished he could hear what the blind man had said but this moment facing Thalok was dulling his senses. Yet he swore he could hear Alan begin to cry.

Before Peter could turn back to check, Thalok spoke to Aiyesha. "Step away from him. He will be first."

Aiyesha went in front of Peter, shielding him. "I am Aiyesha Elnaa of Bel Candar. You will have to go through me, first."

Before Peter could react, Thalok was on her in a blink and grabbed her hand holding the sword by the wrist so she couldn't move it, and gave her a violent shove backward so that she landed on her behind past Day's hindquarters. Mr. Nibbetts squealed. The bridge tipped to the right from her crash and her body froze while she waited for the swaying to pass. The others didn't move either for fear of going over the edge. Aiyesha caught the dog by the scruff of the neck, stopping her from sliding over. Belina yipped a shrill yelp that echoed in the drop below.

"Enough!" shouted Peter, one hand raised toward Thalok, the other holding the rope railing behind him. "Okay. Don't hurt them. Just . . . please. Just leave them alone."

"They will die, too, Peter," said Thalok.

"How—how do you know my name?"

Thalok grinned.

Just as he was about to grab Peter by the neck and crush his windpipe, a voice rang throughout Thalok's mind, stopping him from moving.

Now! Kill him, now!

There was a flash, and the desire to carry out the Void-man's command temporarily weakened. Thalok remembered the Second Main Road in Hillmalen. He remembered the faces in the windows. The Qinorans. He remembered them dying in the Voidman's perverted version of Jakarland.

"No!" growled Thalok and spun around so he was facing away from Peter.

Aiyesha got to her feet and in the span of a second, was behind Thalok, about to thrust her sword into him. He suddenly turned around and knocked the sword from her hand, sending it tumbling over the edge. He grabbed her by the neck and held her against the rope railing. The bridge tipped to the right and everybody scrambled to find footing and something to hold onto. The dog barked, the horses snorted and neighed.

"Never touch me," said Thalok and he squeezed her neck even harder.

Not her! Peter first!

"Quiet!" shouted Thalok.

All looked on, puzzled, not knowing who he was talking to.

Aiyesha clutched Thalok's forearm, and delivered turning-kicks to his ribs, trying to free herself. Her blows were barely felt. He squeezed harder when she hooked him across the jaw.

He grinned, excited that soon he would crush her windpipe and she would breathe no more. She coughed and, just as he was about to silence her, there was a powerful grip on *his* neck. It felt like the fingers would squeeze right through his flesh and touch each other.

When Thalok released her and tried to turn around, he felt a sharp, hard blow to the base of his skull.

"Argh!" he cried and stumbled a few paces away.

The bridge rocked and he turned around. Peter was helping Aiyesha to her feet.

Once she was stable, Peter faced him and stepped toward him, his face like stone, his jaw cast in iron.

Now!

CHAPTER LIV
The Third Sign of Power

Peter's hands shook and he didn't know if his legs would support him much longer. *Treat him like a Slummer, nothing more. He's just a Slummer. Just a Slummer. Not Thalok. A Slummer.* He thought back to the Slummer that had attacked Catina back home and how he had bested the Streetfellow. *Just a Slummer.*

Thalok moved toward him swiftly, to grab him, two gloved hands reaching for his neck. Peter brought his own hands up in between Thalok's forearms and stopped him from grabbing hold. Forearms against Thalok's, Peter circled his arms outward, Thalok's arms falling to the side. Fist clenched like a ball of steel, Peter swung at the Man in the Gray Cloak and connected squarely with the Man's jaw. There were shouts from the group behind him. There was another flurry of motion and Peter saw that Aiyesha had charged Thalok again.

"Aiyesha, no!" he shouted.

But it was too late. Thalok grabbed her and threw her back into the horses. The bridge rocked violently and again all held on until the deep swaying passed.

All except for Thalok.

Peter turned to her. "Get them off of here! We can't stay on here like this unless we want to go over the edge." His eyes met hers. "Please."

Her green eyes glazed over; she bit her lower lip.

"Aiyesha, please," he said. "He's come just for me. I don't want any of you to die because of me. Please, lead them off. You have to."

She took a long look at him, her gaze pleading with him to reconsider. Then—she nodded. Her face became hard. A warrior's face. She moved to the others and worked with Mr. Nibbetts and Alan and Catina to help the horses back down the bridge.

Peter turned back to Thalok. "Wait until they leave, I beg you. Wait until they leave."

"No," said Thalok and he tackled Peter to the bridge's floor.

Thalok's weight was crushing, more than what Peter had expected given Thalok's size. The sky tilted in his vision as the bridge moved. More screams. More shouts from the animals. He could hear Belina's claws scraping against the planks as she tried to maintain her balance.

Desperate, Peter punched Thalok's head—anywhere in the head—as best he could despite the Man's weight. Thalok blocked one of the blows and brought his forehead to meet Peter's. Red and green stars burst before Peter's vision.

Thalok hoisted him to his feet, spun him around and dragged him away from the others.

"Peter!" called Aiyesha.

"Go back!" he shouted at her. A droning hum filled his head. "Get off the bridge!" He watched her through watery vision as she slowly led the others back to the forest. His heart ached at the thought of never seeing her again.

Without warning, Thalok's elbow caught him in the neck and he couldn't breath. He coughed, gasped, summoning his strength just so he could draw in a small breath of air. His lungs felt like they were clamped in a vice. Nothing was getting through.

"P-please . . . " he managed. His arms sank to his sides and his legs grew limp as Thalok dragged him down the bridge.

Not here, he thought. The Sickness was returning. Already he could feel his stomach begin to swim. He tried raising his arms but couldn't. *Breathe, just breathe!* He swallowed; bile rose in his throat. *Stay calm. Just breathe.* He closed his eyes and relaxed a moment, letting Thalok have total dominance. When an inner calm was found, he sucked in air slowly through his nostrils. Slowly.

Slowly.

Slowly. Air filled his lungs. He exhaled, an immediate sense of rejuvenation filling him. He began to breathe through his mouth again.

Over Thalok's cloaked shoulder he watched as the group went back down the bridge. Were they almost at the other side? He couldn't tell. They were too far away.

His heart pounded, his head throbbed, and his breathing was shaky. But he was alive. Adrenaline began pumping through him and Thalok's grip against him didn't feel as strong. He moved his ankles. Then he moved his wrists. Peter recognized this strength. It was the same one that had come to him during the Battle on the Hill. His elbow now bent, as with his knees, all . . . strength . . . was returning to him and the Sickness was lifting.

Mind leading the body, he thought absentmindedly.

He planted his feet firmly against the planks and lurched himself forward so he was standing, Thalok still holding him. Peter knocked Thalok's hands off him and hooked the Man across the jaw then doubled back his blow so that the back of his fist slammed Thalok across the temples. The Gray Man reeled to the side and grabbed hold of the rope railing to prevent himself from toppling over the side of the bridge.

"Argh!" growled Thalok.

Peter felt as if his whole body were made of air, so light, so easy to move. Energy coursed through him and he had to bounce on the balls of his feet just so he wouldn't feel like he would burst. The bridge rocked slightly with his motion.

When the Man in the Gray Cloak stood to face him, Peter came at him again, delivering a steel-like fist to Thalok's middle and another to Thalok's kidney. The Man growled again and claws shot out from the tips of his gloves, two inches long, black and curled. He slashed at Peter and tore five slash marks into Peter's shirt and across Peter's chest and part of his stomach. Peter wailed and kicked Thalok's kneecaps, temporarily causing the Qinoran to lose his balance.

The fight was on.

The horses had obeyed well enough for them to be led back to the beginning of the bridge. Alan wished he could be out there with Peter. All Alan knew, as he sat atop Night, were the sounds of yells and growls as Peter fought the Man in the Gray Cloak somewhere down the bridge.

"Alan." It was Aiyesha. She was at his side and handed him Night's reins and that of Day's.

"Yes?" he said.

"Stay here with the others and make sure they don't leave this spot. I'm going after Peter."

"No, you are not," he told her. "Peter said for us to stay here. He—"

"And have him die out there at the hands of that—that thing! Are you *that* blind? Peter is going to get killed out there."

"The Man in the Gray Cloak—Thalok—came for him. You heard Thalok himself say that. There is no sense of us getting involved. What about Catina? Or Mr. Nibbetts? Or the bloody dog, for the Master's sake? Do you think Peter would want us to put ourselves in the way of harm or do you think he would want us to be safe?"

"Me want to be safe," said Mr. Nibbetts.

"You selfish, foolish creature," she spat at the Flistablare. "You care nothing of others. Only yourself." She addressed Alan. "I will not let him die. If there's anything I can do about it, I will not let that creature take him." She took off to the edge where the land met the bridge.

"Aiyesha." She stopped. "Thalok threw you back each time you went for him. I may not have seen it with my own eyes, but I know what happened. I certainly felt it. He will do the same thing again. He will keep throwing you back. Perhaps this time over the edge. Is that what you want?"

He heard the grass rustle beneath her feet as she turned to face him.

"I would rather that than stand here and watch," she said.

Her footfalls began to fade as she ran off down the bridge.

"Be careful," he said quietly.

Thalok screeched and kicked Peter in the chest, sending him flying back and sliding along the planks. The bridge tipped as he drifted off to the left side. He caught the rope railing where one of the rope supports met the bridge and hung on as his body swung out off the edge. He immediately looked down and the World twisted beneath him.

"Guh . . . " He readjusted his grip on the rope. "Thalok!"

The Man in the Gray Cloak was at the edge of the bridge, standing over him. Thalok kicked at his fingers and Peter's left hand let go. He had only the strength of his right to save his life. Thalok crouched and slashed at the fingers still hanging. Peter twisted himself just enough so that the rope moved with him and Thalok's claws only scratched the skin instead of cutting his fingers clean off his hand. Warm blood trickled over his fingers from the wound. Peter swung his left hand back over so he was hanging on with two hands again.

There was a rumbling down the length of the bridge. Footfalls. Running. Thalok went to slash at Peter's fingers again and just before he did, he let out a wail as a knife pierced him from behind.

"Peter!" Aiyesha was on her stomach, over the bridge's edge, hand outstretched toward him.

He grabbed it and she helped him up. When he was bent over the bridge at the waist, she grabbed the waistband of his trousers, making the task of swinging his legs back on to the bridge a lot easier. The bridge tilted and swung and Thalok stumbled back as he wrestled with the knife sticking out from in between his shoulder blades. Aiyesha had stabbed him in a place that was difficult to reach.

"Are you all right?" asked Aiyesha.

Peter rolled onto his back and caught his breath. "Yes, fine." He looked at the backs of his fingers where Thalok had cut him. Thin, red lines stared back. "Ow."

Thalok, finally grabbing hold of the knife's handle, slowly withdrew the blade from his body with a fell scream.

Aiyesha disappeared from Peter's side and began kicking at Thalok, delivering blow after blow at the Qinoran. Thalok caught her fist and squeezed. Aiyesha grunted as Peter heard the cracking of bone. At least one of her fingers had just been broken. Delivering a knee to Thalok's side, Aiyesha twisted herself so her hand broke free. Her legs struck out and she nailed Thalok in the neck when he moved toward her. This was the girl Peter knew. This was the girl who took out those Voidsmen in Darim.

Thalok grabbed her and threw her to the bridge's planks. He crouched over her, the tip of the knife at her neck.

"No!" shouted Peter and he jumped at Thalok from behind.

The bridge rocked and all went sliding toward the right side, toward the railing. There were shouts back on land from Mr. Nibbetts and Catina.

Thalok dropped the knife as he caught the railing so he wouldn't go over. The knife slid off the bridge and fell to the ground far below. When the bridge stopped moving, Thalok picked Aiyesha up and socked her one good across the cheekbone. There was another snap as something fractured. Aiyesha stumbled back and landed on her behind.

Thalok's strikes are hard, thought Peter. *How can I withstand them better than she can? She's the warrior.*

Aiyesha's eyes rolled back in her head and Thalok kicked her in the face and she fell over onto her side, unconscious.

Grimacing, Peter grabbed Thalok from behind and planted his forearm firmly across the Qinoran's neck. Peter squeezed his arm to himself, choking Thalok.

"This is what you get," said Peter, "for hurting her. For hurting me." He shouted, "For living in my head!"

Peter drove his knees into Thalok's back. Something popped beneath Thalok's gray cloak but Peter did not know what. He squeezed his arm to himself harder. Harder. And harder still. Thalok slid to his knees, clutching at Peter's arm. He drove his claws into Peter's forearm. Peter released immediately and, cradling his arm, stepped a few paces away.

Thalok got to his feet, turned to face him, and grinned. "You killed them all."

Arms crossed under his fury breast, Mr. Nibbetts muttered, "A fool's errand. Why she went off like that is beyond me. Now look at her, unconscious on a swinging bridge."

"At least she did what few would do: risk their life for another," said Alan.

Mr. Nibbetts huffed. Belina was at the edge where the forest met the bridge, ears perked, staring out at Peter and Thalok. The two men stood facing each other. Mr. Nibbetts wished he could hear what Thalok was saying to Peter. The dog yipped and stepped out onto the bridge.

"Belina, no," he told her.

The dog glanced back at him defiantly then padded forward down the planks.

"Belina!"

"Belina," echoed Catina and she got off Night.

"Catina, Rana Ko!" said Alan, hand out. "Gnal la cal."

Catina went to the edge and called the dog by name, whistling and patting her leg, trying to get the dog to come back. Belina glanced back at her and with the same defiant gaze, went further down the bridge. Catina went after her.

"She's on the bridge," said Mr. Nibbetts.

Alan got off his horse and felt his way forward, using the arrangement of the horses as a guide. Mr. Nibbetts grabbed Alan by the shoulder. "You can't see, man. You'll go over the edge."

"Then help me!"

Catina was about fifteen feet down the bridge, calling to the dog. Belina didn't pay her any heed and kept going toward Peter and Thalok and Aiyesha's lying form.

"No. Me am staying here," said Mr. Nibbetts.

Alan made a face at him and went toward the bridge.

"Stupid old fool," muttered the Flistablare.

At the bridge's mouth, Alan felt along the rope railing and planted his feet firmly on the planks.

Mr. Nibbetts didn't know what Alan was saying to Catina but could only assume it was along the lines of, "Get back here."

Alan went further down the bridge. He stumbled and the bridge tilted. He hung onto the ropes and Catina went for the nearest railing as well. The dog slid along the bridge and her left forepaw and hind leg went off the edge.

"Belina!" called Mr. Nibbetts and he jumped off his horse. At the same time Alan called out Catina's name.

Catina was already at the dog's side, helping the canine back onto the bridge. The Flistablare went over to Alan, who was clutching the rope railing, his knuckles white from the strain.

"Please," said Alan, "I am begging you. Go and get them, bring them back."

"Me don't want to go over the edge," he replied.

Alan grunted. "Fool! Do you think of nothing but yourself?" And the blind man went cautiously down the bridge to his granddaughter.

Catina had managed to pull the dog back onto the bridge. She crouched by her side. Alan held out his hand to his granddaughter.

Peter called out to them from further down the bridge, telling them to go back. Thalok swung at him and knocked Peter down. The bridge tilted again and Catina went over the edge.

Alan caught her hand and Catina hung off the edge with Alan's hand the only thing between her and the Master's waiting arms. Catina screamed. The dog yipped and growled.

"Nibbetts, get over here! Please!" shouted Alan.

Wide-eyed and angry, Mr. Nibbetts swallowed his pride and went down the bridge to help the blind man.

"Okay, okay, me am here," he said when he got there.

"Help me help her up!"

Mr. Nibbetts bent down and took hold of Catina's arms. "Me got her." He helped Catina back onto the bridge, her weight, for some reason, less than he expected. When she was on, he slipped and went partly over the edge himself. "Alan!"

The blind man felt along his furry back then grabbed him by the scruff of the neck. But Alan didn't help him up.

"What are you waiting for? Help me up!" said Mr. Nibbetts.

"How does it feel," said Alan, "to look Death in the eye while others who could help you wait? Tell me!"

"Okay, okay, me am sorry. Me am sorry. Just help me up!" His heart raced, hurt, pounded hard inside his chest.

Alan's grip on his scruff lessened and Mr. Nibbetts thought surely he would go over the edge. Then Alan squeezed the fur in his fingers so hard the Flistablare winced from the pain. The blind man pulled and, shortly, Mr. Nibbetts was back on the bridge, stable, the roots of his fur stinging from being pulled on so hard.

"You nearly let me die!" he shouted.

Giving Catina a gentle shove toward the forest, Alan waited for her—listened for her—to get back to the mainland before turning to Mr. Nibbetts. "I hope you learned something. And I also hope that if we have to do this again, you will act accordingly." The blind man then leaned in closer, his white eyes haunting. "Am I clear?"

Mr. Nibbetts nodded and got to his feet. "You're clear." And he went back to the mainland.

Alan didn't follow.

Somewhere behind him, there was action on the bridge and Peter heard his friends' voices.

"Go back!" he shouted, turning toward them.

Just then Thalok swung at him and the dull force of the hit knocked him down. The bridge tilted and, beyond Aiyesha's body, Peter watched as Catina went over the edge and Alan grabbed her by the hand at the last second. Before he could watch to see if she would make it, Thalok picked him up and brought his gray, scaly knee to Peter's face.

"You killed them!" shouted Thalok.

Killed who? "I don't know what you're talking about," said Peter as he wiped the blood from his nose.

"I know you don't," said Thalok in that low tone. "You have no idea why I'm here. Why you must die."

Peter spat out a wad of blood. The taste made his stomach swim. "Then why don't you tell me? Maybe we can reach an agreement of some sort." He knew he sounded foolish, even cowardly, but it was the only thing he could think of to say right now. He hated fighting. His eyes were watery and Thalok's image was distorted, like it had been when he saw Thalok beneath the river that time.

"The Master wants you dead," said Thalok.

What? "That's not true," said Peter. He glanced back and saw Alan standing at the end of the bridge, while Mr. Nibbetts and Catina and Belina were back on the land. *What's he waiting for? Get off the bridge!*

Peter shakily got to his feet. His head swam. "The Master loves everybody. He wouldn't want me dead." *Right?* He honestly didn't know.

"Shows how little you know." And Thalok swung at him.

Peter blocked the blow and returned one of his own. It knocked Thalok to the ground.

"You haunt me and then you try to kill me. Why!"

Thalok wiped a smear of black blood from his face. "So you don't get to the Ark of Light before the Master does, that's why." Thalok's dark eyes lit with rage. "How I hate you. It's because of this foolish quest to kill you that all my brethren are dead! I have my own methods of dealing death, you see, but they're not good enough for the Master, or, as He's more properly known, the Void-man."

The Void-man! The Voidsmen! It suddenly made sense. That's where that slang for the Dembatstayr came from. But why should he believe Thalok?

"What do you know of the Ark of Light?" demanded Peter. He walked over to Thalok and stood over him.

"No more than you do. But the stories are true, Peter. At least, there is some semblance of truth to the stories you've heard. The Ark is real. The Master—the Void-man—doesn't want you to have it."

Me have it? It didn't make sense.

Thalok lunged at Peter's legs and tackled him to the bridge's boards. Thalok's fists came upon him.

In his world of darkness, Alan could see Aubri. Tears ran down his cheeks.

"Why did you go?" he asked her. *Tell me.*

She didn't move. She just stood there, gazing at him, love in her rich blue eyes.

"Aubri, please, why did you go?"

He reached out to touch her and as he did, she vanished and he was left clutching black air. Suddenly dizzy, Alan remembered where he was: on the bridge. His headache returned and his heart felt like it were made of porcelain, so fragile. In a blinding flash of white, his heart shattered and he thought of Aubri once more. He felt the rope railing in his hand, its rough, twisted cord against his palm. Heart searing with heated pain, tears leaking from his eyes no matter how hard he tried to compose himself . . . . How easy it would be to go over the edge.

I could just pretend I slipped and fell over. No one would think it was my choice. I am blind. I cannot see. No one would hold it against me after I am gone. Anything to end the pain. Anything for you, Aubri. To be with you again . . . . Someone was calling his name outside the grief that had its arms around him. He didn't know who and he didn't care.

"Over the edge. You would not even feel the impact," he told himself. A hand over his eyes, he broke down and cried. "You are worthless. You are nothing without her. Just pretend you lost your footing and it would all be over."

Shouts to his right. Two men. One, a Man. The second more Beast than Man. He thought of a palanthora beast. He had never seen one but he could imagine its snarl and sharp teeth. One of the men shouted. Peter. It was Peter. Where did he know him from?

Over the edge. Leave it all behind, he thought. Another pang hit his heart.

Jump. Aubri in his mind. *Jump and you can be with me.*

"No," he said and wiped the tears from his eyes.

Just fall. It will be done with. We can finally be together.

"You are not Aubri. You cannot be. She would never say that."

Heart pounding, Alan fell to his knees and rocked back and forth, hanging onto the rope railing. The bridge rocked beneath him. He felt his body slip on its wooden surface. There was his daughter-in-law, too, lying dead back in Grek. He loved her. He may never have always been there for her . . . but he loved her. He never even got to tell her that before she . . . . *I am sorry,* he thought.

Catina. Her pain, flowing through the bloodline. Her loss, her confusion, her isolation being trapped in a group of people who did not speak her language. Catina. She was the reason he was here, the reason not to give in to the despair, the pain, the blessed relief of ending his life so he could be happy with Aubri.

Catina.

Shinali.

Suddenly, his heart became alive with emotion and his vision filled with color. Mats of blues, reds, yellows, greens, purples and grays flashed before his eyes. Each color represented a feeling, he knew. Blue for Peace, red for Anger, yellow for sunshine and New Days, green for Life, purple for the Master, gray for . . . Thalok.

Peter! Alan got to his feet and a voice behind him said, "See? Told you he'd be all right." It took him a moment to realize the voice belonged to Mr. Nibbetts.

Alan's heart felt like it was being gripped in someone's fist and that that someone was pulling him, by the heart, down the bridge. All of his insides, his Being, reached out, felt down the bridge. Felt Peter. Felt Thalok. Gray flecked with bursts of purple came over his sight.

"Peter!"

There was a shout behind him but he could not hear it. There was another sound in its place. They were words, he recognized. They carried the rhythm of speech. But they didn't make sense. Thunder clapped and his ears rang.

Alan Reached and, within moments, found Thalok.

"Get out!" shouted Thalok as he came into focus against a mat of purple and gray smoke. The Man in the Gray Cloak covered his ears with his hands.

Giving himself wholly to what was happening, Alan Reached further into the Qinoran, losing himself in him. Flashes of purple and gray and black burst into view cyclically, the pattern never changing.

"Leave him alone!" demanded Alan.

"Get out! How did you do that? You're Reaching!" shouted Thalok through the din of rolling thunder. "Ahhh! My head . . . "

Thalok spun in a circle, his gray cloak whirling about him. Alan forgot he was on the bridge. The ground in this . . . reaching . . . place was sturdy, sound. Thalok stumbled toward him, arms outstretched, aiming for his neck. Alan's heart drew forward toward the Qinoran and filled Thalok entirely. Pain, loss, helplessness.

"Let go," said Thalok and grabbed hold of Alan.

The blind man struck at him but the Qinoran was too strong. Thalok swatted at him and knocked him to the ground, but what ground there was, Alan could not see. All he saw were interchanging mats of gray, purple and black.

Thalok stood over him and, springing out of the color-changing mist behind him, Peter grabbed Thalok from behind.

"Peter!" shouted Alan.

His head pounded and it felt like someone was pinning the back of his head to the floor, disabling him from getting up. There was someone else on the ground with him, too, just beyond Peter and Thalok. It was Aiyesha, lying there, unconscious. It had to be. He'd recognized that smell of Spring anywhere.

Thalok growled and Peter delivered a series of blows to the back of Thalok's head and to his kidney region. Then the two disappeared into the mist.

Thalok screamed and his low, gravel-like voice faded into the distance.

He didn't feel the impact. If he were anything but a Qinoran, a creature from the Island of the Dead, he would be . . . *dead*. But Death didn't come easily to those who only existed but were not alive. He lay on his back, gazing at the swinging bridge high up through the gaps in the forest's canopy, against a backdrop of blue with pale gray clouds. Peter and the others were up there on the bridge, though Thalok couldn't see what they were doing.

There was no feeling in his arms or his legs, or any other part of him for that matter. His insides were hollow yet filled with the warm fuzziness of pins and needles. A first for him.

Thalok.

The Qinoran's eyes darted around to see where the voice was coming from. He couldn't move his head.

"Master . . . I'm sorry . . . I'm . . . " began Thalok. A bubble of black blood gurgled in his throat. He hurt too much to even try and spit it out. The black ooze spilled out of his lips and onto his chin and trickled down his jaw onto his neck.

Betrayer.

He swallowed and the World around him filled with purple mist and a rush of warm wind swept over him. He was on the Island of the Dead and the Void-man stood over him.

Thalok's screams echoed not only in that Realm, but in the World as well.

CHAPTER LV
Reflections

Her world split between sight and darkness, Catina rode in front of Alan, his arm around her waist, atop Night. They had crossed the swinging bridge at Tatamound an hour ago. She was going home.

Belina padded along beside her and she wondered if dogs got tired or if they could walk on forever. Catina knew that *she* got tired after days on end on the road. Especially behind her eyes, and, more so, behind her left eye. She thought that since she couldn't see anything out of it, that eye wouldn't need to use as much energy and so wouldn't get tired. But it did and it ached intermittently as they traveled, especially when there was a bump on the ground that Night had to step over, or step on. But she was glad Belina was all right and hadn't gone over the edge of the bridge. The dog was the only one in this group that she felt close to, other than Alan. At least, on the level of understanding what it was like not being able to communicate with others because you couldn't understand what they were saying. Catina saved Belina as penance. By saving her life, she replaced the one she took on that day long ago. Her heart cringed at the memory of the man on the road who tried to harm her.

The others in the group spoke. She wished she knew what they were saying. She would have to ask Alan to teach her some of the Common-tongue if she were going to spend any significant amount of time with Peter and the others.

After the bridge, they had passed through one more forest, a small one, and that didn't take much longer than twenty minutes or so to get through. Over to her right, at the bottom of the small rise in the land they were presently on, was a dirt road. She thought she recognized it as one of the ones she had taken when making her trip to Garathen a couple of months back. But she could also be mistaken. A lot of the dirt roads out in open country look similar if not exactly the same. Just grayish-brown dirt, a mix of yellow and green grass alongside it, and not much else.

The ache returned behind her eye. She put her fingers to it and tried to rub the soreness away. She thought of Rano again and his pouch of Gero and the intense pain she had felt before being able to see through his clothing. She wondered if she could summon the pain again, just to see if she could see through her hand, make sure that what happened that day with Rano had in fact been real. There was no way to know how to begin so she removed her hand and watched the road come closer as they neared it. Yet she couldn't help but wonder if her blindness and her ability to have seen through Rano's clothes were somehow connected. Perhaps Time would share the answer on that one.

The others rode quietly, all travel-worn and weary from the ordeal with the Man in the Gray Cloak. She was glad he had gone over the edge and fallen to his doom into the forest and land far below. But she would never forget his scream, that low, raspy garble that spewed from his mouth as his voice faded while he fell. Then there was that scream at the end that echoed like thunder all around.

It was good to be going home or to some place she could learn to call home. She missed her parents and Lamara. She missed her home on the farm. She missed herself, the Catina that existed prior to everyone in Grek getting sick. That's when it all began. The Sickness came and stole the lives of the only two people she truly loved with all her heart, aside from her real father. So much had changed since then. There had been so much growing up and Catina knew that her childhood had now been lost. There was only those many days on the road, those many lonely nights crying herself to sleep on the tufts of prickly grass alongside the dirt paths that were the route to Garathen.

There was that man she had killed. She still wasn't quite past it. But after seeing so much death over the past few weeks, she also had grown numb to Death's effects. It was all just a part of her life, now.

There came a couple pulses of pain behind her eye, like a heart beat. She to tried rub the hurt away again. She wished she could see through her hand.

It was over. Thalok was dead.

Right? Peter thought so. No one could have survived that fall even if they were not of this World. And that scream, that horrible scream that was like a thousand bats screeching in the night sky, like thunder booming throughout the heavens . . . . Thalok could not have survived.

It was a relief to know he was finally free of the Man in the Gray Cloak. Even Peter's mind felt lighter, less full. He couldn't help himself but smile every so often at the thought of Thalok being gone, and of the now-assured safety of the others. Even more so, he smiled at the thought of going home.

Home. Though just a distant memory, the thought of a quiet night sitting on his veranda sent a warm tingle through his bones. Home. Safe within the Forest-Ring. Home. Now different because the others were with him. Home. A place where he can grow in his friendship with "Alan the Traveler" and Catina. Home.

Peter glanced down at his hands, holding Day's reins. His knuckles were red, the skin raw, a couple of the knuckles crusted over with blood from exchanging blows with Thalok. The thin, red lines over his fingers on his right hand when Thalok had scratched him.

"Wait a moment," he said to himself. *Thalok had tossed Aiyesha back like a rag doll despite any of her skill. How strong was he? She didn't even make a mark on him. Yet . . . yet when I hit him, he fell back. I hit him. I . . . I hurt him. I*—He stared at his knuckles, and then he squeezed the reins hard, testing the strength in his hands. It *felt* normal, regular, but what did that mean? Had he grown stronger? He rolled up the sleeves to his shirt and began clenching his fists, the muscles in his forearms rippling. Those ripples and bulges weren't there before. His forearms had always been thin, with only a faint outline of muscle definition. Now his forearms looked more like the Baker's: thicker, denser; they carried substance and weight.

"What's happening to me?" His voice was barely a whisper and no one in the group seemed to have heard him.

He thought back to Thalok on the bridge and part of his conversation with him.

"You haunt me and then you try to kill me! Why!"

"So you don't get to the Ark of Light before the Master does, that's why."

The Ark of Light. The Master. The Void-man.

Getting to the Ark of Light first, thought Peter. *Does it even exist? Thalok said that the stories are true, in a manner of speaking. What did he mean by that? What part of the stories aren't true? Was all that Pnumar said true?* His head suddenly felt full again. He glanced at the others and things suddenly seemed *big* again and no longer safe. *Thalok was sent to kill me but, in the end, I killed him. I threw him off the bridge, heard him scream on the way down. I still don't know how I did it. I still don't know how I was able to hurt him while Aiyesha could not. She's a better fighter than I am. Far better. Is it because I'm male and she's female? Is that why I was able to hurt Thalok? That can't be because Aiyesha hurt Yaman and Yaman is a man. Gender has nothing to do with it. It's what you can* do.

The dirt road stretched out in a straight line before them. He hoped he was leading them in the right direction. It was afternoon and already the sun was dipping down behind them, in the Western horizon. *The sun rises in the East, sets in the West. East is where we need to go.*

"The Ark of Light," he said. He glanced back at Alan and the blind man was looking *at* him and not just in his general direction, like Alan often did.

Peter turned back in his seat then faced forward. There had been more going on than just some strange fellow trying to kill him. *Strange days.* That's what Alan had said on more than one occasion. And Alan was right. These were strange days. There was the Sickness that plagued them; something that still no one in the group had fully recovered from. There were these bizarre displays of power; from Thalok, from himself. Alan had even mentioned that Catina told him she was able to see through the cloak of one of the Men of Humility. Now, as Peter thought about it, that claim became plausible. After experiencing the surge of strength that he had, something that couldn't be explained, anything was possible. Even Catina's ability to see through solid material.

Later, he knew, he would have to talk to Alan about this. Besides, something had happened to Alan on the swinging bridge. It was almost as if he could see.

The thought of his little place at the end of the Through-way stuck with him as they rode on. Alan looked forward to getting home. His heart, however, was heavy and he was weary with concern for the others, namely Catina and Peter. He was beginning to believe what Catina had said about seeing through Rano's cloak. And as for Peter, in that place of purple and gray fog with Thalok, Peter had grabbed Thalok and pulled him away. Aiyesha's body was just beyond those two men, lying on the floor of the purple murk. That would mean she hadn't been strong enough to beat Thalok . . . but Peter had.

And then there was his own . . . something . . . that occurred, a world of interchanging colors, a world of feeling and emotion and the drawing of one individual to another. Lost in those moments between reality and the mist, Alan had been able to control it, to *reach* out to Thalok. Out here, out in the World, he didn't know how he did it. But he had and, after giving it consideration and practice, thought he could do it again.

What happened back there? It was all feeling. *Aubri. I was willing to go over the edge of the bridge for her; to be with her. To be in the arms of the Master.* He breathed in deeply through his nose. His heart suddenly ached with disappointment. *But you also know that is not true, right, Alan? The name 'Master' is a lie. You knew that the moment you touched the heart of Thalok. You knew everything when you did that. The Master is an illusion, a tool used by the Void-man to mask his true intentions toward the World. You also knew the thoughts of Thalok, his pain, his loss. He is a . . . Qinoran. I think that is what he called himself or, at least, his kind. But he was different. There was a darkness within him that I have never seen before. Something blacker than night. In that place of gray and purple and black, so much was said, so much revealed. There is not just the 'Purple' involved in this. There is a forgotten war that still hangs on, if only in memory and nothing else. The Battle of Then.*

He imagined Peter in front of him sitting atop Day, and wondered what was going through his mind. The blind man no longer felt safe. He had been able to feel the need to kill Peter, the same as Thalok had, the same as the Master—the Void-man—had, when in that place apart from reality. Peter wasn't just the simple poet and painter from Garathen. There was a price on his head, one to be paid in blood.

The Void-man wants Peter gone, he thought. *But he also fears him. I'm going to have to have a talk with that boy.*

That night they set camp alongside the road. They hadn't encountered anyone else while they traveled. And that was pleasant, too. After all the commotion, both on the bridge and in his thoughts and feelings afterward, Peter felt being alone just as a group a fine thing. The bridge at Tatamound was six hours behind them though it felt like what had transpired there happened a lifetime ago. Yet, at times, it seemed like it had just occurred, the rushing intensity of fear and survival still lingering inside him. So many questions, so few answers.

About an acre from the road was a small pond. Mr. Nibbetts had ventured over there, claiming he wanted to be alone and, when he returned, he came back with five fish—small whiskered-fish—clutched by the tails in his stubby brown fingers. Dinner.

Silence was favored around the fire, as if all were afraid that any attempt at conversation would steer them in the direction of events passed. They would eventually talk about it, Peter knew, but not tonight. Everyone wanted distance from it. Everyone, he assumed, were already having conversations with themselves about it in their minds.

When dinner ended and dark set in overhead on a clear sky, the moon wearing a vibrant cloak of white and the stars dotted around it in perfect clarity, Peter excused himself from the others and wandered a ways in the direction of the pond. He hadn't got far when Aiyesha trotted up beside him.

They walked in silence for a time. Aiyesha was the first to speak. "You must be excited about going home."

Peter nodded. "I am. I'm also a little nervous and I don't know why. I suddenly feel detached from it, like I don't belong there." He gave his statement some thought. "Thalok said something to me on the bridge and I can't shake it from my memory." He looked at her. "Like you, I don't agree with what the Voidsmen stand for. Not now. Not since I know where they're coming from. *Who* they're coming from. It's all been a lie, Aiyesha. The Master isn't who we thought he was. The whole World is blind to it, too. I still can't fully figure out why Thalok betrayed him. Thalok said something about the Void-man—"

"The 'Void-man'?"

"A slang name for the Master. That's what Thalok called him. He said that the Void-man killed his people, others like Thalok. Yet if Thalok is from the same place the Void-man is, and if the Void-man would do that to, essentially, people of his own . . . then what would he do to the World? What gets me is that he's shown nothing but love and kindness throughout the Aeons. Now I learn a different spin on that, one that contradicts all he's done, and I don't know what to think." He stopped walking and put his hands on his waist. He faced her. "But I also believe Thalok because Thalok was sent to kill me. Kill me first. At least, that's what I think because I saw Thalok first. Then he'd most likely would have killed you, Alan, Catina, Mr. Nibbetts. He might have even killed the dog and the horses, for all we know. It's what he said to me, too, that's got me worried. He said the Ark of Light . . . he said I have to get to it before the Void-man does. That also tells me that the Master's—the Void-man's—Second Coming is real and that he will come. I hope he doesn't but if he does, and if his getting the Ark is a bad thing, then I have to—have to stop it. Stop him. I have no idea how, though."

Her green eyes were dark this night. "But why you?"

He turned from her and stared off into the horizon. "Because I fear I'm the only one who can. You were there on the bridge with me. You tried attacking Thalok, but he just tossed you aside as if you were nothing, yet I was able to hold my ground. You have no idea how powerful I felt up there on that bridge. I felt like I could do anything, be anything. I was so strong, Aiyesha. I can't explain it."

"Sometimes in battle," she began, "your abilities get heightened, almost to the point of being superhuman. Your sight grows sharper, your hearing, your strength. Even your skill in combat, once you get past the fear, grows in its ability to be executed. Trust me, Peter, I know about that. It may have been that which allowed you to do what you did."

"I don't think so," he said. "Not entirely. Remember when we stopped by the river, before the Battle on the Hill?"

She nodded.

"I went for a bath and as I stood there, looking into the water at my reflection, I appeared bigger. My muscles . . . they were more defined, swollen. They're still like that and I've seen myself naked in a sheet of Linsheum enough times to know what I look like without my shirt. I'm changing."

"I don't have an answer for that," she said.

"Nor do I expect you to. But I have to consider that there is more to me than I always thought. Maybe I'm the only one who can find the Ark of Light? Maybe these are the days where I'm supposed to fulfill a destiny that was mapped out for me at the moment of my creation? I wish I knew but because I don't, I cannot dismiss it as a possibility."

The left side of her lip curled up slightly. "Now you're starting to sound like Alan, so wise and proper."

Peter smiled. "Then I take that as a compliment. He's been great to have around on this journey. I can't wait to get home. I'll show you around once we get there. I built a veranda out against the front of my house a couple of years back. After I rebuild my place, I'll build another one. We can have tea out there. You're also welcome to stay with me, if you'd like. If not, there's always Alan's place. He lives down the street—the Through-way, it's called—at the other end."

"I'd like that. Tea on your veranda, I mean."

Peter's heart filled with a comforting heat. He imagined them sitting out there, looking out onto a sky as clear as the one above them now.

Aiyesha was a wonderful girl to be around.

And what about Talia? What would happen with her once he returned home? He supposed he'd have to introduce Aiyesha to her. That would be the ultimate test, too, to see which way his heart would go. After all, Aiyesha was like a girl he once knew, and a girl he would shortly see again.

An hour later they returned back to the camp. Catina and Alan were asleep, and Mr. Nibbetts, though still up, yawned.

"What took you two so long? Me thought you got lost over there," said the Flistablare.

"We were just out for a walk, my furry friend," said Peter.

"There's more fish, if you'd like," said Mr. Nibbetts. "Catina didn't finish all of hers."

"I'll have it," said Aiyesha, and Mr. Nibbetts showed her where it was.

Mr. Nibbetts. He was friendly this evening. Peter wondered what changed that. Then, suddenly inspired, he went over to Day and pulled out his journal from the saddlebags.

He had something to say.

Destiny Forging

And so it starts,
a subtle pulling,
leading me forward,
taking me to I do not know where.
It wraps itself about me like a chilly cloak
yet it also carries an air of warmth,
giving me purpose.

O, this Destiny Forging.

Fear puts its arm around my shoulder
like an old friend,
whispering, taunting,
making confusion of my thoughts.
Yet Confidence comes
on the other shoulder,
letting me know it's all right to be afraid.

O, this Destiny Forging.

I think on the Ark of Light
and what it means to me,
what it really means to me.
Nothing.
But it cannot be dismissed,
for I was told the stories are true.
And I am burdened.

O, this Destiny Forging.

So where shall I go from here?
Home, that's where.
Home first.
Just home.
But then there'll be choices,
ones I cannot make on my own,
but will have to.

O, this Destiny Forging.

I pray that my heart will know,
know where to go.
That this pulling in my Being will stay true
and not bring me or others to harm.
I pray.
I pray.
I pray to this Destiny Forging.

- Peter Jones

CHAPTER LVI
Journey's End
(And to the Broken City They Returned)

The days wore on and home was drawing near. They traveled by day, getting started around the tenth hour and finishing up sometime just after the nineteenth or twentieth. They camped alongside the road or under the shelter of the outer edge of a forest if there was one. The traveling was kept to the dirt road that ran across the country and only when the road forked off did they take another, one that, if Alan's memory served him correctly, would lead them home. If he wasn't sure, Aiyesha would recall the maps she had studied on the Coast of Seryn and point them in the right direction. They also had Catina to help with direction as they wound up on a path she had traveled when she had come to Garathen on her own. Fortunately, none had gotten sick while they traveled as yet. A blessing to them all.

The episode on the bridge and Thalok's end began to fade into memory for everyone, except for Peter. It was still immediate in his mind. Some nights, away from their bonfire, he and Alan would go for a walk; not far, though, as Alan quickly grew tired of Peter leading him by the arm. They talked about Thalok and what happened, and theories of the Ark. Most of their talks were just repeats of ones previous, with no new ground covered.

Now, as he rode down a road called the Terafin Road, Peter recalled one of their conversations.

"I'm afraid that when I get home, things won't be the same," said Peter.

"In what way?" asked Alan.

They were about fifty spans from their camp, well out of earshot of the others.

"I'm not sure what the others expect of me. They all now know what Thalok said about the Ark of Light. I keep wondering if they're wondering what I'm going to do about it. We're still heading home and, in their eyes, it looks like I haven't made a decision yet."

"Have you?"

Peter studied the blind man's face, the dark blonde bristles of hair along Alan's receding hairline. He wondered if Alan would shave his head again once they got home. "No, I haven't," he said finally. "I wouldn't even know where to begin. I don't know *what* the Ark of Light is never mind where to start looking for it. What about you? What do you think?"

Alan clasped his hands behind his back and strode a few paces past Peter. "I wish I had an answer. This is obviously a decision you are going to have to make on your own. I cannot make it for you. Neither can the others. We still do not know precisely what Thalok meant when he said that the Void-man wanted you dead so you could not get to the Ark before he did. But we also cannot ignore it. As I always say, these are strange days and too many things have gone on that cannot go beneath our notice." He stared up into the sky, as if he could see the stars peppering the tarp of darkness above. "I wish someone would point the way. I know what it is like being lost to the dark. And it is the same thing, here. All we have are clues, theories, but no solid answers."

Peter thought he was stating the obvious but he also realized that was a good thing. It helped to get things out in the open, even if they were things you already knew. Sometimes speaking something aloud helps you to make more sense of it. Perhaps even provide some insight into a solution.

"It just makes me wonder," said Peter, "if there is something *I'm* supposed to do. Or, if this is all chance and it just so happens that I've been pegged to complete a task I know nothing about. But, as you said, some things cannot go ignored. The Void-man's hate for me, for instance. I have loved the Master all my life, and now to learn of what he truly is . . . it's taken all that for a spin."

"But you also once told me that you had faith in the Master because others did. You were trying to find him for yourself, this past while." Alan took a step closer. "Now you found him, for what he really is."

"It makes sense, too, I suppose. Aiyesha's helped show me that. The Voidsmen are affiliated with the Master and look what they stand for. Look what *she* once stood for. She's one of the few, it seems, who can see that it's not worth it, even if there is a 'war' coming, as she was told by that Gasahd fellow. She recognizes it isn't her job to cleanse the World, to prepare it for the Master's Second Coming." He reconsidered. "Then again, it might be worth it. This 'war' can be anything, and we don't know when it will hit. And if the Void-man is tied up in it somehow and if I have a connection to the Void-man, then I'm involved, too. That means I have to do something."

With a slight nod of the head, Alan said, "Yes, you do. And you will, when the time is right."

The mood changed and Peter thought of Garathen. "I want to go home."

"Do not worry. We will be there soon."

They were close, now. According to Alan, if they stayed on the Terafin Road, they should be near the Forest-Ring in a matter of days. Less, if they put in a few extra hours each day. Alan said they would soon be able to see the Forest-Ring off to the South of them, very small, if he remembered the Terafin Road correctly. Peter longed to see the Ring again, sitting there atop the Ranmorahn Plains. They'd be coming in from another side and would have to round the Forest-Ring to the right, to gain access to the same entrance/exit they had taken when they first left. It was also important for them to do that during the day, to avoid any palanthora beasts or Slummers. But that idea, of the safety of going through the Ring during the day, was proven wrong the last time they had ventured through there. The palanthoras had been awake and had nearly killed them. Peter was more confident about their approach this time, though. This time they had Aiyesha with them and Mr. Nibbetts. Aiyesha, combined with a "Changed" Mr. Nibbetts, would be a lethal force against any oncoming palanthora beast.

So on they went.

Alan's estimate had been right; better than right. A day later the vast expanse of the Ranmorahn Plains spanned out alongside Terafin Road. The sun shone brightly in the sky. They had traveled long the night before, so as to get there early the next day. It was now only the eighth hour. They were almost home.

"Do you see it? Do you see the Forest-Ring?" asked Alan.

Peter put his hand to his brow to shield his eyes from the glare of the sun. "No, nothing."

"How long have we been on this road?"

"A long time. Too long," said Mr. Nibbetts.

"We should have been there by now," said Alan.

"I don't see anything. Just field."

"How far to the South is it?" asked Aiyesha. She was riding Day, now. She stroked the mare's mane.

Alan wiped away some of the sweat built up on his forehead. "Not far. Perhaps three or four leagues. From the Forest-Ring you are unable to see Terafin Road, but from Terafin Road you are able to see the Forest-Ring." He turned his head to the right; South. "It should be here, or we should at least be seeing it. Peter, you are not toying with me, are you?"

"No," said Peter. "I wouldn't joke about this. I've been too eager to get here. The Forest-Ring is gone, Alan."

"It is not gone!" Alan got off Night and walked forward a few paces so he was beside Peter.

The Ranmorahn Plains stretched out, the horizon flat and green. Long blades of grass blew in the warm early morning wind. A few small clouds dotted the sky.

Peter scanned the horizon, searching. Even if they were still far away from the Forest-Ring, they'd still be able to see its green bulge somewhere in the distance, even from here. The Forest-Ring was almost perfectly round when looking at it from far away, like a wedding band lying flat on a table. Here, Peter saw nothing.

They stayed by the road for a quarter of an hour, staring out against the Plains, checking and rechecking to see if they hadn't missed it, simply because they refused to believe that an entire forest with a small city contained inside would just suddenly disappear.

Perhaps it was the angle of the sun, but Peter saw a small dark blur, a grayish-black, out on the horizon to his right.

"Probably just a shadow," said Alan.

They waited some more and, as the sun slowly rose in the sky, casting more light, Peter began to believe that it wasn't just a shadow.

"Oh, dear. Give me the horse," he told Aiyesha.

"But—"

"Please?"

She looked hesitant.

"I'll be back. I promise."

"All right," she said.

"What? We have to get off the horses now?" said Mr. Nibbetts.

With a huff, the Flistablare threw up his hands and hopped off Day, groaning all the while.

Aiyesha dismounted, too. When she turned to Peter, her eyes bore concern. "Is everything all right?"

"I don't know," said Peter. He mounted Day and tore off toward the shadow.

The smell of smoke hung thick in the air and the further that Peter got from Terafin Road, the more his stomach churned with worry at what he might find. He rode Day hard, digging his heels into her sides, urging her to go faster. The mare's legs were a blur as she galloped.

The shadow along the ground grew and began to spread out to the left and right of him. When he got even closer, he saw a cloud of smoke hovering a few inches from the ground, maybe a foot or so high. Fire or, at least, it had been a fire. The shadow grew even more and Peter choked at what he saw.

The Forest-Ring had burned to the ground.

So had Garathen. The Broken City was gone, reduced to nothing more than a pile of charred rubble swathed in a fine blanket of smoke.

He crossed what was once the edge of the Forest-Ring and rode along the field of ash, the smell of smoke now poignant to his nose. He covered his mouth and coughed. He couldn't speak. He could barely breathe. Everything was gone. All around him were broken trees, burnt to a crisp, black pieces of wood scattered all over the place. The ground had a film of ash on it an inch thick, if not more. When the wind blew, so did the ash.

Reaching what was once the First Stage of the Forest-Ring, the first of the three stages when leaving Garathen, Peter pulled back on Day's reins. The horse slowed then stopped completely. Far ahead, toppled over frames of huts and buildings lay collapsed over each other at odd angles, the wood black with soot. Scattered in places and lumped together in others, lay the charred husks of dead bodies, some with arms reaching up, others with legs bent behind them in odd positions. Fortunately, since the place where his house once stood was still relatively far away, he felt a detachment from the carnage. But that feeling soon passed and tears welled up in his eyes. The faint smell of cooked meat mixed with the smoky smell in the air.

"I—" he began but could not find the words. *What happened here? They're all—everything, everything is . . . is gone. Burned. Destroyed. Dead.* "I can't be seeing this." But he was and his heart ached.

Only the rocks that bordered the city in places remained, but still were furnished with soot.

He went and got the others and came back with them. They rode together in silence, this time past the First Stage and into what was left of the Broken City itself. The smell that hung on the air made Alan gag, as it did Catina. Aiyesha rode with calm resolve, and if she were feeling anything at this moment, her face didn't show it. Mr. Nibbetts—the one who always had something negative to say—didn't say anything. Peter presumed the Flistablare knew this smell all too well, as the same thing had happened to his people.

It was like riding into Grek all over again, seeing the bodies laid out on the side of the road but this time the pain was sharper, the disbelief more overwhelming. This was Garathen; what was left of it. The remains of the Forest-Ring encircled them, perfectly round, a formation that, to Peter's knowledge, was unique to this part of the country. Alan confirmed for him that there was no other forest or city inside a forest anywhere else, as far as he knew. They had come home and had found death, blanketed in ash and smoke and soot.

Peter took them down the main Through-way, which was now no more than a gray path spanning the distance across town. He glanced to his right, to the place where his home had burned down that night the Slummers came. If there was any sign that the rubble of his old abode still remained, he didn't see it. Wooden structures lay on their sides, walls fallen over, broken in places, holes burned through most of them, the wood black with soot. Black bodies littered the ground, some of the corpses holding each other, the people giving each other one final embrace while they met the end. Peter suddenly envied Alan because he wasn't able to see the destruction.

"How do you think this happened?" said Aiyesha.

Peter glanced around then shook his head. When he spoke, his voice was cracked with grief. "I . . . I don't know. I didn't expect this. I'm sorry."

"For what?"

He didn't have an answer. He thought he would be taking her home to a place that he could show off proudly—not this: the remains of a place he once loved. When he left for Grek over a month ago, he truly had left his world behind. He could see that now.

"Peter?" said Alan, his voice soft. There were tears in the blind man's eyes.

"Yes?"

"Take me home."

He nodded. "All right."

He gave Aiyesha and Mr. Nibbetts a look that told them to stay where they were. Peter got off Day and, gently, led Alan, Catina and Night down the Through-way, to where the remains of Alan's home lay in a charred mess of ash-covered trees and rock.

The front of Alan's hut, the part that stuck out from the rocky slope, was burned to ash. The hollow inside the slope was dark, soot covering its outer walls and floor. Peter wondered if the inside was intact or if the fire had got to it, too.

Alan and Catina dismounted Night, and Peter led Alan by the arm to his home, the humanette following a few paces behind.

"Let me go in first," said Alan.

The blind man left them, ducking his head as he entered. Peter and Catina remained outside.

Off down the Through-way, Aiyesha and Mr. Nibbetts were looking about, Day as well, as if the mare knew that a city should not look like this: all rubble and crumbled boards and smoke. Mr. Nibbetts's and Aiyesha's mouths were moving but Peter could not hear what they were saying. Belina padded around them in circles. He glanced down at Catina and saw the confusion in her eyes. He got down on one knee and put his hands on her shoulders.

"I know you don't know what's going on. I wish you could understand me when I say that everything is going to be all right."

"Fen som meva genli," she said, gesturing toward her surroundings. *It is all different,* is what Peter would have heard if he understood her.

Alan emerged from the hollow in the slope a short time later, his shoulders hunched, his head bowed, blank eyes on the ground. It looked like all the turmoil in all of History weighed on his shoulders.

"Alan?" said Peter.

"Do not go inside," he said and sat down cross-legged, not seeming to care the ash would tarnish his trousers.

Catina came beside him.

Slightly confused, Peter went in. The inside of the hollow was dark and the smell of the dead was thick, like that of an untreated corpse. Only a few feet into the hut, Peter's toe stubbed something hard. He felt it with his foot and discovered it was also soft. A body. Moving away from the door frame to allow more light into what was once a doorway, he saw the vague outlines of bodies, the hollow filled with them.

They must have come in here to escape the flames, he thought. *Poor Alan. His whole life . . . gone. Everything he had . . . gone. These people . . . .* He didn't know if he would be able to recognize them. He wondered if Taimus the Baker was among them or if he was lying elsewhere outside.

Talia.

Peter ran out of the hut and out onto the Through-way. Misty-eyed, he surveyed the street. Rubble and fallen-over market stands, cracked and broken, black with soot, were strewn about. Bodies lay all around, both grown-ups and children. Talia lived on the Through-way. She ran the fruit stand for her father. Peter hurried to where the fruit stand once stood. Aiyesha and the Flistablare were standing by Day not far from it, Belina at their ankles sniffing the ground.

"What's wrong?" called Aiyesha.

He didn't answer and stood over the ash-covered ground and the broken pieces of the fruit stand. Black fruit, shriveled and burnt like lumps of coal, were scattered on the ground. Peter frantically searched the surrounding bodies for any sign of Talia. His heart hurt when he found none that might be her. Maybe she escaped somehow? He hoped so. The bodies all looked the same, just charred skeletons reduced to nothing more than black bone and ash. Tears ran down his cheeks in gray lines through the soot that had built up on his skin from the ash on the air. Peter fell to his knees.

"Talia," he said.

Aiyesha came over to his side and put a hand on his shoulder.

"Was—" she began but didn't finish.

"I knew someone who used to live here. Her name was Talia. I had known her all my life."

"I'm so sorry, Peter," she said. She gave his shoulder an affectionate squeeze.

He wiped his tears away with his sleeve.

"There was a fire here before I left," he said. "Right over there." He pointed to where his house once stood. "It was at my place. I thought then would be the last time I saw anything reduced to ash. Now I've come home to this. Everyone I've ever known or loved have all been . . . . There's nothing here. Nothing." He sat back on his behind and crossed his legs. Elbows on knees, he put his chin in his hands. "I don't even know what to do or where to begin; begin what, I don't know. This couldn't have been by accident." He thought of any possibilities that could have led to a fire of this magnitude but any he thought of were far-fetched. Then again, with all that he'd seen since leaving home, even the impossible seemed *possible*. Lightning? A bonfire that had gone out of control? But even when his house burnt down, the rest of the city was fine. "This fire must have come from the outside, from the Forest-Ring. Something or someone must have set it on fire. But why anyone would want to do that, I have no clue. From what I know, not many people know that Garathen even exists inside the Forest-Ring. To them, the Forest-Ring is just that: a forest." He sighed. "I was so safe here. Now it's all gone."

"If there's anything I can do . . . " said Aiyesha.

He glanced up at her and looked into her green eyes. "Thank you. I—I just need some time alone, to sort this out. Figure out what I'm going to do from here."

Belina yipped and he saw her running toward Alan and Catina. Catina giggled when the dog jumped up on her and began licking her face. Peter stood, dusted the ash off his behind and walked away from the group, their eyes—even Alan's—following him as he passed them by.

Catina walked with Belina, Alan having told her not to wander too far from the group and to be careful where she stepped. She picked a burnt stick off the ground and threw it for Belina. The dog chased it and brought it back, the stick clamped between her teeth. Catina had to tug it away from her before she could throw it again. Belina barked once before darting off after the stick.

Catina wondered if they had come to the right place. This wasn't Garathen but when she asked Alan about it, he explained to her what had happened: the Broken City had burned to the ground.

Belina brought the stick back and Catina threw it for her a few more times before the dog lost interest and didn't go and retrieve it. As Catina made her way back to the group, something on the ground caught her eye, something in the hand of one of the bodies. Covering her mouth from the smell, she went over to it. A hard slap hit her in the chest and she couldn't believe what she saw. There, clasped tight in a Slummer's gnarled hand, was a brown, canvas strap, burnt at its edges but distinguishable enough to recognize to whom it had belonged to. The strap had symbols on it, figure-eights turned over on their sides, running up and down the length of the band.

Rano.

This was Rano's strap. How could he—Before she attempted an answer, she snatched up the strap and ran back toward the group.

Peter was returning to the group the same time Catina was running toward them from the opposite end.

What's she all excited about? he wondered.

She was carrying something. It looked like a black string from where he was. It flapped in the wind. She gave it to Alan when she approached him and began rambling on in Grescalla, sounding urgent, her tongue rolling at high speed.

"Is she all right?" asked Peter when he got to the others.

Alan raised a finger, telling Peter to wait a moment. While he waited, Aiyesha turned to him.

"You all right?" she asked.

"I'll be fine," he breathed. "Just needed to go for a walk. I went out into the Ring to see if I could find any clues as to what happened." He paused. "I couldn't find anything. I also looked for my . . . my friend but wherever she is, well . . . I don't know where she is. I'm going to miss her."

Aiyesha's eyes bore concern.

"I had feelings for her," he said. "I never really knew I did until now. I knew I always cared for her but I didn't realize how much. Now she'll never know. I should have said something . . . but I didn't. Have you ever been in that place before? Ever cared for someone but didn't say anything and then for whatever reason it was too late and you never got the chance to tell them?"

Her lips curled up slightly. "There was this one boy—Jotham, was his name. He always had an eye for me. Every so often when I went into town with my mother and he was there and he saw me, he would chase me around, almost tease me. That was when I was young. Years later I realized he did that because he liked me. I was sixteen years of age by the time I figured it out and for weeks I thought of him. He had grown into a handsome young man by then. When I finally saw him again in town, he was seeing this other girl, Shella. I never got to tell him that I cared for him. But I was also sixteen at the time so I'm not sure if they were real feelings or just an infatuation of sorts. Either way, I missed my chance, so, yes, I know what you mean."

Her account made Peter feel a little better but not really. He wished he could have said something to Talia—anything—just to let her know he cared—that he loved her more than just a friend. While on the road, he had thought of her. He thought of perhaps starting a closer relationship with her when he returned home. Now that hope had become a memory—like Talia.

"Peter, come here," said Alan.

Peter blinked, shaking himself from his thoughts. He went over to where Catina peered up at her grandfather, questioning in her blue eyes.

Alan handed him the burnt canvas string.

"What is it?" asked Peter. "I know it's a string but what about it?"

"It belongs to Rano," said Alan.

Peter's heart stopped dead in his chest and he knew his wasn't the only one.

Rano. Leader of the Men of Humility.

Everyone's attention was on Alan.

"Rano? Why would he have come here?" asked Peter.

Alan explained everything to him, how Catina was able to see through Rano's cape and cloak and to the pouch containing the Gero and the string—the same string Peter now held in his hands—that strapped the pouch to his body.

"That's impossible," said Peter.

"I thought so, too," said Alan, "but do you really believe that? I do not. Not anymore. Look what happened to you, Peter. Your strength. Warding off men at the Hill, Thalok on the bridge. Look at me, able to feel my way into Thalok, destroy his mind, reach into him."

Peter didn't know about that. While on the way home, whenever Peter asked Alan what had happened on the bridge, Alan always changed the subject. Now Peter knew. Or, at least, tried to believe that what Alan was telling him was true. He was still coming to terms with the realization of his own unbelievable ability.

"We all have gifts, Peter, and Catina has the gift to see through things. She cannot control it, at least not yet. Maybe in time. Like yourself and your strength. Even me, with my feelings."

"Nonsense!" shouted Mr. Nibbetts. "This is all rubbish."

"Then you explain to me how Peter fought off three soldiers at the Battle on the Hill or how he was able to fight off a creature who was more powerful than any man I have ever known. Thalok fought off Aiyesha, the greatest fighter I have ever encountered, as if she were a child. Yet Peter prevailed over him and it was not by skill in combat. It was by power, simple strength."

"Me still don't believe it," said Mr. Nibbetts.

"Believe what you would like," said Alan, "but it is true. Catina told me when we first met Rano that she had seen straight through his clothes. I did not believe her at the time but after all that has happened, how can I not? If I expect you, her, Peter and Aiyesha to believe that I can feel my way into a person, I have to believe my own *Shinali* about this. She described to me what the string had looked like and she says this is the same one. I believe her."

"Me, too," said Peter.

"Me, too," added Aiyesha a little more softly.

"So, if it is Rano's and it survived the fire, like a few other things around here," continued Peter, "that still doesn't explain why he would burn this whole place down. There has to be a reason."

Alan's brow knit together as he considered the question. "I only have one thought and that is this: Rano said that he and his men were preparing the way for the Second Coming of the Master. Getting things ready, spreading the Good News. Perhaps he was also abolishing Evil. This is just a thought, mind you, as we have no proof for it, but what if he was aware of the palanthora beasts in the Forest-Ring? What if he knew of the Slummers? What if he burned the forest to rid the World of 'Evil' and was not aware that there were people within. That is the only thing I can think of."

"The Master's caused nothing but problems," said Peter, "and pain. It's possible that you're right. And unless we ever find Rano, we really have no way of knowing for sure. It's just" —he glanced around at the ash-covered surroundings— "why here? Why this? Why destroy?" He sat down.

"Why, indeed," said Alan.

CHAPTER LVII
Carrying On

Dark clouds blotted over the moon like a Rorschach. It was the eighth hour. Night had come early. The wind had picked up an hour ago and whisked away some of the smoke that hovered along the ash-covered ground, helping rid the air of the smell of burnt wood and charred bodies.

Peter and his friends were in the middle of the Through-way, together, sitting in a circle on their saddle bags. Catina had wanted a bonfire and Alan had to explain to her that that wouldn't appropriate right now. No fires yet, anyway. They had to rely on the light of the moon, which was enough, the moon shining down in streaks through the cracks in the clouds. Overhead, high in the sky, a large bird flew over them. Aiyesha glanced up at it.

"Tharadon," she said.

"A what?" asked Mr. Nibbetts.

"A Tharadon," she repeated. "They're used as messengers for the Voidsmen. There's still some that fly free but the one that just passed over us could be one of theirs."

"Spies?"

"No, just messengers. They fly all over the country, from one Voidsmen to another, carrying orders from a superior officer or written reports of the happenings in various camps, on collars around their necks."

"Creepy. No one's safe, it seems." Mr. Nibbetts hugged himself.

And it was true. No one was safe. Peter wondered if any messages were exchanged about them—exchanged about Aiyesha—while they traveled, between one Voidsmen and another. Between General Gasahd and—

Probably, he concluded. *They found us, after all.*

After discovering that Rano was most likely responsible for the fire, Peter and Alan parted from the group and held their own private vigil for the deceased.

Memories of Talia and Taimus had flooded Peter's mind, and his heart. The same went for Barmin Hahdgrove, the man who lent them Day and Night, and Dalin Daregrove, Peter's friend who traded him stationery for poems, and Mr. Ambelton, Peter's neighbor. He fondly remembered those nights when he was invited over to join his neighbor and wife for a hot meal. His stomach growled at the memory. He was glad his Aunt Silvi had passed on four years ago, dying from a strange illness, avoiding the suffering of being burned alive. She had gone to sleep one night and simply had not woken up. A mysterious illness? *Could it*—and the thought left him.

As Peter stood there, the more he wished he had taken the time to get to know each person in Garathen. Despite its small size, most folks were still unfamiliar with one another. He had spent so much time to himself, living in the World of his paintings and poems, not paying attention to the World outside him, a World that, he now learned, was far more vast and complex than anything he could ever dream of. Their vigil lasted an hour and Peter noticed that Alan did not cry. He even asked Alan why there were no tears.

"I am . . . I am dealing with things," he replied. "It is like I had a *feeling* overload of sorts while on the bridge. In all truth, I am feeling kind of…empty of emotion…right now. Perhaps it is just part of the recovery process of this new gift I have."

Peter understood as he felt similar. His arms and legs were tired, always feeling like they tended to do when first getting out of bed in the morning: weak and sluggish.

If any one thing that was good had come out of the Forest-Ring being burned down, it was the death of the Slummers and the palanthora beasts. Now they couldn't bother anyone, or steal people in the night. Who knew how many future lives were saved because of their demise. Not the people of Garathen, because they were all dead, but the unborn generations who would be subjected to the Slummers' and palanthora beasts' nightly hunts.

The Voidsmen. Peter supposed their nightly patrols to make sure everyone was indoors at curfew was over, too. Surely they must have seen the fire, or at least its after-effects. He assumed that it was currently being reported to Command—if it hadn't been already—that Garathen had burnt to the ground and curfew checks were no longer necessary. But if the soldiers returned . . .

Back in the middle of the Through-way, looking around the circle at his friends, Peter said, "We need to decide what we are going to do. We can't stay here. This is no place to lay our heads. We can camp just outside the Forest-Ring, out on the Ranmorahn Plains. We'll be out of the filth and the smell of smoke, out of sight of the bodies."

"Me am getting sick of it. Me smell like a burnt log. Smoke doesn't come well out of me fur," said Mr. Nibbetts.

Alan wrinkled his nose, as if smelling the Flistablare to verify. "I agree," he said.

"We also need to consider where we're going to go from here," said Aiyesha.

The memory of Thalok's voice filled Peter's mind.

So you don't get to the Ark of Light before the Master does, that's why. The hairs on the back of his neck stood on end.

"I have to go," said Peter.

"Go where?" asked Mr. Nibbetts.

Peter breathed in slowly through his nose. He exhaled. "I have to find the Ark of Light. That's what Thalok told me."

"But what is it?" asked Aiyesha.

"No one knows," said Alan. "And therein lies our problem. You cannot find what you do not know. That goes without saying."

"I know," said Peter. "But it has to be done, doesn't it? Thalok said that the Master wanted me dead."

"That is true," said Alan. "When I went inside Thalok during our battle on the bridge, I got a glimpse of what he was feeling. His people, called Qinorans, suffered death at the hands of the Master, or the Void-man, as we now know his real name. If he even has a real name. Thalok betrayed the Master as a result, and revealed to Peter why he was after him. And us."

All turned to look at him.

Alan continued. "We were also to be slaughtered by Thalok because we were with Peter. But Peter was first. It was though the Master could not wait to have Peter dead, even if his passing was ahead of ours by only a matter of minutes. The sooner the better. But now, seemingly, the plans of the Master will change. And they will change because Peter is alive. So are we." He leaned in closer to the group. "We are not safe."

"And the Ark?" asked Peter.

"There is no answer for that question, I am afraid," said Alan. "But it is safe to assume that we will find out all we need to know in due time. Look at how much we have learned during our time together. Astonishing, really."

"Everything is connected," said Aiyesha. "The coming war, the Master, the army, the Ark of Light. And us, having been brought together by pure chance? I'm not so sure. Something brought us together. It was not the Void-man. That wouldn't make sense for he wouldn't bring together a band a people who could possibly lead to his undoing."

"Me want no part of this," said Mr. Nibbetts. He crossed his arms beneath his breast and turned away from the group.

"You are already a part of it," said Alan. "You were a part of it the moment you set off with us when we found you. None of us may have known what was happening, but it was happening nonetheless."

"I think the Sickness is a part of it, too," said Peter. "Either that or it's a remarkable coincidence that a sickness of that kind has come along during theses strange days, where a group of people are thrown into something that is bigger than them all."

"Perhaps you are right, Peter. And as for the Sickness, I am inclined to believe that it is somehow tied in to what has happened to you, myself and Catina. Our new abilities that began manifesting shortly after we had fallen ill."

"What about me?" asked Mr. Nibbetts, his head cocked back toward the group. "Me am dying, too."

"Who knows what's going to happen to you?" said Aiyesha.

"Happen to me? What do you mean happen to me? Me don't want to die!"

"You won't."

"But—"

"You. Won't." Her stern tone kept the Flistablare quiet.

Wow, thought Peter. *Can it be? Can an illness bring on . . . strength? How*—Before he could finish his thought, Alan was speaking.

"We have a responsibility, I am afraid," he said. His white eyes set on Peter, who was sitting across from him. "Especially you, Peter. You were singled out by Thalok."

Peter put his head in his hands then ran his fingers through his hair. When he steepled his fingers on his nose, they smelled like smoke. "I wish I could know more. I hate this feeling of being left out; feeling like I'm outside of something I should already know."

"We can learn on the way," said Aiyesha. She got up and sat closer to him.

He appreciated the warmth of her presence yet he was a little too anxious to enjoy it. He stood and moved to the middle of the circle. "Where do we begin? Like Alan said, it's impossible to find something if you have no idea what it is you're looking for."

So you don't get to the Ark of Light before the Master does, that's why. It was Thalok again. Peter couldn't shake the haunting of his voice.

Belina came over to Peter, circled around him once, and then went over to Catina. She stroked Belina's neck and scratched behind her ears.

"Makes you wish there was a Master to pray to, doesn't it," said Aiyesha.

"Yes," said Alan. "But now we know who he really is. I feel like a fool for being blinded for so long."

"But we were all fooled," said Peter. *Come to think of it*— "Perhaps my, what's the word, 'destiny'?—to find the Ark is linked to my recent questioning of my beliefs in the Master. Maybe I already somehow *knew* that I shouldn't be believing in him, or at least the *him* that he wants us to believe in."

"I am afraid this newfound knowledge about the Master will come back to bite us in the heels, if we are not careful," said Alan. "He will not let us go easy because of what we know and for fear of us telling others who and *what* he really is."

"*If* they believe us," said Aiyesha.

Peter looked off into the ash-lined horizon. Somewhere out there was the Ark of Light. He wished he knew which way to go. *Something will guide us,* he thought. *Something will. Whatever it is, it's brought us together. There is no coincidence in three people with extraordinary gifts being together, plus a warrior and a creature who can go through the Change. Even our horses are an asset. Day and Night are smart and spirited.* He fondly remembered the two horses coming out of nowhere that day when they encountered the palanthora beast in the Forest-Ring. *We're all together.*

He sat back down and surveyed each of them. Alan sat with his legs crossed, his hands in his sleeves, his blank eyes gazing at the ground, sweat glistening off his forehead in the moonlight. Catina was beside him, her legs tucked up beneath her, her ash-smudged dress over her toes, her small hand stroking Belina. Mr. Nibbetts faced slightly away from them, his arms crossed. Peter could tell the Flistablare's mind was torn between staying or going. Aiyesha, beside him, sat with arms on knees, playing with her fingers, one foot tapping.

The Ark of Light needed to be found. Somehow they would find a way. They would be guided. They were a special group with special abilities. If that Tharadon they had seen earlier was a messenger, that meant there might be spies outside of Garathen, Voidsmen who had been following them as they returned home.

The Void-man. Peter wondered what he was thinking and if he was aware that Thalok had failed to kill him and the others. Given what Peter knew of the Master, he wouldn't leave anything to chance. The Master was able to manifest himself in this World in various ways. They weren't safe here.

The clouds parted over the moon, casting light on the group. The Lights of the North were out, misty drapes against the black sky, like smoky bands on velvet. Peter hadn't seen them in months, not since long before he left for Grek.

North. That's where they'd start. Alan said he had first encountered an illness with the same symptoms each of them now had, while up North. But Alan didn't say if any of the people had suddenly been able to do things no one throughout the course of History had been able to do. Either way . . .

North. It was a good place to start.

Without saying a word, Peter stood and brushed off his trousers. He glanced around at everyone one final time. He didn't have to say a word. They knew.

Peter took the first step. The rest followed.

EPILOGUE
The War is Coming

And so begins the quest for the Ark of Light. Five have been brought together to rise up against the Master—the Void-man. His dark secret has been exposed. He is not the Savior of the World. His Second Coming will surely only bring destruction. And with the Power of the Ark of Light, should he find it, Humanity will be at an end, History will unfold as he desires it.

The Ark of Light has called. It has sent out its signal: the Sickness, a tool used to purify the Earth, ridding it of Evil, preparing the World for the final curtain of History to fall. And with the Sickness comes the abilities needed to find the Ark, gifts of extra-ordinary power. But, if the Ark of the Light isn't found in time, the Sickness will claim those who carry it, even the most powerful, and the Void-man will win. He will recreate the World as he sees fit, a perverted imitation of Eden aeons ago.

Men and women, both Human and Creature, have been afflicted with this deadly disease. Yet with this illness comes redemption for a fallen race who have blindly followed a Master who only wishes to rule them.

And so comes a choice. To continue to serve the Master's deception or to follow those who know the Truth. The Purple is rising, anxious to claim back what was lost in the Battle of Then: a place in the Realm of the White.

Scattered throughout the Earth, some of the Black and White remain, awaiting the coming days where Future History will reach a climax and the war will begin.

They wait, watching to see if the Ark of Light will be found.

Peter and his companions have made a choice and with it will come consequences. The Void-man is aware of what has happened and is infuriated with Thalok's failure to kill Peter. A new darkness is stirring on Yem Batu, the Island of the Dead, a force unlike any the World has ever seen. And, when the time is right, it will be unleashed upon the Earth.

The war is coming.

End of the First Volume of *The Ark of Light*

Glossary

The economy of the World has changed since the Battle of Then. There are two systems: one of trade (less common) and one of tradesworth (common). For the latter, the terms "dollar" and "cent(s)" have been lost and are instead called "drops" and "droppers." For the sake of this glossary, here is the comparison between the money system of old and the tradesworth system in the Year 134 of the Fifth Aeon.

One-dropper: one cent
Two-dropper: two cents
Five-dropper: five cents
Ten-dropper: ten cents
Twenty-dropper: twenty cents
Fifty-dropper: fifty cents
Seventy-dropper: seventy cents
Hay drop: one dollar
Stone drop: three dollars
Copper drop: nine dollars
Silver drop: thirty-three dollars
Gold drop: one hundred dollars

It should also be noted that the pronunciation of the months of the year has changed over time. The words are slurred together, but are still crisp enough so a month's name still sounds like its predecessor. See below.

Janwary = January
Febwary = February
Martch = March
Aupil = April
Mae = May
Joom = June
Joolay = July
Arguass = August
Setomer = September
Octomer = October
Nobvomer = November
Deesomer = December

GLOSSARY

Terms:

The following is a list of terms used by the Peoples and Creatures who live in the Time and World of the Ark of Light. Also included are descriptions of the Peoples and Creatures and other words that are commonplace in this far off, Future History.

Age of Enlightenment: During early childhood, usually between the ages of four and eight, Humans and Creatures alike dream of the Master. Though the dreams take place in different settings dependant upon the individual, the outcome is always the same: a deep devotion to the Master and a reaffirmation of one's Faith in Him. See also Master

Armasulia (Arh-mah-SOOL-eya): "Arma" meaning "end," "sulia" meaning "war," it is a celebration centered around the Battle of Then and how the Master saved all people from that battle.

Back Way: A portal powered by the Purple Fog that makes moving about from the Coast of Seryn to elsewhere in the World much quicker. Back Way's, however, are very rare. There are perhaps only a dozen or so known to exist throughout the World, if that many at all.

Battle of Then: The last major battle at the beginning of the New History. All knowledge of the World prior to then was lost to the chaos. Armageddon.

Bauclabba (BOK-lob-ah): Frozen cream mixed with fruit. Found in Darim and other cities.

Being: The term for "soul."

Bertamin (Bur-tah-mihn): An oily substance used on the Coast of Seryn for healing wounds and enhancing blood clotting.

Black: Agents of evil. Demons. Also used to refer to the forces of Hell.

Border: A portal that leads from the World to Yem Batu.

Bush-people: Name for the people of the Calahudron Woods.

Change, The: Something that occurs within a Flistablare that transforms them from near-cowardly creatures to bloodthirsty beasts. An internal shift where survival is all that matters, and the dealing of the death is handed out with no more consideration than squashing a fly. A Flistablare's teeth and nails will elongate to two or three times their normal size, making for deadly weapons. Rage and savagery becomes their only consciousness. A Flistablare is only able to remember fragments of what occurred while in the Change. See also Flistablare

Circle: A group of five or six Dembatstayr that a Tharadon is assigned to for the duration of the bird's life. The Circle uses a Tharadon to carry messages over great distances to any individual(s) they choose. See also Tharadon

Colga (Cohl-gah): An offshoot of Humanity. They are Human in appearance, the only difference being the color of their skin, which is a sickly yellow. They are born to both Human parents as well as other Colga.

Common-tongue: The language spoken by most Humans and Creatures of the World.

Common-talk: Chit-chat; general conversation.

Creature of the Night: A bogeyman.

Crossing: A portal that leads from Yem Batu to the World.

Darimeers: Name for the people of Darim. See also Wandering People

Darmaleg: The Old-tongue once spoken in Darim.

Dayfolk: A Slummer's term for those in Garathen; also used when referring to those who are awake during the day.

Dembatstayr (DEM-bot-STAIR): An army trained on the Coast of Seryn, a coastline next to the Border of Purple Fog that protects Yem Batu, the Island of the Dead. Their purpose is to serve the Master and bring order to a chaotic World, and pave the way for the Master's Second Coming. The term "Dembatstayr" means "Stepping Stone into the Mist," a name referring to the redemption believed to be obtained should you follow and/or believe in the Dembatstayr's cause. See also Guardians, The

Farewell: Term used for a funeral.

Flistablare: Short furry Creatures originating from the Eastern side of the World, having lived mainly in the Tanturee Forest, near the Kilimin Mountains. They stand almost three feet tall, with round bodies covered in matted tufts of brown hair. The hands and feet of the Flistablare are similar to that of Humans, but are brown and wrinkled. They have small heads, with their hair combed tight against their skulls. No ears can be seen but they can hear as well as Humans. They have dark eyes.

Fopphin (Fawp-fin): A small creature that ranges anywhere between one foot to one-and-one-half feet in height. It has big, floppy paws that hang out in front of it, with a small, round face, with large, dark oval eyes and small ears pressed flat against its head. A pair of bucked-teeth protrude from its mouth, hanging over the lower lip like a rabbit. It is covered in dark, fine hair. A very cute creature that makes chirping noises.

Forest-Ring: A patch of woods that surrounds the Broken City of Garathen, hiding it from the outside World. It is surrounded by the Ranmorahn Plains. From the outside, the Ring is so round in appearance it looks like a wedding band turned over on its side.

Gel (JEHL): 1.5 miles; 2400 meters.

Gero (Gee-roh): A shiny black powder used for lighting fires, especially when the wood is wet and getting a steady flame is difficult.

Ghuduff (Goo-DAWF): The Flistablare's word for "good."

Giver of All, The: The bush-people of the Calahudron Woods' name for the Master. The bush-people also believe the Master is female rather than male, "male" being the common belief throughout the World.

Goula (Goo-lah): Race evolved from the primortal cells on the Island of the Dead. They mated with the remaining Black spirits that stayed behind from the Battle of Then, and, as a result, spawned the race of the Qinoran. See also Battle of Then; Qinoran

Grescalla (Grehs-kah-lah): The primary language spoken in the Western city of Grek.

Guardians, The: Former name of the Dembatstayr.

Heraseah (Hehr-ah-SAY): Little creatures that look like tiny chickens with their feathers plucked off. They are without arms and are only found at night. When cooked, they taste like liver.

Humanette (Hew-mahn-eht): A female human being.

Jakarland (Jah-KAHR-land): A realm created around a Qinoran when he or she runs due to the energy given off from their great speed, distorting the physicality of the air around them. When a Qinoran is in Jakarland, they are unseen by any they pass by. It is also used as a means of defense, when engaging an enemy. By creating Jakarland around them through quick movement (i.e. vibrating their bodies), they become invisible to the eye.

League: A length of distance equal to three miles.

Link: The connection Thalok forms to his prey while hunting them.

Linsheum (Lihn-SHE-uhm): A highly polished stone that serves as a mirror, commonly used in Garathen. It is imported to the Broken City once a year. It is manufactured in the Western cities.

Lost Aeons: An indeterminate amount of time—albeit a long one—after the Battle of Then when the Fourth Realm adjoined to the Third.

Master, The: Diety thought to be the giver of love and blessing, the savior of People and Creatures alike. To the People of the World, save a few, His origin at the time of the Battle of Then is presently unknown.

Men of Humility: A band of approximately six men led by a man named Rano, who travel the World spreading the Good News of the Master and, like the Dembatstayr, are on a mission to pave the way for the Second Coming. They annihilate all they view as evil. They are most commonly Men of Velmoras heritage. See also Velmoras

New History: The period of Time after the Battle of Then, when History was said to have started over.

Palanthora Beast (Pah-lahn-thohr-ah Beest): A treacherous creature that lives in the Forest-Ring. It is extremely large and has a slick gray body that moves with great speed and grace. It has long feet that branch out into two thick toes with full, sharp, black nails on their ends. Its upper torso, composed of bulging shoulder and trapezius muscles, hunches over its powerful hindquarters. Its arms hang down almost to its knees, like that of a gorilla, ending with Humanlike hands. It has a long face, the top portion above the nose gray and scrunched, like a Human face slightly compressed. Its has a long jaw with a mouth full of sharp teeth. It has black eyes.

Pnutar (New-tahr): A deep hole on the Coast of Seryn where those who disobey orders or are lagging in the expectations set upon them, are sent. It is sealed with iron bars so the prisoner cannot escape. Table scraps are administered from the Dembatstayr's messhall every two days. The prisoners are, however, allowed to have two glasses of water a day. Generous, by Dembatstayr standards.

Qinoran (KEE-nohr-ahn): Their creation dating back to shortly after the Battle of Then, a Qinoran is the spawn of the Goula and one of the Black. Qinorans are able to sense each other's presence. They also rely on the Island of the Dead for nourishment. All Qinorans save Thalok are confined to the Island. They are neither alive nor dead, but merely *exist*. See also Black; Goula

Ragmarus (Rayg-mair-uhs): The name of the Keeper of the Ark of Light during the Battle of Then. See also Master, The; Void-man, The

Reaching: The act of searching with one's heart over great distances, an ability up until recently only having been possessed by Thalok.

Rigmata (Rig-MAH-tah): A device used for lighting fires.

Rolling-tongue: The nickname for the language spoken in the city of Grek.

Ruggard (Ruhg-ahrd): Another name for "pirate."

Scruffle: Someone who is "scruffy" in appearance.

Silence: An occurrence during intense combat where the World quiets and all that is perceived is the *moment* of battle. Focus on your surroundings and the survival at hand prevails above all else.

Slummer: What the people in Garathen call the poorest of the poor people. They are a strong people with the strength of two or three men, who are more savage than civil in nature. They sleep during the day in the Forest-Ring and come out only at night. They are allies with the palanthora beasts.

Streetfolk: Common word for those without home. A label for those who struggle day-to-day to survive. Similar to Slummers, Streetfolk are simply poor Human beings, nothing more.

Telmari (Tel-mahr-EE): A recurrence in the elephant species, the Telmari is the remergence of the prehistoric Wooly Mammoth. From a sliver of their tusk, a whistle is made, its sound heard only by Tharadons. See also Tharadon

Tharadon (Thair-ah-don): An immense bird with a black beak and long, brown feathers. Used as a messenger to bring letters to people, only giving the letter to whom it was intended. They are summoned by a whistle made of Telmari bone, a sound only they can hear. Tharadons also belong to a Circle, five or six men to whom they are loyal to for the rest of their lives. They know the men both by name and by sight. See also Circle

Tradesworth: The term for "money" in the Year 134, the Fifth Aeon. It is unclear when the term for it had come into existence and the word "money" was lost.

Vanillaberry: White flower with pink markings near its bud. Smells like strawberries mixed with vanilla. Alleviates an upset stomach and is a good source of energy.

Velmoras (Vehl-mohr-ahs): Travelers who preach the Faith of Master to all corners of the Earth. The Master's mark is upon them, a birth mark. They are said to be in tune with the Master. They are typically characterized by their long, brown robes and black, flowing cloaks. See also Men of Humility

Void-man, The: Nearly unknown alias of the Master. The new guise of Ragmarus. See also Giver of All, The; Master, The; Ragmarus

Voidsmen: The slang term for the Dembatstayr, known only to the Voidsmen themselves and a handful of people throughout the World. See also Dembatstayr

Wandering People: Once a name for the nomadic Darmala, those who eventually became the early settlers of Darmalennon. Darmalennon, after a great battle that nearly left the city in ruins, was renamed Darim, both in honor of the past, with a change in name to signify the embrace of the future.

White: Agents of good. Angels. Also used to refer to the forces of Heaven.

Zewlan Berry (ZOO-lahn Bair-ee): A red berry no bigger than a small nut. It is as sweet as sugar.

THE GREAT MAP
(UPPER FELLAMOOR CONTINENT)
RATHERN
BEL CANDAR
BEL HABORR
BEL JINU
PALATAY
THAKARI
DESERT
REL J'AKAAR OCEAN
GREK
WESAFELD
DARIM
GARATHEN
GNORAVEER
SEA OF BLUE WATER
N
W
E
S
0 mi
250
500
0 km
250
500

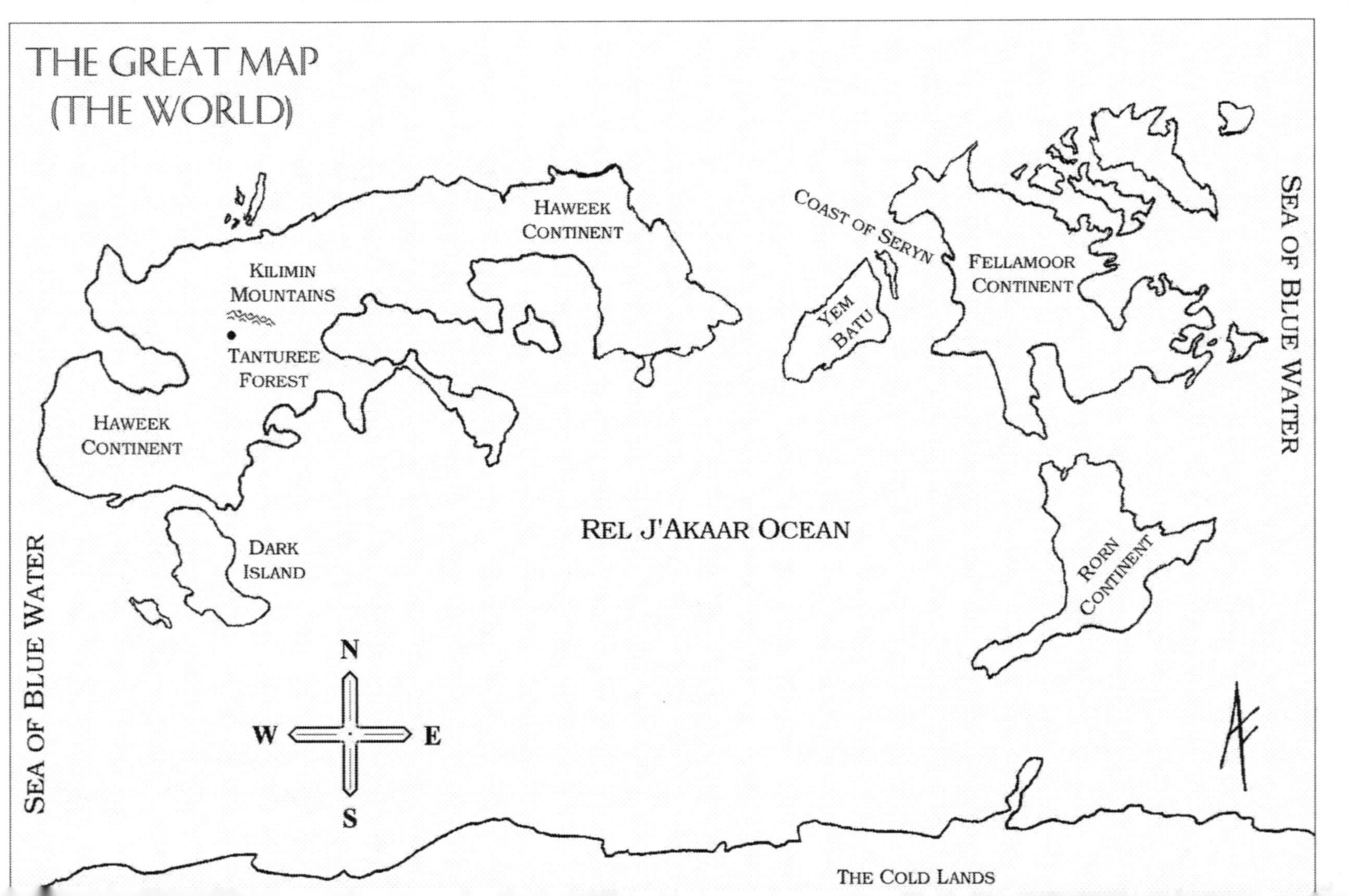
THE GREAT MAP
(THE WORLD)
Haweek Continent
Kilimin Mountains
Tanturee Forest
Haweek Continent
Dark Island
Coast of Seryn
Yem Batu
Fellamoor Continent
Rel J'Akaar Ocean
Rorn Continent
N
W
E
S
Sea of Blue Water
Sea of Blue Water
The Cold Lands

About the Author

A.P. Fuchs writes from Winnipeg, Manitoba with his wife, Roxanne, where they are eagerly awaiting the birth of their first child, due in July. He is the author of eight books, among the most recent *Magic Man*, *A Red Dark Night*, and *April*, a love story written under the pseudonym, Peter Fox. Visit him online at www.apfuchs.com

www.ingramcontent.com/pod-product-compliance
Lightning Source LLC
Chambersburg PA
CBHW060606310726
48982CB00008B/1258/J

* 9 7 8 1 8 9 7 2 1 7 0 1 6 *